About the Author

David McMichael is a doctor. His family now grown up, his main leisure interests are writing, people, history, fell walking, the countryside and wildlife, and all forms of the arts. Having previously lived in London, he now lives on the edge of the Yorkshire Dales and in the Lake District.

To Barbara, for her patience, courage, and enduring support.

David McMichael

SHADOWS IN A PHOTOGRAPH

"The language of Time is not like other languages. It cannot readily be parsed into Tenses: for the Past mingles with the Present, and the Present is already a part of the Future.

… The Past is always with us … like those shadows in a photograph that lie there unnoticed but without which the picture is incomplete."

The lines of verse on 'Kate Kennedy', in Chapter 12, are reproduced from 'Historic St Andrews and its University', by John Read, FRS, published in 1947 by W.C. Henderson & Son, Ltd.

AUSTIN MACAULEY
PUBLISHERS LTD.

A CIP catalogue record for this title is available from the British Library.

ISBN 978 1 78554 684 6 (Paperback)
ISBN 978 1 78554 685 3 (Hardback)
ISBN 978 1 78554 686 0 (E-Book)

www.austinmacauley.com

First Published (2016)
Austin Macauley Publishers Ltd.
25 Canada Square
Canary Wharf
London
E14 5LQ

FOREWORD

There are moments in life, seemingly inconsequential, which later turn out to have been of particular significance. That Friday evening, the day of the funeral, would afterwards prove to have been just such an occasion. And although it is some years ago now, time has not dulled the memories.

It had been a tiring day. Physically and emotionally. The motorways had been even busier than usual, so that the journey in each direction had taken over five hours when it might normally have taken four. Altogether ten or eleven hours of tedious driving. Punctuated only by the funeral.

For some people a funeral seems to generate a spiritual charge as though, like a bolt of electricity, it shocks them from their accustomed complacency. For that all-too-brief hour or two it brings them face to face with the certainty of mortality, leaving a faint shiver of morbid excitement at having been forced once more to peer into the abyss, yet at the same time bringing with it the thrill derived from the primitive herd instinct that once again, thank God, this time it's some other poor guy, it isn't me.

For me, funerals are merely depressing. Even when it's not really personal, when it's not the departure of a loved relative or friend, the ritual seems inadequate. One gazes at a flower-strewn box and realizes that at best it can only be a functional symbol of the person who has gone. Gone. An empty word. Not as in Going – back next year. But Gone – never to reappear. Perhaps to still exist in some vague, imagined spiritual world. Or perhaps simply obliterated, leaving behind only memories which fade, a few written words, and flat two-dimensional images. Not much to show for a lifetime of existence. And, presumably, one can't even hover around to count heads, to see who's come and who hasn't, to learn who cares enough.

But funerals are of course for the benefit of those left behind, not for the departed. It always seems a pity, however, that the deceased can't hear all the good things said about them. It would be nicer if the words of praise could more often come whilst they are still around.

This time the thought of the funeral had been even more wearing than usual. Apart from Peter there would be no one present whom I knew, or come to that whom I'd previously heard of. In fact, so far as I could tell from what little he'd said afterwards there'd hardly been anyone there that Peter knew. And I had only a sketchy idea, really, of why we were there at all.

When Peter had asked me if I could possibly take him, as it was such a long way, he had done so in such a nervous manner as to make it clear that it was of considerable importance to him. However, on the drive up to Cumbria he had told me very little about it – only a few bare facts, revealed with effort. Apart from that he'd been more or less totally withdrawn, responding with terse monosyllables to my few attempts to make conversation. In fact he'd remained like that all day – so unlike the articulate man that I had come to know. My curiosity had been more aroused, therefore, as the day wore on. However, in the end, by mutual agreement I'd opted out of the funeral service; Peter had seemed almost to prefer it that way, as though he'd rather be on his own. So I'd spent the hour pottering about, content enough in the winter sunshine and with the wonderful scenery on all sides.

And that evening, as I mooched around in his study while he briefly busied himself in the rest of the house (drawing curtains to shut out the blackness of night, turning up the heating, and doing the other little things that one does on returning home after a day out in winter) I'd looked around with new interest. It was a room that I had been in only three or four times in all the years I had known him. It was his inner sanctum, the 'den' of the confirmed 'bachelor', the place into which it was a privilege to be invited. Judging by the layers of dust, obvious even to my careless glance, and by the untidy piles of papers and books on every available surface, it was a room that even Martha (who 'did' for him) never entered – except, no doubt, occasionally, with deviousness and stealth. I studied anew the black-and-white photographs, now somewhat faded and yellowing at the edges, which in their plain black frames adorned the walls. His pictures from the past. The groups at school, some of rugby teams in horizontally-striped jerseys and tasselled caps; others of the members of his House, posing self-consciously in rows, and variously wearing expressions which ranged from irreverence to self-importance. In all of them, Peter's lean frame and solemn features were easy to pick out. There, too, mixed amongst them as though they were from one and the same time, were photographs from university: gowned figures lounging in front of the medical school buildings, or cavorting against a backdrop of, here, the Old links of St. Andrews, or there the harbour walls, the wild waves of a wind-whipped North Sea breaking over their ancient stones.

Separate, though, from all these, as though requiring a place of their own, were other photographs. In most of these it was Peter's absence that one noticed. Those pictures gave the impression of having come from an entirely different world – as, in a sense, they had. In these, the figures, individual or in groups, still lounged nonchalantly, and in most instances wore cheerful grins; but the backgrounds were of airfields, Hurricanes and Spitfires, Wellingtons and Lancasters, and the men, mere boys it seemed, were dressed in flying-kit or RAF uniform – the trappings of war.

I'd studied these for some moments, carried back almost physically, in the way that one can sometimes be with old photographs, to a world that I hadn't known. For twelve years Peter had been my senior partner in the practice, during which he had become a close friend, and it was now fifteen years since he'd retired, fifteen years in which I had probably seen even more of him socially than I ever had before; and I realised for the first time, at that moment, that over all those years not once had he ever talked of his past.

As I'd continued my slow, inquisitive drift around the room I'd pondered that fact and the accompanying revelation: that I had never asked myself who he was. I had been content with the knowledge that he was honest, warm and friendly, a good doctor respected and liked by his patients and colleagues, a man to turn to in times of trouble, and a loyal friend. Sure, I knew where he'd been born, where he'd gone to school, and which university he'd been to. I knew that he had been married for some years, at some time or other; but for how long, and what had happened to the marriage, I didn't know. There was a rumour, and only a rumour, that his wife had 'died young'. I was ashamed to admit to myself now that I'd never enquired. I made a mental note to do so sometime, when the occasion was more appropriate. I did know that he'd never had any children; and I knew that neither had he any brothers or sisters, and that apart from the possibility of some distant cousin he had no living relatives. And that was it. I couldn't have told anyone another thing about him. He hadn't talked, and I hadn't asked. And it was from that moment that I had had this sense of guilt.

So much so that I'd been startled when just then his voice had come drifting through from the kitchen.

'You'll have a whisky, David?'

'Beer would be better, if you have it,' I'd replied.

'Sure.' As usual, laconic, not wasting words. And there'd been the clink of bottles and glasses in somewhat overactive fashion as though he were glad of something more with which to keep busy.

While he did this I'd resumed my perambulation around the room, arriving at the cluttered wooden mantelpiece poised above the old-fashioned tiled fireplace. At the end nearest to me stood a long pipe-rack in which resided an assortment of venerable pipes, their once-black stems grey with age, their mouth-pieces gnarled from use, and their polished wood bowls burnt and charred at the rims. Although I hadn't seen Peter smoke his pipe for many a year, these had an air of grace as though, much loved, they were waiting patiently, knowingly, to be taken back into favour. The rest of the busy mantelshelf was occupied by a variety of objects jostling for space, but dominated by two rectangular photographs, faded by age, in plain silver frames. One that I had seen before was of Peter in uniform, his peaked officer's cap set at a jaunty angle in clearly deliberate manner, a self-conscious grin on his face. The other photograph was one that I hadn't remembered seeing previously; and indeed I found it so arresting that I knew that I couldn't possibly have forgotten doing so. It was a snapshot of a laughing girl probably in her late teens, taken perhaps in the Twenties or Thirties judging by the cut of her clothes. It must have been taken on a summer evening, for slanting sunlight cast long shadows across her from one side and slightly in front, making it impossible to tell the shade of her hair, which was short and fell untidily across her face. She was dressed in summer attire, short-sleeved shirt and shorts, revealing a slim athletic figure with well-shaped limbs. Even in that old, monochrome snapshot she radiated sunshine and fresh air, a vivacity and a zest for life which leapt from the frame. It was as though she were ready to step out, as if from suspended animation, to resume her life from where she'd left off. But, unable to make out detail in her features, she seemed not so much an individual as the embodiment of girlhood, of Woman in the flowering of youth. All at once I'd felt deprived that I'd never be able to meet her – never be able to know the excitements, joys and dangers of those times. The whole effect had been incredibly poignant – but at the same time, having experienced just a glimpse of it, strangely exhilarating.

I must have been standing there for some time, gazing at that image and caught up with the emotions aroused by it, before I'd realized that Peter was standing silently behind me, drinks in hand, also staring at the photograph.

'Nice,' I'd said. 'Someone important from the past?'

He'd merely nodded, and turned away, taking the drinks over to the low table between the two leather club-chairs. There he'd stood for a few seconds, his tall figure wilting slightly, his still-handsome features set, as though lost in his thoughts but having to fight lest they overwhelm him. Then, almost brusquely, he'd sat down, gesturing for me to do the same.

I'd done so, taking glass in hand and waited for him to expand, imagining that he would be glad of the opportunity to do so. But he hadn't, instead had stared soberly ahead for what seemed an embarrassingly long time before beginning a conversation on some totally unrelated topic.

We'd talked desultorily for quarter of an hour, until I'd finished my beer; and then, conscious of the fact that he was having to make an effort to converse, and that, anyway, Sue would be waiting at home for me, curious to know how the day had gone, I'd made that my excuse and taken my leave.

He hadn't got up to see me out, which was unusual, merely made a farewell gesture with his right hand, almost a formal salute – but, after all he too was tired after the events of the day.

'I'll see you tomorrow,' I'd said, on impulse.

As though not immediately understanding what I'd said, he'd looked up at me blankly for a moment before replying slowly, 'Yes.' Then, 'Thanks, Dave. Thanks for everything.'

I'd turned briefly to look at him as I reached the door, but it seemed that he'd already returned to his thoughts, for he sat staring down at the carpet, his hand reaching out for the whisky bottle at his side.

As I'd driven away, I couldn't help but ponder about what it must be like to reach the finale of one's life, to know that as winter trudged its weary course it wouldn't any longer automatically be followed by the appearance of spring – thoughts turning to the past, rather than to the future which had almost ceased to exist. And I'd wondered about the girl in the photograph; and pictured Peter sitting alone with his memories, and tried to imagine what those might be.

CHAPTER ONE

A late evening in early January. Cold, damp and pitch black, so that the masked headlights of the truck grinding its way along a Suffolk country lane are hard put to find the soggy verge, camouflaged as it is by the clumps of dead and dying leaves. The only sounds the growl of the engine and the wildly arrhythmic whir of the windscreen wiper as it scrapes ineffectually at the drizzle obscuring the screen, the tempo of its motor and of its passage across the windscreen changing with every change of gear. Only occasionally do the lights bounce sufficiently to briefly illuminate a grey trunk or bough wet with rain, or patches of snow lying by the verge like discarded piles of grubby white linen. After the long hot summer stretching into autumn, and the portentous events accompanying it, with now the first real bite of winter, the overall mood is one of desolation. A desolation so great that it even subdues the relentless excitement and apprehension felt, surely by everyone, in recent weeks. Even the half dozen or so men behind, in the back of the truck, have lapsed into silence; although that may be because of their awareness of the officer sitting in front.

He glances at the corporal sitting beside him. All he can see is a vague profile of the man's face as he stares intently into the darkness, his hands pale on the steering wheel, the tip of his nose grotesquely illuminated by an orange glow each time he draws on the cigarette dangling between his lips. The smoke, ghostly in the dim light reflected back through the windscreen, is acrid, and he regrets having given the man permission to light up. Perversely he is also tempted to bring out his own pipe, but the thought of having to delve, in the cramped cab, beneath his greatcoat to reach the pipe, pouch and matches in his jacket pocket is too much. In any case, it perhaps wouldn't be seemly. And, anyway, he's too nervous.

He stares out at the blackness, thinks again how dreary everything is: as dreary as the past four months of war – a slow tedium, the British Expeditionary Force camped in France, everyone waiting for something to happen. 'The Phoney War', the newspapers have got to calling it: seemingly as spurious as the P.M.'s 'Piece of paper' of only fifteen months ago, his now infamous 'Peace for our time'.

Out of nowhere, from afar, the distant drawn-out rumble of thunder intrudes, and persists: the rumble becoming louder until within a couple of minutes it has attained a throbbing, all-embracing presence within the cab itself, coming up from below and through the roof, drowning all other sound. Involuntarily, in the darkness, he ducks; then, as the clamour becomes a deafening vibration overhead, realisation dawns. He can almost feel the sweep of the wings as the heavy plane trundles in, probably no more than a hundred feet above them – and can visualise the smile which must now be playing on the corporal's lips. His own face becomes hot at the thought.

'Almost there now, sir. That'll be a ferry job coming in, most likely. A Wellington by the sound of it.' The corporal's voice is carefully neutral.

A minute or two later they turn into a gateway let into a wire-mesh fence, stopping at the barrier where a sentry strolls out of the darkness then snaps to attention and salutes as he spots the peaked cap of the officer sitting in the passenger seat of the cab. Papers checked, they drive on.

'I'll drop you off at the Officers' Mess first, sir.'

He grunts his thanks, his mouth dry. It's like the first day at school. Bardolphs. 1926. Almost fourteen years ago. At times it feels no more than fourteen months. The sensations are there, fresh in his mind, and propel him even further back into childhood, almost it seems to the beginning of memory.

* * *

'Peter. It's time to go.'

His mother's voice, floating up to him from a distance, barely registered. Without awareness he brushed it away as he would a troublesome fly.

The tears welled again, and impatiently he also brushed them aside, struggling to maintain his contrived step into manhood. For it was what he repeatedly told himself: that this departure was not only from this room, this house, from all that he had ever known, but also from something else. For in only seven months' time – on 7th November 1926, to be exact: the date was important, a momentous one – he would be thirteen, would become a teenager. Childhood would be left behind. His mother was now his responsibility, rather than the other way round. That realisation had formed over the past weeks until the gradual sense of pride that accompanied it had almost abolished the pervasive fears and feelings of isolation.

Almost.

From outside, muffled by the glass of the window, the sporadically busy growl of motor traffic, trundle of iron-shod wheels and clip-clop of hooves seemed to jeer at him. *You're leaving us. We're not coming. There'll be nothing like this where you're going. It'll all be very different.* Looking out

7

through the window, if he pressed his face close to the glass, he could just see the distant rooftop of the Members' Stand at Lords, and could again recall the click of bat against ball, the muted applause, the warmth of sun against his face, and the comfort of the hand grasping his own; moments of peace and companionship.

Nearer to, the streets of St John's Wood with their friendly familiarity gazed back at him in sympathy – or so it seemed. Windows, reflecting sunlight, smiled their understanding; nodding tree-tops, fluttering the bright green of spring, appeared to wave farewell.

With a sigh he turned away to cast a last longing look at the room which for so long had been his retreat, empty now of all but Dobbin. The big rocking-horse stood in the corner, alone in imagined misery. It had entered his consciousness with the name of Dobbin, bestowed upon it not by his father but by *his* father before him. It had always been understood that, although Peter professed to have outgrown it, it would survive to be passed on in due course to his own children – and, even though he had pretended to be no longer interested, he had in private moments continued to climb upon its broad back to ride the highways, masked and armed, gallant to the ladies and ruthless to the men, to leap trustingly over ditches and hedges, or to laughingly ride the purple sage, careless of Redskins in pursuit. The recent arguments about it with his mother had been repetitive and bitter; but he'd known in his heart that it was a lost cause. Dobbin would stay behind, to drift away with most of the other contents of the home, to be seen no more.

'Peter! Will you come down! The taxi will be here at any moment.' This time the sharp edge of anger in his mother's voice pricked him out of his melancholy. He thinks he can remember a time when she didn't sound cross, but he's not sure.

Unwillingly he walked from the room without a backward glance, down the first flight of stairs to the landing, past that other room, as usual averting his gaze from the firmly closed door, down the next flight to the hall, where his mother waited. She studied him for a moment, then turned her head away, but not before he had seen the tears in her eyes, provoking the return of his own.

* * *

Impressions of space stretch into the night, of concrete and tarmac and of vague angular shapes, dragging him back to the reality of the present. But the child never really goes away, he thinks. Simply retires. Takes a back seat. Becomes a back-seat driver, peering over one's shoulder, telling one how to react, where to go.

To one side, blacker still, are rectangular forms of low buildings, their windows glinting blindly in the dim light of the night sky, giving them a deserted air; heaped sandbags are huddled protectively around their doors as if in an odd attempt to keep out the rain; and beyond these, as a looming backdrop, are the great curving outlines of hangars like the vast tents of some outlandish circus.

They stop at another building, a short distance from the others. 'This is the Mess, sir.'

He climbs out, muttering his thanks. An airman comes round with his holdall and suitcase from the rear, hands them over and salutes. His hands occupied with the bags, he doesn't think to return the salute before the man has turned away. He still hasn't got used to all this.

From inside the building there is the sound of tumult. With difficulty, bags in one hand, he opens the door and pushes his way in, immediately becoming entangled with a black-out curtain hanging just beyond. As he struggles to free himself, blinking in the sudden light, he glimpses a door open across the hallway and a figure emerge accompanied by a crescendo of shouts and cheers. It sounds like a rugby match in there. The figure is that of a stocky man about his own age or perhaps younger, hair tussled, and uniform tunic open and awry. On the sleeves of his tunic he wears the rank of squadron leader. The man glances irritably in his direction.

'For Christ's sake get that door closed!' he snaps. 'The buggers'll be able to see us all the way from Berlin!'

Then he stops and stares. 'Waring?' he says. 'Good God, it *is* you! I wondered if it might be…Peter, isn't it?'

Still in a daze, suspended between his previous world and this, his mind is blank.

'Well I'll be damned! Peter Waring,' the man repeats. 'It's a small world all right. But when I saw the name on the manifest, I thought: that's a name I recognise. Sufficiently uncommon and all that.'

Peter stares at this stranger, this squadron leader who knows his name. He drops his cases. Doesn't know whether to shake hands or salute.

The man decides for him. Comes forward with hand outstretched. 'Of course, you won't remember me. But I fagged for you for just one term. At Bard's. On Founders. It was your first term as a House Prefect, my last term as a fag. In…'30 it would be. Good God! Ten years ago. No wonder you don't remember me.' He laughs. 'Changed a bit since then! Mind you, you haven't, not much.'

Peter tries to gather his wits. The chap must think him stupid, standing there with his mouth open. For heaven's sake, the fellow has even thought it necessary to remind him of the name of the House and the school! Hurriedly he takes the man's hand, frantically searching in his mind for a name.

'Yes of course. I remember you.' He does, now – the name, at least. 'Munro, isn't it? Didn't recognise you, I'm afraid.'

'How could you? I was only a nipper then. You've done well to remember the name. First name's David. A bit of a coincidence though, isn't it, us coming together again like this. And that's not the last of it!'

He doesn't know what Munro means by that last remark. But fragments of memory are coming back. He remembers him as a pleasant, willing lad. A damned good sportsman, too – that's right, he recollected reading that in

9

Munro's last year at school he'd become one of the best wing three-quarters the First XV had ever had. Something else, though… Yes. In his first year at school the lad had been very unsettled. He remembers that was why he'd had a lot of sympathy for Munro. Both in the same boat, so to speak.

Now he doesn't know whether he should be addressing him as 'Sir'! – then remembers that this is the Mess, one doesn't use titles in the Mess, anyway. Unless it's the C.O. But he can't be the C.O., can he? No, of course not. Too young, and not enough rank. Stupid again! The C.O.'s called Wakeham, anyway.

'I'm surprised you've remembered me,' Munro repeats. 'One usually doesn't remember those behind, only those ahead. But I didn't know you'd gone on to become a doctor, that's why I couldn't be sure it was the same Waring. I say, it really is a coincidence, though! The shindig in there is for the C.O., who's going up to Group. And the new C.O., arriving tomorrow – and you won't believe this – is Jim Beal. I'm sure you remember him. That'll be three of us on the Station all from Bard's, and all from Founders, to boot. Extraordinary, isn't it.'

Peter thinks: Munro doesn't know just how extraordinary! – line of succession, so to speak. But the news about Beal is a shock. He tries to echo Munro's enthusiasm, but knows from the other man's expression that it's clear that he hasn't succeeded. In fact it takes him all his time not to reveal how devastated he feels. Beal of all people. And for Beal to be his commanding officer. It's going to be like being back at school all over again – and now he really does feel like a new boy, starting a new life.

* * *

The drive to the station was a blur, the street scenes drifting past beyond a moist curtain of held-back tears, mother and son silent, neither of them trusting themselves to speak. He was vaguely aware of crossing the Canal as they drove down Park Road, of turning into Baker Street and then Marylebone Road, and of passing Madame Tussauds – all familiar landmarks, to be glimpsed for the last time. Here, even the traffic – motor vehicles manoeuvering impatiently and noisily in their attempts to pass the slower horse-drawn carts and drays – took on acute significance, became for him a doleful procession as though it were destined to vanish into history once he had gone.

But, as they passed beneath the great arch at Euston station, for Peter some of the excitement of the journey began to make itself felt. He became a Roman general in his chariot at the head of his legions passing beneath the triumphal arch; and by the time they had obtained a porter with a trolley for their suitcases and followed him to their departure platform a sense of adventure had taken hold.

Their train was not yet in, but coming forward to meet them as they arrived were Uncle Max and Aunt Sheila, here as promised, platform tickets still clutched in hands as though afraid that without them they would be destined to remain as inhabitants of some strange railway ghetto, never again to be released to the outside world. His mother greeted them warmly, clearly grateful to have familiar faces. But Peter hung back. Not really his uncle and aunt, but merely his father's ex-partner and wife, well-meaning but humourless they were a couple who'd never quite endeared themselves to Peter. He returned their greetings prudently, polite enough, but quickly made his excuses to head off and explore his immediate surroundings, lifting a carefully careless hand to his mother's admonition of, 'Don't stray far, Peter. The train will be in soon.'

Already the busy platform had had his head twisting this way and that, his senses bombarded by the sights and sounds of the noisy station. He tried to ignore the throng of people, craning his head between and beyond the moving bodies to stare down the lines of empty tracks, the silvery rails drawing his gaze into the far distance, beckoning his imagination into the unknown. Across the way, the next-door platform was deserted – apart that is from a porter wearing a tattered cap and greasy black waistcoat who was sitting on a flat-bed trolley, idly smoking a cigarette. Beyond the man, however, at the far side of that platform, at the head of a passenger train, was a big locomotive which filled Peter with awe. A black monster, it stood there, wisps of steam escaping with a faint hiss from around its pistons. From its funnel dark smoke wafted lazily up towards the glass roof high above; and from somewhere beneath its great barrel of a boiler came a series of subdued grunts, revealing as it were an impatience to be gone. He imagined that at any moment like some wild beast it would fling off invisible shackles to leap into violent action, pulverising all before it. Through the windows in the line of coaches at its wake figures could be seen moving along the corridors or settling into seats, all with an air of haste as if they, too, felt the urge to be off. And at that moment, as if in response to the crystallisation of those ideas, came a sudden blast from the engine's whistle, a short shrill screech of exultation. A further whistle, this time much thinner, like that from a referee, then served to galvanise it into action. With eructations of black smoke the whole apparatus began to lumber off, its carriages juddering with the effort. Peter watched it slowly gather pace until, wreathed in steam, it had rumbled out of sight. For a moment he felt it had snatched a part of him with it. But then, startled by whirring overhead, he looked up to see a flock of pigeons, disturbed by the noise, spiralling up towards the roof, silhouetted against pale rays of sunlight filtering through the grimy panes – and his spirits rose with them.

Behind him, on the wall at the back of the platform, a large coloured poster caught his eye. In a wooden frame fixed to the blackened bricks, it portrayed a sunny beach with bright umbrellas, bathers and bathing huts, and in the foreground children playing in the sand, watched by loving parents. In the left half of the picture, at a little distance, a train could be seen winding its way round a headland, beyond which could be glimpsed hazy blue mountains. He could almost feel the warm sand between his toes, hear the surf and the excited chatter on the beach, and detect in his nostrils the briny smell of the sea. At the foot of the poster, in bold, flowing letters, was the exhortation, *Come To Sunny Rhyl!* He had no idea where Rhyl was. It sounded foreign; but in the picture it didn't really look foreign. Perhaps, though, it was the name of a country? He must remember to ask.

His gaze drifted, flickering between the intruding forms of the many people passing to and fro, to take in the other features at the back of the platform. Doorways, with signs projecting above them, led into darkly windowed rooms. His eyes skipped from one to the next, reading the signs. *First Class Waiting Room*; *Buffet*; *Second & Third Class Waiting Room*; *Ladies' Waiting Room*. He wondered why ladies needed a separate waiting room – but couldn't come up with any ideas. Further down, a newsagent's stand displayed newspapers and magazines; a crowd of people stood huddled about it reading their news-sheets as though they couldn't spare the time to move away. Arrayed across the front of the kiosk were a number of news-boards, one of which proclaimed, *Miners Stay Locked Out*. Locked out of where? he wondered. And why couldn't they break in? After all, he imagined, miners must be very strong, and had hammers and picks. Even more mysteriously, another board stated, *National Strike Looms.* He couldn't make any sense of that, either.

With a mental shrug he turned his attention to a high-spirited bunch of sailors in their taut, dark-blue uniforms, spilling out of the Buffet Room. He felt himself grinning as they good-naturedly jostled one another, their laughter infectious. Suddenly, though, their mood changed and they straightened, saluting, as a khaki-clad army officer with glossy knee-boots, swagger-cane rigid under his arm, strode by with a disapproving frown. As, subdued, they moved away, their bell-bottom trousers flapping in solitary defiance, Peter's mood, too, had changed, and dispirited once more he watched instead the stiff figure of the officer march away again into the crowd. For Peter this was familiar ground.

Slackly he trailed further along the platform to examine a trolley piled high with cases and trunks also waiting for the arrival of the train. One of the stout-looking trunks was extravagantly labelled, many of the labels showing signs of wear and tear: tattered, stained and distinguished, they proudly bore the names of exotic-sounding destinations. *Cape Town*, declared one; and *Buenos Aires* another; *Bombay* and *New York*. He looked for 'Rhyl' and was vaguely disappointed not to find it. One of the labels said, *Hold – Not Wanted On Board*; and he formed a mental picture of the trunk left in isolation on the quayside as the ship sailed away. He wondered if their own trunks might also be on the trolley, until he remembered his mother telling him that they would be going 'in advance'.

Absorbed as he was, he only gradually became aware of being watched. Looking up, he saw a little girl, aged about five or six, standing a few yards away watching him intently. Surprisingly, in view of the warmth of the day, she was dressed in a thick tweed coat below which her two sturdy legs were encased in leggings of a similar material with buttons all the way up the sides. Not surprisingly, her face was flushed to the colour of a ripe tomato, and to his unsympathetic eye looked not unlike one. Dressed as she was for cold conditions, he began to wonder whether she – or at least her parents – knew something about The North that he and his mother didn't, and his misgivings returned. This mixture of disdain and dismay must have revealed itself in his features, for the little girl abruptly stuck her tongue out at him. He stuck out his own tongue in reply, and made himself go cross-eyed for good measure – and was overcome with a mixture of gratification and dismay when this made her burst into tears.

There was no time to dwell on it, however, as from a distance, above the general hubbub, he heard his mother calling his name. The mixture of anger and anxiety in her voice produced in him a twinge of guilt as he realised he wasn't sure how far he had wandered, nor of her whereabouts in the now considerable throng – the guilt changing to alarm when he became aware at that moment of a train, presumably the one they were to go on, noisily drawing up alongside the platform. It was with something approaching relief therefore that at that moment he was grasped fiercely by the upper arm, and looking up found himself staring into the pop-eyed features of Uncle Max.

'So there you are, boy!' The exclamation, expressed with some venom, clearly proclaimed annoyance rather than relief; so it was without protest that he allowed himself to be dragged roughly through the crowd back to his mother's side.

Events after that moved quickly, their porter appearing out of nowhere (having mysteriously threaded his way through the crowd with their luggage on his trolley) to lead them like a mother hen onto the train and along the corridor to find a compartment with two available window-seats. Moments later he returned with their three cases, which he stowed on the rack above their heads. Then, before disappearing with his gratefully acknowledged tip, he lowered the window for them so that they could talk to Uncle Max and Aunt Sheila, who had manoeuvred their way along the platform and were standing fussily outside their compartment. As he and his mother leaned out, Max reached up to grasp Peter's arm once more, his grip fierce enough to make Peter wince. 'Look after your mother, boy,' he said with intensity, adding, 'and always be proud of your father and of the name Waring. He's been a brave man!'

Embarrassed, and not knowing how to take that, Peter glanced up at his mother, but could read nothing in her expression. Pale and tense, lips compressed, she stared into the distance. Max, noting this, now became yet more flustered. Stumbling over his words, he said, 'Keep in touch, won't you, Marjory. And I'll continue to do what I can with those fellows at the Prudential.'

She nodded gratefully, and was about to say something when, with an abruptness which startled them all, a tinny voice blared out above the general clatter. Seeming to be all around, echoing from the cathedral-like roof, it was almost unintelligible, and Peter could make out merely bits of it: '*The train now standing...the nine-fifteen for Glasgow Central, calling at...Crewe, Warrington... Oxenholme...Penrith and Carlisle. Passengers for Windermere*

13

change at...holme...' Strangely, he found that this fragmented catalogue instilled even greater excitement in him; it would imprint itself on his memory, for years to come, as an evocation of that day.

'Goodness!' said Max, 'that's new! Can't see it catching on, though. Couldn't understand a word of it.'

After that there seemed to be nothing to say. For quite some time they stood gazing around in uncomfortable silence – until, to everyone's scarcely concealed relief, without warning the train began to move, leaving time only for hurried goodbyes. Leaning out, he and his mother waved until Max and Sheila had disappeared from view, then sank back in their seats.

Whilst they'd been standing with their backs to the compartment, three other people had taken seats; and as the train picked up speed, acrid steam and smoke drifting in through the open window, a man got up and with muttered apologies made to close it.

'I'll do that,' said Peter, hurriedly springing to his feet. It must have sounded rude, for his mother frowned at him, but the man merely politely inclined his head, nevertheless hovering in case help should be needed. Indeed, Peter knew that he might have difficulties, having unsuccessfully attempted to do it on the one previous occasion when they'd travelled by train, on their trip down to Brighton for his birthday last year. But that hefty leather strap hanging from the bottom of the window had a primitive appeal, and as he struggled to haul it upwards he could pretend that he was hauling on a flapping mainsail in the teeth of a gale, the only man aboard able to save the ship. Gritting his teeth, he did finally manage to get the heavy pane to the top and secure it by forcing the top hole of the strap onto the stout brass stud on the lower edge of the frame.

'Well done, boy!' said the man – and Peter felt as if he really had saved the ship.

After that, for a while they travelled in silence, his mother sitting with her eyes closed, and the others engrossed in their newspapers. The compartment wasn't very interesting, all subdued browns, with woodwork and seats grimy and smelling of stale smoke; even the photographs in their oblong frames were yellow and faded, so that on the one opposite him he could only just make out the caption, *Central Pier, Bournemouth.* For some time he stared out of the window, fascinated by the villages and fields appearing and disappearing from view through the billowing smoke streaming past, and he became transported by the cadence of the wheels, the ring and rattle of metal on metal. He'd just read a book called *The Thirty Nine Steps* which was jolly exciting, all about spies travelling on trains and so on, and he imagined himself being on such a journey, perhaps in central Europe, secretly going to meet another agent in...in...Budapest: perhaps his father, even, also there on his own secret mission, and Peter arriving just in time to warn him of danger, his father saying, 'Well done, boy!' as together they made their escape.

Deep in his thoughts, he jumped, startled, when the sliding door of the compartment rolled back with a bump, a uniformed steward poking his head through the doorway to call: 'First bookings for lunch?' Peter looked hopefully at his mother, who was now gazing out of the window. It would have been fun to go along to the restaurant car to eat while the countryside rolled by. But he knew they could no longer afford that. They'd brought meat paste sandwiches.

He hadn't yet really come to terms with their change of circumstances. Everything had happened so quickly. One minute his father had been there and then, suddenly, he'd gone. And he missed him. In spite of everything. In spite of the fact that for as long as he could remember his father had been irritable, and sometimes violent – not seriously so, but quick with his hand. Enough to make Peter wary of him. He'd worked out that he would have been six when his father had come back from the war in 1919, but he couldn't remember anything about it. He'd learned since that his father had been badly wounded in the trenches, and also gassed, and that he'd spent a considerable time in hospital before coming home. But to Peter those events had never seemed to apply to the man in front of him, but to some other man, a stranger; and his father would never talk about it. In fact his father didn't do much talking at all, not even to his wife, and had spent long periods away from the house, or else on his own in his Study, where no one else was allowed. He remembered his mother once saying to him, 'Your father wasn't always like this, you know, Peter. It's the war – and what's happened since.' That had made him feel better for a while, allowed him to believe that his father might again become 'what he had once been'. But it had never happened.

There had been good times, such as the cricket matches, and the occasional treat, as when they had that outing to the seaside. But little warmth. He hadn't been allowed out on his own, almost as if his father was afraid for him; but nor had he been permitted to invite friends home, with the consequence that he'd never had any real friends like other boys had. He'd learned to become his own companion. Sometimes he'd wished passionately that he'd had a brother, or even a sister; but, then, from what he'd seen of some of the other chaps who had brothers they seemed to spend all their time fighting.

Perhaps things would be better when he went away to school at the end of the summer; although he was also a bit nervous about that. It was his father's old school, and the way that he had talked about it, on occasions, his father had led him to believe that in his day he'd been an illustrious member of the school. It would be difficult to live up to. It was funny that his father had never mentioned to him that he, Peter, would also be going to school there some day. Yet he'd left written instructions to that effect, together with something called a 'financial trust' to pay for it. His mother had made an exasperated sound when Uncle Max, in the role of family solicitor, had read that out, and Peter still wondered why. He'd tried to ask his mother about it, but it seemed that she didn't want to discuss anything to do with his father. There was a lot that he didn't understand.

'Mother, where will father have gone?' he blurted out now – then inwardly cringed as her face contorted in anger and embarrassment.

'Really, Peter, not here!' she hissed, glancing hurriedly at the other passengers. 'Later!'

That was a word she always used when she didn't want to talk about something. He'd learned that 'later' never came.

The train slowed and drew up at a large station, not like the small stations they'd sped past so far. *Rugby* said the signs. He'd not heard of a place named after a game, before. Some people got off, but more got on, and their compartment became full. Everyone ignored each other and sat in silence. Grown-ups were funny: if it had been a load of boys they would all have been chattering away by now. It was all very boring. He wished he'd brought his book as his mother had suggested, but he had thought it would all be a lot more exciting than this. Perhaps he could go exploring along the train, but there were people now standing in the corridor outside their compartment, and he was certain his mother wouldn't let him go.

With a jerk the train set off again. As they drew slowly out of the station they passed a big round clock suspended from the platform canopy. Half past eleven. His mother had said they would get there 'about teatime'. He inwardly groaned. It was hours yet. He wondered what it was going to be like. His mother had described it as 'wonderful', with lakes and mountains 'and so on'; but she'd grown up there, so she *would* think that. He could only vaguely remember his Uncle John and Aunt Mabel, from when they'd come up to London to visit, when he was eight or nine. For some reason they'd never come again after that. Perhaps because his father had said he didn't like them. Peter could recall the terrible rows between his mother and father afterwards, before their relationship had relapsed into the distant silence which characterised it most of the time. At least they were a proper uncle and aunt, Mabel being his mother's elder sister. And they had a daughter, his cousin Jordan, who was two years older than him; but, in spite of her interesting name, from the little he could remember of her she'd been just as snooty and boring as all the other girls he'd ever come across. He couldn't imagine what it was going to be like living with them. His mother had said that they had 'a nice big house, with plenty of room for all of us, and you'll still have your own bedroom of course'. Still, it wouldn't be like being in one's own home, just staying with someone like that, even if they were his uncle and aunt. Although the more he thought about it the more he thought he could remember his Uncle John being quite nice: a tall, spare man with a rather austere manner but a twinkle in his eye and a good sense of fun. He was a doctor, a general practitioner in the town, with his surgery attached to the house, his mother had said, which might be quite interesting. Perhaps it wouldn't be so bad after all, even if it was a lot duller than London – as his school chums had been at pains to point out when he'd told them. Anyway, he'd be away at school much of the time, so it wouldn't matter.

But that thought did nothing to cheer him up.

The remainder of the journey, however, passed quickly enough in spite of his doubts. They passed canals with locks and colourful long narrow boats, villages and farms, and fields which no longer had green blankets of corn but instead contained cows and sometimes horses, and progressively more and more sheep, all of which at least moved about and therefore for a while were marginally more interesting. But slowly, as they progressed north, the skies clouded and became sullenly grey, the flat land gave way to more hilly terrain and the hedgerows to dull higgledy-piggledy stone walls undulating their way across the slopes; until, by the time they drew into the place called Penrith, where they were to change trains ('for just a short journey now') the countryside in the dwindling afternoon light had become harsher and altogether more forbidding, and the dark clouds had started to deliver cold grey rain. His worst fears were confirmed. A simmering anger within now boiled to a fury, that his father, selfishly following his own path, had reduced them to this. He felt he wanted to cry. He wasn't going to like Cumberland.

CHAPTER TWO

Munro glances at his wristwatch, a gesture of haste rather than a need to know the time. 'Well, come on, I'll introduce you in there, if we can make ourselves heard! – and if you can bear it! Then I must rush off, I'm afraid; something's come up. I'll see you again tomorrow however. Anyway, best of luck.'

He leads the way towards the door behind which the tumult seems louder than ever. Peter's mouth is dry, so that he's afraid he might not be able to speak, especially in that din. He's always hated meeting strangers in any number. And parties. Never quite been able to shake off that overwhelming feeling of shyness and inferiority in those circumstances, always needed time to quietly assert himself and let people get to know him. Too self-conscious by far. Not competitive enough, he knows. He wonders what Munro meant just now by '…if you can bear it' and '…best of luck'. Can he remember those things about Peter, from school, the things he would prefer to forget?

And now this shock about Beal. That's really taken the ground from under his feet. He has to dig down to remind himself that he's a doctor, now – the Station doctor – with the elevated rank of Flight Lieutenant; that he has his own set of achievements behind him. Even so…he knows what this lot are going to be like: 1st XV types to a man, who, having mastered the difficult task of flying planes would now be facing up to the enemy with the same sort of panache.

But now Munro is ushering him into the room, and the sound buffets and blares like an express train. It takes him a moment to sort out the scene before him.

It's a large room, with blackout-curtained windows at one end, and a basic-looking bar down one side at which a white-jacketed steward is calmly lining up tankards of frothy beer. The steward looks at him cursorily, then continues with his task. The rest of the room looks as though a bomb has hit it. A number of chairs – some Lloyd Loom wickerwork, others leather – are piled up in an untidy heap at the far end, leaving the centre of the room clear. Clear, that is, apart from a chaotic scrum of bodies and chair cushions heaving and shifting around the floor as if it were a single entity with a life of its own. Arms and legs clothed in air-force blue stick out in all directions as do several heads which cannot be clearly associated with any particular body parts. Apart from streams of recognisable oaths, the cacophony of sounds coming from this mass of quasi-humanity defies interpretation.

As Peter stands beside Munro, stunned by the unexpected confusion and violence of it all, a section of the mass abruptly peels apart to reveal three individuals sprawled on top of one another.

'Angel!' yells Munro, just about making himself heard above the din.

One of the individuals looks up, then, as Munro beckons him, heaves himself to his feet and, staggering a little, comes forward. Of stocky build and medium height, surprisingly he looks much older than to be expected, his short-cut hair and thin moustache clearly showing signs of grey. His partly undone tie is twisted around towards one ear, his tunic jacket is hanging off one shoulder, there is a red, puffy swelling beneath his right eye which looks as if it will be a real shiner by the morning, and his mouth is spread in a cheerful grin.

'Sorry to spoil your fun, Arthur,' shouts Munro, his mouth close to the other's ear, 'but this is Doc Waring. Just arrived.' He turns to Peter. 'Arthur and you will be bunking together. Now, I must fly – if you'll forgive the pun – having satisfied myself that your two bodies and souls are both once more being catered for! See you on the morn.' And with a wave of his hand he heads for the door.

Struggling with a feeling of having once more been abruptly abandoned in foreign country, Peter searches with barely contained desperation to see whether this man now facing him is one in whom he can find friendship. And is reassured by what he sees. There is at once a ready acceptance in the man's eyes. This is a man he senses will take him under his wing, show him the ropes, put into practice those familiar metaphors, those clichés which underline the common need, in man, for patronage. For a moment he's taken back to that summer of '26, and his new life, when he was taken into the bosom of 'the gang', to become a member, briefly, of what Uncle John later came to christen 'The Famous Four'; and memories come cascading back of all that came before and all that followed.

* * *

The house would live with him, become a part of him, for the rest of his life. A large Georgian house of two storeys in its own grounds at the edge of the town, it immediately captivated him. Tall, rectangular, unfussy, its rendered walls painted a warm summer yellow, it faced the street benignly, its well-proportioned windows almost smiling towards the handsome gates at the end of a short drive. It actively welcomed him. It was called *The Beeches*.

Instead of a normal front door, the sort of front door that he would have expected, the gravelled drive took one to an entrance along the side; but, in Peter's eyes, no ordinary entrance. For a couple of stone steps led up to a spacious glass conservatory filled with exotic-looking plants, a jungle of green misted with the moisture of the tropics; and only when he had gained entry to this, gazing around in wonder, did the elegant front door become apparent to the side.

Once through that front door, the hallway inside proved to be equally spacious, displaying at its far end a wide stairway. This was bordered, on its right, by a smooth, broad banister which led gently upwards to a half-landing where it turned gracefully out of sight. Even from the length of the hall Peter could see that the banister was a veritable Cresta Run of polished mahogany positively begging to be slid down. Furnishings and furniture in the hallway, mostly period oak, were simple and gracious, so different from the heavy, dark Victorian pieces he'd been used to at home.

They were taken into a large drawing-room with an expanse of patterned carpet stretching almost to the walls, where it met a surround of polished boards. Arranged around the room were a number of bright chintz-covered easy chairs and settees, and other items of plain oak furniture similar to those in the hall. To one side a log fire crackled happily in a grate with a marble surround. Opposite the fireplace three tall windows, reaching almost to the floor, were flanked by cream-coloured wooden shutters folded back on themselves; shutters which, when closed and barred, would in his imagination bring a reassuring sense of security, capable of keeping out storm and foe alike. Between the windows, against the walls were hefty iron radiators also painted cream and served by equally robust pipes running the length of the skirting-boards; Peter gawped at these – he had heard of so-called central heating, but only once before had he come across it, and that had been in some public building or other. And, when his eyes lifted to the windows themselves, in spite of the gathering gloom outside he could see a garden stretching endlessly across lawns towards lofty trees. Maybe things weren't going to be so bad after all.

As though divining his thoughts, his uncle came up behind him and, laying a hand lightly on his shoulder, said, 'Do you think it's going to be all right here then, Peter?' – adding, 'We want you to make this your home too, now, you know.'

But as Peter turned, not saying anything, to look up at his uncle, he saw his mother, aunt and cousin in the background, all standing watching him, and he caught a whiff of tension in the group: his mother looked close to tears, his aunt's expression was unreadable, and his cousin was in the act of tossing her head in what seemed to be a gesture of vexation, her single, long plait bobbing in emphasis.

He didn't know what to make of it.

He tried to review in his mind the impressions he'd had when they first arrived. After they'd changed trains at Penrith the journey had been quite short – and definitely encouraging. For it had stopped raining, weak late-afternoon sunshine struggling through, and after a few miles of trundling along the centre of a broad vale the mountains they had merely glimpsed until then had moved closer, rising up as though to peer benignly down on this small expedition below. Not long after that the train had entered a much narrower, thickly wooded, valley through which a river tossed and tumbled its way, first on one side of the train and then the other, crossing and re-crossing under the girder bridges over which the train rattled and rumbled as though about to enter the water itself in its headlong rush. Then, before they'd finally drawn into the country station that was their destination, he'd had a brief sighting of a small town nestling some little way below them. And everywhere the mountains, now no longer crowding in but standing back, as it were, to cradle the town at a respectful distance.

His uncle, aunt and cousin had been there on the platform to greet them, his uncle solemnly shaking his hand, his aunt planting a kiss on his cheek, and his cousin decorously presenting her own cheek for him to hesitantly peck. As they'd waited for their cases to be unloaded from the guard's van he'd had time to study them.

His Uncle John was in fact much as he remembered him: tall, erect, spare of frame in a sober tweed three-piece suit with a heavy gold watch-chain strung across his lean midriff. His somewhat severe countenance, with closely-trimmed moustache, was however countered by that reassuringly humorous glint in his keen blue eyes, just as Peter had recalled.

His Aunt Mabel on the other hand he hadn't remembered at all. She was quite short (her husband seeming to tower over her) and on the plump side, a feature accentuated by the fact that she was dressed (like his mother) in a slightly old-fashioned costume with her skirts down to just above her ankles. Her manner was kind and solicitous, but her features a little pinched with a down-turn to her mouth as though constantly disapproving of something. He was withholding judgement on his aunt.

Not so with his cousin. He hadn't taken to her at all.

Fair and, he supposed, quite pretty, she must be fourteen or fifteen by now, and clearly thought herself almost grown-up. He didn't think so. Her attitude towards him so far had largely been one of amused condescension, but in addition she had exhibited a certain resentment, as if in some way or other he wasn't acceptable. She made him feel unwanted. He'd been confused, too, because her mother addressed her as 'Mary', and her father called her 'Jordan' – Peter had never known anyone with a name like that, the name of a country. His mother, after a moment's hesitation, also greeted her as 'Jordan'. Peter, uncertain, had merely mumbled 'Hello'.

Once their luggage had been collected by the porter and they had trooped outside, however, he had perked up. For there, standing impressively in front of the station had been a brand-new, gleaming black Morris Cowley that turned out to be his uncle's. He hadn't somehow expected this. In London his parents had never had a motor car, yet here was Uncle John in this small country town in possession of his own car. He couldn't wait to get in, to sit on those dark-green leather seats. And when his turn eventually came to do so, the cases having been fitted somehow into the rear trunk, there was plenty of room for him on the back seat, sitting between his mother and his cousin. Furthermore, when his uncle, struggling with the starting handle in front of the car, had had difficulty in getting the motor to start, it was Peter he had asked to get out to adjust the little brass lever on the steering-wheel, following his instructions, until the thing fired – leaving Peter feeling rather important that he'd played a part in enabling them all to complete the journey. Then, on the brief drive down the hill from the station into the town, they'd passed, in succession, parks protected by iron railings and ornate gates, a cricket ground sporting a white pavilion, with a river running by, and tennis courts and gardens; while in the town itself they'd passed shops and hotels – and a Picture House. He wasn't sure what he'd expected of the town – perhaps, vaguely, a village-sort-of-place with one shop and a pub – but certainly nothing like this; and definitely not a cinema!

Then, in the car, bolstered by his renewed enthusiasm for things, he had turned to his cousin and asked, 'Why are you called Jordan?'

'Because that's my name, silly!' she'd replied, looking down her nose at him.

'But Aunt Mabel calls you Mary.'

'That's my first name. My middle name's Jordan.'

'So why doesn't everyone call you by your first name?'

'Because I think *Mary* is boring!'

His aunt, in the front, had sniffed irritably at that; whereupon his cousin had added stubbornly, 'It's only Mummy who insists on using my first name.'

'But Jordan is the name of a country', he'd persisted.

'So? What's wrong with that?' she'd snapped in annoyance. 'One doesn't have to have boring names like everyone else, names like…like *Peter*!'

At this point his uncle, from the driving seat, had intervened.

'Your aunt and I spent our honeymoon in Egypt and the Middle East, Peter, in 1910, and…and, well, it began there. I mean, that's where we…I…came up with the name.'

His cousin had then said, 'Actually, I believe, it was a place called *Petra*.' Giggling, she'd added, 'But I think they thought that would make me sound too much like a dog! Anyway, you're really just an old romantic, aren't you, Daddy.' It had been said laughingly, but there was a bite to it – and, he fancied, a chill in the silence which followed.

It was beyond him.

So now, in the drawing-room of this unexpectedly pleasant house, he didn't really know what to make of it all. And while he was struggling to get his thoughts into order his expectations took another knock, for there came a tap at the drawing-room door and a rosy-cheeked, middle-aged woman in a white overall-dress and pinafore entered with a tray of tea and cakes and, with a nod in the general direction of everyone in the room, placed it on a table in the centre of the room.

'Marjory,' said Aunt Mabel to her sister, 'this is Jessica, our cook. Needless to say we'd be lost without her.'

'Cook' (the name by which, it after appeared, she was usually known) bobbed a half-curtsy to his mother, then turned to face Peter and, with her apple-cheeks dimpled in a smile, said, 'And welcome to thee, Master Peter. I 'ope you'll be reet 'appy 'ere.'

It was a simple gesture that made him feel important. He was a little surprised to find a servant in the house (although he knew, of course, that lots of people had them), and certainly had been unprepared for her paying him any attention. But at that moment he became her lifelong friend.

After tea, having been taken around the rest of the downstairs of the house, they were shown to their rooms. Upstairs, the main landing was even bigger than the downstairs hall, with half a dozen doors leading off it, including that to a large bathroom at the far end. He was delighted to find that his own bedroom overlooked a good part of the garden, which seemed as though it might be considerable, and that in every respect the room exceeded his hopes and expectations. Their trunks had arrived and were waiting in their rooms for them, so that by the time he'd helped to do some of the unpacking, and found places for his own things, it was time for dinner.

He should have been excited at being able to sit at dinner with the adults ('I think tonight of all nights, Marjory, Peter might be allowed to stay up, don't you?' his uncle had said); but the truth was that after the events of the day he was more tired than he would have admitted – so he listened with little interest to the desultory conversation of the grown-ups. His cousin also remained mostly silent throughout the meal, but once or twice he looked up to find her studying him thoughtfully, only for her to turn away when he met her gaze.

There were two other incidents, as well, to once again jar his composure that first evening. With little appetite for the meal, towards the end of the main course he had left part of his vegetables on the side of his plate, which prompted his aunt to say, with some asperity, 'Are you not going to eat your cabbage, Peter? It is home-grown, you know.'

When, reddening, he shook his head, she turned to his mother. 'Perhaps it's as well that you'll now have us to help with his upbringing, Marjory. With Charles gone the situation has clearly got out of hand.'

'Mabel.' The single word, uttered quietly by his uncle, stopped her in her tracks with her mouth already open to say more. She shot her husband an angry glance, her lips compressed into a thin line, but remained silent. Peter's mother, biting her own lip, fumbled for a handkerchief; and Peter, upset at being the cause of this fuss, was overcome by confusion. He caught his cousin's eye, and became even more disturbed on seeing a glint of triumph there.

He felt a bit better though when his uncle went on to say lightly, 'I've always maintained that cabbage is not much more than wind and water, anyway. I don't think Peter is missing anything there!' Then he held up his hand in mock surrender as his wife was about to speak again. 'Yes, I know,

Mabel – you think it an important source of iron. I suspect he would have to consume a whole field of the things to obtain his annual requirements. He certainly wouldn't be fit to live with then!'

Across the table Jordan exploded into laughter, quickly stifled on receiving a glare from her mother and a raised eyebrow from her father; and this time, when Peter found her looking across the table at him, he thought he detected a gleam of empathy in her eyes.

Perhaps there was more to her than he'd supposed.

Yet when Uncle John, clearly striving to lighten the atmosphere, conversationally said to Peter's mother, 'You probably got here just in time, Marjory, for it looks to me as if there's definitely going to be a general strike' – and Peter then blurted out, 'Does that mean there's going to be another war, sir?' – there was another loud guffaw from his cousin which made him curl with embarrassment. Further disconcerted by seeing a frown of irritation cross his uncle's face as he considered Peter's question, he was relieved therefore when the reply came in gentle tone. 'No, of course not, Peter. It just means that a lot of people are going to stop working for a while – and cause a whole heap of trouble in the process. But don't call me 'Sir'; it makes me feel as though I'm back in the army again. 'Uncle John' will do nicely.'

Peter, filled with sudden excitement at his reference to the army, asked, 'Were you in the war, too? Were you an officer in the trenches, like my father? Did you see him there? He was a hero, you know'.

'Whoa, one question at a time, young fella. Yes, I was an officer in the war, but, unlike your father, not in the trenches. I was there as a doctor, you see. Picking up the pieces. And, yes, your father was a hero. He still is. They all were. And, no – going back to your original question – there isn't going to be another war. We've all learned our lesson, this time.'

Throughout this reply, Peter had noticed that his mother had held her clenched hand to her mouth, as though the exchange had upset her in some way. He was aware, too, that Jordan was watching both of them with unconcealed interest. And he began to feel ashamed. It was the first time, he realised, that he'd actually thought of his father as a hero – and indistinctly he recognised therefore that there had been something hypocritical in his expressing that sentiment at this particular moment. Perhaps that was what had upset his mother?

He lapsed into silence after that, preoccupied with his thoughts, responding listlessly whenever his uncle tried to draw him out. Once again he was unsure of himself; and when, later, he lay in the dark in his strange bed in his unfamiliar bedroom, in that condition mid-way between wakefulness and sleep, he pretended to be Richard Hannay from *The Thirty-nine Steps* – then *became* Richard Hannay, alone on a train, stalked by foreign spies, not knowing who they were or where.

And sometime during the night the dream that sooner or later always returned came to haunt him again: somewhere up in the corner of the room, in a hidden cupboard, loomed that featureless presence, so menacingly dark that he tried to open his mouth to scream – only to find that yet again his mouth was wedged by a thing that had no substance, so that he couldn't even cry out.

* * *

The hubbub in the middle of the room has risen to a crescendo again, making conversation impossible for the moment but giving Peter further opportunity to surreptitiously study the other man, this 'Angel', otherwise known as Arthur. His initial impression of his age is confirmed: he judges him to be in his mid-forties at least. He, like Munro, wears the rank of Squadron Leader and displays wings at his left breast. Peter can't work it out. He looks a bit too old to be actively flying, yet is not as senior in rank as might be expected. And didn't David Munro say that he, Peter, would be sharing a room with the man? That surely must be unusual, to be sharing with someone a rank above him? And what was that crack of Munro's about '…body and soul now being catered for'?

But through the din the man is now trying to say something to him, and he looks up, realising that he must have been staring at the other's wings sewn above his left breast pocket: there is something not quite right about them, sort of…old fashioned.

'Sorry,' he says to him in a voice loud enough to overcome the noise, 'I didn't catch what you said.'

'I'm Arthur Stanton.' The man shouts the re-introduction into Peter's ear. At the same time he takes Peter's elbow and steers him towards the bar, adding, 'Welcome to Marwell! Let's go over to where it may be a mite quieter. You must be ready for a pint anyway. I know I certainly am.' His voice is friendly, with a faint Scottish brogue. As Stanton reaches for a beer from the bar top and hands it to him, Peter fumbles for change in his trouser pocket, thinking that he should offer to pay for both of them.

'No, no,' says Stanton, noting the movement, 'these'll go on my tab. Your mess bill can't be set up until tomorrow.'

Flustered, Peter mumbles his thanks. The man must think him really green, not appearing to know that no cash is used in the Mess.

But there is something else niggling at Peter, something that he feels he should understand, that fits in, but that he can't quite get sight of.

Then, 'Why did David Munro address you as 'Angel'?' he asks.

There is amusement in Stanton's grey eyes. 'What else would you call a flying vicar!' he replies; then adds, 'Although some would say that it's because my feet, and head, are so far above the ground!…You know,' he adds, noting Peter's blank expression, 'angel – one thousand feet?'

Realisation strikes. The small, metal crucifix at the other's right breast, in a similar position to his own medical serpent-and-staff-of-Aesculapius emblem, seems now to leap out at him. At once everything falls into place. Apart from the presence of the wings, that is.

'You're the padre!' he blurts, then feels foolish yet again.

25

Stanton laughs out loud. 'Heavens, did David not tell you! No wonder you're looking perplexed. No doubt thinking: What's this old codger doing as a bomber pilot! Actually, the wings are merely a concession to history, I'm afraid. I was a pilot in the R.F.C., in the Great War – even the term sounds like ancient history, now. I suppose we'll have to start calling it the First Great War.'

'Oh.' For the moment he can't quite take in the fact that this man of the church had been flying in the war, can't think what else to say. He recovers, to say the first thing that comes into his head. 'But surely this one's not going to be anything like the last!'

' "Over by Christmas" you mean? Like they said last time? Well, one Christmas has passed, and I fear there'll be a few more before we can say it's over. I know not much has happened yet, but give it time! Just like the last occasion, this is going to be a long haul. I can feel it in my bones.'

'But now that the Germans can see that we and the French mean business, and with the Navy blockading their supplies, they're bound to see sense and come to some sort of accommodation, are they not?'

'Like some of the papers would have us believe, you mean?' says Stanton brusquely. 'Not with that bugger Hitler in power, they're not. There's a megalomaniac if ever I saw one. You mark my words, this war's come to stay! We'll be damned lucky if they're not ruling the roost over us by next Christmas. Especially with Chamberlain and Halifax in power!

'Anyway, enough of that! Let's go and get you settled into your quarters. Most of this lot'll not be fit to carry on any sensible conversation, anyway, I can tell you. You can meet them tomorrow when you're treating their hangovers!'

'Does it often get like this?'

'Only when they're not on standby,' says Stanton with a grin. 'No, seriously, mess rugby is quite a popular pastime when the boys are a bit bored and they haven't the opportunity for the real thing. It allows them to let off steam. Incidentally, don't ask me the rules, because I haven't come across any yet! But this is a special occasion. The C.O.'s been very popular. We'll all miss him.'

'Because he turns a blind eye to this sort of thing?' says Peter, trying to be flippant.

'Turns a blind eye? He's in that scrum, somewhere! Anyway, come on! If he emerges, we'll be stuck; and I, for one, am buggered and ready for an early night. Let's go and find a bit of peace and quiet.'

* * *

He awakened to bright sunlight thrusting its way through the curtains, accompanied by a symphony of sound from outside: a raucous chorus of complaint and mockery, harsh and strident. Clearly the noise of birds, but unlike any he'd heard before. He hastened to the windows to let in the morning. The garden, of which he'd had only impressions the day before, stretched before him, bathed in sunshine; and at the far end, circling above the tall trees that had so interested him the previous evening, a flock of large birds, black against the morning light, declaimed their protests, wheeling and soaring effortlessly, with only an occasional flap of their broad, coarse-feathered wings. That was the sound which had disturbed him: a plaintive sound, yet with notes of exuberance, of delight with the day. It struck a chord with him; and for the rest of his days he would associate it with a certain morning in spring.

As he stood there, wrapped in the scene, there came a confident tap on his bedroom door. He turned, to find Cook already halfway into the room, bearing a tray, which she deposited on his bedside table.

'Aye, you are up, then, Master Peter,' she said. 'We were beginning to think you would sleep forever. I've brought you some breakfast before it's all stone cold.'

'Thank you, Cook,' he said, eyeing with interest the porridge and bacon and egg set before him. But first he had to satisfy his curiosity. 'What are those birds making that sound out there?'

She glanced only briefly in the direction of the window. 'Oh, them rooks! Noisy blighters they are, an' all, 'specially at this time of year. It'll be nobbut somethin'n nothin'. If I 'ad my way I'd do away wi' em!' And with that she was gone.

Slightly taken aback by her irreverent attitude, so different to his own, he watched the rooks for a few seconds more before turning to do justice to his breakfast.

Arriving downstairs a short time later, he found his mother sitting reading in the drawing room. She greeted him warmly, as if particularly glad to see him, but otherwise was even more subdued than she had been the previous evening. From her he learned that his aunt was busy somewhere, his uncle was in surgery, and his cousin had gone off to play tennis with some friends. Somehow deflated by all this, as though deep-down he'd expected them all to be there waiting for him, he brightened scarcely at all at the news that in a short while he would be expected to accompany his mother and aunt 'into town' – generally boring, but his natural curiosity meant that he could look forward at least to seeing what the place was like.

It was somewhat disconsolately however that he went into the garden to explore, only to find that his vague misgivings about that also were justified. Truth to tell, he was downright disappointed, after the lift in his expectations of the previous evening. Certainly the lawn was large, entirely adequate for football or cricket – but limited by the presence of flowerbeds. He could already hear the catalogue of restrictions and recriminations. Anyway, who would he play with? His uncle was about the only candidate, and he seemed to be constantly busy, not only through the week but, it seemed, at most weekends as well. He, Peter, certainly wasn't going to become a doctor when he grew up!

None of it was what he'd hoped for, at all. All right, he hadn't had the chance of friends, very much, at home; but at least he'd had his chums at school during the week. He'd begun to persuade himself that things would be happier here, at last, with his mother's sister and family. Not having any brothers or sisters of his own, he'd always imagined that it would be wonderful to have the close, shared interests of a wider family. Instead of which he could see that his mother and her sister were already circling each other warily, without much evidence of warmth between them, almost as if they resented each other for some reason; and his uncle was having to keep the peace between them. With his father gone Peter had thought that all those months and years of angry quarrels would be behind them, but it seemed that it wasn't to be. Perhaps most families quarrelled all the time? He hadn't thought of that. And as for his cousin Jordan, he didn't fancy her as a surrogate sister. Who else was there that he could call 'family'? He'd got a grandfather living somewhere here in Cumberland, his mother's dad, whom he heard from once a year at Christmas, but whom he didn't remember ever having met (although he apparently had done, when he was smaller). And his mother had another, younger, sister, his Aunt Anne, who lived somewhere in Africa (which had always captured his imagination), but whom he'd never met. And that was it. Not much to call his own. He missed his dad. In spite of everything, he missed his dad.

Now, abruptly weighed down by the misery of it all, he found himself at the bottom of the garden, where there was a mass of green shrubbery and a couple of large beech trees standing against the high boundary wall. On the other side of the wall were more tall trees and beyond them, seen indistinctly through the foliage, the outlines of other houses. And beyond those, above the roof-tops, all about, stood the high mountains, circled around like friendly sentinels watching over the small community below.

Listlessly he began to explore the shrubbery for possibilities of making a den.

'Hello. Who are you?'

The voice came from somewhere overhead.

Looking up he saw, dangling through the leaves of the nearest tree, a grubby pair of gym shoes which led to an equally grubby pair of legs. The next moment, after seconds of furious agitation of branches, the owner of the legs appeared, crouching on a bough a few feet above his head – a boy about his own age, peering at him through the foliage.

The question was repeated. 'Who are you?'

Uncertain how to answer a question like that, he continued to hesitate. After all, who was he? But the boy's gaze, though disconcertingly steady and direct, was friendly enough, as was the tone of voice; so he said, 'I'm Peter. Peter Waring.'

'Hello again. I'm Jamie. Are you staying here at The Beeches?'

'Yes. That is, I've come here to live.'

'To live? Permanently?' The boy's voice quickened with interest. 'Are you a relative of the doctor's?' Then a note of concern. 'I say, you're not an orphan, are you?'

'No. My mother's come here to live, as well. Doctor Webster's my uncle.'

Having recovered his composure Peter was now able to study the boy in more detail. He had a rather determined-looking sort of face, but it was open and amiable. He had dark hair, rather long, curling down onto his collar, and brownish sort of eyes. He wore cotton shorts and a shirt that had clearly been mended on one shoulder. He looked lithe and athletic. Peter decided, all-in-all, that he was all right.

'Your father's not here then?' Jamie went on. 'What about brothers and sisters?'

'No. I haven't any.' All at once feeling deprived, there was a note of defiance in his voice. But when Jamie said in a matter-of-fact manner, 'Same as me, then, I haven't any brothers or sisters, either,' he felt a bit better.

He went on, obscurely, 'I have a cousin, though. Jordan,' – he still found himself hesitating over the silly name. 'But she's a lot older – and I don't think she likes me very much.'

'Jordan? Oh, I know Jordan. We used to play together. She's all right. And she's not much older. She just acts grown-up. It'll be better when she gets to know you, you'll see. She's very pretty, though, don't you think?'

Peter looked at him in surprise. Whilst he had to admit that she probably was quite pretty, he hadn't attached any importance to it. All girls were soppy, at whatever age, and fairly useless. And whilst he had heard older boys referring to how a girl looked, it was usually along the lines of '*Cor, she's a cracker!*' This boy, on the other hand, had said it in a detached sort of a way.

When Peter made no response, the boy laughed. 'I bet you're not the least bit interested in that, though. Anyway, you're quite nice-looking yourself.' And, as Peter stared at him in even more astonishment, Jamie went on, unconcerned, 'My father was killed in the war. I don't remember him. Is that what happened to your dad?'

'No…. No.' He didn't quite know what to say to that. 'He's…just away.'

'Away? Away where?'

How to answer that? Where was he?

'I don't know.'

There was a further pause whilst Jamie digested that; then, 'You mean he's run off? Left you and your mum?'

The tone was more sympathetic than inquisitive, which added to Peter's distress. 'No!' he said vehemently, close to tears. 'No. He made up his mind. 'It's secret, really. He's a sort of…sort of spy. He can't tell us where he is.'

'Gosh!' Jamie's eyes widened in astonishment. He was clearly impressed. 'How exciting. You do see him from time to time, though? Or get letters from him?'

'No.' That didn't sound quite right. 'Well, now and again. But he's a secret agent, you see, working for the government, so he has to be very careful. And he's away for long periods at a time. We had a letter some time ago from…from Budapest. But you mustn't tell anyone about any of this. You have to keep it a secret.'

'Gosh!' Jamie exclaimed again. 'No, I won't. Tell anyone, I mean.' Then, clearly struck by a new idea, 'I expect you'll be coming to my school. How old are you?'

'I'm twelve. But I'll be thirteen in November. How old are you?'

'I'm thirteen. And I'll be fourteen in August.' It was said simply, without airs. Then he went on, 'Will you be starting on Monday?'

Suddenly faced with the issue, Peter felt apprehensive. He realised he would have liked to be going to school here, to the same school as Jamie, rather than away.

'No,' he said slowly. 'I won't be going to school here. I'm to go to my father's old school. Bardolph's. It's a boarding school. In Scotland. It's all been arranged.' Then he added, 'But not until September.'

'Golly!' Jamie was impressed again. 'Won't you be going to school at all until September? That's a whole term and a half! And then going to a boarding school. I've heard of Bardolph's. It's a public school, isn't it? Lucky you!'

Peter didn't feel so lucky. On the other hand, it had clearly earned him considerable respect from Jamie.

But then his new-found confidence was dashed again, for Jamie, abruptly changing the subject, said, 'I think there's a woodpecker's nest near the top of this tree. Come on. I'm just going up to see if there are any eggs. We can go together.'

Peter looked up in alarm. The tree seemed to go on for ever. From where he was standing he couldn't even see the top. There was no way he could go up there. The very thought made him tremble.

'No. No, I can't,' he said desperately. 'I'm…I'm in my best clothes. We've to go into the town shortly. And anyway, I've only got ordinary shoes on.' Elaborately he proffered one of his feet with a leather-soled shoe for inspection.

Jamie looked at him thoughtfully for a few seconds, then said, 'No, you're quite right, it's no good in those.' There was just a hint of disappointment. 'We'll do it another time. I say, though, would you like to join my gang?' There was a muted surge of enthusiasm in his voice.

'Your gang?'

'Yes. Well, it's not much of a gang, really. There's only three of us. Me, George and Bill. You'd make it four.'

'Well, yes. Thanks,' Peter replied slowly. Privately, he wasn't too sure. Jamie clearly was a bold spirit and it sounded as if the others might be the same. As well as climbing trees they probably did all sorts of things that he wasn't used to doing. He wasn't certain that he could manage that. 'Yes, all right.'

'Good, that's settled then. We'll call for you. Tomorrow. After lunch. Say two-thirty?'

'Oh. I'm not…I'm not sure I'll be allowed to play out on a Sunday.'

There was a trilling laugh from Jamie. 'Caterwauling catfish! Why ever not? If I know Doc Webster, he won't object to that! And he'll be sort of like your pa, now, for the time being, won't he.'

Peter hadn't thought of that.

At luncheon, later, absorbed in his own thoughts and doubts, he only half listened to the conversation among the adults. His cousin Jordan was still out with her friends, and he was largely ignored. At least his mother was looking more relaxed, more like her old self, and Uncle John was clearly taking pains to include her in the conversation, to make her feel a part of the family. Even Aunt Mabel appeared less stiff and formal.

Certainly the trip into town that morning had seemed to thaw relations between the two sisters, as his mother had enthused about how wonderful it was to be back again, how little change there had been in the town, and how 'much more peaceful' it was than London; and the chit-chat between them had been along the lines of 'Do you remember this, Mabel? and 'Marjory, do you remember when...', and so on. In spite of his own preoccupations the enthusiasm of their chatter had got through to him and he'd started to take note of what they were saying. He hadn't really given it any thought before, but it seemed that as girls they had lived out in the country, not very far from the town, and so had known it all their lives.

He'd been buoyed up, too, by his own delight with the place. It had been no more than five minutes' walk into the centre of town (even at the pace of his mother and aunt in their high heels and unfashionably long skirts), down a narrow street with a number of houses and shops on either side. This had then opened out into the main street, which in effect was a long, wide market square dominated in the centre by an old town hall: this a small, narrow, two-storey building with a square clock-tower.

It being Saturday there had been a market in full swing, with stalls occupying the whole of the middle of the square, and considerable bustle and hubbub from the crowds there. The stall-holders were, in his view, rather rough-looking folk in working-clothes (some wearing sackcloth aprons, with clogs on their feet), selling a variety of vegetables, cheeses and meats. One stall had fish laid out on oilcloth in glistening array, looking as though it had only just been caught. There was a great throng of customers drifting from stall to stall, stopping to peer at what was on offer, to bargain, or merely to chat with their neighbours. Their clothes appeared to be much more varied than those of the stall-holders: some down-right shabby, others self-consciously fashionable. Some of the customers, like many of the market people, spoke in dialect so broad that he couldn't understand them; a few, in contrast, revealed accents which would have been equally at home in St John's Wood. In the middle of all this stir, the town hall, its white-washed walls and lofty tower bright in the sunshine, stood impassively, a quiet focus in the midst of the tumult.

Soon bored, though, by the limited attractions of the stalls, he had wandered away from his mother and aunt out to the edge of the square, on all sides of which were a variety of shops offering goods ranging from clothes, to wools, hardware, boots and shoes, pencils and paper, and books and newspapers, along with a couple of bakeries, a butcher's, and two grocer's. As well as the shops there were a couple of hotels and not a few pubs, and at intervals, leading out of the square, a number of narrow alleyways which intrigued him. At the bottom end of the square was a huddle of hand-carts parked on their ends, their shafts jutting jauntily upwards like the masts of so many moored boats; and beyond them a couple of horses stood patiently, harnessed between the shafts of their much larger carts. He'd been surprised to find just how many more horse-drawn vehicles, and how relatively few motor cars there were, compared to London.

He'd continued his wander around the square, stopping only briefly to study the contents of some of the shop windows; until he'd come to a boot-maker's, and there he'd stayed for some time, staring in fascination at the contents of the window. For, as well as ordinary shoes and boots, there had been clogs like those he'd just seen worn by the country folk, and boots such as he hadn't known existed: boots with thick soles which curved slightly upwards towards the toe, on the under surfaces of which were numerous small, metal studs and, at their edges, sharp cleats like so many steel teeth. As well as the footwear, there had been gaiters, too, fashioned either of canvas or of shiny leather. He'd studied the clogs for some time. In some ways they were like ordinary working boots, with tough, oiled leather uppers that fastened over the ankle; but it was their wooden soles he found fascinating, for around the edges of them, underneath, were nailed strips of iron. And besides all that, in a corner of the window, were coils of new rope, and canvas knapsacks, and a collection of maps – enough to remind him, if indeed he needed reminding, that at every turn, wherever there was a gap in the rooftops, he'd seen the mountains, waiting.

'You're very quiet, Peter. Perhaps you and I will have to see what we can find to liven things up a bit, this afternoon? What say?'

Uncle John's voice brought him back to the present, to the luncheon table – and he nodded, grateful. But there was something else that he was waiting to broach when the opportunity presented.

His uncle studied him for a moment, a half-smile on his lips, and a quizzical look in his eyes; but when Peter made no other response he turned back to the ladies. Peter was still nervous of those eyes, which seemed so piercing, but he was beginning to learn that behind that stern facade was a good deal of warmth and understanding.

At that point Ethel, the maid, brought in the pudding, and this prompted his mother to say, when she'd gone, 'You're so lucky to have staff like this, Mabel.'

'Well, I don't know whether 'lucky' is quite the right word,' replied his aunt, stiffly. 'With a house this size I couldn't possibly manage without them. And with John's Practice we get a lot of messages to the door and on the phone, you know. Without a maid I'd never have any peace.'

Peter looked at her in amusement; but quickly removed the smile from his face when he saw she was serious. He'd met the maid for the first time, after they'd returned from town, not having previously realised that not only did they have a cook but a maid as well – and then he'd started to wonder when the butler was going appear!

'Cook and Ethel do only work the six days a week, you know,' his aunt went on. 'But at least they have different days off. Before the war the servants lived in, of course, so it was easier to get good staff.' She lowered her voice. 'Jessica is very good, needless to say, but the girl's a bit wanting.'

'And what about the garden?' his mother asked. 'I presume you must have some help there?'

It was Uncle John who answered. 'Yes, I have a chap who comes four days a week, Marjory. Ex-army, and elderly, but a damned good worker. Helps to keep the place tidy, you know, because I certainly don't seem to have the time.' He cleared his throat in an apologetic way.

'Are you...we...likely to be affected much by this general strike if it occurs next week, John?' his mother asked.

'Oh, hardly, Marjory. Probably not at all. But I agree, it's beginning to look as though it'll definitely take place. It can hardly not do, now – the confrontation with the government has reached such a state. In a small town such as this I imagine there'll be very little impact, but for much of the country it could be pretty devastating, I imagine. No trains of course, nor buses, and maybe the post will be affected; but most essential supplies here are local and will no doubt continue much as usual. Could be a different story in major towns and cities. The government do seem to be getting organised, however. It'll be interesting, though, to see trams and buses driven by bank managers, and the post being delivered by stockbrokers! But I would expect it to be all over within a week or two, anyway. Most Britons are too sensible to allow their lives to be disrupted for too long by something like this.' He gave a laugh. 'Thank God! But I do feel sorry for the miners. They've had a rough deal for far too long. Perhaps now someone will take some notice of them.'

The ensuing pause for reflection gave Peter his chance.

'I made a new friend today,' he said to his mother.

'Did you, dear?' she replied absently – then looked at him more sharply. 'How did you manage to do that? Was this while we were in town?'

'No it was here. At the bottom of the garden. That is, in the trees on the other side of the wall. He's a boy about my age. Called Jamie.'

'Oh, we know Jamie,' his aunt said, 'but...'

'There are no 'buts,'' his uncle quickly intervened, 'As you say, we know Jamie. And Peter couldn't find a better friend.'

'But...' his Aunt Mabel began again.

'Mabel,' Uncle John once more interrupted, 'as you've heard me say more than once, 'but' is one of the worst words in the language. It's the 'but's which tend to inhibit the seizing of opportunities, which get in the way of living life to the full. Jamie is very sensible and will make an excellent friend for Peter. That is all we need to concern ourselves with for now.'

This was all too complex for Peter, but he had seen his mother showing increasing concern; and was becoming a little alarmed himself.

His uncle turned to his mother. 'I assure you, Marjory, we couldn't be more pleased if Jamie is going to become a friend of Peter's. We can talk more about it, later, if you like.' He turned back to Peter. 'Jamie won't lead you into doing anything silly, Peter, but I assure you you'll have a jolly exciting time!'

That was partly what was alarming Peter, but he didn't say so. Instead, he said tentatively, 'He's asked if I can play out tomorrow afternoon. May I? To join him and his gang.'

'But tomorrow's Sunday, Peter,' his mother remonstrated. 'I don't know whether... And what's this about a gang?' she appealed to her brother-in-law.

'That'll be George Tyson and Bill Jackson. Both good lads, and also both sensible. Not exactly a gang in the sense that you're thinking, Marjory. And I don't see that being Sunday is material. What better than being out and about in the fresh air? We should have finished lunch by soon after two. And we don't usually go back to church in the evening, I'm afraid.'

He turned back to Peter. 'But if you're going to be out and about with Jamie we'd better see about finding you some appropriate footwear, hadn't we? That's something we could do this afternoon, couldn't we.' He held up a hand as Peter's mother started to protest. 'No 'but's, remember, Marjory?'

And Peter, with growing excitement, put all doubts aside, in spite of the fact that his aunt was still glaring at her husband in a distinctly disapproving manner.

Uncle John really understood about things that mattered.

CHAPTER THREE

The room they are to share is simple but adequate: a couple of beds, a single wardrobe, two chairs, two chests of drawers, and a desk. Peter is content enough. The conditions are much the same as they were in school and college. He's confirmed in his first impressions of Stanton, likes what he sees, feels that in spite of the age difference they should get on well. There is, perhaps, a certain logic in their having been put together. Much as David Munro had said, albeit in jest, their tasks as non-combatants are similar: to try to maintain the physical health and morale of those doing the fighting.

He unpacks his cases, awkwardly turning aside the padre's suggestion that Burton, the batman they are to share, could be sent for to do it for him: he's still not become comfortable with the status conferred on him as an officer. Equally, but in a different vein, he hasn't been prepared for the free-and-easy behaviour in the mess and the disregard of rank that seems to be the norm. From what he's heard, it certainly isn't so in the other two services; indeed, it wasn't so in the O.T.U. where he did his basic training.

As he puts clothes and bits and pieces away, the padre sits on the bed chatting to him, and he's able to ask him about it.

'Lacking in hierarchical protocol, sort of thing?' says Stanton. 'Oh, you'll find plenty of that sort of discipline outside the Mess, believe me. But you're right. It is more free and easy, perhaps, than in the other two Services. Whether it really is peculiar to the RAF, I don't know – it certainly wasn't like that in the RFC in the last war! – but then that was more like an extension of the army, in those days. It does depend to some extent on the C.O., I suppose: some are more rigid, and sticklers for military protocol, than others. But on a bomber station like this the absence of protocol doesn't stop at the officers' mess, either, you know; and there's a good reason for that. Quite a number of pilots now are only sergeants, you see, whereas other members of the crew – for example the navigator – may be officers. But the pilot is always captain of the plane – so, in flight, the rank hierarchy is in effect reversed. A sergeant may be issuing orders to an officer, orders that have to be obeyed. You never get that in the other services – or indeed on a fighter station; although they do have sergeant pilots as well. And there's one other difference between the RAF and the other services: aircrew are heavily dependent on the efficiency of the N.C.O.s and ordinary ranks of the service crews – their very lives may depend upon it – and both crews know that. It's a great stimulus for breaking down artificial barriers, I can tell you!'

As they continue to chat, Peter learns a bit more about Arthur Stanton. It turns out that he, too, had at one time contemplated going into medicine, but the advent of the Great War had seen him volunteering for the army and fighting on the Western Front, gaining rapid promotion ('in effect stepping into dead men's shoes'), but then eventually ending up in the R.F.C. ('anything to get away from those bloody trenches; and in those days you could learn to fly the damned things in about six hours'). After the war, his steps had no longer taken him into medicine, but instead into the church. He doesn't say that this was the result of his experiences in the war, but nevertheless Peter gets the impression he had undergone some sort of spiritual catharsis because of what he'd been through. Finally, he'd compromised and rejoined what was by then the newly-fledged R.A.F. as a padre ('only to find myself, now, taking part in another bloody war!').

As their conversation continues, it's only when Stanton has twice made passing reference to 'Sylvia', that it strikes Peter that the man is married. Somehow, with the schoolboy-ish pranks displayed in the mess lounge, and the overall atmosphere of bachelorhood in the place, he hasn't thought of there being married men here.

'Yes, indeed. In fact we're coming up to our twentieth wedding anniversary. Sylvia is here with me, in a small house that we're renting in the neighbourhood – as do a number of the chaps who are married. I'm given quarters here in the mess, because naturally we're expected to 'sleep in' when the station's on ops or on standby. The rest of the time, we live at home. So, you see, you'll have this room to yourself most of the time. I'm only here this evening because of the Wingco's farewell do – in fact, I shall be heading off home very shortly: I did promise Syl that I wouldn't be late. You'll understand that most of the officers, yet, are regulars who've been in the force for some time. Once we begin to see more and more of the reservists and new volunteers appearing on the scene I've no doubt the regulations will probably change. I can't see the powers-that-be wanting wives hanging around the place. Too distracting, and all that! And anyway, as time goes on it would just become far too fraught.'

Peter is to understand only too well in the months to come what the padre means by that last comment. But as Stanton bids him goodnight and takes his leave, he's simply content that already he seems to have made a good friend.

And later, curled up in his bed, drifting off to sleep in spite of the sounds of celebration floating down the corridor, he's reminded of that other occasion when new friendships were forged.

Keeping safely away from the edge, he stared in fascination at what could have been a toy scene displayed before him. The water, hundreds of feet below, appeared as smooth and shiny as a piece of glass in which were mirrored the mountainsides, the sky, and the rich spring-green of the tree-lined shores. Dotted around on the lake were several wooded islands, seemingly so small that he felt he might lean forward to pick them up between finger and thumb. In places, moving ever so slowly on the glistening surface, were even tinier boats; but also a motor launch moving more quickly so that there trailed behind it a miniature wake. The distance was too great to be able to clearly see people, which added to the impression it gave of being merely a model in a toyshop. Although lunchtime had heralded a change in the fine weather, with cloud increasingly wiping out the blue of the sky, the sun still shone fitfully to paint vivid colour into the scene.

George and Bill were cavorting near the cliff edge, apparently heedless of the vertical drop no more than a yard or two away; but Jamie, who until now had been standing on the rim quietly absorbing the scene, had come back the few feet to join Peter. Peter himself had gone to the edge initially, when they had first arrived, astounded by the view which suddenly opened up before them, but, becoming aware of the vertical drop at his feet with diminutive trees, fields and road far below, and immediately overcome by an abrupt sense of giddiness and a powerful desire to jump, he had backed away.

Silent for the moment, he studied the other two lads whom he'd met for the first time only an hour or so earlier. At first he'd been carried along by the excitement of events. But all at once, now, he felt tongue-tied as the realisation dawned that he was after all a stranger among this tightly-knit group of lifelong friends. They not only were at home here on these mountains, and knew the area intimately, but also had different interests to his, were used to different sorts of activities, and even spoke differently. And they would doubtless have a wider circle of other friends. He was the outsider.

Bill was all right – friendly enough from the word go once Jamie had introduced Peter to him and George. Both Bill and Jamie were slightly taller than Peter, who had been used to being one of the tallest in his class at school, but then they were a year or so older. Bill was heavily built in contrast to Jamie's and Peter's relative slimness, had brown eyes, black hair and a dark complexion as though he'd spent a lot of time in the sun. Like Jamie, he had an air of casual calmness about him as though nothing would really upset him; and the semblance of a smile constantly hovered on his lips.

At least Bill spoke proper English, so that Peter was able to understand him.

George, on the other hand, was almost impossible to understand, speaking at times in what appeared to be a foreign tongue. Short and stocky, he had a mop of wiry red hair which sprouted in all directions, a mass of freckles on his face, and a constantly pugnacious attitude to the world. He and Bill would, it seemed, good-naturedly scrap on the slightest provocation, rolling about in a tangled heap on the ground entirely careless of the effect it was having on their clothes and skin – but evidently evenly matched in spite of their disparity in size. Peter nervously wondered if he too, in due course, would be expected to enter into this violent activity (although, admittedly, they never seemed to actually hurt each other). However, it was noticeable that Jamie never joined in the fray, only watched them with an air of bemused tolerance and resigned amusement. Nor did they show any inclination to involve him in this particular activity, which was reassuring for Peter. But then Jamie was clearly regarded as the leader, slipping easily into the role on almost every occasion. Peter, actually, was more disconcerted by George than by either of the other two, not only because of his rough manner, appearance and way of talking, but also because he had the distinction of wearing clogs – clogs of the kind that Peter had seen worn by the rougher sorts of country folk the previous day and had enviously gazed at in the shop window. The other two wore plimsolls and had looked with approval at Peter's, albeit with some amusement at their newness. But going along the road from *The Beeches* after the three of them had collected Peter it was George who had been able to make that satisfyingly rhythmic clatter, and George who had been able at intervals to idly swing his leg to strike sparks off the paving stones with the iron 'clinkers' on his soles. Peter had decided there and then that he must have a pair of clogs like George's – after all, hadn't Uncle John said, when he'd bought the plimsolls for him, 'These'll do very well for this dry weather, but I fancy we'll have to get you something more serviceable for the wet.'?

George's dad had a farm on the outskirts of the town, where they had gone first – to see the bull that had just arrived, George said, to 'service' the cows, whatever that meant (the others had giggled at that, and Peter had dutifully joined in, not wanting to show his ignorance by asking). He had been very impressed by the farm, however. The stone buildings, a mottled grey splashed by yellow and green lichens, had a time-worn appearance suggesting a presence of hundreds of years. The walls, constructed of slabs of rough slate laid one on top of another so that their edges, facing outwards, appeared at first not to have any mortar holding them together, although when he'd peered more closely he'd been able to see evidence of crumbly mortar deep inside the crevices. The roofs consisted of hefty stone slabs, laid on like slates but far more ponderous, those at the lower edge of the roof being the largest, then becoming progressively smaller towards the ridge. So heavy did they look it was difficult to believe that they hadn't years ago crashed down through the buildings, and indeed the central parts of one or two of the roofs did have a decided sag to them. When he'd asked about these he'd been told that Yes, they did 'settle' with time. He'd also learned, to his considerable amusement, that the roof-slabs had names – 'Dukes, Duchesses, Lords and Ladies' – according to size.

On one side of the yard was the house itself, not very big, with windows so small that they surely wouldn't be capable of letting in much light.

Contiguous with the house was what he took to be some sort of barn. On the other two sides of the yard were more outbuildings. One of these had enormous wooden doors rising the full height of the barn – doors which were impressively bleached, warped and cracked, and studded with iron bolt-heads. The other buildings were smaller, with doors which had an upper and a lower section, so that each half could be opened independently – and it was through one of these doors that George had led them.

Inside, once his eyes had become accustomed to the gloom, Peter had been able to make out a number of pens – solid-walled sections of the building, really – enclosed by stout wooden doors so high that he was only just able to peer over them. And in one of these had been the bull.

Massive and black, it had stood half-turned to face them, its small red-rimmed eyes glaring angrily, its horns tipped forwards as though set for a charge. The thick copper ring through its nose, by which it was roped to an iron bar set into the wall, had glinted equally intimidatingly, reminding them as it did that only its presence prevented this awesomely menacing beast from hurling its immense weight against the door which separated it from them. For a few minutes they'd stood quietly, speaking in whispers, while the bull restlessly shifted its bulk from side to side. Then, without warning, it had snorted loudly, and they'd all involuntarily taken a step back, a collective shudder running through them. Mustering what dignity they could, as one they had tiptoed out, ruefully looking at each other with suppressed excitement once they'd got outside. Peter had been glad to see that all three of the others, including George who might have been expected to be more nonchalant about such things, had been as chastened as he had.

It was then that George had said what sounded like 'Less gaa oop t'fell, shallus?' He was finding that some of the time he was able to understand what George was saying, but that pronouncement had had him baffled. It was only a few minutes later, after Jamie and Bill had nodded their assent, when they'd all trooped out of the yard, taking Peter's agreement for granted, made their way through a small pine wood and thence up the mountainside, that he'd understood the gist of it. The irony was that what had really roused him to indignation, when he'd first met Bill and George, was that George had said, 'Eh, thoo talks queer!' and Bill had said airily, 'Oh, Peter's from London. They all talk like that, down there. You'll get used to it.'

Their progress on the path climbing up the hillside had been varied in the way that (Peter would learn) was typical for such expeditions. Bill and George would argue and tussle, Jamie indulgently looking on but not taking part. From time to time they would all stop to look at something-or-other that had taken their interest, or to gaze back at the scenery which gradually unrolled behind them as they climbed higher; or they would hotly enter into debate on some topic or other on which they all had decided views – although Peter had contented himself, at this stage in the relationship, with simply listening to the others in these discussions. At other times they would try to outdo each other in activities such as climbing small rocky outcrops, or jumping off them, leaping over streams, or racing one another from one feature to the next. As the path had got steeper they had had one such race for a good two hundred yards uphill, in which Peter, to his great relief and satisfaction, had finished not far behind Jamie, who had been the clear winner; Bill, with his heavier build, had lagged a bit behind, with George last – although they'd all readily agreed that he had been at a disadvantage in his clogs on the dry grass. Jamie had proved to be every bit as athletic as Peter had suspected, but not only that, he had a litheness and economy of movement that made the others look clumsy, and made even Peter (who'd always prided himself on his own agility) feel positively awkward in comparison.

'Don't take too much notice of those two,' Jamie now said, interrupting his thoughts. 'It's all show, this pretence of scrapping. Kind of a habit, really, I suppose. And a reminder that they're both boys and have that as a common bond.'

Peter looked at him in surprise. What a funny thing to have said. Almost like a grown-up speaking; the sort of thing his Uncle John might have said. As though Jamie felt himself excluded from Bill and George in that respect – and (in a strangely disturbing way) instinctively lumped Peter into that exclusion.

Jamie must have misinterpreted his expression, for he went on, 'But don't worry, they won't think any the less of you if you don't join in.'

Again Peter was taken aback. What a strange boy this Jamie was turning out to be. Not like any other boys he'd known. It was as though he was identifying with all Peter's innermost thoughts and uncertainties. As though he was mothering him. Peter really didn't know how to take him. One minute he was as carefree as the other two, joining in with all their roistering, and the next he was acting as if he was ten years older, standing apart from them, as sensible and sensitive as any grown-up Peter had ever come across.

'Come on, idiots,' Jamie called out. 'It must be nearly four o'clock. It's time to be going home for tea. Let's go down into Big Wood and see if we can spot those red deer that Bill's dad came across yesterday.'

Peter half expected them to react to being called idiots, even in fun. It should surely have been a signal for further tussling involving all three of them. But they merely got to their feet and nodded in agreement. There was no doubt about Jamie's undisputed role as leader.

At this mention of 'going down' Peter instinctively glanced toward the cliff edge. Jamie must have noted even that, for he now laughed and said, 'Don't worry, we're not going over the edge. Not without ropes, anyway!'

Peter nervously joined in the general laughter at that, but not with any conviction. He half suspected that it implied that they did sometimes do things like that, with ropes.

'There's a path down, further on,' Jamie explained. 'A bit steep, but alright.'

As they continued along the cliff top, the others pointed out features on and around the lake, naming the islands and some of the surrounding mountains. Perched high up on the far shore at intervals were several large houses in their own grounds. Bill, indicating one of them, said, 'That's *Fairview*. Your cousin Jordan goes there sometimes to play tennis. It belongs to Hammy.'

He means Colonel Hamilton,' said Jamie, in answer to Peter's uncomprehending look. 'Bill always uses that nickname for him. If you ask me, it's that habit that's "hammy".'

'Jamie's got a bit of a crush on him,' Bill jeered, 'so doesn't think we should give him a nickname at all.'

'I have not,' said Jamie, hotly. 'I think he's a prig. Anyway, you're only jealous because he looks like Douglas Fairbanks, and Jordan goes there, and it's you who's got a crush on Jordan.'

It was Bill's turn to look discomforted, and he didn't make any reply; and although it was the first time that Peter had seen either of them argue he decided that it was all taken in good part. But he couldn't help an odd glance at Jamie. There was something going on here he couldn't understand. It was all very peculiar. And, anyway, he certainly couldn't see how Bill or anyone else could have a crush on Jordan, and concluded that Jamie must have just made it up in reply to Bill's dig at him, which hadn't sounded believable at all.

Beyond the end of the lake to their right, some distance away, where the valley turned, was another lake, long and narrow, and beyond that the mountains on all sides dropped away into a plain. The light in that direction, to the west, had a particular clarity to it, and Bill, noticing the direction of Peter's gaze, said, 'It's not visible today, but on a clear day you can see the sea from here, and beyond that, Scotland.'

Peter stared even harder on being told that, wishing the cloud away, but no amount of imagination could make anything recognisable appear.

In contrast, in the opposite direction, to the south, the mountains appeared to pile up higher, peak after peak, ever taller, mysterious in their craggy, cloud-cloaked outlines, demanding to be explored.

'Have you ever been up into those mountains?' Peter asked in general, pointing toward them.

He might have been asking if they'd ever been to the local park. 'Yes, of course,' they chorused, disbelief at the innocence of his question evident in their voices.

His embarrassment at his own naivety was only partly lessened by Jamie adding, 'They're much nearer than they look, and quite easy if you know the routes.'

It didn't do a lot for his doubts. He'd heard them use that sort of expression before. He wondered again about this 'path' that they were heading for that was 'a bit steep but alright'.

However, when they came to it, after some initial fright as he saw it disappear over the edge, once he'd got onto it he found that it was in fact as they'd said. Narrow in places and steep in others, requiring hand-holds at times, it wound its way down between boulders, rock-faces and stunted shrubs in a manner which didn't present any real difficulty. And it soon widened into a broad, downward-angled ledge on which grew trees, which seemed to protectively wrap themselves round them so that there was no longer any awareness of the drop below.

As they made their way down in single file, Jamie leading with the others following behind Peter, chatting as they went, he learned that George had an older brother and a young sister and that he intended to follow his father on the farm; and that Bill had a younger brother and that his father was a solicitor. Peter was on the point of blurting out that his father too had been a solicitor, after the war, but he bit back the words before they were uttered. They hadn't so far asked any questions about him, from which he assumed that Jamie had already filled them in with as much as he already knew. But he didn't know whether Jamie would have told them about his dad being a spy, in spite of the fact that he'd said it was secret. Could Jamie be relied upon to keep secrets? Somehow, he thought that he almost certainly could. So to start saying anything about his dad now might just complicate things.

By this time they'd arrived at the bottom of the crag, the path levelling out to meander through the wood; and to Peter's astonishment directly ahead of them spread over the ground beneath the trees as far as he could see was a carpet of blue. At that moment the sun decided to come out, its rays flickering through the stirring foliage overhead and dancing on the scene, highlighting lavenders, purples and mauves. Peter had stopped in his tracks at the sight, never having seen anything remotely like it before, so that George, immediately behind, careered into him. Jamie, hearing the muffled oath, turned, and seeing the expression on Peter's face, said, 'Bluebells. They don't stay long – just a week or two. Fantastic, though, aren't they?'

'Gaan!' George grumbled, as Peter was starting to enthusiastically agree, 'it's cissy for a lad to be interested in a load of old flowers!'

'Don't be daft,' Jamie retorted, with a quick glance at Peter. 'You don't know what you're talking about.'

'Shut up, you two!' Bill hissed. Then, still in a whisper, 'Look!'

He'd sunk into a half-crouch, pointing – and following the line of his outstretched arm Peter was just in time to see a flash of brown disappearing into the far trees.

There was a groan of disappointment from the others.

'What was it?' Peter said.

'Deer. And we missed it! All because those two were arguing about those bloody flowers.'

'Just one on its own, do you think?' Jamie said calmly.

'Couldn't tell. Probably.'

'Expect it was a fallow, then. Seemed too small and brown to be a red, anyway.'

There was a murmur of agreement from the others.

As, without further discussion, they continued on their way, he felt disappointment at their nonchalance. There he was, having just missed seeing a deer in the wild for the first time in his life, and the others were behaving as though it was of no importance at all.

By the time they'd got back to the outskirts of town, however, not having seen any further signs of deer, his disappointment had evaporated, leaving him with only a growing excitement at all the new things he had done and seen and the new friends he'd already made. The others were back to school in the morning, so he had to put up with a certain amount of chaffing along the lines of 'alright for some!' Privately, he wasn't so sure. He was going to be kicking his heels on his own for the next few days. Anyway, he didn't know for sure that they would want to continue having him in their 'gang', whether he'd measured up to their exacting standards.

He needn't have worried. As they lingered for a few minutes outside George's house on their way back into town, he learned that Mr Bradley (who had the bakery where Jamie's mother worked) kept a rowing boat on the lake, which he allowed Jamie and the others to borrow whenever he wasn't wanting it for himself, which meant it was available most of the time. They were planning to take this out for an hour after school on Wednesday, and more or less seemed to take it for granted that Peter would join them if he'd nothing better to do. He couldn't imagine anything better, although he did his best to appear casual about it. And with that, having arranged to all meet by the town hall at four o'clock on Wednesday, they went their separate ways.

Sure enough, the next few days dragged. Monday was washday and – as his aunt and Cook said in disbelief – 'fine for once!' Peter was therefore banished, and thankfully left the two of them plus his mother and Ethel falling over one another in the back kitchen amidst a battleground of soap-suds, laundry, zinc tub and mangle. He decided to do some more exploring.

Ten minutes later, therefore, he had found his way to the road leading down to the lake. This wound past a kind of park with gardens but also other attractions such as an aviary, an ice-cream kiosk, and an obstacle-golf course. The kiosk had for sale other items, including fishing nets on sticks, which interested him – but after a quick count of his few pennies decided that he hadn't enough to splash out on something like that, and anyway there didn't seem to be anyone looking after the kiosk. The whole place was quiet in fact, with few identifiable 'visitors' in this period between Easter and the Whitsuntide holiday, and by the time he'd reached the lake a minute or two later he more or less had the place to himself.

This, his first view of the lake from close to, cast a spell on him. The road opened out and sloped down to one side to merge into a shingle foreshore on which were drawn up a large number of rowing boats for hire, their oars stowed neatly on their rowlocks. Beyond them, continuing along the shore, was a series of four stone piers from which wooden jetties reached out into the lake. Alongside each of these were moored large elegant motor launches each capable of taking dozens of people at a time. The varnished, planked sides of the launches, and the polished brass-work on their decks gleamed in the morning sunshine, the glass of their cabins reflecting the lapping patterns of water and the activities of the many ducks and similar birds busying themselves on the placid surface.

Beyond these landing stages the lake, punctuated by its three or four islands (so much bigger, now, than they had appeared from up on the crag the day before), stretched away so still and calm that the mirrored images of fell-sides, tawny still with winter bracken, might have been painted on. And the lake had its own faint aroma, a not unpleasant odour that somehow conjured up the presence of this large, complex body of water, yet so different from the salt-and-seaweed smell of the seaside – a smell that, with your eyes closed, could say to you: here is a lake.

A man in waders, working at one of the rowing boats, glanced curiously at him before going on with what he was doing; but otherwise, again, there was nobody else about. He hadn't yet got used to the quietness of this small town, the general absence of people. He wandered on, automatically kicking at the shingle as he went, feasting on the images around him, until he came to another stone jetty which formed one side of a deep channel leading into a boathouse. He climbed the steps onto the jetty and walked to the end. The water there was deep, but clear – he could see tendrils of dark green weed wafting lazily about, with small fish, minnows, darting in and out as though playing hide-and-seek. He wished he'd been able to buy one of those fishing-nets. Peering back, within the shadows of the open-ended boat-house he could see, bobbing on the water, the shape of a boat. A narrow walkway extended back along the side wall inside the house, and he wandered along to take a closer look. He thought how wonderful it must be to have a boat of one's own like that. He was tempted to climb into it, but decided it would be wrong; anyway, it didn't look too easy.

Going back to the far end of the jetty he sat for a while throwing small stones at the fish, which darted towards each of the sinking stones in expectation of something to eat. Tiring of that, he then spent some time pretending that he was commanding a destroyer, on the lookout for submarines, and then that he was the pilot of a seaplane coming in to land; but playing these games on his own quickly became boring, and despondency once more took hold.

As always when in that mood his thoughts turned to his father, and anger rose. How could he have thought so little of them that he could abandon them in the way that he had? For abandonment was the way Peter thought of it. Desertion from the line of duty rather than in the line of duty. Not only had he not made any arrangements for sufficient money for their needs before he went, but had left behind various debts, so that the house had had to be sold merely to 'make ends meet' as his mother had put it. All right, so he'd taken care to make financial arrangements for Peter's schooling, in the form of a 'Trust', whatever that was; but even that left the impression that it was done to gratify a kind of pride that his son would be following in his own footsteps. He'd never asked Peter what he wanted. What he wanted, now, was to go to the school that Jamie, Bill and George went to. He didn't want to go away to board at some strange school to be away for weeks on end, where he'd have to live up to whatever standards his father had set, before him. It would be like going to a…a second-hand school. And it would mean leaving his mother. He worried about his mother. So far she didn't seem happy to be living with her sister. There was a kind of resentment simmering in the background, not only from Jordan, but from his aunt as well. Uncle John was certainly doing his best to make them feel welcome, but his Practice took up so much of his time that he was hardly ever there. Peter had been determined that he would look after his mother, so that she wouldn't feel lonely and worried; but the realisation had dawned that for most of the time he wasn't going to be there – and even now, when he was there, he didn't seem to be able to help. It was as though she was in a kind of daze, talking to him but not really with him, not in the relaxed sort of way she used to be before all this happened. But then, he expected, it must be the same for her as it was for him, probably even more so – living in someone else's house, whatever the relationship, and however kind they might be, wasn't the same as living in one's own.

Mind you, before all this had happened the atmosphere at home had been pretty bad. Both he and his mother had become afraid of his father, constantly wondering what sort of mood he was going to be in, whether he was going to be sunk in his black, wordless depressions or in one of his violent rages as was particularly the case when he'd had too much to drink, which was quite often. At least now they didn't have that any more.

But he did miss not having a father. He did miss him.

In that dejected frame of mind he ambled home.

In the afternoon it rained – and continued to rain for the next day and a half. He spent time exploring the large attics at the top of the house, which were reached by means of a staircase from a corridor leading from the main upstairs landing to a back staircase going to the kitchen. These attic rooms had, some years before, been living accommodation for the domestic staff (and, intriguingly, for that reason, there was a second bathroom off that same back corridor) but were empty now, and although they made a good setting for all kinds of games, including the pretence that they were haunted, again they weren't much fun on his own, so that he soon tired of it. He read in his room and in the drawing-room, drew pictures and even painted one or two of them, something he hadn't done since he was quite small. He looked wistfully at the various knobs on Uncle John's new wireless set, but knew that he wasn't allowed to touch that – anyway the reception among these mountains was so poor that it would have been more trouble than it was worth (although he felt that given half a chance he could make a better job of tuning it than Uncle John). He got under Cook's feet, so that even she lost patience; and he even got out his stamp collection, something else he hadn't done for a long time, having lost interest in it years ago. And he remained bored.

But all the time he was sustained by the thought of this boat trip on the lake, so that when by Wednesday lunchtime the rain had finally stopped and a weak sun had even made its appearance, he couldn't wait for four o'clock.

Nevertheless, when he did arrive at the meeting place by the town hall he was a little bit late, the result of some last-minute fussing by his mother, and was therefore taken aback to find that only Bill and George were there.

They were larking about in their usual fashion, but when they saw him coming and turned to meet him he thought there was an air of impatience about them, as if they were, in Jamie's absence, a bit lukewarm about him.

'The boat trip's off for this evening,' Bill said, without ceremony. 'Jamie's had to go to visit a sick aunt, or something.'

The disappointment stopped Peter in his tracks. 'Can't we go without him?' he asked tentatively.

'Without who?'

'Jamie.'

'But you said "him".'

'Yes. Jamie.' He was beginning to wonder if Bill was being deliberately dense.

But suddenly the other two were rolling around with laughter, holding their sides in exaggerated mirth.

Rising panic fought with anger, as he shouted, 'What's wrong?'

'Jamie's a girl,' they spluttered, 'didn't you know?'

His face hot, wishing the ground would swallow him, he said desperately, 'But Jamie's a boy's name!'

George, struggling to straighten his face, came over to lightly punch Peter's arm. 'It's just a kind of nickname, Pete. Her real name is Jane Mary Evans. Get it? "Jay-ME". She's called herself Jamie ever since I've known her. Even her mum calls her Jamie.' His voice roughened. 'Surely it's obvious she's a girl, anyway?'

'Seems obvious to me,' said Bill witheringly, still grinning broadly, 'However, we can't use the boat if she's not there. George and I are going off to play football. Come if you want.'

'No, I'd better go,' Peter muttered, struggling to control tears of humiliation. 'Thanks.'

He turned and walked carefully away, but after some yards broke into a run, the tears finding their escape.

He ran all the way home, anger and frustration driving him on. When he burst into the house he found his mother, uncle and aunt sitting in the drawing room having a cup of tea, astonishment written across their faces at his unexpected entry.

'Why didn't you tell me Jamie was a girl!' he shouted wildly, to no one in particular, wiping at his tears.

'Peter!' his mother cried sharply, 'Control yourself! What on earth's got into you!'

'But it's not fair!' he wept. 'You should have told me!'

His uncle, who had been in the process of filling his pipe, got rapidly to his feet and with a frown came over towards him, causing Peter to flinch, half expecting a clout. But the frown just as quickly cleared, and Uncle John put a friendly hand across his shoulders to lead him to a chair.

'Don't take on so, old chap. It can't be as bad as all that. Now just calm down and let us talk it through.'

'But why didn't you tell me?' said Peter brokenly.

'I'm afraid that was my fault. I was obviously wrong not to do so, and I apologise. It was an error of judgement on my part. But I didn't think it would result in this.'

Through his seething anger Peter heard his aunt sniff contemptuously.

'But why?' he asked again, gaining more in control of himself.

'Let me tell you a simple story,' his uncle said in reply. 'You're walking along beside a shallow, fast-flowing river, and you come across three men – an Englishman, a Jewish man, and an African, a negro – standing talking, all strangers to you. Just then you see a small dog being swept down the river, clearly on the point of drowning. "Look there! We need to save that dog!" you call to the men.

Peter, shuffling irritably, felt his anger rising again. What on earth was the old fool on about? What had this to do with anything?

' "I can't," says the Englishman,' his uncle went on, ignoring Peter's reaction, ' "I've got my best suit on."

' "I can't," says the Jewish man, "I've got to dash off to an important meeting."

'The negro doesn't say anything, but wades into the river and saves the dog.

'Now, which of those three men would you most respect?'

'The negro, of course,' Peter muttered sullenly, still wondering where this was supposed to be leading.

'So you would judge them not by how they looked but by how they behaved?'

Peter shrugged resentfully, not deigning to answer.

'I'll take that to mean Yes. Now suppose I said to you that I respect the Englishman most, because he was well-dressed and looked important. Would you agree with me?'

'No,' Peter said, sounding as irritated as he felt.

'Alright. So you'd stick to your own opinion. That's good. Supposing, though, that beforehand you had decided, not knowing anything about the men, that the Negro was the one to be least respected, because he was different to the others – that's what we call "prejudice", incidentally: making up your mind about something before you've taken the trouble to find out about it – would you still feel the same, afterwards?'

'No. I wouldn't!'

'Quite right, too. In other words, you would have waited to find out for yourself before you came to an opinion, wouldn't you. Now, do you see what I'm getting at?'

'Not really,' said Peter, almost rudely.

'Alright, let me ask you this, then. Do you usually mix with girls, when you're out playing?'

'No, of course not. Girls are soppy.'

His uncle laughed delightedly. 'Well, then? Would you have been keen to join Jamie's "gang" if you'd known she was a girl?'

'I dunno.' He shrugged again. 'I suppose not.'

'And what do you think of her now?'

'She's alright.' He'd said it positively, a form of praise; and enthusiasm suddenly bubbled free. 'As good as any boy, actually.'

His uncle laughed again, and clapped him on the shoulder. 'Well, there you are, then! But don't let Jamie hear you say that!'

CHAPTER FOUR

The earthquake comes without warning. Beginning as a subdued grumble emanating from the very fundaments of the earth, it barrels rapidly upwards until it erupts with demonic force from the high corner cupboard. The room, already unfamiliar, instantly becomes unrecognisable, its walls bulging and sundering into great chasms which threaten to engulf him, their torn edges knocking rhythmically against one another in imitation of the gnashing of giant teeth.

The next moment, struggling up to consciousness, he finds himself still in a strange place, initially dark but then less so, grey unfamiliar objects slowly materialising before his bewildered half-open eyes. Yet the rumbling and knocking continue, though more remote: not so much heard as felt through the substance of what he begins to identify as a bed – and manifest also in the faint rattle of some small object somewhere on a hard surface. The knocking, however, becomes louder and more insistent. By the time he's decided that all this is indeed happening, no longer a dream, it is accompanied as well by a long shaft of light entering space, and by an unfamiliar voice.

'Flight Lieutenant Waring, sir. It's A/C Barnes, your steward. Good morning, sir. I've brought you some tea.'

Of course! Marwell. Barnes, his batman, whom he hadn't yet met. He mumbles something unintelligible, and the door opens fully, highlighting aspects of the room with weak yellow light from the corridor, pouring him back to the present and to reality, the contents of his dream already sliding back into oblivion.

But the vibration and the distant noise still continue.

'I don't know whether you like tea in the morning, sir. All the other gentlemen seem to. And welcome to Marwell, sir.' There is a note of apology in the voice with his last comment, as if Barnes has decided that the words do indeed sound like an afterthought.

Peter struggles to haul himself up in the bed, still dazed and a little disorientated. 'Yes. Thank you,' he croaks. Actually, he can't stand tea first thing in the morning, but it seems tactful not to say so for the moment. He peers up at the man, who is part-silhouetted against the open door. Smallish, slight, probably no more than nineteen or twenty, and clearly anxious to please.

'That noise,' he says, 'what is it?'

His steward places the tray down on the table and strides over to open the blackout curtains. Grey light meanders in, competing unsuccessfully with the man-made light from the corridor.

'Half a dozen ferry jobs just come in, sir. Wimpeys.'

Peter begins to worry that he is still in cloud-cuckoo land. What on earth are 'ferry jobs'? Or 'Wimpeys'?

'Wimpeys?' he asks cautiously. That sounded the more reasonable question of the two.

'Yes, sir. You know. Wellingtons. That'll please the new C.O. It'll just about put the station back up to full strength, I reckon.'

Peter stifles a groan, partly of discomfort at having revealed ignorance and partly in frustration at how long it was taking him to absorb the details of this new, service background. He sits up, and squints through the window. Facing him in the January gloom is a flat terrain disappearing into mist, the part that he can see empty except for a group of heavy bombers noisily trundling in line along a ribbon of snow-patterned tarmac, their props turning lazily as though reluctant to haul their loads any farther. In the half-light and dank atmosphere, mist rising from the ground, the aircraft – with tall tail-planes, lanky undercarriages, and with the bass growl of their engines – look and sound like a line of antediluvian creatures waddling their way across a grassy swamp, their guts rumbling as they go. As his eyes become adjusted to the conditions, through the fog he begin to make out the spectral shapes of hangars, the likely destination of the slowly moving planes. Standing a little apart from the hangars, nearer to, is a huddle of main buildings, included a tall control-tower, its windows gazing blankly out at the greyness. The thought strikes him that until the very recent past all this would no doubt have been, at this time of year, a patchwork of fallow fields, ploughed or farrowed, dormant until Spring. In this corner of the country alone there must by now be thousands of acres similarly given over to airfields, all constructed in haste. Doubtless it will be many years before there will once more be hedgerows and crops – and God-only-knew under what circumstances that might prove to be.

For a moment a cold hand of foreboding grips him, so that he's only half-listening as Barnes goes on to say, 'Squadron Leader Munro sends his compliments, sir, and wonders whether you'd care to join him for breakfast? When you're ready, that is. He says 'no hurry'. I don't suppose there'll be many other gentlemen there, this morning. They're all still sleeping it off at present! It's just as well there aren't any of the squadrons on standby today – but, then, the C.O. had made sure that was the case.'

Still befuddled, Peter has to think for a second who this S/L Munro is, then remembers. An ally in an enemy camp. Along with the padre, of course – he seemed a decent sort.

'Thank you, Barnes. Would you tell the Squadron Leader I'll be delighted to join him for breakfast. In about ten minutes or so?'

Having then managed, with no little difficulty, to assure the steward there is nothing else the fellow can do to be of assistance, he finds his way along to the washroom where, with the place to himself, he showers and shaves. Whilst doing so he does his best to retrieve the last tattered remnants of his dream before they retreat beyond reach – a dream that had so disturbed him it had ended in visions of catastrophe. The setting, he thinks, must have been that first Christmas dinner-dance at the Royal George hotel when he was…what? …thirteen? No wonder he'd awakened with such feelings of distress: he still squirms at the memories of that particular piece of absurdity. And recollection of it prompts him to think that Jordan must have appeared somewhere in the dream – yes, and Beal also. That figures. Beal, whom he will probably have to meet up with later today – that is if, during his first day on the station as the new C.O. he will have time for relatively unimportant ancillaries such as Peter: Beal, too, must be feeling the strain of facing fresh challenges in his new role as Station Commander. But Beal was the sort who relished that sort of thing, without qualms about his ability to do the job. Those two terms of fagging for him at Bards had at the time invoked in Peter a mixture of pride and anxiety. Everyone in his year on the House – and not a few in the year ahead – had told him how lucky he was to have landed that job. Which was what he himself had thought at first. It had given him a particular status among the other first-year fellows. But the others had never had any real inkling of the exacting demands that Beal had made upon him – or, if they had, they hadn't seen it as a problem. Beal had expected nothing less than perfection, or so it seemed. And Peter, therefore, had never understood why it was he'd been chosen for the job in the first place, or why he'd been kept on for the rest of the year. He remembers his school report at the end of that year (a report about which he'd had so many misgivings that in order to get an advance peek at it he'd been driven to steaming open the envelope before eventually handing it over to his mother and uncle – doing the job so clumsily that Uncle John had cast him a whimsical look as Peter had given him the unmistakably wrinkled and battered paper). *Waring is so often on the point of success,* Roberts, his Housemaster had written, *but somehow never quite manages it.* Peter could still see the words standing out on the page in the man's flowing handwriting. *Next year,* the statement had gone on, *he must try to apply himself more diligently and strive to attain more belief in his own undoubted abilities.* Worse still, 'Cannonball' Brindle, the Head, in his comment in the Report, had been worthy of his nickname in his bluntness, so scathing in his sarcasm that it had swept the legs from under Peter: '*If Waring keeps on as he's doing he should make a complete success of failure.*' Peter still wondered how a man of the church could have been so insensitive and so uncharitable as to write something like that. Uncle John had snorted when he'd read the words, and had muttered something about 'that crass oaf!' Peter recalled a couple of occasions after that when his uncle had tactfully tried to draw him out and discover what the problems were. But as Peter himself had never understood his own behaviour, and anyway had felt too wretched and self-conscious to be in any way forthcoming with his uncle, it had ended up being merely an embarrassment for both of them.

His thoughts drift back to Jordan, and the complications she'd introduced into his young life. It must be two years or more, now, since he's last seen her, just before she'd made her big break into the West End. No doubt she would by now be more conceited than ever. He smiles ruefully as he remembers Aunt Mabel's expression of disbelief when Jordan had announced, at the age of seventeen or so, that she wanted to become an actress. Jordan of course had had the idea that she would achieve instant recognition and within a couple of years be called to Hollywood to become a film star; whereas her mother could only think of how horrified all the townspeople would be to learn that the doctor's daughter was going to go on the stage! Uncle John had, as usual, understood that the reality, in both cases, would be nothing like that. Peter suspected that he'd given his blessing to the venture in the belief that Jordan, in the face of failure, would all-too-soon pack it in and come hurrying home. But, to give her her due, she had stuck it out through difficult times over the years (much to everyone's surprise, and without much evident financial support from her father – a deliberate policy on his part), and was now reaping her just rewards.

But, enough – he still doesn't want to think about Jordan. And David Munro would perhaps be getting impatient waiting for him. He hurries back to his room, dresses quickly, his mind still a little clogged by elements of his dream and the memories it has evoked.

* * *

The sun shining hotly on his back was, he decided, a fitting celebration of the first day of the summer holidays, when the others would have as much time to themselves as he had had for all these weeks. It was another of those days that, though without any other significance, he would find perpetually imprinted on his memory. The days and weeks of idly kicking his heels, of tedium, when he perversely wished he were at school, when no amount of suggestions or cajoling by the family could lift him from his apathy, were over. True, he had spent time with the gang on some evenings and weekends, during which gradually their new friendship had firmed, but it wasn't the same as having the prospect, as he now had, of days on end in their company.

He thought back to that terrible occasion when not only had he felt such an idiot at not having realised that Jamie was a girl, but also had feared that as a result of his gaffe the friendship would be over before it had begun. Now, after all these weeks he was just about able to contemplate it without still going hot and cold – even though it had quickly come right. He remembered how he had miserably dragged himself around for a couple of days, mostly staying in his room, until on the Friday teatime Jordan had looked briefly into his room to brusquely say, 'There's someone downstairs to see you, Peter.'

'Who?' he'd asked listlessly.

'Jamie.'

Panicking, he'd protested,' I don't want to see her!'

'Don't be pathetic!' Jordan had said, totally unsympathetic. 'It'll be all right. You'll see.'

And it was. When, red in the face, he'd reluctantly trailed downstairs it had been Jamie, perfectly relaxed and natural, who'd immediately started apologising to him for the mistake, as if none of it had been his fault, seeming to imply that she should have made things more clear, that there was no way he could have known. Of course he hadn't for one moment believed that; it hadn't made him feel any better. But, 'I hope we can still be friends?' she'd said.

For a while after that, though, he'd been disorientated when out with the gang, still able to see Jamie only as a boy; on the other hand, a number of inconsistencies that previously he'd been only indistinctly aware of had finally fallen into place.('She's always been a tomboy, that one,' Aunt Mabel had said, 'even when she was little. That's one of the reasons why Jordan and she drifted apart after a few years; I think it just became too much for Jordan.') Now, though, he was all right. He could accept her as a girl, yet one of the gang – still the leader in fact, still capable of out-running, out-climbing and out-doing all three of them in most things.

From his prone position in the bow of the boat, he glanced over his shoulder at the others. Jamie was nearest to him, rowing carefully in time with Bill, who was stroke, and for a few moments he studied the movements of her slim back as she rhythmically bent and straightened to the task. He could see the action of her muscles and shoulder blades beneath the thin shirt, and the rippling of her spine. Areas of damp were appearing on her shirt and the back of her shorts, as the warmth and effort had its effect. Partly visible beyond her, Bill's bulkier shape and jerkier movements were a defining contrast. Beyond him, George sat indolently on the stern seat, the tiller ropes draped over his shoulders. Catching Peter's glance he grinned in conspiratorial fashion. 'Come on, you two,' he shouted, 'put yer backs into it!'

'It's alright for you,' Jamie grunted. 'Anyhow, it's nearly your turn again.'

Peter turned to once more peer over the prow of the boat, his arm over the side, trailing his fingers in the water. They were going at a fair lick all right, the bow wave frothing and slapping against the planking, the sound mingling with the splash and gurgle of the oars each time as they entered the water, and the hiss and drip as they lifted. For a second or two with each pull the boat would surge eagerly forward, pitching and rocking gently as it did so, then settle as though to take a rest. It was a movement that was at once soothing and restful but at the same time urgent and purposeful. It was the way to travel, all right, to take one into adventure.

Gazing into the depths here in the centre of the lake, the water was a mysterious black, a beckoning void on which was glazed the bright of the sky – but he had no fear: that thin inch of planking could be felt buoying them up, keeping them safe, in a world alone, enclosed by mountains. He could be an explorer charting the unknown lakes and rivers of Canada, savage Iroquois threatening from either shore; or a buccaneer, being taken by his motley crew to find treasure trove on some lonely isle.

Startled, he sprang back as, without warning, a mere five yards away a black head shot, snakelike, out of the water and fixed him with a beady eye. But when, immediately, that head and long neck were followed by the sleek black wings and body of a bird, rising to shake off the iridescent droplets of water clinging to its plumage, he laughed shakily. The others, equally startled by his sudden movement and involuntary cry, burst out laughing when they realised the cause of his alarm; and the bird, as if to emphasise Peter's foolishness, took off in fright.

'What you so scared about!' Bill jeered. 'It's only an old cormorant.'

'Come on, Peter,' said Jamie, immediately businesslike, 'it's time George and you took the oars, anyway, so Bill and I can have a rest.'

Bill, on his feet in a flash, said 'Bags I steer!'

'Sit down, Bill!' said Jamie, an edge of anger in her voice as the boat wobbled violently. 'You'll have us over.'

His response was to deliberately rock from side to side, the boat tipping so that its rowlocks were almost touching the surface.

'Bill!' Jamie snapped. 'Don't be so stupid!'

'Yah!' scoffed Bill. 'Just like a girl, always too careful!'

George's head snapped up, his eyes wide with surprise. Even Bill for a moment seemed taken aback at what he'd said. Peter, dimly aware that something momentous had just occurred, couldn't put his finger on it. He could see, though, the tension in every line of Jamie's body.

She, meanwhile, stared silently at Bill for several seconds, before quietly saying, 'If being careful is not risking other people's lives, then yes, I'm careful.'

'Where's the risk?' Bill blustered. 'We can all swim.'

'You don't know that.' She turned to look at Peter. 'Can you swim?'

All eyes were upon him, and he was tempted to bluff his way out; but he shook his head dumbly.

'I don't believe it!' Bill said, hostility in his eyes as he stared at Peter. He was still standing, but had stopped his rocking movements.

'That's enough!' Jamie snapped. 'We're not all clever-clogs like you! Now why don't you just do the thing properly instead of showing off.'

For a moment Peter thought that Bill was going to hit out at Jamie; but his flare of temper turned at once to sullenness, and without another word he went at a half-crouch to sit on the stern-seat next to George, who moved over to make room for him. George wore a look of embarrassment; but the look that Bill again flashed at Peter was still full of antagonism, making Peter wonder whatever he'd done to deserve that.

'Right, Pete,' Jamie said. 'Now you come and sit next to me, but keep low.'

Feeling somewhat offended that she'd found it necessary, after all these weeks, to remind him of the way to move around in a small boat, nevertheless he quietly did as he was told, sitting down on the narrow bench next to her – and becoming all at once acutely, and strangely, conscious of the warmth and closeness of her as he did so, an awareness that paradoxically became even sharper once she moved away to take his vacated place in the bow. As he adjusted his position, through his thin shorts he could feel the warmth of the seat where she'd been sitting.

For a few minutes he remained in a daze, unable to understand the abrupt change in mood of the group, something he'd not previously experienced in the weeks he'd been with them. But he did, vaguely, begin to realise that whilst he'd allowed his mind to create, in them, a haven of freedom and stability away from the continuing tensions and uncertainties of home, in reality it was just that: a figment born of desire, without foundation. There could be no escape from the disquietudes of life.

However, as he swung away with the oars, following George's lead, his depression soon lifted; rowing was something he had by now become adept at, able to hold his own with the others, another skill by which to build his self-confidence, and therefore to be fully enjoyed.

And the rest of the day was near-perfect, differences forgotten. They landed on one or two of the islands, pretending to hunt for buried treasure. They rowed and punted part way up the river, then tied up to a tree stump, stripped to their underpants and splashed and lolled in pools and shallows, gasping and shouting at the icy coldness of the water. After that, the sun hot upon their bodies, they dried off as they sat on the bank, eating their lunch. It was at that point that a certain self-consciousness reappeared in the group, introducing another provocative facet to the day. The lads had sprawled near to each other, their assorted packages of sandwiches a focal point; but Jamie had chosen to settle down a little farther away, separate from them. That small gulf, a mere hyphen in their usual closeness, served, curiously, to emphasise their intimacy: for they had to look across to Jamie to talk to her, had to reach out as it were to re-establish the bond, thereby underlining its importance. Yet it set her apart, made her different. And that difference began to proclaim itself in other ways. Stretched out on her back on the grass, her cotton knickers adhering wetly to her body, her limbs were clearly more rounded than their own, she was more streamlined than they around her hips and tummy, and her chest had a softness, a fullness almost, that theirs lacked; and the area of darker skin around her nipples was wider than theirs, and more prominent. What's more, all too obviously, where her knickers clung between her upper thighs she was very different to the boys. Peter himself was at first only distantly aware these nuances; but conversation became progressively stilted, and it was noticeable that Bill and George no longer looked at Jamie in their usual careless manner, but did so covertly, quickly averting their gaze whenever she glanced their way – so that he, too, soon became conscious of the increasingly charged atmosphere. It was as if they were all seeing her for the first time – and not yet cognizant of the fact that what they were seeing was change.

If Jamie was aware of any of this she gave no indication; for soon enough she was on her feet rallying them to further action as she dressed. Familiar relationships returned on the back of familiar activities, and by the end of the day the whole episode, for Peter at least, had been forgotten.

* * *

He finds Munro looking quite relaxed, having seemingly finished his breakfast. The room is empty apart from a couple of stewards and a group of six people, five men and one woman, all dressed in white overalls, sitting at a table in a corner of the room. He can't begin to think what a woman is doing there, or indeed who any of them might be.

'Morning, Peter,' Munro says. 'Everything all right so far, I trust?' It's more of a statement than a query, Peter realises, leaving no room for the negative.

'Yes, thanks.' He isn't sure how to address him, so dodges it altogether.

Munro, perhaps sensing his quandary, helpfully provides the answer. 'First names only, in the mess, old chap. No ranks, no formality. Apart from the C.O., of course. He usually gets a 'Sir'. And different outside the mess, needless to say, especially in front of the men. Although you will find that within individual aircrews it's much more informal.'

'Yes. Squadron Leader St…sorry, Arthur Stanton…was saying the same thing, last night. I suppose it's only natural, when they're working as a team.'

'Bang on!' Munro nods his approval. 'Many of the aircrew are volunteers having previously been in ground maintenance crews – they become flight engineers, gunners, and wireless-operators – after further training, of course. They're all promoted to sergeant when they join aircrew, and we've even got, now, some sergeants as pilots. So, you see, there can be quite a range of ranks on board an aircraft. They're all doing essential, complementary jobs, so it would be invidious to be too concerned with differences in rank. The first pilot is always the skipper of course, and that's usually how he gets addressed, as 'Skipper'.'

Peter nods. The topic prompts his eyes to drift back to the group of six at the other table, his curiosity aroused particularly by the presence of the young woman.

Munro, noting his bemusement, says, 'A.T.A. They've just brought in a flight of Wellingtons for us. Quite rightly they're always offered the hospitality of the officers' mess until their return transport arrives, even the women.

Well, Peter thinks, at least I know what A.T.A. is – 'Air Transport Auxiliary', or something like that. However, he's still confused.

But before he can frame the question, Munro goes on, 'And, no, your eyes don't deceive you. That is a woman there! There are, increasingly, quite a number of them in the A.T.A. And damn good pilots they usually are, too. The famous Amy Johnson is one of them – remember her? In fact some of them are a lot better than some of the chaps we get coming straight from the flying-training schools. These girls learn to fly all sorts of different aircraft, from Spitfires through to Wellingtons, and they can often show all of us a thing or two, I can tell you. There was a story a short while ago from one of the fighter stations, where they'd recently been supplied with a couple of squadrons of Beaufighters. I've never flown one, but I understand that they can be a bit of pig; and the boys there were all grumbling about them, and saying how impossible they were to fly. Until, that is, an additional one was flown in by the A.T.A. The chap flying it apparently did a low-level double roll at speed over the field and then made a perfect landing. Imagine their reaction, then, when the pilot stepped out of the cockpit, removed his flying-helmet and revealed 'himself' as a girl with long blonde hair! I gather they all just got on with it after that!'

Peter laughs along with Munro at the spectacle this must have presented; but privately it makes him yet again feel somewhat inadequate at his own pathetic role in this war.

'What happened to my predecessor here?' he asks.

'Doc Thompson? Oh, he got booted upstairs to become Group M.O. in one of the other groups. I forget which. Did you know him?'

Peter shakes his head.

'No, I suppose not. A bit older than you. And of course he was a career officer.'

Peter knows that Munro hasn't meant anything by that particular remark. But his stress on the word 'career', underlining the fact that the fellow had chosen to practice his profession within the R.A.F. even before the outbreak of war (as had Munro – and Beal) serves to emphasise again the impression that those who did so tend to look down on those who have come into it out of necessity: as if the former are the true professionals, and the latter mere amateurs, thereby less proficient.

He's about to voice some mild, and hopefully jocular, form of protest at this, but at that point Munro looks up to call out, 'Good morning, Arthur. Have you come to join us? I'm afraid Peter and I have almost finished our breakfast, but we'll be happy to stay and watch you pig yourself, if you've a mind to.'

'Very generous of you, David, I'm sure,' replies the padre drily, now standing at Peter's shoulder, 'but Sylvia's already fed me. Good morning, Peter. You slept well without feeling deprived at the absence of my harmonious snoring, I take it? I dropped in, really, to see if you'd like me to take you over to your office, as it were, and show you the ropes?'

This evokes a loud guffaw from Munro. ' "The ropes"! That's a strange euphemism if ever I heard one!' He turns to Peter. 'What Arthur is so figuratively referring to is – or, rather, are – your staff over in the Sick Quarters; although I would use a rather more colourful expression than "staff", myself!'

Peter feels prickings of alarm. He's been banking on experienced support over at the medical centre to give him some guidance; now, it is implied, that is the last thing he can expect.

'Don't look so worried,' Munro says, taking pity on him, 'it's not quite as bad as it sounds.'

'Isn't it?' says Stanton, less charitably – although he does soften it with a grin. 'Browning's okay – once you get used to him. But O'Connor...well...let me put it this way, Doctor: do you consider yourself a man of the world?'

'Take no notice,' says Munro, a shade more sympathetically, possibly influenced by some perception of the bonds of the old school tie. 'Arthur doesn't deserve to be called a Christian. What's more, I should warn you further about Arthur. Just because he happens to have a brother who's an intelligence officer at the Air Ministry, who seemingly keeps him informed about matters that even the Chief of Air-staff knows nothing about, he's become a real know-it-all, and an insufferable bore. I should ignore everything he tells you! Anyway, let me explain before he misleads you further. You have two members of staff at your Sick Quarters. Corporal Browning is there to look after admin and the general running of the place. Browning is...well, you'll just have to meet him...suffice to say that he was a don at Oxford before he was called up. History, I think.'

'And if they'd really wanted to win the war that's where they should have left him!' interrupts the padre, seeming to even further deny his calling.

'The other member of staff,' continues Munro, ignoring Stanton, 'is Flight Officer O'Connor – female – who is a WAAF nursing Sister with a Scouse-Irish background. She's in charge of the clinical side of things, the treatment room and the two sick-rooms.'

'And that's where your problems really begin!' says Stanton with relish.

'Shut up, Arthur!' says Munro. Then, with a spuriously considerate expression directed at Peter, 'On second thoughts perhaps this once you should listen to Arthur!' Now he pauses before saying, more solemnly, 'Do you know much about the Irish?'

Peter, bewildered, shakes his head.

'Go on, you tell him, Arthur,' says Munro with a wicked grin at the padre. 'You've a Scottish background, and we both know the Scots and the Irish are all much of a muchness. Anyway,' he adds unkindly, 'your brother has probably had something to say about the matter!'

'Same school or not, don't ever be tempted to regard this man as a friend,' says Stanton blandly to Peter, with a nod in the direction of Munro. 'All right. O'Connor: redhead with a temper to match, a heart of gold, the seductive magic of the Little People, a steely competence at her job, and a first name that is spelt S-i-o-b-h-a-n but is pronounced, in typical Irish fashion, as *Shevaun* – get that wrong and she'll have you gelded in a flash.'

'Speaking of which,' says Munro, '...and I suspect that our padre here, with true Christian guile, was not about to warn you...around the said Shevaun keep your undercarriage well-secured at all times. She must have tried to make a trophy of every man on the station, and believe me, she's deadly! Once she's got you in her ring-sights, with a quick burst she'll have you going down in a tail-spin before you know what's happened. And be warned, her approach is from the beam: you don't see her coming till it's too late. I think Arthur is the only one she's not had a go at. But then he's far too old, of course.'

'Not a bit of it,' says Stanton, 'it's just that whenever I'm anywhere near her air-space I make sure that I wear my dog-collar around my pelvis. The Irish,' he adds helpfully to Peter, 'are very religious, you know.'

Peter, not sure whether to take any of this at all seriously, gives the two men a sickly grin. Believable or not, it has brought memories of the past flooding back, memories that he thought he had more or less successfully buried: of 'Plum', the matron on Founders, that time in his second year at Bards, when he was confined to the sick room with torn quads; of Anne, when she was over from Kenya, and they'd all gone to the Morritt Arms for Christmas; and, of course, of Jordan.

'Well, the sooner I get airborne and come to grips with these two, the better,' he says, adopting an air of mock heroism.

'You might be better to resign your commission here and now,' Stanton says, hanging his head in feigned sadness.

'He can't,' says Munro, 'we're at war. Anyway, I must be off.' He gets to his feet. 'Kind of you to offer to take Peter over to Sick Quarters, Arthur. I was about to do it myself, but it might mean coping with the deadly Shevaun – anyway, I'm sure you'll be pleased to have an opportunity to fill some of those idle hours of yours. And don't forget to re-site your dog-collar!'

He turns to Peter. 'I expect Beal will want to meet you at sometime during the day, depending on what time he arrives and what his schedule is. I'll have a word with the Adjutant and I'll let you know. I'll see you later, anyway.'

After he'd gone, Stanton turned to look at Peter with interest. 'Must be quite something to meet up with not just one but two old school chums like this?' he says. And his eyes betray rather more than just 'interest'.

But Peter is hardly listening. Already he's back in that summer once more, so long ago but now suddenly so real. And the events come crowding in on him, dragging along all those scarcely suppressed emotions.

* * *

So, in like fashion, that first summer had continued. Looked back upon, it seemed to be a succession of days of clear skies and hot sunshine. In reality it was probably no different to most other summers. But the gang had days on the fells, climbing the peaks to gaze, unhindered by haze or cloud, at other peaks, layer after layer, as far as the eye could see – or, from time to time, beyond to the sea, with Scotland or the Isle of Man on the far horizons, like mysterious foreign lands. They explored caves and old mines, woods, rivers and waterfalls, and Peter, tutored by the others, learned the names too of all these. Over the weeks, they saw the bracken grow – new shoots, feathery and pale green, unfurling from the turf to carefully push up through the brown sticks of last year's growth until, by July, it was shoulder high, its distinctive aroma filling the breeze. Lying on their backs they would listen to the songs of larks, striving to be the first to spot their tiny presence hovering high overhead, indistinct against the bleached blue of the sky; and they watched the ravens and the buzzards, identified by their cries as they circled above the high peaks. Once, they saw a fox sitting on top of a wall; if it was aware of them, some two hundred yards away, it gave no indication, but continued to peer around for a full minute before quietly disappearing over the other side. On another occasion they came across a nest of young adders basking in the sun under the cover of a fallen rowan tree, the tiny zigzag markings on their backs already speaking of menace; and the gang, uncertain as to the parent snake's likely proximity or demeanour, having briefly satisfied their curiosity, beat a hasty retreat.

For company, otherwise, mostly they had only the sheep, Herdwicks and Swaledales (Peter quickly learning to recognise the individual breeds), as they grazed in mixed flocks in isolation on the fellsides; but now and again they would spot a hare loping away from them across the steep slopes. However, as the summer progressed they increasingly lost possession of what they had almost come to regard as their right: the sole occupancy of the mountains. More and more they came across other walkers or climbers, in ones or twos, or sometimes in larger groups, until there was hardly a day when they didn't meet such intruders on at least two or three occasions, perforce stopping to chat like all explorers in distant lands. As for the town, no longer were the streets mostly empty except for market days: every day would see groups of several dozen people at any one time in the main streets and square, together with the noisy presence of several cars and even motor charabancs, their rattling and backfiring more than once disturbing a horse to the point of it bolting and on the verge of overturning its cart and contents.

The gang stayed intact, contained and exclusive, Peter no longer feeling that he was merely an addition, to be tolerated, but soon content that he had been fully accepted, now one of them. They pretty well did everything together, without a need to extend invitations to others; and if there was any awareness on their part that this was perhaps too clique-ish and introspective for their own good, it was firmly suppressed. It was then that Uncle John came to refer to them, not altogether jokingly, as *the Famous Four*. But Peter would now and again worry that once he went away to school the spell would be broken, he would return as a stranger, that they would drift away or even reject him. He did dimly realise that he had become emotionally dependent upon them, their easy companionship making up for the remoteness he still felt at 'home' (for even the term was one that he still could not entirely accept, feeling that he and his mother were mere lodgers, having to drift with the dictates of others). His mother's constant wariness, translating into a stiff politeness at all times, rubbed off on him so that at home he was never fully relaxed, being too careful not to offend. His mother and his aunt still seemed to be circling each other in a kind of contest wherein they searched for weaknesses; his aunt's snapped criticisms, from time to time, being met by an almost frightened, tight-lipped silence on the part of his mother. Furthermore, in spite of his mother's undoubted love and attentiveness towards him, Peter felt that even it was so consciously done that it might at times be contrived, with the result that rather than gaining strength from her it was more a matter of constantly feeling that it was he who had to support her. His uncle remained the main source of encouragement in his life, a wellspring of humour and thoughtfulness without which he might have been lost. But Uncle John remained so busy that much of the time he wasn't there – and then Peter found himself increasingly turning to Cook, who in her no-nonsense, homely way could always put things back into perspective. As for his cousin Jordan, she continued to treat him with indifference, and to respond to his mother with a patronising politeness bordering on contempt – unless, of course her father was present, in which case she displayed a spuriously solicitous concern.

It was inevitable, therefore, that Jamie, Bill and George would become for him an extension, as it were, of his family. Bill, brash and confident, was always the challenger and Jamie the pacifier. But Jamie, far from taking Peter's part rather would quietly encourage him to take up the challenge, casually inserting the concept that although he was indeed a year younger than the rest he was still capable of competing with them. And George, too, showed himself capable of a sensitivity that his outward roughness belied. From time to time he would interpose himself in front of Bill's all-too-frequent needling of Peter, inventing an excuse (if, in truth, any such invention was ever necessary) for one of their customary fights – but it was noticeable that on those occasions the struggle was that much more violent, so that Jamie would have to be quicker than usual to intervene, ensuring at the same time that Peter was not drawn into the fray.

Towards the end of that summer two things happened to interrupt the pleasant routine, two things that he felt worth recording in his journal. He and his mother went for a few days 'holiday' to stay with his grandfather. And they went, with Uncle John, to visit Bardolphs School to be interviewed by the Headmaster. The prospect of the first filled him with eager excitement, which in general turned out to be justified; and anticipation of the second triggered nervous foreboding which the visit itself did nothing to allay.

His grandfather (his mother's father, whom he had met only once, when he was so small that he had no memory of it) lived at the seaside near a town called Silloth, on the Cumberland coast. His mother, for some reason anxious about the whole thing, dithered for a week or two as to whether they should go, and it was only as a result of repeated encouragement by his uncle and aunt that the visit was finally arranged. His uncle, finding Peter perplexed by this and becoming anxious, took a quiet moment to explain to him that there had been some 'difference of opinion' between father and daughter, in the past ('as tends to happen', as he rather drily put it), but that 'everything should be all right once they meet again'. And this, on the whole, proved to be the case.

Silloth turned out to be a quiet, small, unimposing sort of a town, nothing like a 'Resort' such as Brighton. However, as they were being taken by taxi from the station, the place contentedly displayed broad, cobbled streets lined by elegant Victorian and Edwardian houses. Those facing the sea did so across an intervening expanse of sandy 'green' running the full length of the half-mile of sea-front, the otherwise dull flatness of which was relieved by small, neat copses of pine trees and shrubs, one or two glass-sided shelters, and a single ice-cream kiosk. The few shops that there were, scattered around the streets in ones and twos, boringly provided only the necessities of life such as food and clothing; but Peter did note one exception, this particular shop pretending some frivolity by displaying (in one small window) bathing-costumes, beach balls and inflatable rubber Lilos, with fishing nets on sticks and brightly painted buckets and spades hanging in its doorway. Although a fine afternoon at the height of the season, the streets were almost empty, and what few people there were had dispersed themselves indolently along the green. The only evidence of anything with a pretence of activity in fact was a short line of half a dozen donkeys plodding their patient way along the green, small children bobbling precariously on the animals' backs, chubby hands nervously clutching the pommels of their saddles. However, screwing up his eyes against the dazzling light Peter did catch glimpses, beyond the green, of a sandy beach and a sparkling sea from which breaths of air wafted hints of salt and seaweed and foreign lands; whilst, overhead, gulls wheeled and soared, wildly screeching their complaints like tormented souls. It was a new, different and, for him at that moment, altogether exciting world.

His grandfather lived some two miles south of the town. Peter had seen photographs of him, but wasn't prepared for someone quite so old. He must have been at least eighty, Peter decided, with a bushy white beard and equally bushy eyebrows and a minimum of snowy white hair around the periphery of a gleamingly brown bald head. Beneath those eyebrows pale blue eyes glowered fiercely but were belied by a kindly manner and the creases of a smile. In spite of what, in Peter's view at the time, was a very great age, he was actively upright and energetic. He wore subdued tweed plus-fours with matching jacket and waistcoat across which was suspended a gold watch-chain; and he exuded a discrete smell of eau-de-cologne and tobacco, the latter reinforced from time to time throughout the day by his taking from an inside pocket a leather cigar-case from which he would extract a large cigar and carefully trim both ends with a gadget fished from one of his waistcoat pockets before lovingly lighting it. Then he would contentedly puff away wreathed in clouds of aromatic but eye-watering smoke. On one such occasion he persuaded Peter to take a puff, something for which Peter never quite forgave him. In spite of that, and although the old man had in him a certain reserve and remoteness, they soon became firm friends.

The house was a large, modern, multi-gabled affair that grandfather had designed himself. Standing on the main road, it had a neat front garden, and at the back led onto a field that too was owned by the old man. Around the edge of this field were parked a variety of caravans. There were a few of the horse-drawn, gypsy kind; some of the new, purpose-built variety that could be towed by a suitably powerful car; two that were not really caravans at all, but converted motor buses; and one that had even been converted from a railway carriage. It transpired that, permanently sited there for a small fee, they all belonged to various acquaintances of his grandfather, the owners coming to make use of them at weekends and holidays. Peter had never imagined such things existed. He was enthralled by them, would have loved to live in any and all of them, and over the ensuing days he spent some time circling the field studying them from all angles, and in some cases contriving, on tiptoe, to peer in through their windows – on two occasions thereby startling both himself and the occupants.

Beyond that field was another field, also belonging to his grandfather; and beyond that lay the furthermost reaches of the golf links, across which a footpath wound its way through clumps of heather and sharp-pointed marram grass, past immaculately manicured greens and over the springy turf of fairways to the sea. A mere five minutes' walk, therefore, (or two minutes if he ran) could get him to the shore, there to play to his heart's content among the tumbled dunes and on vast isolated stretches of sand, becoming one moment a smuggler of brandy and rare silks, hunted by the excise men, and at another an excise man hunting the smugglers.

His grandmother had died long before Peter was born, and his grandad therefore had a housekeeper: a middle-aged, kindly woman not unlike Cook (perhaps, Peter thought, either such women were naturally drawn to work of that kind, or else they grew to become similar to one another because of the nature of their work). The house was clean and tidy therefore, although cluttered by a scattering of books and bric-a-brac that his grandfather had accumulated over the years. The old man in his youth had been, for a while, a professional photographer – at a time when the discipline was still in its infancy. As a result, there were relics around in the form of a couple of box cameras and stands, and (most importantly for Peter) a stereoscopic viewing box with a set of slides out of which, when viewed through the binocular-type apertures, the sepia-coloured figures and scenes seemed to spring to life with a startling three-dimensional clarity.

The four days they spent there, then, passed all too quickly, to the point that he hardly gave a thought to the absence of The Three – Jamie, Bill and George – although he did now and again wish they could be there to join in the fun.

But there was one incident that did, for Peter, mar their stay.

It occurred on their second evening. He had just come into the house towards teatime, and overheard his mother and grandfather in an unusually heated discussion in another room. Dismayed by the extreme vigour of their voices, he'd stopped where he was, hardly daring to breath.

'It is just nonsense, Marjory,' his grandfather was saying, 'you're making him into something he never was.'

'You never gave him a chance, though, did you, father?' his mother's voice cut in. 'You always thought him not good enough for me.'

'Which indeed he wasn't,' his grandfather replied acidly, 'particularly when compared to John. Only – from the beginning – you were too besotted to see that. And too eager always to please him. That's much of your trouble, isn't it, always too eager to please!'

'And whose fault is that!' Peter could hear the bitterness spilling out, her voice trembling, as she carried on. 'As children we always seemed to fall short of the high standards you expected of us, nothing we did was ever quite good enough. However hard we tried there was never any real praise, only criticism. Except for Anne, of course. She could never do anything wrong. And look what happened with her.'

There came a brief silence, before her father said gruffly, 'I only ever wanted you to learn to stand up for yourselves – and make the most of the opportunities life offered you. As for Anne – who was it who turned her into what she had become?'

'That's not fair!' Peter heard his mother reply with even more bitterness, clearly holding back tears. You can't blame Gerald for that – Anne was every bit as much to blame as he was.'

Another short silence; then, from his grandfather: 'Anyway, the truth is, Gerald never gave himself a chance! Head full of fanciful ideas, and his feet several inches off the ground. He always lived in a world of make-believe. Otherwise he might have been able to make more of himself. And taken better care of you and Peter. But he only really ever thought of himself.'

'How can you say that!' his mother cried, 'particularly now!'

'It's particularly now that I can say it . . .'

'But he made sure that Peter could go away to school by having the foresight to set up the Trust, and it can't have been easy to make financial provision for it.'

'That's stuff and nonsense! What other provision has he made! Certainly none for you. And none for Peter other than the school thing. As for that, it's not clear to me that that's going to be any particular advantage to Peter. I think the whole idea is just another example of Gerald wanting to relive his life through his son in a sort of fantasy in which Peter would be required to play the part to perfection, thus expunging all Gerald's failures and mistakes. Thank God . . .'

But by this time, Peter, not really understanding what was going on, but distressed and frightened by the anger in their voices as well as the manner in which his father was being discussed, had run into the room to fling his arms round his mother (whether in protection for her or for himself, he didn't know) – whereupon his grandfather had broken off in confusion, and no more had been said.

However, that night Peter, curling himself into a tight ball in his nest-like hollow in the old-fashioned deep feather-bed, lay awake trying to make some sense of it all. He couldn't begin to imagine his mother and Aunt Mabel as children, however hard he tried. In fact it had barely ever struck him that they themselves must indeed have been children at some time or other. Less still could he think that his father had ever had a childhood. But the things he'd heard his mother accuse her father of in her childhood had struck a chord with Peter, because it was exactly one of the ways in which his father had treated him. At that point it occurred to him that perhaps it wasn't the way in which all fathers treated their children: after all, Uncle John was a father to Jordan as well as an Uncle to Peter, and he didn't treat her like that – even if, in Peter's view, he should in general deal with her a lot more severely!

At one point, that night, he fancied he could hear muffled sobs from his mother in her bedroom next door to his, and wondered if he should go in to her – but he decided she would only be embarrassed, and be upset that she was upsetting him. And finally he fell asleep.

But during the night the Thing in the high cupboard, shapeless and without name, came to haunt him again.

CHAPTER FIVE

When, having finished breakfast, they walk out to Stanton's car, Peter is struck by how much the mood of the place has changed in the half hour since he first looked out of his bedroom window. The mist has largely dispersed to reveal a pallid sun, low in the sky, the rays of which gleam without enthusiasm on the wet surfaces of airfield and buildings, where snow is clearly starting to melt. The main block of buildings, which he'd noted earlier, is perhaps four hundred yards away, the area around it no longer deserted: several figures can be seen moving around it with an air of purpose; a number of sentries, their rifles with bayonets fixed, stand at the sandbagged entrances to some of the buildings; and further out on the field khaki-clad figures man sandbag-encircled gun-posts. For the first time in weeks Peter perceives a semblance of preparation for war – as opposed to that uneasy pretence of peace which has been even more disturbing.

Inevitably his thoughts drift back to that first Sunday in September. With time off from his S.H.O. surgical job at Croydon General, and trying to elbow aside the threat of war, he'd invited out one of the nurses, a pretty but somewhat vacuous girl. It being a glorious day, cloaked in the remnants of summer, they'd gone up to London and he'd taken her boating on the river at Richmond. It had hardly been a success, even from the word go. She perhaps had been expecting something more enthralling than bobbing around on water; and he – probably subdued by nostalgic memories of past boating expeditions on a different stretch of water several hundred miles to the north – had found little to say to her, particularly as her contribution to any conversation had tended to be monosyllabic. And, try as they might, in the end it was obvious that neither of them had managed to stop thinking about the Crisis. So they hadn't even reached that stage of tentative manoeuvrings that would have been normal at the start of this kind of relationship: she'd seemed bored and preoccupied; and Peter himself had been unable to decide, anyway, what he wanted his attitude towards her to be. Nevertheless, with the hot sun and a relaxing scene all around them, in spite of everything it had been a peaceful morning.

So when, suddenly, the calm of the river had been carved into jagged shards by the undulating wail of the air raid sirens, it had been hard to take in. Starting from afar, in the direction of central London, the sound had spread, source by source, wave by wave until it was all round them, chilling in its intensity as well as in its implications; and even when, after a minute or so, the wailing had droned to a muted moan before petering out into silence, the menace of that sound had hung over the water and seemed to have driven away even the warmth of the sun.

Of course, they shouldn't have been taken by surprise: they knew – who didn't – that an ultimatum had been issued to Germany. But, like so many others, he had chosen to believe – because they'd all desperately wanted to believe – that some sort of last-minute accommodation would be arrived at with the enemy. After all, Poland wasn't that important, was it? All the same, they hadn't expected the sirens to sound so soon, bringing as they did the expectation, any minute, of bombs, mutilation and death.

Without a word, taut with worry, both of them wrapped in their own thoughts, Peter and the girl had rowed for shore. But nothing had happened, of course; it had been a false alarm so far as any raid went. But it had proclaimed the declaration of war.

And so, in like fashion, this so-called war had continued, nothing much happening, neither side making much of a move – making it even harder to believe that it was anything more than a prolonged nightmare from which they would all soon awaken.

Immersed in these thoughts as he gets into Stanton's car for the short drive to the H.Q. block, he finds himself having to apologise and ask the padre to repeat what he'd just said.

'I was asking, old boy, what you know about Beal, having been at school with him I understand?'

'Not a lot, now, I suppose,' Peter confesses. 'I haven't seen or heard anything of him since he left school, which would be in '28. He's probably changed quite a lot since then.'

'They say he's a hard task-master.'

'Well, certainly, he was always that. But fair. He's a bit junior to become a Station Commander, though, isn't he?'

'Yes, he is. And only just been made Wing Commander, with this posting. But, you see, he must have joined the RAF when he left school, in '28 you say? And there's no doubt he's had a meteoric rise. Of course, he played rugby for the RAF for a number of years, and that always helps! And I think circumstances, particularly the mushrooming of all these new airfields over the last three or four years, have led to a lot of these appointments at a young age, which would never have been the case in peacetime. Did you know he has a German wife?'

'Good lord! No! That must be difficult!'

'I'll say! Particularly as they'd been wed only a few months when war was declared.'

'It must be difficult for her, as well.'

'From what I hear she's been in this country since '36 or thereabouts. Jewish blood or some such thing, and had the sense to get out while she could. But I gather she was quite famous as an actress and as a film star in Germany, before that. And, I believe, she's stunningly good-looking. All that's inclined to win over a few hearts – and minds.'

'Even so,' Peter says, 'to be leaving one's own country, and everything you know, to come into a very different culture and environment can't have been easy.'

But he isn't, in truth, thinking about Beal's wife but about Beal himself; and about his own first introduction to Bardolphs, and all the misgivings that had aroused in him.

* * *

Ten days after their stay in Silloth, Uncle John took Peter and his mother on the visit to Bardolphs – the visit that Peter had been dreading.

By car, with his uncle's steady driving, the journey took about three hours, which made it seem an awfully long way away. Normally, when he was actually at the school, he knew, he would be required to make the journey by train, which took about the same time, but necessitated a couple of changes – something that he wasn't at all sure of being able to manage on his own.

The school was in Scotland. Not being too clear about the geography, but aware only that it sounded outlandish and remote, he'd eventually been driven to study a map. He discovered that it was, in fact, only the other side of the Solway Firth, which on the map was a sharp finger of sea that looked as if it was trying to prise Scotland away from England. He realised then that when he'd been at Silloth the coastline that he'd been looking at across the wide stretch of water had in fact been the Scottish coast, and that if it had been nearer, or if he'd had a powerful enough telescope, he might have been able to see Bardolphs itself. That thought had, briefly, provided some comfort, to know that it was as it were within striking distance; but then he'd thought of that expanse of cold, wind-ruffled sea, and of how long it took to reach the place by road, and that feeling of reassurance had quickly evaporated.

When, therefore, shortly after a picnic lunch they started down the side of a valley which in the distance opened to the sea, and at the far reaches of which he caught his first glimpse of the school buildings, the remoteness of it all struck him like a sudden icy fist. All his worst fears were confirmed; he was on the verge of panic.

As they drew nearer, and detail emerged, he saw that the school was identifiable as an entity separate from the village. A loose straggle of severe, pale sandstone buildings poised on the lower slopes of the far side of the valley, it had the air of a medieval monastery peering down on the small secular community which was its inferior not only in position but also in privilege. With its assortment of castellations and towers and multi-windowed blocks of buildings (that Uncle John was later to describe as 'Anglo-Scottish Victorian Gothic'), to Peter's eyes it also had the manifestations of a prison. Along its front, on the floor of the valley, were a series of playing-fields. At one end of those, nearest to the village, a white wooden cricket pavilion with a verandah, dignified in the Edwardian manner, exuded genteel memories of the season which had just ended; but the rest of the grounds sported the tall spires of rugby posts which heralded the rough and tumble of the Michaelmas Term to come.

The rain that had been threatening all day had now started to fall in a fine mist-like drizzle, adding to the general gloom. And when, a few minutes later, they drove down the empty, single street of the village, past the small railway station and over a level-crossing to finally turn into the school grounds it was like entering a ghost town populated only by shadows and by the distant echoes of earlier feet. It was with some relief therefore that they came across a lone handyman crossing the terrace, and were able to obtain directions to School House, their destination: until that point Peter had begun to fancy that they might remain permanently lost in the jumble of quadrangles and passageways of the school.

Having not long ago read *Tom Brown's Schooldays*, he had a pre-set image of what a Headmaster would be like. Canon William Brindle came not far short of that image. As they were ushered into his study and he came forward to greet them, the impression was of a large, solemn man with beetling brows, and a full set of neatly-trimmed whiskers. In fact, apart from his greater size he was not unlike the King, whose portrait together with that of Queen Mary could be glimpsed hanging on the wall behind his desk. He was dressed in black, with only his white clerical dog-collar to relieve the severity of his garb, and wore a flowing black gown. Peter was slightly disconcerted that he wasn't also wearing a black mortar-board, until he spotted one sitting on top of a bookcase in the corner of the room. More ominously, next to the bookcase, hanging by its curved handle from a hook in the wall was a long, whippy-looking cane.

The Head greeted them affably enough, shaking hands with Peter as well as his mother and Uncle John; but there was an air of condescension, as though it were a concession that he was seeing them at all. It was then Peter realised that this was probably the case: interviews had no doubt been held during the week, and it was only because of the impossibility of Uncle John getting away other than on a Sunday that they had been granted the privilege of being seen. That fact singled Peter out in a most uncomfortable way. A couple of upright chairs had been placed in front of the desk, and his uncle and mother were invited to sit; there being no third chair available, Peter had to remain standing, which he took care to do at attention, as though on parade – as indeed he was.

He was so nervous by this time that he had difficulty in preventing his legs trembling, and from time to time had to surreptitiously wipe his sweating palms against the sides of his trousers. He was unable therefore, try as he might, to closely follow the ensuing conversation, instead dwelling at intervals on his own concerns. As the Head didn't appear to want to speak to Peter personally – merely shooting glances at him at intervals as if to affirm for himself that what his mother or uncle were saying about him was likely to be correct – this didn't seem to matter. But he was aware it was possible that at any time the man might suddenly pounce to shoot a question at him that he then would be unable to answer; and so fearful was he of that, and of what the consequences then might be, that his concentration lapsed even further. He'd already decided that in spite of the man's religious calling he was someone to be reckoned with, and he was to learn in due course that throughout the school – not only among the boys but among some of the staff also, it was suspected – his nickname was 'Cannonball' (because he was 'big and heavy and equally dangerous').

Like the incoming tide swirling on a beach, therefore, the talk lapped to and fro into his consciousness. At one point the questions from the headmaster were on matters of finance, and 'the Trust' ('...something the Bursar would normally have dealt with...' was said rather pointedly); at others, about 'guardianship', whatever that might be. Sometimes his uncle would ask a question, perhaps interrupting the Head's flow courteously but firmly; at others his mother would, hesitantly and almost apologetically, venture a question, her deferential manner embarrassing Peter as well as further undermining his own self-confidence.

Then, when Canon Brindle started to talk about the 'regime' at school, Peter began to pay more attention. '...we believe that sport is as important as academic achievement in fitting a boy for the outside world,' the Head was saying. 'We have compulsory games every afternoon – except Sundays, of course – either team games, or cross-country running or athletics, according to season. Getting onto a team will bring its own rewards.' Here he paused to hurl a glance at Peter, his expression (in Peter's view) one of challenge tinged with doubt. 'Further classes after tea, of course, then an hour's prep before supper, and another half hour afterwards prior to bed at eight forty-five and lights-out at nine. Much as you will remember, no doubt?' Here he looked at Uncle John, as if assuming that all men of status must themselves have been to public school. 'We do, needless to say, believe in strict standards of discipline, with free use of the cane for the more serious breaches, such as smoking and... er... a number of other things – but I'm sure we all approve of that... ' (here, it was noticeable, he didn't bother to look at Peter) '...but prefects, it must be said, are allowed to administer beatings only with the approval of the Housemaster.'

Peter, with growing dismay, stole a glance at his mother; but if she had any feelings on the matter they weren't revealed. As for his uncle, he merely gave a brusque nod of his head, which might have meant approval, or merely acceptance.

'The whole school attends Chapel,' the headmaster went on, 'for fifteen minutes every morning during the week, and on Sundays for an hour in the

70

morning and half an hour in the evening; and all boys are required to join the O.T.C. – that is to say the Officers Training Corps – training which takes the place of sport on Wednesday afternoons.' His eyebrows came together in a brief frown.

Peter too had seen the smile crossing his uncle's lips – from the way that the head had spoken of them together, almost in the same breath, it appeared that religion and military service co-existed in the Reverend Brindle's mind.

'You find something amusing in that, doctor?'

'Forgive me, Headmaster, it was merely the juxtaposition of the two concepts.'

'You find that amusing? We should remember that men fight and die for God, King and Country, in that order. I take it that in view of your, er, profession, you didn't take part in the Great War?'

'Oh, yes, I did,' said Uncle John quietly. 'Helping to pick up the pieces – quite literally. I presume, however, that being a man of the cloth, you didn't?'

Canon Brindle's only response was to noisily clear his throat whilst taking from an inside pocket a large watch and studying it.

'Now you must excuse me, I'm afraid, but I have things I must do. I'm sure, er, Waring will be successful here, as no doubt his father was before him. I've arranged for Richard Wilson, who is Head of English and also Assistant Housemaster on Founder's, to take you round the school and the House, and he will answer any other questions you might have.'

Coming around the desk, he shook hands with Peter's mother and uncle (but not, this time, with Peter), then opened the door. 'Ah, there you are, Wilson. This is Mrs. Waring, Dr. Webster, and, er, young Waring. I leave them in your good hands.' With a gesture that was clearly dismissive, he ushered them through into the corridor, and promptly closed the door behind them.

The man who came forward to greet them, somewhat effusively, was relatively young, perhaps in his mid-thirties, slim and of medium height, with a thick mop of dark hair flopping over his forehead. Both hands were raised as if to grasp some unseen object from the air; but the right one shot out as he reached them, and it was with Peter that he first shook hands.

'Welcome to Bard's. Peter, isn't it?' He pulled a rueful face. 'I'm afraid this'll be almost the first and last time your given name will be used here. It'll be 'Waring' only, after that. Such are the mores of our glorious education system for the nation's future leaders.' His speech was precise, with a faint Scottish intonation which softened the irony of the content, every word coming out almost in isolation as though he were relishing the sound of it.

He turned to shake hands with the two adults, after which his hands returned to their unusual gesturing movements. It soon became apparent that they were every bit as voluble as his lips and tongue, playing their own descriptive role in his conversation – apart, that is, from those occasions when one or other of them would dart upwards to brush back his recalcitrant hair.

'Come on, then, I'll show you around and answer as many as I can of all the questions that without doubt you won't yet have had chance to put.' He then led them at a rapid pace out of the building, his steps short and as precise as his arm movements were variable.

'I apologise that it will have to be something of a whistle-stop tour, as our American cousins might say, but I'll show you as much as I can.

'As you probably know, there are four boarding houses: School House where you've just been; Founders, where Peter will be, as was his father before him, I believe; Bishop's, (after the founder) which is a little apart from the rest of the school buildings, down on the fringe of the village, but which has the distinct advantage, in the view of many, of being slap next to the school tuckshop; and Benton's (also named after the founder). There are, roughly – the right adjective, that! – a hundred boys in each house, making some four hundred altogether in the school...in case your arithmetic is as shaky as mine!' He threw Peter an impish smile.

He prattled on in similar vein as they continued their tour, his eyes moving from face to face to gaze earnestly at each in turn as though beseeching understanding and agreement with what he was saying. But in spite of – or perhaps because of – his mild eccentricities, Peter had already taken a liking to him.

He showed them the chapel, the science block ('...a place of mystery, peculiar smells, and the occasional explosion – only joking!'), the swimming baths ('...distinctly Victorian – but the water's modern'), and the library ('...the one oasis of sanity'); and eventually they came to Founders, which finally brought home to Peter what life was going to be like for the next few years.

Founders was the only one of the boarding Houses which was contiguous with the main block of school buildings. As Mr Wilson explained, this was due to the fact that it was the oldest part of the school. Originally, a portion of the House itself had been the old grammar school, dating from the latter part of the seventeenth century, to which had been added over the years successive extensions incorporating first of all additional classrooms and then boarding facilities. There had been attempts to follow the initial Stuart architecture, but gradually the designs had drifted, until it had become 'a hotch-potch of indeterminate style' (as Wilson gleefully put it). Like all the other buildings it was constructed of sandstone, which from a distance had looked pastel-soft and almost ethereal; close to, it displayed instead an angry brick-red. Inside was no different: the walls of the corridors, hung with photographs, were of bare stone, and the floors were flagged, so that their voices and their footsteps rang with a brittle echo. So evident was the effect, their guide was moved to comment, 'You will appreciate why there is a strict rule of "no running or talking between classrooms".'

As they came to one particular section of corridor he slowed the pace, saying, 'Now, let's see...your father should be on one of these photographs somewhere here, Peter.' He looked at Peter's mother and uncle. '1st XV around 1900, I believe? Not sure? Ah, well that's what I'm led to

72

understand.' He peered in myopic fashion at a number of the faded pictures (which were all of rugby or cricket teams), stooping to look at the captions at the foot of the frames.

'Yes, here we are! "Waring, G.".'

He stood aside to let the three of them crowd around the photograph he'd indicated; and Uncle John, in turn, put a guiding hand on Peter's shoulder to allow him priority.

Peter stared numbly at the picture, yellowed by age, at the figures in football kit, tasselled caps on their heads, their poses, in the Victorian manner, stiff and unreal, already frozen in time even before the photograph had been taken. Underneath was printed: *Bardolph's School Rugby 1st XV, 1900-01*, and beneath that the list of names.

His eyes drifted to the figure indicated by his father's name, to the young face of a stranger – albeit a stranger whose features were recognisable – and his emotions took a tumble. The brief thrill at seeing his father was mixed with a sense of loss; and the vicarious pride at his father's place in school history was joined by a distant anxiety that this would be the standard by which he, Peter, would be judged – in school at least, and possibly beyond.

He must have been betrayed some of this in his expression, for Mr Wilson said, 'It is odd, isn't it, when you think about it, that sport is the only thing for which our past pupils are feted and remembered …that, and death on the battlefield! We have no public acknowledgement of those who have achieved much in the professions or the fields of commerce, or …' (and here he gave a laugh heavy with his by-now-familiar irony) '…become Prime Ministers. Or, come to that, made a success of their ordinary lives.'

But perhaps he was suddenly aware that he might have strayed onto sensitive ground, for there was a hint of embarrassment as he hurriedly went on, 'Come! Time is short and there is yet much to see.'

They continued into a section of the building that was arranged around three sides of a large quadrangle, seen through the stone-mullioned windows of the corridor, the fourth side being enclosed by tall wrought-iron railings and a gateway on the other side of which was the road. 'This is the oldest part of the school, and we are now in Founder's House, Peter. Perhaps it's a good time to describe some of that to you. The rooms you will see on the ground floor are mainly Dayrooms, to some extent allocated by years – First, Second, Third and so on – with two or three Studies for Prefects. The Dayrooms are where the boys live, in what little free time they have, and also, incidentally, where evening 'Prep' is done, under the supervision of a prefect. Like all the new boys, Peter, you will be in 'Baby' Dayroom for the first year.' He pulled a face. 'Sorry about the name, it is a bit derogatory, I know – deliberately so, I suspect! Each term, when you arrive back at school, your position in the House will be posted on this board.' He took a few steps along and stopped at an empty notice-board fixed to the wall.

'As soon as you get in, at the beginning of every term, the first thing you'll find yourself doing, along with everyone else, will be to rush along here – if you can get anywhere near because of the crush! – to discover which Dayroom you are in, and your 'position', relative to the others, in it.'

With a quick glance at Peter, he addressed his next remarks to the two grown-ups. 'I can see you're a bit mystified. At the end of each term, the Housemasters, together with the Head of House – the senior prefect – decide, in their collective view, what progress each boy has made. General behaviour, academic success, participation in school and house activities, and, of course, sporting achievements are all taken into consideration. Boys who have done particularly well during the term will move upwards for the next term, perhaps 'leap-frogging' over some of their fellows. Others, perhaps because they've blotted their copy-books in some way, will slide back. For some, their relative positions will stay unchanged. It can all be a bit invidious, I know, and quite definitely creates a certain amount of excitement – some would say, anxiety – at the beginning of term. But it is of course intended to encourage competition, and to reward success.'

Uncle John made a thumbs-up sign in the direction of Peter, presumably intended to be encouraging – but, if so, Peter didn't judge it at all effective.

'Anyway, let me show you one of the dayrooms,' the housemaster said, waving an arm in a more deliberate manner than usual as he headed off along the corridor. 'The stairs on your right lead down into the house changing-rooms, baths and showers; and they're used also by visiting teams. They're used, too, from time to time, with the typical lack of imagination of boys, for a quick smoke, a pastime which, I believe, can have distinctly painful consequences.' He turned to Peter with a grin. 'But then you wouldn't ever dream of doing anything like that, would you.'

Peter, with successive visions of his father drawing angrily on a cigarette, of Uncle John puffing contentedly on his pipe, and finally of his grandfather's cigars, could only shake his head.

'No, of course you wouldn't,' – and Peter was disconcerted to be given a conspiratorial wink.

'As you will have appreciated,' the master went on, 'Founders being the only house that is physically attached to the main school buildings means that it is also the one house that is to some extent necessarily integrated with the functioning of the whole school.

'Now, this is in fact Third Dayroom we're coming to, but they're all much alike – when you've seen one you've seen the lot.'

The room he showed them into was a large, square room with a single window on one side. In the centre of the floor, which was of bare, unpolished boards, was a long, battered table above which, at a height of about eight or nine feet, hung a solitary, unshaded light bulb. Lining all the available space around the walls was a series of wooden cubicles consisting of a simple desk and bench-seat, each attached to the adjacent partition dividing one cubicle from the next; and on the interior wall of each cubicle was fixed a double layer of bookshelves. A couple of stand chairs were parked against the table in the middle of the room; and underneath the window, which was the only part of the periphery of the room not taken up by cubicles, was a settee that might at one time have seen better days.

'Is this it? Do you mean to say this is where they actually live?' said Peter's mother in a tone of disbelief.

Wilson cleared his throat. 'I'm afraid so, Mrs Waring. But you must understand that they spend relatively little time in here apart from perhaps on Sundays, and even then they're mostly elsewhere doing other things.'

'Even so...' said his mother faintly. 'I mean, there seems to be nowhere for them to keep their belongings.'

'Well, of course, each boy has his own cubicle throughout the Term. The desk-tops do lift up, so they can put things inside. And there are the bookshelves. And there's room under the desk for them to put their tuck-box.'

'Even so...' she said again.

His uncle, who had been silent all this time, now said, 'You must remember, Marjory, that these are young, vigorous boys. They don't have the same concerns as you or I. And we must all remember that there will be many a lad in this land who would give his eye-tooth to have as much space as this all to himself or these conditions in which to live. Or, come to that, so would have the men in the trenches during the war.' He had spoken in a kindly manner, but there was a note of impatience also.

'Quite right, Dr Webster, said Wilson briskly, but, Peter thought, not with quite the same note of conviction as Uncle John. 'However, if you've seen enough, we must move on.'

He ushered them out of the room and on towards where the corridor disappeared around a corner, saying, 'We've just time to pop upstairs to see one of the dormitories, if you would like?' He didn't wait for an answer, but as they reached the corner he stopped abruptly so that they almost cannoned into him, and indicated a closed door facing down the corridor.

'In there is the prefects' main study. As you are aware, all boys have to fag for their first year. That means that they are at the beck and call of any of the prefects at any time, as a sort of 'batman' in military terms. The usual arrangement is that when a prefect comes out and bellows 'Fag!' down the corridor, usually the last one to arrive is given that particular chore, such as taking a message, going into the village to purchase something or other, or whatever. In addition, each of the fags will be allotted other regular duties such as cleaning the changing-rooms or dayrooms, making afternoon tea for the prefects, or acting as waiter in the dining room.

'However, each of the prefects, of which there are nine on this house, is entitled to choose a 'private fag', who will keep that job throughout his first year, for as long as the prefect sees fit. Private fags are excused all other duties, and do not have to respond to the general call of 'Fag!' But it's no sinecure. They have to act, in effect, as I said, as a sort of batman, looking after their 'officer's' laundry, sports kit, and Officers Training Corps kit – and cleaning rugby boots or 'boning' army boots, for example, is a time-consuming business. It's a good system though – good for discipline, both for the present and for the future.'

Peter, thinking of *Tom Brown's Schooldays*, couldn't see what was good about it; but he had no time to ponder, for they were already heading off towards a narrow stairway which took them up onto the next floor.

At the top the housemaster indicated another closed door. 'That is the House Sickroom, presided over in a most kindly and professional manner by the House Matron, Miss Plumly. The place is locked up, so I can't show you, but inside is a small treatment room, a four-bedded sick-bay and a bathroom, and Matron's own little apartment. It also has the distinction of being the only upstairs area to have hot water and heating: the school governors have been talking for some time about extending the downstairs systems to the upper floor, but I'm afraid that for the time being at least cost is the prohibitive factor.

'As for the Sickroom, the less serious illnesses and injuries are looked after here. If there are too many cases, for example with flu, then the patients are moved to the school sanatorium – which you would have passed on the road into the village – where the Matron is, er, shall we say, even more professional.

'Now, here's the dormitory you'll be in when you start, Peter, which also is much like all the others. I regret to say that it too, like the dayroom I mentioned, rejoices in the name of 'Baby Dorm'. He pulled a face, demonstrating again his own disdain for the name.

The room he showed them into this time was long and narrow, with high windows beneath an even higher ceiling, and a row of iron bedsteads, twenty in all, along each wall. The beds had still to be made up, and with their bare, flock mattresses looked forlorn and uninviting. Beside each bed was a plain wooden wardrobe about five feet high and two feet wide, in front of which stood a small chair. The floor was laid with lino; and the walls were painted in green gloss, now faded and chipped. At the far end of the room, up against the wall, were four washbasins, each with a single tap, and in the right-hand corner next to the basins was a low table. Even to Peter's eyes it was utilitarian in the extreme. He caught Mr Wilson glancing nervously at Mother: but she said nothing, staring straight ahead as though unwilling to acknowledge what little there was to see. Uncle John, as always, kept his thoughts well hidden.

'Well, if there are no other questions, then?...' said the master, a little too hurriedly. Uncle John, after pausing to see if Peter's mother had anything to say, merely shook his head.

'I'll show you the way out, then. You've a fairly long drive before you, I suppose.'

And a few minutes later, after they'd all politely said their goodbyes: 'We'll see you next month, then, Peter. I'm sure you'll enjoy being here, and will no doubt do well – following in your father's footsteps.'

The journey home was done mostly in silence. His uncle, after a few attempts at conversation, wisely left them to their own thoughts. Peter didn't know whether to be perturbed or relieved at his mother's withdrawn mood. He would have been more upset, he knew, if she'd tried to make reassuring noises. In any case, he couldn't yet fathom what his own reactions were. One moment he could feel the cold lump of apprehension, and the next he was stirred by an air of excitement and the whiff of adventure. It must be how men felt when they were about to go off to some lonely outpost of the empire. It made him feel heroic.

He couldn't quite shake off the feeling, though, that by admitting to himself any enthusiasm whatsoever for going away to school he was being disloyal to his mother. He didn't know why. All he knew was that she seemed uneasy about his going away.

It would only be years later that these memories, returning from time to time, would crystallise sufficiently to enable him to understand what it was that had so disturbed him: that his inner self had been reminding him that he had made a pledge that, with his father gone, he would look after his mother. He knew that having to live with Aunt Mabel and Jordan was making her unhappy; how would she get on, without him there to support her?

He was distantly aware, moreover, that he would be leaving behind something of more personal importance: those wonderful weeks of the summer with his new-found friends, who had become for him an extension of family. He somehow knew that he would never again be able to reclaim those exact sensations, those feelings of belonging, of being cocooned in a carefree world, a world of apparently endless sunshine. Again, in later years he would find that he could look back and have a clearer view; for the moment, it was only vaguely that he understood that, for these past few glorious weeks, time had not actually stopped but had merely paused, and would now continue inexorably on its way.

CHAPTER SIX

Stratton has by now stopped in front of their destination, and Peter starts to absorb the detail. Apart from the taller control tower at one end, the buildings in the centre of the block are largely two-storey, of concrete, flanked on either side by similar, but single-storey, flat-topped structures. The whole edifice is resplendent in a coat of camouflage paint in an abstract pattern of greens, browns and yellows which has clearly been recently applied. All the windows are crisscrossed in approved fashion with stuck-on strips of brown paper (which is supposed – optimistically, in Peter's view – to limit the effects of blast), which gives the impression that the buildings are derelict and perhaps up for sale. Fat sandbags providing protection for the doorways are piled one on top of another in a kind of bulwark, so that one is required to enter from the side and then turn at right angles to get through a door.

'To give you a quick idea of the layout, Peter,' says Stratton, 'working from the control tower at the far end are the Crew Rooms, then the main H.Q. block which of course contains the Station Commander's and Adjutant's offices, Records and Admin, the Lecture Room, which is used mainly for briefings, and other offices for bods such as the Intelligence Officer, squadron commanders and the senior WAAF Officer. Below HQ, underground, is the Ops Room, gained by a separate entrance and – strictly – only when in possession of the appropriate pass. That, incidentally, is known by all and sundry as 'The Hole'. The other buildings we passed on the way here, the Nissen huts, were the Sergeants' Mess, and then the quarters for other ranks and auxiliaries. Further on, the other way, out of sight from here, are the WAAFs' quarters…', he chuckles, '…can't think why they put them so much out of the way, can you! …and then the Guardhouse, and finally, beyond them, the fire and ambulance stations.' He grins, and adds, 'Perhaps there was some sense in lumping them all in the same area, after all! And beyond the control tower are the main hangars and workshops, armouries and, finally, dispersal huts. Oh, yes, and, you'll be pleased to know, there is also a Chapel, which is adjacent to the Sick Quarters.'

Scrambling out of the car, he says, 'But come on, you want to see your department. It's not much, I'm afraid, but better than on many stations, where not infrequently it's housed in a cold, damp Nissen hut. One good thing about being posted here, is that Marwell was built between the wars, with proper, centrally-heated buildings, unlike many of the airfields which were constructed more recently and done in a bit of a hurry. So make the most of it while you're here! It could be all much more spartan at your next posting.'

Well, I've been used to that in the past, thinks Peter. And again, sickeningly, it brought back further memories of Beal, and that first night at Bard's.

* * *

He lay, knees up to his chest, trembling with nervous excitement. The dormitory was silent apart from the occasional sibilant snore and the faint sounds of whispered conversation several beds along from his own. He had the uncomfortable feeling that none of the other boys was quite as dismayed as he by their new situation. Rather, pure excitement had seemed to be the dominant emotion displayed by most of them. There had been animated chatter during their rather rudimentary supper, for which together with the rest of the House they'd gathered in the dining room, and throughout most of which Peter had simply listened to the others in numb silence.

There had then been a brief interlude of an hour or so between supper and coming up to the dorm, which they'd spent in the dayroom, swapping names and sizing one another up. Peter, in spite of making considerable effort, had remained inarticulate, shackled to his shyness – but so also, he'd noticed, had been some of the others. He'd found himself gravitating towards them rather than to the majority who outwardly were so much more confident and able to see the whole thing as a tremendous adventure – but he knew that, if he'd felt able to, he would much rather have joined in with the latter.

One boy in particular, clearly lacking any self-consciousness, had taken centre stage, with a ring of others around him joining in the general banter. Smallish in stature, with dark curly hair, an impish face, and a marked Scots accent, his name was Prentice. Without exactly showing off, he had made it evident that he already knew what was what, having an older brother on the House, the year ahead. Because of this, he pronounced, his brother would now be known as Prentice Major, and he himself would become Prentice Minor. Prentice Major was clearly the source of much useful advance information. For example, the Housemaster, T.A. Roberts (whom they had still to meet – but who would be coming around at bedtime, according to Prentice Major), they learned, was generally known as 'Jack' or 'Sailor', depending on whim – because of the association of his initials, and because he walked with a rather rolling gait. In his younger days he had played scrum-half for Scotland for several seasons, which, needless to say, gave him great standing within the school – and was said to account (somewhat obscurely) for his gait.

But the information that Prentice Minor had really been bursting to pass on to the rest of them was that Beal was the prefect who would be in charge of their dorm. Beal, he explained in response to the blank expressions that greeted this purportedly stupendous news, was the hero of the House and, probably, of the whole school. Only now entering his fourth year and the Lower Sixth, and having just been made a house prefect at the early age of sixteen, during the last year not only had he already become a star of the 1st XV, playing as wing forward, but had also proved to be a more than useful bat and fast bowler on the 1st XI, a record that had never previously been matched. Prentice was so enthused by the whole thing that he made it sound as though he, or at least his brother, had been partly responsible for Beal's success; and, it had to be said, his audience had been suitably impressed by the knowledge that they were all to bask in the reflected glory of this exceptional fellow – for (they learned from Prentice) the prefect in charge of each dorm had his own bed in there as well.

When, therefore, a little while later, Beal himself had appeared at the doorway of the dayroom to shepherd them up to the dormitory, he had been greeted with silent awe. He was tall and well-built for his age, with short-cut sandy hair, and blunt pleasant features. His manner was relaxed and friendly, without any trace of bossiness, but nevertheless an air of determination which clearly would brook no argument with any suggestions he might make. Peter couldn't fail to be impressed by him, but more importantly had liked and admired him from that moment onwards.

Beds had been allotted according to age, each boy having his name-label attached to his wardrobe. Peter had been disconcerted to learn that, being the youngest boy on the house, as if to emphasise his position of inferiority his was the bottom-most bed in the room – but then had become puffed with pride, and the immediate focus of attention of the others, when Beal had strolled over and casually remarked, 'Now, that's a lucky bed; that's the bed I had when I started as a new boy.' And then he'd gone on to say, 'Waring, isn't it? I say, I couldn't help noticing, was that your sister with you and your parents, when you arrived?'

'No,' Peter had stammered, red with embarrassment at being the first one to be singled out for attention, 'she's my cousin. And that was my mother and my uncle,' – adding, for some reason or other, 'He's a doctor.'

He squirmed with shame when he thought about it now. It must have sounded pathetic. He couldn't understand, either, why there was this unexpected interest in Jordan. He didn't know why she'd wanted to come in the first place, anyway. It was most unlike her. She'd never previously shown the slightest interest in any of Peter's affairs. Aunt Mabel had been just as baffled, it seemed, and had grumbled at great length about the frock Jordan had chosen to wear – which was a new one, ending just at her knees and, according to Aunt Mabel, 'far too short' – and been equally scathing about her daughter's new shoes with narrow heels at least one inch high, which she'd chosen to wear along with her very first pair of ('extravagantly expensive') silk stockings. Anyone would have thought she was going to a party, instead of simply accompanying Peter to his new school. Aunt Mabel had said angrily that she looked like a 'flibbertigibbet'; Uncle John had merely looked amused; while Peter's mother had appeared cross that Uncle John had allowed Jordan to come at all.

Peter hadn't known what Aunt Mabel's long word had meant, but suspected that he agreed, having for several days been fascinated by glimpses of Jordan practising on those heels, tottering around with bent knees until Uncle John had shown her that what she really needed to do was to make herself stand upright and force her knees back as far as they would go. When Peter had taken a moment to go and look the word up in the dictionary, he had become at even more of a loss to know what his aunt had meant; but by then had lost interest in any case.

So when Beal had followed up with, 'She's a stunner, anyway. Lucky you!' Peter had begun to get some inkling at what his aunt had meant. Although he couldn't begin to think why Beal had thought it lucky for him. All Jordan had done, all the way to school, was to stare dreamily out of the window, hardly addressing a word to Peter sitting beside her on the back seat. However, it had all confirmed him in his decision, made some time ago, to give up trying to understand women. Why, only last month, when Uncle John and he had been full of glee because England had at last regained the Ashes for the first time in fourteen years, with the second innings' opening partnership of Hobbs and Sutcliffe knocking up a glorious two-hundred-and-sixty-one, none of the women in the household had been the slightest bit interested. But then, only five days later, when the papers for some reason had been full of the news that Rudolph Valentino had died, all of them, including Cook, had gone around with tears in their eyes as though they'd suffered some personal loss. Uncle John and he, bonded by mutual bafflement, had merely rolled their eyes at one another over the breakfast table. Peter had seen Valentino only once, in *The Sheik*, and had thought that both he and the film were soppy.

Anyway, after Beal had spoken to one or two of the other boys in the dorm, and then departed, the boy in the next bed to Peter had leaned over and said, 'I say, Waring, don't you have a father, then?'

He'd made his mind up after only a moment's hesitation, replying somewhat loftily, 'Yes, of course I do. But he's away.'

'Away? Away where?'

'We don't know, actually. It can be anywhere...like...like Constantinople, or...or Budapest.'

'Gosh! But doesn't he write, then, to let you know where he is?' The boy's interest was quickening.

'No, he can't...It's secret.'

'Why should it be secret?' There was now growing disbelief and truculence in the other boy's tone.

Again he hesitated only briefly. 'It's part of his job. He's a secret agent, you see.'

His neighbour's eyes had widened in astonishment, and before Peter could say anything else he'd called out, 'Listen to this, you chaps! Waring's father's a British spy!'

Peter hadn't liked the sound of that. Being a spy didn't sound quite …well, honourable. As far as he could remember, Richard Hannay had never been referred to as anything other than an 'Agent'. He had begun to wish that he hadn't said anything about it at all. It could get complicated.

But before he'd been able to say anything more, a party of three people had appeared through the doorway at the far end of the room, and the place had abruptly gone silent. The newcomers had in fact turned out to be Mr Roberts, the housemaster; Mr Wilson; and Jenkins, who was Head of House.

They'd slowly worked their way down the dorm, with all eyes upon them, their small entourage seeming to represent such hierarchical power that you could have heard a pin drop. As they stopped at each bed in turn to have a brief word with its occupant, Peter had had chance to study them.

'Jack' Roberts was a smallish man in his early fifties, with a balding head, steady pale blue eyes, and disconcertingly expressionless features. He'd a bluff, almost hearty, manner, and a gravelly voice. He walked not so much with a roll, as described by Prentice, but with an only-just-detectable sway of his hips – a motion that would become recognisable as an echo of the movement he would teach them when passing the ball on the rugby field. As he talked he would at intervals clear his throat, as though beginning a cough that never quite materialised, and punctuating the end of every third or fourth sentence with this as though it were a full stop.

Mr Wilson of course he'd recognised. But this had been a different sort of Mr Wilson from before. This Mr Wilson had stood deferentially a pace or two behind Roberts, leaving no doubt that the latter was the senior member of the partnership; and he'd hardly said a word. As he'd been carrying a sheaf of papers in one hand and a pen in the other, this time his previously so-expressive hands had also remained relatively still, as though anchored, and even the lock of hair tumbling over his forehead had remained more or less unmolested.

Jenkins, on the other hand, had had no such compunction about overstepping his proper position in the hierarchy. A head taller than Wilson, and a good head and a half taller than Roberts, it was evident that he, at least, saw his position as senior prefect on the house as being equal to theirs as housemasters. Thin and gangling in body, his face had the same characteristics, his eyes being close-set, his nose long and narrow, and his lips somewhat slack above a receding chin. The overall effect was that he seemed to look down on all those around him in a sneering, disdainful manner, while at the same time managing to look more than a little gormless. Whilst Peter in due course would learn that Jenkins' features accurately represented his character, he would also learn that they concealed a razor-sharp intellect, and that he was, to boot, a competent full-back on the 1st XV, and Senior Cadet in the O.T.C. He hadn't become Head of House without good reason.

Finally the three had arrived at Peter's bed, and Peter had found himself subjected to the unwinking gaze of 'Jack' Roberts' eyes. Although the initial impact of this had been to make him wonder if his every thought was being laid bare, he had been relieved to find that the effect was softened by creases around the housemaster's eyes which suggested a sense of humour; and his voice, when he spoke to Peter, hinted at a certain compassion for the situation in which the occupants of Baby Dorm now found themselves.

'Now then, Waring. Second generation, I believe. Who knows, your father might well at one time have been in that very bed!'

That thought, no doubt intended to give him some small comfort, had merely left him with an odd, hollow feeling. But he'd had no time to dwell on it, for the master had gone on to say, 'However, you're not your father, and it's up to you to make the best of the opportunities here and to make your own mark in your own way.'

There had been an almost imperceptible lift of the eyebrows following this pronouncement, perhaps inviting response – so Peter had hastily mumbled, 'Yes, sir.'

Roberts had turned away after that; whereupon Peter had been startled to receive a sly wink from Mr Wilson before he too turned to follow Mr Roberts back down the dorm. Jenkins, however, had paused for a moment to say condescendingly, 'I see your father was First Fifteen. That's something to live up to – if you can.'

There had been no particular inflection in the way that he'd said it. But for Peter, already pondering on what the Housemaster had said, and why he'd said it (the words reflecting as they did Peter's own lifelong doubts about his ability to live up to his father's standards), Jenkins' comment seemed to imply that indeed he wasn't likely to be 'up to it'.

Now, in the darkness of the dorm he had become overwhelmed by an all-too-familiar sense of isolation, of being disconnected from other people, a being apart. Once more he was among strangers, having to strive to bridge that gulf, his few supportive companions left behind. Following the habit of recent years, he allowed his imagination, the process of pretence, to take over, to carry him to a more acceptable world. He drew himself a picture of his father in a foreign land. His father too would be among strangers, hiding in unfamiliar cities and having to cope. Was that the inevitable lot of a secret agent – a spy? He found that he could, after all, embrace the term 'spy'. He decided that it more properly described the condition of that profession: having to hide in shadows, to pretend to be what one was not, having to avoid detection with all its consequences – but eventually being able to emerge into bright daylight holding out Success, yet hiding Failure so that it could slip away unseen. Here in the darkness he could perceive that as being his own future role also, in this unfamiliar place with uncertainties and difficulties to be faced on the morrow; he could conceive it as having to become literate in a strange tongue and having to compete with those already wise in this different world.

Imagining that, somehow comforted him. He might not be able to meet up with his father in Berlin or Prague, but they shared a common state. His father had experienced this same training ground, knew of all its challenges, rigours and privations. That was a common bond. He could pretend that his father would be able to imagine Peter's situation, and would be able to follow his progress every step of the way. Neither of them, in fact, would be entirely alone. That was what his father must have known when, so long ago, he'd made arrangements for Peter to come to this place: that his son, too, would be a sort of secret agent, following where his father would eventually tread, uncovering the secrets of a secret world.

And later, when he briefly awoke to hear the muted sounds of someone, presumably Beal, getting into bed at the far end of the dorm, by the door, he felt only excitement and anticipation for the morning.

And so, as things progressed, as the initial hours slid into days, and the days into weeks, he coped by inhabiting two different worlds. For much of the time the routines and distractions of everyday activity occupied his mind and demanded his attention. But at other times he could turn inwards to his secret life. He could fleetingly pretend that his alternative role, his undercover mission fed by covert coded messages from his father, was to detect foreign agents infiltrating the camp, and thereby thwart their malevolent aims; following which, of course, everyone would be amazed at what had been going on under their very eyes, all would be revealed and he would be regarded with awed admiration. Useful candidates for these foreign agents were not hard to find, and quite often included Jenkins, Blackman the maths master, and even 'Cannonball' Brindle. Sometimes, for variety, he would change the scenario, and imagine that he was a Captain of Cavalry in Arizona, with Apaches up on the hill beyond the stockade; or a member of the Foreign Legion manning a lonely outpost in the Moroccan desert – although he thought, on the whole, that this one would be best reserved until the hot days of summer.

If, now and again, a glimmer of critical self-awareness began to intrude on these diversions, a consciousness that, maybe, they might be diluting his attention to real-life school activities, it was firmly suppressed. For it became not a form of escapism so much as a mechanism for transmuting the physical and emotional state into which, silently protesting, he had been pitched. If the vicissitudes and hardships of his present situation could be seen to be not meaningless, but to have relevance and validity in his life, then he could embrace them. They became a preparation for some future, not yet identified, existence.

In any case, fortified by this private alliance of the real and the imaginary, after the first two or three weeks he discovered that he didn't actually dislike school. Unlike Mason (a namby-pamby, roly-poly sort of a chap who, having run away after only a few days only to be brought back, was so picked upon after that that he ran away again and was then taken away from the school) Peter found himself quite popular, so that he soon made friends. One of these, surprisingly, turned out to be Pearson, whose loud, attention-seeking behaviour had so grated on Peter during the first few days. Pearson, though, once he'd settled in, proved to be lively, yet thoughtful and modest; and having an older brother in school he was a valuable early guide to the mores of this new regime. Another who became his close pal was Chaplin (who never had any hope of avoiding the immediate nickname of 'Charlie'). He was a small, quiet boy with glasses – academic and introspective but with a good sense of humour and a keen recognition of the ridiculous (which also served to identify him with his namesake). After the first couple of weeks the three of them turned out to be doing more and more things together. However, they also shared a general camaraderie with most of the others in the dayroom, for 'baby' dayroom was a microcosm in that first year: there could be no fraternisation with those more senior on the house. At the intermediate level, between Second, Third, and Fourth Dayrooms, yes, there was some mingling between occupants, for they could share with each other membership of the same class or of the same team; but the First Years were Fags, the lowest of the low, not yet able to prove their worth, not yet granted recognition. This lowly status was emphasised, intentionally, by their being at the beck and call of the prefects, often for the most trivial of tasks, and also by their having to undertake any number of menial duties such as cleaning the lavatories and the changing-rooms, or preparing and tending coal fires in the prefects' studies, as well as making their afternoon tea. Failure to carry out these duties in a manner acceptable to the prefect concerned could incur a variety of penalties.

Each of the eight prefects on the house was, however, also entitled to have a 'private' fag. As had previously been explained to him by Mr Wilson, these latter individuals were excused all the duties of the 'general' fags (including the requirement to respond to a call of 'Fag!', as it echoed down the corridors). There was great competition, therefore, at the beginning of the term, to land this relatively privileged position, even though it meant equally hard work tending to the laundry, games kit, and O.T.C. uniform and equipment needs of the 'master', not to mention the endless cleaning and polishing of his shoes, rugby boots and army boots. Being chosen, though, was a matter of luck – and Peter had been out of luck.

If fagging was an integral part of the hierarchy leading all the way up to Prefect, then that hierarchy was itself one of the cornerstones of the overall public school system – the driving force of which also included Challenge, Routine, and Threat masquerading as Discipline.

Peter soon learned that punishment at Bards was handed out freely, in most cases by the prefects, for any infringement of the rules, which, he discovered, were many. They included, for example, such things as: the requirement to have all three buttons of the blazer fastened (unless one was a prefect, or on the 1st XV or 1st XI, or in the Upper Sixth Form); to avoid walking with one's hands in one's pockets (with similar, but not exactly the same, exemptions) and many, many others. In the first weeks, therefore, transgression was as much a matter of ignorance as carelessness or rebellion. Punishments ranged from extra chores, to running a given number of circuits of the House block in a given time, to cross-country runs (to be at once repeated if 'too slow'), and, finally, to canings, generally known, menacingly, as 'beatings'. The latter, carried out by the prefects, were not frequent, perhaps carried out on Founders no more than half a dozen times in a term, but always brought a reverent hush to the junior day-rooms, with the victim, once his ordeal was over, treated with sympathetic awe by his peers – provided, that is, that his deportment remained one of courage and dignity.

During that first term, only one of Baby Dayroom had to suffer this form of retribution: a boy called Hanson who, ironically, being bigger than the average and also a braggart, had shown himself to be a bit of a bully. Rumour had it that the cause of his downfall was being caught in suspicious circumstances with an older boy in the toilets, but this was never quite clear, and Peter was not inquisitive enough to search out the truth. In spite of Hanson's lack of general popularity, for the twelve hours between sentence being pronounced and it being carried out there was an atmosphere of suspense in the dayroom of such degree that it might have been all of them on whom the punishment was being meted. And when, walking stiffly, with a pretence of bravado but a trembling lip and an ashen face, he came back in through the door, there was a collective rush towards him and a murmuring of sympathy. It had to be said that curiosity was the mainspring of this attention, rather than genuine compassion; but when, in a corner, with almost an air of pride, he allowed them to see the damage, there were gasps of respect. In view of his youth he had been given only four strokes of the cane (as opposed to the older boy, his co-criminal, who had been given the usual six), and the four lines crisscrossed his buttocks as angry red welts. On closer inspection (the subject-matter being sufficiently intriguing to overcome any sensitivity there might be) it could be seen that actual pinpricks of blood were oozing along the length of the midline of these weals, which were flanked on either side by deep purple bruising. The enormity of this assault stunned them into silence, but only for a few seconds, and then Hanson was bombarded with questions which he answered with something like his usual cockiness.

It appeared that all the prefects had been there to witness the beating, but it had been Jenkins who had wielded the cane ('standing there, swishing the thing as if he was practicing his Squash strokes, when I went in'). Hanson had been instructed to bend over the back of a chair, holding onto the lower rungs ('....like a carpet over a line.'), and Jenkins had actually taken a run across the room to deliver each stroke. The outrageousness of that, when they heard it, shocked them all; none of them had envisaged anything quite so savage.

But if they were about to voice their universal condemnation of such a practice, it was immediately stifled, for at that moment Beal walked into the room.

'Inspecting the damage, I see,' he said, his voice matter-of-fact. 'Let it be a lesson to you all. Anyway, Hanson, well done. I should pop up and see Matron, if I were you, and she'll find something to put on to soothe those wounds.' And with that he walked out again – yet somehow managed to leave behind the impression that he'd disapproved of the way the caning had been carried out, thereby mollifying their anger at the prefects in general.

They turned then to Hanson, intrigued to know whether he would follow the advice about going up to Matron, but, when prompted, all he said was, 'Don't be bloody daft! Would you?' – and they all emphatically shook their heads.

The threat of force was not of course confined to prefects, as they were reminded on a day-to-day basis; most of the form-masters regularly and enthusiastically used this form of control in one way or another. This ranged from petty methods such as tweaking the short hair at the back of one's head or 'knuckling' of the scalp, through cuffing of the head, to the hurling of a book or the wooden blackboard cleaner at the head of any recalcitrant member of the class (usually accurately, for the teachers who favoured this approach had had plenty of practice). Clearly, the blueprint for discipline throughout the school had to be drawn at the top. And if there had been any doubts as to who was the architect they would soon have been dispelled by 'Cannonball', who took them for Divinity and Latin. For at all times in the classroom he carried his thin cane and used it with carefree abandon on hands or bottom, according to convenience, whether for some minor infringement or merely for displaying ignorance of the subject matter at that particular moment.

Most of the boys in Baby Dayroom seemed to have arrived at school well aware of the conditions that were likely to prevail. After all, they indicated, it was the norm, at least in Public Schools (Chaplin, whose sister was at a convent school, said that, even there, corporal punishment by the nuns was the preferred method of keeping the girls in their place). But Peter hadn't been prepared for it to quite that degree. Therefore he found it particularly difficult to adjust during those first three or four weeks. He could come to terms with the spartan conditions: they fitted in with his secret concept of personal mission, of heroic acts in the face of hardship. But when it came to reality, he had half-admitted doubts about his own physical courage. His father had never talked about his time in the war. But Peter had seen at first hand the effects that it had had on him; and in the past year or two there had been plenty written about some of the horrors that had attended the fighting in the trenches. He couldn't imagine himself in a similar situation; wondered what he would have done when the whistles had blown and it had been time to go over the top. With the thought of facing machine gun bullets and shells, of experiencing the frightfulness of the possibility losing one's legs, or the agonies of shrapnel in the belly, would he have simply curled up and refused to go? Richard Hannay or Bulldog Drummond, in those stories, described the experience of fear, but met it in calm manner, without trace of flinch or hesitation; the main characters in *The Four Feathers* and *The Scarlet Pimpernel* appeared to be cowards, but the reader knew that, underneath, unrealised at first by the world at large, they had indomitable courage. That, for Peter during the first weeks, was the attraction of his own make-believe world. Most of the time he could, without effort, be whatever he wanted to be. He didn't have to face the things that frightened him. At a stroke he could make them go away. But when it came to the classroom or the rugby pitch, there was neither the time nor the opportunity for imagination. Reality crowded in.

In any case, by the end of the first month his outlook on it all had, imperceptibly, changed. Some of the masters, as well as some of the prefects and seniors in house, were more benign. Mr Wilson, for example, might refer to them in class as a 'huddle of heedless horrors' or 'the great unwashed', he might address an individual as an 'irritating ignoramus', but that was the only hint of anger he ever showed, and they all knew from the very words, spoken though they were with a display of venom, that this was an expression almost of affection, and they responded accordingly. Not all the classes, therefore, when imminent, produced apprehension; and for those that did, Peter learned to develop stratagems to cope with them, to keep his head below the parapet, as it were, without seeming to – as he did in everyday activities on the house. He found, too, that he was good at running and also (being a little taller than the average) did well on the rugby field, playing at centre three-quarter or else on the wing – and began to enjoy it. Then, as well, once a week, on a Wednesday afternoon, they had their O.T.C. activities. The very term, Officer Training Corps, with its implication of their already being among the elite, instilled a sense of pride. And for Peter, dressed in army uniform with cap and badge, battle-dress and gaiters, and shouldering one of their new issue of Lee-Enfield rifles, it reinforced that sense of affinity with his absent father, as well as providing a background of realism for some of his games of imagination – as did, helpfully, the tradition in the school for one of the buglers from the O.T.C. band to play (from a balcony on School House) *Reveille* and *Stand To!* first thing each morning, and *The Last Post* to announce 'Lights Out!' at 9 o'clock each evening.

So it came about that the last weeks of that first term passed, in pleasant enough manner, almost unnoticed; and, suddenly it seemed, he found himself on the train home. When, on the last short leg of the journey, he could begin to glimpse the mountains again, there being no one else in the compartment he let down the window and, heedless of the billowing smoke and flying cinders, stuck his head out so he could get a better view. He was filled by a sense of heroism and growing elation. He had come through his baptism of fire unscathed, home to tell the tale. As the metallic click and clunk of the wheels on the gaps in the rails beat out their staccato rhythm it was like the beat of a regimental drum. He could believe he was at the head of his column of troops, leading them to the relief of Mafeking. And once more his mother would gratefully have his support, her miserable isolation ended. And he would very soon be re-united with his old companions.

* * *

Stratton leads the way over to the Medical Centre, but as they are about to go through the doorway he stops so suddenly that Peter cannons into him.

'Hang on, have you introduced yourself to the Adjutant, yet?'

Peter shakes his head in mild alarm.

In a gesture of vexation, the padre thumps his forehead with the butt of his hand. 'Of course, you didn't meet him last night, with all that shindig. My fault, I'm afraid! We'd better put that right before we do anything else. Wakeham, the out-going C.O., has of course probably already left – and, anyway, there's not really much point in meeting him, is there.'

It is just a short walk over to the H.Q. block, and after a quick introduction to the flight sergeant manning a desk just inside they head up some stairs to the where the offices are.

The Adjutant, a Squadron Leader sporting on the breast of his tunic the single wing denoting non-pilot aircrew qualification, proves to be a bluff-looking man with wiry grey hair. In his late thirties or early forties, the lines in his face suggested a normally-jovial character; but this morning he seems pre-occupied, even harassed, a state no doubt aggravated by the clear-cut signs of a good-going hangover. He greets Peter warmly enough, with a few welcoming platitudes and one or two follow-up questions, but it is evident that he is impatient to get on with other matters in hand, and after two or three minutes they take their leave. The presence of an M.O. on the station, new or otherwise, is clearly of little import to him at the present time.

As, at their second attempt, they enter the Medical Centre, a corporal who is busy at a filing cabinet springs to attention in a movement which is both over-elaborate and not quite co-ordinated.

'Stand easy, Browning,' says Stratton. 'This is Flight Lieutenant Waring, our new M.O.'

'Welcome to Marwell, sir,' says Browning, and sticks out his hand.

Peter, still not too confident when it comes to the protocol of dealing with other ranks but feeling that this isn't quite the norm, hesitates for a moment, then takes it. Out of the corner of his eye he sees the padre making no attempt to suppress a grin.

'Well, Doc,' says Stratton, 'I'll leave you to settle in. Browning, here, will show you what's what. Perhaps we might meet later, in the mess, for lunch?'

After the padre has gone, Peter, feeling the need to keep the relationship with Browning on a friendly and informal basis, says, 'And what's your first name, Browning?'

'Bartholomew, sir.'

Peter, unable to remember having ever met a 'Bartholomew' before, struggles to keep his face straight.

'And what do they usually call you?'

'Bartholomew, sir.'

There is not the slightest hint of humour in the man's voice, but rather a touch of impatience, as though explaining something to a child; and the eyes that look back at him from behind wire-framed spectacles are earnest and devoid of any guile.

Peter coughs and says, 'Er, yes...er...of course.' He studies Browning for a moment. Difficult to be precise about his age: in spite of a receding hairline, possibly only a few years older than Peter. Medium height, with an angular, wiry build, an imprecise chin, and an eager, edgy manner as though constantly wanting to be up and doing. Not so much nervous as living on his nerves. With his liquid brown eyes which have something of the imploring about them, his demeanour passive but betraying eagerness, he reminds Peter of a young spaniel.

'You were a tutor at Oxford, I believe?'

'Yes, sir. At Merton.'

'Teaching what? – and look here, if we're to be working here together we can't have you keep calling me 'sir'.'

'No, sir...I mean...Modern History...How should I address you, then?...sir.'

'Oh, I don't know,' says Peter distractedly. 'How about 'Doctor'?'

'Would that be less formal?...sir.'

Peter stares at him suspiciously, wondering if the man is quietly taking the piss; but all he gets is that unwaveringly innocent look. He decides to take a different tack.

'How does Flight Officer O'Connor address you?' he asks.

'Usually as 'Corporal', sir.'

'Usually, but not always?'

'Sometimes she calls me...calls me...' He seems unable to complete the sentence, his suppressed agitation now becoming manifest.

'Sometimes she calls you what?' prompts Peter, gently.

'Sometimes she calls me 'Bart'.'

Peter has to turn away to hide his smile. He decides to abandon the subject for the time being.

'Is Flight Officer O'Connor here?' he asks, with a mixture of anticipation and apprehension, but managing to keep the nervousness out of his voice.

'No, sir, she's having the day off. She'll be back tomorrow.'

Peter experiences a twinge of relief at that, as if he'd just been handed a temporary reprieve – which is immediately followed by intense irritation with himself for being so childish. Apart from the irrationality of his reaction, he more than half suspects, anyway, that Munro and Stanton, with their florid description of O'Connor, have merely been setting him up.

'With a background in History, how did you end up working in the medical field, then?' he asks, as much as a distraction for himself as out of genuine curiosity.

'Well, sir, when I was coming to the end of my six weeks basic training the group was asked if anyone had any experience in nursing or other medical work. So I stepped forward. I reckoned that whatever it was going to be for, it was likely to be better than being a general *erk*.'

'So, what experience have you had, in fact?'

'When I was in the Boy Scouts I obtained my badge in First Aid…sir.'

Peter has to burst out laughing. Not only has the answer been given in a totally ingenuous manner, but the fellow gives no indication of finding anything remotely humorous in the situation. Against his better instincts he decides, though, that he'd better follow up that extraordinary piece of information.

'And how on earth did they respond when you told them that?'

'I didn't tell them, sir.'

'So what did you tell them?'

'Nothing.'

'Nothing?'

'No. I mean Yes. No one asked.'

Incredible as it sees, Peter has no difficulty in believing it. In the present atmosphere of confusion and uncertainty, someone would have been only too glad to have apparently found a suitable candidate for yet another post of relatively little importance. More than a bit like his own posting as Station M.O., in fact. And the momentary gleam in the other man's expression reveals that he, too, has not only come to the same conclusion but is well aware also of the similarity of both cases. He decides then that as already suspected there has to be more to Bartholomew Browning than meets the eye.

The rest of the morning is spent in acquainting himself with what little equipment there is, going through files, and being shown around the premises by Browning. Apart from the outer office, there is a small Treatment Room, an even smaller Consulting Room with barely enough space for a desk and a couch, and two Sick Rooms, which hardly merit the term 'Wards' – one, for WAAFs, containing two beds, and the other, for men, containing six beds. When he queries, with Browning, the adequacy of this arrangement, he is informed that they are in any case very rarely used, and that 'anything at all serious' will be sent on to the RAF hospital at Mildinghall. So much, Peter thinks, for the service's confidence in the Station M.O. and his staff.

CHAPTER SEVEN

Later, joining the padre for lunch in the Mess dining room as arranged, he finds the place pretty well full. The atmosphere is fairly subdued, as befits a bunch of men who show all the signs of still being severely hung-over, but even so the quietness is sundered from time to time by sporadic outbursts of jocularity from various corners of the room. He wonders, not for the first time, how he is going to fit in with this bunch of men who are not only so high-spirited but evidently devil-may-care about most aspects of life. Indeed, he feels a familiar depression begin to steal over him at the prospect of this enclave of strangers wielding the authority of their collective expertise and self-confidence. It's old territory – he's all too aware of that – but he still hasn't learned how to successfully cross it. Then he looks at them again, and it strikes him that they all look so young – are in fact so young, scarcely more than boys. A few look at him curiously as he seeks out Stanton then wends his way between the tables to join him; some nod in friendly enough fashion, or look enquiringly at his tunic to discover his rank and function; but for the most part he is ignored – not, he takes pains to reassure himself, because he is likely to be of absolutely no interest to them, but purely because they are so wrapped up with their own affairs. Nevertheless, as with his meeting with the Adjutant it has the effect of reaffirming his relative unimportance in the scheme of things here in this small theatre of war, and does little for his self-esteem.

Perhaps some of this reveals itself in his expression – or perhaps Stanton is particularly perceptive – for as he greets Peter and gestures for him to pull out a chair, he says, 'You know, it takes a while to get beneath the surface with this lot. You look at them all, even the relatively new ones and you think: here's a roomful of seasoned warriors, confident and professional in their approach to the task ahead. In reality they – or most of them – are a crowd of schoolboys excited by a new adventure; for heaven's sake, some of them had never even been up in the air before, until two or three months ago!

War, for the majority of them, is still – at the moment – a new game, a different challenge to be approached with the same bravado as they've approached every other challenge so far in their young lives. The thought of death or injury is, as yet, still unfamiliar to them; and if the thought is there at all, it is merely as a tiny acknowledgement that it is something that can happen to someone else. Their main concerns at present are with their own performance, with learning new skills, with not 'letting the team down', and – most important of all – with not 'losing face'. Much like the rest of us mere mortals, in fact! All that will change, of course – perhaps next month…perhaps next week. Those few of us with personal experience of war, of its realities, know *that* only too well. But we can't tell that to them – there would be no point, and anyway they wouldn't believe us. They have to learn it for themselves. Our task – yours and mine – will be to help them through it as best we can; and, God knows, that will be a task verging on the impossible.'

Peter nods sagely, for he knows that what Stanton is saying must be true. But his thoughts are again briefly elsewhere, to a period of his own when he had been initiated into yet more of the realities of life.

* * *

The rain, sweeping horizontally in heavy grey curtains, momentarily blotted out the fells on the far side of the valley, making it incredible that the four of them standing watching it could still be bathed in wintry sunshine.

'Come on,' said George, ever practical, 'we're being left behind.'

Obediently they trooped in his wake. He was the one with the most experience, therefore the natural leader of this expedition. Sure enough, the Huntsman in his faded red jacket, his horn slung over one shoulder and his plaited leather whip coiled in the hand holding his long stick, was already several hundred yards ahead, the thirty or so hounds and the half-dozen followers scattered around him.

Peter still couldn't come to terms with how fast the man could move: although not tall, and never seeming to hurry, he covered the ground whether uphill or level at a pace that was difficult to keep up with. Peter made the excuse for himself that his new boots, proud as he was of them, still felt strange and awkward ('it'll take a while to walk them in' was the expression that Uncle John had used when he'd presented them as a belated birthday present); but, anyway, the others were having just as much difficulty in staying with him.

When George had suggested that they follow the hunt, it being right on their doorstep on this particular occasion, Peter had been a bit dismayed. Embarrassment overtook him again now when he recollected how he'd said, 'But I can't ride!'

The laughter from the others had, however, been gentle, even though there'd been the usual derogatory note of challenge from Bill, who'd said:

'Don't be daft. No one goes on horseback here. How could they, with these mountains!'

It had been obvious really, when he'd stopped to think about it. In any case, it didn't really bother him all that much: he was only too relieved that he'd been accepted back as a member of the Four without any reservations. He'd worried that being away at school all those weeks might have created a distance between them. As it turned out, nothing seemed to have changed – apart from Jamie.

His thoughts on that, though, were now disrupted by shouting from up ahead and an air of excitement which communicated itself to the four of them, so that they spontaneously broke into a run. He couldn't make sense of the shouts, dissembled as they were by distance, and anyway huntsmen and hounds had now disappeared from view around a rock spur; but there now followed a different sound from even further away, a drawn-out, keening sort of sound that brought up the hairs on Peter's neck. It had an anguished, haunting quality, echoing from the surrounding fells, yet musical – the sort of sound, he imagined, that might be made by wolves.

'Whatever's that!' he blurted.

'Someone's hallering!' said George, equally excited, and increasing his pace.

Bill, anticipating Peter's look of blankness, explained with unconcealed amusement, 'He means that someone's calling a "view", that is he's seen a fox. What's called a "Halloo" in books. It draws the hounds in that direction; as opposed to the calls you heard from the huntsman immediately before, which were to encourage the hounds to spread out and start searching for a scent.'

By now the gradient was much steeper, so that they had no breath to spare for further talk, but pushed themselves until, puffing and panting, they breasted the top of the hill from where they had a clear view of the fellside falling away from them, and of the valley below. The huntsman could be seen on a ridge still some distance away, a splash of red surrounded by the drab greys and browns of his immediate followers, and, well beyond them, streaming down towards the valley floor in a straggling line, were the dots of mottled white which were the hounds.

Peter and the others, chests heaving, paused to regain their breath. Peter, quite transported by the thrill of this sudden change of pace, also felt a sense of awe. When they'd first gathered at the meet, earlier that morning, he'd been overcome by the sheer, unexpected size of the hounds. For some reason he'd imagined something smaller; and this mass of large, patchwork-coloured dogs in black, white, and tan displayed such power and exuberance that he had initially recoiled in fear. However, it was soon obvious that the dogs' enthusiasm was matched by their friendliness; and he'd then taken delight in holding out his hand for them to snuffle and lick in a show of curiosity and delight. To see them now, though, a united mass responding in such a manner, as if to a bugle call, conjured up the image of a glorious cavalry charge hell-bent on breaching enemy lines – until he remembered that the purpose was, after all, to hunt down and kill a single fox, still unseen. It seemed too much for so little, and his heart went out to that isolated prey.

He was so struck by that last idea that he ventured to express it to the others.

George, phlegmatic as always, gave him a long look before saying, in some perplexity, 'But they've always hunted that way. It's not as easy as you might think. It's not as if the fox is just sitting down waiting for them. You won't be seeing him for dust! And remember, they won't even have got his scent yet, never mind caught any sight of him, and he knows every stick and stone of the country a lot better than what they do.'

'Ignore him, George. He's just being soppy!' Bill, although friendly enough, was still keen to seize every opportunity to needle Peter, and there was a distinctly disparaging note in his voice. 'Pete probably thinks of a fox as being some sort of cuddly toy to take to bed, rather than as the killer he is!'

Peter glanced uncertainly at Jamie. Previously she would have come to his support by now, instead of which she was simply looking at him, her face expressionless. He was out of his depth. He didn't know anything about foxes. And he didn't now know about Jamie. She was different. He couldn't quite understand in what way. It was as though she didn't much care about anything any longer. From being the organiser, the controller, she now just let things go over her head. Previously careful, she was now nonchalant, indifferent, almost devil-may-care. And if the other two had noticed, they weren't showing it.

Perhaps he should have listened more carefully to what Uncle John had been telling him. Asked questions. But no. He couldn't have done.

When he'd arrived home two days ago none of it had been how he'd imagined it would be. The house itself had had that welcoming appearance, as he'd thought it would, reminding him how much he'd missed it. His mother, when she met him at the station, had been affectionate and delighted to see him but, it had to be admitted, was not exactly swooning with delight and relief that he'd come to 'rescue' her from her beleaguered position of abandonment and isolation. She hadn't in any way intimated that she regarded him as her saviour and hero. He'd felt quite let down.

His uncle and aunt had been pleased to see him, of course, as had Cook – in fact she'd been more demonstrative than any of them, particularly when he'd thanked her for the large fruitcake she'd had sent through the post for his birthday: generously 'laced' with glace cherries and covered with almond paste and sugar icing it had made him the most popular person in the dayroom for several days.

Brought back to the reality of home life, he'd been relieved, therefore, to find that his mother and Aunt Mabel were evidently now getting on much better. Even Jordan was genuinely being more civil. She was different in other ways, as well. Following her sixteenth birthday, which was close to Peter's birthday, she'd been allowed (reluctantly by her mother, and less so by her father, according to Cook) to have her hair shingled in the up-to-date style. Without her pigtail and with her hair so short, and her skirts even shorter, above the knee this time (to her mother's, and even Cook's, consternation, but with her father's permission), she looked now quite grown-up. She was even being more civil to Peter. True, she hadn't greeted him with actual enthusiasm, but she'd looked at him with something like interest, and said, 'You've grown.'

It was true. According to the 'Bombardier', their gymnastics teacher (ex-Sergeant-Major Moss was his self-styled title, but he was always known by the lesser soubriquet, at least behind his back), whose responsibility it was to weigh and measure them at the beginning and end of each term, he'd put on just over two inches. So he was now almost as tall as Jordan.

Come to think of it, he'd looked at her with different eyes, this time, too. The interest shown in her by Beal and others at the beginning of term had made him think. He supposed she was really quite pretty, now that he considered it. Exceptionally so. But they didn't know her as he knew her; were they to do so, he was certain, they would quickly lose interest.

But Jamie was different. She might, too, be a girl, but she couldn't help that. He cared about Jamie, he realised. And it worried him that she appeared to have changed from the Jamie he'd got to know before.

That very first day home, once Uncle John and he had got over the excitement of showing him the telephone that had been installed (and Peter had even had a practice with it, speaking to the woman at the other end, at the *Exchange* as it was called), his uncle had taken him aside and said, 'I take it The Famous Four will be meeting up again?'

Peter had nodded, although at that point privately a little uncertain as to how things would be.

'There's something I think you should know, Peter,' his uncle had gone on. 'It's about Jamie.'

Then, seeing Peter's consternation, he'd hurried on, 'It's nothing you need to get worried about. It's just this. You know that Jamie's mother is a widow? Well, she's planning to get married again, and Jane – that is to say, Jamie – is, well, a bit upset. She'll get over it in time, I'm sure. I can't say any more than that, because Jane – Jamie – is my patient, so it's confidential, you understand? But I thought you ought to know, in case you find that she's a bit different from before, d'you see.'

Uncle John had had difficulty in hiding his awkwardness at talking to Peter about it, and in disguising his own sense of upset, with the result that he'd said it all in a bit of a rush; but rather than making things easier for Peter, as he'd clearly intended, from that moment on it had in fact made him anxious about meeting Jamie again.

It was with a sense of relief, therefore, that he now heard Jamie saying, almost dreamily, 'I don't think the fox is a killer – not in the way you seem to mean it, Bill, as though he's evil. He – or she – has to kill to live. Which is what we all do, isn't it?'

'But we don't kill for the joy of it. The fox does.'

'Don't we?' There was bitterness now, unusual in Jamie. 'What about in the war? I don't even remember my dad. I don't even know how he died. But the way they write about it now, all those guns and shells and machine guns and…and suchlike, makes you think that there was some kind of…of hideous delight in it some of the time.'

The change of mood produced an oppressive silence which so disturbed Peter that he became desperate to break it. 'Isn't that the same as what's going on here? All these people and all these dogs trying to kill one fox, and enjoying doing it? And the fox is all on its own, as well, with no one to help it.'

The three of them looked at him with curious expressions, all different. Jamie, he imagined, was perhaps looking at him as though he was someone she'd only just met, with interest, even admiration, so that he suddenly felt two feet taller. Bill merely looked impatient with an accompanying lip-curling contempt, as though Peter hadn't a clue what he was talking about; and George – well he was just the usual, patient, unperturbed George. It was he who this time broke the ensuing silence.

'I think the fox is always on its own, Pete. That's what my dad says, anyway, and he knows a lot about such things. He says that the dog fox is a solitary animal anyway. And once the cubs are pretty well full grown they get kicked out by their mum and have to fend for themselves as individuals. And if they try to come back she'll attack them and chase 'em away. My dad says that the fox spends the rest of its life alone, except for mating, like, or, if it's a vixen, for the few months that she has her cubs.'

Peter felt himself flushing – partly because of the talk of 'mating', which George, living on a farm, seemed to know all about (whereas Peter knew only that it referred to something that was 'dirty' and that one talked about secretly, with furtive excitement); and partly because of the distress and sympathy he felt for a creature destined to live always in loneliness. At least the fox lived in familiar territory, was at home there. A secret agent, on the other hand, a spy in, say, Constantinople, was not only hunted but had to spend his time in a place he didn't know. Desolation overcame him.

As he turned away to cover his discomfort he was startled by a sudden brassy sound concussing the air – an extended single note followed by several short ones, strident yet musical, it bounced off the surrounding crags and echoed off the hills before dwindling down the valley.

Before he could speak, George said laconically, 'It's the huntsman's horn. He's calling the hounds to him. It could mean that the fox has been seen doubling back this way, and he's bringing the pack back to head it off.' Then he added, 'Or it might be that he's decided that they've gone off on a false trail, and he's starting all over again. It'd be worth us getting to him, though, in case they do chase off in the opposite direction.'

Galvanised by the thought, they all began to run in the direction of where they'd last seen the huntsman, who'd now disappeared from view. As they went, Peter recalled what George had said at the outset, that on most hunts you were lucky if you saw the hounds again, once they'd set off, never mind being ever able to spot a fox. Well, at least they were seeing the hounds in full chase, so that was something.

A few minutes later, though, when they'd reached the top of the next knoll, to their disappointment they saw that the principal knot of followers had already moved to higher ground about half a mile away, and there was no sign of the pack. At George's suggestion therefore they decided to sit down and await further developments. As George said, anything could happen and the hunt could as likely come to them as go away.

Finding a level ridge of ground they sat in a line facing across to the opposite fells. The rain in that direction appeared to have moved away, and the mist obscuring the peaks was already breaking up into individual gatherings of cloud repeatedly coming together then parting, drifting and rolling up the slopes in a restless, almost agitated manner as though anxious to be gone. Even as they watched, the sun broke through uncertainly, illuminating an area of hillside and striking silver off thin filaments of streams hurrying their way down to the valley below; and before long the whole mountainside was beginning to clear and the peaks, backed by blue, started to peer coyly over the few lingering ranks of cloud. He was sitting upright, his arms out behind him, propping himself up, and on his left the two boys lay flat on their backs. On his right, close to him, Jamie was also sitting propped up. As they continued to sit in silence, gazing at the changing view, Jamie shifted her position slightly, to make herself more comfortable, and as she did so her hand came into contact with Peter's, so that her fingers rested lightly across his. The effect this had on him took him by surprise: he was all at once overcome by his awareness of her, the feel of her fingers on his magnified to the point where his skin seemed to tingle. His heart began to race and his cheeks became warm. He expected her to immediately remove her hand, and when she didn't he wondered whether to pull his own hand from under hers – though that seemed a rather abrupt thing to do. He glanced nervously at her; but if she was aware of the contact between them she didn't show it. They sat there like that for some time, Peter hardly daring to move. He found it exciting, although he couldn't have said why – and also comforting. It made him feel special. It also made him think differently about Jamie. Of course he was alive to the fact that, being a girl made her different to the rest of them – how could he fail to be aware of that after the humiliating way in which he'd first made the discovery! But it hadn't had any effect on the relationship. She hadn't behaved any differently from the rest of them. But now, all at once, he was all too conscious of the difference. If George or Bill had happened to touch his hand he wouldn't even have noticed. It was disturbing.

Wrestling with these emotions, not wanting anything to change, he barely noticed George abruptly sit up, tension in the movement.

'Listen!' George's voice was gruff with urgency. 'I think I can hear the hounds.'

All four of them silent, Peter could hear at first only faint sounds that hadn't registered before: the tiny tinkle and splash of numerous, far-off streams, the subdued sigh of the breeze ruffling the heather, and the occasional bleat of a plaintive sheep. Then he began to pick up something else. Ebbing and flowing to start with, but becoming more constant, it was like the jumbled, muffled music of some distant woodwind band, the pitch rising and falling, but the confused, disparate notes gradually linking, as the seconds passed, to produce a more coherent tune in which there was no mistaking the theme: it was one of excitement and exhilaration.

'Yes, there!' cried George. 'It is! It's the hounds in full cry. And it sounds as though they're heading this way.'

At that point Bill, who'd sprung to his feet on George's warning, hissed at them, 'Quiet! There's the fox!'

Their heads jerked up to see him pointing behind them, over their left shoulders – but at this point Bill was looking down at Peter and Jamie, an odd expression on his face.

As they all swivelled round to see for themselves, Jamie released Peter's hand, although not before giving it a small squeeze in what seemed to be a conspiratorial fashion. But he'd no time to think about that. It took him a few seconds to identify what Bill was pointing at. Less than fifty yards from them the fox stood in a half-crouch, staring at them. It looked weary, its flanks heaving and its coat, the colour of winter bracken, dark in places, as though wet. To Peter it seemed to be looking directly at him, and, he thought, its eyes held a beseeching expression.

'Let's get the hounds this way,' urged Bill. 'Go on, George, give them a 'haller'!'

'No!' The single word from Jamie was spat out with uncharacteristic venom. Then, more gently, 'No. Let it go.'

There was a stunned silence; but Peter felt a tide of relief and an additional surge of warmth for Jamie.

And the fox, as though understanding what had been said, turned away and went off at a fast trot, finally disappearing from view, cat-like, into a tumble of rocks below an expanse of crags.

With only five days to go to Christmas Day, the weather turned wet and windy, effectively baulking the plans of The Four to meet again during that period. Peter found this frustrating for more than one reason. He was conscious of the fact that there were a couple of unresolved issues: firstly the tensions which had arisen as the result of their disagreement on the day of the hunt, and the way in which it had become evident that Jamie and he had been allies in opposition to the other two in the dispute about their conduct on that day; and secondly the relationship between him and Jamie which, in his eyes at least, had taken on a subtly new face the significance of which he could only guess at.

Following their silent inaction as they'd all watched the fox disappear from view, there had come a sullen anger from George as well as Bill. As George had forcefully reminded them, 'The whole point of a hunt is to catch the fox'. When Jamie had challenged that view against the vociferous arguments of the two boys, Peter had been bold enough to side with her – but when Bill, with naked antagonism, had challenged him to say what other reasons there could be, he'd been unable to come up with anything; instead he'd again reflexly looked towards Jamie to provide an answer. That had left him feeling both ineffectual and dim, particularly as Jamie had wordlessly met his silent appeal to her with a look that, in his eyes, was tinged with contempt. Yet he knew that he'd experienced only joy that the fox had been allowed to get away; and he had half-formed suspicions that the thrill of the hunt, undoubted as it was, appealed to much baser instincts than anyone was prepared to admit.

So now he didn't know how he stood with Jamie. All he knew was that the relationship had taken on a new importance for him. He now believed that her holding his hand – if that wasn't describing it in too strong a term – must have been deliberate. It may have been accidental to begin with, but after that she couldn't not have known she was doing it. There was no doubting it had had a surreptitious almost conspiratorial quality to it. Private and personal, secret, just between the two of them. Maybe she just felt that they shared a common bond? Neither of them had a father; and both of them were suffering stresses in their personal, family lives. And neither of them had a brother or sister, either. Perhaps that was it? Jamie was looking upon him as a brother? That thought gave him a good deal of comfort. He wouldn't mind Jamie as a sister. Not one little bit.

Distracted by his problems and frustrated by the weather, he moped around the house over the next two days, getting under everyone's feet, so that Jordan, who was equally bored, snapped at him even more than usual, her voice, as always, heavy with sarcasm. With Christmas looming, he was getting more anxious about plans for that, as well. They were all to go to *The Royal George*, the principal hotel in the town, for their dinner on Christmas Day and Boxing Day, a tradition that his uncle and aunt had established over the years – 'to allow Cook and Ethel to have both days completely off ', as his aunt had put it. He was led to believe that on both days it would be a fairly grand occasion (by local standards), attended by many people from the town as well as by hotel residents from away. Dress was formal, and following dinner there would be dancing, with a band and 'some games'. Just the sort of thing he hated. Even worse, he'd had to have a new suit for the occasion, his first 'sort of grown-up' one, which, when he tried it on, made him feel really self-conscious (particularly when his mother had said 'You look really nice in that, darling'). So, really, he felt quite down about everything at the present time.

However, on the morning of the third day Joe Harris, the man who gardened for them, delivered the Christmas tree and, with some difficulty but willing help from Peter, brought it into the drawing-room and erected it. Standing in its tub it must have been eight feet high, its tip not far short of the ceiling; and for the first time Peter began to absorb some of the growing excitement as the countdown to the festive season really got under way.

Then, to his immense surprise, Jordan invited him to join her in bringing down the decorations from the attics; and after lunch suggested that he might assist her in putting them up on the tree.

For this purpose they had a pair of tall stepladders which were somewhat rickety, swaying and creaking as one climbed up on them. Peter was appointed therefore to steady them for Jordan to climb (much to Peter's private relief) and to hand the baubles and streamers up to her as she required them. Jordon had on one of her new, light dresses (more suitable for summer than for December, in Peter's opinion – but, in fairness, the downstairs central-heating was on and the house really not at all cold), so that much of the time he found himself staring at her ankles, which were at his eye-level. For once she was being remarkably civil towards him, indeed almost friendly, asking politely for the decorations as she required them, and even remaining patient when he occasionally fumbled them. So, gradually relaxing, he began to take more notice of what was in front of his eyes. As usual, she was wearing silk stockings, and he became intrigued by the way in which the silk clung to, and followed, the contours of her ankles and calves, imparting a smoothness and lustre to her skin which was really quite fascinating. He allowed his eyes to follow the line of her calves up to her knees, below the hem of her dress, finding pleasure in studying the fine curves and dimples of knees as well as ankles, and the changes in muscle tone with her small movements. And he discovered, curiously, that he found all these things really quite interesting.

As he passed things up to her she had to reach down to take them from him, bending forwards to do so. He then realised that as she did so, and also whenever she leant towards the tree, it created a tent-like space in her skirt enabling him to see up the back of her thighs. The shadows up there were softened by light from the overhead chandeliers which, shining through the thin material of her dress, produced a diffusely soft glow with gradations of light and shade as she moved. His eyes, travelling upwards, along the line of her thighs, past her stocking-tops and suspenders, then met a faint gleam of nakedness and beyond that the suggestion of more silk and darker shadow. A strange sensation, like a current, swept through him, and at once became a storm of excitement so great that it caught his breath. He was like a traveller entering dramatic new terrain. He wanted to reach out and embrace all that he could see. His arousal became physical, startling him in its suddenness, so that he looked down to see whether she would be able to see for herself the evidence of his shame – and, alarmed, almost cried out as, at the same time, her voice floated down.

'Come on, dozy. Wake up. Pass me something else.' There was no hint of accusation; indeed, there was perhaps a certain self-satisfaction in her tone.

Then a new voice, tart and critical, intervened.

'Now then, young lady, what are you doing up that ladder in one of your best dresses? You'd be better to be wearing a pair of them slacks you're usually so fond of wearing.'

Confused, his head whipped round, driven by his sense of guilt, to see Cook standing there, arms akimbo, a flush of anger adding to the normal high colour of her features.

'Oh, don't take on so, Jessica,' sang out Jordan above him, unperturbed. 'We're alright. Quite happy, in fact, aren't we, Pete?' – and her voice rang brittle with inexplicable glee.

* * *

Stanton pulls a face. 'I'm sorry, Peter. I have, as you will have realised, a natural inclination to preach! I hope I haven't seemed to be talking down to you. Just thought it might be helpful to understand that everything isn't always as meets the eye in a set-up such as this.'

Peter, his thoughts having been drifting to the past whilst listening to the other man, mumbles his thanks, coupled with a denial of having in any way felt patronised by the padre's potted sermon. And this is the truth. He's grateful to Stanton for giving him a different perspective on things; and even more so for indicating, as he seems to have done, that he understands that Peter too carries his own burden of self-doubt – and, in indicating that, admitting at the same time that he, Stanton, also is personally familiar with the same sorts of uncertainties. But there remains one radical difference between them: the padre might now be in a purely subsidiary supporting role, as is Peter, but he at least has experienced all the terrors and vagaries of front-line war; he has earned the right to the same status as the present combatants, can hold his head high among them. Peter feels himself to be merely an onlooker, an also-ran to all the other officers in the Mess, and therefore, he imagines, not really to be counted as one of them. A bit like cheering-on the 1st XV from the sidelines whilst wishing one had the opportunity – and the ability – to be out there among them to share the vicissitudes and the glory.

Inhibited by these conclusions, it is with difficulty that he takes part in the discussion as it drifts onto more idle topics, with the result that conversation becomes gradually more stilted. He is relieved therefore when, some minutes later, they are joined by David Munro.

'Not stopping,' Munro says energetically without any greeting, 'just bobbed in to tell you, Peter, that I've seen Beal, who arrived about an hour ago, and had a quick word with him. I suspect he's hardly changed from when you were at Bard's together – a bit older-looking, no doubt, but he gives the impression of being essentially the same man. And professes himself delighted to find that there are two other Old Bardians here on the station! Anyway, I've arranged that the two of us will look in and see him later on, if that's okay? About four-ish? I'll collect you at the medical centre.'

Not quite able to share Munro's enthusiasm for all this harping back to Bard's, and the arrival of Beal – indeed, if the truth were admitted, more than a bit taken aback by it – Peter spends a restless afternoon. This isn't helped by his finding very little more to do at the present time in the medical room, with the result that he becomes more and more overtaken by doubts as to how he is

102

to fulfill any sort of useful role on the station. In fact that is what he is. Useless. As most of his life he's been. Exactly as he'd felt that first Christmas in Cumberland, when he'd been assailed by all sorts of uncertainties, not really understanding what was going on.

* * *

When he awoke on the day following the excitement of putting up the Christmas tree the weather turned out to be as bad as ever. For most of the morning, therefore, he hung around hoping to be with Jordan again; but when he finally enquired – ever so casually – of her whereabouts, he learned that she'd gone off for the day with some friends. In a way this was a relief. He wasn't clear, really, why he wanted to see her. As they'd gone on to complete the decorating of the tree, the previous afternoon, moving down to the lower branches, her attitude towards him had reverted to type. She'd become bored and impatient, both with the job in hand and with him, once more treating him with disdain and belittling his attempts to help. In a way, he now disliked her more than ever. But he couldn't get her out of his mind. At breakfast he'd found himself studying her, when he thought no one was looking, observing the cut of her hair, the sweep of her eyelashes and the line of her brow. As she'd got up to leave the table he'd noted how the curve of her hips swung with the movement, tautening under the material of her dress, which clung to her. Turning his head after watching her walk from the room, to his mortification he'd found Uncle John watching him, the expression on his face both amused and reflective at one and the same time.

So, still restless, after lunch instead of returning to his room he wandered into the kitchen. Cook, busy with jars and bowls on the large scrubbed table in the centre of the room, looked up with a smile whilst her hands continued their practised movements as though functioning with a life of their own. Over in the corner by the sink, Ethel, polishing glassware, flashed him a bright smile and broke into an unexpected giggle.

'Hullo, Master Peter,' Cook said, 'have you come to give us a hand, then?' Then, more sharply to the maid, 'Ethel, have you not finished those glasses yet? There's them bedrooms to do yet, you know, what with us both soon being off for two days. Get a move on, girl, and get yourself upstairs, or we'll never be finished.'

As the maid, flustered and still giggling, hurried from the room with a further nervous smile at Peter, he said to Cook, 'What's wrong with Ethel?'

'Eh, take no notice of her. She's just being a silly little girl.'

This short statement was followed by a long pause, as if she was about to say something else but then thought better of it.

He watched her silently for a few moments, trying to make sense of her activities. 'Can I help stir the Christmas pudding, when you do it?' he asked hopefully.

'Eh, Lord save us, that was made weeks ago, Master Peter. You missed it, I'm afraid, with being away. You'd've enjoyed that, right enough, stirring in them silver sixpences and all that. Another time we'll have to see if we can't do it whilst you're at home.'

'So what's that you're stirring in the bowl?'

'This? Mincemeat. For the mince pies. Here, stick a finger in and have a taste. I won't let on.'

'And is that almond paste, in that other bowl? For the Christmas cake?'

'Bless you, that's been done and iced and decorated days ago, as well. This is rum butter.'

'Rum butter?'

'Aye. D'you not know about that? Like as not you won't, coming from London. It's a mix of fresh butter, sugar, rum of course, and a touch of nutmeg and cinnamon.'

'What do you do with it?'

'What d'you do with it? You eat it, of course! Here, have a taste of that, as well.'

He scooped a large fingerful into his mouth, then pulled a face. 'Ugh!'

'D'ye not like that? Ah, well, doubtless you'll come to it in time.' A pause – then, 'There's lots of things you have to come to, gradually, when you're ready for them.'

There was further silence while she busied herself with the mincemeat – then, as if coming to a decision, she said, 'Just you be careful around Miss Mary, Master Peter.'

'Miss M…? Oh, you mean Jordan.'

'Miss Mary,' she repeated firmly. 'You want to look out for that one.'

He looked up in alarm, conscious of the sudden flame in his face, but Cook was looking down, concentrating hard on the job in hand. 'What do you mean?' he mumbled.

Still not looking up, she said, 'I mean that Miss Mary is at an age when she doesn't know what she wants. Her mind and…and other things, are all of a jumble, like. It's one of those things that happens to girls for a year or two. And to boys too, like as not. But it can lead them into all sorts of mischief. As you'll likely find out. But watch she doesn't get her sharp little claws into you! Don't get me wrong, like. I've known Mary since she was a bairn. She's a nice enough girl, underneath. A bit spoilt, that's all, being the only one. And not thinking of anyone else but herself at present. Hopefully she'll come out of that. But for the time being she's a bit of a danger to herself and to the likes of you. The Mistress can't see it, of course, so she's not been checked. Maybe the Master has some inkling, being a doctor and all, but he dotes on her too. So nothing's done. But you take care, mind! And don't say I said so!'

He didn't fully understand what she was on about, but the essence of what she'd said somehow struck an uncomfortable chord in him, and that, together with his uncertainty, made him nervous.

Affecting a nonchalance he didn't feel, therefore, he said airily, 'Oh, Jordan doesn't bother me! She's just a soppy girl. And, anyway, she doesn't even like me.'

Cook looked up sharply, causing him to recoil a little as she held his gaze. 'Now see here, Master Peter, there are things you need to know. You're growing fast – we've seen that this time – and you're a good-looking lad. The lasses'll've already got an eye on you, believe you me. Why else do you think that silly little girl, Ethel, has been simpering around the place ever since you came home this time? And Miss Mary's already said to me that she thinks you're rather handsome. Don't let on that I've told you that, either, mind! And don't let it go to your head,' she added drily. 'As I've said, it's just the way they are at that age. They'll fasten on anything in trousers! Anyway, enough said. And do me the kindness of not letting on to anyone that I've talked to you in this way. It would get me into real trouble. But it needed saying. And no one else was going to do it.'

With deliberation she went back to her preparations, and Peter, his face still fiery, muttered his thanks and made his escape.

Up in his room, both excited and disturbed by what had been said, for the first time in his life he took a good look at himself in the mirror. The face that looked intently back at him seemed to him unremarkable. Fair, somewhat unruly, hair; light blue eyes beneath eyebrows that were a shade darker than his hair; long eyelashes, even darker; a straight, rather narrow nose; and a wide sort of mouth. The whole set in an oval shape with a square chin. An ordinary sort of face. Nothing to get excited about. He continued to study it for a minute or two, before shrugging his shoulders and deciding that Cook must be exaggerating the whole thing. After all, she was well past middle age. What could she know about what was good-looking and what wasn't. Still, she'd meant well, and he appreciated her talking to him like that, in a confidential way – motherly, really, but better than a mother could have done. And it had certainly made him think about Jordan in a different way. He thought of her again, up that stepladder – but the picture now was fading, the detail more difficult to recall.

He glanced out of the window. It had stopped raining. Maybe he would go and see if the gang were around.

CHAPTER EIGHT

When David Munro arrives at four o'clock to take him along to meet Beal, Peter's thoughts are still in turmoil, therefore. He's not able to shake off the emotions aroused by harping back to the events of that particular Christmas. Moreover, he can't seem to rid himself of the feeling that in some way it is linked to the prospect of meeting up with Beal again. Nor is he sure what sort of reception he will get from Beal.

However, when the moment arrives Beal greets him with a considerable show of delight, shakes his hand eagerly and declares what a 'wonderful surprise' it is that they should be meeting again 'after all these years'. Beal then excuses himself for a moment ('while Munro and I talk shop'), giving Peter time to study him while he's deep in conversation. Apart from having lost his youthful appearance, his sandy hair now receding a little at the front and showing signs of premature silvering at the temples, he has, as Munro had suspected, changed very little. Always heavily built even when at school, he is now more thickset, although still looking fit and agile. His greenish-grey eyes are as steady and disconcerting as Peter remembers them, but perhaps now more watchful, as though time has dampened the optimism with which he'd once viewed the capabilities of his fellow men; and his mouth, which had always displayed a determined set, now reveals a certain thinning and tightening of the lips, indicating maybe a dissatisfaction with the world, which hadn't been there before.

'Well,' he says, turning back to Peter, 'so you became a doctor! I must say I wouldn't have guessed it at the time, but I'm not altogether surprised. I'll bet you're excellent at it, too.'

Peter, knowing that Beal would never stoop to idle flattery (or 'flarching', as they would have said in Cumberland), and mumbling some sort of embarrassed reply, then has the wind immediately taken out of his sails by Beal suddenly saying, 'And have you seen Jordan recently?'

He would have been less astounded if Beal had asked him 'Have you seen the Prime Minister recently?' His carefully constructed fences for this meeting are smashed at a stroke. He has fleeting recollections of Beal, on that first night at school, asking 'Was that your sister who came with you?' And of further, casual questions about Jordan from time to time after that. But…after all these years? It doesn't make sense. Yet he knows it must.

Fighting waves of alarm and irrational jealousy, he can only blurt, 'Do you know Jordan?'

He can't understand why the revelation has upset him so. But it is so unexpected. It's as if two people who've had such a perversely significant influence on him in his early life have all along been conspiring behind his back. He knows his reaction is ridiculous. But something from deep down is dictating the script.

The reply, in measured, amused tones, then delivers the ultimate predation, stripping him of any sense of self-worth.

'Yes, of course. Very well. Has she never told you?'

For what seems an age, he sinks into himself, hugging to him the rags of his donned delusions, while the taste of betrayal cloys bitterly in his mouth.

'I can't believe that you didn't know,' continues Beal relentlessly. 'Actually, it was Jordan who introduced me to Anna, my wife – about three years ago, that would be. They knew each other from both being in the theatre, you see.'

Contrarily, that piece of information drops some crumbs of comfort to him. Perhaps the relationship with Jordan has been a merely casual, incidental one. But there again, Beal had said '…*very well*'. And the '*Has she never told you?*' particularly rankles with him, as though he must have been of no significance to her whatsoever.

'However,' Beal goes on, 'I'm afraid I must get on. We can mull over the past, over a jar, later on. Welcome to Marwell, though…' He pauses, and laughs. 'Actually, we're both new boys, and I believe you were here fractionally before me, so the welcome should be the other way round! Anyway, I'm sure you'll look after us all very well, and deal competently with whatever problems the chaps may bring you!'

Peter, determined, in spite of his sour mood, to match the lightness of tone, replies flippantly. 'From what I've seen, they don't need anything from me! They all appear to be having a jolly good time. It seems more like being on holiday than being at war!'

The words are no sooner out than, from the effect they have, they might have been blown away in the silence of a polar wind; and instantly he realises, without knowing why, that he's just stepped over the edge of a crevasse.

Beal's features stiffen, and, his voice icily quiet, he says to Munro, 'Would you mind leaving us for a moment, David.'

Then, having silently watched Munro shut the door behind him, he turns back to Peter. His eyes are pebble-hard with anger, yet manage still to convey a hint of sorrow and disappointment – all familiar signs from the past.

107

'Stand up Waring,' he says, his voice grating, 'and come to attention.'

'I…I don't understand!' says Peter desperately, stumbling over the words.

'And that's the problem, isn't it. You don't understand. And, when you're addressing me as your C.O you'll address me as 'Sir', is that clear!'

'Yes, sir!' Peter stiffens; as he's feared, the years had been stripped away, and with them any semblance of his adulthood.

'I had hoped that with time you would have lost some of your inadequacies. But that appears not to be the case. You give the impression of still being locked up in your own little world with no awareness, half the time, of what's going on around you – and, what's more, with no indication of having any interest in finding out. Well, you might have got by – after a fashion – with that at school, but it won't do here. If you're to be of any use to us at all, you'll need to know what's going on! All the time. In detail. And if you're of no use to us, I'll have you posted out of here before you know what's hit you – if anyone will have you, that is!

'Just as I have to know everything that's going on, on this Station – how the machines, instruments and weapons work, what the conditions are, the tasks of the men, and women, the difficulties, the morale, the concerns of individuals – so do you! In fact, you'll be one of the people I'll be expecting to keep me informed. If you think that your role here as our M.O. is simply a matter of sitting in your office waiting for people to come along with their coughs and sore throats, then you're sadly mistaken: they've all got better things to worry about. And so should you.

'I expect you spent the afternoon with your thoughts and your files in the medical centre, didn't you?'

Here Beal pauses and nods his head as in affirmation, as though not expecting any denial.

'Well – now…here – you'll have to climb out of that mysterious cocoon of yours and play your part in our world, not opt out as you tended to do at Bard's. Throw aside that reticence that seems to limit you all the time, and you might achieve something at last, and have more significance for those around you.'

Peter, immediately smarting at that taunt (as if becoming a doctor wasn't an achievement in itself!), still not comprehending what he's said to start all this, but also burdened by a suspicion that some of what Beal has said is getting uncomfortably near the core of his condition, blurts again, 'But, sir, I still don't understand!'

'Oh, for God's sake, man! Get out there and find out!' The exclamation is as much an expression of weariness as of exasperation. 'Talk to people! Get to know them! Especially the Ground Crews. They often know more of what's going on than do the aircrews; they have the advantage of constancy: their posting on a station is usually for the duration, whereas the aircrews come and go…' Here he pulls a face full of irony '…one way or another.' But that thought seems to finish him, and he slumps in his chair.

'All right, that's enough. Dismiss.'

Peter, only too eager to be gone, salutes, turns smartly, and marches towards the door. His hand on the door, he stiffens as Beal's voice comes again from behind him.

'And, Peter?'

He turns.

'You can do it, you know. Surprise yourself!'

He nods dumbly, and turns the handle.

'And, Peter?'

He turns again, holding down his irritation. But this time there is the semblance of a smile on Beal's lips, and a more forgiving expression.

'You don't salute when you're not wearing a cap.'

Back at his office, he can raise only a muttered greeting to Browning and a brief instruction that he doesn't want to be disturbed. Then he shuts himself in and sits at his desk staring into space. His thoughts as well as his emotions are tumbling over one another. Beal had spoken as though he'd been crassly negligent; and Peter had noted that even Munro had flinched at what he, Peter, had said. Could it be that they are all so blinkered by their tradition of a gung-ho, schoolboyish way of doing things that they can't see the truth: that in order to become more efficient and truly professional, they also need to become more mature instead of this pretence that it is, in the end, all a kind of power game? He wonders, even, if he dare put this point of view to Beal – given the right opportunity. After all, he, Peter, like all medical students (with one or two notable exceptions) had behaved in an equally irresponsible manner much of the time – merely a matter of relieving the stresses of the work – but once they'd qualified, overnight all that had stopped.

But then again, he is disillusioned with Beal: the man has revealed that he isn't as straight and upright as he'd always made himself out to be. His secretive – underhand, actually – relationship with Jordan demonstrates that; and, what's more, he must have had a similar influence on Jordan, or she surely would have mentioned the acquaintanceship to Peter. Or would she? In fairness, he hadn't seen much of her in the past year or two. However, long as he's known Jordan, in spite of everything, he still doesn't know where he is with her. It is something he rarely admits to himself. And doing so, now, creates a knot in his stomach, and hurls him back into more of those memories from the past.

* * *

Suddenly, after all the mounting anticipation, it was Christmas Day. And, all in all, for Peter it turned out to be something of an anti-climax.

People wandered down to breakfast at, more or less, the same time as each other, to be faced, in the absence of Cook, with what Uncle John described as a 'Continental breakfast'. This, it appeared, simply meant the absence of the usual porridge, bacon and eggs, et cetera, to be replaced merely with toast and marmalade. Peter's mother, offering to cook breakfast for them, was firmly put in her place by her sister, who said that it had become 'a tradition' in the household to 'do it this way, thank you very much all the same. Anyway,' she'd added, 'there'll be quite enough cold repast at lunchtime to keep the wolf from the door until you have your Christmas dinner this evening' – which had the souring effect of making it sound as though his mother had been thinking only of herself and her own greed. So that, for a start, was enough to dampen any festive spirit there might otherwise have been – in spite of Uncle John's attempts to instill a bit of life into the proceedings (which were understandably half-hearted, anyway, as he'd already had one telephone call as well as a caller at the door, both requesting visits to patients during the course of the morning). The other 'tradition' was that the opening of presents from under the tree was 'always' delayed until they'd 'partaken' of breakfast. That, too, was a word that Peter had not heard used before – but it sounded far too grand for the poor fare on offer. Also, in previous years he had continued to have his childhood Christmas stocking (actually a pillowcase) by his bedside, to waken up to; so, now that he had to wait like everyone else, he was itching to get to the boxes and parcels on display in the drawing room.

Anyway, the meagreness of the 'repast they had 'partaken' of (he rather relished the pomposity of those two words, mentally adding them to his vocabulary) was such that the moment very soon arrived. Yet, once all of them were gathered around the tree, there was a disappointingly brittle edge to the gaiety, Peter thought, as they politely handed around the brightly wrapped presents. Greeted, as each in turn was opened, with expressions of surprise and delight, it was impossible to tell which of these exclamations was genuine and which was pretended; and irreverently he wondered what effect it would have on the spirit of the proceedings if one were to express disappointment or even downright dismay at one's gifts.

As it happened, he was more than satisfied with his own. From his mother he had one of the new Waterman 'reservoir' pens, which could be pre-filled with ink and carried around ready for use at any time; and – even more excitingly – a proper, full-size, hard-backed diary, bound in red, with the title *Personal Diary-1927* gold-blocked on the cover, and a whole page devoted to each day of the year. Vying with this for sheer excitement, from his Uncle and Aunt was a Box Brownie camera that could be adjusted for 'sunny' or 'cloudy', together with a roll of celluloid film. There was even an individual present from Jordan, which he met with considerable suspicion on seeing the label, but which turned out to be a 'self-propelling' pencil with spare leads stored in its barrel; this imbued him with yet another renewed wave of warmth toward her – in spite of the fact that his attempts at thanking her were met by Jordan with casual disdain.

However, with that particular ritual fairly quickly over, and with the weather still wet, it was a matter of kicking his heels for the rest of the day until the evening's 'entertainment', which he wasn't looking forward to anyway. Staring moodily out of the window he half wondered if he could try out his new camera; but decided that although it had the setting for 'cloudy', that could hardly be said to include 'rain'. So he spent a little while browsing, with minimal interest, through the many Christmas cards displayed around the rooms. Most of the people who'd sent them he'd never heard of. In his imagination he began to conjure up the possibility of one having come from his father, either in code or else written in invisible ink between the printed lines of the card. That would be jolly exciting, and he could spend quite some time deciphering it. But to say that it was unlikely was putting it mildly, and he soon gave up on that particular fantasy. Then he came across one from his Aunt Anne in Kenya. Instead of the usual boring pictures of snow, stage coaches, robins, holly, and so on, this card had a picture of a fierce-looking lion on the front, and inside, in large, flowing handwriting, was the message, 'Will be thinking of you all, shivering in the snow, whilst I'm out in the heat of 'the bush'! – With Much Love, Anne'.

As he was poring over that and thinking how wonderful it would be, in fact, to have snow, Jordan wandered into the room; and, encouraged by the apparent thawing of the antagonism between them, he impulsively said, 'Jordan, have you ever met Auntie Anne?'

There was a gurgle of delight from Jordan. 'She *would* be pleased to be called *Auntie*, I'm sure!' Then, taking pity on him: 'She's not the 'Auntie' type, anyway, I can tell you that! I met her four years or so ago, when she came over for a holiday. She'd be...let's see... about twenty-six or twenty-seven, then. But she may have changed a lot, now. I can't remember her very clearly – I was only twelve at the time – and she didn't stay with us very long. Too keen to hit the bright lights of London, I imagine! In fact, I'm surprised she didn't come to stay with your parents...oh...no...perhaps not!'

He thought there was a malicious edge to that last bit, almost a sneer, which made him bridle. She was obviously referring to his father's bad temper, and his instinct was to spring to his defence – in spite of the bitter memories he carried – but he didn't know how to go about that with any conviction. It did however have the effect of reminding him again of not having his father. His uncle did his best to be a substitute, he realised, but it wasn't the same. There wasn't the same sense of belonging. Uncle John was, at the end of the day, Jordan's father. That bond had to be special, even when there were periods of conflict; so much so that Peter decided, when he stopped to think about it, that he was just that bit jealous of Jordan.

'But I liked Anne,' Jordan was saying. 'Mummy says she's "flighty"; I think she just sets out to get the most out of life! I don't honestly know what Daddy thinks of her; but he always refers to her as the 'black sheep'. I suspect that he, too, has a sneaking admiration for her. But he wouldn't dare admit to it in Mummy's presence! Anyway, you'll probably meet her someday. In the past she's tended to come home for a holiday every few years, from what I've gathered.'

It was the longest and most civil conversation he'd had with Jordan since coming to live here. For once she hadn't been talking down to him.

But, that evening, it all changed again.

It began as he came out of his room, having reluctantly got into his new suit and, still feeling like a tailor's dummy, had done his best to slick his hair into some sort of order. Coming onto the landing he saw Jordan further along, poised at the head of the stairs. She was wearing her new, silver-coloured party dress. Her back was towards him and she was pivoted gracefully on the ball of one foot, her other slim leg elegantly stretched out sideways, the high-heel of her shoe pointing downwards like a spur, as she twisted round to straighten the seam of her stocking. With her skirt and petticoat hitched up so that she could adjust the suspender, in the light from the stairs he could clearly see the nakedness of thigh above stocking and, where her thigh curved into her bottom and hip, a hint of pale pink satin and lace. The silken texture of stocking, skin and undergarments, bathed in the overhead light, flowed in a series of delicate lines and curves, beckoning. The impact was even greater than that of seeing her semi-nude from beneath the step-ladder: then, the overall effect had been one of shadow and recess, a kind of discrete revelation; here, the exposure, although arising from a private moment, gave the impression of being bold and deliberate and therefore more shocking. So absorbed with it was he that he hardly breathed, committing the scene, indelibly, to memory. He was captivated: in an instant what had started off as startlement became wonder, momentary dismay became delight. It was a revelation. He felt instinctively that he had, for the first time, discovered the essence of grace, beauty and femininity.

She looked up and saw him.

For a moment neither of them moved. 'Have you seen enough, then, you nasty little boy?' she snapped, her lips curling in contempt; and, letting the hem of her frock fall, she swept haughtily onto the stairs.

From being briefly transported by exultation, he crashed to a state of wretchedness, unaccountably feeling dirty.

At dinner, later, amongst all the forced frivolity and silly hats, and the music and chatter of the crowded *Royal George* dining room, he remained quiet and withdrawn. His mother, and even Uncle John, after a number of unsuccessful attempts to draw him out and get him to join in the fun, left him to it. Probably they thought he was simply signalling his objections to the whole, boring event, an attitude of which they were already aware. Jordan, sitting across the table from him, being (rather too enthusiastically) the life and soul of the party, coldly ignored him. For his part, he tried not to look at her. Yet, on one or two occasions when his gaze happened to drift her way, he would catch her (as in the past) sneaking a quick look at him; and whenever that happened, as in the past, she would hurriedly look away. He couldn't begin to make any sense of that, which caused him more unease – particularly when he recalled Cook's words.

Between courses he occupied himself with looking around the room. Many of the women wore full-length dresses, although the younger girls had, like Jordan, elected to wear short ones – with more than a few disapproving looks from the matrons present. Similarly, the older men wore evening dress – the tailcoats of which on those who were tall and slim like Uncle John looked elegant enough, but which, in Peter's view, on those of shorter stature appeared merely ridiculous. Much better the short jackets of the dinner suits worn by some of the younger chaps, he decided. A few tables away he caught sight of Bill sitting with his family. He was staring intently towards Peter, as though seeking mutual commiseration, so Peter roused himself to give him an enthusiastic wave. Disconcertingly, Bill took no notice – whereupon Peter realised it was not he who was the object of his friend's attention, but Jordan. And that discovery, even more disconcertingly, aroused in him a sudden inexplicable flash of jealousy.

The meal over, and some of the tables moved aside to clear the centre of the floor for dancing, the band struck up its tedious procession of Viennese waltzes, Barn dances, Veletas and a host of other dances that he'd never even heard of. Listlessly he prowled the back of the room, therefore, then the corridor leading to the bar, hoping perhaps to find Bill, who seemed for the moment to have disappeared. Finding nothing to divert him there, and wandering back to the dining-room he found his way blocked by a couple of youngish women languidly standing chatting in the doorway. One of them was smoking – her long cigarette-holder held so fastidiously between the fingers of her left hand as to give him the impression she was so bored by the thing that, really, she would have preferred someone else to have held it for her. The two of them deep in conversation as they watched the couples on the dance floor, he hovered at their elbow, hesitating for the moment to interrupt them. Not interested in listening to what they were saying, he did nevertheless pay more attention when he heard the one of them say, 'Young Jordan Webster is fairly growing up, is she not?'

'She most certainly is,' drawled the other, 'in more ways than one!'

Following the direction of their gaze, Peter spotted Jordan dancing with her father and looking more than a little fed up as she was steered around the floor in a modern waltz.

'I wonder where she gets her looks,' went on the first woman. 'Not from her mother, anyway, it seems!'

'No,' agreed her companion. 'I suppose her father's quite distinguished-looking, though. And, from what I understand, that's her mother's sister there at the table – she's quite attractive for her age, I suppose. I'd give anything for legs like hers, though – Jordan's, I mean!'

They both went into a fit of the giggles at that, the second woman adding, 'Yes, and the rest! Mind you, she's jolly lucky in this day and age that she has such small tits. She won't have to do any binding, I'll be bound! – if you'll forgive the pun!' Again they both burst out laughing.

Peter was as much taken aback by the term she'd used as by the way they were talking about Jordan. He hadn't thought that women could use expressions as crude as 'tits'; he'd thought only boys did that.

But at that point one of them caught sight of him.

'Hello, young man,' she said tetchily, 'what are you doing there! Practising your eavesdropping?' They both burst out laughing once more, amused at his obvious discomfort.

113

'No. Sorry,' he mumbled. 'That is...excuse me.' And red in the face, furious with himself and with them, he brushed past, heading for the table – only to realise, halfway there, that if he did that they would immediately understand that he was there with Jordan and would be able to give away what they'd been saying. He therefore changed direction, in the process becoming even more furious that he found it necessary to do so.

Seeking some form of reassurance, he peered to see if he could spot Jordan again among the closely packed couples circling the floor. Yes, there she was, still dancing with her father, but looking about her in a distracted fashion, as though searching for someone. It wasn't him anyway, he decided, as her eyes slid past with hardly a pause.

Disgruntled, he headed back to their table, careless now whether the women saw him or not. His mother gave him the briefest smile of acknowledgement before turning back to continue her conversation with her sister. He might as well be invisible, he thought savagely; and when Uncle John and Jordan, having rejoined the table, also went on with some private conversation of their own, completely ignoring him, he became convinced of his own irrelevance.

He was very much taken aback, therefore, when, a few minutes later Jordan clutched at his arm and said, 'Come on, Pete, come and have a dance with me.' There was a brittle gaiety to her voice that he found even more off-putting than the thought of making a fool of himself out there.

'But I can't dance,' he said desperately, pulling back.

She pouted prettily, a small moue that even to his innocent eye seemed contrived, as though she'd been practising in front of a mirror. 'Don't be a silly. It's only a Slow Foxtrot. All you have to do is practically walk round! Come on. I'll show you. It's easy. Just leave it to me. I'll lead you.'

'No,' he said, resisting harder.

'Oh, don't be such a coward!'

It was said lightly, without any real malice, but it had the effect of stinging him into compliance, tamely allowing himself to be drawn onto the floor.

Once there, she drew him to her, taking his right hand and placing it around her waist in the approved manner. Close up against her, although he was only about half a head shorter he felt dominated. Half-pulling and half-pushing, holding him tightly to her (which seemed to be the way that most couples were dancing – as much due to the crush of dancers as to the requirements of the dance) she began to steer him around the floor. With his relatively long legs their lower bodies were much at the same level, so that he very quickly became conscious of the pressure of her belly against his. The warmth of her body through the thin material of her dress, and the contact of her thighs against his as they danced, led him to recall the scene on the landing earlier in the evening. He persuaded himself he could actually feel her suspenders pressing against him, and could detect the slithering of silk upon silk beneath her dress. His excitement became even greater as he became acutely conscious of her leg thrusting between his at each step, forcing him along as much by the press of knee and thigh as by her body and arms.

Perhaps she was as aware of it as he. At first, having bumped and shuffled their way awkwardly through two circuits of the floor, she was silent, her movements distracted as she looked here and there about the room, clearly more interested in the people out there than in him. But now she suddenly looked at him and said, 'D'you think I have nice legs, then?'

The directness of the question, and the way in which it had coincided with his own fevered thoughts, flustered him. It seemed to him, also, that at that moment she deliberately increased the pressure of her thighs and hips against his. It was as if she were not only emphasising the closely personal nature of the question, but implying as well a certain intimacy between them – exemplified by their present embrace and also by the manner in which she was making it clear that she, too, was aware that he, and he alone, had been privileged in the last few days to see as much of her legs as it was possible to see, and more besides.

'No,' he said, his initial reaction being to deny that he'd actually seen as much as she assumed he had; then, desperately, 'Yes. I mean yes!'

But it was too late. She tossed her head in exasperation and stopped so suddenly that he careered into her. 'You're such a childish nincompoop!' she said. 'And this is all so boring. You'd think they would at least have been able to play a Charleston.'

Whether by coincidence or not, they had all this time been keeping to the periphery of the dance floor. She turned now to a man standing nearby, watching them. A stranger to Peter, he was of medium height, probably in his late forties, with suave good looks, slicked-back dark hair, and a pencil moustache.

Pushing Peter away from her, she said to the man, 'This little idiot's just about broken all my toes! You'll dance with me, won't you, Roger?'

'Delighted, my dear!' he said. With a quick look at Peter (a look that briefly contained both amusement and a certain sardonic sympathy before instantly dismissing him) he took her in his arms and without a backward glance steered her with supreme self-confidence onto the floor.

'Bad luck,' said a gloomy voice at Peter's elbow.

He turned to see Bill standing there looking as glum as Peter felt. But he thought he detected also a glint of malicious satisfaction in his friend's eyes.

Who is that man anyway?' he asked.

'That? Don't you even know who he is? That's Hammy!'

'Who?'

'Hammy. The famous Roger Hamilton. Major Hamilton. You know, the chap who lives across the lake. We pointed out his house that time. The place where she goes to play tennis.'

Peter had forgotten. But he knew that he hated her, him and it.

* * *

With an almost physical effort he shakes away the memory at the same time as, to his further annoyance, there comes a tap at the door. Before he can answer, it opens and Munro pokes his head into the room.

'May I come in, old boy?' Without waiting for a reply, he does so and plonks himself down in a chair. 'Don't tear a strip off Browning out there, Peter; I pulled rank on him, I'm afraid.' He makes a face. 'I came in to see whether you'd survived after the Wingco climbed up at you like that with, I'm sure, all guns blazing. Did he shoot you down in flames?'

Peter nods, not trusting himself to speak. But he feels his anger returning. 'I think now, though, that I understand what it was all about,' he says, with growing determination.

'Do you?' says Munro placidly. 'I doubt it. Because you'd really no way of knowing. It was just bad luck the way it developed. And my fault in a way. I probably should have filled you in a bit more. But, to be fair, there hasn't been the time. And given all that, Beal was a bit hard on you to take you to task at all. But he'd no way of knowing, either. If I get the chance, I'll explain all that to him. Put the record straight, don't-you-know?'

Peter stares at him blankly, wondering what on earth he's talking about.

'Let me explain,' says Munro. 'As you know, not a lot has happened since the declaration of war on September third. The boys are simply sitting across there in France waiting; and jerry himself doesn't appear to be in much of a hurry to do anything. But that doesn't mean total inactivity. I do realise that all is quiet here, at present – but that's because we've been standing down for the past three days, firstly because the weather was closed in, and then because we've been waiting for replacement aircraft; you probably saw some of them this morning. And you'll note that I did say *replacement* aircraft.'

Peter begins to experience twitchings of disquiet, but remains silent as Munro goes on.

'You see, from the word go, in September, we've had quite a number of sorties for reconnaissance purposes and also to do with the *Nickel* campaign – do you know about that? No? A daft codename if ever there was one – and a daft idea, if you ask me; but who am I to know, I'm only a chauffeur! It's dropping leaflets over Germany; telling them they're being led up the garden path, that they ought to give old Adolf the order of the boot, that they can't possibly win, and all that sort of tosh! And you can guess what use the populace will be putting to all that paper! It wouldn't be so bad, but it isn't without its risks; after all, jerry doesn't just sit there and say, "Oh, it's all right, they're only dropping leaflets"! The best that can be said for it is that it is giving us some operational experience, which is much needed; but at the expense of the loss of one or two crews.

'Then, at about the beginning of October, someone up top had the bright idea of 'reconnaissance in force': the idea being that if anyone saw anything worth bombing, instead of wasting time reporting it and then waiting for the chaps to arrive, they would be able to bomb it there and then. In other words, instead of sending out aircraft in ones or twos, for 'recce' jobs, they'd send out the odd squadron or two. I should point out here, however, that there's a damper on the whole thing: because we're forbidden from bombing anything where there's any risk whatsoever of civilians being injured. That means, in effect, we're only able to bomb naval craft – and there, too, usually, but not always, only those that are not in port but out to sea.

'Are you still with me? Good. I assure you, I am coming to the point – and, anyway, these are all things you should know about. So we started looking for opportunistic targets in the form of enemy naval vessels – and at intervals we found some, but, by God, they turned out to be tougher nuts than we'd bargained for. For example, in September we attacked warships at *Brunsbuttel* and *Wilhelmshaven* – we weren't involved from here, but Wellingtons from Mildenhall and Honington in this group were – and with very little damage inflicted on the enemy we lost between a quarter and a third of our planes.

'It soon became apparent, though, that that was only for starters. Just over two weeks ago twelve Wimpeys of 99 Squadron at Mildenhall went after a warship off the mouth of the Elbe. But before they could get themselves in a position to bomb they were pounced on by Me109s and 110s. Five of the Wimpeys went into the drink, and a sixth crashed on landing. Beal was leading that raid. Then, a fortnight ago yesterday, I led a couple of flights from my squadron here to join others from Honington and Mildenhall – twenty-two Wellingtons altogether – to target warships at *Wilhelmshaven* once more. Again, Beal was involved. The bugger of it was that when we got there, under clear skies, we couldn't attack the blighters because they were tied up in harbour, which would have meant putting civilians at risk! And on the way back we were repeatedly set upon by a bloody great mass of 109s and 110s. The devil of it was, much of the time they came in at us from the beam – which is a bloody difficult thing to do, because with the relative speeds of the aircraft it requires pretty nifty deflection-shooting. Previously therefore everyone had pooh-poohed the notion that it would ever be done. But jerry managed it alright on this occasion! The thing is, that from that angle our gunners couldn't get a shot at them – which, of course, is what the buggers had worked out. Anyway, out of the twenty-two aircraft which started on the raid, twelve went down – and five of them were from here.'

The words are dispassionate, but his eyes not quite expressionless, the pain glimpsed like the blackness of a night-time window through the chink of an imperfectly closed curtain. Peter sits motionless, frozen and appalled by the casually recounted tale, but also thoroughly wretched on recalling his own words in Beal's office.

Munro, too, has for the moment lapsed into silence, evidently at last struggling with his emotions at the memory of those events. And when he does begin again to speak, his voice cracks under the strain of trying to retain control.

'The thing is, a lot of them were on fire – going down like bloody great torches, so that very few of the crews got out; and of those that did, many went down with their chutes burning.'

He gets up abruptly and goes over to the window, standing with his back to the room. After a minute or so, without turning around he says, 'They're going to have to do something about that. They've tried to keep the craft as light as possible you know, in order to give it more height and speed. The result is it hasn't got any armour, and it hasn't got self-sealing tanks. And it's got a fabric skin water-proofed with dope.'

He swings round. 'Did you know that? No wonder the bloody thing goes up like a bonfire as soon there's the slightest spark. They're trying to come up with some sort of fireproof dope for it, but they're having difficulty it seems.' He gives a hollow laugh. 'Apparently there was an excellent product available, before the war, but it's German! – and no one apart from them knows the recipe!'

Coming over to the front of the desk and sitting down again, he looks steadily at Peter. 'Don't look so stricken, old man. You weren't to know any of this. But you see, now, why the skipper was so rough on you – as I suspect he was. It's more than likely that you weren't really the cause of his emotions, but just happened to be in the way and took the stray flak. Many of those chaps were long-standing chums of ours. And Beal would have had to write all those damned letters; as I did – to wives, parents and fiancées.' This time his voice breaks. 'That's the worst job in this whole bloody business.'

Later that evening, sitting alone in his bedroom, and eyeing without enthusiasm the prospect of his inhospitable-looking iron bedstead, Peter struggles again with his thoughts. He tells himself that earlier on he'd made a passably-good stab at getting to know some of the fellows in the Mess – even though he'd received one or two long looks, later, when he'd politely drawn the line at going off to a pub with them. The trouble is, try as he might, he can't persuade himself that he would be seen as one of them: they are operational aircrew, and he isn't. They are facing dangers and putting their lives on the line in this war. And he isn't. They are all extroverts, living life for the moment; and he can't. They must regard him as dull.

He knows that Uncle John for one – and Jamie for another – would have torn into him for that self-effacing viewpoint; but he's discovered that it is less fraught learning to live with himself as he is than trying to change. Of course, none of these issues have been expressed in the letter he's just written to his mother – a letter that, he knows, will be passed on to his uncle and aunt (and, for all he knows, to Cook) – like all those letters, the many hundreds by now, dutifully written week after week throughout his schooldays and his years at university, and since, which contained only bland, safe items of 'news'. In fact, of course, it was never news, only the same old mantra (which, as the terms rolled by, changed only by his gradually reducing, and finally excluding, the exhaustive account of what the meals had consisted of for that particular week). He must have told them, time after time after time, about his routine activities, spiced only occasionally by something out of the ordinary. It had been a recital that must have been as boring for them to read as it had been for him to write (and how he'd hated, and delayed, getting down to doing those weekly, self-exacted-two-page epistles!). It had to be said that his mother (or, indeed, Uncle John, on the few occasions when he would pen a reply) had never expressed anything but delight and gratitude for the receipt of them; but perhaps, deep down, she had been grateful, too, that he'd never poured out to her his inner-most thoughts, doubts and torments. The accepted precept was that life was much simpler if one merely got on with it instead of resorting to all that anguish. He wonders if men like Munro and Beal (who now have to write all those letters whenever the necessity arises) follow the same principle: a few platitudes and expressions of sympathy – and the unspoken exhortation to just 'get on with it'. But as soon as the thought arrives he acknowledges it as being unworthy: it cheapens the loss, the sacrifice. And, for God's sake, what else could anyone expect the bereaved recipients of those letters to do, except 'get on with it'! It is, these days, what everyone has to do. There isn't any choice.

Finally, wearied by all the soul-searching, he capitulates and retires to bed, where for a while he drifts half-in and half-out of sleep, his thoughts, or his dreams, whichever they are, returning to those scenes in his childhood.

* * *

The weather changed between Christmas and New Year that year, with hard frosts at night and bitter cold during the day. For the first two days the trees and hedges were totally white, frost clinging to every surface like icing-sugar; but as the air dried under the influence of a strengthening breeze this disappeared, leaving branches once more bare with a glittering varnish of hard black. The mountain tops, too, had a powdering of white as though gigantically sprinkled with flour, the borders of the becks and the untidy brown bracken along their banks were scattered with shards of ice glistening thinly in the weak sunlight, and even the blue of the sky had a pallid look.

To the gang it was all-too welcome. After the days of wet and the strictures and excesses of the Christmas period it offered the possibility of adventure. But in spite of the wintry look, even at higher levels there was insufficient snow for any chance of tobogganing, and barely enough for a decent snowball fight; and although the lake rapidly began to freeze over, for their purposes it was painfully slow. More in hope than expectation they made excursions to the lakeside on three successive days. By the third day the ice, like an expanse of dull black glass, stretched a good hundred yards from the shore, encouraging them to venture out onto it. But when, after some thirty yards or so, it started to faintly creak and hiss as though uncertain of its own strength, they would pause, testing its solidity with small stamps of the feet. These would progress to bigger jumps until, reaching the point where they could detect some broad-based, vertical movement of it beneath them, they would retreat giggling towards the safety of land. These retreats to caution would, for a while, lead them to resort to the safer method of bringing out large stones from the shore to hurl them skywards, out towards the furthermost reaches of the ice: if they then landed with a hollow thud (a sound, they imagined, like that of distant cannon shot) – essential evidence, in their view, of the strength of the ice – they would once more venture further out. If the foolishness of what they were doing impinged at all on their consciousness, then their collective brashness would heave the thought aside.

With hindsight it would become apparent that it was Jamie who was the catalyst for this recklessness. Not long ago it would have been she who would have introduced some sanity to the proceedings before they could get out of hand. Now she was impetuous to the point of being neglectful not only of her own safety but that of others. It left the three boys uneasy, without sense of control or direction. Previously they (that was to say Bill and George, with Peter rather lamely in tow) had been able to give full vent to their bravado, knowing that Jamie was there to keep it in check, to shield them from the edge of real rashness. She being a girl, this had been acceptable: she could carry the taint of temerity; they could allow themselves to be reined in without loss of face. It seemed, though, that she just didn't care about anything any longer. Peter was constantly pricked by the impulse to talk to her about it. But he didn't know how to set about it. He sensed that it was something to do with her mother's intention to remarry. Uncle John had implied as much. But his awareness of that didn't help. He wasn't equipped to deal with something of that sort.

He was becoming more and more conscious of the fact, too, that Jamie was indeed a girl. Much of the time he would forget this as she ran and climbed and scuffled and shared adventure with the rest of them. But then there would be a certain gesture, a particular expression to her face or in the way she moved, that would bring the difference home to him. And he had learned by now to be wary of girls, of their ability to one minute raise one up and the next to dash one down. Following the dance on Christmas Night, Jordan had reverted to pointedly ignoring him, and he had taken pains to keep out of her way. He found that, for most of the time, he could put her out of his mind. He didn't want that sort of thing to happen with regard to Jamie. Admittedly, she wasn't pretty like Jordan. It was easier not to think of her as a girl.

Along with the chill of the days came also the chill of realising the holiday would soon be over, and with it the return to school. Whenever he allowed himself to contemplate that, the cold would percolate through to sit like an ice-ball in his stomach. He tried to bolster his resolve by adopting the pretence that he would be returning to a far outpost of civilisation, doing his duty to uphold the fabric and traditions of the empire. Sometimes this worked, allowing him to regard the prospect with some equanimity. Sometimes it didn't. In the past the coming of a new year had always filled him with excitement. This year, too, the very sound of the approaching New Year, the incantation of '*1927*', should have sent a thrill through him with its promise of change and progress. Instead, he counted off the days knowing that each one brought him nearer to departure and a different world. Even the mountains and the lake began to evoke in him a morose nostalgia, as if by his leaving they might disappear; and he began to imagine, in his mother's natural tendency to become more attentive to him in those last few days, that she shared with him a distress, not at his evident nervous misgivings about his return to school but at his approaching desertion of her once more.

The day came with stone-hard inevitability, and towards its end he found himself in the main corridor of Founders, jostling with the others in their attempts to reach the notice-board. Scrambling and tripping over assorted trunks and cases stacked waiting to be carried up to dorms, any apprehension was almost banished by the excitement of the struggle. Once a line of vision had eventually been achieved between the heads of those in front of him, fear fought with anticipation – and relief quickly won as he discovered his new hierarchical level in the House. He'd jumped three places in his relative position in the dayroom, and also therefore on the dorm. Of his two closest friends, Pearson had leap-frogged even further; but Chaplin had fallen several places behind.

In the process of swapping all their various bits of news, the hottest item was that Tomkin, who was Beal's personal fag, had during the vacation contracted diphtheria, had been at death's door, but was now slowly recovering, although not expected to return to school until the following term.

And, the next day, Peter was asked by Beal to take Tomkin's place as his personal fag.

CHAPTER NINE

The carriage heaves and sways so violently at times as to suggest desperation. It is as if the train itself is conscious of the load it carries and the urgency with which it does so, yet is struggling not only to maintain its pace but even to stay on the rails. On upward inclines it rattles and rumbles with the effort. When crossing points its wheels sing, metal upon metal, to Peter's mind sounding like the anvils of war. It echoes and feeds his own sense of alarm and discomfort at being carried into the unknown, crammed in with all these people, like convicts deprived of all rights and volition. The corridor in which they are standing, packed tight with variously-uniformed personnel, thrums with excited voices, the volume of which ebbs and flows as they compete with the irregular clatter of the tracks. It makes meaningful conversation difficult. Even the voluble O'Connor, standing in front of him, her back against him, has gone quiet for the moment. To add to the overall discomfort, wreathes of tobacco smoke, swirling like fog and mingling with the stale smells of all-those-yesterdays'-cigarettes-and-soot, catch the throat; but do provide some counter to the even more unpleasant fug of sweat and other body odours. In fact he wouldn't mind at all if only he'd been able to light his pipe; but the prospect of trying to fill it and the subsequent risk of his being jostled and having the stem rammed down his throat is just too daunting.

For the umpteenth time he wonders what this is all about. No one seems to know. It is all so hush-hush. Beal, when he'd handed Peter and O'Connor their passes and travel dockets, had been no wiser. 'All I know,' he'd said, with scarcely concealed exasperation, 'is that I have orders to provide one M.O. and one nurse within twenty-four hours, each to be equipped with gear and emergency rations sufficient for seventy-two hours, and that you're to report to Dover by sixteen hundred hours tomorrow.'

'Does that mean we'll be back here after that?' Peter had asked.

'How the hell should I know!' Beal had retorted. 'For all I know you could be in France after that. Do you think the Air Ministry lets me into all their little secrets! Presumably you'll get further orders when the time comes.'

'But how will you manage here, without us?' Peter had blurted with growing desperation.

'Oh, for God's sake, Waring! You sound like an old woman. Do you really think you and O'Connor are indispensable? What's anything but uncertain these days! Just follow your orders, as I have to do! Now, get out!

'...And best of luck!' he'd called as a placatory parting shot at Peter's retreating back.

Peter has asked one or two others on the train if they've any more info, but none of them is any wiser. All top secret, as stated. Which does nothing to lift his increasing despondency. He is tempted to again get out their orders, but he's already surreptitiously studied them several times, as though repeated perusal would, by some magic process, all at once provide an answer. Anyway, by now he knows the wording by heart:

'TOP SECRET. OPERATION DYNAMO. F/L Waring,P. and F/O O'Connor,S. to report to Dynamo H.Q., Town Hall, Dover by 1600 hrs 27/05/40. (O/C. Col.R.D.Murgatroyd, RAMC.).'

Terse and to the point, as to be expected. No clues in any of that. The orders are accompanied by their train passes which had designated a particular departure time and platform at St Pancras. He permits himself a wry smile. The passes have, of course, automatically specified a First Class compartment, as is thought only fitting for commissioned officers of His Majesty's forces. The irony is that such a multitude of the said forces have been assigned to the one train (which anyway looks as if it has been cobbled together in a hurry from a few bits and pieces of dilapidated rolling-stock that had happened to be available at the time) that they'd had a struggle to get on it at all. From what he'd seen, the coaches didn't even merit the soubriquet of 'Third Class'. Thank God it wasn't far to Dover; and at this speed would take even less time – if they ever got there at all.

Once more he surveys the masses crammed into the compartments, sometimes two to a seat as well as standing, the rest crammed into the corridor. Mainly other ranks, they consist of men mostly in khaki with the insignia of either RAMC or RASC; but there are scattered among them also a few Military Police – and some women, in the uniforms of ATS, FANYs and QAs. By contrast, those in navy blue or airforce blue are few and far between. What is significant, then, is that there are no personnel that can be described as front-line troops. They are all, in one way or another, from support units. Did that tell him anything? What else is known?

One thing for sure, that those poor buggers in the B.E.F. over in France are, from all accounts, in full retreat and, according to yesterday's press reports, in grave danger of being overrun by German panzer divisions. Can it be, then, that reinforcements are being shipped over? Are there, indeed, any such reserves available? And if so, could this hotch-potch of support units on the train be destined to join them? Hard news has been so sparse in the last two or three days that it is impossible to know what the likelihoods are. He consoles himself that if reinforcements are in fact being sent, they would hardly have included RAF people, much less naval types. Then he remembers that all along there have been RAF squadrons operating from airfields in France – perhaps their own destination is to be one of those?

Another possibility of course is that casualties might have been considerable, and that some of these are being shipped home. If so, that would explain the medical and nursing personnel on the train, but not all these other bods, who are very much in the majority.

Her own thoughts clearly mirroring his own, O'Connor at this moment half turns to peer up at him, allowing herself to lean even more heavily against him as she does so.

'D'you think the codename *Dynamo* has any particular significance, then?' she asks, looking at him – but her voice loud enough to be directed in general to those around them.

'I reckon they go out of their way to ensure the total irrelevance of codenames,' he replies. She merely nods and turns back to again gaze out of the window. He's had to bend his head down to get close to her ear, and become aware of the perfume she is wearing in disregard of regulations: something unsubtle and provocative. But then O'Connor doesn't give a fig for anything, simply takes life by the throat in whatever form it comes at her.

He recalls their first meeting at the beginning of the year. He'd been prepared for some form of virago after the dire warnings from Munro and Stanton, not to mention the more veiled implications from Bart Browning. But when he'd walked into the treatment room and she'd turned to greet him the impact of her had been even greater than he had anticipated. In her mid-thirties, he judged, and only about 5'4" in height, barely coming up to his chin, she nevertheless had seemed to dominate the room.

'B'jaysus,' she'd said without preamble, looking up at him with undisguised admiration, 'you're a right-looking boy, and that's a fact. A lot more of the girls'll be going off sick when they get wind of you, and that's the truth!'

He'd been expecting a formal welcome, and the unexpectedness and sheer effrontery of this had briefly rendered him speechless. Hearing a quickly stifled titter from Browning at the back of the room hadn't helped. He remembered wondering whether it all amounted to some form of insubordination. But then she'd come forward with outstretched hand and a winning smile, and said, 'Welcome. I'm Shevaun O'Connor.' – and he'd thought, What the hell, and had met her with an answering grin.

As he'd shaken hands with her he'd had time to take in more of her appearance, and now recalled that this initial impression had not been all that favourable, either. He remembered thinking on the plus side that firstly she had a good, compact figure (getting his priorities right!), and had attractive hair – cut short, in some lights it appeared to be auburn, in others more a copper beech. But, he'd decided on that first acquaintance, she escaped being unusually pretty by reason of high cheek-bones and a well-defined jaw, which he thought gave her a somewhat hard look – an impression not lessened by her eyes, which were emerald green and looked straight at one in a way which expressed both interest and attack.

Of course he'd revised that opinion since; had come to realise that in spite of her outward brashness she would from time to time reveal small signs of a more caring, thoughtful nature; and then, when she became more relaxed, her features would soften. Importantly, though, she was thoroughly professional and conscientious in her work, and very capable. So, in spite of continued wariness on his part, in the five months that had followed they had become friends of a sort. Moreover, her attitude towards him, after that initial meeting, had become much more correct. There had been very little of the flirting or sexual innuendo such as Stanton and Munro had indicated; indeed they seemed baffled to have him report this fact to them. After a while he'd even begun to feel let down, had begun to wonder whether, in spite of what she'd said to him initially, there was something unattractive about him. Of course, O'Connor and he met up only at work. She lived in the WAAF officers' quarters and so far there had been no social contact between them, therefore. But they worked well together.

Not that there had been a great deal for them to do, initially. The newspapers had continued to refer to it as *The Phoney War*, which had been apt, because very little had happened. At the outbreak, hospitals in the south-east of England, he knew, had been expecting up to 60,000 casualties from bombing alone in the first few weeks. After all, this was to be the 'war of the bomber', they'd said: the concerted belief being that 'the bomber will always get through'. Well, it hadn't yet been put to the test. There had been no enemy bombers over the country at all. Sure, from this end, Bomber Command had been busy in the opposite direction, in fits and starts, and there had been casualties among the crews – he wasn't likely to forget in a hurry the account of their own squadron losses in the raid on *Wilhelmshaven* in December. Some of the other stations had lost a high number of aircraft on other operations, too. But most of the outgoing activity had been in the direction of leaflet dropping over Germany (code-named '*Nickel*', for some reason) and mine-laying in the North Sea (equally obscurely code-named '*Gardening*' – the mines themselves being referred to as '*vegetables*') – none of which had carried a great deal of risk from enemy activity. True, aircraft from Marwell had taken part in raids in general, on enemy shipping and on oil installations, and there had been pretty nasty results for some of the crews on those. But the whole thing nevertheless had taken on the atmosphere of a game, of merely playing at war. It had seemed as though everyone was treading carefully for the moment, even Adolf. More extraordinary still, Bomber Command had actually issued orders that if it seemed there was likely to be any risk to enemy civilians on any raid, the mission had to be aborted.

So the requirements for medical attention at Marwell in the four months he'd been there had been minimal. There had been some repair work to do on a small number of men with nasty-looking but superficial wounds caused by flak; but the few injuries of a more serious nature that had occurred (some of them on the base rather than on ops) had all gone to the RAF hospital at Kings Lynn. No, their main enemy, from the medical point of view, had been the weather.

It really had been an atrocious winter – even, hard to believe, reports of the Thames having been frozen over at one point – and among aircrew they'd had a number of cases of flu, and even some cases of frostbite. It was an irony that now the winter had ended they'd started fitting the Wellingtons with heaters, and issued air-gunners, in their more exposed cockpits, with electrically-heated gloves and boots. He recollected with shame how he'd made a real ass of himself the first week he'd been there. He'd noticed a young rear-gunner from a new crew who were walking into Debriefing after their second mission, during which their plane had been severely shot up, its fabric skin now a network of gashes and holes. Seeing that the man was still shaking and shuddering from fear, he had solicitously (and patronisingly) taken him aside with the words, 'Don't worry, yours is just a normal reaction at first, after something like that. Before long you'll be taking it in your stride. You'll see.'

The youngster had looked him up and down with a look which had first expressed surprise and then contempt. 'Who the h..hell are you?' he'd stuttered in a broad Aussie accent, his teeth chattering. 'It's not b..b..bloody jerry that's g..getting to m..me. It's the f..fucking c..c..cold.' There had been a few sly glances of amusement when Peter had walked into the mess that evening.

Stanton had later told him that interior temperatures of aircraft at altitude could commonly get down to 30 degrees below freezing.

A day or two after that, word must have filtered through to Beal, who'd called him into his office and torn another strip off him. 'I've told you once, and I'll tell you again,' he'd growled. 'Get the hell out there, talk to crew – and ground crew – and get to know exactly what conditions and what problems they have to work under. Otherwise you'll be no bloody good to any of us.'

Anyway, the *phoney war* was over now, with the sudden German *blitzkrieg*, and that was certain! It was difficult to take in how abruptly it had happened, this turnabout. All right, there had been the Norway fiasco last month, when British forces had attempted to invade that country as a sort of preventative *coup* (Churchill's idea, apparently) only to find they'd been adroitly beaten to it by Hitler. That apart, however, things had seemed to be at stalemate, with even whispers from some quarters about a negotiated peace – not that many people would have gone along with that!

But all that had changed in the past two weeks. Strange to think how it had all coincided on May 10th: Chamberlain forced to resign, Winnie taking over as P.M.; and at the same time the Germans, without warning, sweeping into 'neutral' Belgium and Holland, and now into France, with all the stunning impact of their previous invasions. The suddenness of it had taken everyone by surprise. Everyone, it seemed, except Bartholomew Browning, who had muttered on a number of occasions, 'Look at the history. Look what the Germans did at the onset of the last war. Look at what Hitler did this time in Czechoslovakia, Poland and Norway. That's what will happen again.'

And, that's what everyone then began to say, once they had the advantage of hindsight, that the allies had been made to look absolute fools. 'Anyone could have seen, surely,' that jerry, with their track record, weren't going to take any notice of declared neutrality from countries like Belgium and Norway? And there the French had been, foolishly, with all their forces in strength sitting smugly and securely (and, as it turned out, uselessly) behind the Maginot Line; and the much more meagre British Expeditionary Force (what an archaic term that title had turned out to be, as well!) equally smug on the Belgian border thinking that Belgium's neutrality would act as a buffer, or at least provide ample warning of any attack. And now Holland had capitulated, and Belgium could do so at any moment, so the allies really had their backs to the wall! The consequences didn't bear thinking about. What was the British strength over there? Something around quarter of a million men? If they and the French couldn't hold out, what then? Britain couldn't afford to lose all those men and armaments, for without them there'd surely be little hope of repelling any subsequent invasion. And invasion would be sure to come if the Frogs capitulated. Already, he knew, around the countryside workmen could be seen hastily removing signposts and obliterating the names of villages and towns – so that, as Arthur Stanton had put it, 'if the buggers can't be held off, at least they might get lost!'

The more he thinks about the possibility of Britain being overrun, the more the sour taste of panic begins to rise in his throat. The same sensations must be there in Government, too. He wonders if they've smelled defeat. Almost all of the government had apparently been at the 'Service of Intercession' at Westminster Abbey yesterday – the full Cabinet, and most of the Commons and Lords as well as many of the senior military – willing God to be on our side! So the thought must be there. Yet it doesn't bear thinking about. Those few days in Berlin with Hans four years ago were enough to bring home to him what it would mean. Surely it isn't possible? It's a nightmare.

His thoughts drift back, as they have done on a number of occasions in recent months, to the peace but also his own personal turmoil in that summer of '27. From this present perspective he can see himself not as himself but as a different person, someone he'd once known. But someone he had known, at least – not like those photographs of his mother and Uncle John in their youth, in which they'd appeared to be people he'd never known. The world he was familiar with, the world he'd carefully constructed for himself, had been overturned by that discovery. Pretence had gone; and reality had been hard to take. Gradually, regret and self-pity had been driven out, replaced by anger. Anger that his father had not only, in the end, rejected them, but that he had entered their lives in the first place. If he hadn't, everything would have been so different. He would have had a father, a different father – probably Uncle John in fact! – one who would have been there for him, one whom he could have admired and modelled himself on. One he could respect. Not someone who had run away.

* * *

The summer of 1927 would prove to be one of the worst and wettest for fifty years; and survived in Peter's memory as a summer of sun-drenched experiences. The clues to this paradox were to be found in his Journal for that year, but not wholly explained.

From the moment he arrived home (the term 'home' consciously used by him as a practical description rather than yet being fully acceptable) following the completion of his first year at Bardolph's, it rained. Not, on the whole, particularly heavy rain, but incessant rain, day after day. In the Lake District the terrain took on a brooding, hostile demeanour. The rivers flowed, a sullen brown, with swift and silent menace, yet leaden as though forced on only by the immense weight of water following behind – until, that is, they reached some more swiftly downhill course, when they would loudly erupt, white with fury. The mountains were obscured for much of the time: only now and again would cloud break and roll along the fellsides, like smoke from enemy camp-fires, briefly allowing crag faces, as grey citadels, to peer through with aggressive countenance.

At first the Four took the weather in their stride, donning oilskins and going forth. But venturing out soon required more than determination; it required inventiveness with regard to finding outdoor pastimes sufficiently intriguing as to make the prospect of getting wet of little consequence. After a number of days of arriving home soaked through following only a few hours of exploring the fells, woods and old mine workings (the latter proving to be no drier, as water dripped through the roofs), hunting for birds' nests, or rather listlessly playing various adventure games, the gang admitted defeat. Resorting therefore to card games, charades, and other equally boring (it had to be admitted) indoor activities – interspersed with an occasional (when, that is, their collective pocket money was up to the occasion) foray to the Picture House to see a Charlie Chaplin film, or a Tom Mix western – all this too quickly palled.

Quite soon, therefore, many days would go by without any of the four meeting up. (The truth, anyway, was that actually they were now growing away from childish things, although this wasn't apparent to them at the time.)

So it was, by the same token, that Peter's entries in his journal became less and less frequent – because 'nothing happened'. (His uncle, some time ago, had found a children's version of Pepys' Diary for him to read, but he'd found those sorts of entries of 'ordinary day-to-day events' boring, much preferring the modern 'adventures' described by Scott and Shackleton in their journals – and for the same reason continuing to think of his own writings as a 'journal' rather than a 'diary'). And of the entries he did make, some were in the form of a compromise, made out of a growing sense of embarrassment at the blank pages staring him in the face.

At breakfast each morning Uncle John was in the habit of reading out from time to time bits from the newspaper that he presumably thought might interest everyone else because they particularly interested him (but in fact trying everyone's patience in the process – including, normally, Peter's). Peter, however, began to selectively take more notice of some of these items – those that he grudgingly deemed worthy of inclusion in his own journal. Among these were the reports that 'someone called Segrave' had driven a car at the unbelievable speed of over 200 miles an hour, beating by a considerable amount Malcolm Campbell's world record earlier in the year; that there were now, for the first time in Britain, more motor cars on the roads than there were horse-drawn vehicles; and that Hollywood was about to release a film in which people could actually be heard to speak.

Nevertheless, more and more of his pages remained blank; and, mostly, all that had been entered (and, by the same token, remained in his memory) at the end of that period were those few brief spells when, mercifully, the weather had relented, allowed summer to put on its proper raiment and encouraged proper 'adventure' to take place.

It is the Wednesday of the third week in July. Unbelievably they have woken to a clear sky, and by mid-morning the Four are out on the lake with the sun high, glaring fiercely against a backdrop of intense blue, and the temperature already up in the seventies. Peter is lolling in the stern of the boat, the cords from the rudder loose in his hands, for direction doesn't matter, is purposeless as long as they don't actually hit anything. Bill and George are rowing, dreamily, taking no particular care to co-ordinate their strokes, the water dripping from their blades in a manner as seemingly lethargic and haphazard as the movements of the oars themselves. Jamie lies prone, in the front, taking no notice of the three boys, her arm over the side, idly trailing her hand in the tiny waves frothing from the bow. If Peter peers along the side of the boat he can see her fingers like pale fish moving beneath the surface. Below her hand, rays of sunlight strike chords of green and gold in the water, shimmering like some fine material caught in the cold currents beneath. Deeper still, here in the centre of the lake, is the darkness, where light cannot penetrate; and Peter shivers, in that moment longing for the friendlier shallows of the shore. Then, as he peers further out, looking across the breathless surface of the waters, sky and shore are so perfectly reflected that with little imagination the four of them could be floating upside down in an azure sky surrounded by up-ended viridian hills; but on the near side, in the shadow of the boat, looking down into the blackness of invisibility, they might just as easily be suspended in a void, held up only by some unseen hand. Perhaps his own life is like that? An existence in two disparate worlds, neither of them real? His life at school, part ritualistic, part make-believe; and his life here, at 'home', created and directed by others.

Is that what has also happened to Jamie? Since the four of them met up, as it were by instinct, earlier in the day, she has again had very little to say. They miss her liveliness and leadership. The reason for their lack of purpose is not just the unaccustomed humidity and fierceness of the day. Jamie's mother has remarried, back in May, and Jamie's unhappiness at this is clearly eating at her from within. The three boys have not talked about it. There is no point. Cause and effect is clear enough, even to them. At a basic level they can understand it, even if they're not equipped to analyse it. But Peter feels it acutely. It's not just that he sympathises with her unhappiness from a distance; it is more than that, it has become a part of him, a common bond, a pain that is shared. He hasn't thought it through, but indistinctly understands that it is something to do with a father lost.

His thoughts drift back to the school term just gone. A term for which his School Report, like the previous two, refers to his lack of application, talks of 'failure to achieve potential' – failure of which not only is he himself only too well aware, yet unable to redress, but which perversely he finds himself embracing. Even where success is within his grasp, he seems unable to break out of his own private world, to fully take part. It's as though, whatever sphere he is in, he sees himself as being there purely as a disinterested observer.

In this summer term, just past, he was chosen to play on the Colts cricket XI – unusual for someone in their first year at school. At first he was excited, the object of praise and admiration. It brought back warm memories of his father and him sitting together at matches at Lords, of playing with bat and ball in the garden and in the park – memories of those few occasions when they had been able to share something at least. But gradually, in those matches at school, those recollections had come to haunt him, reminding him that, unlike the other fellows on the team, he never had anyone there of his own to cheer him on, to enthusiastically applaud that leg-cut to boundary, or that taken catch, to proudly congratulate him when his innings was done. And then there seemed no point.

After a few weeks he'd been dropped from the team; following which there had been the awkward glances from his friends – even from Pearson (still on the team) whose expressions of sympathy had been strangely constrained – and, from others, one or two cruel little jibes fuelled by previous jealousy. Beal had been more forthright: 'For God's sake man, waken up! You're throwing away the chance to really make something of yourself.'

At this point, though, his ruminations are interrupted by Bill – whose voice is in the process of breaking, so that his utterances are frequently fragmented into squeaks and rumbles.

I say, we're not far from Hammy's place, now. Has Jordan gone there to play tennis today, Pete?'

The question suddenly switching, halfway through, from uncertain baritone to high-pitched falsetto, the others suppress grins – George and Peter know that their own turn will come.

'I'm not sure,' Peter replies. 'Probably.'

Jordan has taken to ignoring him once more, and he has done his best to keep out of her way. But for the past couple of weeks she has been moping around the house with her bottom lip stuck out in a pout as big as a pocket, her disgruntlement displayed for all to see, making it clear that she regards the bad weather as a personal slight to her and her alone. Part of it, though, has also been the reception accorded her casual announcement one evening that she thinks she'll take up acting as a career. From Aunt Mabel's reaction you would have thought that she'd just stated that she was going to dance naked in the streets. Even Peter's mother had looked aghast. Peter himself thought it sounded jolly interesting – he might even be able to admit to some association with her, under those circumstances. As for Uncle John, his response was all too predictable – although on this occasion Peter wasn't too sure whether his expression had been one of amusement or bemusement. He'd said very little, merely nodded sagely as if to indicate, Peter thought, that the idea was worth considering – in the fullness of time. Later, however, in Jordan's absence, when he'd had to withstand the force of his wife's fury along with accompanying charges of 'cowardice' and other such sentiments, he'd calmly pointed out that his daughter had, anyway, 'very little talent for anything else', and had gone on to say, 'She's certainly got the looks for it. Besides which, she's been acting all her life. She's probably a natural.'

So when Bill goes on to suggest that they row over there to find out, Peter isn't any more enamoured of the idea than are George and Jamie: George because, being entirely practical in his approach to life, he cannot understand Bill's preoccupation with Jordan when she has never shown the slightest acknowledgement of him; and Jamie because at present she hasn't much enthusiasm for anything, much less an idea that she would regard as silly at the best of times.

Faced with a blank response, Bill perseveres, urging, 'C'mon, it'll be fun! We can pretend that it's…it's a Red Indian encampment, and we're a party of Rangers creeping up on it for a surprise attack, like in *The Northwest Passage*.'

Having read that book and enjoyed it, Peter warms to the idea. Jamie merely snorts in disgust. And Peter then also begins to realise that they really are getting too old for these sorts of games. What's more, he, too, understands Bill's ulterior motive.

Nevertheless, more as the result of an apathetic lack of resistance to the proposal than any true conviction, ten minutes later they are quietly hauling the boat up onto the shingle below the bluff on which *Fairview* – Colonel Hamilton's house – stands, and are beginning to enter into the spirit of the enterprise. Bill, of course, leads the way, followed by George, then Peter, with Jamie tagging along behind, as they silently make their way in single file up the steep path. Peter turns to see if Jamie is, in fact, following. She glances up at him, catching his eye, and makes a funny face in conspiratorial fashion, as though she knows that Peter, as well, is too sensible to think much of this idea. To Peter, though, it again implies that particular intimacy between them which makes him feel special.

Already they can hear the burble of voices up near the house; at least two: a male voice and a female one. As they creep nearer, more detail can be distinguished: there is the rhythmic *phut-phut* of a tennis ball being hit, punctuated by shouts of excitement and gusts of laughter. The shrubbery here is jungle-like, difficult to see through, and damp, the undergrowth greasy beneath the feet after the recent rains. It all adds to the atmosphere of the game, of tracking through exotic country in pursuit of savage foe.

But a few minutes later they are all four struck by the abruptness of silence: the sounds from the court have vanished.

Perhaps they've been discovered! As one they shrink to the ground, fingers to their lips. A glance at Jamie reveals that even she is taut with excitement. After a minute of hushed apprehension, during which nothing happens, hesitantly they edge forward again, carefully parting the dank foliage until the garden, with lawns leading up to the house, comes into view. The grass tennis court, enclosed by its high wire-netting fence, is about fifty yards away over to the right, and is empty. A couple of tennis rackets and three or four balls lie deserted on the grass at one end of the court. The four peer around nervously. Could the erstwhile occupants of the court be creeping up on them? – the hunters hunted?

Then drifts the sound of voices, more subdued than before, from beyond the court, where there stands a small wooden gazebo. Bill, gesturing for them to follow, sets off in that direction, in a half-crouch, keeping to the shrubbery.

'Bill!' hisses Jamie, 'leave it!'

When he takes no notice, Peter and George, after a hesitant glance at Jamie, follow. She hangs back for a moment, then, with a shrug, reluctantly also follows, conveying the impression that she has decided that it is less likely to become calamitous if she's there than if she isn't.

As they work their way round in an arc, keeping to cover, the front of the gazebo begins to come into view, and just inside it they can make out two figures, a man and a woman, standing close together, both dressed in tennis whites. But it is only when they have stealthily crept further round that they can finally identify them as Jordan and Colonel Hamilton. For initial seconds they are too stunned to fully comprehend what they are seeing – Peter finally doing so probably more tardily than the others. Roger Hamilton and Jordan are in a close embrace, kissing fervently, the colonel's usually-immaculate dark hair ruffled by Jordan's agitated hand as she strains against him, rising onto her toes to do so. His own left hand is at her waist, grasping the hem of her tennis skirt which has been pulled up so that she is largely exposed from the waist down, her tensed lower limbs startling in their nakedness – nakedness that is heightened, rather than lessened, by the sight of her cotton pants pulled taut around her bottom and crotch. Even more shockingly, his other hand is half hidden from view, searching between her thighs. From the couple there now come only odd moaning sounds. So complete is their passion that the four onlookers could probably walk up to them and they might never be noticed.

For long moments they crouch there, unable to believe what they're seeing. Peter can feel himself trembling, almost frightened by the scene in front of him, and by the violence of the emotions it has released in him. All four are avoiding one another's eyes, but Peter takes a quick glance at the others: Bill's face is contorted in rictus fashion, his normal olive skin distinctly pale, eyes suffused and seeming to protrude, hands partly raised and balled into fists; Jamie is calmer, her face expressionless, but her cheeks are flushed as though she has a fever; George is impassive – but nothing ever seems to disturb George.

Jamie, after long seconds of silence, breaks the spell. 'Come on! Out of here!' she demands in a whisper which is almost too loud. Her voice, even though pitched low, has all the decisive tone of command that it once had.

Back at the boat, Bill explodes. 'That dirty, filthy bugger!' he rages.

'Bill!' says Jamie sharply. 'Watch your language!'

'But he's an old man!' he goes on wildly. 'How could he do that to her! And why couldn't she stop him!'

Jamie laughs, a mirthless sound. 'He's not old! Probably only fortyish. And jolly good-looking. It seemed to me that she was thoroughly enjoying it, anyway! Maybe she even started it.'

The three boys look at her in astonishment. Peter sees that he's not the only one unable to believe what she has just said. Everyone knows that girls just don't enjoy that sort of thing. He looks at her with growing curiosity, which then becomes mild dismay. Can it be that she is peculiar in some way?

A flush is creeping over Jamie's face and neck as she meets their collective gaze which has become almost hostile. 'Anyway,' she says, 'not a word of this to anyone!'

'But she's under-age,' Bill protests, aggression vying with the need to assume an air of superior knowledge. 'I've heard my father talk about that. He'll know what to do. Hamilton will end up going to prison. That'll serve him right!'

'Bill!' Jamie snaps, now also angry, 'don't be so childish! Just think of the scandal and what that would do to Jordan. And to Doctor Webster and…and his family.'(Here she looks directly at Peter.) 'Leave it alone! She's sixteen, anyway; will soon be seventeen. Most certainly old enough to know what she's doing – and to take care of herself.'

Somehow she doesn't really seem any more convinced by what she has said than do the boys. But they all appear to recognise the truth of the likely results of any meddling by them; and there is therefore tacit acceptance of the need to keep quiet about it all. The latent atmosphere of hostility remains, however, together with their unsettled mood, and having returned the boat they abandon the rest of the day, each going their separate ways, alone with their individually disturbed thoughts.

The next few days are dry, albeit cloudier and cooler. The gang meet together, but their activities lack direction and enthusiasm. Jamie has lapsed into despondency once more, now accompanied by a new restlessness. She is irritable and quick to find fault. It seems that her personality itself is undergoing change. The episode of Jordan and Hamilton is never mentioned. Peter is glad of that, because he has been afraid the others would bombard him with questions about Jordan. He's done his best to avoid his cousin altogether; at mealtimes, when her company has been unavoidable, he's hardly looked at her, fearing that his expression might give something away. On the occasions when he has allowed himself to glance her way, when he thinks she's not looking, he's looked at her with new eyes, as if she too, like Jamie, has metamorphosed into a different creature – one that he understands even less than before. Even his mother and Aunt Mabel have, in his eyes, taken on a slightly different aspect, as though by association. At times, at night, he is tormented by images of Jordan with Hamilton, or memories of her standing exposed at the top of the stairs or high on that step-ladder; and those images bring with them strange and worrying effects.

On the Wednesday, though, George injects new excitement into the group by announcing that the weather evidently set fair for another two or three days, his father is the next day to start bringing in the hay that he cut at the weekend. They're all invited to take part – 'the more the merrier,' as his father had put it.

* * *

His recollections, in danger of becoming far too nostalgic, are however now cut short by an awareness of O'Connor pressing back against him once more. A realisation within the carriage that they must now be nearing their destination – and with it, in a sense, their destiny – has resulted in things becoming quieter as people retreat into the privacy of their own thoughts. But for O'Connor, to all intents and purposes unbothered by whatever might be flung her way by life's machinations, this has merely offered her the opportunity to more easily chat to a good-looking naval officer standing nearby. Her movement against Peter, therefore, as he by now well understands, has been an unconscious gesture on her part of both power and provocation, an instinctive signalling of the possibility of her availability for whoever might challenge and win the day. He understands it – that innately for her this is her primitive defence against the world – but as she allows her buttocks to rest unnecessarily firmly against his thighs he reflects again on his difficulty in coming to terms with the predatory nature of some females.

His Aunt Anne. How he remembers her! If O'Connor is bold in her approach to men, she has nothing in comparison to Anne, who had seemed to have no scruples at all. He'd been exposed to her only on that one occasion, when he'd just turned 15, when she visited for two weeks at the end of 1928; but if he is now a bit wary of members of the opposite sex, as he has to admit he is, then part of that has to be laid at his Aunt Anne's door.

* * *

The Websters for some time have been in the habit of once in a while going away for Christmas, always to the same place, to a hotel in Yorkshire. This is one of those years. 1928. This year, of course, Peter and his mother are included in the arrangements, as well as Jordan, who will be home for the Christmas break.

There is no little consternation, then, on several counts when, at the beginning of November, a letter comes from Anne to say that not having been over for a number of years she is planning to come for two weeks at Christmas and she trusts that this will be 'convenient'?

Peter, being away at school when this bombshell lands upon the household, is distanced from most of the uproar that ensues – but in due course is given a lucid (and distinctly amused) account by Uncle John. It seems to Peter that his uncle has something of a reluctant soft spot for this younger sister-in-law – in spite of, or perhaps because of, her family's general disapproval of her. When Peter arrives home for the holiday, though, no one will talk about her in front of him, and he is reluctant to ask questions, even of Jordan; she, of course, as has been evident to Peter all along, dotes on her memories of Anne – which is enough on its own to make him suspicious. He does however manage to ask Cook what it is about Anne that makes her so disowned by her two sisters. But even Cook is reluctant to say more than that 'she drinks too much for her own good', smokes too much, is known to swear, and 'has too much of an eye for the men'. This little liturgy simply serves to intensify his curiosity, particularly as he doesn't exactly understand what is meant by that last remark, only that by implication it has some sort of darker meaning.

When, a few days later, then, he first meets her, it's a bit of a let-down. She seems very ordinary. Younger than he expected, though – he'd automatically been prepared for someone looking a bit like his mother. In fact she does look a bit like his mother – but as his mother was in that photograph all those years ago, when she was young. Only then does he remember that there is a ten or twelve years difference in their ages, and that she must be still only in her late twenties or early thirties. She has the same fair colouring as Jordan. Not as slim as Jordan, nor as pretty, but attractive all the same, with a nice figure and good legs.

Everyone greets her pleasantly enough, if a little warily – apart from his mother, that is, who for some particular reason at first remains distinctly cold and aloof. As for Anne, she's very lively and behaves a bit too effusively for Peter's liking, especially when she eyes him up and down in a calculating sort of way before hugging him enthusiastically and planting a kiss on his mouth. Then, with her hands on his shoulders she leans back, studies him appreciatively for a moment, and says, 'Well, look what I've been missing all these years, a nephew as handsome as you!' Her breath smells of spirits, even at that time of day, which is even more off-putting. His uncle looks on amused, his mother distinctly crossly, and Aunt Mabel perhaps even more so – it seems that as the eldest of the three she assumes some sort of parental responsibility for Anne's behaviour.

Over the next few days, though, Peter warms to her. He doesn't see a great deal of her (especially after Jordan arrives home two days later, after which the two go off together, kindred spirits, whenever they can), but whenever she's present there is an air of excitement and adventure. You never know what to expect of her, what small outrage or breach of decorum she will gleefully inflict upon them. It seems as though the untamed spirit of Africa has come with her.

The potential problem posed to the Christmas arrangements by her unscheduled arrival has been solved by their being able to find room for her at the hotel. The only remaining difficulty therefore is that of transport. Uncle John's car has room only for five. Anne solves that in her typically carefree manner.

'That's all right. It doesn't take more than an hour and a half, does it? I can go on Peter's knee, in the back. That'll be all right, won't it, Pete. We'll like that.'

Peter's not so sure. She looks as though she'll be no light-weight. But it seems there's no alternative: they'll be travelling on Christmas Eve, so a taxi for that distance is out of the question, and the journey by train much too complicated. The two older women look uncertain, even wary, and Jordan for some reason a little vexed; but Uncle John nods his assent, so that settles it. The luggage that can't fit in the boot can go on a roof rack.

To the delight of the younger members at least, the day before they're due to set off there's a light fall of snow, enough to cover the ground, and on Christmas Eve everything is still white. Their route will take them across the north Yorkshire moors, to a place called Greta Bridge which is where the hotel is situated (Peter has looked it up on the road atlas), so there's a sense of adventure about the trip. Like a proper expedition, he thinks. As suspected, it's a bit of a squash in the back of the car, with Anne on Peter's knee at one side, Jordan in the middle, and his mother at the other side. But at least there's headroom, and with six of them in that small space the interior of the car is not quite as cold as it would otherwise have been; and at first Anne's not as heavy as he feared. Uncle John isn't able to get away until four o'clock, so that it's already dusk by the time they leave.

To begin with there's a good deal of lively chatter among the grown-ups, voices raised against the noise of the engine – apart from Jordan, that is, who unaccountably appears to be in one of her more sulky moods. Peter mainly just sits and listens. But as the grey light of evening changes to an anonymous black, the only glimmer being that reflected from the white blur of the snow by the roadside, in the darkness people sink into the silence of their own thoughts. He had thought that his aunt Anne, in spite of her apparent enthusiasm for travelling on his knee, would sit stiffly on his lap, both of them bundled up with coats, making the journey uncomfortable for both of them. But she has taken off her coat, and made him take off his, spreading both coats over them in the way of an eiderdown. After that, she has just sort of sunk comfortably into him, her body somehow accommodating itself to his, murmuring, 'Now we should be nice and warm'.

He, though, is taut with confusion, not knowing how to arrange his legs or where to place his hands beneath the coats. At one point, as Anne adjusts her position, he puts them on either side of her chest, and finds his palms against her breasts. For a second he doesn't quite register the significance of this rounded buoyancy beneath his fingers, and when he does he hastily jerks his hands away expecting an instant rebuke. But Anne's only reaction, in the darkness, is to bend her head so that her mouth is close to his ear. He can smell the drink on her breath. 'Just relax,' she whispers, 'it's alright.' And taking his hands in her own she calmly and deliberately places them back on her breasts, leaving her own hands resting on the backs of his as if denying him any possibility of removing them. He becomes rigid with astonishment, not knowing what is going on and what is expected of him. And as he absorbs this new sensation, of the slight judder and bounce of her bosom beneath his hands with every jolt of the car, this rigidity rapidly spreads to involve a predictably more obvious part of his anatomy. 'Just relax,' she murmurs again into his ear. But so preoccupied is he now with further areas of awareness – her bottom curving into his lap, her thighs against his own, every nuance of her felt (with his now heightened sensitivity) through the thin material of her dress – that this is the last thing he is likely to be able to do. Normally he would be totally, exclusively aware of Jordan sitting squashed close to him, her thigh felt against his; but all his attention is on Anne. He wonders if Jordan has any awareness of what is going on, begins to wonder if in fact there might be a conspiracy between her and Anne, sort of testing him, seeing how far they can manipulate him, exert their power over him.

The remainder of the journey passes, for him, in a mild state of shock and a fog of uncertainty. He cannot believe what is happening, at times wonders whether he is indeed in some kind of dream summoned up by himself. Anne remains mostly silent, and might at times be asleep; but every so often she will move his hands, which she companionably keeps loosely enclosed in hers, to some other place, to nestle in the warm recess of her own lap, or to rest on the tops of her thighs, as though seeking, for him as well as for herself, fresh sensations. And after a time he does relax, gains the confidence to simply accept the excitements and delights so amazingly offered to him in this unabashed manner.

For some time, though, he doesn't dare move – either because he is anxious that such movements might be misinterpreted or else, more importantly, because he is afraid that any change will break the spell. But after a while he begins to get pins-and-needles in his legs, which then start to go numb. He shifts his bottom a little, experimentally – holding his breath in case it should cause her to alter her position and sit more distantly. But she simply adjusts with him, moulding herself, it seems to him, to fit in with whatever minor changes he has made. On one such occasion she whispers, 'Is that better?' That brief inquiry, murmured and private, is imbued for him with all the intimacy of their situation – at that moment he is the object of her total interest and concern.

He therefore becomes gradually more adventurous, finding that movements of that sort bring their own, fresh, enchantments: change draws more attention to detail such as the way her fingers will at times intertwine with his in a new form of intimacy; now and again he detects the outline of a suspender or an edge of her bra, or feels the slip and slide of her dress over her underwear, so that he can imagine her partly undressed. And for part of the time – their two pairs of hands resting on her thighs – her dress has ridden up so that the silk of her stockings is beneath his palms. He is certain that she will do something about that, and indeed she does – but it is to briefly guide his hands up and down on her legs in a kind of friendly caress, as though providing for each the opportunity to absorb the other's body-warmth.

This however creates for him a torment of indecision. Does she expect him to continue such activity of his own volition? And more boldly? He is whisked back to his time in the Sick Room, in the summer, and his fantasies with Plummy. Is this the same? Is he at risk of his imagination leading him into danger? He doesn't know; and Anne gives him no clue. He plays safe and does nothing. But he wonders if she will think less of him for that, no longer worthy of her attention.

The journey then is all too quickly over. What might have been one of lengthy boredom has been transformed into one of revelation and wonder. He is ready to worship his remarkable aunt Anne. As they draw to a halt outside the hotel, and stiffly climb out of the car, he half expects that Anne will continue to hold his hands and dwell on him lovingly. Uncle John peers at them and says, 'Have you two survived all right, then, crammed like that in the back?'

Anne glances at Peter with a brief smile. 'Oh, yes,' she says, 'we survived very well, didn't we, Pete?'

And turns away to converse with the others. That is all. It might never have been. From near-ecstasy he is pitched into despair.

CHAPTER TEN

His musings about the complexities and predatory nature of his Aunt Anne lead him back to O'Connor. There are no such ambiguities about her approach, which as always is direct and extreme. But he still hasn't altogether decided whether that is truly her, or whether that too is all pretence. Just as he hasn't decided why it is that he addresses her by her first name, yet always thinks of her as O'Connor.

As though taking her cue from his thoughts, she turns now, her mood mainly one of excitement, and puts her hand up on his shoulder – and even that simple action has to contain elements of caress and possessiveness. 'I think I've just seen the sea,' she says. As a statement it borders on the inane, yet appears complex, for it seems to be formulated as a question, as though accompanied by lurking doubts that have nothing to do with whether the sea is nearby (which is only to be expected, as they must by now be approaching their destination). She provides the solution to that small enigma in her next comment, which is immediate. 'I wonder if it's likely to be rough?' Then, 'I'm a terrible sailor…And I can't swim.'

Well, well. Fancy that. An Irish girl from Liverpool, and afraid of the sea! Who would have thought it. Particularly where Shevaun O'Connor is concerned. So she does have chinks in her armour, after all.

The naval officer, also quick to pick up on it, but ahead of Peter in one respect, is the first to reply. 'I don't think you need to worry. I might well have to take ship, but I can't think that you're going to have to. Whatever your role is to be in this little affair, it'll be on this side of the Channel, I fancy'.

The navy having been the first to come to her deliverance, she removes her hand from Peter's shoulder and turns to continue the conversation with her rescuer, leaving Peter once more with his thoughts.

He, too, can now see the clear light of the sea where, at moments when the terrain drops away from the now-slowing train, the horizon merges into sky – and he is taken back to Silloth, to ebbing early-morning tides, and the gathering of fish for breakfast. When the tides were right, they would of an evening, under Uncle John's direction, set lines and hooks on posts positioned well out on exposed stretches of sea-washed beach that would in the coming hours be covered to a depth of several feet by the incoming tide. He would show them how to look for sandworms, digging down beneath the telltale casts, an activity which in its own right had all the thrill of a treasure hunt. With sufficient worms for their purpose they would (sometimes by the fading light of the setting sun) then work their way along the lines, baiting the hooks – taking great care, as Uncle John would frequently remind them, that the bait 'should be worms and not fingers'. The urge next morning to be up with the sun and down to the beach to discover what bounty the outgoing sea had left was irresistible: the subsequent breakfast (from flounders or plaice so fresh that they flapped in the pan as though still alive) an experience so exhilarating as to be never forgotten.

That recollection makes him wonder now about his mother, aunt and uncle – and Cook – and how they are getting on with the latest food-rationing. On station, at Marwell, as service personnel he and the others are fairly protected from the worst rigours of rationing, but he knows by the correspondence from home that, though living in a rural area, and with some of Uncle John's farmer patients slipping them produce from time to time, the small weekly allowance of some foods is not easy to get by on. Indeed, he realises guiltily, he is so far removed from the vicissitudes of rationing that he is hard put to remember what the weekly allowance is. Let's see: quarter of a pound of butter per person per week, he thinks. The same for bacon or ham. Twelve ounces altogether of sugar, jam or sweets. And now, in the past six weeks, a mere 1s 10d worth of meat. And one fresh egg per week, if they are lucky. They are beginning to learn about that in the mess – some of the scrambled egg presented to them now is concocted from dried eggs imported from America (fresh eggs being reserved for the aircrews on their way to, or return from, missions), and pretty revolting it is too.

He smiles when he pictures what Aunt Mabel must have been like on receiving a food parcel from her sister Anne in Kenya, last month. As reported somewhat gleefully by Uncle John in his most recent letter, her reaction had been one of delight and outrage all at the same time. 'It's like being a pauper and having to depend on other people's charity!' he'd reported her as saying – although she'd been unable to prevent herself from gloating over its contents, it seemed. According to Uncle John she wouldn't have minded so much if it had been from anyone but Sister Anne of all people.

Anne again, and all the revelations about her that had encroached upon his young life. Leaving him still with a confusion of emotions ranging from fond indulgence to resentment and hate, each mood sometimes piling on him in such rapid succession as to be fused into one.

He still sometimes churns inside whenever he is reminded of her, as though her complexes have been capable of becoming a part of his own, infectious. But with the passing of the years he's been able to view that whole episode on that particular Christmas more objectively. It hadn't, after all, really been incest. Not very much had actually happened. He hadn't, afterwards, in any way felt himself abused. In any case, he doesn't think that Anne has regarded herself as a member of the clan any longer, and most of her family probably prefer it that way. Her defection from them at a relatively young age has been absolute: mental as well as physical. She had, that Christmas, not felt any real ties or obligation to any of them.

It should have been a picture-book Christmas, and the fact that it hadn't been, for him, had, really, if he's honest, been nothing to do with Anne.

* * *

The Morritt Arms is as Christmassy as it can get: a Georgian coaching inn out in the country, roaring log fires, holly and mistletoe, tinsel and streamers, warm lights, gleaming old furniture, copper and brass – and snow on the windows and ground. The sixty or so guests, mixed, of all ages, are friendly and lively. There are walks to the rivers and through woods, hide-and-seek and snowball fights, and trips by car or bus to nearby villages and towns. The meals are sumptuous and seem to come in quick succession; there are crackers and paper hats, music and dancing, fancy dress and games. And he hates it.

That is something that has never really changed. He's always been shy of large gatherings, of strangers and parties, of dressing up and 'games'.

But that's not the problem on this occasion, he tells himself. The problem, he thinks, is Anne. One minute he decides he's in love with her, ridiculous as it seems; the next he reminds himself that he can't be, that she is, after all, his aunt – even though she doesn't behave like it and is so relatively young. But he can't understand her attitude to him. It's not even like it is with Jordan, who is at least – more or less – consistent in her disdain of him. Anyway, he is (for that moment) no longer interested in Jordan: all his thoughts are on Anne.

She, that first evening, takes almost no notice of him, as if she has either forgotten about their closeness in the car, or regrets it. Admittedly, very soon she's had so much to drink, and is behaving so outrageously that the family despair, doing their best to pretend she's not with them, although everyone knows that she is. She flirts shamelessly with most of the men, whatever their age or status; her laughter becomes shriller and louder; her behaviour less and less controlled. Her sisters are flushed with embarrassment and anger; even Uncle John's patience is taxed beyond its limits; and Peter himself is overcome with disappointment and shame. Only Jordan seems to find some amusement in her aunt's antics, and this from a distance and with a malicious glow. Eventually Anne reaches the point where she is hardly able to stand, and Peter's mother and Aunt Mabel contrive to lead her off, only mildly protesting, and get her to bed.

The following morning, however, Christmas Day, up amazingly bright and charmingly contrite (although it is clear that she has little comprehension of what had taken place the evening before) she downs a good breakfast and plays her part in the ritual festivities. Even more surprisingly she remains sober for the rest of that day, and the next.

But towards Peter her behaviour remains capricious. One moment she is giving him her undivided attention, perhaps gently teasing him in a coquettish way; the next she is looking through him, as if he no longer exists. She will make a pact with him that for a certain game that is being arranged they will enter as partners; and when the time comes he finds that she has teamed up with someone else. She will invite him to dance (something he normally hates to have to do, but which, with the prospect of partnering her, he looks forward to) – but it is never for, say, a Quickstep which he could manage to do, but will be for a Charleston, or a Rumba, which he finds impossible and in which he makes an absolute fool of himself. He is consumed by jealousy and self-loathing, mopes around feeling sorry for himself, and is generally wretched. She has taken over from Jordan in the role of tormentor. He begins to hate her; but the next moment she will be all sweet contrition, and he changes his mind. He notices Uncle John giving him long, quizzical looks, and suspects that he understands something of what is going on, but that he is unable to find common ground on which to broach the subject with him.

Then, on the day after Boxing Day, something happens. The arrangements are that they are booked to stay until New Year, with Uncle John going home to see to his practice for three days mid-week before returning for New Year's Eve. But on this particular evening, prior to his departure, Uncle John, Aunt Mabel and Peter's mother, together with Jordan, have been invited out to dinner to the nearby house of some old family friends. Anne (possibly through the connivance of her sisters) has not been invited, and nor has Peter.

Later that evening, Peter, who has gone to bed and is reading, hears a tap on his door. Before he can speak, the door opens, and Anne is standing there, leaning unsteadily against the jamb. She is dressed in a pink bathrobe and fluffy mules, and evidently is returning to her room after having a bath. He can smell the gin on her breath all the way from the door.

'Oh, good,' she says, 'you're not asleep, then.' Her voice is thick and her speech slurred.

Surprised, pleased and at the same time apprehensive about this turn of events, he croaks his reply.

'I wanted to talk to someone,' she goes on. There is a pause as she struggles to clear her thoughts. She amends her statement. 'I wanted to talk to you,' – and nods affirmation, evidently thinking that sounds better. 'I haven't been very kind to you, have I?' Again a pause and a nod, as if to confirm to herself that that was what she intended to say. Her words are indistinct, and he's having to concentrate to get their meaning.

She's still clinging to the doorpost, her legs buckling a little. He doesn't know how to deal with this. What will he do if she collapses on the floor? Her robe, tied loosely with a sash, is beginning to gape, exposing some of her breasts and legs. In a moment, he thinks, she's going to be stark naked! His mouth is dry, he tries to look away, but continues to stare, fascinated.

She begins to notice the fixity of his gaze, and looks down. A slow smile spreads across her face. 'I don't suppose you've ever seen a woman naked before, have you?' she says, and, fumbling, deliberately unfastens the sash. The gown falls away, and he's staring at a generous portion of her breasts, firm and full, the nipples and pink area around them much larger than he expected; then, entranced, his eyes slide down to the triangular eminence of hair between her thighs. For as long as he can remember he's been intrigued by what girls might be like there. Now he knows, and is transfixed.

'Is that nice?' she says, after long moments; and with both hands draws back the sides of her robe so that her hips, waist and breasts – the breasts that she'd encouraged him to hold, in the car – are fully exposed, and the nudity that until now he's only been able to imagine is displayed before him. He thinks he's never seen anything so beautiful.

But she's had her hands away from their supports on the door for too long, and has to clutch at them again.

'Whoops,' she says, 'I think I'd better lie down,' and shakily launches herself towards his bed. The door is still wide open, and only then does it strike him that anyone could pass at any moment. He springs out and hurries to close it. When he turns round she is already sprawled on her back in his bed and attempting to pull the bedclothes over herself. Her robe is lying on the floor.

He is appalled. 'You...you can't stay there, like that!' he says, his voice high with desperation. 'Supposing someone comes.'

'Oh, don't be such a silly! You sound just like Mabel.' She giggles. '...Your other aunt! ...Who's going to come? Anyway, there's plenty of room for both of us. Come on. I'm not going to bite!'

He hesitates, beginning to feel the cold of the room striking up through his feet.

'Come on,' she encourages again. 'It's quite safe. Well...' she laughs, a silly, self-satisfied laugh of delight, '...almost.'

Still he hesitates, torn between inclination and caution.

'Come on!' she repeats, now cross, which seems to make her stumble less over her words. 'I've said, I just want to talk to you.' – and when he doesn't move: 'I'll scream if you don't come,' and she opens her mouth as if at the point of doing so.

In sudden panic he dashes to the bed, and as she draws back the clothes for him, scrambles in.

'That's better,' she says, putting her arm around him and drawing his head to the crook of her shoulder. He quails for a second as he comes into contact with her nakedness, the cotton of his pyjamas doing nothing to impair the warmth and smoothness of her skin.

But, in the absence of any reaction from her, he begins to relax just a bit.

They lie in silence for a while, until he begins to think she's fallen asleep. That's no good. It must be well after nine. The others could be back before long; and his mother, whose room is next to his, not infrequently looks in on him if she's been out.

'What's Africa like?' he asks, for something to say, to waken her up.

She stirs. 'Miles and miles of bloodiness, that's what it's like,' she mumbles, '…not at all what it's cracked up to be.'

He smiles, that she can still use that Cumbrian expression. 'Don't you like it, then?'

'Oh, it's as good as anywhere…I suppose. Nowhere's perfect.'

'I bet you get lots of sunshine, though.'

'Well, it's certainly…hot…I'll grant you…that. And, yes, there's a lot of shun…sun…given that there's a whole lot of Africa. But Nairobi…where I'm living…is more often cloudy than not, even though it's almost on the…the equator. But it's at shix…six… thousand feet, you know. Helpsh to keep it that bit cooler.'

She's sounding drowsy again, her speech more slurred than before. He tries to think of something else to say.

'Why did you go there?'

She makes an effort to rouse herself, changing position as she does so. He can feel one of her nipples, surprisingly, pressing into his ribs. 'Oh, that's a long story. I don't think you'll want to hear that.'

Once more for a short time they lie there in silence. He can hear her sniffling, almost as if she's crying. It's something that people often do, he thinks, when they're drunk. He has to think of something to make her leave – even though part of him doesn't want her to. But the consequences, for both of them, of her being found here don't bear thinking about. Perhaps he should simply tell her to go?

Before he can screw up enough courage to do so, she suddenly says, 'I killed my mother, you know.'

The abruptness and shock of it freezes him. 'I don't think that can be right,' he manages to get out after a short delay, his voice rising to an unmanly squeak.

'I don't mean actually, you understand. She died when I was born.' Her voice is less befuddled; now she simply sounds tired.

'But that's not your fault, is it.'

'Isn't it? That's not what others think. If I hadn't been born she wouldn't have died. I wasn't any substitute for my mother.'

He's out of his depth here. 'Are you sure other people think that? Who else thinks that?'

'Oh, everyone really. My sisters and my father and…well, everyone. They always have.'

'That can't be right,' he says again. 'I'm sure you must be wrong!'

She ignores that, saying instead, 'And I've done other things…a bad thing.'

His interest is now fully aroused, curiosity wrestling with dismay at what she might be about to reveal. 'What sort of thing?' he manages to get out, his mouth dry.

Before she can reply there comes the sound of voices and footsteps in the corridor. They both hold their breath until the people, strangers, have passed.

'I'd better go!' she says. 'This would only make things worse.'

She struggles to get out of bed, not on her own side, but flopping across him so that her nakedness weighs wonderfully down upon him. She pauses half way, in order to re-gather her strength, it seems, and looks blearily down on him. 'Sorry!' she says, and giggles. Then, 'You're a nice boy, Pete. You'll drive the girls wild, before long – probably already do,' then continues her unsteady progress.

Stooping to pick up her robe she almost falls, and he rises to get out to help her, but with a vaguely peremptory hand she waves him back. As she fights her way into the gown, finding difficulty in identifying the arm holes, he has time to watch her. Strangely he discovers that her nudity no longer holds for him the overpowering eroticism that it did when her gown first fell away, but that he is able to simply admire and study her body with a degree of objectivity. It's as if his mind, independently of his emotions, is trying to commit every detail to memory.

At last, having made herself look once more reasonably respectable, she weaves her way to the door, blows him an unsteady kiss, and disappears.

The next morning, after breakfast, unexpectedly she declares, without any explanation, her intention to go off to London. The protests from her family are shamefully insincere. Having said her goodbyes to the others, she comes over to Peter. His emotions are in such turmoil from all that has happened that he's having to hold back the tears. Kissing him briefly on the cheek, she murmurs, 'Good luck. And don't think too badly of me, Peter, will you? You'll probably hear the stories about me in the years to come.'

* * *

That was the last time he was to see her.

He's thought of her often, though, over the years – in spite of the later revelations of those 'other stories'. Has wondered what has become of her. Letters have been few and far between: very often only a card at Christmas. The last they'd heard she was living with a chap somewhere outside Nairobi. He's felt – still feels – the need to talk to the family about the things she said to him that night, about her conviction (misplaced, he was certain) that they'd always regarded her as unwanted. But he's never known how to set about it; and has felt wretched whenever he's thought about it, that he's done nothing in that direction. But then, how could he, without further opening old wounds.

O'Connor, evidently having now tired of her naval officer, nudges Peter sharply in the ribs. 'Come on! Waken up! Where have you been! We're almost there.' O'Connor can't abide it when people are taking no notice of her – particularly when it comes to men. Possibly the same had applied to his aunt Anne, would explain much of her behaviour. But he now knows she was – no doubt still is – much more complicated than that.

He's pondered, too, many a time, on the inconsistencies in her behaviour, has wondered if her apparent scorn for others had been a symptom of her own lack of regard for herself. But for all her faults and annoying quirks, she'd had a way of enlivening any gathering; whenever she'd been present the tempo had lifted, and boredom banished. Then too, he is convinced, she had a generosity of spirit constantly fighting to get out, but held back by her own self-contempt. And all for no good reason – other than perhaps that particular one. No one else though had consciously created the milieu in which her doubts and sense of unworthiness had burgeoned. Was it simply that events, disconnected from people, could take on a life, a continuing energy of their own? And that to have sunshine without shadow there had to be a totally featureless, and therefore dull, terrain? That the brighter the sunlight reflected from one side, the darker the shadow on the other?

He glances down at O'Connor. But she's now staring moodily out of the window. Still wondering what's in store for them perhaps, as they all are. Or still brooding about the sea?

And in his present mood that thought takes him back to that summer when he was still only fourteen.

* * *

Further weeks of weather as dark as Peter's thoughts in that turbulent summer eventually give way, in the middle of August, to a more settled spell; and the decision is made for the family to spend a week at the seaside, with Grandfather in Silloth. Peter and his mother are to stay with his Grandad, and the Websters will stay in one of the caravans, there being insufficient room for all of them in the house. Peter's muted enthusiasm for this arrangement – after all, the prospect of staying in a caravan for a week would have been infinitely more exciting – is noted by Uncle John (of course), who makes the suggestion that one or two of his friends might be invited as well? Peter brightens at this: but it turns out that Bill will already be away with his family; and George, now fifteen and regarded therefore as being an adult, is required to help on the farm. Jamie, however (who has just had her fifteenth birthday – celebrated, it would seem, without any party and in some gloom), when invited, jumps at the idea. In answer to Aunt Mabel's objections that it perhaps is 'not appropriate' for Jamie to be invited to stay as Peter's friend, she being a girl and all that, Uncle John patiently reminds her that, after all, for many years Jamie had been a close friend of Jordan's as well. Arrangements are duly made, therefore; and it is only when this has been done, and the point of departure is close, that Peter realises that his growing excitement at this new arrangement is a bit more than that: the anticipation of spending a whole week in the company of both Jordan and Jamie, on his own as it were, is creating within him something more akin to agitation.

In the event the weather turns out to be as tumultuous as his emotions, for they arrive (in a chauffeur-driven charabanc hired for the journey in order

146

to accommodate the six of them and their luggage), in the middle of a thunderstorm. In spite of (or because of) this, Uncle John directs the chauffeur to drive straight on across the field to the caravan, where he and his family, with their cases, can be deposited first, before taking the others back to the house. It is with poor omens, therefore, and no little complaining from Aunt Mabel and Jordan, that (against a black sky riven by sheets of lightning, and hesitant but enormous drops of rain which promise to become a deluge at any moment) their holiday begins.

Perhaps the gods had merely been testing them, however, for against all odds the days that follow are days of hot sunshine, so that by the final day Peter, lying on the sand on his own in a hollow of the dunes, giving in to a lassitude brought on by a substantial lunch and the heat of the early afternoon, is, very briefly, content. That contentment is dependant, however, firstly on his ability to avoid too much dwelling on some of the events of the past days, and secondly on his managing to shut out the knowledge that within another week he will be back at school. In the distance he can hear the sounds of the two girls frolicking in the shallows, their voices ebbing and flowing like the sibilance of the surf. If he were to crawl to the top of the dune he would be able to watch them; but he is deterred by the thought that they might see him. In any case, he can see them in his mind's eye. He's thought of little else all week: both of them in plain navy-blue swimming costumes, the cotton snug on their bodies, particularly when they've been in the water, every subtlety of line clear for him to see, and not much left to the imagination. The only thing is, he has insufficient information on which to base his imagination. He can see the early swell of their breasts (Jordan's small and globe-like, perfect to modern eyes; Jamie's already more ample, and thus more mobile and therefore, in his view, more exciting) and the intriguingly large prominence of their nipples beneath the thin material. But he has no idea what these things actually look like. As for what goes on between belly and thigh, he cannot begin to conceive what might lie there. In their near-nakedness the physical differences between the two girls are more obvious, too, than has been apparent before. Jordan is much slimmer, with narrower hips and long smoothly-shaped legs; Jamie more curvy, the muscles in her arms and legs more discernible, but nicely shaped all the same – and, in Peter's eyes, actually more attractive, particularly when she moves. But having said all that, it had to be admitted, she isn't nearly as pretty as Jordan.

Nevertheless, as he lies there, gazing up at the blue of the sky, recollections drifting along with the scattered fluffy clouds, he's taken back again to the events of two mornings ago. It had been early, the sun up but presenting only that quiet outside brightness that is the promise of a brilliant day; and hardly had he registered that fact, still drugged as he was from sleep, than he'd been startled by the realisation that someone was climbing into bed with him, and he'd yelped in sudden alarm.

'Sshh,' Jamie had whispered, snuggling down in the bed, 'you'll waken everyone!'

'What are you doing here?' he'd managed to croak, finding difficulty both in keeping his voice low and in annunciating the words, his mouth suddenly dry. He could still recall how soft her body had felt up against him, through her thin pyjamas, yet at the same time firm and strong – so different a sensation to that from contact with other boys in the daily rough-and-tumble.

'I couldn't get back to sleep, so thought I'd see if you were awake,' she'd replied, quite matter-of-fact, as though there was nothing unusual in what she was doing.

Strangely, the answer had satisfied him at the time; but since then whenever he's gone back over it he's realised that it hadn't really been an answer at all. Jamie's casual manner, though, had easily persuaded him to accept the situation, and they'd settled down, talking in half-whispers. Thinking about it now, though, he still can't quite decide exactly what effect it had had on him: there'd been warmth and reassurance, certainly, but also nervousness on his part, not knowing what was expected of him. Sinking into the yielding feather-mattress of the single bed, they'd been unavoidably thrown together, and almost immediately, in perfectly natural fashion, Jamie had turned toward him, her top arm flung across his chest, her face close to his, so that he could feel her breath against his cheek and the silkiness of her hair against his neck and brow. He'd also been conscious of the weight of her breast on his arm, and of the smoothness of her tummy against his hip. As they'd stirred and adjusted position from time to time, he'd become more and more aware of this. If that wasn't enough, there'd been, too, something subtle about the scent of her, close to – not so much a perfume as an indefinable fragrance, an elusive fresh-air smell that he'd never been aware of before. All this had added up to a degree of intimacy which was entirely new to him: physical demonstrations of affection had never previously been a part of his experience.

In this manner, though, at moments, they'd chatted quietly about this and that. At times they'd drifted into drowsy silence, both of them, it seemed, just taking comfort from this unforeseen familiarity. It was then, at some point after one of these periods of silence, when they'd started comparing notes about school, and Peter had been telling her about his friends Pearson and 'Charlie' Chaplin, about Beal and about his housemaster, 'Sailor' Roberts, that Jamie had abruptly interrupted his flow of talk to ask, 'Have *you* got a nickname?'

He'd not known how to answer her.

Jamie, intuitive about his silence, had gently tickled his ribs, chiding him, 'You have, haven't you! Go on, you can tell me.'

He'd felt himself flush, was sure that she would feel the heat of it against her face; and anyway she'd reared up on one elbow, and was peering down at him, her features alight with curiosity. 'Come on, Peter,' she'd wheedled, 'just for me! I promise I won't tell.'

'*Wary*,' he'd mumbled, feeling even more wretched.

Her expression had at once changed, to one of concern and contrition.

148

'Oh, that's not fair. Understandable, I suppose – given your surname. But not fair. *Wary* means sort of 'fearful', doesn't it? I don't think you're that, at all. Cautious, perhaps.' Then, coming to a decision, she'd added, 'I shall call you *Cautious*. Just between you and me. No one else to know.'

In one sense he'd been pleased about that – in another, a bit doubtful. He wasn't sure that being called *Cautious* was altogether complimentary either.

Shortly afterwards, though, hearing someone go along to the bathroom, she'd said in a hasty whisper, 'Gosh, it must be time to be getting up! I'd better go. Goodness knows what they'd think if they found me here with you!' And, taking him unawares with a quick kiss on his lips – managing to make it seem both casual and explicit – she'd hurried off with a whispered, 'See you at breakfast!'

When she'd gone he'd lain there for a short while, dazed but basking in the glow of the events of the past hour or so. Her departing words about 'Goodness knows what they'd think if they found me here with you', together with the kiss, and the 'private' nickname she'd bestowed on him, however dubious, as well as again making him feel special had seemed to have all sorts of other implications which he couldn't altogether fathom.

Now, as he continues to lie on the sand, gazing up at the sky, playing the game of trying to spot, against the endless bright backdrop, the black dots that are the skylarks that can be heard singing up there, he wonders if life itself is going to be like that: hints and clues that something is so, but no clarity to it, nothing easily coming into focus. Perhaps, though, like identifying the larks, the solutions to problems may be easier to see a second time round?

But emotional difficulties seemed to have a habit of striking when he's least prepared. Only the day before, when the girls had gone off somewhere on their own (deliberately – to provoke him, he thought), he'd found an old photograph album of his grandad's and had been sitting disconsolately leafing through it when he'd come across some snapshots which had really shaken him. For they were of his mother when young and an equally youthful Uncle John: not his father, but Uncle John! His mother could only have been in her late teens, youthful and slim – and really quite pretty, he realised with a jolt of surprise. He'd never thought of his mother in those terms before: of her ever having been young, that is. Or pretty. It came as a shock. (It was a bit like meeting a stranger, but a stranger with a certain familiarity, as though one might have met somewhere before.) After all, a parent was just...a parent. Not someone with a past, a history all of their own. The concept sat uneasily, changed the tone of personal ownership, made it less intimate, less exclusive.

But what had really taken him aback was the apparent relationship between these two people in those photographs. In some of the shots they were standing or sitting close together, holding hands or gazing into one another's faces; in others, where there was less awareness of the camera, they were laughing and playful, as if they were there on their own, unaware of whoever had taken the photographs. It made him feel like an intruder, privy to something from which he should rightly be excluded. It was as though, in an eddy of time, he was witness to an act of deception. For their relationship, captured on film at different times and at different places, had clearly been close and, more than that, projected an impression of permanence. Devastated, he didn't know how long he sat there, turning the pages to and fro, as though his repeated glaring at the pictures might provoke some explanation.

And, gradually, another question had taken shape. Who had taken the pictures? Could it indeed have been his grandfather, in whose ownership they now rested? And what were the implications of that? For he, too must have been well aware of whatever relationship had existed at that time.

'Ah, you've found some of the old photographs, I see.'

His grandfather's voice, coming at that precise moment, it seemed out of nowhere, had raised the hairs on his neck. He'd whirled round to find the old man standing there, his attitude and tone suggesting that he, too, had unexpectedly come up against a problem.

But if that was the case, he had immediately rallied, visibly bracing his shoulders.

'Must have been around 1910, when I took those,' he said. 'Or perhaps a year or two earlier, because your mother was about twenty – and John, therefore...let's see...yes, around twenty-three or twenty-four, because, if memory serves me, he was just about to qualify.'

'You took those, grandfather?' The question had sounded trite, echoing what he'd just been told. But of course it had carried with it a whole host of other, unspoken questions.

If he'd hoped that his grandfather would therefore be more forthcoming – and he wasn't at all sure that was what he wanted – then he was disappointed. There was a silence that seemed to stretch for ever, the old man clearly struggling to come to a decision. In the end, he'd simply said, his voice gruff, 'Yes...well, my boy, when you've finished with it put it back where you found it, won't you?', and had departed, leaving Peter once more with feelings of rejection, as though he'd no right to know about his mother's past.

Since then he's constantly been wrestling with indecision – whether or not to ask his mother about the pictures, or perhaps alternatively to ask Uncle John. But he's been unable find the courage to do that, even though he can't name what it is he's afraid of. He's almost beginning to feel at times as though he's in danger of losing his already-tenuous hold on the parameters of his world.

The switchback of his relationship with the girls over the past week hasn't helped, either. One moment one or other of them makes a point of individually seeking him out, bringing an unexpected degree of warmth and camaraderie, albeit just for that moment; and the next, when the two girls are together, they're forever teasing him. Much of their banter is pleasant; at least they're paying him some sort of attention. But behind it all the sly comments which he doesn't quite understand, the whispered conversations between them when they think he's not looking, and the giggling about some joke or other from which he's excluded, are unsettling – as is the flattery, which never rings true. It's as if they are competing, one against the other, in their attempts to gain his attention, only to then discard him, as if to say they don't really care. He's well used to that with Jordan; but his relationship with Jamie, up to now, has never been like that. She's simply been a pal, with not the slightest hint of unkindness or dishonesty.

The more he thinks about it, the more he feels like crying. Also, his perceptions, anyway, of the girls have become even more muddled. One minute he visualises Jordan, childlike and artless at play on the beach: and the next minute the picture changes to that of her at the top of the stairs, skirt raised provocatively. Then again, he has been mystified by the guile in her face when, on occasions this week, she has studied him, lips parted and head tipped to one side. He sees Jamie, reliable and uncomplicated, one of the gang: then immediately imagines her presence next to him in bed, or sees an altogether different light in her eyes when she suddenly looks at him, along with Jordan, in that peculiarly challenging way that they have adopted toward him from time to time.

He closes his eyes, for a moment just taking comfort from the warmth of the sun on his face. He thinks back to that first day, when the week seemed to offer so much. To the morning which had dawned hot and sunny, when he and the two girls – having been trying their best for the past hour to get away from the adults (Peter and Jamie both amused to note how ready Jordan is to abdicate the status of adulthood when the need arises) – are hurrying their way towards the beach. Even as they leave the second field and follow the path leading across the golf course, the anticipation of all three is scarcely contained. Although still unable to see the sea, nevertheless it makes its presence felt, annunciated in that distinctive clarity of light, by a certain something in the air and by the smell of salt and seaweed mingling with that of gorse and heather. Bare-footed and bare-legged on the sandy path, they are pricked by spikes of marram grass and sea-holly, but hardly notice. For very soon they are among the high dunes, the sand hot between their toes. And seconds later they are bursting through to the open beach fringed by gentle surf and wet from the ebbing tide, their laughter carried out to sea.

But now, a week later, those innocent recollections are nudged aside as he considers how he has come to view his mother and uncle in a new light, as different people, even, from all the days before. Particularly on this their final day at the seaside. At midday his mother and Uncle John had turned up on the beach, carrying a hamper between them. This was a picnic lunch for all of them (brought as a peace-offering for their uninvited appearance, no doubt). Aunt Mabel, it seemed, had declared it 'too bright' to be going to the beach, and had elected to stay behind. For Peter, putting all this together – the voluntarily shared task, the absence of Aunt Mabel, and his memories of those photographs – has served to renew the vague misgivings that he has about their relationship. Misgivings that he can't begin to get into any sort of focus. Those uncertainties had been temporarily sidelined by the contents of the hamper, which had been thoughtfully substantial and which had been demolished in probably a tenth of the time it must have taken to prepare them. But, lunch finished, he'd been unable to take his eyes off the pair of them, his mother and uncle, one speculation after another bobbing up in his mind.

And now that he's on his own the anxieties have continued to grow.

He tries to shut out the thoughts, and begins to doze. Time is suspended as he drifts….until all at once he is brought back with a cry of startlement as something heavy, cold and wet plonks upon his waist. His eyes fly open – to find Jamie sitting astride him, peering down at him, a smile on her lips and water dripping from her hair.

'Come on, lazy-bones!' she says. 'It's time you came back in the water. It's lovely and warm now.'

With her weight settled upon him, her thighs pressing against his chest, and still mildly winded by the manner of her arrival, for a few moments he is unable to speak. In any case, the surface coolness of her body seeping into his tummy and the novel sensation of being trapped by her in this way is both pleasant and exciting, and he doesn't want to break the spell. He is conscious of moisture, draining from her wet costume, trickling down his flanks. For seconds neither of them speaks, Jamie gazing down at him as if studying his face.

Then, 'You have incredibly blue eyes,' she says.

He doesn't know how to reply to that, and says nothing.

To his disappointment she suddenly rolls off him, but then lies down close to him, their bodies touching. 'Mmm, you're lovely and warm,' she says.

Something indefinable has occurred in the atmosphere between them, though, all at once causing him to become tongue-tied. With growing desperation he searches for something, anything, to say. Then it strikes him that she has known the Websters all her life, has grown up with Jordan. The two families have lived in the same small town together for two or more generations. She will no doubt have heard talk from time to time, the inevitable retelling of any small scandals from the past. She might be able to provide some answers for him.

Haltingly, with growing embarrassment, he explains about the photographs and some of his uncertainties about them.

Having listened to him without interruption, for a while she remains silent. Lying beside him, he can't see her face but wonders if he's offended her in some way, or even whether what she knows is too awful to tell him.

Then she says, slowly, 'I'm not sure that I'm the one you should be asking. Can you not ask your mother about it, or Uncle John?'

Unable to trust his voice, he shakes his head.

The small movement seems to decide her, for she says, 'I don't know much, but, from what I've heard just since you came up here to live, your mother and John Webster when they were young had become sweethearts even though he had become engaged to, or was on the point of becoming engaged to, your aunt Mabel. Apparently there was a terrible bust up, as you can imagine, and of course it was all the talk of the town.'

She hesitates. 'Are you sure you want to hear all this?'

He's not sure that he does, but it would be worse not knowing, and gruffly he says 'Yes'.

He's aware of Jamie taking a big breath as if steeling herself to continue, and she then plunges on, 'But worse was to come. For within twelve months your father came along. He'd trained as a solicitor, from what I've heard, but had got bored with that and joined the army. He was evidently very handsome, already a first lieutenant, very dashing in his uniform and all that, and it seems he swept your mother off her feet. You can imagine the uproar there must have been at that! Her father – your grandad here – who had been terribly upset about what had already happened between your mother and her sister, but had stood by your mother, now refused to have anything more to do with her. Disowned her, if you like. She and your father ran away to London and must have got married sometime after that. Fences must have been mended here, I suppose, between your Aunt Mabel and Uncle John, for in due course they, too, got married as had originally been planned. Rumour has it that your grandfather helped Uncle John to set up in practice – to help to make amends, I imagine. And the rest you know.'

But he is no longer really listening. So much has become clear, but so much has become muddled. He could never have imagined that his family could be so complex. So much has he taken in, but so little is he able to accept. And so much has been concealed from him. More than ever he feels like an outsider. More than ever he feels betrayed. He is sure he's about to be sick. He struggles to his feet and blindly he begins to run. Behind him he hears Jamie's voice, 'Peter, wait!...' But the rest is obscured by the sound of his own sobbing.

Back at school, after that summer, he'd found himself consciously avoiding trying to emulate his father. Whatever his father had achieved at Bard's, he wanted not to achieve. His school work had suffered – and so had his sport. Because of his stature and fleetness of foot, he'd found that rugby suited him; his agility had made him a natural centre three-quarter. Against his inclinations he'd gravitated onto the school teams, therefore. But his heart hadn't been in it. No longer had he yearned for his father to be there on the touchline, to cheer him on. Rather had he become aware that he was in danger of following in his father's footsteps, or at least that he would be seen to be doing so. And he'd drawn back. He understands all that, now. And why it was that everyone, eventually, had despaired of him. There was 'no making anything of him'. He'd 'no ambition' was what they'd said. Beal, by then Head of House, in his last year at school, had had more forthright views.

Peter himself, at the time, had had no understanding of this process. The disappointment revealed, on repeated occasions, on the faces of his mother and Uncle John, had made him disappointed in himself. The disdain at his failures so clearly evinced by his cousin Jordan (who, though, herself had not particularly shone at school), and (less so) by his Aunt Mabel, had reinforced his own sense of lack of worth. Only Cook had treated him, consistently, during his holidays, as though he would one day conquer the world. And only later, much later, would he himself begin to understand some of the forces that had been at play. A deep part of him, that part hidden from conscious awareness, had at the time recognised that achievement was necessary for self-respect and for respect and admiration of others, and that the two were interdependent. But whenever that impulse had tried to surface a perverse side of him had applied the brakes, persuaded him that this was not a direction in which he wanted to go: if his father could so neglect him, he'd argued, then he would deny his father any opportunity for pride in, and ownership of, his son.

However, with time, there was one thing that he'd come to learn that he wanted to do, and could do. He would become a doctor.

As for that summer that had just passed at that time and the one before it (those summers which at the time seemed to go on for ever – and seemed as if they might go on being repeated for ever), it was so soon over, not to come again. For by the following year Jordan had gone to RADA in London; and, much more significantly, Jamie, by then sixteen, too had gone away, also to London, to learn German and French and be trained in secretarial work. George had become fully employed on his father's farm; and with the gang broken up, Bill, who had never really been Peter's friend, also went his own way. The Famous Four had been no longer.

* * *

O'Connor digs him in the ribs once more. 'For God's sake, Doc, come back to us! Where have you been? Can't you see we're there!'

O'Connor, never complains – she accuses.

Sure enough, they're drawing into the station, the platform already busy with military personnel.

As, minutes later, they get out into the street, shuffling along in the midst of the crammed mass of others, they find a similar crowd already there, also mainly service people, heading with difficulty in various directions and having to thread their way between a variety of slowly-moving army trucks, ambulances and the occasional motor-cycle despatch-rider. There is an atmosphere of purpose, but despite the size of the throng it is strangely quiet.

And from a long way off, out of a bright clear sky, comes the subdued sound of thunder.

CHAPTER ELEVEN

A cold hush had settled on the room. All eyes are fixed on the figure up on the platform. Colonel Murgatroyd isn't in himself an especially imposing figure; his rather high-pitched voice would normally sound unauthoritative. But the import of what he is saying imparts to him, in this instance, a particular stature. Certainly he is commanding their undivided attention.

'...enemy armoured divisions coming – totally unexpectedly – through the Ardennes, had forced a major crossing of the River Meuse by the fourteenth and then advanced an astonishing one hundred and fifty miles in ten days to reach Arras, after which, out-flanking us to the south, they reached the coast near Calais. Our forces, faced with that situation, had been expected to move north towards the Somme, but when it became clear to General Gort that virtually the whole of the forces available to the B.E.F. were in serious danger of being further surrounded from the north and also totally cut off from the coast he decided they should make a dash for a town called Dunkirk, which is midway between Calais and Ostend and has a small harbour. I'm telling you all this because, although it is not, strictly speaking, within our remit, it is important that you understand what it is, here, we have to face.'

Peter glances around the council chamber. Apprehension and disbelief are etched on the faces of every one of the hundred or so people here, many of whom are women. They've all been aware, from the daily news bulletins since the 10th of May, how serious the situation was likely to be; but confirmation of this now has wrenched away what little hope they've been clinging to.

'When all this became clear, two days ago,' the R.A.M.C. colonel goes on, 'a decision was taken that we must at least try to evacuate as many of them as we can. To this end the Royal Navy immediately despatched all available ships, and the first of the evacuated troops began arriving here and to other nearby ports yesterday evening – and others have been coming in today.

'You will be aware that we have something like two hundred and fifty thousand men there. Also – because of the...er...awkwardness of the...er...shall we say, political situation – the P.M. has assured the French that we will in addition take off as many of their troops as possible.'

He pauses as there is a collective gasp from the audience.

'That's right. We're talking about perhaps a third of a million or more men altogether, not to mention all their equipment – tanks, guns, motor transport and ammunition. Clearly an impossible task! So much so that there is no question of being able to save any of that equipment, and it is thought that we will do very well if we manage to save as many as forty thousand of those troops – roughly half of which will be ours and half of them French.'

Again he pauses in the face of the reaction from his audience – not so much a gasp as a collective groan.

O'Connor, sitting on Peter's right, not sounding at all afraid, murmurs, 'Bloody hell! I wonder if I could be allowed to become an Irish national again!'

Someone behind them mutters, 'Well that's it then. We can expect jerry to invade us at any time. And precious little left to prevent them!'

Peter, whilst experiencing a stab of fear, feels a rising irritation at that defeatist attitude and starts to turn round intending to say, 'For God's sake put a sock in it! – what about the Royal Navy and the RAF!'; but O'Connor, sensing his mood, jabs her elbow in his ribs and says in a loud voice, 'Oh, leave it be – he's not worth it!'

Peter, knowing she is right, reluctantly turns back and gives his attention to Murgatroyd again.

The colonel, the murmuring in the room having settled, continues 'I see I don't have to spell out the implications of all this. Which brings me to the point, why have all of you been brought here: doctors, nurses and medical orderlies? To answer part of that I'm now going to hand over to Lieutenant Saunders, who has just come off one of our destroyers on which some of the first of our troops have been brought back.

'Lieutenant Saunders.'

A young naval lieutenant, looking decidedly weary and dishevelled, takes the centre of the platform, clears his throat and, in a hoarse voice, begins: 'I hope you can hear me alright? I've been doing a lot of shouting in the past twelve hours!'

Receiving a subdued and sympathetic chorus of assent, he goes on, 'Right. Well, the situation over there is absolutely bloody! When we left, about four hours ago, there must already have been many thousands of men on the beaches, and thousands more pouring in all the time. The harbour at Dunkirk is really quite tiny, and can only take the smallest of ships. Fortunately the beaches – which are sandy – are fairly broad, even at high tide, and shelve gently. That has the disadvantage however that only small boats can get anywhere near the beach. Troops waiting to be embarked are therefore having to wade out, in some cases up to a couple of hundred yards, in order to be taken into the boats. Needless to say, jerry is not being idle all this time, and there is constant strafing by fighters not to mention repeated bombing, mainly by Stuka dive-bombers. When we left early this afternoon there were already orderly lines of men forming, wading out into the sea virtually up to their necks – almost as if they were queueing for the cinema, if you'll excuse a small joke under these circumstances – waiting patiently to take their turn in the boats. They, therefore are sitting ducks and taking considerable casualties; as indeed are the small boats, as well as the destroyers, frigates and other ships of various kinds waiting offshore to take them on board. Our own ship was hit several times by machine gun and cannon fire from Messerschmitts, and we took a bomb on our fo'c'sle which fortunately didn't do much damage. Quite a number of the men that we took on board were wounded, and others were suffering from burns of various degrees, and, in some cases, from ingestion or inhalation of oil mixed with seawater.

'From what I heard, our defensive perimeter, yesterday, had been out at Lille, about fifty miles from Dunkirk; but the retreat was taking place at a very rapid pace so no doubt the poor blighters on the beach will be subjected to shellfire as well, before too long.

And that's about all I have to report, sir,' he concludes, spreading his arms in a helpless gesture towards the Colonel. 'And I'm afraid I must now get back to my ship. We're doing a very rapid turn around.'

Yes, please do get on your way, Saunders, and thank you for sparing a few minutes to come along and give us that on-the-spot information. I'm most grateful to you. And best of luck!'

Hardly waiting for the naval officer to hurry from the room, the colonel turns back to his audience, holding up his hands to silence the subdued chatter that has broken out.

'What Lieutenant Saunders didn't have time to tell us – and possibly didn't know about – is that over the past forty-eight hours the navy has sent people to scour all the harbours and marinas along the coast, and up the coastal rivers, to commandeer as many seaworthy small boats as they can lay their hands on, and hopefully to get some of the owners to volunteer to sail them. Bloody dangerous business for anyone who does go across, of course – if you'll excuse the language – but the more boats they can get, the more men we'll be able to save.

'The other latest official bit of news, also, is that as of first thing this morning the allied perimeter has contracted back to the area of Ypres – and there's a ghost from the past! – which is only twenty-five miles or so from Dunkirk. So you'll see that the numbers of men concentrating on Dunkirk over the next twenty-four hours or so will be immense; and that, particularly if they get all these small boats organised, the numbers arriving here may also be very considerable. Incidentally, for the moment at least, there seems to be no question of surrender – thank God! But God only knows what the outcome will be.

'Anyway, that's enough spouting from me. You've got the picture. Our role here in Dover can only be a sorting one – or *triage* as our French friends would call it. In a few minutes, Major Armstrong and his staff at the back there will organise you into your parties. But basically what will happen is this. As the troops are landed from the ships, and possibly some from the small boats, they will be streamed.

'Firstly, into those who are perfectly able to be entrained as soon as possible, without the need for further attention, to be transported to holding camps. This will be handled largely by contingents of the R.A.S.C. and Military Police.

'The remainder will become the responsibility of all of you. Some will be suffering merely – and I say 'merely' – from severe fatigue, shock and hunger: remember many of them will have been making their way towards Dunkirk, on foot, at a rapid pace, over several days during which they will have had precious little to eat, or even drink, and certainly no sleep. Others, having been immersed up to their chests in seawater for long periods waiting to get into boats, may be suffering from hypothermia.

'Of the remainder, as you have already heard from Lieutenant Saunders, there will be a mixture of wounds and burns of varying severity, as well as respiratory difficulties due to inhalation of oil. Incidentally, it has to be said at this stage that, regrettably, the most seriously wounded who cannot easily be transported will have to be abandoned over there for the Germans to deal with – which, we can only hope, they will do with humanity.

'You will be divided into units, therefore, organised in a 'cascade' pattern. Initially, casualties will be met by teams of medical orderlies, each of which will also include one nurse. They will rapidly sort out those who are 'walking wounded' who can be directed to make their own way to designated treatment stations, which are clearly identified within a short distance of the harbour area.

'The next tier will consist of teams of nurses, with a doctor attached to each team. Their role will be to quickly place casualties into one of three categories: firstly, those who require urgent surgical treatment and who are unfit to travel any distance, and therefore are to be treated at nearby hospitals; secondly, those who are still fairly urgent but who can be transported to hospitals further afield such as London; and finally, those who will require major surgery, but who are stable enough to undergo a rather longer journey.

'In addition, there will be one sub-group in each of those first two categories: that is to say, those who require immediate stabilisation procedures such as pain relief, splinting, re-dressings, or immediate transfusion. That will be organized to be done near to the quay area.

'Patients in each category will be clearly labelled, using appropriately coloured labels; and there will be fleets of ambulances or stretcher parties at hand to assist in their transfer.

'All that, of course, is the ideal. None of us can pretend that it will remain so cut-and-dried. We don't know how many men we will have to deal with, at what rate they will arrive, nor whether we will be here for twenty-four hours or for several days. As far as possible we will provide facilities for you for something to eat and drink and somewhere for you to rest at intervals – but I'm afraid that, once again, I'm quoting the ideal.

'Finally, we don't know if we will be subjected here to air attack by the enemy, although informed opinion is that they are likely to concentrate all their activities on the Dunkirk beaches; I must say that makes sense. However, you should all have your gas-masks to hand. So far, in these hostilities, there has been no suggestion of the use of gas; but if there should be anything of the sort, warning will be given by the sound of rattles and whistles as in the last war. Needless to say you should have your tin hats with you, as well – that is, if you have them!

'Go to it, then. I will hand you over to Major Armstrong. And the best of luck to all of us!'

Peter, awakening with tingling in his right arm, discovers that O'Connor is laid across it. He moves cautiously, so as to reposition it without waking her. The vast shed in which they are resting is in darkness apart from subdued lighting at the far end where there seems to be still some activity; but there is blackout up at the high windows, so that it's not possible to conclude whether it is daylight – although of course, when he thinks about it, there was no likelihood whatsoever that they would be allowed to sleep beyond dawn.

He feels as though he could sleep for ever. His limbs and body ache with fatigue: he knows now a little of what those soldiers coming off the ships must be experiencing, never mind their additional burden of fear and pain. It seems like many days since they'd been gathered in the Town Hall preparing themselves for this; yet not much more than forty-eight hours has passed.

Now that his eyes have become accustomed to the gloom, he makes an attempt to see his watch, but there is insufficient light. It had been after 03.00 by the time they'd staggered wearily to this corner of the huge Customs shed, each carrying their one grey army blanket – hardly sufficient to keep out the chill of the concrete floor: and it had been O'Connor (of course) who had suggested that they use one, doubled over, as a kind of groundsheet, and share the other to cover themselves. He suspects that, not having had any sleep for two days, they would have slept whatever the conditions. The fair-haired Q.A. nurse who'd gone, at about quarter to three, to waken the three other nurses on the team (Daphne, he thought she was called, but there hadn't even been the time to properly learn their names) had reported that she'd had the devil of job to rouse them: but no wonder, when they'd been allowed a bare two hours in which to rest.

Muted sounds now coming from the far end of the building suggest that the half-strength teams are still occupied to some extent, and he tries to crane his head to see what the activities are; but he is in danger of disturbing O'Connor – and at this distance it isn't possible to make out any detail. Certainly, by midnight the numbers coming in had diminished considerably, as they had done the night before.

Although, across at Dunkirk, they'd hoped to take advantage of the cover of night, it was evidently just too dangerous to have too many smaller boats milling around in the dark, and even the destroyers and frigates had to move with extreme caution. By first light, of course, the full influx would begin again. As would the strafing and bombing of those poor sods in the town and on the beaches. From the reports coming in, the rear-guard of allied troops on the far outskirts of the town were putting up a terrific fight, but casualties were said to be high, and the perimeter to be contracting hour by hour. It was surely just a matter of time until they could no longer hold out.

Lying there in the semi-darkness, much-needed sleep now strangely elusive, he again goes over the events of the last two days.

Many of the casualties landing at Dover have in fact suffered really quite severe injuries – so much for the grim forecast that such cases 'would have to be left behind'. The sheer numbers of wounded have also been a surprise: much greater than anticipated – but then they seem to be landing far more men in general than had been expected. They have dealt with a certain number of civilian wounded, as well – from those redoubtable volunteers with their small boats, who have turned out in droves. Many of the rescued troops have commented on how fantastic had been the turnout of private boats – they had described everything from motor boats and launches, yachts and pleasure boats of various kinds, to Thames tugs, barges, fishing boats and even lifeboats from ships tied up in the London docks. From all accounts, not all of the smaller craft had been seaworthy, either, and one or two of the rescued soldiers had had to be rescued for a second time. Peter has been filled with awe and pride at some of the things he's come across among the wounded, in civilians as well as military. There had been one fourteen-year-old boy who'd gone out from Rye with his dad in their small motor boat and had reached Dunkirk, only to be sunk by a nearby exploding shell – he'd been brought ashore with compound fractures in both arms, pale and tearful, with no idea of what had happened to his dad, but clearly proud of what they'd done.

This pride, though, has been apparent in some form or other in many of those they've had to deal with over the past two days, including some of the more severely wounded. Mingling with the dwindling expressions of fear and horror on all those grey, bewildered faces, there had been the light of self-respect. They may have been a beaten army, was the impression given, but individually they were not defeated. Glinting from those eyes, many otherwise dulled by pain or from the morphine given for relief, has been a spirit of defiance.

But there has been something else besides. A seething anger at what had been allowed to befall them, at their inability to have upheld the honour of the British army, at the fact that they had been forced into unseemly retreat, that they had let the country down.

And an even greater anger at the R.A.F.

This last factor had gutted Peter and O'Connor and the few other RAF types there, so totally unexpected was it. Time and again, when their uniforms had been noted, there had come from the soldiers words of fury, accompanied by strings of expletives. 'And where the fuck was the bloody R.A.F.!' was typical of the accusations hurled at them. After this had happened on several occasions, they'd begun to get sly glances from their other medical and nursing colleagues; glances that had at first been sympathetic, then become curious, and finally frankly hostile. It was impossible to believe the RAF hadn't been there to play their part in all this. There must be some explanation. But they themselves had no answers. They had had simply to try to ignore it and get on with their own tasks.

He tries now to push it out of his mind, to recapture sleep, but capriciously that continues to elude him. He makes another attempt to see his watch, and change position. Once more, O'Connor stirs, muttering in her sleep, and he holds his breath, reluctant to be responsible for wakening her before it is absolutely necessary. He has been so impressed, and not a little surprised, by the tenderness and concern she has displayed in dealing with all those injured men, mixing compassion and sharp humour with consummate ease, and not allowing either to interfere with professional objectivity. He'd previously had inklings that there was a soft centre to her hard-bitten exterior; and the last two days have confirmed it in no uncertain way. Prior to this, he'd found it all but impossible to get beneath that brittle veneer. All attempts to do so had been turned by her, by her resorting to her usual flippant asides and scornful sexually-charged innuendoes. But earlier that day, as they were wearily sitting together getting a bite to eat during a brief lull, when her defences clearly were down, he'd got through to her.

'Did you ever live in Ireland?' he'd idly asked, for something to say to take their minds off the unrelenting awfulness of the previous few hours.

He'd thought for a moment that she was going to make a typically caustic reply. The corners of her mouth had turned down in familiar fashion, she'd looked at him with those green eyes, now dulled by tiredness, and had lifted her chin defensively – and something completely unexpected had happened. Tears had started to roll down her cheeks. Impatiently she'd brushed them away, and he'd braced himself for the usual salvo of sarcasm.

But she'd quietly said, 'No, I never did. More's the pity. Particularly as I was born there.'

'So, other than that, you're a Liverpool lass through and through?'

She'd shaken her head emphatically at that, the copper glinting in her hair. 'No, I'm an Irish colleen through and through.'

He'd stared at her. There had been something about the fervour with which she'd made that plain statement.

'And proud of it?'

'And proud of it, to be sure!'

'Yet you joined the British armed forces?'

'Ah, well, anything to get away from Liverpool, you know. Besides, not all Irish hate the British.'

'You for one.'

'Oh, I hate them alright.'

He'd looked at her in some perplexity. She wasn't making sense. What he'd been thinking, probably, was that this was a typically Irish contradiction.

Something of that must have shown on his face, for she'd put a hand on his arm and said sardonically, 'Not all of them. Not you, Pete, so you're quite safe! Just some of them.'

'Which of them? And why?' he'd asked, intrigued.

'My husband, for one.'

'You've been married?'

'To be sure – that's how I came to have a husband, you understand! Anyway, why so surprised? I bet you'd thought, No one could possibly want to marry her!'

That was more like the usual O'Connor.

Slightly flustered, he'd said, 'But he wasn't British?'

'Oh yes he was, the pig! He may have had an Irish name – that's what took me in – but any Irish blood he once may have had was long disappeared.'

'And he was no good?'

'And *that*'s an understatement!'

'Ah. So what happened to him? Are you divorced?'

'I wish I was! But I'm Catholic, you know. They don't exactly approve of divorce. It sends you to hell, or something, they'd have you believe.'

'But you don't believe that?'

'Who's to know what to believe. But, no, of course I don't. But I wouldn't be able to take Communion any longer.'

'And that would matter?'

'I don't know…Yes, I think it would.'

'So you still believe in God?'

'I don't know that, either. Yes, I suppose I must. Ridiculous, isn't it, given all this!'

That had raised the spectre of his own doubts, doubts that he didn't really want to face.

So he'd turned the focus back onto her.

'You never had any children?' As soon as he'd said it, he'd wondered why he'd asked it in the negative – and immediately wished he hadn't. She'd looked for one moment as if she were about to cry again.

She'd turned her head away then, her reply so soft that he'd had difficulty hearing it.

'No, I never had any children.'

Once more, uncomfortable, he'd changed tack. 'What about brothers or sisters?'

'Oh, yes, plenty of them. It was all my dad was good at.' She gave a hollow laugh. 'So many, I hardly remember their names!'

'And your parents were Irish?'

'My mother was Irish. My father was…well, you've guessed it.'

'Yes,' he'd said ruefully, 'I begin to see. So, what did they do, your parents?'

'*Do*? There's a good middle class expression for you! – Do! I'll tell you what my dad did. He drank. A lot. And, when he wasn't too drunk to get there in time, now and again he got employment on the docks. The rest of the time, I seem to remember, he spent the time knocking the living daylights out of Mam and the rest of us. If you mean 'work', my Mam did it all, going out to work as a skivvy six days a week, besides feeding and clothing all of us until we were just about big enough to do it for ourselves. She died when I was twelve – 'consumption', they said; but I think she was just worn out, in body and spirit.'

They'd fallen silent after that. There hadn't seemed to be anything else to say; although he'd felt guilty about it, thinking that he ought, somehow, to be able to find words of comfort. Anyway, very shortly there had come another rush of casualties, and any opportunity had been lost.

Now, lying close to her in the semi-darkness, he reflects on how differently he's begun to view her after that short conversation. He realises that until then he had viewed her as someone slightly alien, and therefore threatening – he and she had different backgrounds, different personalities, different ways of speaking. But they had, after all, something in common: fathers who had rejected them, or who, in one way or another, hadn't been there; and mothers who, in individual ways, had borne their own sets of problems through life to such an extent that it had created in them a certain remoteness from their children, an inability to fully engage. As a result, both he and Shevaun O'Connor were burdened by that sense of isolation in this world.

At this point, however, these maudling thoughts are abruptly halted by the unsympathetically brisk voice of the R.A.M.C. sergeant attached to their group. 'Rise and shine now, ladies and gentlemen! Dawn is almost upon us, and work calls.'

Half an hour later, the trickle of casualties that had been coming in throughout the deepest hours of darkness has once more turned to a torrent. Peter wonders how long it can continue. In one sense, in spite of the numbing fatigue that now assails them all, he feels some elation. It is by now obvious that many more men have been brought over from France than had at first been thought possible; and the wounded, although running into many hundreds here at Dover alone, are turning out to be only a relatively small proportion of the total. But the effect of seeing all these thousands of exhausted, battered and bruised men hour after hour for the best part of three days is taking its toll on him. He's felt so useless. He is accustomed to feeling, as a doctor, that at times he is only too impotent in the continual battle against disease and injury; but in this instance, when he is merely observing and sorting, and not in a position to actually do anything other than that, he finds it even more demoralising. And there have been so many tragedies: men dying in front of his eyes, and nothing he can do; the most terrible mutilations, where a part of him almost hopes that the man will not survive; the small boy with the broken arms, whose hope was that his father was somewhere safe and alive but whose eyes betrayed a different conclusion; and others like him.

By now they've accumulated so many casualties that the various sheds being used to temporarily shelter them can accommodate no more and collections of them are scattered around the quaysides. And it is while he is moving from group to group at the behest of one or other of the nurses, that he sees a figure whom he seems to know. Slumped against a wall, hatless, the man's right arm is supported in a newly-applied sling; the epaulettes of his stained and torn battledress carry the three pips of a captain, at his shoulder is the regimental badge of the Gloucestershires, and pinned near them on the left side is a yellow label denoting 'non-urgent surgical'. Peter can't see all of his features, the man's head lolling sideways onto his chest, but a shock of dark hair, matted by sea-water, falls across his face in a familiar way. In his mind's eye Peter can almost see a hand coming up to brush it back. He moves nearer.

'Mr Wilson?'

For a moment he can't believe this is the man who'd been his Assistant Housemaster on Founders for those five years, the English teacher who'd always seemed to have pacifist tendencies in spite of having taken on an officer role in the school Cadet Force.

Richard Wilson opens his eyes, and looks up wearily.

'It's Waring, sir. Peter Waring. Founders, '26 to '31. You probably don't remember me.'

Wilson, with considerable effort, draws himself up and manages a smile that is tired and apologetic. 'Waring. I thought it was you. I've been watching you on and off, moving around – may I say competently and economically – and with compassion. That's so important, isn't it? Particularly now. Thought of coming over to say hullo, but somehow couldn't just raise the energy, you understand. I always knew, when you elected to read Medicine, that you'd chosen the right path – just as, I think, you knew it too?'

Yes. It was true. He hasn't really thought about it until now. It had always just been there in his mind, that he would become a doctor. But yes, he'd known it was the right path. And Richard Wilson had noticed.

'So how are you, sir? Sorry – silly question! What I mean is, what are you doing here? – which is an equally daft question! What I mean is, what are you doing in the army in the first place?' Thoroughly flustered now, Peter attempts to recover. 'What I meant was, that you…well…seemed to…'

'Not agree with wars? No, you're quite right. But then which of us does?' He winces as he tries to ease himself into a more comfortable position, and attempts another smile, which ends as a grimace. 'But then I suppose some people must, or none of us would be finding ourselves in this situation.'

'So why did you…well…' He doesn't quite know how to finish the sentence. As a teacher Wilson would have been exempt from call-up, so the presumption was that he had volunteered.

'Join up? Good question. I've wondered about that myself. Particularly now. It's a bit of a long story – but you remember Canon Brindle? Yes, of course you do. *Cannonball*. Well named. Now, he did believe in war! Those who haven't been personally involved in one are often the ones who do, I've noticed. Well, Cannonball observed that as I was one of the fit young men well qualified to fight for King and Country, as he put it, he thought it would be a good idea if I were to do so. Made it clear that failure to do so would be the act of a coward, and that he had no room for cowards on his staff. "Sets a bad example", I seem to remember was how he put it. So, clearly I was out on my ear – regardless. Silly as it sounds, in a rash moment I decided to take up his challenge. And here I am.'

He closes his eyes again, either wearied by the effort of talking, or else overcome by renewed realisation of the futility of it all. It is difficult to reconcile this man, at present reduced to battered immobility, with the youthful teacher with the exuberant hands that Peter remembered from so few years ago. He can still see Wilson bouncing into class, hands and hair all over the place, and saying with fondness, 'Right, you bunch of feckless philistines, let's see if we can cram a crumb of culture into you, shall we?'

And, immediately, that picture is replaced by another – one that makes Peter grind his teeth in shame and remorse.

There had been a period in their second year, lasting much of the term, when 'Charlie' Chaplin, with those mild eccentricities which set him apart from others, had become the object of bullying by one or two in the dayroom, others then beginning to gang up against him, as was so often the case in such situations. Pearson, stalwart as ever, had done his best to defend his friend, but, outnumbered and isolated, had failed. Peter, intimidated by the majority, to his everlasting regret had done nothing.

Eventually, Mr Wilson, perceptive as ever, had picked up on the situation, and had taken Chaplin off to his study and grilled him sympathetically but unrelentingly until Charlie had confessed all. Following that, a new side to Wilson had emerged when he had harangued the whole of the dayroom in no uncertain terms, not issuing any punishments, but making them analyse for themselves how it was that their own inadequacies had led them to that behaviour. Having taken that reasonable approach he had then described in explicit terms the dire consequences that would ensue if the behaviour were to continue. It had been enough.

But then it had been Peter's turn. He'd been taken aside by Wilson, whose words, in the privacy of the master's study, had been ones of sorrow and understanding rather than of anger. One sentence remained indelibly printed in Peter's mind: 'Two of the most difficult but most important lessons in life are: to learn to have the courage to stand up and be heard in the face of injustice; and to remain loyal to one's friends'.

From then on his respect for Richard Wilson had grown immeasurably.

He bends now to peer at the scribbled note on the yellow label: *Shrap wound e comp fract R humerus.* God knows how long ago it had been sustained; the sleeve of Wilson's tunic is torn but has not been cut open, so it is unlikely that a dressing has been put on. As with all of the casualties in the present situation, there is barely enough time give any proper attention to even the most seriously wounded, never mind those in the Yellow Label category. But there must by now be considerable risk that it is infected, with all the consequences that might follow.

'When did you cop that lot?' he asks.

Wilson opens his eyes with difficulty. 'Sometime yesterday morning, I think. There were so many bombs, so much going on, it's hard to remember. Chap next to me was killed, so I got off lightly.'

'Is it giving you much pain?'

'No. It did at first, but I can't really feel it now, it's just a sort of numb pain. If that makes sense.'

'And when did you last eat?'

'God knows. Seems like weeks ago. Probably three or four days, in actual fact. There was a little group of five of us, separated from all the rest, had to make our way through jerry lines.' He pulls a face and becomes silent, as though recollecting some horrific experience.

'That must have been frightening business?' Peter says gently.

Wilson's face crumples as if about to cry...or laugh – Peter can't decide. Wilson then starts to shake his head, as though in disbelief. 'Strangely enough it was very easy,' he says. 'But there was this one occasion when we came round a corner and met this German motor-cyclist sitting on his bike having a quiet fag. He swung round, rifle in hand...and I shot him with my revolver. It just happened. I hadn't time to think. I looked at him afterwards, lying there, dead. He can't have been more than eighteen. He might have stepped straight out of my English class.'

He shakes his head again, tears in his eyes. 'One moment he was there, alive, enjoying a quiet moment – and the next he was dead. And I was responsible for that.'

'But you didn't really have any choice,' Peter says.

Wilson looks up blearily. 'There's always a choice. Anyway...anyway, the next day we reached the beaches. And here we are.'

'It must have been pretty awful over there? On the beaches?' Peter says, wanting to get the man's mind off that one episode.

Wilson manages a weak smile. 'Important as it can be, I don't remember ever teaching you the value of understatement! It was unadulterated hell. But thank God for the sand.'

'The sand?'

'Yes. Soft sand. It cushioned the explosions, you know. In fact I think quite a number of shells and bombs didn't go off. But it was still hell! And that's not over-stating it. I can still see the dead and dying, hear the screams and moans and the pleading for help. But there was nothing any of us could do. We hadn't even any water. And, by the end, the stench of decay, of blood, and the sight of bodies drifting untended in the sea...someone described it as smelling like a charnel-house on a hot summer's day. And that was pretty accurate, I imagine.

'And yet...and yet...there was something glorious about it, as well, you know. There was very little panic. Everyone, when it came time for them to go out to the boats, patiently waited their turn. In lines, as though queueing to go into a football match. No pushing or trying to get there before anybody else. No one pulling rank. Often the reverse, in fact. The British tommy at his best.' He pulls a face. 'Living up to our reputation, I suppose! – always at our best in the face of defeat. Winning isn't what's important, it's *how you play the game*! Isn't that the rule?' There is more than uncharacteristic sarcasm in his voice now – there is a distinct hint of rancour, as if he's scented the whiff of betrayal. And then anger flares; he shakes his head in bewilderment. 'Is this, in the end, all that your father and mine, and millions of others, gave the best part of their lives for?'

However, it is only a moment before the glint of enthusiasm returns to his eyes. 'But, I say, did you see that troop of Guards come off one of the destroyers here, earlier on!'

'No?'

'Incredible! Just as if they were coming on parade! Boots polished, brasses shining, in perfect order, and ramrod discipline…of course we didn't see their wounded come off.

'And that reminds me. I met Jenkins, briefly, over there. You remember Jenkins? Head of House your first year, I seem to recollect. Yes, I see you do remember.' He gives a rueful smile. 'I don't suppose you took to him any more than I did. A real bastard he was!' He shakes his head in dismay. 'I shouldn't say things like that. Particularly now. It may be those particular characteristics which will, after all, save the bacon for all of us.'

Here he slumps into what appears to be a reflective silence; then after a few seconds, seeing Peter's patient look of enquiry, rouses himself to explain: 'He's a major in the Coldstreams, now. Regular army, of course. When I saw him he was leading a company of them back to form part of the defensive rearguard. To let the rest of us, those who could, get away. Quite likely facing death – but as determined and cocksure as ever.'

But at this point a nurse is tugging at Peter's sleeve. 'Can you come and look at this one urgently, doctor, please.'

Awkwardly, Peter hurriedly shakes Wilson's left hand. 'Sorry. Must go. You should be off pretty soon. All the best. And I hope we can meet up again, soon.'

Wilson nods. 'Before you go, though: I've waited nearly ten years to say sorry – must do it now.'

'"Sorry"?'

'Yes. You see, I was aware of your…difficulties…at school. With regard to your father. The ghost of him hanging over you, and all that. So I looked him up. In the school records: reports and all that sort of thing. And I always meant to have a word with you about it. Never did. Didn't quite know how to put it. And lacked the courage, I suppose.'

Peter, startled, finds his knees begin to tremble. Of course – Wilson as housemaster would have known the facts with regard to his father. He felt his face flush.

'What could there have been to say,' he mumbles.

'Only this. I've had time to think of the words over the years. Your father was a good man. But no one is perfect. And when we strive to walk in a man's footsteps – particularly our father's – we can all too often find ourselves following a false prophet. But equally, if we go out of our way to avoid pursuing that trail we can find ourselves on ground that is even more uncertain. When you've had time to think about that I'm sure you'll begin to understand what I mean. I'm only sorry that I didn't manage to say something of the sort to you all those years ago.

'Anyway, good to see you again, Waring. And well done, in spite of everything. And best of luck – to all of us! We're going to need it, now.'

Four days later, on the 2nd of June, Peter and O'Connor, having been given orders to return to their unit at Marwell, are making their way towards the railway station, hardly able to walk from exhaustion, when an R.A.F. truck pulls up alongside them and the driver leans out. 'Want a lift to London, sir, ma'am?'

Thankfully they climb into the back. The past six days no longer seem real. It has been a dream-like continuum of work with snatched intervals of food and sleep. Their brief periods of rest at night had continued to follow the same pattern, with Peter and O'Connor bedding down together. If anyone had noticed, things had been far too chaotic for thought or comment; and there had been no renewal of the mood of intimacy or of discussion between them as had occurred that first day – as soon as their heads were down they'd been asleep.

By now the numbers having gone through Dover must have reached tens of thousands (and word is they have been landing at Folkestone and Ramsgate as well). But at least over the last three days (once it had become apparent that there were going to continue to be far more evacuated troops – and casualties – than had been anticipated) things had become better organised. So Peter and O'Connor had been transferred to one of the Surgical First Aid stations that had been set up in Dover to try to temporarily improve the condition of the more seriously wounded before they were moved on; that at least had lessened for Peter the sense of powerlessness inherent in mere *triage*, even though many of the injuries were so horrific that he'd despaired for the soldiers concerned.

But his thoughts had kept returning to Wilson, wondering how he had got on; and to days at Bards.

Now, as they sprawl numbly in the back of the truck, Peter to his surprise feels O'Connor search for and grasp his hand. He quickly turns his head to look at her. She looks steadily back, the only expression in her eyes the sudden desire for comfort and companionship in the face of what they have seen and what is to come.

And as they drive through the town, they pass a small contingent of Queen Alexandra nurses coming from the station, red capes swinging as they march; and he closes his eyes, and is transported back, away from these troubled times, away from the Kentish fields and the chalk cliffs, to a wilder northern scene.

CHAPTER TWELVE

Another gust of wind clutches at the long line of students straggling in both directions along the stone pier some hundred feet below, the wind madly tossing their academic gowns so that for a moment all the eye sees is the red of those garments. From this distance it could be a parade of scarlet-clad medieval monks. The jetty, forming the northeast side of the small harbour, is known to have been there for centuries, and at some time in the past to keep out the worst of the winter seas its outer half was raised by its present seven feet or so, resulting in two levels. The walkers in the procession (which traditionally follows the Sunday morning service in the ancient University Chapel) therefore climb steps at the far end of the pier in order to make the return journey along the not-very-wide upper section as custom demands. That walkway, slightly insecure even at the best of times, is today made more precarious by the buffeting wind and by the spume flung up from the hurrying waves as they sweep in to crash against the outer wall. This spray, glazed by the low October sun, hangs briefly before falling like a silver curtain over the walkers, who just have time to pause and weave (in sometimes alarming fashion) to avoid the worst of the wetting. Yet from the shouts and laughter drifting up on the vagaries of the wind it is clear that, so far as any dangers are concerned, those in the procession are, in the ways of students, as indifferent to the situation as are the elements.

Up here, on the seaward edge of the priory grounds, the wind from the North Sea is bitingly thin, and Peter draws his own gown more closely around him. Of heavy, woollen cloth, the Scarlet Gown worn by undergraduates is unique to the University of St Andrews – but it is more than just an academic symbol, it is a garment of great practical use, serving as a comfortable loosely-fitting topcoat as warm as any, and equally useful as an additional blanket, so often welcome during the cold winter nights.

Because of this general usefulness, it is worn much of the time by many students; and, anyway, is required to be worn in Chapel, for dinner in Halls, and on all formal occasions.

Standing beside Peter, Hans is muttering good-naturedly as he fiddles with the small optical instrument he calls a 'Light Meter'.

'Grey seas, grey buildings, grey pier, grey clouds, and striking through it all this slanting sunshine and those bright red gowns!' he says. 'It is – how you say? – playing havoc with the exposure.'

Peter looks at him with some amusement. Hans's *Rolleiflex* camera (with a view-finder to look down on that is so much larger than on Peter's own camera), and his preoccupation with exposure, shutter speed and aperture, are all novel aspects of photography to Peter; with his Kodak camera he simply decides whether it is cloudy or sunny, and depresses the lever.

Hans Kolber is here, for two terms only, as an exchange student from Dresden University, where he, too, has completed two years' study as a medical student. On his arrival, seven days ago, he was treated with suspicion and even antagonism by many of the undergraduates in St Salvator's Hall. That was perhaps understandable: 1918 may in many ways seem a long time ago when seen from the perspective of 1933, but it is, after all, only fifteen years since the end of the Great War. A good proportion of the students would have lost fathers or uncles at that time; and the tales of atrocities committed by the Hun, so prevalent in those years, still adhere to the popular psyche. Hans, only too well aware of this latent hostility, and finding himself among strangers in a foreign environment, is still clearly very nervous in these first days of term, which makes Peter nervous also. Now, however as they have got to know a little more of each other, things are beginning to settle down, and other students, noting Peter's ready acceptance of this unwanted German intruder, as they see it, have softened their approach as well.

Fortunately Hans's English, although strongly accented, is very good. Initially, Peter had been wary when the Warden of St Salvator's Hall asked Peter if he would consent to being Kolber's 'Senior Man', since (by chance or by design, Peter didn't know) they were to have adjacent rooms in Hall. Now, however, he is glad he accepted, and day by day is warming more and more to his task. Hans, a big, burly young man about Peter's age, now that he is relaxing is showing himself to be a warm-hearted individual with a good (if rather strange at times) sense of humour. With his dark, curly hair, somewhat chubby features, and brown eyes he is not at all like the stereotype of the flaxen-haired, blue-eyed, stern-visaged Hun; in fact, of the two, Peter thinks ironically, it would be he himself who could be mistaken for a German.

Having to explain so much to Hans about things here has been good for Peter, as well: it has meant that he has had to take a more enquiring look at the town and university which, he has to admit, although he is now starting his third year, he has rather taken for granted until now. He remembers how strange and lost he himself had felt in that first term. He had thought that having spent five years away from home at Bard's, he would have taken this new environment in his stride. But being at university was different. Apart from having had to make a whole new set of friends, something he found ordeal enough, there possibly could have been the added difficulty of having to live in relative isolation in digs on his own. Being in a Hall of Residence at least allowed him to be with other students. But, having said that, he was in a room of his own and had to organise himself throughout each day: whereas at school everything had been organised for one, and everything had been done in a group.

For the first few weeks in his first year here therefore he had suffered from feelings of considerable loneliness and depression. It is the recollection of this that has prompted him to accept the challenge of helping Hans through what could be an even more daunting prospect. Peter himself by now feels at one with the university life here, and will miss it when, at the end of this year, they go on to Queen's College in Dundee to do the clinical studies, even though it is only across the Tay. He is now enjoying writing his journal again, too, having let it lapse in the first year or so at college as well as during the last year or two at school.

While Hans is still concentrating on getting a satisfactory photograph of 'the Pier Walk', Peter turns to look back at the town. It is well named, he thinks, the 'auld grey town'. From the ruins of the 12th century St Rules Church and Cathedral, which is where Hans and he are standing, the three main streets – North Street, Market Street and South Street – fan out slightly to run from east to west. To the north of North Street lies The Scores, a residential street starting at the ruins of the castle, above the harbour, and ending at the Royal and Ancient Club House and the Old golf course. It is a town – strictly speaking still designated a City – which is full of character and interest but, it has to be said, in appearance somewhat dour. He had all along absorbed that fact, but had not consciously registered it until he had asked Hans whether Dresden was anything like St Andrews? Hans had hesitated before answering, clearly struggling between the desire to be honest and the need to be polite.

'Well…Dresden is much larger, you know? Several hundred thousands of people. So the university is less…how do you say?…less dominant. The centre part of the city, too, is old. Some of it, like this, is medieval, but much of it seventeenth and eighteenth century, baroque and rococo, very beautiful I think. Of course, St Andrews also is beautiful. In its own way.'

Peter had smiled at that. Hans was a nice man. Not at all overbearing and boastful in the way that he had half-expected.

'Do you come from Dresden, then?'

'No, I come from Berlin. That also is very nice, I think. But much bigger, you understand. Like London? I saw a little of London, on the way through.'

A pang of nostalgia had hit Peter at that. His mother and he had revisited for the first time in the summer after he left school, before coming up to university. They had stayed at the Regent Palace Hotel, recently built at the heart of Piccadilly Circus. He had thought at first that they were going to have to stay with Max and Sheila (now that he was grown-up he no longer thought of them as 'uncle' and 'aunt'), a prospect that didn't thrill him at all; but Uncle John (coming to the rescue as always) had pointed out that the hotel in question was really very reasonable, particularly with money still in short supply following the slump of '29. And, anyway, he thought that , in view of Peter deciding to do Medicine, some of it should be his 'treat' ('as a form of commiseration', was how he'd put it, with the usual twinkle in his eye). Peter had suspected that Aunt Mabel had been not too pleased by the arrangement; but that had been how it had been left.

Now, as Hans and he begin to walk back towards their residence he thinks again about that trip to London. They had, at separate times, met up with both Jordan and Jamie. Jordan then just out of drama school, and struggling (in the prevailing economic climate) to find any work, was nevertheless still more grand than she'd a right to be (financially supported as she was by her father). Jamie, on the other hand, was still just...well...Jamie. But she had by now become a woman (suddenly, it seemed, as it were in Peter's absence) which he'd found most disconcerting: he'd been visualising her exactly as she'd been when she'd first left for London four years previously.

He wonders about her now. What she might be doing. They've lost touch over the years. Last he heard, she was working for a City bank, making use of her languages. Strange how, from time to time, all at once he misses her dreadfully, wishes desperately that she was here with him – or, perhaps, that the old times, that brief interlude when they were children, could be recovered and then never end. And he finds himself dwelling yet again on that summer when Jamie had unaccountably been so despondent; and the developments from their having been invited to join in the haymaking at George's dad's.

* * *

Peter comes to with a start, with something tickling his ear and a weight on his lower chest. Then his nostrils are assailed by the sweetness of new-cut hay, and he knows where he is. He must have nodded off for a moment. It is still hot, even in the shade, and he can feel the dampness of sweat clinging to his neck. Unable to move his upper body, he contrives a sideways glance down the length of his own cheek and chest. Jamie is lying on her back, at right angles to him, her head, which is pillowed on him, lolling so that her face is turned towards him. She is fast asleep, her quiet respiration creating a slight vibration of her lips every time she breathes out. She has quite full lips, he notices, with a smooth, soft surface. He tries to control his own breathing, so as not to waken her. Beneath her closed eyelids he can detect a slight movement of her eyes, as if she might be dreaming, and there is a small trembling of the lids. Her lashes are surprisingly long and luxuriant, he decides, and dark. But then her hair is dark, as well, particularly at her temples, where it is clinging to her skin, damp with perspiration; elsewhere it is thick and wavy, and more chestnut, what he thinks of as the colour of new conkers. In her faded aertex shirt and well-worn khaki shorts she gives the impression that she is out-growing her clothes, which indeed she is: around her shoulders and breasts the thin material is stretched so that the shape of them is clearly seen. It may not be the fashion to have such relatively pronounced tits – some young women, he'd heard, even binding theirs so that they didn't show – but personally he thinks they look kind of…comforting. He smiles when he thinks back to when he first met Jamie, only fifteen months ago – if she'd been as she is now there's no way that he could have mistaken her for a boy! In fact, he realises when he thinks about it, she's become altogether more…rounded. Her legs, stretched out on the hay, and much the same colour, being weathered to a pale golden colour with an almost invisible covering of even paler downy hair, are not as slim as Jordan's: more muscular, but still finely curved in what is clearly a more athletic manner.

He hasn't until today realised just how strong she is. The way she'd hefted that hay up onto the cart during the morning had taken him by surprise, as had his own difficulty in doing so. He hadn't realised how heavy it could be, particularly on the end of one of those long pitchforks. He'd said something about it to her, hiding his envy with a joke, and she'd said, 'Yes, well I've done it before; you haven't. There's a technique to it. You have to swing with it. You'll soon learn.' But he hadn't; and after a while George's dad, noticing his difficulty, had set him onto raking, adding, to Jamie, 'Thoo too, Jane. If tha gaas on lek thet tha'll've muscles like a lad, 'n thet'll niver do!'

It'd been a good morning, though. Getting up at half-past five was admittedly difficult, but once out in the fields, with the sun already warm and golden over the rim of the mountains, a variety of birds voicing their own delight with the day, and the faint additional sounds of bees and other winged insects busy about their tasks, it would have been impossible not to have shared in all that rejoicing. Even the big shire gelding, harnessed between the shafts of the hay-cart, had seemed impatient to be doing, scraping the ground with those great 'feathered' hooves and vigorously shaking his long mane.

There had been three hours of hard work, raking and forking, at times climbing onto the cart to help distribute the hay, at others going with the load, balanced somewhat precariously on top some twelve feet from the ground, as it was taken, swaying and jolting, on its way to the barn. That bit, particularly, had been fun, as well as providing a welcome rest for aching muscles and weary feet; then, with the morning having become rapidly warmer, it had been a relief to enter the coolness of the stone-built barn – Joseph, the carthorse, quite unperturbed, having been turned round so that he could back the load in through the tall, arched doorway. Once inside, though, the work had started all over again, as they had to stack the hay. At first it hadn't been too bad, but as the stacks grew higher they'd had to fork the hay upwards from one to another in a series of 'steps', so that eventually it had required several actions to get one forkful to the top. It couldn't be done in just any old fashion, either. As they worked upwards, thick bundles of hay, tied with twine, were placed in the middle of the stack, and as the stack grew around them they were hauled gradually upwards. George had explained that this was to provide a 'chimney' in the centre of the stack. If the hay wasn't entirely dry, in storage it could sometimes get hot to the point of setting on fire. This way, any such accumulation of heat could escape through this central vent. Peter thought that was clever; but with muscles that he didn't know he had bunching and complaining in no uncertain manner by this stage, he'd wondered why someone couldn't invent something like the escalators in the London tube, able to carry the hay up onto the stack without all that forking.

Temporary relief from all this heat and hard work had come at around nine in the morning, in the form of breakfast. The dozen people involved with the hay-gathering – which included a couple of neighbours, George's older brother, two schoolmasters, and even the local vicar – all retired to the farmhouse where, in the large, cool kitchen they were treated to home-cured ham, eggs, black pudding, fried bread and fried slabs of golden lentil pudding, accompanied by chunks of freshly baked bread. By this time made ravenous by all that exertion and fresh air, they had really pigged themselves – which, with hindsight, had been a mistake, for within a short time they were expected to go out to resume their labours.

The rest of the morning had become still hotter, the shimmering heat bouncing off the stubble and burning their skin, so that whenever possible they sought what little shade there was, and almost quarrelled to take their turns to go with the hay back to the barn. The mountains receded into a somnolent haze, the surface of the nearby lake glittered with an unsympathetic glare and the very air itself, heavy with the scent of cut grass and wildflowers, seemed breathless. It was with considerable rejoicing, therefore, that George's mother and sister were greeted when they arrived, at around midday, with baskets of bread and cheese, along with jugs of lemon barley water, which meant that the workers had at last the excuse to retire to find individual pockets of shade. Peter had by this time already identified what he hoped would become his spot: a pile of hay that had earlier tumbled off the cart and lay forgotten under the shade of a small beech tree by the gate; and it was here that Jamie had found him.

He is beginning to get pins-and-needles in his legs, feels he must move, but is reluctant to do so. There is something pleasant about Jamie lying here with him, just the two of them. The others are with a small group that have found shelter on the far side of the hay-cart, about thirty yards away. Experimentally he carefully eases his bottom to one side; and curses silently as Jamie's eyes flicker open. For a moment there is consternation there, then signs of recognition immediately followed by those of contentment.

Peacefully she lies there for a few more seconds, not saying anything. Then: 'Sorry, I must have fallen asleep. I was dreaming.'

She sits up; and at once he feels bereft, as though something good has deserted him: he is acutely conscious of the warmth at his chest and side, where her head and shoulders have lain. She looks around, quickly taking stock of things, then turns back and looks into his eyes: for a moment there is bafflement there in her eyes, then it clears. He hasn't, before, really studied her eyes. They are more hazel, he thinks now, with flecks of brown and gold which seem to dance when the light catches them.

'I was dreaming about my father,' she says.

To his surprise she lies down again, this time resting her head against his shoulder so that her hair is brushing against his face. Her hair smells faintly of grass and flowers and summer air. She has turned her body so that it is lying alongside his and inclined towards him. He is conscious of her bare legs cool against his, and of the softness and warmth of her body weightily on his own. The sudden intimacy of it all overwhelms him, and his heart pounds.

'Do you miss your father?' she says.

He is tempted to make the usual response, that his father will be returning soon, once his secret missions are completed; but this time it doesn't seem right. After all, Jamie's father will never return.

'Yes,' he replies, 'very much.'

Is that the truth? He remembers shouts and anger, actual blows; at times cold indifference or disdain; the terror of that day when he realised that his father, unannounced, had gone away. Has it all been lies? Has what he's secretly wished for all these months – the opportunity to go back and begin again – all along been his driving force, however unrealistic it might have been?

Is that what has fed his need to invent and pretend?

But he's not yet ready to accept the unacceptable. That he knows.

'I do miss him,' he repeats.

'Yes,' she says. 'So do I. Miss mine.'

He can feel the wetness of her tears through the cotton of his shirt.

* * *

'It is strange, is it not,' says Hans, breaking into his thoughts, 'this term, *Bejant*?' Hans, because it's his first year at St Andrews, has, with slightly peculiar logic, been designated a *Bejant*, the term used since time immemorial for first-year students, or 'freshers'.

Peter, having just this week researched the answer to that question, is able to say, nonchalantly, 'Yes. It's thought to come from the French, *bec jaune*, or 'yellow beak'. Refers to a nestling, I suppose – and so, a first year student. As I think you already know, the university was founded in 1410, and therefore is the oldest in the country after Oxford and Cambridge; and Medicine, in one form or another, has been taught here since the sixteenth century. So some of the traditions harp back to the days when Scotland had strong associations with France.'

'And this *Kate Kennedy* that I hear about? Who is she?'

'*Was*,' Peter corrects him, now revelling in his lately-found knowledge. 'According to legend she was the niece of Bishop Kennedy, who in 1450 founded St Salvator's College – the one you can see along there, in North Street. She was said to have been very accomplished and very beautiful. In the spring there is 'Kate Kennedy Day', with a procession. It is said to be a very old festival – although there is some uncertainty about it all, as there always is with these things. Anyway, I expect you will be here to see it for yourself.

'Actually,' he adds, with a sudden impulse for honesty, 'I looked all this up the other day, thinking that you might be asking about it! There's a couple of verses quoted about her, and about the origins of the festival, if I can remember them. Let's see … *'I was maid here 'ere you were man or boy; I shall be maid when you no more can be; I shall not perish – nay, I shall enjoy while years exist; I am Kate Kennedy'*. And then it goes on: *'I am your past delight, your beauty lost; all that you saw and all you failed to see; plaything and price, the purchase and the cost – I am them all; I am Kate Kennedy'.*'

Hans laughs, delight in his voice tinged with friendly irony. 'Very sentimental for a very unsentimental sort of town!'

'Quite. And don't ask me what it all means!'

'And next term I am to give you half a kilogram of raisins, do I not?'

It is Peter's turn to laugh. 'Not literally! Again, just tradition. But, yes, the custom is that the bejant 'pays' his Senior Man for taking care of him – supposedly with a pound of raisins – hence it is called *Raisin Monday*. And the Senior Man gives the bejant a receipt – which is often quite elaborately designed. But don't expect anything elaborate from me!'

By now they are approaching the residence, and Peter, remembering that he has an anatomy *viva* the next day, and that he still has quite a lot of swotting to do for it, says, 'I'm sorry, but I'm afraid I have to do some work this afternoon, so I'll have to leave you to your own devices.'

'*Devices*'? What are they?'

'Sorry! I mean, you'll have to amuse yourself for the afternoon.'

'Quite all right. That is no problem. I will take some more photographs, while it is fine. Normally, here it rains much, is that correct?'

'No, actually. In winter it is often quite dry – and sunny. But also often very cold. St Andrews is about as far north as Moscow, you know.'

'No! Really? That sounds too cold! But you make joke, do you?'

'No. Really. But it's not so bad, in fact. Because Britain is in the Gulf Stream, you understand. It's not uncommon at night, though, to see the Northern Lights.'

'The Northern Lights?'

'The *Aurora Borealis*.'

'Ah, yes. Good heavens. I have never seen that. I wonder if it will be possible to photograph it. It is, I believe, quite beautiful?'

'Yes indeed. I have seen them several times. Sometimes like ghostly mares' tails blowing in the wind, and, once, like translucent coloured fronds waving in the water. We must look out for them when the sky is clear. Sometimes it is only for a few minutes, and at others it can last for an hour or more.

'Anyway, what I was going to say to you, Hans, is that on Sunday evenings a few of us often congregate in one or another's room. Just for a chat, you understand, and to smoke and perhaps have a few beers. I am sure you would be very welcome to come along this evening, if you would like to?'

'Thank you. I would like that.'

'Good. I will see you at dinner, then.'

Later that evening, Peter, lounging on Martin Birkbeck's bed, carefully tamps down the recalcitrant tobacco in his pipe, puts another match to it, and with some satisfaction squints at the resultant smoke as it curls up to add to the clearly-visible grey level suspended below the ceiling. With all of them smoking, apart from Hans, the room has got decidedly fuggy.

Having been preoccupied over the last two or three minutes with getting his pipe going again, he has been content merely to listen to the conversation between Hans and the other three, which has jumped rapidly from one topic to another. That is one of the advantages of being in a hall of residence, he has long ago decided: the diversity of academic disciplines and interests that one is necessarily thrown up against. Martin, for example, is a divinity student, in his final year; Barry Hepworth a third year medic like Peter and Hans; and Sidney Green is doing an M.A. in English Lit. Peter counts himself lucky that he has happened to land up at St Andrews just when the university has expanded its residential system. St Salvator's Hall, built only three years ago, between North Street and The Scores, near the new Graduation Hall, is already affectionately known as 'Sallie's'. The study-bedrooms admittedly are small – enough space, just, for a bed, desk, chair and bookcase, chest-of-drawers and wardrobe. And the only source of heat is a coal fire (with one smallish bucket of coal being allowed per evening, and up to two per day at weekends). But it is close to the centre of university life; and the common room and dining room downstairs are warm, being centrally-heated. In any case, it is all so much more comfortable and civilised than were the primitive conditions at school.

'So, how does the medical teaching here compare with that at Dresden?' Sid Green is asking Hans.

'Of course I haven't yet had much time to compare,' Hans answers carefully. 'Here it is very good, I think. One difference, though, is that here we study only anatomy, physiology, pathology, bacteriology and materia medica.'

'*Only,* the man says!' snorts Barry Hepworth, his fellow medic, in mock indignation. 'Well, it's quite enough for me, I can tell you!'

'I don't know what all those are, or what they entail, but certainly it sounds quite enough all at once, I must say,' agrees Sid.

'Yes, it is plenty of work,' replies Hans passively. 'But what I mean is that in Dresden we go into the hospitals at a much earlier stage and start seeing patients. Here, there are three years passing, almost, before the patient will be seen.'

178

'But what's the use of seeing patients until the basic medical sciences have been learned,' argues Barry. 'You don't have any basis for understanding what you're seeing. You have to know about diseases, what is normal and abnormal, before you can hope to understand what it is you're seeing in wards or outpatients.'

'Up to the point – is that how you say it? – yes, that is so. On the other hand, once you start to see patients and their illnesses, even though you don't understand what is going wrong, it gives you an…an incentive to find out. It makes you want to go and find out the reasons why people become ill, what the causes and mechanisms are. It is no longer just dry facts in a textbook.'

'Yes, I can see the logic in that,' says Martin. 'I sometimes wish that Theology had something more concrete, more practical, that one could get one's teeth into! But you are enjoying it here, all the same?'

'Oh yes, because it is so different from Dresden. And the Scottish language…no, accent is what I mean…the accent is so…so amusing. I have difficulty understanding it at times. And some of the staff are so…so…droll – is that a good word?'

'A very good word!' laugh the others. 'We know exactly what you mean!'

'On Friday, for example,' says Hans, 'we had lecture from the Professor of Pathology…what is his name, Peter?'

'MacTavish''

'Yes, that's right…MacTavish! A strange, Scottish name! Well, this Professor MacTavish is very old, I think. And he smokes his cigarettes all the time, even while he lectures. But he doesn't stay up at his desk, he sits at the front bench and turns around to look up at the class. Do you understand?'

'What Hans means,' interjects Barry Hepworth, finding the non-medics looking mystified, 'is that he tends to sit with the class, at the front. I think your lecture theatres at St Salvator's College and St Mary's are much the same as in the Bute Medical Building, are they not? The lecturer's desk on a dais out at the front, and for the audience steeply-tiered benches with desks, but on the front row a bench only, without any desk? Well, Prof. MacTavish tends to sit on the front row, swivelled around to face the class, with his elbow on the back of the bench. All very informal, you see.'

'You go on and tell it, Barry,' prompts Hans. 'You will do it better than I.'

'All right, if you like. Well, as Hans says, the prof is smoking all the time, one cigarette after another – sometimes you can hardly see him for smoke. And once in a while he has a prolonged coughing fit. And sometimes when that happens it goes on and on until he's totally incapacitated and quite blue. Now if you're sitting more than halfway up in the theatre, towards the back you understand, all you see is him gradually sinking down, coughing away, until he altogether disappears from view beyond the desks on the second row. At that point, for those sitting towards the back, bets start to be taken as to how long it'll be before he resurfaces – or even whether he'll ever reappear at all! But – up to now, at least! – a clawed hand eventually appears,

179

to grasp the back of the bench, and he hauls himself up, bit by bit, gasping for breath and red in the face. Whoever has the time for when he is able to start speaking again wins the bet.'

'And do none of you medics rush forward to help him?' asks Sid Green in amusement.

'No fear, we're all too busy timing him!'

'God save us from all doctors!' Martin Birkbeck says cheerfully. 'I bet it isn't like that in Dresden, is it, Hans.'

'No,' says Hans solemnly. 'Things are more disciplined, I think, in Germany.'

'They don't seem to be any too disciplined at the moment, from what we read,' retorts Martin. It is said good-naturedly, but there is a sharp edge to this divinity student's voice. 'Or perhaps I should say "*over*-disciplined" in some respects!'

'Yes, who is this Hitler fellow, anyway, who became Chancellor at the beginning of the year?' asks Barry. 'I didn't seem to have heard of him before that.'

There is a snort of disgust from Sid Green. 'You're all alike, you medics. All you ever think about is beer, women and rugby! Don't you ever read the newspapers? There's been plenty of interest – concern, I should say – about him in the last two years or more. He sounds a proper maniac! – if you'll forgive me for saying so, Hans.'

'Oh, I think you are quite wrong, though, about Herr Hitler,' Hans protests mildly. 'He seems to get...how do you say?...a bad press...over here. But he is to be quite good for Germany I think.'

'Hans, how on earth can you say that!' exclaims Martin. 'Look at his record even before he became Chancellor – which, incidentally, I think he did by very devious means. And just look what he's done since! In March, for example, what did he do but put into place his so-called "Enabling Bill", which in fact gives him full rein do just whatever he likes...'

'Hold on, though, Martin,' Peter interrupts, conscious that they are in danger of offending Hans. 'That was passed by their parliament in proper democratic manner, surely, wasn't it?'

'In an atmosphere of terror, you mean, with hundreds of Storm Troopers marching outside shouting "full power...or else!". So there was no opposition at all – and anyway, the socialist and communist members had all been outlawed, so they weren't even present!'

'Only because of the burning down of the *Reichstag* building the month before,' Hans says, beginning to sound upset. 'That was a terrible thing, done by a member of the communist party, you understand? A Dutchman. He was found on the scene, you know.'

'Very convenient, too!' retorts Martin, with sarcasm. Peter has never seen this side of him before. 'It's a wonder the Jews weren't blamed for that, as well. They're being blamed for everything else. It seems!'

'But it is not just Germany in which the Jews are unpopular,' says Hans. 'They are unpopular in other countries, too, I think. In England also, is it not so?'

'Certainly they don't allow Jews into my father's golf club at home,' contributes Barry. 'Never have, as far as I know. I think that applies to a lot of clubs and organisations. You're quite right, in general they're not very well liked.'

There is an exclamation of disgust from Martin. ' "Don't allow them into the golf club"! Have you no idea at all what's been going on in Nazi Germany in the past twelve months! Good God, Jewish businesses are being boycotted, using intimidation; their shops and houses are being smashed; they're frequently badly beaten up in the streets in broad daylight, just because they're Jews, and no one raises a finger to stop it. They're being hounded from office, being dismissed from university posts; in April they sacked all the Jewish teachers from all the schools in Prussia, for heaven's sake! – all of them, mind you! And now, didn't you see in the papers recently, many of them are being carted off to so-called *Concentration Camps* – "for re-education", they claim, whatever that might be! And these are all Germans, remember – men and women who have been German for as long as there's been a Germany, many of whom have contributed greatly to the economic, cultural and artistic richness of the country.

'But it's not just the Jews, anyway. Trade unions are now banned, as are all the opposition parties. German citizenship is now dependant on being a member of the Nazi party – I even saw a few weeks ago that all doctors now have to be members of *the Party*. That's not democracy – that's dictatorship of the worst kind!'

'Some of what you report is true,' says Hans, now rather agitated, 'but I don't know from where it is you hear the rest of it? I have not read most of those things.'

'That's because the German press is now totally gagged!' retorts Martin. 'If they try to speak out, as many have, they get closed down. And when I say 'closed down' I don't mean a polite notice on the door! – I mean their presses are destroyed, their workers beaten up, and their editors and journalists taken away and never seen again. As for where I've heard it, for months and months now there have been many reports about it all in the British and American press and no doubt in many other newspapers around the world as well. But not for very much longer, I imagine. I see that all foreigners now have to obtain a police permit before they're allowed to *leave* Germany, which obviously is aimed at reporters – what's that if it's not intimidation!'

'I must say you seem to be very well informed, Martin,' says Peter. He does his best to quell his growing alarm at not only what Martin has been telling them, but also at what effect it's going to have on his relationship with Hans. 'How is it you know all these things?'

'Simply by reading the papers, my dear chap. The trouble is that most people are like you, with all due respect. They don't want to know what's going on over there. And I include the politicians, or the majority of them, with only a few exceptions – because they don't seem to know what to do about it. But some of us recognise pure evil when we see it, and, believe me, in Germany that evil is now growing and growing; and what is happening in Germany will, sooner or later, affect us all.'

'Really I must protest!' says Hans, his voice this time raised in anger. 'It is, I think, that you do not understand what is happening in Germany. For years now we have been trodden underfoot, with loss of our national pride and without sense of direction. We were unjustly accused of starting the war, which we did not any more than anyone else. We have been made to pay large sums of money to France, Belgium and Britain for the reparation as it is called and, because of that and poor government and the actions of the Jews and Communists, in recent years we have seen the value of the *Reichsmark* plummet. Ordinary Germans were sick of it, I can tell you! And then along comes Herr Hitler, and soon we have our pride again, and money is stable, and there is more full employment, and once again Germany can become great. He is a true *fuehrer*, I think. The first we have had for a long time.'

'What is a *fuehrer*?' asks Barry.

'A leader,' contributes Sid knowingly, promoting his credentials as the more cultured, English Literature, member of the fraternity.

Hans looks at him with surprise and pleasure. '*Sprechen sie Deutsch*, Sidney?' he says.

'Well, no, not really,' replies Sid, somewhat abashed at being unexpectedly challenged in this way. 'Just a little, you know. From school.'

'Ah,' says Hans, disappointed. 'But yes, it is a leader. But in German it is more than that, I think. It means more a great leader, perhaps – no, not quite that…how do you say?…an heroic leader. Yes, that is it.'

Again, Martin intervenes, having to make an effort to remain calm, it seems. 'And that's the worrying part about it. To any sensible outsider the man's clearly a raving, hysterical lunatic – you only have to see his speeches on the newsreels at the cinema to know that. But ordinary Germans don't seem to see that. It's as if the man's got you all mesmerised. And yet one could go on and on about the truly abominable things he's been doing.'

'Yes, what about that wholesale banning and public burning of books, in May,' Sidney offers. 'Those that were said to be 'un-German' but which embraced hundreds of authors, including people like Erich Maria Remarque – you know: '*All Quiet on the Western Front*'. And now I see that a decree has been passed that the importing of banned books is to be punishable by death. By *death*! Can you believe that?'

'I agree, that is extreme,' Hans says. 'But I think is just to press home…is that the expression?…to press home that the days of defeatism and corruption of the German culture are over. It is merely an empty threat, would never be carried out for such a small offence.'

'You think not?' asks Martin in patent disbelief. 'Then what about the new laws, passed in July only, that there is to be compulsory sterilisation of all those with physical deformities, blindness, deafness, and mental deficiency! What about the regulation that anyone attempting to escape from the Concentration Camps – where they have been imprisoned without trial or even legal charges, merely because of their race or their political views, remember! – 'will be shot without prior warning'. What about this business of *non-Aryans*: all officials in Germany with that designation being ordered to 'retire', and marriage between Aryans and non-Aryans now forbidden. Are they, too, 'empty threats? It's absolute madness – madness with deliberate, evil intent. It could never happen in this country – there would be instant revolution. This Hitler fellow has now taken on so much power there's no stopping him. He's got you all in a stranglehold. There's no going back. Unless someone gets rid of him – and I can't see that happening now!'

'What is an *Aryan*, anyway?' asks Barry.

'Strictly, it means Indo-European,' Sidney says. 'Thought to be the ancient stem of European languages and culture. But I don't suppose our friend Adolph thinks of it that way! – the 'Indian' bit would probably frighten him to bits! – although he has pinched their good luck emblem in the form of the swastika! I think in this case they simply mean Nordic or northern white European. Ideally, blond and blue-eyed, isn't that right, Hans? Which would mean that, in this room, Peter is the only one of us who would properly qualify! Ironically, I don't suppose Hitler himself would qualify! – nor Goebbels, Hess or Himmler, for example.'

Hans, silent for past minutes, for the first time is looking uneasy. 'The Fuehrer has blue eyes, you know,' he says. 'And my father, who has met him, tells me that he is most charming and intelligent.'

The others look at him in astonishment, astounded by the fatuousness of the remark. Peter, from what he has learnt of Hans in the past week, cannot believe that he could all at once sound so naïve. He wonders if in fact all Germans are perhaps like that.

Out of the sudden silence Barry, for something to say, asks, 'What does your father do, Hans?'

'He is a Professor of History at the University of Berlin.'

'Is he! So what else does he have to say about your Mister Hitler?'

'I have not heard him say anything else about Herr Hitler. Not, anyway, in the past year or two.'

'Ah! So is his job safe at the University?'

'Oh yes,' replies Hans seriously. 'We are not Jews. We are good German Catholics.'

The enormity of what he has just said does not seem to have struck him. But Peter gets the impression, from the emphasis he gave it, that he is anxious only that they should all believe him.

Martin, too, is looking thoughtfully at Hans. Carefully he says, 'Does your family have friends who have been…affected…by what has been going on in the past year?'

'Oh no!' says Hans, sounding alarmed. 'We do not have such friends.'

'But you do know of people who have been affected?' Martin persists.

'Not people we know. But yes, people I have heard of.' He hesitates. 'Fritz Busch, for example. He is...was...the Musical Director at the Dresden Opera House.'

Waiting in vain for him to expand on that, after a moment Martin prompted him, 'So what happened to him?'

'I remember reading about that several months ago,' Sidney interjects. 'Members of the S.A. stormed into the Opera House – in the middle of a performance, if I remember rightly – and took him away! Is that right, Hans?'

'That is correct, yes.'

'So is he a Jew?' asks Martin.

'I believe he is. But there was talk of some corruption or other.' By now Hans is looking quite distressed, so much so that Peter worries he might even break into tears.

'So what happened to him?'

'I am afraid that...I do not know.'

'What's the 'S.A.'?' asks Barry.

Martin looks at him witheringly. 'Is that all you can say!'

The *Storm-troopers*,' Peter offers, 'the *Brown-shirts*.' – and is immediately a little ashamed of himself, realising that all he is doing is trying to show that not all medics are so ignorant of current affairs.

'Yes,' says Hans, looking grateful, as though Peter, by mentioning the S.A., has somehow endorsed their legitimacy. 'They are what might be called the police wing of the Party.'

'Nazi thugs, you mean!' says Martin sourly. Then, 'I'm sorry, Hans, I'm not going out of my way to insult you – or Germany. It's only that many of us over here cannot believe what is going on in your country at present, nor can understand that your people, who otherwise are so cultured, can have allowed it to happen. And after what happened this week, it's beginning to frighten the living daylights out of us!'

'But Germany does not harbour aggressive thoughts towards England...that is to say, Great Britain...or to France, come to that,' Hans says earnestly. 'I assure you, that is not so.'

'Is that why Hitler has walked out of the disarmament conference in Geneva this week, then?' challenges Martin. 'And declared that Germany will no longer be a part of the League of Nations!'

'Yes, that is wrong, I think. I quite agree.'

'And why Germany is increasingly re-arming,' Martin persists.

'Well, you know, the Fuehrer strongly believes that Germany has been treated unfairly at the Treaty of Versailles, and in the years since – as do the German people. He has said, this week, has he not, that he has peaceful intentions; he was quoted as saying, "equality, not arms, is our aim". That is only fair, is it not, fifteen years after the end of the war?'

'And you believe him, in spite of all that the Nazis are doing to their own people?'

'The German people do not want war. Not after last time.'

'I should think not!' Barry says with gusto. 'Not after being so soundly defeated!'

'I say, steady on, Barry!' Peter puts in, now thoroughly disturbed by the way they're treating their German guest.

Hans has got to his feet. 'We were not defeated! It was an armistice only, arranged by the politicians, without permission from the military. That is why they, and the German people, have felt so betrayed! Germany, too, lost millions of men – millions! – in the war. And for what?'

'Good question!' Martin says quietly. 'One that perhaps should have been asked by your Generals, and your Kaiser, before they entered into war.'

'Anyway, I assure you, we Germans do not want war. There cannot be further war between us. Did I not read that at Oxford University in February in their Debating Society they voted "that under no circumstances would they in future be prepared to fight for King and country"?'

'And more shame on them!' Barry mutters.

'So you see we are like-minded' Hans says, ignoring Barry's riposte. Anyway, I must now go to my bed. Thank you Martin for your beers. And good night everyone.'

As he turns to go, he adds stiffly, 'I will see you in the morning, Peter?'

'Yes, of course, Hans. Goodnight.'

Once the door has closed behind him, Peter says, 'You were a bit hard on the chap, weren't you, Martin?'

'Yes, not very Christian!' Barry guffaws.

'That's as maybe,' Martin says. 'But perhaps some of it will have rubbed off.'

'Is all that true, though, what you were saying?' Peter asks. 'Or just the papers making a drama of it all?'

There is an expression of exasperation from Martin. 'Of course it's all true! We'd better believe it – before it's too late. This Hitler chap is another Napoleon in a different guise. An uncle of mine is in the British Embassy in Berlin. That's how I know – even though he doesn't say so much – and that's why I've taken such an interest in it all. This uncle of mine is worried sick. But not many people seem to want to listen. Hitler is going to re-arm all right – has already started to do so. Why else do you think he's walked out at Geneva. And imagine what an absolute nightmare it would be having to live under a thoroughly evil dictatorship like that! It doesn't bear thinking about.'

'I tell you one thing, though, Martin,' Sid Green says, 'for a churchman you've been born three hundred years too late.'

'What do you mean?'

'Well, you'd have made a damned good member of the Inquisition!'

CHAPTER THIRTEEN

Peter covers his ears as, from outside, the subdued snarl and shudder of aero-engines lift to an earth-rumbling roar from the several Wellingtons moving off in line towards the runway. So he only just hears the tap on the office door, which in any case opens before he has time to answer. Arthur Stanton's cheery features appear round the edge of it.

'Welcome back, Peter,' he says, voice raised above the din. 'Sorry I wasn't here to greet you last night. Glad to see you've survived alright!'

'Hullo, Arthur. Come on in. Good of you to call.' He gets up to go to close the window.

'Oh, might as well leave it, old man. They'll be gone in a minute. It's a shame to shut out the warmth of that sunshine.'

'Is there a 'flap' on, or something?'

'No, just test flights. Ops tonight. Why the whole squadron are doing their test flights as a group, though, I can't think – unless David wants to try some new manoeuvres. He's always coming up with new ideas.'

'Oh, it's David's squadron, is it.'

'Mm. Anyway, how did you get on? Was it grim in Dover?'

'It was grim, Arthur. The condition of most of those men was indescribable. They'd been under more or less continual bombardment for hours at a time at Dunkirk, in many cases for days. And if that wasn't enough, virtually all of them had had practically nothing to eat or drink for the whole of that time, and little or no sleep. And the state of the wounds of some of them was appalling; of course they'd had virtually no attention, not even any attempts at a dressing in many cases. Many of the wounds were already horribly infected; and a lot of the men still in shock from blood loss. And those are just the ones who were able to make it across. God knows what the others were like who had to be left behind. One just hopes that jerry would properly look after them.'

'So how was morale?'

'Surprisingly good. They were all weary, of course, physically and mentally, and very shaken – but resolute. And angry: with jerry, with top brass…and with us, I'm afraid.'

'With us?'

'With the RAF.'

'Ah…How come?'

'The boys weren't much in evidence, it seems. At least, that's what was said. Far too many of the men spoke their minds in no uncertain way when they spotted my uniform! I think they felt we'd just left them to their fate. The Navy were the heroes – and the civilians with 'the little ships' as they were calling them; there's no doubt they were magnificent, and must have sustained their own share of casualties as well. But the RAF's name was mud – or worse!'

'But we were there, I know! And in considerable force. Striking at communications and whatnot. There were several sorties from here every day, and from probably nearly all of the southern stations, I should imagine. But of course, when you think about it, we'd be bombing well away from the beaches – knowing how inaccurate much of the bombing is! – so most likely it wouldn't be noticed.'

'I expect they were mostly referring to the Fighter boys, anyway. Evidently there were plenty of Messerschmitts and Junkers strafing the beaches, but not a Hurricane, Spitfire, or even a Defiant, to be seen.'

'Mmm. I do happen to know that we did have fighters over there but, again, they'd be intercepting before jerry got to the beaches, so they wouldn't be seen.' Stanton hesitates. 'But…strictly between you and me…I believe we didn't have many there.'

'Why on earth not?'

'Well, think about it, Peter. We all know that the invasion is bound to come, now. We've been soundly defeated in France – for, however much this is dressed up as an heroic retreat, which no doubt it was, it's still a defeat. We've saved a hell of a lot of men – I've heard that it's somewhere in the region of quarter of a million or more! – but we've also lost a lot; as well as all those arms, munitions and heavy equipment. It can only be a matter of time now before France capitulates. So we're on our own. And if jerry gets across here – whatever brave words Winnie can come up with, we're lost! We have to stop them *before* they land on our shores. So we'll need all of our planes and pilots, which, God knows, are few enough anyway.'

'But that'll be the Navy's job, surely? They must be more than a match for the German navy if it comes to a confrontation.'

'No, you're wrong, Peter. Not on their own, they're not. That's a misapprehension far too many people have been labouring under for far too long – including some of our military planners; particularly those in the Navy itself! Capital ships are far too vulnerable to air attack – and to mines and submarines. There *has* to be air superiority. And that goes for jerry as well. He can't get invasion forces across the Channel unless he has it. Our fate depends upon whoever wins or loses the war in the air. Fortunately some of the brass have realised that – and, most importantly, C-in-C Fighter Command. For that reason he's been holding back fighters from the battle for France – and that included Dunkirk – in spite of very considerable pressure from on high – and from the French…Mind you, I haven't told you any of this! I'll say one thing for 'Stuffy' Dowding, though, he's crystal clear in his

187

thinking, and he's tough and resolute. Not many men could have withstood that sort of political pressure.'

'Is that his nickname?' Peter is slightly incredulous that an Air Chief Marshal of Dowding's stature could be referred to in such derogatory terms. 'Have you ever met him, in fact?'

'Only the once. I must say he's not exactly charismatic! Comes as quite a surprise to find that he's not the epitome of your gung-ho, extrovert Fighter type. Quite the opposite, in fact. A pretty complex character, I should think. But in my view absolutely the right man for the job. Certainly doesn't suffer fools gladly, though.'

They lapsed into silence, each with his own thoughts. A sudden cold wind of fear blows through Peter as, for the first time, he really considers the implications of invasion. He remembers once again the discussion, that time when Hans was in his first week at St Andrews, and Martin Birkbeck had really laid into Hans. And recollections come flooding back of that week with Hans in Berlin in '36, when, in spite of (or perhaps because of?) Berlin being a showcase to the world, the stark tyranny of Nazism had been only too plainly – blatantly – clear. He suppresses a shiver. What will happen to them all, to civilisation itself, if the Nazis win the day and occupy Britain as well as the rest of Europe? He thinks about his mother, about Uncle John and Aunt Mabel, and Jordan – and Jamie. What would be their fate?

Is it this chill fear that makes him now retreat from the unimaginable to the trite; and for Stanton to respond in the same vein?

'Will you have a cuppa, Arthur?'

'I don't mind if I do!'

Peter groans theatrically. 'You've been listening to that Tommy Handley fellow, on the wireless, haven't you!'

' "Itma"? Of course. Haven't you? Hasn't everybody?'

Not for the first time Peter feels himself to be something of a social outcast, different to other people: others sometimes find things funny that don't begin to amuse him.

'We only have tea, I'm afraid. Not managed to get any coffee, needless to say.'

'Tea, of course. Nasty continental habit, coffee, anyway.'

Peter goes to the door and pokes his head into the outer office. Browning is sitting at the desk engrossed, as usual, in paper-work; whether to do with the RAF, or something of his own, Peter never knows.

Browning, looking up as he hears the door, dutifully jumps to his feet.

'Can we have some tea, Bart,' Peter says, taking customary secret delight in his corporal's facial expression as he hears the abbreviated form of his name.

'Sir,' Browning replies in the careful, militarily terse manner that he somehow manages to make sound respectful and disdainful at one and the same time. It always reminds Peter of the kind of tone too often used by your typical waiter at a London restaurant.

'Make it three,' Peter adds, on impulse, 'and come and join us.'

'Sir,' says Browning, without any noticeable change in expression.

'Where's the awesome O'Connor, then?' asks Stanton, as Peter comes back in.

'Day off. But, you know, Arthur, she really came up trumps at Dover.'

'Well, you should know, from what I hear,' says the padre with a grin.

'What do you mean?'

'Sleeping with the enemy, and all that!'

'Oh, that. My God, doesn't news travel fast here! As I'm sure you're aware, it was entirely a matter of convenience rather than unrestrained lust. I should have been so lucky! In fact, I don't think either of us would have been physiologically or mentally capable, never mind the physical encumbrances!'

'Only joking. I do know that, only too well,' Stanton replies, suddenly sober.

'But I mean it, Arthur, beneath that hard shell there really is a different Shevaun. She's a lot more sensitive than she makes out.'

'I don't doubt it, old chap.'

Peter throws him a suspicious look, but can see that Stanton is serious – more than that, it is something the padre has known all along, long before Peter had discovered it for himself. It makes him feel crass.

'What is it that makes man go to war!' he says vehemently, all of a sudden, with the image of the Dunkirk survivors and the futility of it all.

'Now there's a question,' says Stanton. 'Must have been asked thousands of times without any ready answers. I suppose young men go readily enough to war because of the opportunity it presents for adventure, and because they see it as glamorous – and themselves as immortal. Old men perhaps are prepared to initiate war because, in contrast, they know that mortality is nigh, particularly for themselves: death is no longer a question of If, but one of When and How. It could be that war enables them to cast off a certain jealousy of the young, who still have youth – and to whom, on the contrary, death is seen only as a remote concept in the distant future. War removes that disparity. It is after all noticeable that it is so often the old who make war, and the young who have to enact it...although this particular war, intruding so much onto the home front, could I'm afraid be a lot different to previous wars in that respect. And – to be really cynical – maybe for older men war introduces a zest to life where it no longer existed. But, no, I don't know why men create wars.'

Peter looks at him in some surprise. As Stanton himself admitted, it is a particularly cynical view, especially from a clergyman. But then, as he is beginning to learn, Stanton is no ordinary cleric. And the man's experience of war has to have affected his viewpoint.

But at that moment Browning, who, unnoticed, had just brought in the tea, speaks up.

'As often as not, wars aren't made, they happen,' he says.

The unexpectedness of it make Stanton and Peter both quickly look up at this corporal, standing there with a tray of tea, who has the temerity to voice an opinion. They then look at each other with rueful expressions,

189

simultaneously understanding the conditioning that has made them react in this way. In this instance, they've suddenly remembered, they are the amateurs and Bartholomew Browning, Oxford history don, the expert.

'Sit down, Bart...Bartholomew,' Peter says. 'What do you mean by: "they happen"? You make it sound as though there's no human input at all.'

Browning, cautiously taking a seat, blinks nervously behind his spectacles as though suddenly aware that he's made himself the focus of attention in a way that he hadn't wanted. He gives the impression that he's spoken without really intending to. He takes a hurried drink of his tea, spluttering slightly as he discovers it is too hot.

'Well,' he says slowly, 'if you imagine the prelude to war – all wars, really – as being like a jigsaw of many pieces that are capable of being put together to make a number of very different pictures according to how the pieces are placed in relation to each other, and in what order, that might give you the idea.

'Take the Great War, for example – a perfect example – where in the simplest terms, it was the assassination of Archduke Franz Ferdinand and his wife on their visit to Serbia that triggered the whole thing off. Quite obvious really, because he was the heir apparent to Emperor Franz Joseph of Austria-Hungary; and the latter couldn't be expected to tolerate an outrage of this kind from a footling little country like Serbia – although in reality it was nothing to do with the Serbian government, but entirely the work of a small group of disaffected students. So, of course as we all know, the Emperor Franz Joseph got a bit belligerent, which then dragged in Germany, and everyone else got sucked in.'

'Yes, but they were all decisions by individuals,' Peter interrupts. 'It didn't just happen.'

'But, you see,' Browning says earnestly, 'we now believe that no one actually wanted the war to happen. It just did. And that was because of a whole panoply of complicated events in the past.'

Peter is shocked into silence. The implications of what has just been said are too awful to accept. He looks at Stanton, who is staring at Browning with great intensity, disbelief all over his face.

'Go on,' says Stanton quietly, but there is almost menace in his voice. Peter inwardly cringes. For someone like Stanton, who'd fought through the War, both in the trenches and in the air, who'd seen first-hand the horrors and the immense loss of life, to be now told that the war hadn't even been necessary must be like a knife in the guts.

His own anger rising at Browning's insensitivity, he starts his reprimand, but Stanton interrupts with a restraining hand on his arm and, still staring at the other man, says again, 'Go on. Explain.'

Browning briefly screws up his eyes and licks his lips uneasily, as if only belatedly realizing the impact of his statement on these two officers. Hurriedly he says, 'We have, now, all the documented facts for this, but you do have to realise that not all historians agree on the interpretation of historical evidence. As someone once said, "*History* is all that has been found to survive the grave; but the *motives* of man are buried much deeper". History so often hides behind a false face.'

'Go on,' repeats Stanton tetchily. 'Just give us the version that you believe in.'

'How much do you know about the European alliances at the turn of the century?' Browning asks, pauses, takes one look at Stanton's face, and hurries on. 'Right. Well, during the last part of the Nineteenth Century and up until the Great War, the main military powers in Europe were France, Germany, Russia, the Austria-Hungarian empire and, to a lesser extent, Italy...as I'm sure you know. Great Britain in a sense stood apart: as well as being cut off, as it were, from the continent, we had, relative to the others, only a small standing army, although we did have the most powerful navy – and of course we had our extensive Empire. Also, we had little or no vested interest in what went on in Continental Europe, so long as it didn't affect our other worldwide interests. Throughout that period, peace was largely maintained by a series of military alliances, which acted as a deterrent to aggression by any single country. Over time these alliances became more and more complex – but I'll keep the explanation as simple as I can.'

Peter and Stanton, relaxing a little, exchange amused glances: Browning, warming to his theme, has changed: no longer the nervy out-of-his-element corporal, he has taken on the stature of someone who is confident of his material and of his ability to marshal it.

'The first of these alliances,' Browning continues, secure in this world of his own, 'was in 1879, between Germany and Austria-Hungary: each would come to the aid of the other if attacked by Russia.

'Three years later, Bismarck in Germany drew Italy into the alliance, when it became generally referred to, therefore, as The Triple Alliance. The terms of it weren't straightforward, however: the Alliance between Italy and Germany, for example, would apply only against France, and not against Russia – and there were other provisos, as well, which I won't bother you with. However, from Bismarck's point of view, the alliance was designed to protect Germany from either France or Russia. But both France and Russia were equally nervous of Germany. So in 1894 an Alliance was formed between France and Russia...'

Here he pauses, and asked solicitously, 'Are you still with me?'

'Yes,' Peter and Stanton reply solemnly, the latter adding, '...just about.' Browning's patronising tone is so innocent it is impossible to take offence.

'Good. Well, there were, at the same time more or less, a number of other minor alliances between various countries which don't really come into it – for example between Great Britain and Japan – but the thing about all of these alliances, great or small, was that there were any number of uncertainties about what each country's obligations would be in the face of unforeseen circumstances. And in addition, to muddy the waters even more, over the years there were forged a series of so-called *Ententes* (which in effect meant that they had a loose agreement to support one another without any hard obligation to do so) such as that between Great Britain and France in 1904 – and later, and more importantly, Britain's vague pledge to support Belgium's neutrality in the future. But all of these were extremely blurred in their implications.'

But surely,' Peter says, 'as you've pointed out, they were all intended to prevent war rather than bring it about?'

'Exactly. They were pacts of defence, not of aggression, and designed to prevent war. But, you see, that's where the element of control started to disappear.' His voice is beginning to rise as he warms to his theme. 'What we have to understand is that by the turn of the century all of these other countries had universal compulsory military service of one degree or another – Great Britain was the only country that didn't. But whatever the exact pattern of that military conscription the principle was the same – that when that service was completed those men then became "reservists", liable to be called up whenever the need arose. This meant that all those countries – apart from Britain – had millions of men available that they could "mobilise" within a few weeks should that country have to go to war. And that's an important factor in what eventually happened, as you'll see. Incidentally, the same need was there, of course, for thousands of horses, and provision was made for their "mobilisation" as well from their peacetime tasks. But I'm sure you know all that?'

'Yes,' says Stanton, a shade impatiently.

'No,' says Peter, a little ashamedly. 'I'd no idea of any of this.'

Browning looks from one to the other as if a little perplexed as to how to continue.

'Go on, man,' Stanton says. 'You have our full attention. I for one am agog as to where all this is leading.'

Browning swallows hard, then takes a breath. 'Well, that was the political-military set-up, if we can call it that. Each country wary of the others, flexing its muscles within uneasy alliances, and striving to maintain the policy of "balance of power". What real frictions that existed were quite small ones, and usually to do with border pressures: Russia unhappy about Bulgarians in Constantinople because of the potential for their control of the Straits; Austria unhappy about Serbians on the Adriatic; that sort of thing. In all the small individual countries of the Balkans there was, though, also considerable nationalistic fervour for independence – a fervour that had little chance of being translated into success, given the might of the Austro-Hungarian Empire which held sway over them. For that reason Austria was constantly irritated by Serbia and the other Balkan countries, fearing that they might foment unrest in their fellow nationals residing within the borders of the Empire. But the preoccupation with the Balkans was solely Austria's – it was never Germany's.

'With regard to the purely military set-up, however, there were a number of more serious flaws. On the face of it, all military planning was entirely defensive in nature; but that planning for defensive war, over many years, was entirely theoretical and purely habit, if you like – an essential pastime for professional soldiers and sailors in times of peace. You have to remember that no staff officers, from the Generals downwards, at that time had any actual experience of fighting a large war. In all cases, however, particularly in Germany, there had come a widespread belief that the best form of defence is *offence*; equally, that the element of surprise, of attack before the enemy is fully prepared, is essential for success. Fieldmarshal Schlieffen in Germany in particular had laid down plans for that country which were a product of the concept that the nation that could mobilise the most men in the fastest time and achieve the most speed in the offensive was likely to be the victor.

'But in the German case especially, because of the rigidity of the plans, mobilisation once it was under way could not easily or safely be slowed down or stopped and then restarted should the need arise. Once it had been initiated it would become a juggernaut with a momentum of its own. In that sense, therefore, military planning had become separated from political objectives. Even if the need for war was being only tentatively considered by the politicians it was liable to set off a process that would become unstoppable – and the opposing forces would fight only for victory, without any other precise political goal.'

'Are these just your theories?' Stanton demands, 'or is this now an accepted view of the beginnings of that…that nightmarish, ungodly conflict?'

'I would say that it's now a widely accepted view among certain historians,' Browning replies carefully, 'and one that I accord with. An awful lot of documentary evidence for it has come to light over the years. All that can change of course with the passage of time and further knowledge.'

'I still don't quite see how all this fits in with your premise that wars – particularly that war – "just happen",' Peter says. 'Surely it was still deliberate declaration of war, justified or not, that set if off?'

'Well, no,' Browning says. 'It seems not. That's the trouble. The evidence suggests that it happened more by default, that the actual declarations of war were the product of personality flaws in a small number of leading characters caught up in the systems I've referred to.'

'For heaven's sake, Browning!' says Stanton, exasperated. 'You're surely not trying to suggest that all, or indeed any, of these nations were led by a group of incompetents?'

'Not at all, sir. Of course not. Just by men with normal human weaknesses. Perhaps the common problem is that in a time of crisis a leader has to lead. He cannot allow himself to prevaricate too much or he will be deemed weak and a failure. Therefore he must often act before he is in a position to judge the best course of action – with consequences that are largely the product of luck. If you then add another ingredient to the pot, that is failure of communication, or more precisely failure of adequate consultation, then you have a recipe for disaster. Couple that with a series of self-fulfilling military systems and you have the certainty of disaster. And that's exactly what happened.

'At the time of the Sarajevo assassination the Austrian Foreign Minister was a chap called Berthold – Count Berthold. Now he was only too well aware that he had a reputation for being somewhat weak in looking after Austria's interests – just as Austria itself was regarded by its ally Germany as being a bit weak-kneed; after all, Germany was by far and away the most militaristic of all the nations, and had been since the Second Reich was established in 1871. So Berthold, conscious of his reputation, bombastically sided with those in Austria who proposed war with Serbia – not because he was an enthusiast for it, but because he fully expected that it would never actually come to that. He did however consult with various people, including the Prime Minister of Hungary, who went along with what he proposed, but for various reasons insisted that war should only begin if first approved of by Germany.

'Thus, a process was set in motion. Berthold, displaying "strength", therefore proposed to Germany that Austria should now forcibly eliminate Serbia from the power struggle in the Balkans – probably expecting that Germany would never agree. But the Kaiser did agree – perhaps because he and his ministers felt a need to match the firmness shown by Austria; certainly because Kaiser Wilhelm, as well as being a distinctly aggressive character, personally was outraged by the assassination of a fellow sovereign ruler. And also because they all suspected that Austria's outward show of belligerency was in fact merely bluff and would come to nothing in the face of Russia's inevitable interest in the proceedings. In any case, the German Chancellor at the time, one Bethmann Holweg, was not at all averse to a localised war between *Austria* and Serbia only, he having decided that it was unlikely that Russia would intervene in the face of Germany's alliance with Austria. Such a course of action would, he must have decided, after all improve the military standing of Germany's principal ally, Austria, and therefore bolster the strength of their alliance.

'There then followed a short period of vacillation by the Austrians. They did, though, serve Serbia with an ultimatum couched in terms that would be extremely difficult for the Serbian government to agree to – although in fact they almost did agree, quibbling only at the last minute with some of the detail.

'In the meantime Russia – well aware of events and with no desire to see Austria increase its power-base on Russian borders – was of course also trying to decide what to do. The Tsar of all the Russias had absolute power in his country: final decisions rested with him and him alone – an awesome responsibility for someone of rather weak character. Remember, too, that he was a cousin not only of the Kaiser but also of King George V in Britain; and he did several times confer with both of them. But it seems that that family relationship was of not much help in the situation that confronted them, much as one would have liked to think that it might have been.

'Anyway, as things progressed the Tsar did eventually, and with much prompting from his ministers and others, ordered *partial* mobilisation on only the Austrian border, so as to present a deterrent – only then to be told by his generals that, for practical reasons of organization, *partial* mobilisation was not an option: it had to be all or nothing.

'Meanwhile Germany, increasingly alarmed that the situation was in danger of getting out of hand, sent diplomatic notes to Russia and France warning them not to mobilise or Germany also would have to do so. It seems that this move had been genuinely intended to be of a cautionary nature, and not a threat; remember that Germany herself for decades had been somewhat fearful of attack by either France, on one of her borders, or by Russia on the opposite border.

'*France* however saw it as threat, and it therefore had the opposite effect to that intended: it initiated the first steps to mobilisation, bearing in mind that in the case of France the process could be made to pause at any chosen moment.

'Russia on the other hand hadn't appreciated that *different* viewpoints prevailed between herself and Germany: in her case, mobilisation was merely seen as a *prelude* to the possibility of war; whereas in Germany, because of the exigencies of the Schlieffen plan of "offensive defence" to be carried out with the utmost speed, once Germany had mobilised it wouldn't be stopped and war would inevitably follow within two or three days.

'Given that misunderstanding, the Tsar, still dithering, was finally stung into action by a casual remark by one of his ministers along the lines of "making decisions of this sort can be very difficult" – and, probably only to show that he could make such a decision, he promptly ordered *general* mobilisation! The irrevocable slide to war had begun.

'With the prospect of Russian troops heading for the border, and France beginning her own tentative mobilisation, Germany swung into action. She declared war on Russia, and asked for a guarantee of neutrality from France. The Schlieffen Plan – kept secret, of course – had always been for Germany to attack France first and, once that country had been neutralised, then turn her attention to Russia. The French reply was deemed to be unclear; so Germany, with no time to be lost, then declared war on France on the false pretext that France herself had already infringed German territory. Because of Germany's short border with France (which the French had got well fortified), for strategic reasons the German plan had always been to swing the attack north through Belgium – naturally enough with or without that country's permission! But Belgium had a strong fortress at Liege. Now remember that for Germany and the Schlieffen Plan, speed was of the essence. Therefore by the time Germany had demanded "permission" of the Belgians (which would of course have been refused, anyway) she had already crossed the border – Liege was quickly taken and the German army headed rapidly for the French-Belgian border! The Great War had begun.'

Silence follows. Stratton is sitting with his head in his hands. Even Browning himself now seems stunned by what he has been telling them. Peter simply sits, equally incredulous, and stares at the man, his thoughts whirling at the enormity of it all.

'So you mean to say,' Stratton eventually says, disbelief in his voice, 'that none of these countries actually wanted war, but that it happened despite that?'

'Not war on anything like that scale, certainly. Austria had been quite keen on her small war with Serbia, expecting, quite rightly, that it would be an easy one. And Germany at that stage hadn't any objections, particularly as they themselves weren't for one minute likely to be involved. Austria, as it happens, who had in a sense started the whole business, was the last to enter the war, and then reluctantly! But no, we have to now conclude that until it actually happened it had all been a question of bluff and counter-bluff; of human frailty; of individuals – and nations – flexing their muscles and flaunting their views of their own self-importance. Mind you, Germany had over a good many years progressively become very much a militarized state, and when that happens sooner or later it has to be justified. And the only way to do that is by war, by one means or another.

'Finally, though, it wasn't even so much a matter of bluffs being "called", but of politicians and military being overtaken by self-perpetuating systems. What had been set up to prevent war actually precipitated it. Diplomacy would probably have worked, that is up to the point when Germany demanded that Russian and France should not mobilise – a demand that could never have been safely met given the concept that "the fastest to mobilise, wins"; and the belief that "the best form of defense is offence".'

Stratton groans, an expression of anguish and frustration, and gets to his feet to pace restlessly up and down the room. Peter has never seen him like this. He is normally so calm and outwardly relaxed. Browning, too, is now looking agitated, polishing his spectacles with almost frantic intensity. Perhaps he is regretting that he's come out with any of this; after all, he's been expressing views – albeit ones shared by other historians – that, as far as Peter knows, have never yet been widely spread before the general public.

'What I can't understand, though,' he says to Browning, 'from what you've told us, is how Britain came to be involved. I'd always thought that we'd been in it, as it were, from the beginning.'

Before replying, Browning carefully replaces his spectacles on his nose, and squeezes his eyelids together several times as though to check his vision. 'Not at all,' he says. 'We were very much clinging to the coat tails of it all. Or, as someone was said to have put it, "all for a scrap of paper!" It was the somewhat uncertain pledge that we'd previously given to Belgium, that we would defend her neutrality, that dragged us in. The Cabinet were against our involvement, as were the Commons in general, in spite of some talk of "honour".

'The German army had begun its crossing into Belgium early on the morning of Monday 4th August, 1914 – which happened to be a Bank Holiday in Britain. At that stage there had been numerous appeals by France for help from Britain which we'd responded to only by stating that the Royal Navy would certainly protect French vessels in the Channel – substantially, nothing more than that had been offered. However, later that day Sir Edward

Grey, who was our Foreign Secretary, possibly in collusion with the Prime Minister, Asquith (although it's not certain that he was even involved) sent an ultimatum to Germany requiring them to honour Belgium's neutrality "or else" – it's not known whether the exact consequences of their failing to do so were spelled out. The Cabinet were informed of the ultimatum, but not previously consulted; and the same applied to the Commons – the King wasn't even informed until afterwards.

'At this stage there had been no request for help from the Belgians; and there had never been any prior intimation to France, or Germany, of what Britain's reaction might be in the face of war on the Continent. Probably the assumption had been in Germany that we would stay out of it; as indeed had always been the assumption of the general public in this country.

'It was as if our becoming involved had been purely the result of a rush of blood to the head, if you like, on the part of only one or two Ministers. Nevertheless, when there was no favourable response from the Germans within the ten hours of the ultimatum, the Privy Council met and, very reluctantly, authorised a state of war with Germany.

'And there you have it. Somewhat simplified, perhaps, but that's the essence of it.'

Stratton comes back to his chair and sits down heavily, his face drawn. 'I still cannot believe it,' he says. 'All those millions of men!'

They sit in silence for a while. Probably no one can think of anything else to say. Browning himself looks, if possible, even more distressed; to Peter it seems almost as if he might suddenly be blaming himself for the substance of what he's said rather than merely the recounting of it. All at once he looks like a corporal again. It's odd, Peter thinks: you take an intelligent academic like Bartholomew Browning, a man who is highly qualified and much respected in his own world, you stick him in uniform, make him a corporal and give him the duties of a lowly clerk, and that's how he behaves. It's as if he's instantly transmuted. He's been told: 'This is what you are now.' So that's what he becomes. But then, in a military hierarchy he doesn't have any choice.

To break the spell, Peter says, 'All right, Bart, you've made your case: man thinks he's in control but isn't really. What about this present war? You're not going to say that this one 'just happened'? Not with Adolf and his cronies on the rampage.'

Browning gazes back, owl-like. 'This one's still too close. An historian requires distance between himself and the object of his study, time for things to come together, to be clearer. But there are certain recognisable patterns that one can discern. The mainspring of this war is of course the Great War itself. I suppose,' he adds thoughtfully, 'we're going to have to start referring to the 1914-18 war as the "*First* Great War." Anyway, all this stems from that war – or at least the shadows of it. If that one hadn't happened, it's arguable that this one wouldn't either. Of course, at all the crossroads of life, when a decision is made on each occasion, voluntarily or otherwise, to take one path as opposed to another, you can never be sure that eventually you're bound to end up in a different place: it may be that the end-point will be the same, except that you've arrived by a different route.'

'You mean,' Stanton puts in with mild sarcasm, 'that if Germany had won the last war there wouldn't have been any need for this one.'

Browning blinks at him in startled manner. 'Yes, I suppose that might be true. But I didn't mean that. What I meant was that Germany's defeat and subsequent economic distress – largely due to the hefty financial reparations she was forced to make to the allies, but aggravated by the world stock market crash in 1929 – added to their other grievances.'

'But they started the last war, just as they've started this one,' Stanton says with some vigour. 'They simply paid the consequences. That could never be any excuse for what has happened since.'

'No,' agrees Browning. 'But you see, they always claimed that they didn't start the last war any more than Russia, France or come to that, us. They would say that they were simply dragged into it like the rest of us. And, they claimed – or the military did – that they weren't actually defeated, that it was an agreed armistice.'

'What utter nonsense!' Stanton explodes. 'It would have been only a matter of weeks before they would have been totally beaten, and they knew it; why else would they have agreed to the armistice!'

'Of course. But the point is *they* didn't – and don't – see it that way, irrational or not. And they were allowed to march home with their arms and with banners flying; so, much of the populace began to see it in the same light as did the military. Therefore, when the terms of the Versailles Treaty were revealed they felt betrayed. Add that to the loss of status – and of territory, with the break-up of Austria-Hungary, the loss of the Sudetenland, of German-speaking areas to what became Czechoslovakia, of the Polish Corridor cutting off Bavaria, etcetera – and the tinder was laid for the bonfire of their so-called National Socialism. Hitler was merely the spark to set it alight.'

'So it's all our fault? Is that what you're saying?' snaps Stanton impatiently. 'We are responsible for those thugs that trample across everything that's decent and civilised and who are now on the point of trampling us under foot in the same manner.'

'I'm not defending them,' says Browning mildly. 'I'm only explaining the processes.'

Peter, with his distaste for confrontations, now hurriedly intervenes. 'Do you think Hitler could have been stopped at some point, then?'

'By the Germans or by us?' Browning answers with a slight frown.

'Well, both?'

'By the Germans, perhaps. But there are elements of the policies of National Socialism which seem to provide answers to much of their ills, which have sufficient appeal to allow them to turn a blind eye on the nastier aspects of the Nazis. They probably hope that all that will tone down once certain objectives are achieved. A sufficient number of Germans are only too happy to have someone else to blame for their woes, and the Jews and

Communists serve as well as any in that capacity; after all, a distaste in many people for those two sections of society was never confined to Germany! But by the time a sufficient number of people in Germany at that time had perhaps begun to realise that in the Nazis they had a tiger by the tail it was too late: Hitler already had them by the throat, and isn't going to let go. Once he'd swept away all semblance of democracy and was now able to rule by terror there was little anyone could do. It's history repeating itself, as it so often does; it's the sort of thing that happened in the Russian Revolution, and in the French Revolution before it – and in countless other cases. I remember one of my tutors saying, "The importance of History is not the shadows of the Past that it describes, interesting though they may be, but rather the substance of the Future that can be revealed." We never seem to learn that lesson.'

'So what about the war this time? Could it have been prevented just a few years back, if we'd learned lessons from the past?'

'Who knows? It seems to me that throughout his political career Hitler has achieved everything by a mixture of low cunning and stealth. He's made threats – threats that, as demonstrated only too readily by the activities of the Brown-shirts, he and his accomplices are brutal enough to carry out – and then has waited for others to make concessions. We and France hadn't the resolve to be able to do anything about it when he annexed Austria, nor when later he marched into the Sudetenland. The same thing happened when he made demands with regard to Czechoslovakia two years ago. We and others gave way, persuading ourselves to see it his way, hoping that if we made concessions he would become more reasonable; so we threw Czechoslovakia – a country that we had been jointly responsible for creating in the first place – to the dogs. It's small wonder that he expected to be able to get away with the same thing in Poland last August. He was probably as dismayed as we were, when he didn't! It could almost be construed as a miscalculation on his part. After all, he's gone public since to say that he has no quarrel with Britain'.

Stanton has got to his feet. 'I should stop there, Browning. And I wouldn't let anyone else hear your views! It could be construed as treasonable under the present circumstances. I have been interested in what you've had to say, but take my advice: stick to history in future.'

He turns to Peter. 'I must go. But I'll see you in the Mess this evening?'

Peter can't ever before recollect hearing Stanton so terse. The man is clearly upset by Browning's views. But he wonders nevertheless why he is making the point that he is staying on Station this evening. Then he realises.

Of course. Stanton, as padre, always makes a habit of staying on Station on the nights when crews are on operations. The war that Browning reckons should never have been, and certainly that no one wanted, is all at once very personal, with all its consequences.

CHAPTER FOURTEEN

Peter, sitting alone in the Mess lounge that evening, taps out his pipe and spends the next couple of minutes carefully refilling it. I'm smoking too much, he thinks. It is one of the perks of being in the services: tobacco is fairly readily available, with none of the shortages and rationing to be found in the civilian sphere. On his last visit home, before Christmas, he'd taken some up to Uncle John, who'd accepted it with expressions of gratitude but had then said, 'But don't bring any more, old chap. It makes me feel uncomfortable. It's alright for you fellows fighting the war to have these benefits, that's fair enough; but not for the rest of us taking it easy.' When Peter had muttered that he personally wasn't fighting any war, his uncle had said, 'Don't you believe it. It may be quiet enough for you at present, but it won't be long before you're in the front line like everyone else, if my experience is anything to go by.' Peter had thought privately that being in the RAF as a doctor was hardly the same as being a doctor in close support to the trenches, as his uncle had been; but he hadn't said so.

He sits back and puffs disconsolately at his pipe, getting little pleasure from it on this occasion. He wishes now that he'd never phoned up to find out about Richard Wilson. It isn't helping having to sit here on his own in this empty room, either – a bit eerie, in fact, without any of the usual camaraderie, and he regrets having sent the steward off: he would at least have been someone to talk to. He wishes too that Arthur Stanton would come. It is Arthur's habit, though, to have supper with his wife before coming back to the Station on these ops nights, and Peter fully understands that. But it isn't usual for all four squadrons to be away at once; usually at night there are at least a few fellows left in the Mess. The habit of the crews, previously, had been to take off in penny numbers on night ops, at whatever time, within reason, suited them, to follow their own chosen route to reach the target area at the appointed time; and from the operations point of view it could be said to make sense – less easy for jerry to spot the odd plane on its own at night.

But Beal has now put a stop to that, and all the Flights take off together; the brass had evidently decided that it was tidier that way, or something of the sort.

Out of habit he looks across at the clock on the mantlepiece, but as always its hands point to 8 o'clock. That stands for 8 a.m. *Alpha* and *omega*, the boys call it: alpha for the morning of the day already dawned, with all its uncertainties; and omega for the morning of the following day, when destiny has played its hand. He consults his watch. 11.30 p.m. They should be over the target by now. Northern France, David Munro had said, striking at enemy communications, bridges, roads, railways, that sort of thing, in support of the remaining British divisions who are swinging north trying to link up with the French. But Arthur has confided that it is pretty well regarded as a lost cause and that those units also will shortly have to be evacuated before they too are in serious danger of being cut off.

His eyes slide back to the clock – or more particularly to the quart tankard of beer standing next to it. An odd sort of talisman if ever there was one. The tradition is that the last crew to arrive back, thereby completing the safe return of all the squadrons, will share it; if one or more crews fails to return, the beer will be thrown away – like the lost crew members, it will 'go for a Burton'. Peter permits himself a grim smile: the full version from which the truncated expression derives is 'gone for a Burton Ale' – so, whether they've realised it or not, this particular ritual has connotations of 'ashes to ashes…'. Not only that, if all is well it is as if they are *toasting* the last crew back, who by the simple act of returning have reaffirmed the faith of the whole group in their ability to all go out and all come back; but they are doing it in advance. It is, then, by a curious twist of instinctive thinking, more in the nature of a bribe than a reward. Strange how so many of the chaps have to go through these superstitious rituals before going out on ops. He knows that many of them will virtually refuse to fly if for some reason they don't have with them their favourite lighter, coin or scarf, or whatever other item their fancy has fixed upon – sometimes, he knows, it is their wife's or girlfriend's knickers! It is common too, he's learned, for crews to have a team ritual such as the rear-gunner urinating on the rear wheel before boarding the kite, or the navigator kissing the tail-plane. It is even rumoured that on one occasion a crew had come round and landed again because they'd omitted to go through this performance. But he is no longer surprised by any of this. He now knows that their apparent *sangfroid* is contrived; their easy nonchalance a front. They would have to be stupid not to realise the dangers they face. Already losses on some missions had been frighteningly high, particularly among the Blenheim squadrons of 2 Group who seemed to have come in for a lot of the operations in past weeks. No youngster at the dawn of his adulthood, with all before him, is going to be relaxed about the prospect of missing out on life. Instead they face the risks with as much bravado as they can muster. The Team is everything. They are interdependent, the survival of one held in the hands of all. They can't let the side down, and can't be seen to lose face: it isn't the *experience* of fear that worries them, it is the possibility of showing it. That would be even worse than 'shooting a line', which is regarded as contemptuous enough – probably because they all realise that the fellow doing that is covering up for his own self-perceived deficiencies; and if that is how he sees it, then that is very likely how it is, making him a danger to them all. But fear is common coinage; it comes with the job, it is what they all trade in – it is vulgar to show that you have it, for to do so makes things more difficult for your buddies.

Of course, there are a good many among them who live for the moment; men of a character for whom the opportunity for excitement and adventure makes it all worthwhile. For those types the rush of adrenaline is sufficient to brush aside any fear. War has provided them with this once-in-a-lifetime chance to pit their prowess and their wits against a worthy opponent and, with luck, to cover themselves with glory. They are to be the heroes of the day, to be regarded with awe. Perhaps they choose to believe, as Stanton has suggested, that they are immortal. They are a self-selected group, volunteering for the role as opposed to being there out of a sense of duty. For them it is a game, no different from rugby or cricket, except that there is more at stake.

Impelled by Beal's semi-contemptuous prodding that he should get closer to the men he serves, Peter had at first frequented the crew-rooms as crews prepared for their missions, just as he had attended the briefings. But he soon learned that on those occasions he wasn't welcome, he was seen as an intruder. They didn't want to talk, except to each other. They'd already closed in on themselves, into what would become for the next few hours their own private world, a shared experience that was exclusive. They didn't want any outsider along as a kind of disinterested spectator reminding them that, for some, the world that night would remain a relatively safe place. They certainly didn't want to open their hearts, to admit to the fears that were so carefully buried deep. Anyway, Peter thinks, it is like the half hour or so before an important rugby match: the team together in one place, each member contending with his jittering muscles, dry mouth and racing heart and that hollow feeling in the stomach which makes one feel hungry and nauseous all at the same time. On the first occasion the experience is almost intolerable: one simply wants to run and hide. But with experience one learns that once out on the pitch, a job of work to be done, a responsibility to be fulfilled, nervousness disappears to be replaced by concentration on the task ahead and the excitement of the action.

For those remaining behind during these raids, however, the waiting becomes increasingly fraught. As the hours and minutes tick by towards the crews' expected time of return the tension becomes almost palpable. Right now, Peter knows, Beal will be pacing his office, postponing with difficulty the point at which he will go to the control tower to await the eruptive crackle of the RT announcing the arrival of the first of the aircraft back over England. Stanton has warned Peter that Beal doesn't welcome company during that last spell of waiting; even the men and women on duty in the tower know to keep silent until the moment actually comes for that initial radio call. Then will come murmurs of relief; but still the nerve-wracking wait until, ten or fifteen minutes later, the first has landed and, over the next half hour or so, each one in turn has been safely counted in. For even their arrival over the airfield is no final reassurance: too many crash on attempting to land, the consequence either of aircraft damage or pilot injury during the sortie.

Peter and Stanton, therefore, along with those aircrew who are on stand-down, have got into the habit of drifting toward the debriefing hut as E.T.A. draws near; or on occasions will go out to join the ground crews anxiously standing by at the hangars or on the tarmac – for they also, to a man, feel an affinity with the aircrews they serve, and a responsibility for any failures in the aircraft they service. And, as the safe landing of each aircraft in turn is announced, all present will exchange brief grins of delight – almost immediately stifled, for attention has then returned to the next one to come.

At times, though, the wireless message from an incoming aircraft will carry more ominous tidings: of desperate damage to the plane, or of serious injury to a crew member; then Peter and perhaps O'Connor, and often the padre too, will be required to hasten to stand-by at the medical unit so as to be able to be taken swiftly with the ambulances to the crippled plane.

For those waiting to carry out debriefing on the first crews as they arrive, however, there is then quick confirmation of how things have gone. If the first few crews enter, fatigued and cold as they are, in ebullient mood, with wisecracks and friendly scuffles, the likelihood is that all is well. If, on the other hand, at first there is a silent wariness, an unwillingness to meet people's eyes, a surly reluctance to talk, then it is almost certain that one or more of the squadron has been seen to go down. The loss of some other crew is more than the loss of friends: it is a reminder of one's own vulnerability.

The cohesion within each of the crews had surprised Peter at first. There are six to a crew on Wellingtons, often of different ranks, and with disparate though complementary tasks: pilot and co-pilot, navigator, wireless operator, bomb aimer and gunners. (The last three roles require some 'doubling up', with twin tasks, for there are three gun positions to be manned: rear, midships, and nose.) As Peter had initially been told, the pilot might in some crews be a Sergeant and have, say, a Flying Officer as his navigator or even as an air-gunner, yet is always 'skipper' and in command. And this is one factor which has done away with the hierarchical structure, making it easier for each crew to become like a family, a close unit. Not only do they fly together, but their recreation will be taken together, they will drink in the pubs together; their loyalty will be first and foremost to one another. Each crew will normally remain together for the duration of their 'tour', which consists of thirty or so sorties; and sometimes they will even manage to come together for a second tour. Only if something drastic happens will that pattern be broken – and the one or more replacements will have to work hard for a while before they are properly assimilated into the 'family': more often than not, though, they will be joining a crew by invitation or by recommendation. Not only that, but each crew will have their own, identifiable aircraft until perhaps it becomes unserviceable, and this too strengthens their sense of identity.

Some time ago Peter had asked Munro how, and when, members of each crew were chosen, and the answer had surprised him.

'They choose each other, old man. Halfway through their training at O.T.U. when the individual specialties start to train together, at some point they're invited to make up their own teams. By then they've had the chance to get the measure of one another with regard to both competence and personality, and they just sort of drift together by inclination, or by direct invitation, one to another.'

Peter had revealed his astonishment, saying that he had fully expected that the decisions would be taken either by the senior instructors or by the pilot in each case choosing his own crew.

'It is a bit unusual,' Munro had said, 'I quite agree. It just happens to have evolved that way. And it seems to work.'

'You're looking very morose, Peter. What's up?'

Stanton's voice jolts him into consciousness. He must have nodded off. In dismay he looks at his watch. 12.15. That's all right. Another thirty minutes or so before the crews can be expected back.

'No, I'm all right. Must have just dropped off for a moment.'

He sits up, then stoops to retrieve his pipe, which must have fallen onto his chest and with his sudden movement has rolled onto the floor.

The padre sits down and lights a cigarette. As he usually does for these occasions, he is wearing his clerical collar and shirt, which is in pale airforce blue – much more friendly than the black and white jobs, Peter has decided, and wonders why all clergymen don't adopt something similar.

'Actually, I suppose I was feeling a bit fed up,' Peter confesses. 'The other day at Dover I came across my English teacher from school. A chap called Richard Wilson. One of the better beaks at school. He'd been wounded a few days previously. Nothing too bad, just a compound fracture of his arm.'

' "Compound"? Remind me.'

'An open wound over the fracture; the importance of it is that there's always the risk of infection getting into the fracture site. Anyway, this afternoon I got Browning to track down which hospital he'd been taken to. Turned out to be a hospital at Redhill, in Surrey. So I rang them to find out how he was. It seems that he died yesterday. Septicaemia. I wish I'd never phoned, now.'

Stanton makes a sympathetic sound with his tongue. 'Oh, bad luck. I'm sorry. It's a bit hard to have come so far only to succumb like that.'

'I'm afraid there would be a lot more like him. Their wounds had been left unattended for so long, in many cases.'

'I thought they had something now to combat infections like that?'

'Yes. That's right. "M & B". *Sulphonamide*, it's called. Made by *May and Baker*, hence the tradename. I don't know a lot about it yet, though, and I think it's still in short supply. There's also recently been some talk in the

B.M.J. about progress in the development of an active ingredient from *penicillium* – the stuff that chap, Fleming, isolated a few years ago. They're working on it in America. Great hopes for that in the treatment of infection, I believe. But I suppose it'll be some years before we can say that we really have a sure-fire cure for infections.'

'Yes. That really would be something! One could then really begin to believe in the age of miracles. But, to change the subject – and while I still remember! – I forgot to tell you this morning that Beal is throwing a Mess party tomorrow evening. Wives, girlfriends, brothers, sisters – especially sisters – and even parents, all invited. So, if you can find someone to bring along? Girlfriend for example?'

'No. No one at present, I'm afraid.'

'Well, you do surprise me. No matter. You'll just have to invite the conquering O'Connor, then! Make you the envy of all the chaps. You'll have to keep a close rein on her, though, or she'll be going off with the first bloke who makes a pass at her! But then, you should have the advantage of the others, having so recently slept with her.'

Peter chucks a cushion at him. 'Poor Shevaun, she does have an unfair reputation. And I bet she's not done anything really to deserve it.'

'Don't let her hear you say that! She depends upon that reputation for all the good things that come her way – and there have been plenty of those!'

'Any particular reason for this shindig of Beal's, then?'

'Oh, it's no shindig! Much more decorous than that. Dress uniform and all that sort of thing. And the ladies all dressed up to the nines. Grrr! Wonderful! But no, no particular reason as far as I know. I suspect he thinks it may be the last opportunity for quite some time.' There is a pause as both he and Peter dwell on the implications of that. 'Also,' Stanton goes on, somewhat hurriedly, 'with the whole squadron on ops this evening, and none of them likely to be out again tomorrow, it's more certain that everyone will be able to come.' Again there is sudden silence, this time more awkward. Stanton grimaces, realising what he's said: it reminds them that the members of the Mess have still to be counted in from tonight's raid.

The talk about the Mess party causes Peter to dwell again on the incongruities of the Service system. The Sergeants, who mostly make up the crews out there tonight, are rarely invited to the Officers' Mess. They have their own Mess, which again is exclusive to them: the only time commissioned officers are invited there is at Christmas, when, by tradition, the officers go in to serve the sergeants' Christmas dinner. Even now, the 'class' barriers could be broken down only so far. It is all so artificial. Take Browning, for example. Outside in Civvy Street, as an Oxford don he would be 'accepted' anywhere. But not here. Here he is 'only' a corporal.

From there his thoughts drift back to Richard Wilson. All at once he can picture him so vividly, as he was at school: full of enthusiasms, his body seeming to be going in several directions at once; with a biting but not unkind sense of humour, and a sensitivity to the needs of his charges that was not usual in a public school. Wilson – who somehow had become C.O. of the

Officers' Training Corps at school, and had ended up dying in uniform in the service of his country, yet who had had a leaning towards pacifism. A man who, given time to consider, would probably have chosen to surrender his own life rather than take that of another, in particular that young German motorcyclist – and who, by some strange irony, had forfeited his own life in any case.

And here, moving from a twinge of vicarious guilt, he is struck by a pang of conscience of his own: he realises all at once that, other than those facts, he knows nothing about the man. When Peter was at school Wilson had still been single. But did he now have a wife? And children? Here was a man who had had a subtle influence on five years of Peter's life, yet to Peter after all these years he was still little more than a cypher.

He looks at his watch again, more out of habit than a need to know. This waiting is awful. But the transient urge to be out there on ops with them is, he suspects, entirely spurious. Many a time he's wondered how he would measure against them. Would he, if fate had decreed it, have been able to do what they do with such apparent calm? Would he ever be tested, would he ever know? Does he want to know?

To take his mind off that, 'Have you recovered from Bartholomew's homily this morning?' he says to Stanton.

'Oh, it was hardly that! Quite erudite, I thought. With regard to its accuracy, I don't know – and perhaps don't care to! It's not an easy thing to have put one's life on the line so many times, and to have endured so many hardships only to be told it wasn't really necessary. Better if he'd kept quiet. A plague on all historians, I say! They're like vultures, up there, waiting – high above the blood and gore of everyday life – finally coming down, when all the turmoil is over, to pick the bones clean.'

It was said more with resignation than with rancour; but when Peter reflects about the effects that that war had had upon his own father, and consequently indirectly upon himself, an edge of bitterness cuts across his own thoughts.

He hesitates. 'I've wondered several times,' he says, 'how it is you went through all that and yet...'

'...Decided to do the work of God', as it's usually put?' Stanton finishes for him – he must have caught Peter looking at his dog collar. 'You might well ask! I've wondered about it myself, many a time. I suppose it was mainly a reaction to it all: that there must be something more to life than the shambles created by mankind.'

'But you do still believe in God? – silly question! But do you? In spite of it all?'

'That there is a God? I've never thought that there isn't. But I am sometimes afraid that God has gone away, that he no longer cares. But there, you see, I've fallen into the trap that so often I warn against – only to myself, mark you, never to my flock! That is to say, that we think of "God" in human terms. We dutifully trot out the message that Man is made in the image of God. What we're really saying is we've created a God with the face of Man.

We've created "God" in *Man*'s image. We're so egotistical! And I'm talking about all religions, not just the Christian ones.

'In fact, the more you think about it the more you realise that virtually all of the world's major religions are still actually pagan.' He pauses to cast a long pensive look at Peter, who is aware he must be looking totally bemused by now, indeed is beginning to wonder if his friend is not altogether mentally sound.

'It's true,' Stanton persists. 'Think about it. What is the essence of paganism? Ritualistic practices, without doubt. Well, aren't the five major religions all extremely ritualistic?

'But more than that, all the pagan religions of the past were, and are, polytheistic. Well, look at Christianity. Do Catholics and Protestants share the same God? – how can they when each side believe that the only way to salvation is to adhere to their particular God, their particular beliefs. And that's *within* the same basic religion, before one even begins to consider the antipathy between Christianity and Islam, for example, or indeed Christianity and Judaism, never mind Hinduism with its actual plethora of gods – or at least God in a variety of forms. Maybe Buddhism is the nearest of the five to have a broader view of deism in general – but then *we* don't believe that they have an actual *God* at all.

'However, to return to my original theme, that of God in our own image, take the Lord's Prayer, for example. Just look at the metaphorical images in that, and their implications. The word 'Lord', for example: someone who has control over our lives, who can dictate to us. 'Father' similarly: the power to provide for us, to nurture us or to punish us. 'Kingdom': much of the same, only more so. 'Forgive' and 'Deliver': pleas by us to God, with the implication that not only does He have total power over us but that, like us, He chooses whether to use that power or not; in other words, like us He can be capricious! We have created for ourselves a God that acts on whim, who is nothing more than a super-human; not only that, but 'He' is male – and, for us, of course white! For some other religions He is very much a wrathful God, a vengeful one – as indeed He was, spectacularly so, for Christianity in the past, with the message of purgatory and hell thrown in for good measure!'

Peter doesn't know whether to be alarmed or elated. He's never heard a clergyman talk like this before. It sounds...cynical.

'Yet you say you've never *not* believed in God? I mean...what sort of God do you envisage?'

'Ah, don't expect me to tell you that!' Stanton replies cheerfully. 'Anyway, this is strictly between you and me! Professional confidence and all that. So far as the chaps go, those that want my services, I toe the party line! Tell them the sort of things they want to hear: the comforting sort of things.' He looks sharply at Peter. 'I say, I hope this sort of chat hasn't upset you? That you're not now regarding me as an out-and-out hypocrite. I'm afraid I've always taken you to be an agnostic. Am I wrong?'

'I don't *know* whether I'm agnostic!' says Peter, using the pun to grasp for a leavening of humour. 'I've never thought about it much. Until now. But,' he persists, 'you must have some idea of what it is you do believe in?'

'Yes, well if you look at the world around us, there is miracle enough. And there clearly is order in nature, and in the universe. We seem to be such a speck in it all, though, don't you think? I just can't believe that mankind is at the centre of it all – indeed I hope we're not! Surely the Deity, whatever form that takes, must have a more expansive plan than that. But our understanding is so tiny that there's really no point in speculating, is there?'

'Doesn't it worry you, though, doing a job like yours yet having so much uncertainty?'

'Is your job any different?' Stanton challenges. 'I've no doubt that all your undergraduate teaching in medicine was from a position of certainty? But that you are finding, with experience, that certainty in what you do is becoming less and less?'

Peter nods ruefully. It helps, however, that someone else understands that.

'Don't worry about it, though,' says Stanton kindly. 'I remember the words of one of my tutors at clerical college. What he said was, "Maturity is not achieving a state in which one is certain of one's views and attitudes, but it is the arrival at a place of understanding that there is always another point of view". And someone from the class said to him, "But that surely is uncertainty, and uncertainty is the enemy of decision." And do you know what he replied – and I've never forgotten the words – he said, "But without uncertainty you cannot make a decision: the decision is already made for you. Is that not called prejudice? The shadows of the walls of yesterday preventing daylight from entering the corners of today?" I've thought of it many a time, particularly when one is tempted to take the easy route and simply accept what one has always been led to believe.'

'Did you pray to God for help, though, in the war when things were really bad?'

'Damned right I did! Along with all the others, atheist or otherwise! When it comes to the crunch we choose to believe in whatever is convenient at the time. No doubt the Hun was doing exactly the same! Must have been dashed difficult for God to choose between us!'

Peter is by now faintly shocked by what he is hearing. It doesn't seem right for Stanton, wearing his clerical collar, to be so irreverent. Does smack of hypocrisy, after all, he decides. He's disappointed. Is that one of the effects of the Great War, that it has turned those who had survived the experience into cynics? Like his father.

'Was it really so terrible, that war?' he asks, without thinking.

Stanton looks at him keenly. 'You've asked me that before,' he says. 'Yes, in the trenches it really was horrific. As much from the conditions as anything else. It never seemed to stop raining – perhaps, after all, God had it in for both sides! There was deep mud, water, stench, rotting corpses – and rats – everywhere. Not to mention lousy food, typhus and trench foot.

Frequent shelling, and the constant threat of a bullet from a sniper. Constant fear, of course, but one became numbed to that; at times one felt one would almost welcome death. What one really feared was mutilation. Going over the top was a nightmare; but that wasn't all that often – in fact I had to do so only once, at Ypres. There were patrols into no-man's land, which were very scary, particularly if one had to lead them – as I had to several times. Worse in the dark, as they usually were, than in daylight: you imagined that every shell hole you slithered into contained a jerry with his bayonet at the ready; or that a flare would go up at any moment and make you an instant target for the machine guns. No, being up in the air, flying, had its own dangers, but at least you had a little bit of control over your own destiny. Mind you, for a long time they wouldn't even give us parachutes. Did you know that? Seemed to think that it would make us funk it, if we had the means of escape. Can you believe it! So the greatest fear for us in the R.F.C. was of being burned. And I suppose that's not a lot different today, is it.'

Again, that enquiring look, after which he goes on to say, 'But your father was in the War, Peter, I seem to remember you telling me. Did he talk about it at all?'

'Very little. And not at all to me. But I don't suppose I asked. As a child it all went over one's head. There was no comprehension about it.'

'No, of course not. How could there be. But somehow I have gained the impression from you that your father must have suffered quite a lot, as the result of the war?'

'He was wounded twice. And gassed. And then…well, shell-shock I suppose. So-called. Just had enough, couldn't take any more, I expect.'

'Mm. Saw plenty of that. "L.M.F." was the other term – and, God forgive us, still is! Wouldn't you think we'd've learned more than that by now! I mean, what a goddamn awful term to use on blokes who have given their all, been through so much that their nerves are totally shredded. Did they teach you about "Lack of Moral Fibre" at medical school, or on Officer Training? – the psychological mechanisms, and so on?'

Peter shakes his head.

'No, I bet they didn't! The trouble is, half of the cases don't even reach a quack – if you'll pardon the expression. The tag is pinned on them by some senior operational Johnny who either has never had a nerve in his body, or else is so far gone he can't remember what it was like on the front line – if ever he was there in the first place! And I'm afraid that even some of the service M.O.s collude with that. Gets the bloke out of people's hair, of course, but the poor blighter's stuck with the slur, because most people equate it with "dishonourable discharge due to cowardice" – usually people who've never had cause to test their own courage. Has no one come up with an acceptable medical term to describe the condition?'

'Not specifically, no. I suppose the nearest would be chronic melancholia – or "Nervous Depression" is the newer term. Or else the diagnosis might be "Chronic Nervous Asthenia." '

Stanton snorts. 'Fat lot of use they are! They sound to have the same sort of inference as L.M.F. So did your father recover all right?'

'Not really, when I think about it now. I don't recollect the time that he came home, out of hospital, that is, in 1918. Too young. I was only five, and couldn't remember him at all before that, so there was nothing to compare it with.'

'*It* being?...'

'He was always very moody. Not easy to be with. Full of enthusiasms one minute, and very down the next. And an explosive temper – I remember that well!'

'You say *was*. How is he these days?'

Peter doesn't reply. Can't reply. He resists the memory. But relentlessly and unbidden, the scene begins to take shape.

1925. November 15th. His twelfth birthday.

Miserably, he is sitting astride Dobbin, disappointment, self-pity and remorse fighting for supremacy. For the umpteenth time he is going over the events of the past hour or so.

The day had started well enough. His father had insisted they had breakfast before Peter was given his presents, but that was usual, he's used to that – and at least his father had been in a good mood. Nevertheless he'd been hard put to curb his impatience until, breakfast over, his father had left the room, presumably to fetch Peter's present. The minutes had ticked by, and even his mother had been starting to look anxious. Finally he'd voiced his concern; and his mother's reply had done little to reassure him: 'I expect he's still wrapping it, dear. You know what your father's like, always at the last minute!'

He'd been faithfully promised a dog this year. How could you wrap a puppy!

Eventually his father's voice had floated down the stairs, sounding almost as excited as Peter felt. 'Right, son, come on up. I've something very special up here for you this year!'

He'd taken the stairs two at a time, and tumbled into his father's study. His father had been standing there, a battered cricket bat in his hands. Puzzled, Peter had peered around the room, unable to see his present, and then looked at his father.

'I...I don't understand,' he'd stammered. 'Where's my present?'

'*This* is your present, son,' his father had replied; and he can still picture the pride and pleasure written all over his father's face.

He'd stared at his father, dumbfounded. 'But I already have a cricket bat,' he'd stated, disbelief and anger causing his voice to rise. 'And you promised me a dog!'

Then it had been his father's turn to look dismayed. 'Steady on, old chap,' he'd said quietly. 'Wait until you see what sort of bat it is! It's not just any old bat. It's one that was used by Jack Hobbs in the 1921 Test Match, and is signed by all of the England and Australian teams. It took some getting, I can tell you! Here, take a look at it.'

Peter remembers brushing it aside, hardly able to see it for tears in his eyes. 'I don't want your silly old bat! I wanted a dog. And you promised me!'

At that, his father had become angry too. 'Your mother and I decided that a dog was not a good idea, living in London. And it's time you learned to be grateful for what you've got, boy! Most lads would give their eye-teeth to own a bat with the history this one has.'

'I don't care!' he'd yelled. 'It's not a dog! I hate you! I wish you'd never come back from that silly old war!'

He'd realised immediately, of course, that he'd gone too far. He'd seen that the wound had gone deep. He'd also known what the consequences were likely to be, was flinching even as the words came out. And although he feels sorry for what he'd said, understanding the effect it must have had on his father, he can feel the emotion, the truth of what he'd shouted at that moment.

His father of course erupted with anger, grabbing his swagger stick from its habitual place of honour on top of the bookcase and lashing with it at Peter's legs and arms. He admits to himself, though, that it hadn't really hurt, even though he can still feel a slight smarting on his legs; it was the split-second anticipation of it, and his horror at the raw fury that had been uncovered between the two of them, that had triggered his reaction. 'I hate you!' he'd screamed again, 'you're not my father!', and had fled from the room.

Perhaps he'd expected his mother to take his part. He doesn't know. But she must have heard the whole thing, or at least the parting words; for he'd found her, when he'd arrived downstairs, totally unsympathetic. 'That was a dreadful thing to have said to your father!' she'd shouted at him, adding her own anger to the sum total. 'You must know he loves you. And he was convinced that you'd be so proud to have that bat. You know very well, too, that your father cannot stand scenes of that kind, not…not the way he is now. You'll go up to your room and stay there, Peter. There's no lunch for you today!'

And now, sitting in his room, the more he thinks about it the more he begins to feel some contrition. After all, he can picture the faces of the chaps at school when he shows them that bat. And perhaps his parents will have second thoughts and he'll get a dog for Christmas. He decides that he doesn't, in the end, know why he said all those awful things to his father, or even what he meant by them. He begins to cheer up. He'll say he's sorry, once he's allowed out of his room.

The sound, when it comes, is a familiar one. That of a motor vehicle backfiring in the street outside. Except this time it's louder. Could almost be in the house. The silence, after it, seems equally loud. Then the sound of feet on the bottom stairs. Hasty feet. His mother's. Followed by the equally hurried but heavier footfalls of the new maid, Mary. A door opens down on the landing below. There comes a voice he hardly recognises, in a long drawn-out moan: 'No..o..o!' Followed by a scream, a different voice –

Mary's. He flings himself at his bedroom door, hurtles down the stairs three at a time. His mother is standing in the part-open doorway of his father's study, her hand still on the doorknob. She's very pale, her eyes closed, her body rigid but swaying. Behind her on the landing Mary stands, her eyes wide, the knuckles of one hand clenched in her mouth. There is an acrid smell, like the smell of fireworks on Bonfire Night; and a whiff of something else that he can't identify. He heads for the doorway, but before he can push at the door his mother's arm comes across and bars the way. 'No, Peter!' she commands, her voice shrill. Then, more gently, but still firm, 'No, Peter, don't go in there.'

Past the half-open door he can see his father's left hand stretched out on the floor as if reaching for an item under the bookcase. On the wall above there is a splattering of grey and red.

He lifts his head. Stanton is looking at him oddly. How long has he been waiting for Peter's answer?

'He committed suicide,' Peter says. 'On my twelfth birthday. After we'd quarrelled. He shot himself.'

The time of pretence was over.

CHAPTER FIFTEEN

'So, did Arthur bring you his head on a plate, yesterday evening?'

Peter hastily turns his attention back to the speaker. For a moment – gazing round the Mess at the groups of chaps in their dress uniforms and the women (mostly young, pretty and all dressed up) and listening to the subdued buzz of civilised chatter (thinking how very different it is tonight from the more usual drunken and bawdy rowdiness of most nights in the Mess) – he's lost the thread of their conversation. Totally mystified by Sylvia Stanton's remark, though, he still doesn't say anything; simply stares at her in perplexity.

She laughs, a pleasant sound. Even that has traces of her Scots intonation, so much more definite than her husband's. 'I've suggested to him several times that he might bring you home for supper. After all, we only live in the village – ten minutes away – so I wouldn't think anyone could object even if you were on duty. But it seems he keeps forgetting to do so. If you haven't already discovered it, my husband's a man who can carry only one priority in his head at once: everything else gets overlooked. So I'm afraid that yesterday evening he had to put up with a bit of flack from me. Anyway, you must come sometime. I've heard so much about you.'

Pleased by this attention, and flattered by the way Stanton has evidently been talking about him, he can only tumble out his thanks.

'I mean it. You remind him, as well. There may not be much more opportunity.'

This last was said a shade glumly, and Peter raises his eyebrows enquiringly.

'Arthur's on at me about me going back up to Edinburgh,' Mrs Stanton explains. 'We still have a flat there. But it's utter nonsense. If there is going to be an invasion it won't matter, in the end, where I am.'

'Perhaps he's more concerned about the likelihood of bombing in the coming weeks?' Peter suggests carefully. He doesn't want to consider the possibility of invasion.

'Yes…well. How does he think I would feel if I'm up there, safe and sound, and he's down here with bombs falling around him. Anyway, I've told him I'm not going – I won't hear of it, so that's that.'

He looks at her in amusement. Slight, with an open, friendly face and a quiet manner, she nevertheless clearly has a formidable will. Her hair, cut short and wiry, is showing streaks of grey, and he reckons she must be about the same age as Arthur, in her mid- to late-forties.

'From what I hear they're going to ban the wives of aircrew from living near the Station, in any case,' Peter says, thinking at once that his comment was more than a bit tactless. Hurriedly, therefore, he stumbles on: 'Apparently it's been decided that it's bad for morale. Whose morale, that of husbands or wives, they don't say. In any case, I can't see their reasoning. They're all going to worry about one another whether they're a mile away or a hundred miles away.'

'Exactly. Perhaps people like you should tell them that. But I don't think they could make wives who are already living in the area move, anyway. They wouldn't have the power to do that, would they? Surely it'll only apply to new people posted to the Station?'

'I really don't know. Wartime seems to give governments the excuse for an awful lot of powers. I mean, look at the authority given to Ernest Bevin as Minister for Employment – it seems he now has the legal right to move anyone to any part of the country to do any job under whatever conditions of work and pay he chooses. That's absolutely draconian, isn't it – regardless of whether he actually uses those powers. Anyway, at least you don't have to worry about Arthur when the squadron's out on ops.'

He regrets that, as well, as soon as the words are out of his mouth. It, too, is a crass thing to have said.

She looks at him thoughtfully, seems about to say something, then it's as if she's changed her mind. He decides he isn't doing too well with Sylvia Stanton; she must think him an absolute ass. He was expecting her to retort that the same applied to him: sitting back in a safe cushy job while others put their lives on the line.

Instead, she says quietly, 'Do you know there's hardly a day goes by when Arthur doesn't wish that he could be up there with them. I thank God that he's deemed to be too old for that to be possible, otherwise I think he would have abandoned the church and volunteered as a pilot again.'

There isn't any hint of reproof in her tone of voice; but it is there, in the content of what she's said. Arthur had already done his bit, in the last war. Peter has no such excuse, she seems to be saying. Not for the first time he finds himself wondering whether he isn't, in a sense, a *line-shooter* himself: wearing uniform, with a significant rank, pretending to be one of the combatants doing his bit to defend king and country, but in reality nothing of the sort. He feels himself going scarlet; and she must have noticed, for she

214

tactfully looks away as she adds, 'But the jobs that he and you are doing are equally important, you know – just as are all the other support services, the WAAFs, ground-crews and so on. These boys, brave as they are, I'm sure are partly sustained by your being there.'

He isn't persuaded of that, doesn't feel any better for her generous comments; but decides to change the subject. 'You're a teacher, I believe?'

'Yes. I was lucky; I managed to get a job quite quickly, in the local school.'

'You like children.' It is a statement, made out of sudden conviction, rather than a question.

She smiles at him and nods.

'And you have two of your own, Arthur tells me.' With a twinge of conscience he realises that he'd never actually asked Stanton anything about his children.

'Yes. No longer children, alas. Our daughter, Beth, is a nurse – at Westminster Hospital, in London. And our son, Alex, is an accountant by profession, but now in the RAF – as a pilot in Coastal Command.' She pulls a face.

He nearly says, 'At least he's relatively safe' – but stops himself in time: it would have been unforgivable to have made the same mistake yet again. Anyway, he is beginning to learn that flying aircraft is never safe, whatever the conditions; and she would be worrying about her son, regardless.

'Where is he stationed?' he asks.

'A place called Silloth. It's up in Cumberland.'

He brightens with pleasure. 'Oh, I know it well. I grew up in those parts, in the Lake District; and my grandfather lived at Silloth. We used to spend holidays there with him.'

For an instant he is transported back to those days, can smell the sea-borne breeze, feel the prickle of marram grass and the warmth of sand between his toes. 'How's he liking it?'

She pulls a face again. 'Says it's a bit quiet. "Dead-and-alive" was actually how he expressed it in his letter – although I think he was referring to the flying activity as much as the place.'

Peter's spirits dip. She'd added the last sentence a shade hurriedly, probably only out of politeness. But he's no right to think that his own childhood enthusiasms would be shared by anyone else; nor, even, if he were to go back there now, that he would feel as he used to. Nevertheless he can't quite shake off the wave of home-sickness that has rolled over him, a nostalgia for the past. In recent years he hasn't been too good at keeping in regular contact with his mother and with Uncle John, the two people who remain the most important for him. Why is it, this ability to so easily lose touch?

'Are you close to your son and daughter?' he asks on impulse.

She laughs. 'I like to think so. But I doubt that they feel the same about Arthur or me. We get a letter from one or other of them once a month or so, if we're lucky. But they're leading their own lives now, had been doing, even before the war. It's only to be expected. You must know that, probably can more readily see it from their point of view.' It is framed more as a question than as a statement.

It is his turn to laugh, somewhat wryly. 'That's what made me ask the question. A certain guilt in that direction.'

'Oh you mustn't feel guilty about it. It's inevitable, is it not, that parents and children see each other in a different light from one another?'

'Is it?' he says. He hadn't thought about it before, but he can see that she might be right.

'Well, yes,' she goes on, giving a rueful little smile. 'After all, parents have watched their children grow up, and have played a part in the process. What they see in the grown-up child is a sort of *collage* of all the years and phases that have gone before, from infancy to adolescence. It rather inhibits their seeing their offspring as a fully-fledged adult. Besides which, they know a great deal about their son or daughter as they were when they were children, but very little about them as adults. The child's life has changed and has moved away, as it were.

'In contrast, the child has only ever seen the parent in adult form, behaving in a controlling adult way – or perhaps, at times, in rather less-than-adult ways! That's a very limited picture they have of us. Not only that, but just as we, as parents, have difficulty in seeing our offspring except through parental eyes, so our children have some difficulty in throwing off their childlike views of us. After all, so often we've conditioned them over all those years to behave like children, with one rule for them and another for us. It's no wonder they so often have difficulty in maintaining relationships with us. A part of them is still concerned with the process of shaking us off, of ridding themselves of our influence over them; but another is harping back to the need for guidance and emotional support from us, as happened in the past – particularly during the rougher parts of their lives. Of course, I'm generalising. In many cases this is never an issue: in others it is there, but of no great importance.

'The sad thing is, when one comes to the inevitable losing of a parent, it's always a bit like an amputation, whatever the relationship has been.'

She pauses. Then, 'But from what Arthur has told me I think you already know that?'

For a moment he doesn't trust himself to speak. Fortunately, at this point, anyway, he has no need to formulate a reply, for Mrs Stanton turns to greet a girl who has come over to join them. He is able to briefly study the newcomer as the two women touch cheeks, and the introductions are then made. He likes what he sees: not just that she is vivacious and pretty, with a trim figure, but that with it there is a certain serenity about her face and manner. He therefore self-consciously turns on the charm as they shake hands.

'This is Peter Waring, Athena,' Sylvia Stanton says. 'Peter is the new – well, relatively new, now – station medical officer. Peter, can I introduce

Athena Brown. Athena is a nurse at the local hospital, and is David Munro's fiancée.'

He'd had no inkling that Munro was engaged, and his twinge of disappointment at the news that she is already spoken for is disguised by his expressing genuine surprise.

'Hullo. Well, I'd no idea. Congratulations. I must say he's kept very quiet about *you.*'

Catching, out of the corner of his eye, an amused grin from Sylvia, he thinks: Whoops! Put my foot in it again – and the girl herself looks momentarily taken aback before laughingly saying, 'Well, I'm not sure how to take that!'

Her handshake is firm, however, and there is excitement in her as she holds onto his hand for a few seconds longer than necessary, saying, 'I've heard all about you, however. David fagged for you at school, I believe. He's never previously talked much about his schooldays, but in recent weeks he's done so quite a lot.'

He can still picture Munro on the rugby field, in his second year at Bards already playing at stand-off half for the school *Colts* XV, and doing so brilliantly. From there his sporting career at school had taken off – mirroring Beal's before him in some respects as he rose to become captain of the 1st XV and to play also for the 1st XI. After Peter had left he'd continued to follow Munro's school career in the twice-yearly Old Boys' Magazine, doing so with a mixture of envy and spuriously proprietorial pride. His own school career had been anything but distinguished. In fact the only distinction he could lay claim to had been that he had been made a House Prefect in his final year, and that, in his own estimation, only by reason of staying on in the Sixth Form in order to qualify for entry to medical school. And now that he is prompted to think of Pearson again, as well, he feels ashamed and not a little sad that he hadn't maintained contact with him afterwards.

But all in all he is mystified by her having said '*I've heard all about you*'. He can't begin to think what Munro would have found to say. Perhaps she is merely being polite. People say these things without meaning them.

Distracted by these thoughts, he is chastened to find that for the last few seconds he's missed what she'd been saying – clearly noticed by her, as evidenced by a trailing-off of her words. Using as an excuse the buzz of conversation from others around them, he has to apologise, therefore, and ask her to repeat what she's just said.

'I was saying that David hadn't expected you to remember him, but that he recalled only too well the encouragement you'd given him during his first year at school.'

That comment really floors him. He can't begin to think what is being referred to. The shreds of his charm offensive vanish altogether as he is left open-mouthed and speechless, no doubt looking like a complete idiot. Even Athena Brown herself is beginning to look doubtful.

'I'm not confusing you with someone else, am I?' she says anxiously.

'No...no. It's only that I can't recollect having helped David particularly, in any way.'

And that sounds bad, as well – almost as if it was unlikely that he would have bothered to help him. He can see that he isn't making a good impression here. Goodness knows what she'll be reporting back to Munro.

'Well, perhaps you're just being too modest.' She doesn't sound convinced, almost disappointed in fact, and her manner has become distinctly diffident as she adds, 'Anyway, I must go and find David. I don't know where he can have got to. Nice to have met you.'

That's me dismissed, he thinks.

After she'd had a brief word with Sylvia Stanton and walked away, Sylvia turned to him and said, 'You're not too good at receiving praise, are you?' There is humour, kindness and sympathy in her voice, but also scrutiny. He can almost see the glint of professional interest in her eyes.

He doesn't reply; has to think about that somewhat novel suggestion.

After giving him a moment, she adds gently, 'Forgive me for saying so, but I somehow get the impression that it's because, much of the time, you are uncertain that you deserve it. Could I be right?'

How on earth can he be expected to answer something like that, he thinks, panicking. 'I hadn't really considered it,' he mumbles, managing at the same time to sound more than a little ungracious.

'Well, forgive me again, for speaking to you like a dowager aunt, but being humble and modest can be attractive to other people, you know, but it can become quite a handicap for oneself. It can...well, get in the way of one's sociability. There again, others can see it as false modesty. And that's not so attractive.'

She waits again for some response from him, and when it doesn't come – he standing there tongue-tied and flustered, like an awkward schoolboy – she adds firmly, 'You're a very likeable man, Peter, whether you realise it or not. You're clearly capable, approachable, and dependable. People always like that. From what I hear, you make a good doctor, as well, which is an achievement in itself and gives you standing in any gathering. Can I suggest that you accept those things, and don't hide your light under a bushel quite so much?'

Her words devastate him. He's never before met anyone so direct. In one respect he is grateful for what she's said, it having had the effect of making him feel better about himself; but at the same time it has brought home to him his recognisable inadequacies. He tries to think of something to say to make light of it, but before he can do so she lays a hand on his arm and says, 'I hope I haven't offended you? It's rather patronising of me, I know. But I felt it needed saying.' She laughs. 'It must be the frustrated mother in me.'

He manages to say, 'No, of course not. Thank you.'

But they lapse into silence, turning to watch all the activity in the room, a certain tension between them.

There is a definite restlessness in the room tonight, anyway, felt rather than seen. On the surface there is light-heartedness, gaiety even: last night's raid had been successful, not quite so much in terms of what they'd achieved, perhaps, but in the sense that all the aircraft had returned safely, with little damage, and what few casualties there were had been light – a couple of men with flesh wounds caused by shrapnel, and one case of relatively minor burns. But at the back of everyone's mind is still the thought that has to be hanging over them all: what will the next few days and weeks have in store? It isn't so much fear as uncertainty. A bit like facing a major surgical operation, perhaps: knowing that all control over one's immediate destiny has been taken away; oppressed by uncertainty as to what will be involved; having doubts about how one will stand up to the pain and distress of it all; and not knowing what the outcome will be. But, he thinks, in the situation in which they now find themselves there are two crumbs of comfort: as before an operation, there is knowing that there is no choice in the matter, it has to be gone through, the die is cast; and secondly, in this case one isn't on one's own – they are all, the whole nation, in it together. And it is astonishing how quickly people can move from a state of recoiling from the unthinkable to one of facing the inevitable.

Nevertheless, as he watches the room, now quite crowded, the cigarette and pipe smoke beginning to thicken, he thinks he can detect that particular underlying uncertainty in their faces and in their voices. There is a certain brittleness to it all. Perhaps the formality of the occasion, and the presence of women in the Mess, are serving as a reminder that they can't all the time go on pretending that it is just a serious kind of game. Reality is edging in. The white-coated stewards winding their way between knots of people, trays of drinks held aloft, are a reminder of normal times, but a reminder also that those times might soon cease to exist. Permanently.

He glances cautiously at Mrs Stanton. Is she thinking the same sort of thing? She, like Arthur, like his mother, aunt and uncle, and so many others, have experienced war before, directly or indirectly. But never the threat of invasion. What must they be thinking, now?

Aware that the silence between Sylvia Stanton and himself is beginning to hang heavily, he searches for something to say. He still isn't awfully good at casual conversation with people he doesn't really know; and (whenever he's reached the point where he suspects the other person would welcome someone else with more sparkling repartee) he is even less good at finding the means of politely moving away without having to resort to an obviously lame excuse.

But it is she who breaks the silence.

'It was thoughtful of you to invite Shevaun, this evening.'

He looks at her in surprise, then across to where O'Connor is standing at the far side of the room, three young Pilot Officers, new arrivals to the station, hanging onto her every word. With her mahogany-red hair, and in a somewhat startling emerald green, low-cut dress (no doubt thankful that, being a guest, she is excused from having to be in uniform), she certainly stands out, certain to draw any uncommitted chap into her sphere. Noticing Peter looking in her direction, from across the room she slips him a sly wink.

'You know Shevaun?' he says, the surprise still in his voice. He hadn't thought that Mrs Stanton would even know that O'Connor is his guest. He supposes that Arthur must have told her.

'Yes, indeed. Very well. Fellow Celts, and all that.'

Thinking back to the slyly derogatory remarks made about O'Connor by the padre and by David Munro when he'd first arrived at Marwell, he wonders if Sylvia Stanton is familiar with the notoriety O'Connor has on the station.

'She's a friend of yours?' he asks cautiously.

She gives him a cool look. 'If you mean – as I think you may – do I know about her reputation – yes I do. But tell me. You work with her, and I believe you were together at Dover for the Dunkirk evacuation. What is *your* assessment of her?'

He doesn't know how to answer that. Sexy and provocative? Certainly. But that would sound – would *be* – trite. Of easy virtue? He doesn't really know, not having any direct evidence to go on. Uncle John's words, from all those years ago, come back to him, as they quite often do. Perhaps that's what she is getting at. Prejudice.

'Direct,' he says carefully. 'Professional and proficient in her job. Not very tolerant – but caring. On the surface devil-may-care, but underneath uncertain, wanting to be liked.'

'Honest? Loyal?'

'Both of those, certainly.'

'Well done.' She lays an approving hand on his arm. 'We'll make a doctor of you yet.' It is said in kindly, ironic fashion, with a smile. 'Not many people who know her – who think they know her – understand her in that way. I'm not sure that Arthur does, entirely. I suspect he mildly disapproves of my friendship with her. But she's very misunderstood, is our Shevaun. And I'm glad, for her sake, that you at least realise that.'

He isn't entirely clear as to why she is glad about him specifically; and he's surprised himself in the way that he had summed up O'Connor just like that, because he hadn't consciously given it any thought. But he feels pleased.

'She tells me that you talked quite a lot, during those few days in Dover,' Sylvia Stanton says.

He looks at her suspiciously, but there is no archness in her expression.

'Yes, I suppose we did. When there was time.'

He visualises again of all those broken bodies and splintered minds, of the shattered limbs, infected wounds, the torn and bloodied salt-stained uniforms. And, above all, he remembers the hundreds upon hundreds of faces: faces which reflected pain and bafflement, fear and anger, fatigue, and distress at the loss of comrades – and those eyes in which lingered the apparent certainty of death unexpectedly lifted, but lurking still to haunt them. And he thinks again of Richard Wilson. He hasn't yet had opportunity to tell Beal or Munro about him.

'So she told you something of her background?'

It isn't really a question; it is merely a seeking of confirmation.

He nods. 'Yes. Some.'

'You'll understand, then, if I say to you that under all that brashness Shevaun is actually quite a frightened and lonely person?'

Is she? He finds it hard to believe. But it is possible, he supposes. He doesn't say anything.

'And that is why she spends much of her time searching for approval and affection?' She is choosing her words with care now, her eyes steady on him: 'Particularly from those whom she might consider to be in authority over her, professionally or socially?'

Good God, she's lost him. What on earth is she getting at? Surely she isn't implying, as she seems to be, that O'Connor might be seeing him as some sort of father figure, is she? For heaven's sake, he is several years younger than O'Connor. If anything, from his point of view it might well be the other way round: he has to admit he is still in some awe of Siobhan O'Connor.

'I'm not sure what you're getting at,' he says. 'I can't say I've noticed her doing much seeking of approval from anyone.'

'Well, what else do you think flirting is? And I'm sure you've seen her doing plenty of that.'

'Yes, certainly. Although I'm not sure I'd have called it flirting. It's a bit too challenging to be called that.'

'I think you'll find it amounts to the same thing. A girl flirts when she wants to draw attention to herself, to be admired and desired by a man whom she finds interesting. It may be because she's hoping to strike up a serious relationship with him, of course. But you must have noticed that some women do it to any fanciable man, as a sort of game. And if they're conscious of doing it, but at the same time vaguely resent having the urge to do so, as may well be the case with Shevaun, then it can carry with it a certain hostility. Now do you see what I'm getting at?'

'I think so,' he says slowly. 'You're saying that Shevaun's shows of antagonism, contrary to appearances are actually directed against herself?'

'And against the father who wasn't there for her, the husband who wasn't there for her, and possibly against herself for not being able to produce the children she would dearly have liked to have had.'

Privately he thinks that is a bit fanciful: it smacks of amateur psychology.

Politely, he says, 'That sounds a bit deep for me. You must have studied this sort of thing in the past.'

She laughs. 'No, merely been around for quite a few years, keeping my eyes open, and thinking about what I see.'

'So, were you...warning me, before, about Shevaun?' he says, hesitantly, still puzzled.

'Yes, I suppose I was. But not for your sake. For Shevaun's. You can look after yourself!'

It is his turn to laugh. 'And you think Shevaun can't?'

'I'm certain she can't.'

'But why should she be in any danger from me?'

'Because she's becoming infatuated with you.'

'Oh, come off it! Whatever gave you that idea? Apart from anything else, she's several years older than me.'

'What's that got to do with it? – and, incidentally, you won't do very well with the ladies if you start throwing their age back at them! I happen to know she admires you. You're a good-looking lad. And you're a doctor.'

'Now it's my turn to say what's that got to do with it.'

'And it's my turn to say come off it! You're not that naive, I'm sure. Half the stock heroes in penny romantic novels are doctors! Granted, Shevaun is not exactly an adolescent with her head stuffed with such romantic nonsense. But don't you see? In the professional sense at least, most patients tend to imbue their doctors with parental powers. If you're feeling unwell, and afraid of the outcome, it's a natural tendency to put your trust in the doctor – wisely or not, as the case may be! And what's that if it's not a child-parent relationship? Didn't they teach you any of that at medical school?'

'No they certainly did not. I'm not sure that any such thing had ever crossed their minds.'

'Well I hope I haven't frightened you to death! But think about it. And can you see now what I'm driving at?'

'I think I do,' he admits reluctantly. 'But what do you suggest I do?'

'Nothing. Be yourself. But just be aware of the possible complexities. Anyway, I'd better circulate, or the vicar's wife will be getting a reputation for being standoff-ish! – which is something you should be doing for the same reasons. I've enjoyed our chat; and I'm sure we'll be thrown together again before the evening's out. And remember, invite yourself for supper sometime!'

After she's moved away, he watches enviously as she calmly attaches herself to another small group of young men and women, starting up a discussion with them in the most natural way. It is another thing he's always found difficult to do, never quite knowing how to come up with an opening gambit that will serve to insert him into the existing circle of conversation; mostly he will simply stand awkwardly on the fringe, hoping that someone will be generous enough to turn and include him in the talk – and sometimes that does happen. It's his shyness again, of which he's only too well aware. All right on the whole with people he knows well; but awkward to a fault with relative strangers. He understands now that that is why he's always hated parties. He has made an effort to change, in recent years, but without much success. The trouble is – Mrs Stanton is right – it does make people regard him as standoff-ish, which in turn, he's decided, makes them less inclined to include him. By now he knows all the fellows in the Mess, and quite a lot about them. And they have accepted him – but never really include him, he is certain of that. Right enough, they rib him, along with each other; but from a distance as it were. If there is a sing-song with a pint or three around the piano, he will join in; but somehow he is always at the back, and his heart never quite in it. It is as if he is quite important to them, cheering from the sidelines as it were; but never regarded as a member of the team. He'd mentioned it to Arthur, on one occasion, who'd told him not to be silly, it didn't mean anything: that along with the C.O., the Padre and the Adjutant, the M.O. would always be set a little apart, as being a part of the 'establishment'. But it isn't the same thing. One can understand the C.O. being accorded the respect of his position, and to a certain extent the adjutant as well. However, Arthur, regardless of his being padre and in spite of the age gap, is treated like one of the boys – but then Arthur has his Wings.

At that moment a hand is clapped on his shoulder, and he turns to find David Munro who has a broad grin on his face. 'I saw you'd met our Sylvia, Peter,' he says. 'Quite a breath of fresh air, isn't she?'

'Certainly is. About Force seven, I would say.'

'Oh, very good! I like it. That's Sylvia all right. Comes hard and fast out of the west and just about blows you off your feet. Means well. But can be a bit too direct at times – and a bit too directive. Comes from being a schoolteacher, I suppose. I bet she was having a go at you about the awesome O'Connor, was she?'

Startled, Peter looks at him suspiciously. 'How did you know that?'

'Easy. Sylvia has a soft spot for O'Connor. Tries to mother her, look after her. Can't think why. Shevaun's as hard as nails. But you had a short chat to Athena, as well, I believe.'

He feels himself flush. 'Yes. She seems very nice. Congratulations. But I'd no idea you were contemplating marriage.'

Munro drops his bantering tone. 'I'm not sure that *contemplating* is the right term, really, under the present circumstances. It's more a matter of commitment. It's something I've intended to talk to you about. Do you think it's fair to get married when…when there's all this uncertainty about?'

Peter experiences a surge of alarm. Why on earth does David think he is capable of answering a question like that? 'What does Athena think?' he asks cautiously.

'Oh she would get married tomorrow if she had her way. But I don't know. I haven't said any of this to her, of course, but how can I guarantee her any sort of future, or security.'

Peter is silent. He thinks of the anxiety he feels whenever any of the crews are out on a raid, men he hardly really knows, and – let's be honest – barely cares anything about. What must it be like for wives? Then he looks at the worried, intent expression on David's face. He makes up his mind.

'Does Athena worry about you when you're on ops?'

'Yes I suppose she does – I hope she does! But we've never really talked about it. I know she tries not to show it. Sometimes, I'm sorry to say, I don't always tell her when I'm going on ops – thinking it's better for her not to know. I simply pretend that I'm just on standby. Then I feel a heel, think: What if I don't come back, someone has to go and tell her and I hadn't even bothered to let her know I was going, not given her the chance to *think* 'Goodbye', even if she wasn't going to say it.'

'And do you worry about her worrying about you?'

'Before we set off, yes – but most of us worry about all sorts of things at that stage. Then when we've actually taken off there's the job in hand, other things to think about, and all that vanishes, pushed aside. Of course there are plenty of times when we're scared shitless, but that's different! Only when it's all over, things have gone more or less smoothly, we're on our way home, the excitement is dying down, then I start to think 'That's another reprieve!' And I begin to worry again, that something might at the last minute go wrong, and I imagine Athena sitting there still wondering if I'm going to make it this time.'

He gives an embarrassed laugh. 'Of course, that's big headed of me. She's probably fast asleep in her bed all the time, without a care in the world.'

'Would it be any worse if you were married?'

Munro's brow creases for a moment, then clears. 'No, I don't suppose it would.'

They pause, lapse into silence, musing on the implications of that, the clatter of conversation in the room wafting over them.

'Tell me,' Peter says, 'what do you think is the likelihood of jerry invading in the next few weeks or months, assuming that France falls, as seems certain now?'

'I'd put all my money on it – at least, of them trying to. What else can Adolf do? He's no choice. He can't just sit there doing nothing.'

'That's what Bartholomew says. Says that Hitler would be too afraid of having to face two fronts at once, that sooner or later he'll have to deal with Stalin, and that he has to deal with us first. Which would also effectively remove any possible potential threat from America.'

'Browning? He's a dark horse. But surely Hitler's got a non-aggression pact with Russia?'

Yes, but – according to Browning – one or other is almost certain to break that sooner or later. And I must say Browning does seem to talk sense most of the time. As he says, a study of history helps you to foretell the future – or something along those lines. But the consensus seems to be that if there is going to be an invasion the RAF will bear the brunt of it in the preceding weeks?'

'Surely. The Germans have to obtain air superiority before they can move. If they lose it, we will be able to bomb their invasion forces with impunity before they even reach our shores. If they do have superiority, the reverse is true: they can bomb our defences into oblivion.'

'And what are the chances of them gaining that superiority?'

'God knows. Pretty good, I should say. They have superiority in numbers. And they're more experienced in modern air tactics, I suspect – they had plenty of practice in the Spanish War. Their only disadvantage is that their fighters, more especially the Me 109s, are at present rather short-range, even flying from France.'

'Meaning what?'

'Meaning that the bomber is of course a weapon of offence – and ground-offence only. The principal defensive weapon in the air is the Fighter. And we're very much on the defensive. They have to knock out Fighter Command over here before they can comprehensively obliterate us in Bomber Command, and be said to have gained real advantage; and their most formidable weapon for doing so is the 109, as we have discovered to our cost over France and Germany. It's the only fighter they have at present that is a match, and more, for both the Hurricane and the Spitfire. Contrary to what was generally thought before the war, bombers are useless for daylight raiding if the enemy has a considerable fighter presence over the target area – that's another lesson we've had to learn the hard way! Bombers on their own, are not really able to protect themselves from fighters like the Messerschmitts (and I mean both their 109s and their 110s) – or, in their own case, from Spits or Hurricanes. Both their bombers and ours ideally need to be protected from fighters by fighter escorts. But the 109, flying from central France, has only about ten or twelve minutes' combat time at the most, by the time it reaches, say, London. That could be to our advantage. But it all depends on numbers of aircraft. And numbers of pilots – as well as their quality and experience. And I would say they're probably better off than us on all those counts.'

'So we really are up against it?'

'We really are.' Munro narrows his eyes. 'But what are you getting at?'

'I think you know what I'm getting at. God knows, life is one great big risk at the moment. I can't see that your being married or not is going to make any difference to the fears you may have – that surround us all. Athena's not going to worry any less about you because you're not married, nor you about her. For heaven's sake marry the girl and put her out of her misery!'

As soon as he's said it he begins to wonder if he has the right to give advice like that. He'd said it on impulse, from a gut-felt certainty, and has surprised himself. He finds Munro studying him thoughtfully, as if doubting the validity of what he's said. Then the other man breaks into a grin and punches him lightly on the shoulder.

'By Jove, you're right! Thanks, Peter. I knew I'd be able to count on you to say something sensible. By the way, I've been meaning to ask you, how's Taffy?'

'Taffy?'

'Williams. The mid-turret gunner from B for Bertie. The chap with the burns, from last night.'

'Oh, yes. Fine. They're not too serious. We'll keep him in for a day or two, though. It's just the risk of infection, and the need to change dressings frequently for the first seventy-two hours. Easier when we've got him in the sick bay. He's going to be off duty for a couple of weeks, anyway.'

'So, who's looking after the Sick Quarters tonight? I see O'Connor's here.'

'Oh, Browning – who else. He's quite capable; and he knows where we are.'

At that point, becoming aware that the jangle of noise in the room has abruptly subsided to a low hum, they both turn to see what has brought this about. Many people's faces are turned towards the door in the far corner, and following their gaze Peter sees Beal standing there, evidently having just arrived. But it isn't his presence alone, forceful as it is, that has stemmed the flow of talk and had heads craning in his direction. It is the two women accompanying him, standing a little behind him in the doorway, who have drawn their attention. And in the first glance Peter can see why. Both fairly tall, coming up to Beal's shoulder, one on each side of him, one as dark in her colouring as the other is fair, each in a simple dress, they positively radiate glamour and beauty. Either alone would have been sufficient to turn heads; together they are a knockout.

'Wow!' says Munro, at Peter's shoulder, 'Beal sure knows how to find them.'

Peter, for a few seconds can't find breath to answer. He feels as though he's been kicked in the stomach, his pulse races, and he breaks into a sweat. Angry with himself, he curses silently. He hasn't set eyes on Jordan for the best part of three years, and hadn't bargained for the effect she could still have on him. It is probably just the unexpectedness of it, he tells himself – but without conviction.

'I wonder if the other one is German,' Munro is saying.

'Why on earth should you think that?' Peter manages to reply, 'With such dark hair.'

It is Munro's turn to look mystified. 'The brunette? She's German. That's Jim Beal's wife, Anna. She's quite a well known actress, you know? But I meant the blonde. She looks German.'

'Oh, I see. No, she's not. I know. She's my cousin.'

Munro peers at him, obviously wondering if he is having his leg pulled. Once he's decided that Peter is serious, he is clearly impressed by this piece of news.

Meanwhile, Peter with difficulty tears his gaze away from Jordan, who hasn't yet seen him, and studies Beal's wife. Of course he should have realised that the second girl had to be Beal's wife.

'She's stunning,' he says, not really intending to voice his thoughts aloud.

'She certainly is. That was clever of you, having a cousin like that. You've kept her under your hat! But I need to watch it – here's me almost a married man!'

'No, I meant Beal's wife.'

'Oh, yes, her too. Unusual. You're quite right: one certainly wouldn't suspect her of being German, looking at her. Jewish of course. Her maiden name was Hannah Bloemburg. I happen to know because I was invited to the wedding when they got married last July. Beal and I were stationed together at Watton at the time. Apparently her stage name in Germany, though, was Anna fon Noyman – spelled v-o-n N-e-u-m-a-n-n. Clearly that wouldn't have suited very well here, so after she came over – in '38 I think it was – she evidently changed it to Anna Newman. I heard she was making quite a name for herself in films in Germany before she had to leave. Doing well, here, too, I understand. Getting her name in lights – in a manner of speaking, the blackout and all that! – in the West End,'

'I suppose she did well to get out of Germany when she did, anyway.'

'I'll say. I don't suppose she'd much choice, but I think she just managed it in time. Otherwise it would have been the concentration camps, I imagine. Quite bold of Beal, though, I must say, hitching up with her – she being both German and Jewish. At that stage, before the war, it could have harmed his career. Ironically, now it doesn't seem to matter so much: it tends to be seen as having rescued her from Nazi tyranny – although of course he did nothing of the sort. Mind you, you can understand him falling for her; and he was never one to shirk a challenge. He's been a good catch for her, too, of course: having it known that she has an R.A.F. Wing Commander tucking her under his wing must be something of a safeguard in her situation. She might not have been quite so well received otherwise.'

Peter is mildly surprised by the somewhat cynical tone of Munro's account; it is a side of the man's character he hasn't seen before. But his thoughts are really elsewhere. It had struck him, on their first meeting at Marwell, that Beal had taken a certain malicious delight in telling him he'd been seeing something of Jordan – arousing suspicions that the fellow was very much aware (no doubt from Jordan herself) that it would awaken pangs of jealousy in Peter. Well, the memory of that is having the same effect again now. But suppose Jordan and Anna, both actresses, had become friends before that? That might mean that Beal had only met up with Jordan through Anna; entirely coincidental, as it were. Beal's implying that he'd been having a relationship with Jordan could then have been merely pretence. Somehow that idea makes him feel better. He isn't going to fool himself. Try as he might to expunge the tendency, he has to admit he still has this thing for Jordan, even after all these years. But he knows it is purely physical. He can't think of her without still seeing her that first Christmas, exposed, up that ladder. The mere memory of it still has the power to arouse him, to make him want her. Yet, always, after every such occasion she had then set out to emasculate him – he now realises – with her taunts and contempt. He's never understood why; and for that reason he'd gone on trying to persuade himself that he disliked her as much as ever.

He'd have to go over and speak to her, nevertheless. Not only was it unavoidable: he faces the fact that from the moment of surprise at first seeing her a few minutes ago the urge to do so has been growing uncontrollably. Annoyed with himself, it is with something akin to hate that he glares again in her direction – and finds her staring across the room at him with equal intensity. In the most natural of movements she lifts one hand in a small gesture of recognition and, after a brief word with Beal and his wife, she begins to move in his direction. He watches as she makes her way towards him across the crowded room, her progress made easy by people instinctively moving out of her path as if she were some celebrity. In the past she would have walked proudly, in an almost preening manner, all-too-conscious of heads turning her way; this time there is no evidence of any such self-awareness, her movements merely graceful, her carriage modest. Is this simply the result of her drama training, or is it possible that with maturity she has changed – in this and in other ways?

Out of the corner of his eye he sees Beal and Anna watching her progress, small smiles of amused admiration on both their faces. And then she is at his side – and it he who is self-conscious, aware of everyone looking at them, as she leans up to kiss him at the corner of his mouth.

'You look gorgeous in uniform,' she murmurs in his ear. Then, standing away to appraise him, she says out loud, 'Hullo, Peter. You look well.'

Flustered, not knowing whether to feel flattered or irritated, he mumbles something in reply before introducing David Munro to her – who has the grace to look equally flustered as she bestows on him one of her sweetest (and, no doubt, much practised) smiles. However, after no more than half a minute of polite chit-chat with Munro she makes her apologies to him, takes Peter's arm and says, 'Come on, darling, I want you to meet my friend Anna.'

As he allows himself to be led away, irritated that she's commandeered him in such easy manner as well as being more than a little rude to David Munro, he is also bemused by her use of the endearment to him. He is certain that the nearest she'd ever got to such intimacy with him in the past had been to address him by name. However, as he is telling himself not to be foolish, that it doesn't mean anything, that actors and actresses called each other 'darling' all the time, she clutches his arm and, a note of pleading in her voice, quietly urges, 'Peter, I must talk to you in private sometime this evening. Please.'

At this point, a few more steps having taken them to Beal and his wife, both of whom have by now moved further into the room, he has no time to dissect what she has just said. Such is his confusion (tinged with alarm), though, that he doesn't pay proper attention to the introductions until Anna Beal, taking his proffered hand and peering mischievously at her husband, says, 'Oh, I say, darling, can he be my doctor as well?'

'No he bloody well can't,' Beal replies with mock sourness. 'You'd have to join the WAAFs for that to happen, and be stationed here. I can't think of anything worse.' He grins at Jordan, and then at Peter – but this time with a suggestion of a sardonic glint in his eye.

His wife, still holding onto Peter's hand, turns then to Jordan. 'Don't ever get married, darling. Husbands are such spoilsports. You ought to just continue to have handsome doctors as cousins: I'd find all sorts of interesting new illnesses to have if I were in your shoes.'

Peter, conscious now of Beal's mocking gaze fixed upon him, finds himself almost babbling in his desperation to find something to say to take the attention away from himself. 'How did you girls get to know each other, then?'

He knew it was trite, but couldn't help but blurt it out. Jordan, looking at him with something like the old amused contempt, leaves Anna to answer the question.

'The theatre – you know? We were in the same show together. About eighteen months ago. Only little parts.' She laughs – a low and musical sound – not at him but at herself. Her voice, which anyway is unusually deep for a woman, has an attractive huskiness to it, and holds only a hint of accent to betray her otherwise perfect English. Her speech in fact reminds him of Hans: her words are clipped in the same way – but whereas with Hans they would come out in rather staccato fashion, in Anna one word runs rhythmically into the next with only the slightest hesitation between, almost as if she is testing each one, then savouring it before moving on. Her appearance, close to, is also unusual, and slightly disconcerting. Her eyes are a chocolate brown, the irises so dark that they seem almost to merge with the pupils, giving her a wide-eyed look as though from perpetual astonishment or as though she might have instilled belladonna. They are swept by long, black lashes and bridged by eyebrows which are thick but finely shaped and arched. Above, a broad brow leads down to a nose which, though reasonable small and delicately moulded, is somewhat prominent. With high cheekbones, a full-lipped mouth, and her face framed by a curling mass of lustrous, raven-black hair that looks as if it would resist all attempts to fully tame it, the overall effect is dramatically bohemian and startlingly beautiful.

'Perhaps you should let go of him now, Anna *mein lieber*, this handsome doctor of yours?' Beal interjects, his words bantering in tone but with an edge of impatience to them. Peter, so absorbed in his study of her, realises with surprise that she is indeed still lightly holding his hand, which she now releases – as Jordan, too, teases her: 'Yes, Anna, let him go; I found him first, remember.'

All three are smiling at this, but all three are looking in his direction, and Peter has the uncomfortable feeling that it is he, and not Anna, who is the butt of the joke.

'Anyway, I must continue to circulate,' Beal says, lifting a quizzical eyebrow at Peter – who understands what that means: he, too, should be doing the same. He's already noticed Arthur Stanton and Henry Matthews, the Adjutant, discretely doing just that. Padre, adjutant, medical officer, and commanding officer are all in the same boat when it came to a social occasion such as this, with many guests present: it is expected of them that, representing the Establishment, they will politely carry out the social niceties.

'You'll join me in a minute or two, won't you, Anna?' Beal adds, as he moves away.

'Of course, darling. In a few minutes.' Behind his retreating back she makes a little face, as if to say, what a bore! But it gives the appearance of being all pretence.

'So why haven't you been to see me in London, Peter?' Jordan says, giving one of her carefully pretty pouts (that, at least, hasn't changed). 'Jim tells us you arrived here at Marwell at the same time as him. I'd no idea you were so near – no one bothered to tell me.'

'I don't suppose they thought you'd be interested,' he replies on impulse – provoking her into giving him an unusually thoughtful look. 'Anyway, I didn't know how to get in touch with you.'

They both know how lame a reason that is. Their eyes meeting, they seem to be for the first time reappraising one another.

'So where are you living in London?' he continues, a shade hurriedly.

'I have a flat in Harley Street. It's...' She laughs. 'Of course, you'll know where that is – I forget. Anyway, it belongs to an old college chum of Daddy's. It's above his consulting rooms. Anna and I share it – during the week, that is, when Anna's up in town.'

'Jim and I have rented a cottage a few miles from here,' Anna explains. 'So I come down here whenever I can. I'm in work at present – which is lucky in one sense, but not in another – so it's mainly just Sundays, now.'

'Oh? What are you in?'

'Anna has a leading role in *Private Lives*, at the Adelphi,' Jordan says, as if she presumes he might have known that. Peter would have expected her to display a certain jealousy at Anna's evident success – but there is only pride and excitement in her voice. He is only now beginning to realise just how much Jordan has changed; then the old suspicions surface, making him wonder whether it is, after all, merely consummate acting.

'What about you?' he asks.

'Me? I have a very small part in an Ivor Novello musical. *The Dancing Years*, at the Palace Theatre. It's not much, but better than nothing.'

'Oh Jordan, how can you say that!' her friend expostulates. 'Don't take any notice of her, Peter. It's quite an important part, and a very successful show. She's done very well to get it. You must try to come and see her in it, if you get half a chance – and, if you're inclined to, come and see *Private Lives*. If you let me know when, I can send you some tickets.'

'What sort of houses are you getting, in general, with everything that's going on?'

He's addressed the question to both of them, but it is Anna who, after a pause, answers. Jordan has become oddly subdued.

'Not too bad, considering the absence of foreign visitors in town. I think Londoners are so desperate to escape from their worries at present, to find something to take their minds off things, that they're flocking to the theatres, and the cinemas, in droves. But I suppose we must expect that soon there will be some curtailment of how many performances we can put in during the week.'

'But you've enjoyed being in London?' he asks, directing the question at Jordan.

To his surprise, for a moment she looks quite frightened: he might have been asking some dreadfully personal question such as 'Are you pregnant?' or 'Is it true you're also working as a prostitute?' She quickly recovers, however – leaving him puzzled as to what raw nerve he's hit. Is this perhaps connected with the thing she 'must' speak to him about?

'I was,' she says, 'but it's got a bit wearisome now. There are no street lights or shop lights, of course. After dark, it can be quite frightening, and actually dangerous with cars and buses unable to use proper headlights. Shop windows are so taped over, in many cases, that you can't really see into them; and there seem to be sandbags everywhere – you can hardly get into some doorways because of them. Now they're digging up the parks – trenches or something – and siting big guns all over the place, with barrage balloons and all sorts of other great metal things. You can't get a decent meal anywhere, any longer. They're even talking about taking down all the street names. It's all quite horrible!'

Her voice, initially low, has been rising all this time, the words beginning to almost run away with her. He looks at her in astonishment. He's never seen her like this before. She's always been so in control of herself. He glances at Anna, who has put a hand on Jordan's arm, her face betraying both concern and a certain impatience; catching the movement of Peter's head she surreptitiously makes a face at him in a gesture he finds hard to interpret.

'Well, I'd much rather be in London than in Berlin,' she says lightly, 'At least in London we are free.'

This, rather than placating Jordan, seems to make matters worse, for she begins to tremble a little, as though suddenly cold.

'You lived in Berlin?' he asks Anna, mainly in an attempt to divert the conversation – or perhaps to duck out of having to deal with a situation he doesn't understand in a Jordan he no longer recognises.

'I come from Berlin,' Anna replies, evidently equally glad of the diversionary tactic. 'Do you know it at all?'

'I was there for a week, in the summer of '36, staying with a college friend.'

'Really? For the Games, was that?'

'Yes.'

'And did you enjoy it, in Berlin?'

'Ye..es,' he answers carefully. 'It was…different.'

She laughs, a shred of bitterness attached to it. 'I bet it was. That's one way of putting it. I was still there, in Berlin, in '36. It was certainly 'different' for me, for my family, at that time. We must talk about it sometime. But I must go now. I am receiving black looks from my husband. He will be having me cashiered, or whatever it is you call it. Delighted to have met you; perhaps we might have time to talk again before Jordan and I leave? Anyway, you must come and see Jordan and me in London, remember.'

He watches her for a few seconds as she walks away to join Beal across the increasingly crowded room. Fine legs, but a heavier figure than Jordan: less svelte, but more sensual, hips and breasts almost voluptuous. One could suspect she has gipsy blood in her.

'So, have you committed her to memory now?' It is teasingly said, Jordan clearly having recovered her usual spirits; but she still has that ability to make him feel guilty and gauche at every turn.

His hostility must have shown as he turned, for she catches her breath and takes an involuntary step back, her eyes nervous for a second. It is another novel experience for him, the momentary sense of power intense. Moreover, although she appears to quickly regain her customary poise, her tone is conciliatory as she says lightly, 'Well, are you going to show me your quarters, if that's the right term for where you sleep?'

Of course: he remembers she has this pressing need to talk to him about something. He has a nasty feeling that it is going to be something medical. Why else would she be so fawning all of a sudden. Good Lord, he hopes it isn't going to be a request for him to carry out an abortion. What else could she be so keen to ask his advice about?

Seeming to misinterpret his hesitation, she playfully follows up with: 'Or are you afraid you might be compromised if you invite me to your room?' She laughs. 'I would have thought, on the contrary, it would no end improve your reputation in the Mess. But perhaps it's against regulations?'

He looks at the sea of chattering faces around the room, and imagines that he can see in them a bogus gaiety beneath which skulks a more realistic apprehension. It has elements of a wake: the determination to embrace life in defiance of promptings of death. He decides that her renewed brightness is equally brittle.

Without a word he takes her arm and guides her towards the door; meekly she allows him to do so. This subtle change in their relationship is taking him by surprise, however. And as they cross the room he is very aware that a number of faces are turned in their direction, including that of O'Connor, her eyebrows raised in mocking query. When, the corridor deserted, they reach his room without being seen, a further sense of the clandestine is added, bringing with it a whiff of eroticism.

The door having closed safely behind them, she stands and briefly takes stock. 'It's a bit spartan,' she pronounces, sounding almost disappointed.

'I'm used to that,' he says airily, 'from school and college. Anyway, what else did you expect?'

'There's no need to sound cross. I was only commenting.' Then, noting the additional furniture, she adds, 'So who else shares it with you? Some good-looking young pilot?'

'No. The padre – who's in his mid-forties. Not your type.'

'You don't know what my type is. For all you know I may prefer older men.'

'Quite,' he says, flatness in his voice, an image of her with Hamilton, all those years ago, rearing up before him, arousing him.

There is suspicion in the quick glance she gives him; but after a moment she then sits down on the bed, bouncing experimentally – negligently showing a generous expanse of silk-clad leg in the process. 'Ugh,' she says, 'it's jolly hard!' – and sprawls back onto it, arms flung above her head, china-blue eyes looking up at him from under drooping lids.

His pulse quickens, his mouth suddenly dry. Lying on her back like that, her thighs arched over the side of the bed, her body beneath the thin dress is thrown into relief and seems to be thrusting invitingly up towards him. Still not able to trust his own judgement in such matters, nevertheless he is beginning to believe that her 'need to talk' to him 'in private' has perhaps been merely a ploy to get him alone. A surge of lust is watered down by tricklings of suspicion and alarm, however: he's seen her in these seductive moods in the past; and, anyway, he's no idea how to handle the situation.

'I've been seeing an old friend of yours recently,' she says, her voice husky.

His interest quickens at that. 'Jamie?'

She sits up then, propping herself on her elbows and staring at him in annoyance as if he's somehow spoiled the effect she's been trying to create. 'Jamie? Good lord, no. Why Jamie? I haven't seen her for years. No, I mean Bill.'

'Bill?'

'Bill,' she says irritably. 'Remember? Bill Jackson.'

The atmosphere has suddenly changed. Old anxieties and feelings of intimidation stemming from his early relationship with Bill sweep over him, and are accompanied now by an unexpected rage of envy. Bill had always had a thing for Jordan; perhaps, now, it is reciprocated.

'Oh. *Bill*,' he says, trying to keep his voice casual. 'Where did you bump into him?'

'At the *Savoy*. He's stationed near London – and not far south of you here. At Church Wealdon. He's in the R.A.F. too. A fighter pilot, no less. Very dashing.'

He is hard put to suppress a groan. That was all he needed to hear. It seems he is to be oppressed on all sides by gladiators, emphasising his own effeteness and impotence in this war.

'I thought he went into law?' he says carefully.

'Yes, he did. But he learned to fly at university, apparently. And then was in something called the Volunteer Reserve. So he got called up. Well, actually he didn't, come to think of it. I remember him telling me he volunteered – when he'd decided there was almost certainly going to be a war. Wanted to be in right at the beginning, he said. Typical of him. Clever of him, too, to know there was going to be war, when the rest of us thought there wouldn't.'

Oh yes, that's good old Bill, he thinks sourly – always cocksure and so often right!

But, abruptly, her expression of enthusiasm has slipped away. Her eyes close and her shoulders slump. Without warning, tears began to roll down her cheeks.

Alarmed, he goes over and sits down next to her. 'Are you alright?'

'That's what I want to talk to you about,' she says pathetically.

Is that it, has Bill got her pregnant? he thinks angrily. He takes hold of her hand. 'Come on, then – let's be having it.'

'I'm afraid, Peter,' she sniffles.

He's never seen her like this before, either, looking vulnerable. His heart goes out to her. 'There's always a way round things, you know.'

She looks at him blankly. 'What do you mean?'

What did he mean? It was a daft thing to have said; a platitude. There is no way round this bloody war, for a start.

'I mean things are not always as bad as they seem.'

He squirms inwardly. That was equally trite. Pull yourself together he tells himself; he's never been able to think straight when he is with her. Anyway, he's having to feel his way carefully through this conversation, still not sure where it's leading. 'It's a matter of making decisions,' he continues, with some desperation, 'simple as that. Have you talked to…to him, about it?'

'Daddy? Not really talked. I wrote to him about it, but he wasn't a great deal of help in his reply. Made one or two suggestions, but said only I could decide. He was a bit matter-of-fact, really, although reading between the lines I think he was rather disgusted with me. That's why I've turned to you. Mummy's no good with something like this – and I couldn't think of anyone else.'

He is reeling now. It is as if they are talking at odds. He has a nasty suspicion that perhaps they are; but doesn't feel that he can go back to the beginning and enquire what she is talking about.

'If you don't stop to think about it, what's your first instinct? – to…to carry on with…with it?' he asks uncertainly.

'Oh, definitely. It's just that I'm so scared all the time. But if I don't carry on now I might never get the opportunity again, might I?'

He thinks that is as unlikely a premise as he's ever heard, but thinks it best not to say so. Instead he makes an effort to get onto firmer ground. 'What is it exactly that you're afraid of?'

'Not so much death – although obviously I'm not keen to die just yet.' She gives a shaky laugh. 'But to be mutilated would be dreadful. I couldn't bear that.'

This is getting out of hand. What on earth is she thinking?

'That's ridiculous,' he says sternly, 'there's little or no risk of anything like that happening these days.'

It's her turn to look at him oddly. 'What are you saying? That you don't think they'll come?'

'Who?' he replies, now thoroughly perplexed.

'Who? The Germans of course. Who else!' She gets to her feet. 'You know, you can be very strange at times, Peter. What do you think we've been talking about?'

Flustered, he is catching up rapidly now. He takes a short cut. 'So, you can't make up your mind whether to stay in London and carry on with your…your career, is that it? Is that all?'

'What do you mean, 'is that all',' she retorts. 'It's not an easy decision.'

'All right, so what do you think would happen if everyone decided to bail out and go home?'

'That's more or less what Daddy said. He told me that fears should always be faced, that they're always worse in imagination than in reality.'

He grins. 'I remember him saying much the same to me, once, years ago. I'm sure he's right. Anyway, we don't know that London will even be bombed at all. Certainly *we*'ve been going out of our way to avoid civilian targets, so far, and I should think the Germans will do the same. They'll probably stick to military targets...' He gives a mirthless laugh, '...like airfields.'

Privately – remembering Warsaw, and Guernica before it – he isn't so sure.

'And what about the invasion? What then?'

'Well, if they succeed, and get as far as London, the whole country's lost. It won't matter where you are. We're all in it together. And that, perhaps, would be the time to go home.'

Appearing altogether brighter now, she looks at her watch. 'Heavens, I must go! Anna and I have to catch the quarter to nine train back to town; it's the only one, and Jim has to stay here.'

She pecks him on the cheek. 'Thanks a lot, Peter. You've helped a lot. You've been a brick. There's my phone number. Don't forget to come up to town to see me.'

He nods his acquiescence. As flighty as always, she is giving the impression that she is going to be in London for a bit longer anyway. But he's no idea whether she's actually come to a decision. It's as if she's simply put it out of her mind. They might never have had the conversation they'd just had.

And, afterwards, he sourly concludes: That's me – not a gladiator but a brick.

CHAPTER SIXTEEN

He finds it difficult to sleep that night. He feels weary, but his brain won't let go. Too many memories have been awakened, too many emotions aroused. Although he is usually grateful when he has the room to himself, this evening he finds himself wishing that it had been one of the days that Stanton slept in the Mess: he would have welcomed having him to talk to.

Try as he might, he can't stop thinking. As soon as he manages to push one image aside another will shoulder its way in. Now and again he drifts into some sort of sleep, but that doesn't help: the images are still there, but instead of remaining clear they become intermingled and confused, become more disturbing.

At one point he must have drifted into deeper sleep, seemingly erotic, for he awakens suddenly, with an erection and vague images of 'Plummy' of all people, the Matron on Founders. Then he remembers, and lies there thinking about it as he has on a number of occasions over the years – although not for some considerable time now. But it's no less disturbing for all that.

It was the summer of his third year at Bardolphs, when he was not yet sixteen. The inter-house athletics. He was one of the runners representing his house in the 100 and 200 yards, in which he hadn't exactly covered either himself, or his house, in glory. He'd also been entered for the long-jump; and, stung for once by the gibes of his fellows and by the expression of disgust on the face of his Housemaster (who had gone out of his way to give him a kindly and well-meaning pep-talk before the competition began), this time he'd put every effort into it. With one jump to go, he was lying second. It was with gritted teeth and as much determination as he could muster, therefore, that he accelerated down the track, hit the board perfectly at speed and thrust himself forwards and upwards – and was immediately struck by a searing pain in the front of his right thigh. He hit the sand feet first and crumpled in agony. It felt as though a sword had struck him down.

The doctor diagnosed torn fibres in his femoral muscle, '...not too bad, but he must have complete bed-rest for four or five days'. He thus found himself the sole occupant (it being summer) in the small four-bedded sick-bay which was part of Matron's suite of rooms upstairs.

Miss Plumley, a compact woman in her forties, had been Matron for 10 years and therefore well-versed in the ways of boys between 13 and 18 who, almost totally deprived of female company for the duration of each term (the female domestic staff having been chosen specifically, it was rumoured, for their lack of feminine allure) tended to fawn on her modest attractions. With her trim figure, nice legs, and pleasant face, and more importantly her undoubted, if somewhat maternal, femininity, it had to be said that she provided a not-unreasonable role-model on which they could focus their adolescent yearnings. A very few of the more unscrupulous types on the house had been known to boast of conquests in that direction, varying in description from the minor to the florid; most of their listeners, having worked through an initial response driven by wishful thinking, sensibly dismissed these accounts as mere fantasy. But she did therefore carry, to the boys around her, an aura of desirability that would be totally unjustified in the outside world, and at intervals showed signs of being intuitively aware of it. Out of earshot she was known by all (including, it is suspected, by both Housemasters) as 'Plummy' – a soubriquet that carried connotations not only of her physical attributes but also of the affection with which she was regarded.

To Peter, however, confined in solitude, and bored to tears – visits by friends being strictly limited (a rule set indiscriminately, for fear of epidemics) – she was simply all kindness and concern, successfully combining an I-stand-no-nonsense approach with a motherliness that contained just a hint of playfulness. The prescribed bed-rest was rigidly adhered to, to the point where to his considerable embarrassment he had to ask to go to the lavatory, whereupon she took him there in a wheelchair even though it was only a mere ten or fifteen yards.

What soon becomes a much greater ordeal for him, though, is the massaging of the injured area with the oil of wintergreen that the doctor has prescribed. At first it is altogether pleasant. Although initially disconcerted when, on the first occasion, she stands there patiently for a moment, bottle in hand, and a half smile on her lips before saying teasingly, 'Come on then, let's have those pyjama trousers off, I can't do it through those!', he soon forgets his awkwardness, for while her hands are gentle and soothing they are at the same time impersonal. She chats to him throughout, in desultory fashion, about this and that, in a way that requires no great deal of input from him, so that he is free to enjoy the sensation which is a novel one and which (apart from the occasions when she presses a bit too hard, causing pain – for which she always immediately apologises) is comforting. But the embrocation is carried out four times a day, takes several minutes, and seems to take longer each time.

And he gradually becomes aware of other things. He begins to find that whenever she elicits tenderness sufficient to make him wince, and turns her face to him with a sympathetic smile and a husky, 'Sorry, did that hurt?', he experiences a brief surge of excitement. She sits sideways on the edge of the bed to carry out the treatment, sometimes with her back to him, and sometimes facing him. Since, most of the time, she is not looking at his face, he is able to study her, dwell on the many subtleties of her body as she applies the liniment. She routinely wears a white cotton nurse's tunic that buttons all the way down the front. The light material is close fitting and reveals all the nuances of her movements: the way her back flexes and stretches, rotating first one way and then the other; the quiver and bounce of her breasts as her arms move past them in the repetitive bending and straightening necessary for the massage; the rhythmic tautening of the muscles of her legs and hips counter-balancing the action of her upper body. She must be aware of his study of her, he knows, but does nothing to acknowledge it. The effort of her movements and the awkwardness of her posture on the bed require her to adjust her position at intervals, and this in turn results in a tendency for the hem of her tunic to ride up above her knees. Every now and again she will pause and get up slightly to pull it back down. But as time goes on she is less concerned to do this, and more and more on these occasions he is treated to a view of greater and greater lengths of thigh, particularly when, it seems, she has allowed the bottom button or two at the front of her tunic to remain undone. He begins to ask himself whether her progressive lack of care in all this could possibly be deliberate in order to provide the entertainment for him that it undoubtedly does, but is forced to dismiss the idea as being too preposterous.

In between sessions, though, at intervals he allows his imagination full rein – but this brings a problem, for he finds that his fantasies begin to carry over into the next session. At first, all too conscious of how exposed any subsequent arousal on his part would be, he manages, more or less, to contain these thoughts.

But then something else happens. As the sessions continue, and his leg becomes less tender, her massage becomes firmer, and goes on for longer – but more than that, it begins to take in a larger area, and as it does so it seems she becomes more silent, and he is left to absorb the sensations without distraction. Before long it has progressed to the point where her finger tips are brushing the soft skin on the inner part of his thigh near his groin. His response, immediate and priapic, can no longer be denied. Concealment is impossible, his pyjama jacket quite inadequate for the role. She must know what is happening, if alerted only by the sudden tension in his body and by the barely suppressed groan of panic that escapes his lips. But he doesn't know if she's looking, for he's lying there with teeth gritted and his eyes closed in mortification. He's aware that her breathing, normally increased by her exertions, becomes quicker and more obvious, but the massage continues in the same manner for several minutes in otherwise total silence, the stimulation unrelenting in its testing of his control.

Afterwards, on his own, and accustomed to inhabiting a world of make-believe, he repeatedly created for himself imaginary scenes in which the acts of Matron became more and more wanton; and with the passage of time, months passing into years, reality and fantasy had become so intermingled that he was no longer able to distinguish between them. He knew that the sessions continued in the same manner, with similar results, on several occasions, accompanied by increasingly generous displays of Miss Plumley's legs and by growing, wordless tension between them; but did she out of her generosity and with her reserves of feminine compassion, on that and subsequent occasions lean to relieve his physical and mental torment, or was that merely the product of his overheated imagination? All he had become really certain of, in the end, was that by the fifth day, when he was beginning to get up and walk around a little, she had arrived with the liniment and handed it to him with a carefully expressionless face, but a hint of amusement in her eyes and heightened colour in her cheeks, and said, 'Here, I think it might be better if you were to do this for yourself from now on.'

The memories are indelible – and accompanied by a hovering sense of guilt at the uncertainties that he has allowed to enter into those memories; but also a growing awareness that the episode has over the years contributed to his uncertainties with regard to the behaviour and attitudes of women in general, and what to expect of them.

He turns over and tries to shut his mind to all these ruminations, and to get some sleep. But try as he might, it won't come. A picture of Jordan would drift into view, achieve some substance, then gradually absorb features of others: Anna Beal, Sylvia Stanton or Athena Brown – even, on one occasion, those of Jamie, although he has difficulty, somehow, in getting her face into focus.

In the end he gets up and sits in the chair, smoking his pipe; better to be wide awake than in that twilight of sleep.

It had been a shock, seeing Jordan like that: unexpectedly. He feels as though he's been kept in the dark, cold-shouldered. He suspects that she had in fact been aware that he was stationed here, and that she would therefore be seeing him – but no one had thought to inform him of that in advance. But there again, why should they? It wouldn't have entered Beal's head to do so, even if there'd been opportunity. There'd been nothing deliberate about it: it was quite clear, now, that if there had ever been anything between Beal and Jordan it was long over. Thinking it might amuse her (with regard to the way in which things had oddly come full circle), he'd been tempted at one point to tell her about Beal's interest in her that very first time, when she'd come along on his first day at Bard's – but suddenly there'd seemed no point: too much had happened in between, and it was no longer relevant.

He is convinced there has been a subtle change in Jordan since he'd last seen her three years ago, although he can't quite put his finger on it. Mind you, she'd been even more of a prig, then, than she had all the years he'd known her – so beautiful in her maturity; knowing it, and revelling in it. That had been on the occasion of his trip to London, courtesy of Uncle John, as a 'present' not long after his graduation. He can still recollect the excitement of having the town to himself, to do as he pleased, almost as if it was there for his own exclusive use. He'd seen the city through new eyes.

Now, remembering, he can vividly capture again the sights and smells and sounds of that time, those sensations that had been so new compared to any that he'd bothered to take notice of in the days of his childhood there. The impressions that, suddenly it seemed, were so peculiarly London. Bowler hats and furled umbrellas; the elegance of women (and men) dressed up for their day in town; the busy streets, with cars, cabs and buses noisily manoeuvring to retain their little piece of space, whilst trams clattered and swayed unperturbed and inviolable along their own allotted tracks (and trolley buses, new to Peter, crept up silently on one with only an occasional sigh). Other sounds come to mind: the unmistakably-cockney voices of cabbies, bus conductors, barrow-boys and flower-sellers, enlivened by cheeky humour; the lunch-time chatter from a corner pub; the thin, tinkly strains of a barrel-organ insinuating themselves, fragmented, into the roar of traffic; and, now and again, the distant deep rumble of an Underground train. But it was the smell of London, in particular, that had gripped him; a *potpourri* of odours that he'd not been able to isolate or identify. Now, when he considers it, he comes to the conclusion that it must have been an amalgam of scents from cafés and *patisseries*, department stores, and shops selling leather goods; of the perfumes of passers-by; of the elusive fresh fragrance of parks and plane trees; of the altogether more functional smells of oil, rubber and exhaust fumes; and, most particularly, of that distinctly characteristic smell emanating from the depths of tube stations that everyone, mistakenly, referred to as 'ozone' but for which he's never seen any satisfactory explanation.

The other thing which had boosted his confidence on that occasion had been his initiative (with some prompting from his mother and Uncle John) in contacting both Jordan and Jamie, in advance, and arranging to take them out together for a meal one evening and then to a concert at the Albert Hall (in the gallery, which was all he could afford). Looking back on it, he can't understand why, at the time, it had seemed such a formidable undertaking; but he suspects that his diffidence had been because he'd always been junior to both of them, in age and in physical and emotional maturity, and that this had continued to reinforce the child in him. But on that occasion, perhaps for the first time in his life, the Child had been nowhere to be seen: he'd no longer been merely playing a role; the Adult, he decided, had fully taken over.

He'd stayed (again, through the generosity of Uncle John – he could never have afforded it himself) the three nights at the Imperial Hotel in Russell Square, a stately red-brick building in Victorian Gothic, the interior of which had an understated, slightly shabby elegance which suited him perfectly. Virtually all of the clientele were middle-aged or older, which (he'd convinced himself) served as a perfect counter-point to his own youth and vigour. But, for this particular evening, he'd arranged to meet the girls outside the Coventry Street Corner House, at 5.15. Jamie finished work at 5 o'clock, and thought she could steal a minute or two and, with luck, get there from the City by that time. Jordan was at present 'resting' in theatrical terms, which was something she seemed to be doing a lot of in those days, but (she'd said) although her agent had arranged 'a couple of auditions' for her earlier in the day, she too should be able to make it by then.

So, with the afternoon to himself, he'd had plenty of time to bath (all the bathrooms down the corridor being free at such a relatively early hour), shave (followed by a splash of cologne, which he'd bought specially for the occasion), don his best suit and his graduate tie, put on his shoes (which he'd arranged with the hall porter to have well-polished for him) and stroll self-importantly past the Museum into Bedford Square, then via Charing Cross Road to Leicester Square and the rendezvous, taking in all the sights and sounds as he went, and fondly imagining that all eyes were upon him in his distinguished progress. He cringes now when he thinks about it.

Jamie had been the first to arrive, prompt and breathless. It was, by now, several years since he'd seen her, and he hadn't quite known what to expect. Whenever he'd thought of her, at quite frequent intervals over the years, the image that came to mind had always been that of her in her teens, energetic and strong. He would relive their outings together on the lake and on the fells; that special time that scorching day of harvest-making; and those hot, lazy days by the sea at Silloth. And he could still clearly picture her that very first time, a 'boy' with muddy legs and plimsolls, up a tree. Strangely, too, his visions of her had often been coupled with the remembrance of perfumes: of fresh air and salt sea, of gorse and bracken, and of something sweeter and more subtle. He associated her with excitement of a pleasant kind, with happiness and contentment. But her features had, somehow, become indistinct – more a product of his imagination than of his memory.

So, when she'd arrived, he'd been a little surprised to instantly know her. Nothing had changed. The years might never have intervened. There had been the same calm, controlled energy, the same unadorned happy face highlighted by those lively hazel eyes and framed by that unruly chestnut hair. She'd still radiated enthusiasm, interest and kindness. But, attired in a plain, light green summer dress, she'd been no longer a girl. She'd still had that athletic-looking body, reaffirmed by the precision and economy of her movements, but by now had the fuller curves of a woman. He can't think, now, why he was so taken aback by that – after all, he quickly works out, she must by then have been 24.

It had taken her an instant longer to recognise him; and once she'd done so, and hurried forward, there'd been a moment's hesitation between them, neither knowing whether to shake hands or what. She'd solved it with characteristic spontaneity, reaching up to hug him and kiss him lingeringly on the cheek.

'My, how you've grown!' she'd said, laughing, and just a little flustered. 'I hardly recognised you.'

241

As the minutes had ticked by without the appearance of Jordan, they at least had had the opportunity to catch up with one another. He'd learned that she was still working for a City bank, translating German and French for them, with occasional trips across to the Continent to act as interpreter. He'd talked enthusiastically about his still-novel experiences on the wards, lightening it with humour and, to his delight, making her laugh. And while they'd talked he'd been able to study her. He'd forgotten (or perhaps had never quite realised) just how attractive her features were, in a quiet sort of a way: she had good bone structure, a delicate retroussé nose, nicely shaped lips which turned up at the corners as if she was always on the point of breaking into a smile (which, indeed, she was) – and of course those wonderful dancing eyes framed by long lashes and well-defined eyebrows. He still remembers how, at that moment, he'd felt that he could never tire of looking at her.

He'd noticed out of the corner of his eye that she, too, kept taking long looks at him (whenever she thought his attention was elsewhere), as if seeing him for the first time; and that she was constantly, almost absentmindedly, touching him – resting her hand briefly on his arm, picking a piece of fluff from his lapels, or brushing an imaginary hair from his shoulder. It had been most unlike her – a nervous kind of gesture – and he'd been certain that she was not fully aware that she was doing it.

But as the time had got to 5.30, and still no Jordan, he'd begun to fret, worrying that his carefully-laid plans (for a meal, with sufficient time to get to the Royal Albert Hall for the start of the performance at 7.30) were about to go adrift.

Jamie, noticing his growing agitation, had done her best to placate him. 'You worry too much, Peter,' she'd said. 'It's not important. It's just nice being together again. And if Jordan doesn't turn up, then I can have you all to myself!'

And Jordan had finally turned up, a good twenty minutes late, with the lightest of apologies made in a condescending manner as though bestowing an award upon them. And he'd forgotten until then just how gorgeous Jordan was; and had managed only to simper foolishly. And, after the briefest of polite greetings to Jamie, she'd been all over him for the rest of the evening – not physically (always in fact keeping a small distance between them) – but in terms of giving him all her attention.

Still anxious about his schedule, he'd hurried them in for their meal. It was his mother who had suggested one of the Corner Houses as being within his budget ('Their reputation is for "elegant dining for the middle classes" ') – and the Coventry Street one, at least, had lived up to that reputation. Entering from the street, he'd been immediately enthralled by the *delicatessen* which occupied a large part of the ground floor: counter after glass-fronted counter had had white ceramic dishes containing the most wonderful selection of savouries, cold meats, salads, sweets and cakes – of every conceivable variety – seducing the senses with their cocktail of aromas; and, although he'd been back on two or three occasions since, the recollection of that first impact could still, now, bring a rush of saliva to his mouth. The interior of the building had also impressed him on that first visit: everywhere there had been gleaming marble, on walls, ceilings and staircases, with shining rails and fittings of chrome and polished brass – it might almost have been the Dorchester or the Ritz they were entering.

Inside, with a slightly bewildering number of restaurants to choose from, he'd elected to go for the *brasserie*, which had turned out to be a good choice, the room bright with red check tablecloths. The food had been excellent, yet relatively inexpensive, with fast, friendly service from smartly uniformed waitresses; and throughout the meal there had been pleasant background music from a string trio formally attired in evening dress. In all, the ambience had more than justified the description of 'elegant' – and had left him with a satisfyingly warm view of his own apparent largesse. Slightly intoxicated therefore by this self-induced sense of bonhomie he had allowed Jordan to dominate his attention for most of the meal as well as afterwards on the crowded, clattering and swaying tube train to South Kensington (from where they'd walked up to the Albert Hall), and then throughout the concert. He'd failed to notice – or had chosen to ignore the fact – that Jamie had become progressively sidelined for the whole of that time. And it was only some time afterwards, and subsequently whenever he'd brought it to mind, that he'd really become aware that she'd gradually become silent as the evening wore on, withdrawing not only from the conversation but into herself. When, at the end of the evening, as they'd gone their separate ways and said their farewells, and Jordan had said brightly and carelessly, 'There's my phone number – give me a ring sometime', Jamie in her turn had slipped a piece of paper into his hand and said quietly, 'That's my address, Peter; write to me from time to time and let me know where you are, and what you're doing, won't you?'

And, to his lasting regret and shame, he never had – excusing himself, whenever he'd allowed the remorse to surface, that he'd never been good at writing letters, anyway.

But as he sits, now, in the darkness of his room contemplating Jordan's fickleness, he's once more reminded that Jamie had been the best friend he'd ever had, and he'd let her down – just as he'd let Chaplin down, that time at school. He wonders where she is, and what she's doing. '*Jamie?*' Jordan had said with scorn, '*I haven't seen her for ages!*

He sighs. He thinks about what Sylvia Stanton had said about relationships, earlier in the evening. That, and her reference to Silloth, sets his mind going now in that direction. After his grandfather had died, during his last year at school, he'd been back there only once. He tries to remember whether he'd been otherwise sad at his grandad's death. Had his affection for the old man really been for the place rather than for the person? They'd never actually been close, (his grandfather had been too private a person for that), and the first thing that comes to mind whenever he does think of him is the stilted conversation they'd had on the day he'd found that photograph. His mother, though, he knows, had been terribly upset for some weeks by the loss of her father. But when he'd thought about that in later years, having tried to talk to her about his grandad, he'd begun to suspect that most of her distress, too, had been because certain issues between her and her father had remained unresolved and she had slowly come to the realisation that the opportunity for a reconciliation between them had passed beyond reach.

Is it, he thinks, that kind of thing that makes the finality of death, generally, so unacceptable? Is that why people worldwide seek some form of Heaven? A looked-for concept where everything can come right, all the mistakes and misunderstandings be corrected; a concept of divinity which is so much cosier than that proposed by Arthur Stanton, albeit possibly much less realistic. He still doesn't know what his own beliefs are on that. All he knows is that for most of his life, on and off, he's prayed to God intuitively rather than on any thought-through basis. It has been an intimate thing, personal between him and God. He cares little for the ritual of church or chapel. If he stops to think about it, he's always been impatient with the views that God might be either vengeful or compassionate, as the mood takes Him, or that He might somehow be influenced by the entreaties sent up to Him. There is no logic in that, and no evidence, in Peter's view, to support it (although it has never stopped him from time to time making his own personal pleas to the Almighty). Nevertheless, to have to view God in non-human terms, as Arthur Stanton was suggesting, is still more discomforting (scary, even) and no more logical. Anyway, what is the point in having a God at all, with the promise of some sort of heaven, if not in human terms? But, to come full circle, that thought alone also implied a belief that 'God' was a creation of mankind's, rather than the other way round. Yesterday morning the padre had virtually accused Browning of sedition because of his views; but couldn't the same be said about Stanton himself, given his ecclesiastical role? He wonders if Sylvia Stanton knows of her husband's thoughts on the God he represents; and wonders yet again to what extent those views might have been born of his experiences in the Great War.

And so his thoughts drift to his father. For years he'd avoided facing the truth about his father. He isn't sure what had brought about his revelation to Arthur the previous night; for a revelation it had been, to himself as well. For as long as he can remember he'd chosen to hide the truth in fantasy (which, he now sees, had been easier than facing up to facts), until the fantasy had become for him the reality. He has now begun to understand, however, that as a consequence he had all along avoided asking the sort of questions he should have been asking. Who was his father really – not as a figure but as a person? What had made him the way he was? And what sort of a person might his father himself have wished to be, given more of a chance? Or with more application. What kinds of influences had dictated the outcome for him, other than the obvious ones of the war? What had he been like before that particular experience? It strikes him that when it comes to fundamentals he has known nothing about his father: his own flesh and blood, the fount of his very existence, had appeared out of the mists of time, and disappeared back into them – a figure fixed in outline, like a cardboard cut-out, with certain recognisable features but no other dimensions. And all he had ever done, with regard to his father, was to create for himself a make-believe figure to suit his own needs; or, more accurately, to block out his own inadequacies.

And, now he thinks about it, it has been no different when it comes to his mother. For the past ten years or so he has tucked into some remote recess of his mind his reluctantly gleaned knowledge, sparse as it is, that there had been dramas in her early life which must have significance with regard to her present relationships. Understanding those, and perhaps being able to explore them further with her, would doubtless have enriched their own relationship, mother and son. But his own immediate needs had come first. Over the years he has stumbled to the conclusion that it would prove too difficult for both of them to attempt to cross into that foreign country. As a result, she has remained for him…what? Just his Mother. A largely iconic figure: because she's always been there for him, unchanged; because for the whole of his life his interest in her has been confined to her fulfilling that limited role – an interest in what she has done for him, and what she could continue to do for him. Her other roles in life, her own personal wants before and in the future, had not been seen by him to be his legitimate concern.

And the pity is, he thinks, you can never go back. Time lost can never be regained. The opportunities have been there, and for a variety of reasons he has chosen to ignore them. He can't now go to his mother and say: 'Tell me all about your own life, about how you met my father and then lost him; tell me about all your triumphs and heartaches; about your relationships with your parents and your sisters; tell me about what you think of me.' It would be too contrived, wrapped in an artificiality which would be certain to wither any spontaneity, or indeed any response whatsoever. Or would it?… But the impulse to try to implement such a course of action shrivels as soon as it is born. A sudden frontal assault of that kind would inevitably invite the question, 'Why this sudden interest?' and would be the death of intimacy.

So, would it, after all, in the end, be the usual thing: the arrival at the deathbed in search of those few posthumous crumbs that could be salvaged from disparate friends and relatives who might be there, in order to try to construct, belatedly, some context and meaning for one's own life?

But this is no good: he is slipping into middle-of-the-night melancholy without even the legitimacy of having first of all been asleep. And he is feeling chilly. Yet his bed seems no more inviting than it had an hour ago. He wonders if his pipe is worth relighting, and tentatively sucks at it – receiving a mouthful of cold ash for his pains.

Right, he would go back to bed.

Once there, however, his mind still refuses to switch off. He begins to think of Anna; then of Germany, and Hans. Somewhere he has a photograph of himself with Hans, taken during the last few days of their time together in St Andrews. He can still visualise that picture, the two of them in their gowns, standing together arm in arm, with, in the background, the ruins of the Cathedral and of St Rule's Tower casting long skeletal shadows across long-forgotten graves. If he remembers correctly, they'd both been plastered at the time – rather holding each other up than being purely companionable in their stance. This was the night that, on parting, Hans had said to him, in a slurred voice that was as solemn as it was confidential, 'My maternal grandmother was Jewish, you know.' Peter had a vague recollection of peering back at him through eyes that were having difficulty in focussing and saying, equally solemnly, 'No – Really? I didn't know.' What he can remember clearly, however, was the sudden look of fright on Hans's face, as if he'd only then realised just what he'd said.

After that, each having gone their separate ways, their only contact for the next three years had been by card every Christmas, a few included lines indicating something of what they'd been doing over the previous twelve months. So he'd been more than a little surprised to receive from Hans, in the spring of '36, an invitation to come to stay with him and his family in Berlin for the last week of the Olympic Games, in August. By then, fortuitously, they would both be qualified, and free agents until they started their first hospital jobs in September. As Hans had put it, in his impeccably written English, *It is, I think, too good an opportunity to miss.*

And so it was.

And so it was that he'd boarded the Golden Arrow at St Pancras, that August, bound for the Continent and Berlin (his first foray abroad) with money in his pocket (this time 'borrowed' from Uncle John on the premise that, now graduated, he would, in the fullness of time, be able to pay it back), and a suitcase containing some new clothes bought specially for the occasion…and so it was…

He's on the train, and it's stopping at a station. He can't see a name. In fact he can't see the station. Just knows it's there. Perhaps it's night-time. He can't tell. But somehow he knows they've just crossed into Germany. A moment ago all the people in the compartment were English. Now they're all German. They're dressed ridiculously: all the women in dirndl skirts and low-cut blouses embroidered with spring flowers; the men in short *lederhosen* exposing fat white knees. They're all staring at him. Sometimes, for a few seconds at a time, they look at him with amusement, sometimes with hostility. The train has stopped. There comes the *tramp, tramp, tramp* of feet along the corridor of the train. The door of the compartment crashes back. Startled, he jumps. The other occupants simply smile. Two men stand there. Dressed in grey military uniforms. No, in black. Each with a red armband, on which a black swastika floats in a white circle, first this way up and then that. Their peaked caps have a death's head badge at the front. The metal skulls start to grin at him, as both men say, simultaneously, pointing, 'You must be a Jew!' 'No,' he cries desperately, 'see, I am Aryan! I have blond hair and blue eyes.' The men sneer. Everyone else sneers. 'Hah!' the men exclaim. 'See, you speak English. All English are Jew-lovers. That is the same as being one.'

He comes to with a start, taking a moment to realise he's back in his room at Marwell; must have nodded off for a moment; must have started to dream. Something about a train, something about his trip to Berlin, something he didn't like. He wonders how long he's been asleep. Probably not long. He ponders whether to get up again, whether to switch on the light; but continues to lie there in the darkness, the excitement and the nervousness reborn, the recollections now flooding back, so fresh it might have been only yesterday.

He'd been unexpectedly – foolishly, really – impressed by how different from England had been the countryside through Belgium and into Germany. There'd been nothing conspicuous about crossing the border, apart from the fact that the train had stopped to let officials aboard; but it had become clear that there were noticeable differences between those two countries. As the train had sped past villages and towns, stations and farms, Belgium had seemed to have an easy-going nonchalance about it, a sort of *laissez-faire* attitude that most things could be left to look after themselves, and, if not, well, tomorrow would do. Germany, on other hand, had been so clean and tidy, so spick and span, that it was almost obsessional – everything had looked ordered, as if by command, nothing out of place; and the people, therefore, suitably grave. And in Germany there had been flags – on almost every building, it seemed; red flags with a black swastika on a white circular background. He can still see those flags, remember how sinister they'd looked; and he thinks again, as he'd thought then, how could they take an ancient oriental icon of good luck and manage to turn it into an emblem of evil? And there had been the uniforms. It had appeared that one man in ten (and not a few women) wore some form of military-style uniform.

As he lies there in the darkness with his recollections, all at once it feels so real, as if he were back there. He's looking out onto the platform as the train draws into the busy station, the scene festive, except for the fact that those red banners give the impression of glowering down on the more timorous Olympic flags, and the name-boards sliding past the carriage window positively bellow – BERLIN. There's a kaleidoscope of impressions. Of Hans, just recognisable, on the platform, waving, younger sister Ursula and brother Bruno by his side. Ursula, it turns out is sixteen; and Bruno fourteen. Ursula has pigtails, and simpers; Bruno wears the uniform of Hitler Youth, and scowls. Neither speaks a word of English. That's how he remembers them being for the whole of that week. Hans is as he was in Scotland, but more reflective; and perhaps more arrogant on this, his home soil. He has a car waiting, and they drive down *Friedrichstrasse* past the newly rebuilt *Reichstag* building and the Brandenburg Gate, turn into the *Unter den Linden* and along the fine wide street bisecting the *Tiergarten*, chatting as they go. Hans's English is more hesitant than it was three years ago, but still good enough; which is just as well, because Peter has no inclination to attempt more than a few words of German.

The Kolber family lives in a big, old house in Charlottenburg, a well-to-do suburb to the west of Berlin; which is perfect – for the brand-new, purpose-built Olympic Stadium is conveniently close by. Hans's father is big, burly and heavily moustached, with glacier-blue eyes, a duelling scar on his left cheek, a Party badge in his lapel, and a patronising manner; Peter suspects that he has to make considerable effort to tolerate anything non-German, particularly people. He does, however, speak passably good English and, it turns out, is moderately well-disposed towards the British – '*as is Herr Hitler himself*', he impresses on Peter at one point. The mother is surprisingly young-looking. Thin, blonde and shrewish, with a shrill laugh that contains no humour, she at no time makes any attempt to speak even one word of English – which at least saves Peter from having to try to make conversation with her. There is something odd about her relationship with Hans and his siblings, as if that is how she sees them: as 'siblings'. Not only is there no noticeable warmth between her and them, there appears to be a wariness on both sides. It is only on his third day that Peter learns that she has only recently become married to Herr Professor Kolber; that she is the family's newly-installed stepmother. It takes him another two days (and several *steins* of lager on Hans's part) to learn that Herr Kolber had divorced his wife, Hans's mother, the previous year (under new laws formulated for exactly that purpose, for maintaining 'racial purity'); she has gone to live with her widowed mother in Osnabruck and, Hans assures him, the two of them are planning to emigrate soon to America '*where they will feel more at home*'. He looks searchingly at Hans on receiving this bit of information, but can detect neither irony, guilt nor regret.

After that, in spite of the warm summer weather, he always feels that little bit chilly in Berlin.

The seven days there constitute a week of contrasts. The city is, of course, full of visitors from abroad. There had been attempts by some countries to organise a universal boycott of the Games (for which Berlin had been chosen as the venue before Hitler had come to power), or to have them re-sited. But the lure of the Olympics had been too great for the former to have been successful; and the practicalities too insurmountable for the latter. And so there is bustle, and excitement, even gaiety, with virtually all nations represented along with their concomitant differences of physical appearance, language, behaviour and dress. But the burghers of Berlin, though clearly eager to take this opportunity of impressing the world with what they see as the undoubted superiority, in all things, of the *Third Reich*, perversely seem to have made little concession to the possible sensibilities of this influx of strangers.

True, the streets and gardens are decorated with bunting and flowers, there are bands in the parks and concerts in the halls, entertainers in the squares, and fancy dress: there is a gala atmosphere everywhere. Shop windows in the main thoroughfares sparkle with the latest in clothes, jewellery and luxury goods; street bistros and restaurants positively seduce one to sample their fine fare; and the lakes, boating ponds, walkways, glades and cafés of the *Tiergarten* tempt one to absent oneself from the Games to while away the days in indolence. Everything is perfect. At a glance.

But after a few days you begin to notice certain things.

The citizens of Berlin appear to be of a type, to have a certain uniformity of appearance. They are all, without exception it seems, clearly northern European. Darkness of skin (or swarthiness, say, of features) is confined, they would have you believe, to those who are merely visiting; and whilst such people are invariable treated with the utmost courtesy, as though by diktat, the politeness is accompanied by a scarcely concealed suspicion bordering on contempt; the visitors are kept at arm's length, and the smiles have a definite reserve about them.

Then there are the shops in the *Unter den Linden*, wonderful shops, freshly painted; but on the walls above the windows of some can just be made out the ghost-names of previous owners, not quite completely obliterated: names such as *Bloemburg Gebr., Juwelieren*, or – over a tailors' – *Jakob Rosenthal und Sohn, Schneideren* ; and with that discovery comes the realisation that not only have those particular shops at some time in the recent past been 'reappropriated', but there is an absence of shame about the process such that no one has bothered to ensure that all evidence of this has been removed.

And there are those uniforms. Peter has divided them into two categories. Those that are military, officer-style, whether in *Wehrmacht* field-grey or *SS* black, their owners firm-jawed, tight-lipped and alert, their manners as invariably correct as their uniforms are well-tailored, their jackboots well-polished, their heel-clicking impeccable, and their eyes hard; and those that are civilian – men with grey faces and grey suits, always with Party badge on show, their owners slack-mouthed and blank-eyed, with a tendency to be officious and suspicious. Once he's come to recognise these latter as a type, he casually asks Hans about them – who shrugs dismissively, muttering something about them being '*gestapo* or some other such Party official', and is quick to change the subject. But from none of the residents of the city is there ever any expression of the inappropriateness of these people, uniformed or otherwise, being so conspicuous at a gathering such as this.

However, in spite of his misgivings about Hans, his family and their mother-country, he and Hans enjoy the week in each other's company, reminiscing about their brief time together at medical school and swapping notes about all that has happened since. For they still share something in common: their enthusiasm for the practice of medicine and their pride in belonging to that universal brotherhood with its high sense of ethics and its strong belief in its vocation.

This bond between them had surprised Peter when he'd first become aware of it soon after Hans had arrived at St Andrews; until then, he had thought that it was a thing unique to himself, an entity felt but not clearly recognised and certainly not focussed upon. It had been Hans who had articulated it, declaring without reservation or self-consciousness how 'privileged' they were to be able to embark on this 'noble enterprise'. Peter wouldn't have dared express his thoughts in those high-sounding terms, not even to himself, and had initially been embarrassed when Hans had done so – even to the extent of finding it necessary to excuse it on the grounds of the German's limited command of English and his 'foreignness'.

But the more he'd thought about it, the more he'd realised that was exactly how he himself felt – and no doubt many of his fellow students also, if they'd only had the balls to say so. It was as if they were being allowed, for those few years, to participate in a world of particular privilege, a closed world in which they approached the truth of life itself. They, with their tutors, were a band of like-minded people certain of their calling and of its vital importance to their fellow Man – and were filled with excitement and a certain awe at this discovery.

As it was, the tradition was more one of playing down that aspect of it. The medical students of the Thirties had a reputation: for rowdiness, beer-swilling and rugby-playing, for taking nothing too seriously, least of all their studies; it was a reputation that was, to a lesser or greater extent, well-founded for many of them – a reputation that had accompanied the student body in the past and would doubtless do so in the future. The truth also was that they worked bloody hard. They had no choice in the matter: the workload was such that the majority would fail unless they were prepared much of the time to burn the midnight oil. The first two years were taken up with the study of anatomy and physiology, together with the rudiments of pathology, bacteriology and pharmacology. In anatomy they had to undergo a ten-minute oral examination every two weeks (failure of which meant that they were required to re-sit that section); in all of the subjects they had a written and practical examination at the end of each term; and at the end of the two years they had to sit their intermediate professional examinations, the so-called Second M.B., Ch.B. They were given two goes at that, three months apart, and failure to pass on the second occasion meant re-taking a whole year – a very considerable additional expense for whoever was footing the bill! Only after qualifying at Second M.B. were they able go on to the study of the principal disciplines of Clinical Medicine, Pharmaceutics, Surgery, and Obstetrics with Gynaecology, together with a host of other subjects such as Ophthalmology; Dermatology; Diseases of Ear, Nose and Throat; Child Health; Orthopaedics; and Psychiatry (still in its infancy).

So it was, that during the two terms Hans had spent with them at St Andrews, Peter and his British colleagues, unlike Hans, were still many months away from seeing their first live patients. Hans, on the other hand, had already been exposed to some extent to the activities of hospital wards in Germany – a distinction (carrying with it, as it did, a cachet of professional sophistication) which made him the envy of the others in the class.

Indeed, the Prof of Bacteriology at Queens College in Dundee had pressed for some time for exposure of the students to 'proper medicine' in the early stages of the course, claiming that this would provide some focus and sense of purpose for the study of the basic medical sciences; but his theory had been decried by his colleagues, who argued that there could be no understanding of people and their illnesses until the basics had been acquired. Hans, therefore, with his tendency to arrogance, had at first been actively disliked when he'd adopted these superior airs. Nor had he helped his cause when he'd allowed himself to be openly appalled by what he'd regarded as a flippant approach to things in the Dissecting Rooms.

The proper study of anatomy required detailed dissection of the human body, to the extent of six hours per week for every member of the class. The Dissecting 'Rooms', housed in the Bute Medical Buildings in the grounds of St Mary's College in St Andrews, consisted in fact of a single, large room containing a number of 3-foot-high bed-shaped tables the surface of each being covered by a sheet of metallic zinc. On these the corpses reclined, having already been fished out of their preserving tanks of formalin, for each session, by the time the students arrived. This task was performed (in somewhat mysterious fashion, so far as the students were concerned) by the Attendant, a likeable but rather lugubrious man whose pale skin and thin physique made him look (the students swore) equally cadaverous, qualifying him for their nickname of '*Doppelganger*'.

At the time of his first day in the Rooms, Peter, like most of the rest of his fellows, had very little familiarity with death – a frog or rat pinned out on a dissection board in zoology was in fact by and large the sum total of their experience. To be faced, suddenly, with a dozen or so cadavers displayed face-up, greyish-white and lard-like, but otherwise intact – and emphatically people who were dead – was shocking in the extreme. The realisation, following immediately, that they were expected to start cutting up these people was almost more than they could take. Instinct and natural youthful resilience took over, however, being the only answer; and within an hour each team of six had given a name to their personal cadaver (which would remain 'theirs' for the one-and-a-half years' duration of the course).

They work three to each side of the cadaver. Each term is given over to a particular section of the body: Upper Limb, Lower Limb, Head and Neck, Thorax and Abdomen. The team of three on each side therefore has its own area of dissection, and only when it comes to thorax and abdomen do they have to do some 'sharing' with their opposite numbers. The scene is one of industry, but with a fair amount of chatter – some of which is about what they are doing, and some of which is about other things. No doubt if someone were to come in from outside (which no one is allowed to do unless they have a legitimate interest in being there) they would receive a distinctly macabre impression. Of a number of bodies laid out in obscene manner displaying various degrees of mutilation, white-coated students bent to their grisly task as they slice and probe at the flesh before them. Other figures – who are in fact anatomy 'demonstrators' – flit ghoul-like from table to table to point out this or that. Yet gusts of laughter issue from time to time from one group or another. And the acrid whiff of formaldehyde pervades the air.

The students in the class during Hans's first term at St Andrews don't see it like that. Now that they are in their fourth term, dealing with Head and Neck, they are old hands who take it in their stride. They may grumble about the minute detail in which they are required to learn their anatomy, but it is all good-natured – that's how it is, was always so. But unconsciously they continue with the attitude which allowed them in the early days to cope with the enormity of what they do: a cheerful irreverence, a brash humour.

With Hans coming into the class halfway through the one-and-a half-year anatomy course, there has had to be some accommodation made, and he has joined Peter and Barry Hepworth on their corpse – a youngish female whom they have named 'Mae' in view of her buxom appearance that they have likened to that of Mae West, the Hollywood film star. Hans is appalled when he learns this: declares that it is disrespectful to the dead in a way that would never be allowed in Germany. In vain do they protest that it is nothing of the sort – more an expression of identification with, almost of affection for, this dead woman who inadvertently has come to play her part in the training of future doctors, and who would otherwise remain nameless. The fact is that the system itself, in the wake of the Anatomy Acts, has built-in respect for these individuals, most of whom, without known relatives, would have been destined for a pauper's grave (there being only very few people who Will their bodies for 'medical research'). Their identities are known by the staff of the Department of Anatomy; and when the time comes for the proper disposal of their remains they are given a Christian burial, at a funeral attended by representatives of the department. This fact is deliberately made clear to the students at the beginning of the course; as is the exhortation to 'respect the dead'.

None of this mollified Hans. Clearly the British had dubious standards.

When, at a later stage, it was explained to him in passing that British doctors are not really 'Doctors', since their qualifications in medicine and surgery are *baccalaureates* – that their title of 'Doctor' is purely a courtesy title, he was even more mystified. Again, when told that this was for purely historical reasons, that all British universities regarded the medical degrees as being equal to a doctorate, and treated it as such, he was not convinced – particularly when he learned that once someone had achieved the specialist qualification for surgery, the F.R.C.S., he would be addressed as 'Mister' once more.

They laugh about it now, from the perspective of an interval of three years, as they spend the mornings sitting around the pavement coffee shops in the *Tiergarten*, ogling the girls as they stroll by in their summer frocks, or listening to the bands playing in the parks (mostly Wagner, Strauss and Lehar – 'the Fuehrer believes Wagner to be the best exponent of Germanic music'). Hans takes pains to point out that now that he is qualified, the correct form of address for him in Germany is Herr Doktor; and that should he ever obtain a second doctorate, such as in Law ('heaven forbid that I ever would!') he would have to be addressed as Herr Doktor Doktor. The unspoken implication is that as a system it is much superior to the distinctly muddled one pertaining in Britain.

The afternoons are spent at the Games, for which Hans has obtained tickets for the whole week. Peter is duly impressed by the Olympic stadium, as he is intended to be. Of ultra-modern design, in sparkling white concrete, it displays lofty stands which seem to offer up the oval arena in the palms of cupped hands, as if to say 'This is what *The Third Reich*, with its confident healthy youth, can offer the world'. Indeed there are, on the walls of terraces and walkways, colourful posters depicting vibrant images of German youngsters marching, tanned and happy, through an idealised countryside (the Nazi banner held triumphantly aloft), or performing deeds of athleticism. 'This is the birth of a new era,' the posters appear to proclaim.

The stands are packed with people of all nationalities, flags flutter, military bands play; day after day the stadium is a cauldron of excitement as the finals of field and track events run their dramatic course. Hitler himself appears on most days, a remote figure in his concrete bastion high above the arena. Dressed always in the same drab light-brown suit, and surrounded by a sea of uniforms, his features indistinct beneath the high peak of his military cap, he is like some alien bird looking down on the proceedings, as if from a man-made eagle's nest. Above and behind him, on a slender column, sits the vast saucer in which burns the Olympic flame; and on tall poles the flags of nations, forming a backdrop to this tableau, day after day hang lifeless as though paying homage to *Das Fuehrer*. At the other end of this royal Rostrum, on a 10-foot plinth, there rears what will become for Peter an icon lying across the interface between his memory and imagination: it is as a giant swastika sculpted in concrete that he later recalls it.

On Hitler's appearance on each occasion, the bands strike up with *Deutschland, Deutschland uber alles*, and a great section of the crowd rises to its feet, right arms out-stretched, chanting *Sieg heil! Sieg heil!* Hans joins in with gusto; Peter, momentarily infected with the same surge of excitement, is tempted to join in – until he understands that what he is witnessing is nothing more than mindless ritual, a form of collective hysteria. Let Hans and his countrymen follow the piper – it has nothing at all to do with him.

Unfortunately, Teutonic chauvinism is not sufficient to carry the day. German athletes do well, buoyed by an atmosphere of constant fervour for their crusade; but (as if the gods take delight in their own perversity) for the first time in the history of the Games it is a black athlete, a pleasant and charismatic young negro named Jesse Owens, from the U.S.A., who sweeps the field, winning Gold in the 100 metres, 200 metres and high jump events. More importantly he carries with him the international crowd. It is indeed the dawn of a new era – but, to Peter at least, only too obviously not that of Aryan superiority.

Taking photographs with more enthusiasm than skill, he begins to see the whole proceedings in the same way that he sees them when looking through the viewfinder of his camera: a mere reflection of the real, in diminished form. On one such occasion, as the sun behind the Rostrum descends toward the nadir of the day, painting the daylight-white of the stadium in a golden glow, he perceives that it throws across the arena, in distorted form, the shadow of that swastika; it is then, looking up, that he sees, in the gathering dusk which has thrown the array of national flags into profile, the blood-red standard of the new Germany standing out among the others. And for a few seconds (perhaps as he briefly dozes in the oppressive heat of this particular evening) it seems, as he continues to watch with growing horror but no surprise, that the flag begins to spread and melt before his eyes, flowing down the pole and across the arena in a crimson tide; and as it does so it emits a rustling and a slithering sound, like that from the movements of a giant snake.

He awakens in blackness, the clamminess of sweat on his lip and brow. For a moment he is still in Berlin, but on his back, unable to move. Then relief floods in: he knows he is in his bed at Marwell, has only been dreaming.

But the silk-like slithering sound continues. Inside the room. Dregs of fear from his dream clog his throat. 'Who's there? Is anyone there?' he manages to say.

O'Connor's intonation is unmistakable, even in a whisper. 'Shh – you'll alert the whole damn place. And for pity's sake don't put that light on.'

'God in heaven, Shevaun! What are you doing here?'

'*Shhh*! Right this minute I'm taking my clothes off. And kindly move over – it's getting just that bit chilly.'

'For Christ's sake, Shevaun! You'll get us both court-martialled! How did you get in without being seen, anyway? How did you get past the sentries? And how did you know which was my room?'

'I asked,' she says drily, the sarcasm gentle. 'As for the sentries, I managed to give them the slip, no difficulty. And I do wish you wouldn't blaspheme like that. It doesn't suit you.'

'But supposing someone had seen you,' he says, panic growing, '...or does so when you're...you're leaving. How will you explain that?'

'Well, I've come to get you to sign an authorisation for morphine for one of our patients, haven't I.'

'But we haven't got anyone in the ward requiring morphine at present.'

'No, but they don't know that. And aren't likely to ask. Just so long as they don't catch me without my clothes on. That might take a bit of explaining.'

'They might ask to see the authorisation, though.'

'Yes, that's alright. I've got it with me. I must remember to get you to sign it before I leave. And if push comes to shove, Bartholomew will play along – he's very quick on the uptake, particularly where I'm concerned. Knows me only too well! Anyway, stop making difficulties. And move over!'

He groans. He had a quickly passing image of one night in his ground-floor room as a houseman in hospital, in bed for an early night to catch up on sleep. Of the window opening, and a figure creeping in, illuminated by the lights outside. One of the Staff Nurses from the ward, still in uniform – making straight for his bed and, without ceremony, climbing in, her dress riding up, all white thighs, suspenders, undies and black stockings. From outside the window, giggles and guffaws and muffled cheers from two of his colleagues and assorted nurses, her bet won, but not in a hurry to leave.

Lust leaps.

But before he can stop himself, the question slips out. 'Why are you here, anyway?'

Shevaun stops in the process of tugging back the bedclothes. 'I can't believe that's a serious question. Is it?' There's a mixture of suspicion and amusement in her voice. 'No. It can't be. Move over.'

She's naked, her skin carrying the coolness of the summer night. Everything is compact, generous and rounded, as he's always imagined it would be. He thinks of Anne. But Anne had been drinking. Shevaun hasn't. Instead there's a musky perfume, not at all subtle. And not within service regulations he thinks incongruously. He can't quite take in that this is really happening. But his arousal now is achingly complete. He no longer cares. He begins to fumble at his pyjamas. Impatiently she pushes his hands away, does it for him, and they are skin to skin. His hands are trying to feel everything of her at once.

Suddenly he's conscious of her rearing up on one elbow, peering down at him. 'This is your first time, isn't it?' she demands, disbelief in her voice.

Unsuccessfully he tries to lie.

'Well, well,' she murmurs, all smugness and delight. 'Who would have thought it. And here's me thinking my days of virgins were over.'

Demoralisation having temporarily banished lust, another injection of realism follows in the form of a sudden thought. 'Shevaun, I haven't any...any...'

'French letters?' she contributes brightly.

He winces at the common, slightly vulgar term. 'Yes. No, that is. Condoms. I haven't any.'

'That's alright. I can't have children.' It's said in reassurance, but he thinks he can detect the faint note of regret in her voice.

'Are you sure?' nevertheless he asks doubtfully.

She stiffens against him, moves away. 'Do you think I don't know about something like that?' Then she relents, snuggles against him once more, her sunny nature coming to their rescue. 'It's alright. I'm sure, to be sure. More's the pity. Anyway, let's take our time. There's no hurry. We have a couple of hours yet before daybreak.' She kisses him on the cheek – a chaste, sisterly kind of kiss. 'You asked why I've come. The answer, really – if one ignores the obvious – is: I don't know. I was feeling lonely. Kept thinking of all those poor boys from Dunkirk. And those who didn't make it. And – like everyone, I suppose – thinking about all the tomorrows, and if they'll ever come. Is this the end of our cosy way of life? Is it, do you think?'

Again she lifts her head to peer at him, as if he has the answer.

'No, don't answer that. I don't want to know.' She gives a shiver, pulls him to her. 'Anyway, in reply to your question, the truth is I've always fancied you. Simple as that. Not so much 'whether' as 'when'. And I thought: no time like the present! Impulsive, that's me. Will that do?'

She reaches up and kisses him on the lips, her mouth soft and fragrant. 'Anyway. Here, let me show you what a woman likes. This woman at least.'

For some seconds he doesn't understand what it is she's setting out to do. She's turned her back on him, and then, with a fair amount of squirming she's wriggled herself into a position where she's lying face-up, spread-eagled on top of him, her head resting on his upper chest and shoulder, her face close against his. The generous globes of her bottom are positioned – gloriously – on his lower belly, her legs aligned along the outside of his. It's not like anything he's ever heard of; he cannot think what she's trying to achieve.

He soon learns. She takes his hands and guides them, slowly and gently, along her curves and into her recesses, again and again, sensuously, with growing excitement on her part as well as his. Exposed, as she is, above him, both his arms and hers are free, without hindrance or constraint. She entwines her fingers in his, so that they become as one, until it is no longer clear who is leading and who is following, increasing the pressure here, reducing it there, moving at one moment, pausing another, speeding up and slowing down. It is like that time in the car with Anne, except that here she is naked and it is done with clear intent. The moans begin, kept low, at first lazily but then with muted urgency, and at times he doesn't know whether it is her or him. Suddenly she twists and turns, so that her breasts are crushed against him, her lips to his lips, pelvis thrusting wildly. For a moment she pauses, impatience unrestrained, does something frantic – and all at once he's inside her. He's never imagined that excitement can be so intense, sensation so extreme; he's floating outside himself. For long seconds that are timeless they fight each other, compete to reach the heights; and then collapse, joined. And all at once there's something else. He's warm and safe. It's like being home.

CHAPTER SEVENTEEN

The countryside stands breathless, could be thought to be holding its breath. Leaves hang lifelessly on branches, shrinking almost, as if anticipating a new heat to the day – for already, at this relatively early hour, warmth is heavy in the air, unusually so even for mid-August, and through the golden haze of morning there is a glitter to the pale blue of the sky as if portending a fierceness to come.

It reminds him of London, two weeks previously: the city waiting, anticipating the worst but not quite knowing what to expect.

And in other ways, besides, he has a sense of *déjà vu*. The destination is different, the mode of transport and his present companion also; but the purpose is much the same as that of his dispatch to Dover six weeks ago: he is being loaned out. This time he'd had more sense than to complain – apart from the fact that Beal had been ready for him, probably expecting him to do just that – on this occasion the need and purpose had been clear-cut. There'd been nothing secretive about it, as there had been on the trip to Dover. Beal had been blunt yesterday evening, not allowing a shred of sympathy to shine through – and indeed why should he have felt any: risk to life is, these days, the currency he deals in whenever he issues orders to those under him.

'You are to temporarily replace the station M.O. at Church Wealdon, Group 11, Fighter Command, Peter,' he'd said. 'He was badly wounded in the raid there this afternoon, and all Fighter Command's M.O.s are already hard-pressed. They've promised to find a more permanent replacement fairly soon, though, so you'll probably be there for only a day or two. But – apart from the fact that all Group Eleven fields are under pressure – Church Wealdon is a Sector Control station, so they're likely to cop some more from jerry in the next day or two…No doubt our turn in Bomber Command will come in due course. Church Wealdon say they're coping without their doctor for the moment, so tomorrow morning will do. I'll have a car and a driver ready for you at 0600. Best of luck.' The last had been casual to the point of terseness. Whether Beal, by this indifferent approach, had been trying to play down the risk, or whether his thoughts had simply switched immediately to greater priorities, Peter didn't know. He suspects the latter.

However, his quick, well-hidden, dismay had been not at the knowledge that he was suddenly to be pitch-forked into the front line with all its attendant dangers. What had disturbed him was the realisation that Church Wealdon was where Bill Jackson was stationed; and even that, in itself, wasn't what had perturbed him, so much as not being able to fathom why any of that should bother him in the slightest, anyway. After all, Bill and he had been friends. Hadn't they? Why, then, this slight twisting of the guts at the thought of their being thrown together again?...But he knows why. He has only to think back to Bill's attitude that evening at the Savoy a fortnight ago.

Distractedly he now glances at the WAAF corporal driving him, studying for a moment the gleaming patterns of light being projected onto the side of her face by the rays from the early morning sun filtering through the passing trees. 'A/C Saunders, your driver, sir,' was how she'd introduced herself. He seems to remember her first name is Connie, having seen her as a patient three or four weeks ago – but isn't sure enough to use it. A pretty girl. However, conversation between them so far has been sparse, limited largely to discussions on the niceties of the map-reading – all signposts, as well as place-names at hamlets and villages, having been removed, navigating their way through these minor country roads is proving far more difficult than they could have imagined. But although that requires concentration, he knows that it isn't the whole reason for the silence between them. There is a certain uneasiness on both their parts, he imagines – which he attributes to the experience when, some three or four weeks ago, she'd come to see him at the medical centre, complaining of severe dysmenorrhoea. This had as a matter of course necessitated a vaginal examination, carried out with one finger by reason of her still having a partially-intact hymen. At that point, although merely a matter of routine for him, there had been understandable tension in the girl, which, strangely, on this occasion had transmitted itself to Peter – probably because O'Connor, in sardonic mood, standing at the girl's head to hold her hand while he carried out the examination, had been making faces at him. What would normally not have had any sexual connotations for him had therefore begun to do so, causing him in turn to become self-conscious. Now, here they are, alone in a car together, on a lonely country road with the world not yet stirring, with that brief act of necessary intimacy their only thing in common. He muses again, as he has done on occasions in the past, on the peculiar nature of the relationship between patient and doctor (so often both total strangers to one another) whereby the one allows the other a degree of invasion of both body and mind that they would probably not have granted to any other living soul except maybe a lover – and then, meeting socially, manage to behave as though none of it has happened. It truly is a partnership of a unique nature, incorporating absolute trust on the part of the one and a particular responsibility on the part of the other. Yet, in the vast majority of cases, the morality and ethics of the relationship is understood by both parties, the rules clear-cut.

Why then all this uncertainty in other forms of social relationships?

His own perplexities in that area seem to parallel to a small degree the general confusions in the country over the past weeks. In Britain, in the days following Dunkirk, culminating a week or two later in the capitulation of France, there had been a paradoxical satisfaction, joy almost, in the commonly heard cry, 'Right, we're on our own now – no more allies to bother about!' For there had settled on the country an awareness of common purpose, a single goal: survival. For a few days it had become that simple. Let the bombs come! – and the invasion! Churchill had summed it up in his inimicable way when, in the middle of June, he'd said in the Commons: 'The Battle of France is over. I expect that the Battle of Britain is about to begin…'

Peter had happened to be in London on that particular day; and, following the broadcast, the Prime Minister's words had been on everyone's lips it seemed – in tube trains and buses, in bars and restaurants, and on the street – so that they and their import had resonated in one's mind. Peter had been so moved by it that he'd written the heart of the speech down, copied from the newspapers, and still carried the piece of paper in his pocket. It was amazing how the content of it had galvanised people, removing in a single sweep any thought of defeatism. And it had sent an unequivocal message to 'Herr Hitler'. He now knew what he had to do. And all those at home knew, collectively, that they faced the greatest challenge of their lives.

As if to reinforce this, the U.S. Embassy had been advising all four thousand or so American citizens in London to leave as soon as possible; and now the Ambassador himself, Joseph Kennedy, decidedly no lover of Britain anyway, had taken his leave – evoking in no uncertain terms the picture of a sinking ship. Indeed he had so much as said, 'Britain is finished'.

But the bombs hadn't come. People had waited, and wondered. 'Why doesn't he come?' had been on everybody's lips. The rumour began, born of hope, that Hitler had no intention of taking things any further with Britain – that, having occupied virtually the whole of continental Europe, he would now leave well alone. Even Arthur Stanton was passing on the intelligence (presumably from his brother) that Hitler still wished to reach an accommodation with Britain, with whom he 'had no quarrel'. But men of common sense and integrity knew that no such thing was possible. And indeed crews from Marwell and elsewhere on ops had increasingly begun to report concentrations of German invasion barges on the canals and rivers of France and Belgium.

When therefore at the beginning of July the *Luftwaffe* had begun to attack British shipping in the Channel and shortly afterwards to indiscriminately bomb a number of south coast ports, there may have been a sense of dismay, but there had also been an accompanying sigh of relief. Better for it to happen than waiting for it to happen.

Nevertheless the roller-coaster of people's emotions had gone on after that. There had been Hitler's speech of reconciliation towards Britain in the

Reichstag on the 19th July, which had made some people raise their hopes – fortunately, though, and sensibly, within a few hours it had been curtly, and publicly, rejected by the Cabinet. (Thank God, Peter had thought, that we have such pragmatic and resolute men at the helm.) That had been followed by another lull, and once again people had begun to clutch at straws: perhaps the Germans 'wouldn't have the "bottle" for it?' they said. But a few days later had come the report, in the American press, of Hitler's further furious speech in the *Reichstag*, telling the British public all they needed to know. '*They ask, "Why do you not come?"* ' he was reported to have ranted. '*I say to them, "Do not worry. We come! We come!"* '.

At last, therefore, they all had known. The die was cast – or, in David Munro's words, the 'gauntlet thrown down'. (Stanton had cast his eyes ceiling-wards in mock exasperation at that bit of dramatism – but perhaps it had, after all, encapsulated the right attitude; and, at the end of the day, it was Munro and his kind who were going to have to do the stopping).

But still there had come yet another lull, during which the most dramatic event had been merely the dropping, by the Germans, over the southern counties, leaflets entitled 'A Last Appeal to Reason'. Evidently, from all reports, the citizens of those counties had vied with each other in suggesting ways in which the pamphlets could be put to best use – with one particular suggestion, in these days of paper shortage, being the most popular.

A few days ago, though, the storm had finally broken. The *Luftwaffe* had suddenly carried out very heavy raids on Portsmouth docks and all the R.D.F. stations along the south coast. A number of the latter had apparently been put out of action, which had created a considerable alarm in people such as Munro and Stanton – people 'in the know'. Peter had heard the term 'RDF' often enough, but certainly wasn't 'in the know'. All he knew was that the initials stood for 'Radio Direction Finding'. When he'd asked, even Arthur Stanton at first had been reluctant to say much, but had finally grudgingly hinted that it was 'much more than that…an important element in the tracking of enemy aircraft approaching our coasts'. More than this he hadn't been willing to say – if in fact he even knew.

Then, over the past two days had come the heavy raids on fighter stations all over the south-east, and the situation had suddenly become desperate. But at least the confusion was over. They knew where they were.

Which is more than can be said for his own state of mind. His confusion had started with the Night of O'Connor, as he is now inclined to think of it. No, in reality, a few hours before that, with Jordan. And not even then, if he's honest in facing up to his own half-hearted analysis of the situation. For it had begun with Anna Beal. But he'd become aware of that only some considerable time later. After that evening in London, in fact. And even now, the faces and figures of all three women at times became merged, so that on occasions during his waking hours, as well as in his dreams, he has difficulty in separating one from another. That worries him. He's started to wonder whether there is something wrong with him, some fatal flaw in his make-up, so that he is destined to always remain fickle, to fall for every attractive woman in turn who happens to cross his path, with no hope ever of constancy, of a stable relationship. For God's sake, at the back of his mind, right this minute, he is even beginning to entertain romantic notions about this pretty WAAF driver sitting next to him! It's ridiculous. Frightening.

His thoughts return to O'Connor, to that night (those two hours or so, anyway) of sex (making love was how he'd thought of it at the time – but not any longer). Interspersed only by brief interludes of sleep, it had been more than he could have anticipated in even his wildest imaginings: there had been animal urgency, but tenderness too; variation and inventiveness (all, it had to be said, on the part of O'Connor), yet the pretence (at least) of affection also. And when, at last, she'd stolen away before the first true glimmers of dawn he'd lain awake basking in the afterglow of what had taken place, devastated by the wonder of it all, and believing that this must truly be love, for what else could it be. But, in the cold light of day, his relief at learning that she had indeed regained her own quarters without being detected had been more than tempered by the discovery that she didn't, that workday morning, greet him with the scarcely-veiled light of love and gratitude in her eyes that he had expected, but rather with a cool amusement suggesting that, in her view at least, the episode had been of no importance. And this relative indifference had been manifest ever since; even her usual (slightly cynical) flirting with him had become less evident, as though she was consciously keeping him at arm's length. Gradually, then, he had recoiled from a position of (adolescent, he now has to admit) infatuation with her to one of sulky coldness.

In fact it is like it has always been with Jordan, all over again. It makes him wonder whether he's for some reason unlovable. Now that he thinks about it, no one in his life has ever shown him, in any physically demonstrable way, any real affection. Apart from his mother, that is, and to some extent Uncle John – but they don't count; and, anyway, that has always been in a remote sort of fashion. O'Connor had been the first – he'd thought. But clearly that show of affection had been merely pretence on her part, for her own gratification. He's decided he hates women. They are, when all is said and done, unreliable and unpredictable. It explains why all along he's continued to think of O'Connor by her surname and never by her first name; this had previously disturbed him a little, but he realises now that it must have been his instinctive wariness of her that has brought this about.

At this point, though, confusion overcomes him once more, for he becomes aware that in the space of these few moments of musings he's come full circle: from being undecided which of the women at the immediate periphery of his life he most yearns for, to which of them he hates most. And back again. For he now finds his thoughts drifting once more to Anna Beal. Cross with himself, he almost groans out loud. Years ago, on several occasions Bill had said to him, 'Your trouble, Pete, is you think too much. Just get on with it!' At school Beal had said something similar. And they are right.

But Anna Beal…

It was Anna who'd asked him to London on that second occasion, on the last Sunday in July. Two weeks previously when, by invitation, he'd gone back-stage to see her in her dressing-room after her performance at the Adelphi, she couldn't have been more insistent in getting him to come that second time. *'Oh, you must come,'* she'd almost pleaded with him. *'It's our usual Sunday evening 'do' across the road at the Savoy, but Jim can't be there – some tiresome meeting or other – and I've absolutely no one else I know, to escort me. I'm sure, if I have a word with Jim he'd lend you his car, so it would be quite easy for you. You're the only other person I know who fits the bill.'*

Uncertain about all that at the time, in spite of the guarded sense of flattery *('...I've absolutely no one else I know...')*, he'd been even more uncertain when it came to it. He could see himself being thoroughly intimidated by the whole thing. And Anna's attempt to overcome his hesitation by reassurance had only made matters worse: *'Jordan will be there, and so will Bill – I believe he's an old friend of yours too – so you see there will be people there that you know.'*

However, in spite of his misgivings he had gone, and by then it had become too late to change his mind...

He's deliberately come early to London, straight after lunch, thinking it would be pleasant to spend the late afternoon wandering around town. It's yet another wonderful summer's day. Incredible how the weather's done this: a second miraculous summer after the one before, with that extraordinarily harsh record-breaking winter in between. Ridiculous as the thought is, he's pondered on more than one occasion 'Is God trying to tell us something?' It's so hard to accept that they can be at war while nature at the same time is at its most benign and beautiful.

But at war they are. Yet here in London, so far, he's not seen much evidence of that. Two weeks ago, his visit was brief: in by train for the evening performance (theatre ticket courtesy of Anna), then straight back to Marwell. No time to take in much of what was going on. This time he's seeing it all with different eyes. He's parked in Hyde Park, alongside Rotten Row. Because of the strict petrol rationing there are so few private cars on the streets that parking's been delightfully easy. He gets a slightly suspicious glance from a passing policeman – but of course, as he's already found, his RAF officer's uniform is a passport to anywhere. As he's locking the car, a couple of horse riders, splendidly dressed, canter by on a couple of equally splendid horses. He gazes after them in some perplexity, somehow taken aback at this suggestion of people being able to carry on their lives as though nothing were any different. Driving in, he's imagined the very buildings to be holding themselves stiff and upright, braced for the onslaught to come: a concept engendered perhaps by the evidence of some precautionary measures having been taken in the form of sandbags around many a doorway, and criss-cross taping of windows; indeed, he'd passed a Lyons tea-room (closed, it being Sunday) with its windows protected by new wooden shutters. He'd expected, too, that the populace would be walking around in an arrested state of apprehension. There are relatively few people around for such a sunny Sunday afternoon as this, but as he strolls across the park, past the Serpentine, those that he sees all seem happy and relaxed.

However, en route he has passed, scattered untidily through the main body of the park, loosely fenced off, all the material panoply of war. There are anti-aircraft units, the long phallic barrels of the guns pointing obscenely into the air. Barrage balloons, tethered and floating at about a hundred feet, sway impatiently on their hawsers as they tug toward the sky. Here and there girdered structures (like hurdles for some extreme athletic race) are arranged haphazardly wherever it has presumably been deemed there is sufficient space for a glider to land. And, at intervals, scattered around, there are the dark outlines of slit-trenches dug into the ground, incongruous in their puniness.

He lingers now for a while at Speakers Corner, listening to the would-be orators on their 'soap boxes', they, and the sparse crowd listening to them, as outrageous and irreverent as ever. But he soon tires of the familiar banter, and heads off down Park Lane, back towards Hyde Park Corner. Part way, on impulse, he turns off to Grosvenor Square. At first, he's not sure what his intention is in doing so. Only when he sees the quietly imposing building of the American Embassy does he realise that this has been what has drawn him. But why? Is it the unspoken prayer that the United States might see its way to enter the war in defence of the civilised world – an action that would tip the scales in no uncertain terms? He knows that this as remote a likelihood as could be – the U.S.A. wants no truck with Europe these days. For a few minutes he stands at a distance, gazing at the building, the *Bald Eagle* emblem above its doorway imperious, all-powerful – and aloof. Apart from the uniformed guards at the entrance, who give the impression of being more symbolic than functional, there is no one else around; and he finds himself once again taking out the piece of paper on which is written the core of Winston's speech. His lips moving soundlessly, he reads it to himself. '*The Battle of France is over. I expect that the Battle of Britain is about to begin... The whole fury and might of the enemy must very soon be turned on us. Hitler knows that he will have to break us in this island or lose the war. If we can stand up to him, all Europe may be free and the life of the world may move forward into broad sunlit uplands. But if we fail, then the whole world, including the United States, including all that we have known and cared for, will sink into the abyss of a new Dark Age made more sinister, and perhaps protracted, by the lights of perverted science. Let us therefore brace ourselves to our duties, and so bear ourselves that, if the British Empire and its Commonwealth last for a thousand years, men will still say, "This was their finest hour"*'.

Then conscious that he must look as forlorn a figure as he feels, as well as slightly ridiculous, he turns on his heel and continues on his way.

Reaching Hyde Park Corner, he pauses to stare across at St George's Hospital – the large rectangular building, with all of its many windows taped across, looking at that moment like a heavily-bandaged accident victim itself. How will they, and the other hospitals, possibly cope once the bombing starts? It has been estimated that there will in all likelihood be tens of thousands of casualties within the first week or two alone, not to mention the very many cases of hysteria and acute mental breakdown that will invariably arise. Of course, the estimates could be wrong: the thing is, there is no practical precedent on which to base their calculations – Guernica, Warsaw and Rotterdam apart. This is going to be a different kind of war to the Great War: this time civilians will be at the sharp end of it in a way that has never occurred before.

Turning into Piccadilly, he is surprised to find a much greater number of people than heretofore: the sort of crowd that one would have come across on any summer afternoon in peacetime. The reason becomes immediately obvious, for lining the railings for a hundred yards or so on the Green Park side of the street are the usual Sunday artists' stands, attracting little clusters of passers-by just as they would have done were there no war to occupy people's minds. But the make-up of the crowds is different in one respect, he perceives: not only is there a much greater proportion of military uniforms than would have usually been the case, but many of the uniforms are less familiar. Having crossed over to mingle with the crowd on the park side of the street, he begins to discover just how many other nationalities there are: the drum-shaped military caps of Free French compete with the polygonal ones of Czechs, and other uniforms are those of Netherlands and Norway. Whilst on the shoulders of the tunics of a good number of soldiers and airmen in British uniform are sewn the names which indicate the diversity of their origins – Poland, Canada, South Africa, Australia, New Zealand, and Czechoslovakia. For the first time, really, it sinks in just how global this war has become.

He spends a little time browsing among the drawings and paintings on display, for a short time enjoying with others the pretence that all is right with the world. Then he comes across an area where a group of three pavement artists are at work, the men individually kneeling or crouching on the paving stones as they draw and rub with their variously coloured chalks. One of the men is in the process of completing his latest creation, a semi-surrealistic view of what seems to be a city dissolving and melting in a sea of flames – out of the centre of which arises, phoenix-like, in ghostly fashion, a structure that looks very like the dome of St Pauls. Peter gazes at it for a number of seconds, making sense of it, gradually taking it in – then a cold shiver runs down his spine, and he hurries on.

Continuing on his way in the direction of Piccadilly Circus, by the time he's reached the entrance to the R.A. the number of people on the street has again dwindled to a mere handful. So the young woman approaching him out of the Academy courtyard is immediately obvious. Slim, with good legs, and quite nicely dressed, she walks with an exaggerated sway of her hips, meeting his gaze with a bold look which at the same time manages to look wary. Heavily made-up, she would nevertheless be pretty were it not for a dissatisfied set to the corners of her mouth. Only when she speaks does he recognise her purpose. 'You after a nice time, darling?' she says, her voice low and cajoling.

Foolishly startled, having not instantly appreciated what she is, all the same for a brief instant he is tempted; his new-found frustrations with O'Connor have left him more strung-up than he'd realised. But almost immediately he sees her as yet one more in the line of predatory females who seem to have been the sum total of his 'romantic' experiences so far, and dumbly shakes his head. Any lingering regrets he squashes with the thought that, anyway, she more than likely has the clap.

A fleeting look of annoyance crosses her face, then, with a careless shrug of her shoulders as if to say 'plenty more fish in the sea', she turns away and, with a cautious glance up and down the street (no doubt to make sure no bobby has come into view), returns to her lair in the entrance-way. Still feeling a bit of a wimp, in spite of his arguments to himself, his eyes follow her with a certain lingering lust. Also there is something slightly odd about the appearance of her legs. After a moment he realises: of course, like most working girls these days who cannot obtain or afford silk stockings she has painted them to an uncertain tan and drawn a darker line down the back of each leg to look like a seam.

His mood still unsettled, he reaches the Circus. Here, once again, there is more of a throng, and again a preponderance of people in uniform – it seems they constitute the *faux* tourists of this London summer season – and they, and the general appearance of the place, do nothing to lift his spirits. *Eros* has been taken away and his stand closed in by a soulless wooden palisade which in turn has been decorated with those other all-too-familiar reminders of the war: posters. '*Support Your Spitfire Fund*' exhorts one; and '*Dig for Victory!*' another. The smaller ones he has no need to approach – already commonplace on walls and in buses, trams and Tubes, they say things like '*Walls have ears!*' and '*The Enemy is Listening*' (this one with a cartoon of Hitler and Goering, looking ridiculous in uniform, sitting two seats behind an innocent couple on a bus).

More than ever he has this empty feeling in his stomach. It could be of course that he's just hungry. He consults his watch. 5.15. They're not due to meet at the Savoy until 6.30. Just time to get something to eat. Sunday, though – the Corner House will be closed, won't it; Soho restaurants not yet open, if at all. Then he remembers the Regent Palace Hotel, across the way – maybe the *brasserie* will be open: if not, he'll no doubt manage some sort of snack in the lounge there.

An hour or so later, feeling somewhat better, but still with some qualms, he's making his way up to the weighty Rolls-Royce-like portal of the Savoy Hotel – an establishment that he's had no pretensions of ever having visited in the past. Anna had described it as 'our local, just across the road' (from the Adelphi); but then, laughing at his expression (he not quite knowing how to take her remark), had gone on to elaborate, 'Actually, not only is it handy, but it's one of the few places in the area to have an air-raid shelter, down in the basements. We've come to think of it as our bolt-hole.' As he walks up the steps he can't help feeling just a shade overawed, though, by the doorman, top-hatted and in liveried coat-tails, standing at the top with the sort of superior demeanour that epitomises the exclusivity of the place. But the man, respectful to the point of almost standing to attention, touches the brim of his hat in a form of salute and opens the door for him – and it suddenly strikes Peter that he himself, in RAF officer's uniform, now represents a new kind of aristocracy.

Some fifteen minutes later finds him sitting with Anna in a corner of a large cocktail bar, the room opulent with colours of gold, silver and red, and with the sparkle of crystal. The place is crowded, mainly with young people, many of whom are in uniform. Waves of shouts and laughter crash and eddy against the sides of the room – a sea of agitation and forced gaiety driven on by deep currents of uncertainty, he senses – and this makes it difficult to sustain a sensible conversation. Anna's mouth, as she tries to make him hear, is therefore disturbingly close to his ear. He's feeling both excited and relieved all in one go: the one because, close to, she's even more thrilling than he remembers; and the other because he's just been through the mill with Jordan and Bill, and Anna has rescued him. It is his appreciation of the form of that rescue, too, that has boosted his infatuation with her to the point of yearning; for he understands that although she had been deep in conversation some paces away from him, seemingly oblivious to the noise around her, still she had been aware of him enough to pick up on his growing distress, and had cared enough to excuse herself and come over. Then, putting a possessive hand on his arm, saying, 'Come, Peter, you are supposed to be my escort for this evening and I think you are neglecting me!' she had led him away.

Now, direct as ever, she says, 'So what was that all about?'

What had it been all about? He finds it difficult to say.

When he'd arrived and made his way to the bar, although the place was already packed and quite rowdy, he'd quickly found Anna, Jordan and Bill standing together talking. Anna had greeted him warmly, with decorum, allowing him to take quick stock of Bill, whose appearance and attitude, he decided, had changed little over the intervening years – but Jordan, smelling of drink, in an instant had come over to him exclaiming 'Peter, darling!' rather too loudly, and had been all over him in most uncharacteristic fashion in a way that he recognised as being fed by a private agenda of her own. Once he'd managed, with some embarrassment, to free himself from her clutches, he'd been able to shake Bill's hand and study him at more length. At that stage Bill had been friendly enough, even if his handshake had been firmer than necessary and his grin somewhat patronising, and there had followed several minutes of polite, meaningless chit-chat.

Then, 'Well, you've changed quite a bit since we last met!' Bill had said, at the same time ostentatiously putting his arm around Jordan and drawing her to him. He'd made it sound, Peter thought, as though the change hadn't necessarily been for the better. It was at this point that he'd seen that

Bill, too, had already had quite a lot to drink. He was swaying slightly, and rather exaggerated in the way he was being so possessive about Jordan. So that's it, Peter had thought: he's still got a thing about her, and is jealous; and she's milking it for all it's worth!

'You haven't,' he'd replied, hoping it sounded as sophisticated and cool as he'd intended it to be.

And it was true. Bill, in uniform, every bit the Squadron Leader fighter pilot, was the Bill of old, come to fruition, the swaggering buccaneer. Bigger and broader, of course, about Peter's height, in other respects he was unchanged. He still had that swarthiness, as though originating from the Mediterranean, still had that perpetual half-smile, somewhere between amused condescension and a sneer, still that darkness of complexion which seemed to reflect the slight darkness of his nature.

'And fancy finding you in the RAF as well,' Bill had gone on to say. 'I couldn't believe it when Jordan told me.' Then: 'I see you've managed to achieve a rapid rise in rank, as well,' nodding at the three bands on Peter's sleeve. 'Well done.' And the sarcasm had been obvious enough to negate any pretence of repartee.

He'd felt himself flush, anger rising, but had, he hoped, remained nonchalant as he replied. 'Yes, it comes with particular skills and expertise. As you know.'

'Ah yes, more than one way to glory.' The sneer this time had been unmistakable, the gloves off.

This is becoming ridiculous, Peter had thought, we've only just met for the first time for goodness knows how many years and we're already behaving like children again. But this time we know what it's all about. He'd noticed Anna raise a surprised and quizzical eyebrow at this little exchange; whilst Jordan had been looking on with interest, not quite understanding in her befuddled state what was going on, but stimulated by the growing atmosphere between the two men. Anna, having silently registered her quiet dismay, had, he thinks, at this point moved away to talk to someone else. And it was then that he'd walked into the trap.

Too eager, as always, to mend bridges, he'd said, 'I must say I envy you, flying, being able to make a more positive contribution in this war. Much more glamorous than the work I do.'

'Glamorous? Is that how you think of it, Pete? Yes, I suppose so, in a way. But it's not that easy. It's like...rugby. Anyone can learn to play, after a fashion. But being good at it is a different matter. As you must know, it's a question of ability, of hand-eye co-ordination, of awareness, of reaction times, and, not least, of boldness. It's not for everyone, you know. It wouldn't do for you.'

The last remark had been made lightly, but for all that had been disparaging enough for Peter to want to hit him. The trouble was, though, that he suspected that Bill was only too correct in that respect. He'd found Jordan looking at him curiously, the pupils of her eyes dilated with excitement as though she was actually expecting that he would hit out at Bill.

And he'd tried to take them back onto safer ground, to the past.

'Do you hear anything of George, these days?' he'd asked. At the same time he'd had a fleeting image from the past, of Bill, George, Jamie and himself on the lake that time, of discovering Jordan with Hamilton, and of their joint dismay and disbelief at what they'd witnessed that day.

But it was a different image that Bill had dredged up, one that he hadn't wanted reminding of.

'No, not for some time. He tried to join up, I believe, but they wouldn't have him. Something to do with that damaged leg.' Then he'd looked at Peter in a knowing, challenging way.

And, hauled from some dark oubliette of his mind, the memory, almost obliterated, had hit him with all the impact of the unforeseen. Resisting, he'd been dragged back into the private recesses of his mind to that occasion – one of those uncommon ones when the three boys found themselves without Jamie there to guide and moderate their activities.

They've been scrambling up a steep fell-side, one of those craggy scree-littered slopes which start off being difficult enough but which then, almost unnoticed, very quickly require the use of hands as well as feet. They've paused for breath, Peter taking care that he keeps his eyes away from the dizzying incline below his feet, when George, glancing up to identify their best route, says (in translation), 'Look there! There's a crag-fast ewe up there with a lamb in tow. I reckon it must be one of Josh Cowperthwaite's.'

They follow his gaze, and see what he means. The sheep, not yet sheared, has followed a line of grazing until it has ended up on a narrow grassy ledge half-way up a forty foot crag, where it has found it can go no further but equally is unable to turn around or to back off. Its lamb, no more than three weeks old, has followed behind and is huddling into its mother's rear legs. The ewe has been standing there stolidly, as is the way of sheep, probably for some considerable time; and the lamb is becoming increasingly agitated, the mother glancing round at it in an uneasy manner.

'They'll both have fallen off there afore long, the way they're going!' says George. 'Bill, you know the Cowperthwaite farm, don't you. How about you dash down there and get some help. Meanwhile Pete and I'll try and hold them.'

Peter, anxious about what George means by 'trying to hold them' watches as Bill hurtles off in leaps and bounds down the steep slope, as always totally heedless of the possibility of his losing his balance and tumbling headlong – while George calls after him, 'They'll need a rope.'

Then, turning to Peter, he says, 'Pete, you see that other ledge on the left, running towards the one the sheep are on, at about the same level? Do you think you could work your way up to that, while I go up behind them to the back end of the ledge they're on? The idea is that we box them in, so they don't try to move. But when they see me coming up behind them they may take fright and try to go forwards, where it'll be even more dicey – if you're ahead of them they'll be less likely to do that. But don't attempt to get too close, or they might panic.'

Peter privately thinks there's little likelihood of his trying to get 'too close' – from what he can see, the ledge George has in mind for him is only several yards long and a good twenty feet from where the sheep are – but swallowing his misgivings he simply nods in what purports to be a nonchalant manner.

But when (after a scramble that he finds more demanding than he would have liked) he gets to the ledge, he discovers that it's a lot narrower, even at its nearer, broader end, than it looked to be from below. No more than a couple of feet across, in fact. And on its inside is an almost vertical rock face five or six feet high. Can George really be expecting him to go out onto that? He hardly dare look at the outside, but the drop there must be a good twenty feet. Also vertical.

George, however, some twenty-five or thirty yards away, on the far side of the sheep, is making surreptitious beckoning motions at him. Although his signals are subdued, so as not to alarm the sheep, the urgency implied by them is clear enough. Biting his lip, and trying not to look down, Peter therefore edges out onto the ledge, finding handholds where he can. After a few yards, though, all at once he finds he is no longer able to put one foot past the other without it dangling out over space; and the top of the cliff face on his inside is now just too high to reach for a handhold. Shocked by this abrupt realisation, spread-eagled against the rock he clings with his fingertips to whatever little prominences he can find, hardly daring to move, his hands clammy, and sweat breaking out on his brow. Slowly he turns his head to look across at George. The ewe, perhaps fifteen yards away, unconcerned, looks back at him; and some fifteen yards beyond her, equally unconcerned, George is standing with his hand up, as if to say, 'Don't come any further'. He has no intention of coming any further. What is worrying him is how he's going to get back. He daren't move, feels as though he'll never be able to move.

Time passes. It seems a lifetime. Probably in fact only ten minutes or so before, out of the corner of his eye, he sees George silently gesticulating, his finger pointing downwards towards the foot of the fell. Peter turns to look, then wishes he hadn't. For a moment he thinks he's going to come off. He sways dizzily, an impression of space falling away from him and him falling with it. Eyes closed, he clings desperately to the rock, his whole body trembling. But in that split second of looking down he's seen what George has seen – figures making their way rapidly up the fell-side. Thank God! For once in his life it's not just an expression. It's a fervent prayer of thanks. He stands there frozen, wondering how long he can maintain this posture before everything gives way and he hurtles off. Seconds tick slowly by, then minutes that seem like hours. He's vaguely aware, when he dares move his head at all, of people moving past to his left, not far away. He realises they may have to go a good deal higher than this to get above the sheep, and then presumably come down by rope. But he's not interested in that. Only that they be quick.

269

His concern is no longer how they're going to get the sheep off, but how he's going to get off. After some time he's distantly aware of something happening to his right, beyond the end of his ledge, of a figure dangling in mid-air on the end of a rope. But most of the time he's got his eyes closed. He's in an absolute funk. He realises that. He's disgusted with himself. But he doesn't feel there's anything he can do about it. Then, somewhere above, there are distant voices; a little after that, a subdued cheer. Then silence. For a moment he thinks, wildly, that they've all gone away and left him.

Then comes a voice a few yards from his left. George's voice. A cheerful voice. 'Come on, Pete. Have you gone to sleep on us? You can come off now. They've got them both.'

Somehow he finds a voice. Not his own voice. Someone else's voice. 'I don't think I can move,' it says.

There's a silence. Then, 'Don't be daft,' George says. 'Stop playing games.'

'Really,' he says, irritation rising above his fear. 'I daren't move!'

George's reply contains a mixture of perplexity and mild concern. 'There's nothing to it,' he says. 'Just come back the way you went on. Just retrace your footsteps. Come on. The others'll be here in a minute.' There's a tinge of embarrassment now in his words.

Peter doesn't care. Anger dominates now – mostly because George can't seem to understand. 'If I move, I'll fall off,' he says between gritted teeth.

'Don't be daft,' George says again. 'Here, give me your hand.'

He feels George's hand brush his own, and flinches. It's almost as if George is trying to prise his fingers away from the rock. From safety. As if George is trying to kill him.

'No!' he says. 'Don't!'

But George somehow has hold of his hand now, and is tugging gently. 'Come on,' he says, 'it's easy.' Peter, desperate, resists.

Careful!' George exclaims. 'You'll have us both off!'

He's not sure what happens next. There's a more positive pull from George, Peter tries to move away, there comes a muffled curse from George, then a yell, and suddenly his hand is released. He opens his eyes to a slithering, scuffling sound, a further yell, and then a thud followed immediately by a scream. As though all at once released from a vice, his head whips round. George is nowhere to be seen. It takes only a second for the awfulness of it to strike him. George has fallen.

The rest is confusion. He doesn't know how he gets off the ledge, only that it happens quickly, as if he's up till now been imprisoned in a block of ice, mind and body, and that suddenly it's been cracked apart. Fear is the dominant emotion. No longer for himself, but for George. Unsustainable self-recrimination will come later.

As he reaches the safety of a grassy slope there are further shouts and the thud-thud of rushing feet coming down the hillside above. Some twenty feet below, at the bottom of the cliff, he sees George's inert body. He hurls himself down the incline, feet moving as rapidly as his thoughts. Terror drives him. Please God, let George be all right! As he reaches George's crumpled body, he hears a series of groans. Instant relief is smothered by further immediate fears. Only when he hears George's fervent curses does he begin to give thanks to the Almighty.

People come up behind him, adding their curses to George's own litany of expletives.

'George! Are you alright?' someone calls anxiously.

'No, I'm not,' George manages to reply between groans. 'I've broken my bloody leg!'

'What the bloody hell happened?' someone else asks in somewhat belligerent tones, while others rush to attend to George.

Peter opens his mouth to explain...what? That his craven weakness had led to the injury – perhaps crippling, even fatal – of his friend? But no sound comes out.

He sees George look up; tries again to speak, without success.

'My own bloody fault,' George says. 'I was just being daft.'

Peter, trying to hide his extreme discomfort, looks around – and sees Bill looking at him thoughtfully, the expression on his face difficult to read.

An eternity of time, it seems, but in reality only a few seconds, in which that whole dreadful scene had passed once more before his eyes: for he hears Anna say to him again, 'What was that all about?'

The din in the room is still such that they're having to sit with heads close together in order to hear what the other is saying, and perhaps it's this sense of physical closeness as well as Anna's sympathetic and concerned tone which breaks down barriers. For, having over all these years steadfastly refused to acknowledge to himself the actuality of those events, he now finds himself, in a welter of self-denigration, admitting to her the facts of his cowardice on that day, something he's never before revealed to anyone. He tells her the whole story, knowing as he does, almost masochistically, that it will result in him losing her respect.

But instead there's warmth and understanding in her eyes as she says, 'Oh, I think you are too hard on yourself. I would have been absolutely terrified in that situation. There is no way that anyone would have been able to get me to do what you did in spite of your fear. And you cannot blame yourself for what happened to your friend George. We cannot blame ourselves for the mistakes of others, even if we are interacting with them. Each of us is responsible for our own part of the...the...equation – is that the right word?'

'But don't you see, if I hadn't pulled away from him he wouldn't have fallen.'

'But if he hadn't tried to make your decisions for you, even though he was trying to help, it wouldn't have happened either. But I do understand how you feel. I have similar concerns about myself.'

'You do?'

'Yes. You see, when I left Germany at the beginning of '38 I tried to persuade my parents to leave with me. But I failed to do so – my father said that their whole life's work was there in Germany; and in any case, he was as German as the next man, and it was his duty to stay and work for a better, more sane Germany. And of course my mother refused to leave without him. You realise, of course, that we are Jewish?'

He nods, and says, 'But, equally, you can't blame yourself for having failed to persuade them. I'm sure you did your best.'

'Yes, I did. But, don't you see, if I'd refused to leave without them, perhaps they would have agreed to come as well. They were so very anxious for me to leave while it was still possible. In that respect, it was my cowardice that made me come away regardless. But in my case, I knew what I was doing – and, if I'd been honest with myself, I knew what might be the consequences for them.' Her voice breaks a little at this point, and she takes a deep breath, spreading her hands in a gesture that seems to express apology. 'But once we had to start wearing those damned yellow stars, so that we were like…lepers…so that everyone stared at us as though we were unclean…like animals from some lower order…I just couldn't stand it any longer. I had to get away, otherwise I think I would have gone mad.' Her eyes brim with tears, dark pools into which he can imagine himself falling, and instinctively he reaches out to grasp her hand.

After a respectful pause, still holding her hand, inert in his own, he says lightly, 'What does your father do?'

She laughs, a mirthless, bitter sound. 'He was a Professor of German Literature at the university. That's ironic, isn't it – that for years he'd been seen as a highly respected expert on German culture?'

Reluctantly he picks up on that, not really wanting to, suspecting that he knows the answer he'll receive.

'You say *was*…?'

'He was sacked. Of course. Simply because of being a Jew. Before I left.' She looks at him tiredly, eyes now dry as though suddenly bereft of tears.

'And what does he…where is he…are they…now?'

Her gaze remains steady, full of patience. 'I don't know. I haven't heard from them for over six months. I write, frequently, through the Red Cross, but it's like posting letters into a void. It's just silence. I've tried writing to other relatives, too, an uncle and aunt, and a cousin, but the result is the same. I don't even know if the letters ever get there.' Her voice breaks again. 'If only I could hear something, however bad…but simply not knowing, is…unbearable. You see, in the months before I left they were already taking many people away…Jews, Slavs, Communists, people of that sort…that sort – you see, even I have learnt to speak in that way! No one knew where they were going. There was talk of 'Correction Camps' – but no one knew where or what they were; and there was never any news of those people afterwards.'

'It must have been dreadful.' Even as he speaks, the words he's used sound thoroughly fatuous.

'It must have been, for them. We never really asked. I'm afraid that we, along with all the others, never dared to protest, or even voice our concerns. There was a wall of silence, behind which we all hid, thankful only that on each occasion it hadn't been our turn, that once more we had been spared. But not infrequently, in the middle of the night – it was always in the middle of the night! – there would be the sound of lorries out in the street, shouts and the rush of feet, and hammering on doors. The hammering on doors was always the worst part! – one was never quite sure that it wasn't one's own door. Then, very quickly afterwards – hardly any time at all, almost as if people were bundled away just as they were, no time to collect personal things or to take a last look around – there would be the sound of those people, our neighbours, being taken out into the street and loaded into the lorries and driven away. We never dared look, simply lay in our beds listening, and thinking, and lying awake for the rest of the night. We, I and my parents, had so far been spared – I suppose that my father perhaps still had some respect in the city, even though he'd been dismissed from his post; and of course I was already quite well-known, on the stage and in films. But all that would have…did…change. We knew that sooner or later our turn would come.'

By now she is crying openly, her tears rediscovered, rolling down her cheeks.

For one disgraceful moment he is embarrassed, looking up to see if anyone else has noticed, concerned that they may think that he is responsible for this. But all around him others are still engrossed in their own worlds, mindless of any small dramas within their throng.

Discomfited by his own inadequacy, however, he doesn't quite know what to do or say. He finds himself saying, lame as it is, 'Were you very close to your parents?' As the words come out, they sound not only inadequate but inappropriate. Why on earth did he say something like that? Was he in fact thinking of his own relationships rather than Anna's? Was he indeed still searching for some framework with which to understand his own relationship with his mother – and father?

She doesn't seem to see anything wrong with the question, however. Dabbing carefully at her eyes with a small white handkerchief, she says, slowly, thoughtfully, 'I suppose I was. I think maybe all Jewish families see themselves as close. I don't know. One doesn't think much about it until…afterwards. Up to a certain age one takes one's parents for granted, doesn't one? Sometimes they are kind and solicitous, sometimes cross and impatient – they are just…there. Initially you take to them all your little hurts and wants, fully expecting that they can make things better; and sometimes they resolve them for you and sometimes they don't. But then, as you grow up, there are things you begin to keep from them, private things, things that you don't feel able to share with anyone, or that perhaps you are more inclined to share with your friends rather than your parents. And, thoroughly self-centred at that age, in your teens, you still don't see your parents as individuals who have their own lives, their own secrets and problems. You're not interested in them from that point of view – only as people who can still, occasionally, do something, emotionally or materially, for you. Only when you, suddenly perhaps, find them no longer there, do you begin to think about these things. But by then it's too late. At least, that is how I see it – but then it may be that that is only me, that others do not have that experience?'

Again she breaks down, the tears flowing unashamedly down her cheeks. This time, he has no thought of what others might be thinking, only that he desperately wants to put an arm around her, to comfort her. But he knows he can't do that.

Through her tears she says, 'I cling to the hope that my parents are all right, that they are at least still alive. But I fear they are dead. I know only too well what the Nazis are capable of doing to Jews. And I know that my sense of loss will not diminish with time, but only grow – for there are too many unresolved issues left behind. And I know too that if the Nazis manage to come here I also would succumb, for I could not live with that, even if they allowed me to.'

'Don't worry, there's no fear of their coming here!' he says stoutly – and thinks, Do I really believe that? Isn't that what had been thought for the rest of Europe?

Hurriedly he goes on, 'You must feel lucky to have Jim, in all this? He must be a great support.'

She gives him a look that is almost startled at first, then flares, the fire of the gypsy in it. It's as if in an instant she has changed roles, no longer dependant but strong and spirited. He's as startled as she had briefly seemed to be. He realises his words must have sounded patronising.

For a few seconds she doesn't speak, the embers of her anger still visible in her eyes.

Then, not answering his question, she says, 'You admire him a great deal, don't you.'

Her speech is slow, thoughtful, the precision and accentuation of her words more obvious again, the foreign intonation coming through; and the words are phrased as a statement rather than as a question.

'Of course. I think everyone does.'

Again the thoughtful silence on her part, until, coming to a decision: 'He's not any less human than the rest of us, you know.'

His quick laugh of disagreement has a rueful note. 'Perhaps not, but he gives a very good impression of having more attributes than several of us put together!'

'Oh, certainly. He is very talented, and wise, and kind and brave. All of that. And I love him dearly. But you mustn't turn him into a…a paragon. It would do him an injustice. He has his own share of doubts and disappointments to carry through life, just like the rest of us.'

'He does?' He can't keep the incredulity out of his voice.

She shrugs – an unexpectedly Latin gesture. This is followed by further hesitation, her inner struggle all too obvious before she says, slowly, 'I don't know why I'm telling you this – Jim would be furious if he knew – but he's spurred on always by his fear of failure. None of what he is comes easily, in spite of what you think. And I admire him for that. But he too needs support, and it's not easy to give – or, rather, it's not easy for him to accept. He denies the need to himself, never mind to others.'

This time disbelief renders him speechless.

Perhaps his silence prods her into further explanation, creates the necessity of justifying what she claims, for she goes on. 'All his life he's struggled to please his father. It's been the mainspring of his existence. And all his life he sees himself as having not fully succeeded. Mind you, I don't think his father understands any of this, any more than Jim does. He probably would be horrified if he knew. It's not that he's critical of Jim. It's just that he takes for granted everything that Jim has achieved, and probably in his whole life has never praised him. Or demonstrated any affection. The consequence is that Jim sets himself impossibly high standards – and in his own view always falls short of them – and although he doesn't expect those around him to achieve the same, he is critical when they fall too far short.'

He wants to ask, Is he critical of you? – instead, he says, 'What does his father do?' It's always an inane question, he thinks, asking what someone 'does', so rarely relevant to understanding the person under scrutiny – except that it somehow puts things into context.

'He's something high up in the Foreign Office.'

'And do you get on well with him?'

'I've never met him.'

The flat statement, made without inflection, floors him.

'But you seem to know so much about him, about his personality?'

'Only what I've gathered from Jim. On and off, he talks about him a great deal. I know for example that he flew in the Royal Flying Corps in the last war, that he was capped – is that the right word? – for Scotland at rugby on a number of occasions, that sort of thing. All, it seems, with great distinction.'

He detects a certain resentment simmering there, in the way she says that. Curiosity alone would have made him ask his next question. 'How come you've never met him?'

'He doesn't approve of me, of our marriage. It's my being Jewish, you see – as well as being German.' She laughs, a dry sound. 'A double fault you might say! – although he might have tolerated the latter, at a pinch. So, he refuses to meet me – wouldn't come to the wedding.'

He flinches a little at these further revelations, but is so wrapped up in her, in the way she holds herself in such quiet dignity in spite of the lingering resentment – which imparts a smouldering quality to her beauty – that he's not as shocked as he might have been.

'And his mother?' he asks tentatively.

'Oh, his mother's a dear. I get on well with her. But I see little of her. Again, his father wouldn't approve you see. But to give his father his due, he did pull strings – is that the expression? – he did pull strings to prevent me from perhaps being interned. Mind you, I suspect it was from a need to preserve the family honour rather than out of a desire to help me as a person – or, come to that, to help Jim.'

For a moment he doesn't understand: what influence could the man possibly have had in preventing the Nazis from interning her? Then he realises: it's *this* country she's talking about. Of course, she would be regarded as an enemy alien.

Nevertheless he can't keep the astonishment out of his voice. 'You might have been interned?'

'Of course.' She raises an elegant eyebrow, all that's needed to convey amusement at his innocence. 'You don't know about internment?'

'Well, yes...' he flounders, his confusion amplified by the fact that all this time, because of the level of noise in the room, they've had to carry on the conversation with their faces close to one another, '...but I hadn't thought that...'

'...it would apply to someone like me?' she supplies. 'Let me tell you about Internment.' Her dark eyes flash with anger – and he has to remind himself that it is not, actually, directed at him.

'There are three categories of *enemy aliens* in this country, that is to say Germans and Italians. 'Class A' are those who are regarded as being clearly hostile and a threat to this country. They were immediately interned at the outbreak of war. 'Class B' are those who are not seen as being hostile – and they include of course very many who fled from Nazi Germany because of persecution – but who have been in this country only since after 1936. I of course come into that category. The authorities began to round up Class B aliens for internment at the end of June, on the fall of France. I in fact received intimation that I might be interned, at the beginning of last month. Jim was furious of course, as was I, and it was then that he managed to get his father to intervene.'

When she appears to brood silently on this for long moments, he asks, 'And Class C?'

'Class C are those who became resident in this country before 1936. They, so far, have not been earmarked for internment.' Again anger flares. 'What nonsense! Both they and so-called Class B are in the same boat. They have, virtually all of them, fled from Germany for one reason or another. There is no difference between them. It's all bureaucracy! As if the difference of a few months is of any significance! They were hounded and persecuted in their own country, and now the same has happened to them here.'

'I don't suppose they're actually being persecuted here,' he reasons mildly. 'After all, the authorities will want time to sort out any that might be working as spies. Surely it's reasonable that they're put under supervision until they can be vetted?'

'Oh, you're as bad as Jim!' she says crossly. 'He thinks that having been 'spared' myself I should just keep quiet about it all. Should be content to be simply grateful that his precious father had put in a word for me! Even hinted that my kicking up a stink would reflect badly on his own prospects for promotion in the RAF. But have you seen the conditions in which these so-called Internees are being held?

'No, of course you haven't,' she continues crossly, without giving him time to reply. 'You're like the rest, not interested in those who are merely foreigners and Jews.'

She makes as if to rise, about to leave, and in a panic he puts a restraining hand on her arm. 'Anna, wait,' he says urgently, 'calm down. Just tell me about it. I want to know.'

She looks at him suspiciously, then evidently decides he's sincere. Speaking with passion, she says, 'Many of them have been sent to temporary transit centres in the North of England, or Scotland, preparatory to their being sent on to your Isle of Man – or even, I believe, to Canada. I have made two visits to such places in Lancashire, and seen them for myself. They are being put into old mill buildings, that sort of thing, places that are dirty, cold and even verminous. The food is awful, they have few clothes with them, and even fewer personal possessions. They're not even allowed newspapers or wirelesses. Many families are split up, women and children to one centre, men to another. No contact between them, and not knowing when they will see one another again. For all they know, they will be imprisoned like that until the Nazis come – all ready and waiting, no work for the Gestapo to do other than executing them! Can you imagine it? Here they are, thinking they have escaped all that and found freedom, only to find that it's a lie! It's...it's an injustice, I tell you. Something should be done about it. But I am in no position to do anything.'

'Can Jim not do anything to help?' he asks hesitantly. 'Or his...father,' he adds lamely.

She looks at him scornfully, as though he hasn't been listening. 'As I said, Jim thinks I should just lie low and let things take their course, that by kicking up a fuss I am just drawing attention to myself – and him. But I cannot do nothing. If I do, I'm as guilty as the rest...as have been all those in Germany who have done exactly that.'

He searches desperately for something to say, to find some words of comfort, and all he can find is his own sense of helplessness in the face of her pain and hostility. But in the silence that follows, a private silence emphasised by the heedless hubbub of those around, she suddenly relents. Leaning into him she surprises him by planting a lingering kiss on his cheek.

'Thank you, Peter, for listening to my woes. You carry with you an air of...*verstandnis*...of sympathy – something I'm not too used to at the present time. You will come and see me again, won't you? Promise?'

Several things happen at once to abruptly wrench him from his ruminations. A loud and vindictive roar, hitting the car with the violence of a tornado and punching painfully at his skull and eardrums, is accompanied by a short series of metallic thuds, like hammer blows, on the roof. At the same time the car swerves violently, tipping onto its side amid the sharp sound of crunching metal and breaking glass. He feels himself flung bruisingly sideways across the steering wheel, and the next moment is lying staring up at the sky through a broken window, the soft unprotesting form of the WAAF driver beneath him. Dazed, with a pain in his side and still unable to comprehend what has happened, for a few seconds he lies there before experimentally turning his head to look around him, his gaze arrested by the odd sight of a series of round holes in the roof (now the 'side' of the car), through which he can see the movement of what looks like foliage. His ears are still ringing, but the initial noise has receded into the distance – a noise that he now identifies as the sound of aero-engines at full throttle. Then he understands. They've come under attack. Must be alongside the airfield – for now he can hear machine-gun fire, distant explosions and the sound of klaxons.

'Are you alright?' he asks, trying to turn himself around so as to take his weight off the girl. He can smell petrol. With effort he manages to twist around, find the ignition key, and turn it to the 'off' position. Then, by reaching up to grasp the back of the passenger seat he succeeds in hauling himself to a position where he can stand in a half-crouch, facing the near-vertical surface of the roof, his feet planted on the front and central side-pillars of the car: he's never before considered how cramped it might be trying to stand in a car tipped upon its side.

'Are you alright?' he asks again. Having got his balance, he peers down at the motionless body of the girl, lying in a crumpled heap against the side of the door, her head lolling up against the back edge of the window frame close to his right foot. There is blood on her face, and shards of glass in her hair. With a curse he registers that she is unconscious, and railing at his own stupidity he bends down into an even more awkward crouch, his feet either side of her, in order to reach her neck to feel for a carotid pulse. She stirs slightly at his touch, but her eyes remain closed. Unable to find a pulse, nevertheless he is reassured by her slight movement. He is worried, though, that in her present position she'll be in danger of having her breathing obstructed by her tongue. He must try to move her. Getting himself into a situation where he can do that, however, proves difficult. In order to steady himself as he moves, he places his hand lightly on the side of her chest – and his hand comes away with the stickiness of blood. Swearing, he manages to turn her round sufficiently to be able to see what is going on – and continues to curse loudly: the front of her tunic is soaked in blood which is dripping into a rapidly darkening puddle on the floor.

In a panic, numbed by a total feeling of helplessness, he looks wildly around, but all he can see is an empty road alongside which runs a wire-mesh fence, presumably the boundary fence of the airfield: but there are no buildings, and no other signs of activity, the now-dwindling sounds of gunfire and explosions some distance away.

He looks down at the girl, whose face is now ashen; and as he does so her eyes flicker open, with no signs of recognition. 'Sorry,' she murmurs in a whisper so low he can hardly hear her. And her eyes close again.

CHAPTER EIGHTEEN

To any casual passer-by this particular afternoon the scene around him or her might have had all the attributes of an idyllic pastoral one. Bright sunlight glinted on parched grass which from time to time was ruffled almost imperceptibly by a slight breeze; and lush dark foliage, promising shade, hung gracefully on distant trees. The young men at the outer edge of that very large field, who sprawled singly or in groups on the dry ground, or lounged indolently in easy chairs outside nearby wooden huts, would, from afar, have looked like any other youngsters enjoying an idle moment on yet another perfect day in this long hot summer. Only as that mythological walker drew nearer, mysteriously unaware of the circumstances of this place and time, would they have seen that these young men were strangely garbed in thick uniforms of a darker colour than the deep summer sky, wore bulky calf-high boots, and that some were further encumbered by outer vests of bright yellow – all peculiarly unsuitable to the heat of this day. And they would have noticed that although they laughed and joked from time to time, for the most part they were remarkably silent. On closer inspection the reason for this silence would have become apparent. For they would have seen that although some were quietly reading, and others asleep, many of their young faces were taut with tension and made older than their years by lines of fatigue. Yet, as they continued to study them they might have begun to detect that beneath that weariness there still existed a gleam of determination, as well as the glint of desperation. It was as if the primal anxiety of a nation was crystallised in them – the product of an intuitive awareness that it was at this juncture, in the weeks that had come and the weeks that perhaps were still to come, that the day would be carried or would be lost.

For Peter, sitting on the grass listening to the young Pilot Officer chatting to him, the afternoon felt equally unreal. In spite of all the deaths he'd been professionally exposed to over the years, he still couldn't come to terms with the fact that Connie Saunders had died that morning (and he was conscious that, in now thinking of her by name instead of as his 'WAAF driver', he was sentimentally personalising their relationship). His wanting to deny her death was, he knew, partly due to the difficulty of accepting that he'd been unable to do anything, had simply had to look on helplessly as she died; partly due to an irrational feeling of 'guilt' that, in the lottery of life, it had been she who had caught the bullets and not him; and partly to the knowledge that, of all the ironies, hers had been the only death in the attack on the airfield that morning. Then, too, it had been some time before he'd been able to report his own incident, and arrange for a team to go out to retrieve her body – for having found his way to the main gate, after she'd died, he'd been immediately caught up in the turmoil of the aftermath of the raid. So this had added to his sense of guilt, almost as though he'd somehow continued to neglect her even after her death. But, he sternly reminded himself, during the morning his priorities had had to be other casualties, even though these had been surprisingly light: a few burns and relatively minor shrapnel wounds, a member of ground-crew with a broken leg, and a pilot (who'd been on the point of taking off when his Hurricane had been caught by the blast from a nearby bomb) who'd miraculously escaped with mild concussion and a broken arm.

However, as he gazed across the aerodrome, watching the work-parties frantically filling in craters on field and runway and towing away damaged aircraft, the sense of shock of it all had not yet worn off. Off to one side, at the far end of the field, the dark windows of the control tower also seemed to be watching; and, making a low line on either side of that, the station buildings, from which he'd just come, looked as though they were still recoiling from the morning's assault. Blackened in places, like bad teeth among a row of white ones, they appeared to be fixed in a rueful grin. Further round, one of the big hangars stood crushed and broken, like a torn-open can, smoke still drifting from a gaping hole in its roof. He glanced at his watch. Still only 1400 hours. Yet the morning's events seemed to belong to yesterday. And during those few hours he'd been aware of still-serviceable aircraft of all three squadrons variously being scrambled on a several occasions – at lunch Bill had told him that between them they'd flown a total of 93 individual sorties that morning. Coming on top of all they'd had to endure over the previous days, it was no wonder they were all exhausted.

In all this noise and turmoil, though, he'd found himself captivated by the music of the Merlin engines as Spitfires and Hurricanes took off and landed, or on the odd occasion swept overhead across the field. It was a sound so different from the workhorse rumble of the bombers – this was an altogether more thrilling note, with a mellow depth and richness to its growl, yet containing also, it seemed, higher tones of triumph and set purpose. It made him wish that he could be one of those privileged to fly them. It was a sound that seemed to sum up the age into which they'd been precipitated; one to capture the brightness of the knife-edge of excitement and danger on which they all now precariously had to live.

But, as he looked around at the young men scattered about him, (some flat on their backs, soaking up the sun; two reading and re-reading newspapers as though not really taking it in; another leafing through the pages of a letter as if committing the contents to memory; one fellow staring blankly into space as he fondled the ears of his dog), he very much doubted that he could ever have become one of their kind. For, he knew, all of them were simply waiting: waiting, on edge, for the abrupt jangle of the telephone through the open window of the hut. Tension permeated the group, eroding what little relaxation they had hoped to achieve. He felt his own eyes turn to where theirs so often drifted, to the open doorway of the hut, where, fixed to the frame, hung a large brass fire-bell. Beneath it a familiar notice proclaimed, '*When you hear the bell, run like hell!*' The flippancy was typical, the bravado of youth making light of the otherwise unacceptable: actually, these are merely boys masquerading as men, he thought. To his own suddenly-jaded eyes the thing simply looked chillingly ominous.

For the past few minutes he'd been only half-listening to the excited prattle of this particular young pilot next to him, but something the lad now said caught his attention.

'I believe you're an old friend of Squadron Leader Jackson?'

He looked at the boy in some surprise. Where on earth had he gleaned something like that?

'Yes. From when we were in our early teens. But we'd lost touch in recent years.'

Now why had he found it necessary to add that last bit?

'He's a smashing bloke, isn't he.'

He looked at the youngster silently for a few seconds. The lad's bubbling enthusiasm was beginning to grate on him, particularly as Bill's parting words to Peter had been, '...He's still on a high – just see if you can't calm him down a little, will you.'

That was something that, so far, he hadn't managed to do. Which was doubly irksome: firstly because he knew that it was in the boy's own interests that he should learn to approach his task in a more deliberate manner; and secondly because Bill had first of all said to him, 'I'll leave you with Andy Cameron for a few minutes; you've something almost in common, because Andy's put on hold his studies as a medical student in order to do his bit with us.' His stress on the word *almost* had hit home, as Peter knew Bill had intended it to.

Yet Bill had changed, much more than he'd been able to appreciate at their first meeting two weeks ago, with all the hostility involved in that. Most obviously he had grown a moustache, its pencil-thin line across his upper lip giving him more than ever the look of a buccaneer (and Peter had wondered briefly about the reason for that particular affectation). More significant, though, had been the change in his features. Gone was the familiar lift of the corners of his mouth, which had always made him seem as if he was about to break into a sardonic smile – to be replaced by lips set in a determined line. Gone too was the gleam of perpetual amusement in his eyes; instead, they'd taken on a wary look, devoid of emotion, and around them had appeared frown-lines of concentration as though constantly peering into the glare ahead. Perhaps it was all down to tiredness, as revealed now in the unusual greyness of his skin and the flatness of his words. But no, he *had* changed. All at once he seemed older than his years. His boyishness had gone.

And he'd actually been pleased to see Peter this time, now fully sober and without the distractions provided by Jordan. As though reaching for another familiar link with the past, there had been more respect, more kinship, in the way Bill had approached him. Apart from this recent mild dig, the air of challenge had disappeared.

They'd met up at lunchtime. Astonishingly, in spite of all that had gone on that morning, at around one o'clock Bill had turned up at the Medical Quarters, greeted Peter ('Couldn't believe it when I heard it was you who was coming over as relief M.O.'), and calmly invited him to join him in the Mess for lunch – as though nothing untoward had happened in the previous hours. But, as Bill had explained, his squadron had for the moment been downgraded to *Available* status – which meant that, should they be called into action they would be given up to twenty minutes in which to get airborne. 'Plenty of time, old boy – and we've learned by now that the only way to retain one's sanity is to get back to normal whenever the opportunity arises. Of course,' he'd added, 'we might be put back onto *Readiness* at a moment's notice, in which case I'd have to abandon my soup spoon in mid-air and hare back to Dispersal.'

But their meal had been uninterrupted ('Perhaps jerry's taken time off for lunch, as well,' Bill had said), so there had been time for Peter's many questions. He'd learned, for example, that there were three squadrons stationed at Church Wealdon – one of Spitfires and two of Hurricanes – making, variably, around 50 fighter aircraft in all. However, its status as a Sector Control airfield within 11 Group, Bill explained, signified that the combat control of all fighter aircraft, about 16 squadrons in all, from all the airfields within their 'sector' – that was to say the area immediately north-east of London – was their responsibility.

'I must say that, on the whole, so far, it's a system that's worked very well,' Bill had said. 'They can say what they like about 'Stuffy' Dowding, but he's been a damned good organiser in charge of Fighter Command, and this system's all down to him. But, for us, it's Park who's making it work.'

'Park being A.O.C., Group 11?' Peter had asked.

'That's right. A much more approachable type than Dowding, it has to be said. Dowding's your typical dour Scot, whereas Air Vice-Marshal Park's an affable, blunt New Zealander. Did you know that he flies his own Hurricane around the place? Sort of drops in on one without any warning!'

'Yes, so I've heard.'

'Mind you, it isn't to snoop. He's just keeping in touch with what's going on, face-to-face as it were. A morale-booster, if you like. And it does work. The chaps appreciate it. But Dowding has the reputation in some quarters of not caring, and I don't think that's true from what I've seen of him and heard elsewhere – I think he cares a great deal about those serving under him, particularly his combat pilots. I think he's just not capable of showing it. And, personality-wise, I'm afraid he's a fairly humourless sort of bloke, which means that there's not much affection for him. But, by God, he gets what he wants and gets things done. It's down to him that we've got the R.D.F., you know, against considerable opposition – although it has to be said that Churchill backed the scheme to the hilt. On the other hand, Winnie put considerable pressure on 'Stuffy' to send Spitfires out to the battle of France, no doubt in response to similar pressure from the French and our own army brass. And 'Stuffy', give him his due, dug his heels in and refused to budge, risking his position and his career in doing so. And we would have been in a sorry state now, if he hadn't. Over the last twelve days we've been losing Hurricanes and Spits considerably faster than they can be replaced. And in that same period Fighter Command has lost, in total, 154 fighter pilots. Did you know that? You don't get much of that in the news.'

He'd suddenly looked more drawn than ever, and an uncomfortable silence had followed, until Peter, more anxious than he'd ever been, had tentatively asked, 'So what do you think are our chances?'

Bill had looked at him without speaking for a few seconds, then, his voice heavy, had said, 'Dicey, at best. So far as pilots go, they're churning them out as fast as they can, and even 'borrowing' from Bomber Command – even from Fleet Air Arm. But the net result of that is that we end up with an even smaller proportion of pilots who have had combat experience – whereas the Germans gained a certain amount of experience from the Spanish war and from their blitzkrieg on the Continent. No, to be honest, I think our only hope is that the German High Command make more mistakes than we do. And they've already shown that they are capable of that by apparently having called off so soon their attacks on the R.D.F. stations. If they'd continued with those we'd've been really scuppered.'

'What exactly does R.D.F. do?' Peter had asked at this point.

'You don't know? No, I don't suppose you would. It gives us advance warning of their raids – by as much as 15 minutes, which is all the time we need. Not only that, but it tells us, very roughly, numbers and altitude, as well. Don't ask me how it works! It's remarkable, really. Something to do with reflection of radio waves, as I understand it. It only works out to sea, though – so thank God, once again, for the Channel. After that, once they've reached our coast, it's up to all those guys in the Observer Corps to keep us in the picture. But by then we can be airborne, and directed to the right area and height. It also gives us an indication as to how many squadrons need to be scrambled, and from where.

'And who decides that?'

'Well, initially, Fighter Command H.Q. at Bentley Priory, not far from here. But in practice, so far, it's been almost always over to our Group 11 control at Uxbridge, with Park making the decisions. From there it's then handed down to whatever Sector Control stations seem the most appropriate. It had been expected, before the shindig actually started, that most of the raids would come over the North Sea – but originally of course no one had thought that France could fall in the way it did. So Group 12, immediately to the north of us, had, previously, been expected to bear the brunt of it. A chap called Leigh-Mallory is the A.V-M. in charge of 12 Group. A very competent sort of a man, and sure of his own competence to the point where he pushes and pushes to get things done his way. So I suspect he's a bit pissed off that his boys aren't at the sharp end, the first to be taking on the raids, as it were. Of course they're involved, but not, so far, to the extent that we are, here in 11 Group. Mind you, all that could change pretty quickly! Leigh-Mallory, though, thinks that we're doing things all wrong here. We – that is to say, Park – put up individual squadrons in whatever numbers are thought necessary, and likewise disperse them as seems fit. Leigh-Mallory is all for banding several squadrons together, into what he likes to call a 'Big Wing', so that the jerry bombers can be hit really hard, in force. He thinks that would be far more effective not only in terms of damage done, but also from the point of view of undermining enemy morale. There's probably something to be said for it. Certainly quite a number of experienced senior officers are in favour, including one of his own Wingco's, a chap called Bader, who's a pretty pushy type himself, to put it mildly. The trouble is, getting several squadrons to find each other at a rendezvous over some map reference point takes time – wastes time, some would say – and we just don't have that luxury. The whole objective should be to get to the opposition's bombers before they reach their targets, surely, rather than afterwards. That's Park's view, anyway, and I think most of us in the Group would agree. The argument grumbling on as it does is unsettling, though, and we could do without it at a time like this. However, that's why the whole shebang is more or less being run from 'The Hole' at Uxbridge. I'll take you over there if we get half a chance – it's not far – and, anyway, there's someone there I'd like you to meet. But you can get an idea of how the system works, by going into our own Sector Control ops room here at Church Wealdon. I'll take you later; it needs a special pass, plus password, to get in.'

After that the conversation had switched to reminiscences of their days together as boys, and the Famous Four.

Bill had laughed at that; he hadn't heard the expression before. Peter meanwhile, having got over his mild surprise that it was Bill who'd chosen to lead them down the path of nostalgia, was filled with sudden longing, could see again sun glinting on water and mountains and smell bracken and gorse.

'Have you been home recently?' Bill had asked, sounding almost wistful. It was amazing how much he seemed to have mellowed in only a few short weeks.

'Not for a while. I had four days leave early in the New Year, and used that to go and look at them.'

It had been strange, that visit, even more like stepping back into a previous, now unrecognisable, life than had been the case with holidays from school or university. Uncle John had been in the midst of dealing with an epidemic of winter ailments, and hardly ever there; his mother had been over-solicitous and no more capable of relating to the life he was leading now than she had been to his life at school or college; and Aunt Mabel and Cook had been constantly bickering about dealing with meals, given the exigencies of rationing. Truth to tell, he'd been relieved to be able to come away again – and then, for a day or two, his conscience had pricked him about that.

Bill had been about to say something else at this stage, as though on the point of making an announcement, but just then the tannoy had blared out '*312 squadron to Readiness – 312 to Readiness.*'

'Blast!' said Bill, his features taut, 'Here we go again.'

As he'd jumped to his feet, knocking over his chair in his haste, he'd called over his shoulder to Peter, 'You'd better come along. With luck it'll be a false alarm, and I'll have chance to introduce you to some of the chaps over at Dispersal, and show you the ropes there – and if not, you'll have chance to see how well we function.'

As it happened, his seemingly optimistic forecast of a 'false alarm' had for once turned out to be correct. Within ten minutes of their arrival at the dispersal area (Bill having driven the car as though, in Peter's view, he was at the cockpit of his Spitfire) the squadron had been stood down to 'Available' once more. Bill, swearing volubly, had been seen to slam down the phone and storm out of the dispersal hut, irritably flinging aside his Mae West, his black mood reflected back on the faces of his squadron members in a series of delighted grins and calls of 'Temper, temper!' and 'Down, boy!' Peter, taken aback by their disrespect, had expected some backlash, but Bill had merely treated them to a ferocious scowl and two fingers, even when someone had called out, to general guffaws, 'The butcher thwarted again!'

'Insolent lot!' Bill had muttered to Peter, but there had been no sting in his remark, and beneath his stern exterior his delight in the camaraderie had been obvious.

'Come on then, I'll introduce you to some of this shower,' he'd said – then gone on to explain 'In spite of the show they put on, just now, it's not good for morale when we're put on five minutes readiness like that only to be immediately stood down again.'

Before they'd gone any further, however, they'd been interrupted by the arrival of a short, stocky Warrant Officer, whom Bill had introduced as 'Chiefie' Hodson – 'Chiefie's in charge of our ground-crews, and I defy you to find a better man or better mechanic anywhere.' Hodson's modestly delighted grin at that had lasted a bare two seconds before he'd put on a graver countenance to announce some problem or other with the engines on three newly-delivered Spitfires. It was then that Bill, once more foul-tempered, had delivered Peter into the company of Andrew Cameron, before going off with the warrant officer to discover what the problem was.

And, Peter realised with a start, the lad was still chattering away as if there were no time to be lost, and he'd not really been listening to him again. Then the thought struck him with chilling speed: How many more minutes or hours would boys like Andy Cameron have left to chatter in this way? Was the lad himself only too well aware of this – hence his eagerness to talk? And he hadn't even bothered to do the youngster the courtesy of listening to him.

Racked with new guilt, and making a determined effort to push aside the image of Connie Saunders' grey, lifeless form, which kept floating in front of him, he asked: 'What on earth decided you to interrupt your studies to come and fly fighters, like this?'

As soon as he uttered the words he became conscious of how spineless they sounded, reflecting badly on his own comparatively safe role in all this.

But Andrew Cameron didn't appear to see anything wrong with the question. Instead, with unabated enthusiasm he said, 'It wasn't a difficult choice. Once I realised that what they needed was experienced pilots and not yet another inexperienced doctor, the choice was made for me, if you see what I mean?'

Peter, wincing inwardly at the boy's ingenuous choice of words, managed to say, 'And how much experience had you had as a pilot?'

'Oh, a lot. I got my licence at 18. You see, my dad has a pilot's licence, so I'd learned early. And since then I've done over 200 hours in the air. As soon as I joined up they put me through my paces, and then immediately transferred me over to a familiarisation course on Spitfires.'

'So, how did you find that?'

'Wonderful. A bit tricky to begin with, of course. They're so much faster than what I've been used to. But now I feel as if I've been flying them for years. Squadron Leader Jackson took me up yesterday, after I arrived, flying as my wing man, and said I handled it very well. And this morning, he asked me to fly as his wing man, which was a real honour.' His eager grin was briefly replaced by a crestfallen look. 'Unfortunately we weren't able to see any action. I did ask him if I'd done all right, though, and he assured me I had. Just gave me a few bits of advice.' Again, his features became more thoughtful, then brightened. 'He doesn't say a great deal, though, does he.'

'They referred to him as "the butcher" just now,' Peter said, evading the unspoken question. 'Why was that? Do you know?'

'Oh, don't you know? One of the fellows told me it was because they say he "just goes in and chops 'em up, no nonsense". He already has seven kills to his name, I believe. But I expect you know that.'

He didn't know that, and the notion struck him like a thunderbolt; he couldn't equate it with the Bill he'd known of old. Then he remembered the frequent fights between Bill and George – friendly tussles in name, but with a combative robustness to them that at times spilled over to deadly purpose.

Changing tack, he asked, 'What stage were you at, at medical school?'

'Fourth year.'

'Where was that?'

'Edinburgh.'

'So, only one year to go. Wouldn't it have been better if you'd gone on to finish, first?'

286

'Yes, my dad said that. I'm afraid we rather fell out over it, which fairly upset my mum. But the war might have been over by then, and I'd've missed my chance. Anyway, it's now that they need pilots.'

There was no arguing with that. But Peter couldn't help but feel there was a hole in the argument somewhere.

'What does your dad do?'

'He's a surgeon. In the Infirmary in Edinburgh. That's what I'm going to do, as well.'

'Do you have any brothers or sisters?'

'A sister. Jean. She's just 17. Still at school.'

'And any girlfriend?'

'Oh, yes. Fiona. Let me show you.' He fished into an inside pocket to pull out a dog-eared photograph and held it out for Peter to inspect. It showed a slim, pretty girl standing in shadows beneath an apple tree, sunshine picking out blossom on the boughs. The girl, lively with laughter, was sticking out her tongue at the camera.

'Not very complimentary,' Peter said. 'Looks as though she didn't really want her photograph taken!'

'No, well they never do, do they. Always say, "But I look a mess!" But we've known each other since we were children. Always been friends, you see.' He gave a slight squirm of embarrassment. 'Neither of us ever had any other sweetheart. We're planning to marry once I've qualified.'

'So what does she think of you taking time off to do this?'

He became silent for a moment before answering. 'She didn't say much. There were a few tears, of course. But I could tell she was proud of me. Well, certainly will be once I've shot down a few jerry, anyway.'

'Right, Doc! That's that lot sorted.' Bill's voice interrupted their conversation at the same time as his shadow fell across them. 'Come on, I'll show you some of the set up, while there's time.'

Peter, scrambling to his feet, shook hands with Cameron. 'Well, thanks for the chin-wag. Enjoy yourself.' He grinned. 'And love to Fiona when you write!'

As they walked away, he said to Bill, 'Seems a likeable sort.'

'Very.'

'And, as you say, certainly enthusiastic.'

'Mm.'

'I see what you meant about trying to calm him down, though. Not easy, however; he's so keen.'

'Yes.'

'But very capable, I imagine.'

'Mm.'

Once they'd picked their way between the groups of men scattered about the grass, exchanging a few words as they went, they walked in silence for some seconds, Bill leading them away from the dispersal hut towards where a number of Spitfires were parked at the end of the runway. Beyond them could be seen a series of concrete bays with six-foot-high walls on three sides, but open to the field. It was apparent that each bay had space for one plane, and that the bays were grouped in threes, with perhaps a hundred yards of separation between each set.

Bill, following the direction of Peter's gaze, said, 'Those are where the aircraft are stowed when we're on 'Release'. They'd've been better if they'd been built as singles, but nevertheless so far, if we're caught with our pants down, as we were first thing this morning, they seem to be providing pretty good protection during raids, just as they were intended to do. Certainly far better than keeping them in hangars. This way, they can be wheeled in and out pretty quickly, too, and of course provided we've got sufficient warning we're better to have all our planes up in the air if we're about to be attacked.

As they arrived at the sixteen or so Spitfires standing several yards apart, in lines, a number of ground-crew in dark blue overalls sprang to their feet and stood to attention. One of them, sergeant's stripes on his sleeves, marched up and saluted smartly.

Bill, returning the salute, gave a broad grin, and said, 'To what do I owe this honour, Ginger? Right, carry on, all of you.' He turned to Peter, still grinning. 'They're just showing off because you're here. They usually ignore me.'

'Don't believe a word of it, sir,' the sergeant said to Peter.

'No, I won't,' said Peter solemnly.

'All set up, still?' Bill asked the sergeant.

'Yes, sir. Difficult, this waiting, though.'

'Isn't it.' He turned to Peter. 'The usual form is that once we go to 'Readiness', that is to say no more than five minutes before we have to be airborne, the crews start up the engines using these electric starter trollies that you see already plugged into each aircraft,' ...here he indicated the wheeled boxes standing beside each plane... 'the pilots hare over as fast as they can, pick up their chutes that you see sitting on the tailplanes ready for them, are helped into them by a member of ground-crew, who then also helps them to get strapped into the cockpit, and after that it's simply a matter of 'chocks away' once we get clearance to go.'

He turned to the sergeant who was making no attempt to suppress a broad smile of his own. 'Yes, alright, Ginger – I know! That's the theory. Doesn't always work like that, though, does it.'

'No, sir, it certainly don't.'

'The trouble is,' Bill said to Peter, 'more often than not we get scrambled without any warning – and they didn't pick the term 'scramble' without good reason! At times it can be a right old shambles. Alternatively, it's not unheard of for us to be on 'Standby' – that is to say the pilots sitting in the cockpit with the engines turning, ready to take off at two minutes notice – and still to be sitting there quarter of an hour later. That plays havoc with both the engine and one's nerves, I can tell you!'

Peter thought privately that, as far as he could see, Bill didn't seem to have any 'nerves', but one never could tell, and anyway he thought it diplomatic not to say anything along those lines. Instead, he said, 'It must be a great aircraft to fly,' – and immediately thought how puerile that sounded. (But, he had to admit to himself, he was thrilled just to be standing next to it: close to, its lines seemed to match in every respect the throaty refinement of its engine notes.)

In any case Bill answered in all seriousness, 'Yes, it is. Wizard! Nothing to quite match it – except, in some respects at least, the 109s. They come close. Unfortunately!'

'In what respects do they differ?' (He thought that at least sounded a reasonably intelligent question.)

'Well, they're about on a par for speed and climb rate, although the 109 probably has the edge on both those; but the Spit can be put into a tighter turn, which is a distinct advantage. It means that if you've got the know-how – and can stand the pull of the extra 'G' – you can get inside him more readily than he can you. Where he has one clear advantage, though, is in one of the best 'escape' manoeuvres we have available to us when some bastard is on your tail, which both sides use: that is, a half-roll on top of a loop, and nose-down into a dive. It's a move that creates considerable negative G, which means, as you know, that the pilot is liable to blackout for a few seconds; that, of course, applies to jerry as well. But in both the Spit and the Hurricane it also means that the engine tends to cut-out briefly when you least want it to, whereas in the Messerschmitts they don't have that problem.'

'Oh. Why is that?'

'Seems to be something to do with the design of the fuel feed system. Ours have a carburettor with a float mechanism, so that in negative G the fuel supply is interrupted for those few seconds. Their planes have some sort of system whereby the fuel is injected straight into the chamber, and that isn't affected at all. We could do with copying it, I can tell you! But it isn't that easy. It never is.'

From both of them there was pause for thought, during which Peter took a closer admiring look at the aircraft. Noticing for the first time seven small swastikas neatly painted on the fuselage beneath the cockpit, he realised that this was probably Bill's own plane.

'Is this your aircraft, then?' he asked.

'Yes. George Alpha Sugar.' He grinned. 'That's what the boys say about me, that I'm just one big gas-bag.'

Studying it further, Peter noticed a number of small patches on the rear section of the fuselage, the significance of which struck him with distinct chill. He made no comment, but Bill, noticing the direction of his gaze, said, 'A little present from the rear-gunner on a Dornier, yesterday – but by then they were already on their way down! There's only been time for temporary patches so far – but you'll do a better job if we do get a lull, won't you, Ginger?'

'Certainly will, sir.'

Peering at the leading edge of the left-hand wing, Peter then asked, 'I can't see any ports for your guns.'

'No. But if you look more closely you'll see they have little canvas patches stuck over them, as well. Helps to prevent the gun mechanisms from icing up at altitude. They open up when you fire, needless to say!'

'Four machine guns on each side, is that right?'

'Correct. Point 303 Brownings. Three hundred rounds in each. Rate-of-fire up to twelve hundred r.p.m. Gives us about fifteen to twenty seconds fire-power in the combat zone.'

'Is that all?' Peter was astonished.

'Sure. What did you expect? It means in fact that we tend to fire in two-second bursts – or those of us who are experienced, do; the novices often let fly at first, and are out of ammo before they know what's happened.'

'I don't know how you manage to hit anything!'

'It's not easy,' said Bill drily. 'Like shooting pigeon, you're aiming off all the time in two dimensions. It's probable that about three-quarters of enemy planes shot down are by only one third of our pilots – although often it's not easy to be certain who's responsible for what in the general melee up there. The thing is, you've got to get in close. What we could really do with is a couple of cannon, like the 109s – they provide a lot more punch at a greater distance. As it is, our eight guns are routinely set up to converge their fire-power at three hundred yards, but most experienced pilots have them reset to about half that. We try to instill a set of rules into the new boys. Firstly, get in close and get out fast. Secondly, always, whenever possible, come out of the sun – but remember that the 109s will be trying to do the same, coming up your arse, so it's always vital to keep looking over one's shoulder. And, thirdly, never ever fly in a straight line longer than is absolutely essential. But the bods at Operational Training don't seem to have cottoned on to that. Do you know that the standard procedure is to fly in sections of three planes in 'V' pattern, that we call 'vics', the full squadron being in a tight formation of four or five 'vics' in line astern, even when going into combat? They don't seem to have heard of *Me*109s! They still seem to imagine that the enemy bombers will be flying along tamely waiting for us to come along to shoot them down, perhaps protected at most by a few relatively sluggish *one-one-o*'s. It's absolute idiocy! Flying like that, wing-tip to wing-tip, on its own requires all one's concentration simply to avoid collision. Anyway, we've soon bloody well ditched that, I can tell you. We've retained the four Sections for organisational purposes – red, yellow, blue and green – but have taken a leaf out of jerry's book, and have taken it upon ourselves to fly a much looser pattern of two pairs in each section: each pair made up of leader and wing-man, the main task of the latter being to keep an eye out for enemy fighters – as well as our own! – and to keep a watch on the leader's tail. And it seems to be working – up to a point. The trouble is it so often becomes a case of every man for himself.'

By now, Peter was secretly convinced that he wouldn't have been cut out for this sort of role, and was filled with admiration for those who were prepared to take it on. Bill's description of the niceties of combat flying brought home to him that the fighter boys' swagger was not, after all, just mindless posturing; that the top button of the tunic undone, and the apparent affectation of the silk scarf did, after all, have a practical purpose to it – and 'fighter pilot's twitch' that he'd read about in a medical officers' pamphlet, did, in reality, have a very understandable cause.

'That youngster, Andy Cameron. I take it that with his experience he should get on all right?' he said.

'The way things are going, the chances are he'll be dead in two weeks,' Bill replied. It was said without any inflection. Peter almost staggered. Was this some sick joke of Bill's? But he could see from the other's grim expression that, in spite of the matter-of-fact manner in which he'd spoken, he was absolutely serious.

'But...but he told me that he had over two hundred hours experience,' he managed to get out.

In Tiger Moths. He's had nine hours...no, now just over eleven hours...in Spitfires. That's all.'

'But that's the same for all of the new arrivals, isn't it?'

'Yes. But out of the seventy or so inexperienced pilots that the O.T.U.s are churning out each month, the way things have gone so far, approximately half will be lost within another four weeks. Altogether, to date Fighter Command have been losing getting on for a hundred pilots, dead or seriously wounded, each *week*; and that includes what is now a diminishing proportion of experienced pilots.'

'But Cameron's an experienced pilot.'

'But not on Spitfires,' Bill said irritably, 'and not in combat. He flies well, but carefully and according to the book. To survive up there you have to have an instinct for it. The aircraft has to be an extension of you. You have to be able to fly it without thinking about it, so that all your attention can be on what's happening around you. You have to have instantaneous reaction and total awareness. Compared to the hard core of experienced fighter pilots, at best most of these new guys are like...like someone coming to play on the 1st XV for the toughest match of the season, having had one game on the 2nd XV. Some of them, with talent, given time will learn the skills and go on to become brilliant. But they have to be lucky enough to survive sufficiently long to be able to reach that degree of proficiency. And take it from me, Andy Cameron is not one of those I would put my money on. Up there, in combat, he'll be like a fish out of water.'

Appalled by Bill's callousness, Peter said desperately, 'In that case, surely we can do something for him?'

'What do you have in mind?' Bill replied flatly.

'Well...I don't know. Couldn't I designate him as psychologically unfit, or something?'

'In that case you'd better do it for all of us!' The anger was sharp in his voice.

'But we can't just watch him go to certain death like that.'

'Oh, for God's sake, Peter!' Bill exploded. 'What the fuck do you think is going on here! Almost every time we take off we know that probably some of us are going to our death. Don't you think we give thanks to God – whether we believe in Him or not – every time we land again safely? Death and mutilation is the coinage we're dealing in. We may seem flippant at times, but fear is constantly with us. And if it comes to it, most of us would choose death rather than being mutilated or badly burned. I know I certainly would. Andrew Cameron has chosen to do this – and can only be respected for it – but he has, simply, to take his chances like the rest of us. If the odds are stacked up against him, then that's tough! – he's in no worse position than the majority. Now, for Christsake leave it!'

By this time Bill was shaking with barely suppressed anger; and at that moment there came the urgent clamour of the fire-bell over at the dispersal hut.

'Oh Christ!' Bill exploded again. 'Get those bloody engines going!' Then, waving frantically towards the figures starting their clumsy run towards the aircraft, he bellowed, 'Archie, grab my vest, will you – it's on the ground there!' One of the running pilots, lifting an arm in acknowledgement, dipped briefly in mid-run and without breaking stride held up a yellow Mae West for Bill to see.

'Good man,' yelled Bill; then: 'And you, Waring, get out of the bloody way!'

CHAPTER NINETEEN

Peter glances nervously at the C.O. A heftily-built, square-jawed, hard-eyed man with, so far, little evidence of any sense of humour, Wing Commander Burrows is the last person he'd have wanted to accompany him to the station Operations Room.

As he'd approached the camouflaged, concrete-protected building, Peter, silently reminding himself of the password, had noticed the rank of the officer in front of him, and guessing whom this might be had deliberately hung back. But at the entrance the man had turned round as he was displaying his pass to the sentry and, seeing Peter, had waited. Having casually returned Peter's salute (at the same time gesturing an impatient dismissal at his attempt to come to attention), Burrows had subjected him to a keen, two-second appraisal, noted the insignia at his lapel, and said, 'You must be the temporary M.O., then?'

'Yes, sir. Waring, sir.'

'Come to have a look at the power-plant, have you?'

'Yes, sir,' Peter had gabbled (wondering for a moment whether he had after all come to the wrong place). 'Squadron Leader Jackson has obtained a pass for me. He was going to accompany me himself but he's...er...otherwise engaged.'

'Quite so,' the C.O. had commented drily, without so much as a flicker of a smile. 'I believe you're a friend of Bill's, from days of old?'

'Yes, sir.'

'They tell me you've been doing a good job. Well done. Anyway, come on. In Jackson's absence, perhaps you'll allow me to show you what goes on. It sounds as though something might be brewing again, so you've timed it well. I hope you've remembered the password?'

Now, in the ops room, as the C.O. silently busies himself with taking stock of the situation in front of him, Peter, a little taken aback by the fact that Burrows already knows something about him, as well as by the confusion of

293

activity in the room, finds himself reviewing the events of the previous afternoon.

After his abrupt dismissal by Bill as his squadron scrambled, and as all three squadrons, one by one, had taken off from various points on the airfield, he'd all at once felt totally superfluous. Not only that, he'd felt diminished.

It hadn't lasted long.

Ten minutes later the klaxons had sounded, and around the station buildings and in the distance across the field tin-hatted figures had been seen running in all directions – some to the shelters, or to various places of duty, others to man the Bofors and Lewis guns and heavier 13-pounder anti-aircraft guns in their emplacements dotted around the perimeter. Shortly after that the first of the German planes had appeared, grey shapes high in the sky: Stukas and Dorniers with their long narrow fuselages, and at their periphery, for all the world like sheep-dogs tending their flocks, a dozen or so twin-engined Me.110s (Peter, absurdly, admitting a certain pride in being able to now recognise one jerry plane from another, prompted by the numerous recognition charts plastered around the place). The dull drone of their many engines had sounded ominous in the sudden hush that seemed to momentarily lie across the airfield, but almost immediately the tremendous din of anti-aircraft fire opening up had broken the spell with a sound like the simultaneous slamming of a hundred doors. Then had come the bombs. At first heard only as a distant *crump-crump*, as though nothing to do with the present proceedings, all-too-quickly the ground had started to tremble with the violence of explosions, and all at once the air had become filled with noise, the suffocating darkness of dust and smoke, and the searingly bright anger of flame. To Peter, crouched in the doorway of a building, not knowing whether to retreat inwards or to rush out, it had seemed as though it would never end. But when he tried to remember all that had happened during the long few minutes of the raid, he had only a dim recollection of running figures, of flying debris, of the crash of heavy objects all around, and of the sting of sand and gravel against his face. He could recall, he thought, at one point being flung backwards by blast, but had no memory of picking himself up, and indeed no certainty even that he'd ever left his sanctuary by the door. There had been no sense of reality, in fact: in one realm of time it had gone on for ever; in another it had been over as soon as it began. The guns had stopped, the yellowish cloud of dirt and debris had swirled and cleared, and briefly the only sound to break the sudden silence had been the creak and trickle of settling rubble, and the faint drone of departing planes – and one long sigh, a release of breath, which may have been his own.

And even that respite had existed in a separate quantum of time, for in its place had come, abruptly, the chatter of machine guns, the thud and whine of ricochets, and the roar of enemy fighters as they'd sped low across the field. Simultaneously the defensive clatter of the Lewis guns and the *bop-bop-bop* of the Bofors had joined in the uproar; while, high above, in a confusion of vapour trails, had been seen Spitfires, Messerschmitts and

Hurricanes tangled, to the tune of their own guns, in their own private dance of death.

But he'd had no time to dwell on that either, or on what had just passed, for casualties had been heavy. In the frantic minutes that followed he, the two nurses, and four medical orderlies – two of whom had minor injuries of their own – together with as many volunteers as they could muster, had gone around dealing with the injured as best they could. There were three dead that they'd been quickly aware of; but at that stage how many more lay dead or injured under the rubble of buildings they'd had no way of knowing, for damage had been extensive. The discovery of one of the dead, a young WAAF, had shaken them all, for when they came across her mangled body it was minus legs: these had been found shortly afterwards, a little distance away, still sheathed in torn and ragged stockings. However, they'd had no time to dwell on the horror of that: they'd had to work fast simply to provide basic first aid, at the same time sorting out those who'd have to be taken off to hospital and those whom he would afterwards be able to deal with himself – several with a variety of contusions and lacerations and two with not-too-serious burns.

And all the time they were working they'd all been only too conscious that the Spits and Hurricanes could be landing at any moment, and that it was more than likely that there would be work for them to do there, as well.

However, his awareness of that still hadn't prepared him for the particular episode they'd had, in fact, to face. And, when the memory of it now floods back, it takes an effort of will to prevent himself from shuddering.

But he is saved from having to once more think about it; for the C.O., evidently having completed his perusal of the situation, is bringing him back to the present.

'Now, Doc, let me explain what's going on.'

Whilst wrapped up in his thoughts, Peter has been automatically taking in the scene before him without fully registering what it is all about. The room they are in is high-ceilinged and perhaps 50 feet across. Most of the floor space, some six feet below the gallery where the C.O. and he are standing, is taken up by a large, square map-table around which several people, mostly WAAFs, are gathered. The outline map painted on the table, he's seen, is a large-scale depiction of their own immediate area of southern England, divided into sectors, and of the adjacent Channel coastal area of the Continent; and placed at intervals on the sides of the table, he's noticed, are clusters of small wooden blocks on top of which are fixed upright frames containing various symbols. Now and again one or other of the WAAFs – all of whom are wearing head-phones – will pick up one of the blocks and slide a new or different symbol into its frame, and will then place it into a fresh position on the map table.

The gallery to his left takes a right-angled turn to occupy the whole of the left-hand wall, and along this are seated a dozen or so men in uniform, mostly RAF, but some army, all of whom are beginning to pay increasing attention to the map-table below them. Filling the whole of the wall opposite to them, to Peter's right, is a complex array of light-bulbs, labels, columns and squares, which he has been absent-mindedly studying for the past minute without making much sense of them. On the fourth wall, opposite him, is an outline map similar to that on the table, which evidently, from the symbols crayoned upon it, is there to provide up-to-date weather information.

But, as the C.O. now proceeds to talk him through it, the detail begins to make sense.

'The Plot Table below,' Burrows says, 'is fairly self-explanatory. It centres of course on our Sector, that is to say us and the three other airfields in our immediate area. But it takes in the other Sectors in the Group as well, together with the appropriate areas across the Channel. It enables us therefore to get an overall picture of *Luftwaffe* movements into our Group region, and of the Group response to them. At present we're receiving information from Group Operations at Uxbridge; and they in turn are receiving info from Fighter H.Q. at Stanmore Park. But it does look as if another raid is brewing – which is hardly a surprise – and there should soon be an indication of from which direction that is likely to come.'

'This information is via the R.D.F stations?' Peter says, keen to show that he isn't altogether ignorant about it.

'Initially, yes. That is until they cross our coast. Then it's all up to the Observer Corps people. By that stage the Filter Room at H.Q. at Stanmore will have made a decision as to whether the intruders are Hostile or Unidentified – because they could at times be some of our own chaps returning home. But at that point information from Observers begins to pour in from the numerous points scattered around, and, if they're deemed to be Hostiles, we begin to get estimations of numbers, types, direction and height. Before that, of course, Group, prompted by H.Q., has already started to respond by putting appropriate squadrons on Readiness or even Stand-by.

'There is definitely something building now, though, as you can see from the table – and it would seem to be heading our way.'

Peter, glancing around, can see that all eyes are indeed fixed on the table below them, where the half dozen girls, using long sticks like those used by croupiers, are intent on placing more and more blocks onto the table and pushing them into position. In one sense it is like an outsize game of chess, except that all the pieces are moving in one single direction, coming over the outline of the south coast and moving north. But even as he watches, other pieces are beginning to be placed on the table, from north, east and west, and one by one are being edged forwards in the direction of those moving inland, clearly in opposition; and from the corner of his eye he can see, on the board to his right, more and more bulbs lighting up, as though signalling increasing interest there.

'Christ,' says Burrows at his side, 'the blighters are really pushing the boat out again. There must be a couple of hundred Hostiles already.

'You see the symbols on the blocks, or counters, there on the Plot Table? The 'H' of course denotes Hostile. The Triangle is for Friendly, in other words, most of the time, our own fighter squadrons, each identified by its own squadron number – but now and again they could denote some of our own bombers, caught up in the situation: it wouldn't do to be going up and shooting them down, as I'm sure you'd agree! The numerals on the plot counters indicate estimated numbers in the Hostile groups – for example that one there, '40+' – and below that, '12' for estimated altitude in thousands of feet, or 'angels'.

'Now, if you look at the 'Tote Board' to our right, you get an indication of how we're responding throughout our Sector as shown by the Squadron identification numbers. You can see that they're arranged as vertical columns, one for each Squadron.

'Now look at the lights, arranged in horizontal rows, across the board, so that there's a vertical set for each squadron in the Sector. They immediately convey to us the present and changing status of each squadron. Our own squadrons here in Church Wealdon, six in all, are shown in the columns to the left, and of course those are the ones of immediate interest to us – at present all are on 'Readiness', that is to say they can be airborne within five minutes. But we also get an overall picture of what's happening throughout the Sector, because we have to control that as well. For instance if you look at the column eighth along, 425 Squadron, d'you see how there's a progression of bulbs lighting up in a downward direction? And that the colour has changed from orange to red? That shows that particular Squadron has now moved from 'Standby', to being in the air and in process of moving to their ordered position.'

'And who controls that?' Peter asks.

'As I say, we do, from here. But the involvement of each Sector, and the numbers of aircraft asked for at any one time are under the direction of the Group Controller at Group Ops at Uxbridge, with Air Vice-Marshal Park no doubt in overall control. And it's only from that point onwards that the Sector Controller for each sector takes over.'

'The 'Sector Controller' being…?'

'Here, for example, if you look at the group of bods on our left, the Squadron Leader in the centre, Tim Johnson, is our Controller. In other words, a senior officer with considerable flying experience and, hopefully, as in Johnson's case, considerable combat experience. And the right personality, needless to say – it's no good having a chap who's likely to get into a flap himself.

'Anyway, it's definitely hotting up in our direction, now, so I think we should move over to the Controller so I can get a better idea of what's going on. Come along. But speak only if spoken to!'

Peter, following the C.O. at a discrete distance, is now able to study the 'Tote Board', as Burrows had called it, in more detail. He can see that there is a described state of readiness for each and every squadron in the Sector, in a progressive direction from top to bottom of the board. The topmost row is labelled *Released* – which he knows means that they are 'out of circulation' for one reason or another at the present time. It is somewhat comforting therefore, given the C.O.'s misgivings about the degree of threat they are currently facing, to see that there are no lights on for any squadrons in that category. The next two below are already familiar: *Available* and *Readiness*; and *Standby*, the fourth category, he knows means the pilots are actually sitting waiting in the cockpits, engines running, so that they can be in the air within two minutes. Next comes *Airborne* – 'moving to ordered position in the air'; followed by *Airborne* – *in ordered position*. The final three categories, towards the bottom of the board – *Enemy Sighted*, *Ordered to land*, and *Landed and Refuelling* – are also self-explanatory. But he finds himself thinking that there is no indication of what is happening to the squadrons after *Enemy Sighted* is displayed, when, presumably, they are in action. Why, he wonders, is there no category on the Tote Board for that, when they are actually in action?

And even as he studies it all, lamps are lighting up further and further down the board until, he sees, every squadron in the Sector has been mobilised into one category or another. Only then does the full impact of the system hit him. It is as if one is in the dress circle of a theatre watching a drama unfold in front of one; a part of it, yet not involved. In this case, though, the drama is strangely silent, as in a dream, there being no speech or sound from the actors themselves, nor even their physical presence, leaving one with only an acute abstract awareness of what they are about. And in that instant the thought weighs upon him that this room can be seen as a microcosm of all that is going on in the wide skies above, that upon this stage and others like it, over the next few hours and days might be played out the future of Britain, Europe and, possibly, the whole world.

Meanwhile, he notices, on the Plot Table the blocks carrying 'H' for Hostile are ever more numerous and drawing nearer – propelled with calm detachment by young WAAFs wielding their croupiers' sticks, for all the world as though directing some form of baccarat – or, indeed, manipulating their icons of death, disaster, and of young men gambling their very lives, in a macabre form of ballet. Calm as they seem, surely for those girls, as for him, their hearts must be beginning to pound and their mouths be getting dry?

And now, he observes, the lights for all their own Sector squadrons are at '*Standby*', glaring it seems with a particular impact of their own; and at the same time the Controller begins to speak into the microphone standing in front of him, his voice calm, cultured and deliberate, each word annunciated with clarity.

'Squadrons three-one-two, four-zero-niner, two-one-seven, one-zero-fifer, one-one-niner, two-two-four, and three-one-eight: scramble! I repeat, all squadrons scramble. Vector two-two-zero; make angels one-fifer; repeat, angels one-fifer; rendezvous Croydon. Eighty plus Hostiles now ten miles south-west of Sevenoaks, height niner thousand feet – angels niner. Watch out for Bandits upstairs. I repeat, possible Bandits above you. Over.'

A few seconds later, with a suddenness which startles Peter, the tannoy high on the wall crackles into life, as each squadron commander acknowledges and repeats the orders; and with a curl of excitement he recognises, among those impassive voices, the equally casual voice of Bill.

Now those half dozen lights on the board take on a particular persona. No longer are they mere cyphers but instead have developed an entity of their own, inhabited by men whose lives, for this brief duration, are only on loan. One or two of them he's got to know – and one of them, it seems, he's always known. And as those lights change from one category to the next, representing the changing condition and situation of those men and their planes, from his position of relative safety here on the ground he imagines (with a convulsion of shame for that idle pretence) that he is up there with them.

One by one, shortly it seems, each squadron commander from the Church Wealdon sector, Bill among them, is reporting in phlegmatic tones over the tannoy that his squadron is now in position in the Croydon area, as ordered; and one by one the lights on the board change to represent that situation for all to see. After which, whilst it can be seen on the Plot Table that squadrons from other sectors have also now closed up on the Hostiles, for many long seconds all that issues from the tannoy here on the wall is the hiss of empty static.

He stares at the Controller, whose eyes are fixed first of all on the Plot Table (where 'Hostiles' and those other squadrons are, it seems, jostling for the same piece of space), then flickering up to the silent tannoy. The man can be heard quietly muttering, 'Come on, come on – you should be seeing them by now.'

Peter sees him glance up at the C.O., as if to say, Should we contact them?

'Give it a few moments longer, Tim, do you think?' Burrows murmurs, clearly thinking along the same lines.

Tension permeates the room, silence and immobility its envoys, the only movement to break the tableau being that of one or other of the girls as she leans forward to adjust the position of one or other of the counters on the table. Otherwise all eyes from the floor are fixed on the figure of the Controller up here in the gallery.

The sudden blare of the tannoy, therefore, when it comes, seems explosive, making several of them jump. And the voice is recognisable as Bill's, relief and rising excitement now identifiable in his tones.

'Hostiles identified, one hundred plus, to the north west and below. Dorniers and Heinkels, I think. Going around for the buggers now. Tally Ho!'

In spite of his own excitement at that, Peter winces a little at Bill's melodramatic use of the hunting call, thinking that such facetiousness is uncharacteristic of him. Whether the C.O. has noticed his reaction, he doesn't know: but Burrows turns to him and says, 'The *Tally Ho* may seem a little over the top, but it's the accepted term to signify that the squadron commanders up there have now taken over their own control – for obvious reasons. We've done our job – now it's up to them, and all we can do is listen and wait. We keep our frequency open so that the boys have instant access to us, should it be necessary, but the last thing we want to do at this stage is distract them. However, we can listen in on their internal frequency, if you'd like to do that? Here, put these earphones on, and flick down that switch there. I've set it for 312's frequency – that's Bill Jackson's squadron.'

With a nod of thanks Peter does so, hurriedly adjusting the phones as a confusion of sound assaults his ears. At first he can make nothing of it: it is simply a jumble of noise – voices, engine noise, the occasional stammer of guns, and the squeak of static, all fighting for space. But gradually elements of this turmoil become clearer, so that he can pick up individual voices and start to tease out snatches of talk that are interspersed with long seconds of relative silence. '*Whizzo, Harry! – you got him!....watch out for that tail gunner, Green Two....*'. Then, a couple of minutes later, a single voice, more urgent – possibly Bill's, he can't tell. '*Bandits three o'clock high!...109s I think...out of the sun...Blue Section, break, break break!*' This is followed, over several minutes, by more confusion of noise, interspersed with fragments of identifiable obscenities. Then a different voice: '*Behind you, Blue Two! Break, break*!', and rising on top of it, more urgent, definitely Bill's voice: '*For God's sake, Cameron, break left! Oh, Christ....Come on, man, get out!...Oh, shit!...*' There follows more jumbled sounds, but by this time Peter, unable to listen longer, his mind filled with all-too-vivid images and untenable dread, is already tugging off his earphones. He takes a quick look at Burrows, who has been standing there also listening, with a single phone to his ear. Whether or not he's been listening to the same action, or was on a different frequency, Peter doesn't know – but the man's features are devoid of expression. And Peter stands there unmoving and unable to move, not wanting to stay and not daring to go.

Grey mist, wafting from overhead and drifting wraith-like among trees, is met as sudden impenetrable clumps in dips in the road. At this early hour on this August morning it gives (falsely, one hopes) an impression of autumn. It also deadens all sound, so that all that can be heard is the hum of the motor and the soft drumming of the tyres on the tarmac. He's glad he's had the presence of mind to put on his greatcoat, but even so, in the open-top car, it is decidedly chilly. Even the wildlife seems to have decided to stay in bed: not so much as a bird to be seen anywhere. Bill, at the wheel, now once more seems relaxed and content with his lot (in spite of Peter's *faux pas* a few minutes ago) just as he's been ever since he'd burst into Peter's room, without ceremony, first thing, declaring, 'Come on, you lazy sod. It's a wonderful morning – all closed in! There'll be no flying for the next two or three hours, anyway. Time for some breakfast, then you're coming over to Uxbridge with me. There's someone there I want you to meet.'

And he'd held up a hand to Peter's beginnings of protest. 'It's no good arguing, or declaring that your patients need you. I've already checked, and everything there is under control. Besides, we're only going to be half an hour away, you can be back in a jiffy. In any case it may be the only opportunity we'll get.'

Peter, still trying to ignore the chillingly possible implications of that last remark, now wonders again what is so important about his being taken over to Uxbridge. It's the second time his friend has said 'There's someone I want you to meet'.

Neither can he understand Bill's ability to bounce back so cheerfully in the light of what had happened yesterday. A short while ago, in the face of Bill's relentlessly bright chatter about all things trivial, he'd tentatively tried to broach the subject of the death of Andy Cameron. It ought, after all, in his professional judgement, to be brought out in the open. No good bottling these things up, is it?

He'd chosen his words carefully, trying to keep his tone neutral – to match the seemingly blasé attitude of the pilots themselves. 'Very sad about Cameron, don't you think,' he'd said.

'Yes, it's sad. And yes, I was right after all.' But Bill, picking up the unspoken thought from Peter, hadn't looked at him. His words had had the hard varnish of anger and contempt, and silence had followed. And Peter, even while noting the furious tightening of the muscles at the other man's jaw, had realised with dismay that far from being preoccupied with the loss of yet another pilot whom he hardly knew, all Bill's concerns would be with what had befallen his close friend Archie Sinclair the day before yesterday. For Peter had learned over the weeks that this was something all pilots fear more than anything.

Thus the picture of that, the final image from that first afternoon, the image above all that he's been trying to wipe from his memory for the past thirty-six hours, swims before him once more in all its horror, every detail from beginning to end as vivid as if it is happening all over again.

At first he's slow on the uptake, not yet aware of the significance of what he's seeing. But the orderlies around him know. It's their stopping what they're doing which first catches his attention. He turns to watch what they're staring at so intensely, and all he sees is a single Spitfire, some distance away, approaching the field, coming in slowly at about two hundred feet. Coming in to land, just like the others, he thinks. So why the particular interest? He's about to say something when one of the orderlies speaks. 'That's Mr Sinclair's kite, isn't it?'

'Aye,' murmurs another; then, still staring towards the plane: 'Come on, man, get it down before it's too late.'

Then Peter hears what they're hearing, the stuttering of the engine, and sees what they've already seen, the plume of dark smoke streaming from the engine cowling. And more, a flickering of brightness lapping along the fuselage and curling up over the wings.

'He should bale out!' someone says.

'Don't be bloody daft – he's too low…and too high.'

Now the plane starts to drop, not in an angled glide but falling, as of its own free will, like a broken branch carried in the wind.

'That's it,' someone breathes, 'bang it down and get out quick.'

But already flame has announced its name, in bright red and orange waves billowing up so that the body of the plane can no longer be seen – in the time it takes to draw breath it is no longer an aircraft coming down but a ball of fire falling from the sky. This inferno hits the ground and spins, wings and tail-plane briefly glimpsed like the flailing limbs of some mad scarecrow flung into a fire, the whole contraption rotating and sliding with a screech of metal until, finally, it comes to rest – and from all directions people are running, not away but towards it, disregarding heat, and Peter runs with them. Then from out of the conflagration, glimpsed through smoke, a figure bursts, not human but one of fire in the shape of man, two elongated torches held aloft for arms, head held back as in a scream; it takes several steps, then falls and rolls, and other figures now are there, with garments flung, bending low and rolling with it.

By the time Peter arrives the flames have been extinguished on Sinclair – it takes an effort of will to personalise this creature, this victim, with a name – and he has been dragged, screaming, some safer distance from the fiery mass that was his plane. Now he lies, no longer recognisable as a human being, his body shuddering with his moans – that is the description by which Peter thinks of them, but they are more primitive than that, they constitute a sound compounded of anger, terror and intolerable pain, an animal sound, a sound that signifies a realisation that in a single swift swordstroke of time there has been banishment beyond the human pale, to isolation in the netherworld, alone, where none can follow. Once, when driving after dark with Uncle John, a badger had rushed out from the hedgerow and beneath the wheels of the car. Following the double bump as the car had passed over the body of the badger they had stopped and got out – in time to see the animal scurry, soundless, back through the hedge into the adjacent woodland. And whilst they'd stood, wondering how it could have survived to be able to do that, there had come the sound, this very same sound, of fury, insufferable pain, and disbelief – mercifully, after a few seconds, cut short. At that moment he'd felt that he'd personally experienced some of the abrupt agony of that poor creature. And he experiences that same torment now.

With hands shaking in his haste he reaches into his satchel for a syringe, needle, and vial of morphine, his mind racing, wondering how best to give it, whether he'll be able to find a vein. At the same time a part of his mind, professionally detached, is automatically assessing the situation. Sinclair's head is a featureless black sphere from which shrivelled shreds of scorched skin hang grotesquely; his eyes cannot be seen for swollen flesh, although one feels that if it were possible they would be wide open in horror; there is no visible nose, nor ears, nor hair; only his teeth can be seen, gleaming in macabre fashion, revealed either by rictus or because his lips have been burned away. In places, in that thing that has so lately been a face, Peter fancies he can identify the striations of exposed muscle. Sinclair's leather flying jacket, although burned through in places, nevertheless can be assumed to have to some extent protected his upper torso and arms, but not so his hands, from which he must have at some point discarded his gloves – his arms now lie bent across his chest in the manner of a funerary effigy, a position seeming to be at once protective and resigned to fate, but this serves only to accentuate the obscenity of his hands. His hands are red globes of raw flesh, blackened in places, and in others streaked with silver grey where tendons, bones and sinews are showing through; and already his hands are affected by heat-contracture, so that they are tightly clenched, as in spasm, or as seen in late stage of severe rheumatoid arthritis.

By now the station ambulance has arrived, with medical orderlies, and soon one sleeve of Sinclair's flying jacket is cut away (the action releasing, from the clothes beneath, the reek of unburned aviation fuel) followed by the material of his tunic and shirt. Fortunately the skin beneath is unharmed, protected by the layers of clothes, and the elbow can therefore be straightened so that Peter can get at the antecubital vein. The needle enters the vein first time, a full third of a grain of Morphine Sulphate is slowly injected, and gradually the sounds of anguish fade and cease. The collective sigh from those around is clearly heard.

'I phoned the hospital late last night. The word is that Archie Sinclair stands a good chance of surviving.' In his effort to show he understands how Bill must feel about Sinclair, the words sound a little forced.

Bill laughs humourlessly. 'That really would be his final bit of bad luck.'

'There's a chap called McIndoe, at East Grinstead, who's got together a surgical team who are beginning to do wonders with burns cases now, you know. Funnily enough, his first name is Archie, too.'

'Sinclair will be delighted to know that, I'm sure.' The sarcasm in Bill's voice is heavy with bitterness. 'One Archie remaking another. And can they give him back his good looks, his success with the girls, his delightful sense of humour, and his carefree attitude to life?…No, I thought not. In spite of what you say, Cameron's the lucky one, you know. Did you hear that he went down in flames? Best not to survive that, after all.'

There is nothing for Peter to say in reply. How can he argue an alternative, he who is safely away from the risks these fellows are exposed to?

Perhaps in the end Bill is right about Andy Cameron. A quick death preferable to a ruined life. But need life be unacceptable in an altered state? Different, certainly; but in his short professional experience he's met a number of examples of people overcoming very considerable disabilities to successfully get on with whatever life still had to offer them. Admittedly McIndoe's premise in the remedial surgery he carries out is merely to achieve 'maximum possible functionality': does that include consideration of cosmetic results as an inherent part of 'functionality'? And, anyway, in spite of what he's just said to Bill, he's no idea what sort of results McIndoe is getting in trying to rebuild faces. In the case of some people, their looks are essential to their being able to function (and he is startled that Jordan immediately comes to mind – and even more so by the realisation that it is true, that up to now in her life that is all she has had to offer).

But what would Fiona, the mischievous, pretty girl under the apple tree, have had to say about that in Cameron's case, if he'd survived in the sort of state that Sinclair was in? Would she still have accepted him without a face and hands? Or would her anguish have been greater in that case than in this – of having lost him altogether? For, now, the shadow that has been cast over her will with time surely pass; she will at least have the opportunity to rebuild her own life. Not so Cameron's parents. And not so Cameron himself.

But, then, he reminds himself, what future does life have for any of us at the present time, even assuming our survival?

He can't, though, rid himself of the thought of what Andy Cameron will have missed – it could be said, had thrown away. For it brought back memories of his own student days: the camaraderie of a kind of brotherhood, not reverent, but united in a consciousness that what they were doing, in their learning, was something special – 'privileged', as Hans had once said. At least Cameron had had a taste of that: the latent poet in him would have appreciated the romance of that – just as it had in his view of his role as a fighter pilot.

He shouldn't have been surprised by his discovery of that in the young Scots medical student, but he had been.

Wearily slumped in a chair in the mess, smoking his pipe, the previous evening, still thinking about events overseen and overheard in the Operations room that afternoon, he'd been at first taken aback by being approached by the youngster's batman with the request that he help in clearing out Cameron's things. For one thing, he hadn't been able to understand why it would be expected that he would do such a thing – nor why it had to be done that evening, with what seemed like such indecent haste.

'Some of the gentlemen have a thing about it, sir,' the man had explained. 'They think that for a replacement gentleman to move into the room, without it having been done, will put a sort of jinx on whoever occupies the room, and that the sooner it's dealt with, the better. It's just a sort of superstition, I suppose, sir – but understandable, perhaps? Usually the Adjutant accompanies us for that task, for reasons of decency; but he's fully occupied this evening, and suggested I ask you.'

So, dreading the prospect, he'd felt obliged to go along.

It turns out to be a task every bit as grim as he's expected. Whilst the batman – a somewhat lugubrious character in his thirties, whose name is Larkin – gathers clothes, both uniform and civvies, and packs them into a couple of canvas holdalls, it is Peter's job, it seems, to go through 'the more personal effects'.

'The normal procedure is for clothes to go to the registered next-of-kin, sir, which in Mr Cameron's case are his parents, and for the more personal effects to be gone through by an appointed officer such as yourself and a decision made as to what is the best disposal of them.'

Peter, in spite of himself, can't help but be faintly amused by the (admittedly sensible) way in which service protocol is applied even in a situation such as this: clearly experience has shown that to bundle everything, uncensored, off to perhaps rather staid grieving parents is a possible recipe for even more grief and disillusion. But there is nothing of that sort among Cameron's trinkets and papers.

There is a Will. Written it seems in Cameron's own hand, somewhat hastily, and un-witnessed, it bequeaths everything to his parents *apart from my Edinburgh University silk scarf, which is to go to my future fiancée Fiona* (giving her full name and address), *along with my lasting love.* There are a number of photographs, mainly of Fiona (which, Peter decides, should go to his parents, and they can then decide what to do with them), and also a number of letters from Fiona, carefully tied together with red string, which he puts aside, unread, to go back to Fiona. Among these is also a sheet of paper on which is written, with much alteration and crossing out, what turns out to be a piece of poetry. He's about to say to Larkin, I say, there's a poem here by Mr Cameron – but thinks better of it, hesitates, then decides not only that it should be read but that he has an obligation to do so. It is headed *The Empty Chair*:

Who sits there in an easy chair,
face to the sun, in the open air,
girded for the high skies chill,
yet cold, although the hot sun's glare
would normally bring him gladness?

Others lounge, converse and joke,
and thus put on that essential cloak
to clothe their real unquietness;
hoping to cross in a single stroke
that gulf from child to manhood.

Who sits and ponders tomorrow's mail?
-will his girlfriend write; and will this evening's ale
give him the peace he longs for?
And Scamp beside him wags his tail
at the touch of the restless fingers.

Who sits and waits for the sudden bell
(a starting sign, or a final knell?)
through the open door of the nearby hut,
accompanied by an urgent yell,
a strident call to "Scramble!"?

Comes a clumsy run to Merlin's roar
and spinning blades, to white coils of war
up in the cold blue yonder,
perhaps to peer through the beckoning door
beyond which the rest are waiting.

A burst of his guns, a quick acclaim,
a rapid climb to hard fought fame,
a new star in the watching heavens:
but there comes unseen a devouring flame.
And Scamp will wait untended.

Who is it sits in that old armchair?
I don't see his face, but I know he's there,
along with a thousand others.
So, remember them if you're called to prayer:
Without them the world had sundered.

He dwells for a few moments on the possible significance of those few words. Could it be that Cameron had had some prescience of what was to come, that in spite of his brashness plain common sense had told him what was likely to be awaiting him? But he takes a hold on himself, doesn't want to believe in that scenario.

He glances at Larkin, wondering whether to share this scrap of writing with him – but no, it wouldn't be appropriate, it has been privately written, not intended for public eye; and Larkin looks a distinctly practical sort, not given to sentimentality. But what to do with it? He decides it should go to Cameron's parents rather than to Fiona; he was after all their son, and they have a right to this part of him.

Now, decidedly chilly as well as being buffeted by the slipstream in the open car, in another attempt to get things back onto a brighter note as well as to rid himself of his far-too-morbid thoughts, he says, 'Did you hear on the news last night that report of Winston's speech in the Commons yesterday? That was a jolly good phrase he came out with, wasn't it?'

Bill laughs. ' "Never in the field of human conflict has so much been owed by so many to so few...",' he quotes, with over-emphatic irony. 'I suppose so. Apparently some chap in the Mess said that he must have been referring to our mess bills!'

It is in lighter mood, therefore, that some minutes later they arrive at Group H.Q. at Uxbridge. It is like any other R.A.F. station except that, Peter thinks, the security seems that much tighter.

Having drawn up outside the Admin block, Bill says, 'I shan't be long – hopefully no more than five minutes. There's someone I have to see; and at the same time I'll get us passes for us to go and look at The Hole.'

Good as his word, he is out in short time, muttering, 'It looks now as though the weather's clearing from the south, curse it, so we may have to make this quicker than I'd intended. Anyway, let's go.'

The Hole, it turns out, is simply the Group Operations Room, and the name given to it becomes clear once they've entered, for it is some fifty feet underground, down a steep stairway. Peter can't begin to think why Bill has been so anxious to bring him here – particularly as on the way down he's murmuring, 'It's the Beauty Chorus I've really brought you to see. It'll be a revelation, I promise you.' Peter has heard the term before, facetiously applied to the girls who operate the plot tables, so Bill's comment only serves to mystify him more than ever.

The room itself turns out to be very similar in layout to the ops room at Church Wealdon, the only differences being that it is larger, with more staff, and the Control gallery is separated from the plot room by a glass screen – Bill explaining that it had proved necessary because of the level of noise generated in the plot room.

As they stand and watch, it becomes clear that the tempo around the plot table is indeed growing, and Bill starts to become restless, muttering, 'We'll have to be getting back shortly, I'm afraid. But do you see why I've brought you?'

His gaze is fixed on the room below, but he keeps glancing at Peter as if waiting for him to make some comment. Peter can't for the life of him think what he is on about. There are some fifteen WAAFs and four men actively engaged down there, just as they had been at Church Wealdon although on a grander scale, but from where he is standing, to one side, it is more difficult to see them clearly because of reflections in the glass. He remains mystified. Taking his cue from Bill's comments on the way down the stairs, he can see that the girls are indeed quite attractive, but that is certainly no reason to drag him here. Then one of the girls glances up, catching sight first of Bill, whom she seems to recognise, then seeing Peter. For a moment she stares, then seems to sway a little, putting her hands onto the table in front of her as if to steady herself. One of the other girls says something to her, and after staring up a moment longer, she appears to recover and looks away. But not before he's begun to recognise her.

'Good God,' he says, 'it's Jamie, isn't it. What on earth is she doing here?'

Bill grins at him. 'I thought you'd be surprised. Come on, though, we'll have to go. I'll fill you in on the way back.'

Peter follows him to the staircase, glancing towards Jamie several times as he does so, but she is obviously engrossed again in what she is doing and doesn't look up.

Once back in the car, he can't keep the excitement out of his voice. 'What's she doing here?' he repeats, rather inanely.

'As you see,' Bill replies drily. 'She's stationed here. Has been for the past three weeks.'

Sudden doubts assail Peter. 'Are you…is she…are you two…?'

'Going out together, as one might put it? Good God, no. And don't let Jordan hear you make a remark like that, or I'll never hear the end of it. But I have been over here and had a chat with her, chewing over old times. No, it was always you Jamie had a thing for, anyway. Jordan's more my cup of tea. It would be difficult, with Jamie, in any case – *not fraternising with "Other Ranks"*, and all that. But she'll be getting time off. You could always arrange to meet up on neutral ground somewhere, as it were. That is, if you want to. I have the number for the WAAFs Quarters here at Uxbridge, so you could get in touch with her sometime. For old times' sake. Anyway, I thought you'd be interested to see her.'

But Peter is no longer really listening. He is struggling with conflicting emotions – emotions that he can't fully understand. As an aside almost there is dismay and the familiar jealousy, after Bill's apparent confirmation of his closeness to Jordan. But there is also a peculiar sense of delight at the discovery that Bill has no such closeness with Jamie. For, Peter knows, he's always regarded the friendship between Jamie and himself as special.

CHAPTER TWENTY

Sitting in the busy lounge of the Regent Palace Hotel, observing the general bustle of the place, the comings and goings of people, some in a hurry and some in a flurry it seemed, he couldn't quite shake off an irrational impatience of his own. He glanced at his watch. Not yet 4.30. Having already been here for twenty minutes, it felt as though she was late. But she wasn't. Perhaps thirty minutes by tube, she'd said – and "should be able to get away by four o'clock". Anyway, even if she were a bit late, that would still give them plenty of time to do some 'catching up' with one another before meeting up with the others at six o'clock at the *Savoy*, as arranged.

So why this uneasiness? Was it because he was so eagerly looking forward to this meeting? Was that creating a sense of guilt after the terrible events of only four days ago? Making him feel disloyal? But disloyal to whom? Certainly not to O'Connor, whose pragmatism would never have let her acknowledge that one ever owed anyone anything. O'Connor had always had a healthily robust approach to her relationships, it seemed. And her relationship with him had been no different in that respect. He knew that now, having thought about it. It was only this tendency of his to sentimentalise things that had ever led him to believe otherwise. He should have had a more realistic view of O'Connor from the beginning. One more akin to that of Munro, who more than once had referred to her as "Flight-y Officer O'Connor".

He ought really to be grateful, therefore, that his friendship with Jamie had always been on an uncomplicated basis. Best friends, was the way he'd always thought of it. Even better than being brother and sister. That was why he was so looking forward to seeing her again, why he'd been anticipating this for the past ten days, since the visit to Uxbridge. And that was why his feelings about Shevaun didn't come into it. But his uneasiness stemmed too, he knew, from an awareness of his having sadly neglected Jamie in recent years. He hadn't written, as she'd asked him to do that time. He hadn't even bothered to find out where she was living. Good grief, he hadn't even known that she'd joined the WAAFs. What was she going to think of him with regard to all that? Anyway, no good worrying about it. He was soon to find out. If she bothered to turn up. But good grief, this was Jamie he was referring to, had there ever been a time when she couldn't be relied upon?

So he relit his pipe, which he had ignored over the past few minutes, and sat back to let his gaze wander around the bustle of the lounge.

The atmosphere of the place seemed to refute any idea that anything was amiss with the world. Were it not for the relatively sober monochromes of the many and various military uniforms scattered among the different styles and hues of ordinary everyday dress in the room, it might have been a scene from any afternoon in peacetime. He knew that the Hotel, with its prime position just a few steps off Piccadilly Circus, had been established for many years as a social hub for middle class Londoners and tourists alike; and since the onset of war that pattern had actually increased. It was not difficult to see why. Apart from its conveniently central position, like its stable-mates the Corner Houses it displayed an ambience derived from the best of modern design combined with the stylishness of bygone Edwardiana – all at prices which were no great challenge to the not-so-wealthy. Joe Lyons had certainly hit on a good formula. The hotel's main Restaurant, Grill Room, Brasserie and Salad Bar all provided a variety of menus with good food decorously served at reasonable cost and able to meet most requirements, all in surroundings of warm-coloured carpets and fabrics set against backdrops of white marble and polished brass. Elegance itself.

But the heart of its success as a West End rendezvous was undoubtedly this capacious lounge situated immediately off the entrance foyer. Unremarkably furnished with neat wickerwork armchairs and low tables, among which were interspersed palms and other potted plants, in spite of wartime restrictions it still managed to provide a friendly atmosphere and waitress service of tea, coffee, and cakes, with a reassuringly familiar background of music-to-relax-to from a string trio at the far side of the lounge. And it was still a great place for people-watching; and that was what many were doing, sitting on their own, spending a restful half hour watching the world go by.

It had also, though, a well-deserved reputation as a good place for pick-ups. He'd already seen a demonstration of this, when, at the next table to his, an attractively-dressed young woman sitting on her own had been joined at the table by a man wearing the uniform of an officer in the Czech army. He'd clearly been a complete stranger to her, and had politely asked, in passable English, whether the other chairs were free, whereupon she had nodded her assent in what had appeared to be a disinterested manner. However, within five minutes, both sitting in silence gazing around the room, she had pulled out a cigarette and then had appeared to be unsuccessfully hunting for a lighter in the depths of her handbag. With only the slightest of delays he had offered her a light, they had had three or four minutes conversation, and then had got up and walked away together. As he'd watched them go, their slim backs straight with consummate self-assurance, it was with envy that he had done so. He couldn't imagine himself ever being sophisticated enough to be able to do that. But immediately it had set him thinking about Jordan, the old pangs of longing taking hold once more. It was the sort of thing she might do, wasn't it? She was presumably used to playing all sorts of roles, anyway – as Uncle John had once said, in fact she'd been doing that all her life. These were funny times. The future was so precarious that many people's attitudes had changed, their morals less fixed. Since there was a realistic likelihood of being dead tomorrow, a new urgency had entered the business of living. It was now idle to plan ahead; each day had to be lived for itself, experiences seized upon whenever they presented. Perhaps, after all, that was what Shevaun O'Connor had always so clearly understood, not only as a result of the war but all her life – which had itself been a kind of war.

He himself had begun more particularly to understand this in the past days, since his return to Marwell. He had seen the bomber crews with new eyes. It was strange really. He'd had less than a week at Church Wealdon, but it had transformed his view of things. To borrow from Bill's analogy, he'd begun to see the fighter boys as the backs of the rugby team, fast-flying and glamorous: whereas the bomber crews were the forward pack, the workhorse of the team. And they were having every bit as hard a time as were the Spitfire and Hurricane pilots, if not more so. In the past week he'd built up the habit of going along to the pre-ops briefings, sidling into the back of the room once the crews had assembled, sitting there unobtrusively (he hoped), and sneaking out again before they dispersed. He'd persuaded himself that his purpose was to be able to appreciate the stresses to which they were subjected; but had finally had to admit to himself that his real reason was that as time went on he was feeling more and more excluded, that he was not really taking an active role in this war. He wasn't *one* of them. Not really in the same war. And, perversely, he envied them. Because of that, in his imagination he'd come to identify with them, begun to feel what he thought they must feel. On those occasions at the briefings when there was a collective sharp intake of breath as the target for the night was revealed – it might be say to docks or oil-installations which were known to be well-defended – then he too would draw a breath in. From behind, he watched them as they absorbed what the briefing officer revealed to them, he tensed when they tensed, and sweated when they sweated. He was full of admiration for them when, from a distance, he watched as they trooped into the room, seemingly careless of what they had to face, jostling and joking, for all the world like teams about to take part in some likely-to-be-enjoyable game. But when the reality sank in, when fear, albeit well-concealed, began to appear in individuals in a dozen ways, he felt that same fear, to the pit of his stomach, and doubted whether he would ever have been able to face up to what they faced up to night after night. Then he would feel ashamed, knowing that his sensations were spurious, that without actually having experienced, if only once, what they were experiencing, he had no right to pretend to identify with them, nor could he begin to understand their condition.

Whether, when he thought about it, this alteration in his view of their situation was entirely the result of his few days away from them, in a different environment, (as well as his two episodes of being exposed, briefly at least, to enemy fire on the ground) he didn't know. For the direction of the air war had also abruptly changed, certainly so far as the bomber crews were concerned. Once those few German bombs had been dropped (seemingly inadvertently) on London on the 24th of August, and Churchill had promptly ordered the retaliatory raid on Berlin for the following night, the change had been clearly signalled. Everyone had been for retaliation, the cheers had been unrestrained; but deep down everyone had understood that certain limits had been removed, that from henceforth more would be required of them. The targets at Berlin had been put forward as industrial ones, but by now the operational crews were beginning to get an inkling of just how inaccurate much of their bombing was, so they weren't really taken in by this. They knew now that the gloves were well and truly off. Further raids of that sort, on major cities, would become increasingly common, with all the additional hazards and with rising fury in the way the war was fought. Losses among the crews had already escalated. What had started as an adventure for them had become a bitter job of work. And the whole country waited with bated breath for the bombs to begin to fall on London and other major cities in Britain.

But all that, anyway, paled into insignificance compared to the growing certainty of imminent invasion. It would have to come soon. If Hitler was to cross the Channel he would have to do so before November, or else postpone until spring. And he had only to finish off the air-defences and the way would be clear. Many folk still clung to the hope that the Navy and the Army would be able to keep him from the shores, but without air defence it was hope born of desperation. Deep down, everyone knew it.

It was at this point in his deliberations that he saw her, threading her way between tables. And thoughts of the war immediately receded. Wearing a light, creamy, summer dress, she looked slimmer than in the past but otherwise unchanged. In that instant he was transported back over the years, and all he could see was a vigorous teenager with lean shapely limbs and soil-stained shorts and shirt – and, for one uncomfortable moment, a 'boy' with delicate features and longish hair.

Then, as she approached, giving him a little wave of recognition as she spotted him, his eyes were drawn to two young women standing over a man sitting five or six tables away. What had caught his attention was the vehemence with which they seemed to be addressing him. Indignation suffused every line of their bodies. The man, who was youngish and wearing a double-breasted suit, stared silently up at them as if mesmerised. He was too far away for Peter to be sure of his expression, but it appeared to be one of astonishment or perhaps incomprehension. It made one wonder what on earth was going on. Jamie meanwhile had drawn level with the table and was waiting to pass, just as one of the women leaned forward in order to say something further to the man. At that point Peter saw Jamie turn and speak briefly to the women, whereupon they both took a step back, as though involuntarily; then, clearly flustered, but with a peremptory toss of the head from one of them, they hurried away. Jamie gave the man a quick smile without giving him time to say anything, before coming over to Peter.

His first inclination was to ask her what all that had been about, but it was lost in the moment. As she stood next to him, looking up at him, he felt as though she'd never been away. There were the same flecks of autumn colour in her eyes, the same sparkle of amusement, not at something or someone, but with life in general. Yet, in spite of a hint of a smile playing on her lips, her expression was solemn – although her obvious delight at seeing him was apparent from those eyes, the tilt of her head, and the way she inclined her body.

'Hullo, Cautious,' she said. 'The uniform suits you.'

It was a simple statement, with none of the guile which had characterised Jordan's approach a few weeks ago. It was a form of greeting that echoed what he himself felt: that between them time and distance would never matter. There might be a certain sorrow that their friendship had been allowed to lapse, she seemed to be saying, but there was no need for forgiveness: there was nothing to forgive. They would always simply pick up where they had left off, as if there had never been a separation. They would acknowledge the intervening changes and then move on.

Then she reached up and kissed him on the cheek. The tenderness with which she managed to imbue that gesture without it inferring anything more, together with her use of the private nickname she had bestowed upon him so many years ago, filled him with warmth such as he'd not experienced for a long time.

'Would you like something to eat or drink?' he asked.

The banality of that silly greeting of his own was not lost on him, and it was a relief therefore when she said, 'Oh, no, let's go outside, shall we? It's such a lovely day. Like mid-summer. It's hard to believe we're almost through the first week in September.'

She looked at him quickly, and he suspected they were both thinking the same thing: that it was also hard to take in that it was one whole year since the declaration of war. But he didn't say anything; instead they walked out of the lounge and into the street in silence – not the silence of awkwardness, of not knowing what to say, but in companionable contentment, two pals relaxed together. He couldn't think of anyone else he'd be able to do that with…except perhaps Uncle John.

Outside, brightness and heat bounced up from the pavements, not oppressively but with comforting warmth, as happens when one first sits out on a sun-bathed beach before the body begins to object to the uncompromising rays. It seemed to foretell of days of sunshine and pleasantness to come. But at *Swan & Edgar's*, opposite, the largely-boarded-up shop windows, reflecting as it were the same state as was the 'Eros' site across the way, were a bleak reminder of the true state of the day.

Crossing the Circus through light traffic they strolled down the Haymarket, still without speaking but holding hands as if it was the most

313

natural thing to do. He knew where they would be heading – St James's Park – and felt no need to confirm this with her, convinced that this was in her mind as well. Their inclination would always be towards seeking some semblance of countryside.

'So, you're stationed at Marwell, I believe?...'

'So, how did you end up at Uxbridge?...'

They'd both spoken together, and laughed in delight that their attunement could extend to that. But was there in addition a hint of mutual accusation that they'd never kept in touch?

'Go on,' she said.

'No, I want to hear all about you first. I thought you were still working for one of the City banks?'

'So I was, until shortly after war was declared. But then they were looking for people fluent in German. I never discovered quite who 'they' were; but I suppose they simply trawled through the appropriate city institutions for suitable people. There was no compulsion, but a lot of persuasion. And once one had agreed, one had to sign up to the Official Secrets Act. They made me a WAAF – one of the first in fact, as they'd only just come into existence – because, I think, they realised that having one in uniform was the best way of having the greatest control.'

'So what did they have you doing?' he asked with interest.

'Well, I don't think I'm really supposed to tell, but in effect we were listening-in to German wireless transmissions, both naval and *Luftwaffe*. At a place called Bletchley Park – but I didn't tell you that.'

'You mean they could listen in, without any difficulty, just like that?' he said, astonished.

'Well, no, not just like that. The info came for translation, to us, the translators, in two ways. Open speech, which we, the German-speakers, listened to direct. That was largely of the order 'What's for tea?' kind of thing, and deadly boring. More commonly what we were given were directives and exchanges transcribed onto paper – still in German, of course – obtained from Morse messages, which had either been open ones or more usually had first to have been decoded.'

'Sounds interesting.'

'Don't you believe it. It was deadly dull routine. Most of it was not of the slightest significance, and the few pieces that were of interest had all been in code. The people on decoding quite often had to have basic German in order to do their work, so, much of the time, they came to us merely for detail or to help iron out difficulties. By the time we were involved, not infrequently a day or so later, it was no longer of any relevance. I think only once in six months or so was I involved with one that probably made a difference, and that was information about U-boat movements in the Atlantic.'

'So that's why you left?'

'You bet. I was bored out of my mind. So, after a few months I applied for something more active, as it were. They tried to persuade me otherwise, but I kept badgering, and in the end they gave in. What they really need at

Bletchley is faster decoding. That would make a difference. They're working hard on it. I haven't told you any of this, needless to say.'

'Of course not.' And they laughed.

By now they'd arrived at Trafalgar Square, and he squinted up at the remote figure of Nelson atop his column – accorded such veneration in his day that he'd been placed well out of reach of mere mortal man. That had been the last occasion when the country had been under threat of invasion, and quite clearly the popular relief at deliverance had been very considerable. Yet he couldn't believe that the menace on that occasion had been anything like as sinister as the present one. Already scaffolding was being erected against the fluted column, presumably to protect him from the effects of shrapnel and blast from bombs – a risk almost certainly as great as those at Trafalgar. He glanced at Jamie, wondering whether to share these thoughts with her; but, no, to what purpose? – it would only serve to sour the moment.

As of one accord they turned now under Admiralty Arch into the Mall, passing without comment the ugly blockhouse that had newly been built. To their left, Horse Guards Parade was strangely silent and empty, the only movements being those of several khaki-clad guards, tin-hatted, with bayonets fixed, placed at intervals around the square. Their workaday battle-dress denied any semblance of ceremony; but he wondered what it was they were supposed to protect and from whom – they certainly didn't look as if they were capable of being in any way effective against, say, a squad of jerry paratroopers. Yet, as Jamie and he walked further into the park a glimpse over the rooftops of barrage balloons down-river, their silver skins sparkling in the sunshine, incongruously suggested more of a festive air.

Finding a vacant bench by the lake they sat down. The park was busier than he'd expected. There were any number of nannies still, as though nothing had changed, regally pushing their small charges in big glossy prams, or else trailing toddlers on reins, like pet dogs, clearly determined that water, mud and children should be kept firmly apart. However, some had brought bread for the ducks which greeted this doubtlessly now-infrequent treat with excited squawks; and Peter found himself wondering whether the Ministry of Food, across the way, would entirely approve of this use of scarce resources. There were also, inevitably, a number of men in uniform, nearly all foreign. Strolling along in relaxed manner, many of them with a girl on their arm, they might have been on holiday, tourists in uniform if you like. Not for the first time he gained the impression that this could almost be said to be the official view of them: it was good that they were here, they would be treated with the utmost courtesy, but it was important that they didn't actually get in the way of the proper soldiery. Mind you, he knew only too well what a vital role many of them were playing in the R.A.F. – Czechs, Poles, Canadians, South Africans, Aussies and New Zealanders, and even a handful of Americans.

He noticed a number of them glancing at Jamie as they passed, regardless of whether they had a girl with them or not. Why this should in any way surprise him, he didn't know. He glanced at her himself. She was sitting quietly with her face tilted toward the sun, the autumn tints in her hair

315

glistening in the light. Her features, pleasant and fresh, too had a sunny glow; her figure in the lightweight dress still had the trimness and athleticism that he remembered so well. He supposed, when he thought about it, that she was really very attractive.

All at once aware that he'd allowed his thoughts over the past few minutes to get in the way of conversation, he now said, 'I've been meaning to ask you, what was all that business in the Regent Palace lounge, as you were coming over toward me?'

She laughed. 'Oh, that. I couldn't believe it! Those two girls – who spoke all *la-de-da* as though they'd never known a day's work in their lives – were actually berating the chap because he wasn't in uniform. It was quite incredible. I know it happened to some extent at the beginning of the last war – but in this day and age? I ask you! To say it was mindless is putting it mildly.'

'From where I was sitting they seemed to be trying to give him something, though? What was all that about?'

'Goodness knows. An envelope of some kind, I think. Probably contained a white feather!'

'But you said something to them?'

'Yes. I said I knew the gentleman, and that in fact he was a Squadron Leader in the R.A.F.'

'And is he?'

'I haven't a clue – I've never seen him before. But it certainly shut them up.'

'So did he say anything to you, afterwards?'

'Not a word. Didn't seem to know what was going on. Probably doesn't speak English. He's probably a German spy!'

They had a good laugh about that; and then he said, 'How do you like being in the WAAFs, then?'

She shrugged. 'It's alright. Accommodation's acceptable, food not bad. It's just the uniform.'

'The uniform?'

'Well, the undies, really.' She laughed. 'You wouldn't understand. But the standard issue of bra and knickers is like something out of a medieval nunnery – although, come to think of it, *they* probably didn't wear *any* underwear. 'Passion killers', the girls call them. Most of the time we manage to get away with wearing our own knickers and bras, and just keep the standard ones for presentation at kit inspection. Fortunately they haven't yet got around to inspecting what we actually wear underneath! But, surely, being a station M.O. you must already have noticed this for yourself!'

He had and he hadn't – had noticed the variations, but hadn't appreciated the significance. Strangely he was feeling slightly uncomfortable with this line of conversation with Jamie. So he changed the topic.

'Have you been home lately?'

'Just a long weekend, about eight weeks ago.'

'What a shame, if I'd known perhaps I could have got off too. We could have had a walk together, visited old haunts.'

She looked at him quizzically. It had sounded a bit naive. What he'd meant, really, he supposed, was that perhaps they might do that another time. It seemed as if she understood that – but maybe doubted his sincerity? Or wondered about the implications, if any? For a brief moment he wondered about that himself.

'That might have been a bit difficult,' she said quietly. 'To arrange, that is.'

'Anyway, how were things at home?' he said hurriedly.

'Alright. Not much has changed, as I'm sure you know. In a general sense the war passes them by. Apart from the rationing, of course. And the evacuees.' She laughed. 'To hear some of the townsfolk talk, you'd think that was the most terrible aspect of the entire war! Poor little mites. A lot had come from inner-city slums, and although the few I came across had already been there for several weeks, they looked thoroughly bewildered.'

'Oh, give them a few more weeks and they'll probably be most reluctant to ever go home again.'

That sounded thoroughly condescending – and assumed an awful lot – so he hurried on: 'Do you get on any better with your stepfather, these days?'

'My stepfather died. About two years ago.'

'Oh. I'm sorry. I didn't know.' He should have known, should have maintained contact with her. Some friend he'd been! If he was honest about it, he hadn't put much effort into supporting his cosy concept of a supposedly special relationship with Jamie, over the years. All at once that saddened him.

'Is your mother well, then?' It, too, sounded inadequate. He should probably have expressed some sympathy at her mother being widowed for the second time in her life. But he'd been thinking that Jamie had never really got on with her stepfather, to put it mildly.

'Yes, she's well, thanks. Worries about me being down here, I think – as I'm sure yours does about you. And they must worry a lot about the overall situation, just as we all do.'

She gave a half laugh containing a hint of irony. 'Seems quite content to be on her own again.'

He was tempted to ask about her relationship with her late stepfather – something that he and the others had wondered about often enough, but, faced with her silence on the subject, had never dared ask.

Instead, he said, 'And did you see anything of George?'

She looked at him curiously for a moment before replying. 'No. I didn't see anything of George.' There was a note of surprise in her voice; and a slight edginess to her reply. She paused. Then: 'You know, Pete, we can't go back to the past, much less stay in it. We have to move on. Relationships change, and we have to recognise that, and learn to accept it.'

It was said gently. There was nothing patronising in the way she'd said it; but then he wouldn't have expected there to be, from Jamie. Even so, he

317

felt like a child again, being led by the hand. And he couldn't quite understand what she was getting at.

'Anyway,' she went on briskly, 'enough about me. What about you? What are things like at Marwell? You had a raid there, recently, didn't you?'

'Yes.'

He grew silent, remembering.

He's walking across the tarmac, heading for the Sick Quarters, after lunch. The place is quiet after last night's sorties to *Bremerhaven*, the two dozen or so crews sleeping it off. (Thank God they'd all come back unscathed; but equally the trip had apparently been totally devoid of success, the target completely cloud-covered when they'd arrived.) A small section of WAAFs are marching smartly two by two towards him, led by a WAAF corporal. She salutes him as they go by – the girls, on command, performing a slick eyes-right in his direction. He returns the salute, suppressing a grin, and resists the inclination to turn round to watch them go. Not far behind them Warrant Officer Mitchell is crossing the apron, coming his way, in no great hurry, almost sauntering, but nevertheless spruce and alert, his thin moustache seeming to bristle with military pride. He too salutes, though more casually, and stops, making no attempt to stop the grin which spreads across his face.

'Afternoon, sir. It's grand to see the lasses swinging their hips like that, is it not? And they do a grand job.'

'Afternoon, Chiefie.' He looks at Mitchell with some suspicion – it's as if the man has read his thoughts. 'Yes, it is. And yes, they do.' Instead of turning to watch the departing WAAFs as Mitchell is doing, however, he pretends a certain objectivity by letting his gaze drift in the direction of the far side of the field. Towards the distant perimeter a small group of men can be seen working, presumably on the Wimpey that pranged on landing the previous evening – but it is too far away to see what they're doing. As he watches, squinting into the afternoon sun, his view is obscured by a sudden flash of flame and a plume of smoke from a fire that he hadn't noticed until now, just in front of the plane. How odd, he thinks, wondering what the dickens they're doing. At once though, in the same area three more orange mushrooms erupt in line, all close together, the ground trembles, and a series of muffled explosions reaches his ears. The first tinglings of recognition stir within, then jerk him into action as Mitchell beside him bellows, 'Attack! Attack! Hit the trenches!' – and, more frantically as the line of WAAFs thirty yards away marches steadfastly on, 'You bloody stupid women, get in the fucking trenches!' The next thing he has Peter by the sleeve of his jacket and is forcibly dragging him to the nearest of the slit-trenches twenty yards away. They tumble in, Peter conscious of Mitchell giving him an almighty push at the last moment, so that he bangs his knee on the way in and ends up face down, spitting out moist earth. He lifts his head to draw breath, and thrusts his face into the ground again as a blast of sound hits them with painful impact, then another, and another. For long seconds they lie there, physically unable to move as wave after wave of uproar assaults them: explosions, at times agonisingly close, the scream and roar of aircraft low overhead, and the incessant thud and whine of bullets – all blending in an unholy mixture which numbs the ears and dims the mind. Then, abruptly, comes silence, marred at first only by the ringing in one's head and ears, and then, too, by cries and moans from near and far. Peter lifts his head and sees Mitchell cautiously peering over the rim of the trench. The man grunts, then stands. 'You alright?' he asks, purely as an aside.

Peter stands too, unsteadily, swaying slightly.

'Take care, sir,' the Warrant Officer cautions. 'There may be a second wave close on the heels of that one.'

Peter stares around him. Smoke hangs in grey veils through which can be seen, here and there, flickering flames like the remnants of dying bonfires. One of the hangars has caught a direct hit, and over to their right a couple of aircraft are burning fiercely. But, miraculously, the main buildings appear to be more or less intact. Figures are beginning to emerge warily from one place or another, uncertainty manifest in their movements. From a distance comes the urgent clanging of a bell – fire-engine or ambulance, he cannot tell – moving nearer, and this jolts him into the need for action, his head clearing. He has a sudden memory of the line of WAAFs being sworn at by Mitchell just as the raid announced its presence, and he looks around in panic, expecting to see figures strewn on the ground – and lets his breath go as he finds none. Then, some fifty yards away, close to a still-smoking crater, he sees a head and shoulders appear from the ground as someone begins the process of levering themselves out of a trench. Peter follows suit, intent on climbing out, but Mitchell puts a restraining hand on his shoulder, begins to say, 'I should give it a few...', but breaks off as, for the first time, the siren starts its wail – not the reassuringly constant note of the All Clear, but the gut-wrenching undulation of the Warning. And Mitchell, staring across the tarmac, cries, 'What the hell?...Oh my God, no! Go back!' He's looking in the direction of the main buildings, his body beginning to bunch for action. Peter follows his line of sight, and glimpses, through a drift of smoke, a familiar figure in white, skirt lifting over shapely knees as she sprints desperately across the tarmac, haversack flung over one shoulder, short coppery hair glinting in the sun. She's heading in the direction of the crater that just now caught Peter's attention, and immediately he understands, begins to heave himself out of the trench as Mitchell shouts again, 'O'Connor, M'am, no! Go back! It isn't safe yet!' Peter now is on his knees, out of the trench, getting to his feet, when, with one bound, the warrant officer joins him, cursing fluently, turning to look behind him even as he reaches Peter's side. The next moment they are both crashing back down into the trench, Mitchell's arms wrapped around him; and as he twists and falls he glimpses the thin grey profiles of twin-engined *Messerschmitts*, flying low, approaching fast, flame spitting from their wings, and hears, blending with the roar of engines, the spiteful hiss and thud as bullets strike the ground. A few seconds later and they're gone, can be seen as dwindling shapes soaring up into an indifferent sky. A pause, a moment of held breath, then Mitchell again cautiously raises his head.

'They're gone,' he says. 'Come on.'

Once more they scramble out, begin to run towards where they last saw O'Connor. Ahead, other figures too emerge, bit by bit, from trench and dugout, some to stagger or crawl, clothes torn and black, stained with blood; and anguish reigns. The extent of some of the injuries becomes apparent as they draw close. Stretcher-bearers appear, and an ambulance, and Peter knows that duty calls. But first…

O'Connor lies face down, not moving, blood seeping ominously across her back. Gently, with Mitchell's help, he turns her over. Her eyes are open, looking up at him without expression – in death somehow a softer green. Her tunic, no longer white but crimson, no longer neat but tattered, gapes in places to reveal her hideous wounds. What had she said, when he left for lunch? – 'Now don't be long. I need you here.' Not 'we', but 'I'. Simple words, but from Shevaun somehow filled with dare and promise. Now she's gone, and it's as though a part of him has gone too.

More devastated than he could have imagined, he carefully closes her eyes, rises, and turns to help those whom he can.

'Was it bad?' Her voice, coming from afar, entered the space gently, tinged with concern.

'Yes. Not good. Six deaths, including a couple…three…WAAFs. One of them a friend…a colleague, actually…well, yes, a friend.' And he started telling her all about Shevaun O'Connor, about her reputation on the station, about her true character and her background, about their days at Dover at the time of Dunkirk, about her desire for children she'd never been able to have, and now never would. But he didn't tell her about that night they'd had together. That was personal, private, sacred to the memory of Shevaun. Jamie put her hand on his, a gesture both of intimacy and consolation. And something else. It was if she knew. That there was more to it than that. Something that he couldn't quite admit to himself.

All she said was, 'I'm sorry.'

And somehow she made it sound as though she had a private grief of her own.

CHAPTER TWENTY-ONE

Having lingered too long in the park, Jamie and he arrived late at the Savoy, shortly after 6.45 in fact, eventually finding the others in the lounge adjoining the River Room, which was busy but not quite as crowded as he'd seen it in the past. Aware of Jamie's slight nervousness at this sudden grandeur, and a little flustered himself by their lateness, he hardly had time to identify just who was there of the 'usual crowd', gathered on the far side of the room, before his eyes were taken by the sight of Jordan, dressed to kill, sitting on Bill's lap. As Jamie and he crossed the floor towards them, Jordan, who no doubt had seen them as soon as they entered, raised a languid arm in greeting; and Bill, looking up, treated them to a broad self-satisfied grin. As well he might. For Jordan, wearing a scant, low-cut dress which had risen well above the knee, was draped intimately all over him. Further disconcerted at being unexpectedly faced by this scenario, Peter, for a few seconds, among the general greetings which followed, overlooked the fact that, apart from Bill and Jordan, Jamie was not known by the others, and omitted to introduce her. When, tardily, he did so, prompted by a squeeze of his arm from Jamie and a sardonically raised eyebrow and peremptory jerk of the head from Jordan, in stumbling hesitation he used her given name of Jane. On hearing, with no little surprise, his rather awkward use of her 'Sunday' name this evoked a muffled giggle from Jordan and a mirthless smile from Bill. What Jamie herself thought of it he didn't dare to think.

Thoroughly put out by now, and struggling therefore with a sudden bout of all-too-familiar self-consciousness, he remained confused, lost for words, not knowing which way to turn. It was Sylvia Stanton who came to his rescue, coming over to take Jamie by the arm and lead her away in a flurry of conversation, pausing only to give him a non-too-sympathetic smile in passing. His relief at her intervention almost overcame his surprise at seeing her there: he had been led to believe she was on her way to Edinburgh.

But rooted to the spot and tongue-tied, he was still the centre of attention. There appeared to be a blur of faces staring in his direction, all, it seemed to him, rapt with curiosity at his predicament.

Mortified, and silently cursing himself for the way he continued to allow Jordan to have such an effect on him, through the mist of his embarrassment he began to identify a number of other faces: Arthur Stanton, David Munro with his fiancée Athena Brown, and Anna Beal. Wildly he looked around expecting to see Jim Beal, anticipating the contemptuous expression that he might expect to find on his face, also – but of Beal there was no sign.

And it was Arthur this time who came across to relieve him of his stress – at the same time clearly having to suppress, not very successfully, his own searching look as Peter met his gaze.

'Glad you could make it, Peter. But I've a bone to pick with you.'

Alarm displaced Peter's discomfort. What now?

'With me? Why is that?'

'For telling my wife that her rightful place is by her husband's side. But for you, she'd have been safely in Edinburgh by now.'

Peter had no recollection of telling her any such thing, and denial was about to spring to his lips, when pause came for thought. He could imagine that Sylvia, trying hard to find anything to support her cause, might in her desperation have used his name as that of an ally. Certainly he remembered the conversation with her about her going away; but he couldn't think that he had ever said anything along the lines that Arthur had just quoted. In any case, in spite of the sternness of Stanton's tone there was the hint of a twinkle in his eye – and, Peter suspected, a note of relief in his voice.

'I may have said something about there perhaps being equal merit in you both continuing to face things together,' he told Arthur carefully, not feeling the slightest guilt at the lie. 'Do you, really, disagree with that? Apart from each other, each of you worrying about the other and not there to comfort and reassure one another?'

'No, I suppose you are right,' the padre said with a rather-too-elaborate sigh. And now there was more certain relief in his voice. 'In any case, there's no doing any good with her now. She's made her mind up, and that's that. Anyway, let me get you a pint, and a drink for your Jane, and then you can tell me all about this surprise bonnie lassie you've brought along with you this evening.'

Left to his own thoughts while Stanton concentrated on attracting the attention of the waiter, and with his equilibrium by now returning to normal he was able to take more stock of his surroundings. The whole place was buzzing. As expected, military uniforms were there in plenty, but also richly-gowned women, and any number of smartly dressed, generally older, men – civil servants, diplomats and business people, he supposed. What Stanton was wont to call, with no little disparagement, 'the great and the good'. Of course, he was well aware, the Savoy now had an even greater attraction as an evening venue because of its cellars which were available as safe shelters in the possible event of air raids. The swell of chatter and laughter was as normal as it would have been with any such crowd in the room, even under the circumstances of war; but beneath it, tonight, he imagined he could again detect a familiarly brittle bonhomie and bravado. Yet, when he thought about it, more than that: a more obvious sense of camaraderie. An air of 'we're all in this together'. It was even noticeable among the waiters and waitresses: although still attentive and courteous, they no longer had the formal stiffness of yesteryear; they were more willing to exchange banter with the guests, to place themselves on much the same level – or, more accurately, in the same boat. A common threat was able to produce, it seemed, a common identity. He'd already seen this around town. The Londoner (or, more precisely, the Cockney element of London) had always had this chirpy demeanour, an irreverent type of humour that was no respecter of persons. But now it had more warmth to it, it seemed to embrace those at whom it was directed. It was as if they, the true Londoners, were saying, 'Now we're prepared to accept you as one of us, for shortly you too will be sharing in the struggles and uncertainties of our lives. And you too will be learning what it is to face hardship and deprivation.'

A few minutes later, having set Stanton straight (with some difficulty, it had to be said) about the nature of his relationship with Jamie, he caught the eye of the subject of their discussion. She was standing with Sylvia over by one of the big windows which overlooked the river, and the appeal in her eyes was obvious even at this distance. Well, he could understand that Sylvia Stanton might be proving a bit overwhelming, even for Jamie, so he excused himself to Arthur and hurried over.

'Now then, I've been hearing all about your little secrets,' Sylvia said, 'but I'm sure you two want to be alone for a while, so I'll leave you for now.'

But as she moved away she took Peter's elbow and drew him aside. 'I suppose Arthur told you about my change of plans?' she said in a low voice.

'Yes.'

'And did he mention one of the…er…reasons I gave for doing so?'

'If you mean that I was the one chiefly responsible for your change of plans, yes he did,' said Peter, adopting a stern tone of voice.

'So did you let the cat out of the bag?'

'Nearly – but no, I didn't,' replied Peter with a grin. 'Feel free to take my name in vain anytime.'

She gave his arm a squeeze. 'Well done. And thank you. I'm in your debt.' She lowered her voice further. 'And I think your girlfriend is delightful.'

'Oh, she's not my girlfriend,' Peter said hurriedly, 'just an old friend'.

'Oh? I was under the distinct impression…' She tailed off uncertainly, giving him a keen look. 'Oh, well, foolish me. I've clearly got it wrong.'

But as she moved away he could see she wasn't convinced.

Mystified, he moved back to join Jamie.

'Sorry about that,' he said. 'Just a little bit of conspiracy.' And he explained about Stanton and his wife, adding, 'I'm sorry you got landed with her like that. She can be a bit direct.'

'I think she's very nice. And her directness is one of the things I like about her.'

'So what were the "little secrets" she was referring to?'

Jamie laughed. 'Oh, this and that. But don't worry,' she added teasingly, 'nothing you wouldn't want your mother to know. Sylvia was pulling your leg.'

He had the feeling there was more to it than that, but Jamie was quite relaxed, and he still wasn't clear what he wanted to find out. So he remained silent, and instead they turned to peer through the mesh of sticky-back paper across the plate glass window, looking out over the river. The sun was just going down to the west, up-river, spreading an orange glow over the darkness of the water and placing daubs of red onto the metal hull of a single barge still making its slow way upstream; and wherever the surface of the water was ruffled by wind and tide the reflected crimson took on the appearance of flickering flame. Soon, as darkness spread, all such traffic would cease: denied the ability to show navigation lights it was no longer possible for them to travel after dusk. He still hadn't got used to seeing the city in total blackness: shop windows like funeral parlours, silent and forbidding; West End streets dead without their neon signs; public buildings unlit, like mausoleums; and theatres morgue-like, as though closed down – which indeed some of them were. On really dark nights pedestrians and the few vehicles still on the streets moved with great caution, each wary of the other. It reminded one of the extreme fogs of the past, the pea-soupers with visibility down to a few yards – except that in the fogs, however dense, there had always been the ghostly glow of headlamps to warn one of the creeping presence of cars or buses. Now, with headlights and traffic lights all visored, even tinier glimmers of light were all there were to tell you of their presence. Bearing in mind that hospitals for the past few months had been geared to expect thousands of casualties from air-raids upon the city, the irony was that air-raids, as yet, hadn't come, but the number of deaths and injuries from people being knocked down in the street had increased fourfold.

'Bill seems to have finally caught up with his grail.'

The density of Jamie's remark, cutting into his thoughts, had him floundering for a moment; but as he automatically turned to look towards Bill he understood what Jamie was referring to. And had there been a certain regret in her voice, and was there an unusual intensity in her gaze in that direction? For Jordan was still sprawling on Bill's lap, all wispy dress and golden limbs, he and she clearly besotted with one another. Well, it should have been no surprise. Bill had always carried a candle for Jordan; and he was debonair, dashing, and now one of the modern heroes. Why wouldn't she fall for him.

But had Jamie herself, secretly, always had a thing for Bill?

'Yes,' he replied, affecting disinterest.

The disgruntlement in his voice must have been apparent, however, for Jamie gave him a sharp look.

'Did you know that Jordan is now working at the *Windmill*?'

There could have been expected to be an element of spite in that remark, but there was no hint of that. From Jamie there never would be.

'The Windmill Theatre? No!'

He was genuinely shocked, not so much by the content of the news as by the fact that he hadn't known.

'Yes. Bill told me a few days ago. The show she was in closed down, as so many have; and of course the Windmill is one of the few that has continued to stay open throughout the evening.' She laughed. Openly, without sarcasm. 'Which is no surprise, with all these men in town.'

'You still see Bill, then?'

Again she looked at him in some surprise, probably because of the tangential nature of his remark. And again there was an enquiring light in her eyes. Had there been an edge to his voice?

'Yes, of course. He tends to look me up when he's in the vicinity of Uxbridge.'

Well, he reminded himself, she's known Bill longer than she's known me – all her life in fact. So it's natural enough.

'So she's been reduced to doing striptease, then? Do Uncle John and Aunt Mabel know?' Even he could hear the thin vein of spite running through his remarks, and immediately felt ashamed.

Again Jamie was looking at him oddly. After a pause, she said carefully, 'You're still quite…keen on Jordan, aren't you?'

He tried to laugh it off. 'What do you mean, "still"? What makes you think I was ever keen on her?'

'Oh, little things. The way you talked about her. And the way, on occasions, she talked about you.'

The last caught his attention. He wondered what she meant by that.

What he said was, 'But I don't even like her – well, not particularly, anyway.'

'But that has nothing to do with it, has it.'

'Doesn't it?'

'You know it doesn't. At least, I hope that's something you understand. For your sake, as well as…' She tailed off.

They lapsed into silence while he thought about that, tried to unravel what she was getting at. He just didn't understand women – and this was the first time that he'd ever really considered putting Jamie into that context. Which was a disturbing thing to conclude.

'Anyway,' said Jamie, introducing a false-sounding brightness to her voice, 'to go back to your previous remarks, she's not in fact doing striptease, but employed as a singer and dancer – albeit fairly scantily dressed, I suppose. But that's alright, isn't it?' By now there was a lighter, teasing tone to her words. 'And no, I don't think her parents know about it.'

'They'd certainly be shocked if they did.'

'Well, Aunt Mabel maybe – and Cook, of course! But I think Uncle John would be quite tickled. I get the impression that he's never had any unrealistic expectations of her!'

'How is it you know what it is she's doing there, anyway?' he asked suspiciously.

'From Bill, of course.'

'You mean he's been to see her?'

'Of course. Wouldn't you? I imagine it's been quite a feather in his cap with 'the boys', having a girlfriend in the chorus at the Windmill!'

By now his emotions were churning again, resentments coming to the fore, and it was some relief therefore when Jamie now changed the direction of their thoughts.

'Tell me, who's the exotically dark woman sitting over there?'

'Anna? – Anna Beal.' And he began to tell her about Anna, and about Beal, and then about David Munro, and the connections between himself and the two men.

'How wonderful,' Jamie exclaimed. 'So there are the three of you here, all connected through Bardolph's. As well as Bill, and Jordan, from home. Quite a home from home, in fact!'

'And you.'

'Well, yes. And me. But I'm really just on the fringe. Until now, anyway.'

'Until now,' he said. And out of the corner of his eye he could see her giving him a long look. But he was still gazing at Anna Beal. Every time he saw her anew he saw her with fresh eyes, as though having to be reminded just how entrancing and exciting she was. And every time he would think how lucky a fellow Beal was.

'You like *her* too, don't you,' Jamie said quietly.

'Too? Anna? Oh yes, she's great fun. But also got considerable depths to her.' Why had he introduced that remark? Would Jamie think that he was contrasting her to Jordan? He said the next thing that came into his head.

'She's Jewish, you know…as well as German, that is…'

'So?'

'So…' he stumbled, '…so…it's just that she's very dependent on being married to Beal…' What was it he was trying to justify? '…otherwise…otherwise she would have ended up in a refugee camp…or even worse…if…if things come to the worst…'

But Jamie, laughing, stopped him by putting an affectionate hand on his arm and saying, 'Oh, Peter, for heaven's sake stop there before you get yourself completely tied in knots! You can, still, get yourself in an awful muddle, can't you. You sometimes get too involved in things – in people – do you know that? You make it sound as though you're the cause of Anna Beal's problems and responsible for her. Which clearly you are not… But perhaps would like to be?'

He turned angrily towards her, humiliated by the last remark – but it was Jamie gazing at him, affection and sympathy in her eyes, the years of close companionship distilled there; and his anger died. He couldn't imagine ever getting cross with Jamie. And as he tried to push aside this new image of himself that she had conjured up – an image which somehow was confused with memories of O'Connor – and as he was trying to think of a suitable retort, he saw Anna Beal waving at them, calling them over, aware of their sudden attention on her. The others were all sitting down now, along with Anna, arranged in a loose circle around a couple of tables, and they moved to make room for Jamie and him. He realised that since his arrival he hadn't yet spoken a word to either Bill or Jordan, and that perhaps he had subconsciously been avoiding it; and at the same time it struck him that nor had Jamie and Jordan exchanged greetings, even though it must be a considerable time since they'd last seen one another. And now it was Jamie who spoke first.

'Hullo, Jordan. Long time no see! How are you?'

Jordan gave a half wave, a small circular motion of her hand, at the same time giving a slight shrug of her shoulders, her mouth making a little moue. It could have been interpreted as dismissive, as though, at the moment, she wasn't particularly enthusiastic about seeing Jamie.

'Alright, I suppose,' she replied. 'Thanks. Not exactly happy, though.' Her petulance now changed to naked anxiety. 'Do you think they're really going to start bombing London?'

Her question ended up being addressed to the gathering at large. And it was met by a pause in the conversation. She had voiced the thought they'd all been trying to avoid. But it was Bill who almost immediately answered, making no attempt to disguise the enthusiasm in his voice.

'Oh, I should think so. Adolf's already said so, hasn't he, in no uncertain terms! Anyway, it's to be bloody well hoped so.'

There followed a few seconds of shocked silence. Jordan sprang away from him as if stung, disbelief etched all over her face. Peter himself couldn't believe what he'd just heard. Bill, he thought, in spite of his superior expression looked infinitely weary, and Peter wondered if finally he was cracking under the strain.

Stanton spoke first. 'Terrible as it sounds, Bill's quite right of course.'

The others looked at him in astonishment – everyone except Bill, that is, and David Munro, who was nodding sagely.

'You see,' Arthur went on, 'jerry's been knocking hell out of our airfields for the past few weeks. Particularly the fighter fields. It seems unlikely that we can stand much more of that. We're getting low on kites, particularly Spits and Hurricanes – and, what's more important, low on pilots. Isn't that right, Bill?'

Bill merely nodded, his fatigue suddenly showing through for all to see.

'Even the bomber squadrons are in disarray,' Stanton continued, 'and we badly need those at present, as well. So it's vital that we get some respite – enough time to bring in new kites and new pilots, as well as, even more importantly hanging onto as many of our experienced pilots as possible. Otherwise we're going to lose this damned war. So, you see, if the *Luftwaffe*'s attention is drawn away from the airfields to towns and cities, that will give us the respite we so desperately need.' He looked, now, at Jamie. 'You must know as much as anyone about that, Jane, working at Uxbridge?'

Peter wondered how he knew about that – so far as he was aware, it certainly hadn't been mentioned this evening. It struck him that there must be a whole grapevine of information, at certain levels, that he wasn't party to.

Jamie, for her part, for once in her life momentarily seemed slightly taken aback. But she quickly rallied. 'It's true,' she said, 'that at Group Control we've become directly aware of the rate of attrition on our own fighter strength…' Here she paused, glancing uncomfortably at Bill. 'That's a terrible phrase,' she went on hurriedly. 'When one's been doing the job, listening to it all, for even a short time, one learns to wall oneself off from the reality. Official jargon helps.' She lifted her chin. 'What I mean is, watching the frightful loss of planes and…and pilots – day after day; knowing, at times, that there are absolutely no more reserves to draw on at that particular moment; then one…we…all of us doing the job, all too often go away with feelings of utter despair. And yes, if it means that towns and cities have to suffer, along with the civilians in them, yet that can result in the airfields and service people in them having more time to regroup, then I think that must be a price worth paying.'

She looked directly now at Jordan. 'I'm sorry. I know that the thought of being bombed is a frightening one. But this is war, and that is a fear that most of us here have already had to learn to live with. And the boys who have to go up there and risk their lives time after time have to live with fear that is far, far greater than we can comprehend – and I'm sure I speak for the bomber crews as well as the fighter pilots. I know that they will all tell you – will pretend – that there's nothing to it, that 'it's a piece of cake!' but we all know, really, that that rings hollow.'

There followed an uneasy silence. Peter, whilst admiring her courage and honesty in speaking like that, wondered if she had this time said too much; some things, perhaps, were better left unsaid? Athena Brown was looking, almost tearfully, at David Munro, who, concentrating on some invisible speck on the table in front of him, was refusing to look at her. Sylvia Stanton, though, was staring at Jamie with frank admiration; whilst Arthur, beside her, sat, head bowed, looking thoughtful. Peter looked across at Anna Beal. She too was staring at Jamie, but with an expression he found unfathomable. As for Jordan, she stared back at Jamie with a face which openly betrayed a mixture of fright, anger and sheer venom. Bill, meanwhile, still uncharacteristically silent, although looking at Jamie with some amusement, appeared, too, to be struggling with inner thoughts.

It was Anna who broke the silence, her voice suddenly hard, her whole attitude one of hostility.

'Why is it that it is now, suddenly, so terrible, this idea of being bombed, of the bombing of civilians? You – we – have been bombing German people for some little time now, have we not?'

They all stared at her in astonishment. Peter, for one, with no little alarm. He had never before seen this side of her.

Eventually Arthur Stanton said, carefully, 'But it's not quite the same thing, Anna, is it. We haven't intentionally been targeting civilians.'

'But the result is the same,' she said, with a small toss of her head. 'We know that it has been said recently that the accuracy of the bombing is very poor. You've all said so. All the time, innocent people are killed and injured – the old people, and women and children. What is the difference?'

'The difference,' Bill said aggressively, 'is that the German people aren't *innocent*, as you put it. It was they who started this bloody war. Remember?'

'No, they didn't,' said Anna in spirited fashion. 'It was Hitler and his Nazi thugs who started this war. The German people never wanted this war. Not after the last one.'

'And who was it that brought the Nazis into power, then? It was the German people! They carry that responsibility!'

'Yes they do. But so do lots of other peoples. What were the British and the French doing when the Nazis were bullying their way into power? Nothing! What were they doing when Hitler and Goebbels were making scapegoats of the Jews and persuading people that the Jewish people were responsible for all the wrongs on this earth? Nothing! – because secretly they were all half-inclined to believe that anyway. And what were the Allies doing when the Nazis were so busy re-arming, in contravention of the Armistice, and then walking unopposed into Austria and then Czechoslovakia? Nothing! There are many Germans, not all of them Jews by any means, who all along have been appalled and ashamed by what has been going on, but who have been so intimidated and made to feel so alone and helpless that they have been unable to do anything. They would have welcomed some intervention from outside. It is not just the German people who are responsible for this situation. Many other people also are responsible, for ever allowing it to get to this.'

'So you'll be all right when Hitler swarms in here, won't you, Anna? Because you're obviously first and foremost a German!'

It was Jordan who'd spoken, viciousness in her tone. Peter winced. There was terror also in her voice, terror at the thought of invasion, and clearly it was this that was driving her – but even so, to speak to Anna in quite that way, Anna who was first and foremost her friend…?

And Anna visibly recoiled.

'No, *liebchen*,' she said quietly. 'In German eyes, first and foremost I am a Jew. In Nazi Britain it is you, with your Aryan good looks, who will be all right. There would be nothing for you to worry about – provided you did as you were told. It is people like me who need to be afraid. What they would do to us – to people like me, Jews and Slavs and Gypsies – what they already do, have been doing for years, is…unspeakable. You have no idea. Can you begin to imagine what it is like to grow up labelled as being not only inferior to those around you but offensive to them? To be regarded as less than human? To have to wear a yellow star on your clothing so that there can be no doubt about your origins? To be vilified and spat at in the streets, sometimes to be kicked or even, all too often, beaten to a pulp? To see your fellow countrymen have their businesses smashed and stolen, others driven out of office, and your neighbours disappear overnight, God knows where, and to have to go to bed every night wondering when it will be your turn? And, during all this, to know that it is unjustified, that it is all the result of ignorance and prejudice, and to realise that no one – no one – is going to lift a finger to stop it?

'So, the fact that we are also German is of no help – rather will it condemn us. And if they conquer this country, they will find that they do not have to search us out, for the British authorities have already done that for them! They will find us, most of us, neatly gathered up in prison camps and designated as 'aliens', all ready and waiting to be taken off to slaughter. And if the Nazis – my fellow Germans – have their way and come to this country, do not imagine that it will be anything but unpleasant for all – and more than unpleasant for many.

'But let us hope, shall we, that it does not come to that?'

Surprisingly perhaps, she'd spoken calmly throughout, but the intensity of her words had hit them like a sledgehammer. Peter could see reflected in the faces of the others some of the discomfort and shame that he himself now felt, not least of all because, in spite of what Anna had said to him in the past about conditions in Hitler's Germany, he'd never really stopped to give it a great deal of thought. It was as if the process of fighting the war had been sufficient in itself to occupy one's thoughts without really understanding what it was all about. To be sure, Churchill's reference to "dark tyranny" had had a fine ring to it; but now, to Peter, it began to take on more deadly substance. And a shiver ran through him.

As for Jordan, he was relieved to find that she too now revealed a sense of shame. In a small voice she said, 'I'm sorry, Anna…I didn't mean…'

And Anna cut her short: 'I know you didn't, *liebchen*. We are all afraid.'

It was Jamie who stepped into the uncomfortable silence which followed. Addressing Stanton, as though simply continuing her response to the question he'd put to her some minutes ago, she said, 'From the German point of view, as we've been saying, it will clearly be a big mistake if they turn away from our airfields now; but the biggest mistake they've made, I think, is in not continuing to go for the R.D.F. stations – they are our eyes and ears.'

'Absolutely right!' Bill spoke up. Although his voice still carried with it his current amusement with Jamie, Peter could see in his eyes the respect for her from days of old. 'Jerry would have done well to have had you on Luftwaffe Intelligence, Jamie! – sorry, *Jane*.' He turned to the gathering. 'An old nickname from the past slipped out there.'

Jamie, throwing Bill a friendly grin, turned back to Stanton, however. 'But you said, earlier, something about the bomber squadrons: that we "badly need them at present". What did you mean by that? I've always thought of them as more of an attacking force than a defensive one.'

'Quite right,' said Stanton, clearly relieved to have the conversation get back onto more familiar ground. 'Of course. But…' – and here he stopped, and turned to David Munro as if relinquishing the response to that particular question to someone who could talk about it from his own personal knowledge.

And Munro, nodding in recognition of that, replied. He spoke quietly as though it was important to confine this particular piece of information to their own group, even though the background chatter and clatter in the room was in any case sufficient to drown out most of what they were saying.

'In the past ten days or so the Channel ports, rivers and canals on the other side have been filling up rapidly with hundreds and hundreds of invasion barges. So we're using all the daylight hours we can find to try to knock hell out of them. It's not much fun, I can tell you, because they're heavily defended – but vital!' He looked over his shoulder, more from instinct than anything else, as though checking for eavesdroppers; then, conscious perhaps of his own guilty reaction, added, 'But I'm not telling you anything that you're not already indirectly aware of – the powers-that-be have been warning us for days that the invasion could come at any time. If the church bells ring it's not a wedding, but jerry come to call!'

His lame attempt at a joke rattled around in further silence, descending like a cold mist upon their little group.

But from Jordan there came a squeak of fright which she hastily turned into a cough whilst at the same time reaching out to grasp Bill's hand. Bill, though, Peter noticed, was looking at Jamie. And as Peter tore his eyes away from Jordan – all shapely limbs and vulnerable femininity – to follow the direction of Bill's gaze, he saw that Jamie in turn was staring in his own direction, her eyes searching his face. For long moments he met her gaze, trying to fathom what was in those eyes. Friendship, of course. Warmth, as usual. But something else, something that he couldn't define. Sadness perhaps. It reminded him, with a jolt, of that time when they'd dozed together that hay-time, under the shade of a tree in the heat of the day; reminded him of her eyes then, when she'd woken up – golden eyes, eyes which had shared with him a sense of loss. Now, after long moments with their eyes locked, he not knowing what was expected of him, out of his depth, he felt obliged to look away. And as he did so he caught Anna Beal looking first at him and then at Jamie, and in her eyes too there seemed to be a sweet sadness.

What occurred next seemed to Peter afterwards, when he stopped to think about it, as uncanny – following so closely on the heels of what they'd been discussing. For, percolating into the general hubbub of the room there came the far-off sound of the sirens. . .

It takes several moments for the assembly to register what they are hearing, but once that has happened the silence within the room is profound. The only sound in existence is that wailing lament. Coming initially from afar, gradually the refrain is taken up across the whole city until its terrible symphony fills the space. The tones, rising and falling, on the one hand are relentless in their repetition, tedious in nature. But, visceral in their effect, alien in form, they seem to carry with them all the woes of the world – a cacophony of grief, fear, pain and anguish.

For long moments no one speaks, no one moves. Then a number of expletives crackle across the room, breaking the spell.

'Christ!' says Bill, 'I'll have to get back! The buggers aren't wasting any time, are they.'

Peter raises an eyebrow, a gesture of enquiry. Bill has already said, earlier in the evening, that his squadron is on stand-down. Although the blackout curtains have been drawn long ago, it is clearly by now pitch-dark outside, and Bill's is not normally used as a night-fighter squadron.

Bill notes the gesture, and explains. 'This may just be the beginning of a softening-up process, but come dawn God knows what may happen. It could just be the start of their big push!'

He turns to Jordan. 'You'll be all right, sweetie? You'll get back with Anna?'

Peter winces at the endearment, then says, 'Don't worry, Bill. I...we, will see to the girls.' His voice sounds cracked, not forceful as he's intended it to be. 'Then we'll have to get back, too, I suppose.' Even that sounds lame, he thinks, coming from him. It's a reminder that he's not one of the essential heroes – and also, as has just been explained, if they're attacking the city it's not likely they'll be simultaneously attacking the bomber stations.

Already the heavy guns can be heard opening up from somewhere in the distance, the confusion of thuds felt as much through the feet as registered by the ears.

A voice cuts across the melee, clear and authoritative. One of the hotel staff used to being listened to. 'My lords, ladies and gentlemen, would you kindly make your way down to the shelters. Members of staff will show you the way.'

Peter can't help grinning at the form of address. Even under these circumstances the formalities have to be maintained, the assumption sustained that only the elite are to be found within these precincts, their every need to be attended to.

But then comes the sound of far-off explosions. Different to the door-banging thuds of the guns, they split the air with a softly-vicious *crump-crump-crump* which vaguely rattles the windows and walls. There is an instinctive movement of people towards the windows, several people calling out, 'Switch off the lights, someone, so that we can open the curtains.'

'Oh! I say!' – the voice of the *maître d'hôtel*, now higher-pitched and less certain, rises above the hubbub – 'Gentlemen! Ladies! Caution, please! The glass, you know! – if there's any blast.'

Needless to say, no one takes any notice. The curtains are drawn back and people crowd in, Peter and the others among them. Outside, against the black of the sky, buildings across the river seem to be flickering with an eerie rose-coloured glow. Heads turn to look down-river, the source of the light, and are met with a scene that brings an immediate hush. A mile or so away, in the area of dockland, dense clouds are billowing up into the night sky. Part black, part angry red, touched by the ghostly pallor of a full moon, at frequent intervals they are joined by great gusts of sparks blown upwards as though by the force of giant bellows. And as they watch, numbed into silence, they see the redness from this inferno spread from bank to bank, across the darkness of the waters, as though the river itself were running with flame.

CHAPTER TWENTY-TWO

Quite unexpectedly, some two weeks later he heard from Jamie again. He shouldn't have been surprised. For, as they'd all departed in some disarray from the Savoy that Sunday, Jamie had said to him, 'Now that we've at last made contact again, Peter, we must keep it going. Stay in touch, won't you?' And he'd replied, 'Yes. Absolutely.'

He assuaged his twinge of guilt at hardly having given it another thought in the meantime by reminding himself – as if anyone needed reminding – of all that had occurred in the days that followed.

They had left the Savoy without waiting for the All Clear. Having been assured by Anna with absolute firmness (accompanied by timid silence from Jordan) that the two girls could safely travel by tube to Oxford Street without any help from him, after some hesitation he had given in to her and joined the Stantons, along with David and Athena and squeezed into Arthur's small car. In spite of the enforced intimacy, for the whole of the hour's journey they had hardly spoken. It wasn't difficult to know why. The weird way in which the air raid had come so soon after their conversation on that very subject had stunned them. Anxiety (no, more truthfully, fear) had been the dominant emotion as a result, of that he was certain. The fact that he hadn't been able to see their faces, in the darkness of the car, didn't matter – their silence and the tension in the air had been enough. He'd known, too, that it hadn't been the bombing in itself that had made them afraid. It had been the knowledge that the coming of the raids on London (and, no doubt, other major cities in short order) had to be a precursor to the invasion. And no one seemed to know how prepared was the nation to meet it. Following the losses at Dunkirk, in spite of Churchill's fine words there must be serious doubts that the available defence forces would be adequate. Furthermore, as both Stanton and Bill had pointed out so often, air supremacy was everything if the sea-borne landings were to be prevented. And, it seemed, there were still too many uncertainties as to whether that had in any way been achieved. All right, so it had been claimed that the numbers of enemy aircraft shot down had been considerably greater than those of our own. But Stanton had muttered once or twice that 'those statistics can't be relied upon' – hinting, Peter suspected, that this was something gleaned from Arthur's well-placed brother.

One thing was certain, viewed now two weeks later: the general morale of the populace had been remarkably good in spite of the fact that for most of the past fortnight German air raids on London had continued, day and night, with little pause. And Jordan, too, had evidently dug deep to find reserves she didn't know she had. True, there had initially been several panic-stricken phone calls from her, but, surprisingly, later she'd been much more controlled as though even she was learning to take things in her stride. What's more, there had been no talk of taking flight and returning home. Still more remarkably, she'd evidently kept going in to work (where, just as astonishingly, the shows had continued every evening) – even during the first few days when her distress had been at its greatest. Perhaps, after all, there was more to her than he'd previously been prepared to concede. It surprised him what strengths people could find within themselves when put to the test. No one had known what effect such violent bombardment would have on the populace, and one could have been excused for thinking that inevitably it would result in a rapid disintegration of function and morale. But, in spite of all the all-round death and destruction, from all the reports it seemed that (so far at least) most people had continued to carry on with their day-to-day lives as best they could.

In those first few days, though, Jordan had pleaded for him to come and see her, but with things as they were no one had been permitted any leave at Marwell, so it had been impossible. The fact that she'd turned to him in her distress had however done wonders for his morale – even though he'd conceded, in more realistic moments, that it was likely that it was Bill she would have really wanted to turn to at such a time – but clearly it must have been equally impossible for Bill to get away. Nevertheless he now saw her in a warmer light than he had for some time.

Hitler and Goering having concentrated all their attentions on London, however, had meant that there had been no further raids on any of the bomber stations (nor, unbelievably, on any of the fighter stations) just as Bill had forecast. This had meant that the squadrons at Marwell had been able to play their part in the business in hand without any interference at this end at least. But the 'business' in question had more often than not consisted of trips to the French and Belgian ports to strike at the vast numbers of invasion barges accumulating there – a task that had been formidable for the crews in the face of very fierce defence, and chilling for all in its importance. However, it did seem that the bombing by the RAF, together with the magnificent performance put up by the fighter boys in what was now commonly being referred to as 'The Battle of Britain' (borrowing from the P.M.'s phrase) was having some effect – for, only two days ago the invasion alert had been downgraded from '*imminent*' to '*perhaps still soon*'. Initially, the day after that first blitz on London, that 'imminent' alert (under the as-usual-inexplicable code-name '*Cromwell*') had come to all services with such suddenness that it had caused something close to panic, even though it wasn't exactly unexpected. And, apparently, in some parts of the country it had been misinterpreted to the extent that local authorities had caused church bells to be rung, warning the population. But by now, everyone was agreed, jerry was rapidly running out of time – with September nearly over, sea conditions would probably remain reliable enough for no more than another two or three weeks. With a bit of luck therefore the threat would have passed – for this year at least.

But at what cost? The fighter stations, he'd heard, had suffered dreadful losses. The only thing that eased the pain of that was the knowledge that they'd clearly managed to hand out much more punishment than they'd taken. At Marwell, too, along with so many other bomber stations, the losses had been very considerable. He'd lost count of the numbers of familiar young faces now absent from the Mess, the numbers of bodies brought from returning aircraft for him to certify death (purely a grim formality), the numbers of men with fearful burns or wounds that he'd had to try to patch up before shipping them off to hospital. Bomber Command, too, had undoubtedly played their part in 'The Battle of Britain' – or the Battle *for* Britain, as he personally thought it should more properly be called (and, indeed, the battle for Europe; and perhaps for the World). Well the battle wasn't yet over, not by a long chalk – but perhaps, now, there was at least a glimmer of hope?

So, with Jamie's phone call (asking him whether he could yet 'get away for half a day?') he did feel able to say that 'yes, perhaps, he might, sometime within the next week or two'. It seemed she'd like him to join her on a visit to a cousin of hers, who lived out in the northern suburbs of London. She made it sound important, but gave no details; however, he promised to call her as soon as he could.

In the end it's the middle of October before Jamie and he can both manage to get away on the same day. In the meantime there have been a number of phone calls from her, and he has learned something of the purpose of the visit to this cousin of hers. Her cousin's name is Daphne, she is in her early thirties, and is the daughter of Jamie's mother's sister. She is married to a pharmacist who has a business in the City, and they live in Southgate, in north London. They have one child, an eight-year-old boy named Tom. And, it seems, it is he who is at the centre of the problem. For, with the coming of the blitz, together with the possibility, still, of invasion, his father is determined that they should take advantage of the current offers by the Government of evacuation of a certain number of children to Canada – offers which are not likely to be available for much longer. Daphne is equally desperate that her son should *not* go, that being separated from his parents would be far more damaging than anything else that might happen to him. And in her desperation she has looked to Jamie for help in persuading her husband of this. Jamie, for her part, feeling this is more than she can cope with, has turned to Peter for additional support. He in turn has tried to argue that he cannot see what earthly use he would be, a mere stranger. Not to be put off, Jamie has suggested cajolingly that afterwards they might also go on to a cinema in nearby Finsbury Park, where they are showing *The Northwest Passage* (adding, as further incentive, 'It's in colour').

They've arranged to meet at 2 p.m. under the clock at King's Cross station at which time his train gets in. Jamie will be arriving there by tube, and from there it is convenient for them to continue on the Piccadilly line to Southgate. His train is, as usual these days, late, although only by ten minutes. But, as it turns out, it is he who is standing waiting for Jamie.

As he stands there, patiently smoking his pipe, he muses for a moment on the news that had been sprung upon them in the Mess a week ago, that David Munro and Athena had been married, in secret, in a Registrar office, the previous day. Once the ribald comments and recriminations (to the latter of which David's response had been, 'What? – Do you think I would have wanted any of you shower there to spoil the occasion!'), they'd all repaired to the local pub for a shindig, where they'd been joined by Athena herself as well as Sylvia Stanton ('for moral support' as she and Athena had put it) as well as one or two of the other chaps' 'floosies'. Peter couldn't help think it had been a strange way to 'tie the knot'. But then these are strange times. And the delight he feels for them, that they've gone ahead, is countered by envy – for, he thinks, it must be nice to be so wrapped up with someone to the extent of being a part of them, of sharing life with them.

Suddenly he's very conscious of having no such relationship, his thoughts inevitably turning to Jordan; and he's torn by the knowledge that she's now so close to Bill.

To divert himself from these thoughts he turns to his accustomed pastime of studying people as they hurry to and fro on the concourse fronting the platforms, or as they simply stand around and wait, as he is doing. It intrigues him to wonder who they are and why they are there, what minor or major incidents in their lives might be contributing to their presence here. It is strange, too, that once they are on the move they are always in a hurry, as if Time, once decisions are made, might suddenly not wait for them. But people no longer give the impression, as they would have done only a week or two ago, of constant nervousness, of living on a knife-edge; for in the past few days jerry seems to have given up the daylight bombing raids, a clear sign that they too, like the R.A.F., have been finding them too costly. Only when dusk comes – all too early now that they are well into October – only then do people begin to take on again that wary look, as though constantly listening. For every night now, he understands, for the past weeks, has come the stomach-churning wail of the sirens. Then fear grips the city. Remarkably, not outward fear, from what he hears – nothing that shows – but the inner turmoil of 'Will it be my turn this time, or, worse, the turn of those I love?' And so often the blessed relief of the even-toned All Clear is brief only, for an hour or two later will come again the warning lament of the Alert. Only when dawn comes can people relax and stir themselves to face another day, to go out into the world, not knowing whether their place of work still exists, not knowing how others have fared, whether family or friends have suffered loss of home, loss of limb, or loss of life. Suddenly it is civilians (so-called – but already becoming a pointless term) who have been thrust into the front line, sharing as never before all the dangers to which, previously, service men and women alone have been exposed.

Then he thinks of Anna, of all that she and her family and her neighbours in Germany have gone through; he remembers the sufferings and depredations of countless peoples exposed to invasions and occupations over millennia; and he understands it has always been thus. It is the nature of war. This is nothing new.

It is with quick joy, therefore, that he sees Jamie hurrying towards him; and he fleetingly recalls another railway station on another occasion, and a journey which had initially filled him with foreboding but which had led to a meeting with a non-too-clean tomboy-of-a-girl up in a tree. And immediately all is right with the world and he is reassured.

She greets him breathlessly, full of remorse. There was a brief 'flap' on, which in fact came to nothing, but for a while she'd been anxious that she wouldn't get away at all. But now she's here, wearing a light woollen dress and cardigan and her usual wonderful smile. He wonders for a moment why she's bothered to change out of uniform; and instantly reminds himself that he's still in uniform, as she's expected he would be, and therefore they couldn't have been seen together in cinema or restaurant if she were still in uniform. He pulls a face to himself, angry at the idiocy of officialdom. As always she's quick to notice.

'What?' There's anxiety in her tone.

'Nothing,' he reassures her. 'Just a passing thought.' And to change the mood he tells her about David and Athena's marriage; then she too is delighted.

They head back towards the tube, and as she walks in front of him in their approach to the Lift he thinks how wonderfully well whatever she wears seems to show off her athletic figure. She's in moderately high heels, and has on silk stockings which define her legs (and which give the impression that she's regarded this as something of a special occasion, for they must be in very short supply by now). Her walk strikes him as being as purposeful and poised as ever, but he's never before appreciated just how graceful her calves and ankles are. And there's something else. He's followed her often enough over the years, running and climbing, to have noted the strenuous motion of her hips as she moves, but he's never before recognised just how delightful those movements are: vigorous, yes, but with a smoothness and rhythm which at the same time is really quite subtle. And there's one more thing to notice. It strikes him that, always, he's been used to seeing women girdled and corseted beneath their outer clothes, their bottoms moving in one solid piece as they walk. And Jamie is different. For with every slight swing of her waist each separate curve of her bottom follows with a freedom of its own. She's not wearing a corset. And now he grins. How typical of Jamie. She has the conviction – and the confidence – to be able to defy convention, and to hell with whatever anyone might think!

At that moment she turns round to say something to him, catches his expression, and says, lightly, 'If I didn't know better, I'd think you were ogling me!'

Full of confusion at this new, flirtatious side of her, as well as at being caught out, he mumbles a quick denial.

She laughs. 'Now I'm disappointed,' she says, and turns away.

And, in spite of her laugh, for a moment he almost believes she means it.

Underground, as they sway and rattle along in the noisy carriage, they mostly sit in silence. This is largely because conversation, as always, is difficult because of the racket; but Jamie seems unusually silent, as though lost in thought. It's as if, for a moment, their usual easy camaraderie has sidestepped. At one point he leans over to her, mouth to her ear, and reiterates the point he made a few days ago: 'I don't know what use I can be in this venture'.

She turns to face him, moving her head away a little so she can look at him quizzically. Then she leans in to him, her lips almost touching him, her breath warm against his skin, and he's conscious of her perfume, light and fresh.

'Why *is* it you never do yourself justice, Pete? I chose well when I coined the nickname 'Cautious' for you. Yet, others see you as reliable, concerned, and as having good judgement. Authoritative, even. Do you know that?' It's said with a smile, but there's an underlying impatience amounting almost to waspishness.

'Do they?' he says fatuously, unconvinced. He doesn't know what to make of this. He's never before seen her in this mood. He wonders if she's teasing him.

She stares at him a moment longer, as though about to say something more. Then she looks away, with a gesture of exasperation.

They complete the rest of the journey in silence once more. Unsettled, he moodily stares at the litany of names of stations on the board above the windows opposite: Finsbury Park, Manor House, Turnpike Lane, Wood Green, Bounds Green, Arnos Grove, Southgate. He counts them off, suddenly impatient for the journey to be over. The names beyond Finsbury Park hadn't existed in his childhood, in the days when on occasions he would ride the trains, mole-like (on a penny ticket that would have taken him only to the next station), never coming above ground until once more back at St John's Wood. He fancies that he can recollect reading about these places on their first appearance, can see again their idyllic images portrayed on Underground posters. They had seemed to proclaim the march of progress, commonplace green fields being converted into cosy suburbia – the new middle-class utopia to lay to rest the horrors of the Great War. 'Homes Fit For Heroes' had been the slogan. Well, it hadn't lasted long. And he's overtaken by old emotions, of his father and all that went with that, of his mother and the complications of her life. And he turns to glance at Jamie, again remembering those times when, for the two of them, those emotions had been shared.

Above ground, at Southgate he's impressed by the clean lines and elegant modern design of the circular station building, built only a few years ago. From there it's a short walk down the curiously-named *Ossidge Lane* to the crescent of white, flat-roofed, semi-detached modern 'sunshine' houses where Jamie's cousin has her home.

Daphne turns out to be a fair-haired, slightly-built woman in her early thirties. Quick and nervous in her movements, she's as unlike Jamie as could be. She greets them at the door, then takes them through to the living room at the back of the house, a bright sunny room overlooking a small neat garden. A number of dining chairs line the walls, for the centre of the room is dominated by a Morrison Table Shelter: a large iron rectangular cube painted a dark green, making the room look even smaller than it actually is. On one of the chairs sits a young boy; fair, like his mother, with a pale complexion. He too appears nervous. More than that, Peter thinks, he looks distinctly forlorn. This must of course be Tom, and as his mother introduces him she places a protective arm around his shoulders. Tom doesn't look at her, but seems to shrink slightly beneath her touch.

At that point Tom's father appears from the kitchen. He introduces himself in a hearty manner. 'Harry Barton. Good of you to come, doctor.'

He's just rather too bluff for Peter's taste. He looks somewhat older than his wife, is of medium height and rather portly. He has a ruddy complexion, a small moustache, and an early-receding hair-line. Peter is left with the impression that the man is just a bit too full of his own importance. Having shaken hands with Peter more forcefully than is necessary and kissed Jamie on the cheek, he too goes over to Tom and places an affectionate hand on the top of his head, as he might do to a pet dog. Tom appears to shrink even more.

Peter inwardly cringes, wishing now that he hadn't come, and slightly taken aback that Jamie has thought to 'sell' the *doctor* bit to them. He feels more than a bit cross with Jamie for doing so. The whole scenario reminds him all-too-uncomfortably of his own first interview with Cannonball Brindle, at Bards; and he's beginning to feel that somehow he's being cast in the role of 'headmaster', here to pass judgement – surely an impossible role, given what he's seen so far of Tom's father. He wonders whether Tom knows why they're here, whether his parents have discussed any of these issues with him.

His private question to himself is perhaps answered when Harry Barton says, 'Why don't you go out into the garden to play for a while, son, while we grown-ups talk.' His tone of voice is of the sort 'I'll-brook-no-argument', and to emphasise the point he gently propels the boy, by his head, in the direction of the kitchen door. Tom goes, reluctantly, with an anxious backward glance; and his mother begins to look more distraught than ever.

Silence follows. Peter expects Harry Barton, or his wife, or more probably Jamie, to start the conversation, but finds them all looking expectantly in his direction. He wonders what sort of a build-up Jamie might have given the Bartons about his visit; and experiences a distinct irritation that just because he has the title 'Doctor' in front of his name he's somehow expected to cure everyone's ills. But immediately he feels ashamed. That after all is the responsibility that goes with the honour of the title; that is what he has been trained to try to do. It is a respect that has to be earned, that he has to try to justify.

'Tom seems a nice lad,' he says cautiously. 'But subdued? Is he always as quiet as this?'

'No,' says Daphne Barton, a bit too quickly. 'He didn't used to be.' She looks defiantly at her husband, who gives her an angry glare in return.

Peter fears that there could be a vindictive argument between them at any moment; and Jamie standing beside him makes a small placatory movement, clearly expecting the same.

'Could we perhaps sit down?' he says, trying to introduce a calming note to the proceedings.

'Yes, of course. I'm sorry. Please do.' Barton gestures towards the chairs, and they all sit down.

Peter studies the Morrison shelter, taking in the robust steel corner frames, and the quarter-inch steel top. Three of the sides have their steel-mesh side-pieces in place, giving it the appearance of a cage; the end facing into the room is open, and there is bedding in place on the floor inside.

He nods towards it, saying, 'That looks useful. I take it you don't actually use it as a table, though?'

Daphne laughs. 'No, we don't. We did at the beginning, but it's easier now to keep the side-pieces up, which means we can't really sit around it. It's mainly used by Tom as a play area. It becomes a tank, or a submarine, or a bomber – I don't know, all sorts of things, depending upon whether he's on top of it or underneath!'

This is a new side to her, suddenly more relaxed and more interesting; but Peter glances across at Harry Barton as he grunts in a way that is hard to interpret.

'So do you sleep in it?'

'Only when the siren goes,' Barton says.

'That surely can't be often, out here, can it?'

'To date, one or two nights a week,' Barton replies somewhat tetchily. 'You see, the armaments factory at Enfield is only a mile or two to the north of us. Jerry heads for that quite often. Only last week a parachute-mine dropped just three streets away. Flattened two rows of houses. Dozens of people killed. One family – wife and two children – belonging to someone I know. Poor chap's devastated.' It's said defiantly. The man making his case with regard to Tom, Peter thinks – or else defending his own position, as if to say 'I'm in this war as well, even though I'm not in uniform'. Well, Peter can empathise with him there, it's a discomfort similar to his own. Barton, in a 'reserve' occupation as a pharmacist will have had no choice in the matter either.

Daphne, as if picking up on this, says, 'Harry does fire-watch duties in the City two nights a week.' It's said with a certain anxiety as well as pride.

'But you still have to go to work the following morning, not having had any sleep?' Jamie now says. She too has seen which way thoughts have been drifting, and is doing her bit to bolster the man's morale. Peter looks at her gratefully.

'Yes, but that applies to an awful lot of us these days, doesn't it.' He actually sounds quite modest about it, and looks at Peter. 'That must always have applied to you, as a doctor.' Then he looks at Jamie. 'And must be so for you, in your present job, as well? And some nights, when I'm on duty on some roof-top or other, I can manage to get a bit of shut-eye, anyway.'

Peter begins to warm to him. 'Must be dangerous work, though, exposed out in the open like that.' He keeps his voice neutral, not wanting to be seen to be patronising.

Barton shrugs. 'I suppose so. So far we haven't had any incendiaries to cope with, although we have been trained to deal with them. But they tell us it's likely to be just a matter of time. And that could get more difficult. But in the first two weeks or so of the blitz we were exposed to all that in the City during the daytime, anyway. It's not really any different.'

'But then you weren't out in the open,' his wife points out.

Barton shrugs again. 'It doesn't really make much difference. As they say, your number's either up or it isn't. It's all a matter of luck.'

Peter decides the time has come to wade in. 'So what about this business of Tom emigrating?'

'What about it?' Barton says. Peter is expecting him to be belligerent, but there's hesitation in the man's voice. His wife is looking at him expectantly; her lip is trembling as if she wants to say something but daren't, and her eyes are moist.

'Jamie says your wife and you cannot agree about it,' he says cautiously. 'Is that right?'

'My wife is putting our own interests before those of our son,' Barton says, his voice gruff.

'Oh, that's not fair!' Daphne bursts out. 'It's grossly untrue!' She turns to Peter. 'What Harry can't see is that Tom being away from us is likely to be far more harmful to him than anything he might risk here. And...and he might never see us again. What about that ship with all those evacuee children on board going to Canada that was torpedoed last week, whatever it was called...'

'The *Arandora Star,*' her husband supplies.

She gives an impatient shake of her shoulders '...it doesn't matter what it was called! Those children all drowned! What good did it do them! Or their parents!'

She begins to weep.

Jamie moves across and puts an arm around her, then looks steadily at Barton, challenge in her eyes.

'What is it that worries you about him staying here?' Peter asks.

'The obvious. That he might be killed. Or what will happen to him when the invasion comes.'

'*If* the invasion comes,' Peter corrects him. 'And that seems much less likely now. At least for the next six months. As for his being killed or injured, the risks of that are really quite small, you know. He might just as easily be run down by a bus, or be drowned on his way to Canada, as your wife has pointed out.'

'Alright, but on the other hand the way the Atlantic convoys are being knocked out by the U-boats at present we might all be starving to death over the next six months. At least he wouldn't have to suffer that.'

Peter can see they're getting nowhere. He remembers the conversation he had with David Munro about whether he and Athena should marry or not; and Sylvia Stanton's stance on an issue similar to this.

'Is it possible, do you think, that you're allowing your own fears to be transplanted onto Tom?' he says.

Barton glares at him angrily. But Peter thinks he can detect uncertainty in the man's eyes.

'And what about Tom?' he presses, 'Have you asked him what his views are of all this? All we've heard so far are your worries about him. What of his worries about you? Don't you think he'll be desperately worried about the two of you, if he's away from you? Will be terribly afraid that something's going to happen to you? After all, if the decision is made that he should be sent away to another country, doesn't that send the message that something dreadful is likely to happen here?'

'Well, isn't that the case in fact? It seems more than likely. Anyway, Tom's too young to make a decision of this sort.'

'Is he? But he too will be suffering the consequences of whatever decision is made. Do you not think he has the right to be involved?'

Barton doesn't say anything.

Peter's becoming aware that he's beginning to allow a certain bias to creep into this discussion; that his own views are floating to the fore. He strives to achieve a bit more balance.

'Anyway, I do think it's wrong for us to be talking about something so vital behind his back. The poor lad must be feeling really shut out, as though he's already been discarded, abandoned if you like.' He hasn't chosen the words deliberately, they've popped out instinctively. Nevertheless it seems to have had its effect: there is now doubt in Barton's eyes; and his wife is nodding vigorously.

Peter decides to drive home his advantage. 'He must know something of what's going on. Do you think we should invite him in and at least include him?'

Without a word Barton gets up and goes outside. When he returns, gently shepherding Tom in front of him, the boy looks apprehensive in the extreme. His face is even paler than before, and his eyes big and round.

'We've all just been talking about the war, Tom,' Peter says briskly. 'What do you think of it?'

343

'What d'you mean?' the boy asks, suspicion written across his face.

'Well, do you find it boring, or exciting, or frightening – or what?'

The boy shrugs. 'I dunno. Exciting, I suppose,' He brightens considerably. 'I've got a jolly good shrapnel collection already. Would you like to see it?'

'Rather!'

Tom dashes off, and less than a minute later is back, carrying a wooden cigar box as securely as though it were a parcel of eggs. Proudly he opens the lid to reveal a dozen or so bits of jagged metal. Mainly linear, varying in size from about two to four inches or more, each piece is protectively bedded in scrunched-up newspaper. Most of the pieces are dark in colour, many streaked with rust; nevertheless their edges are sharp with a glittering brightness. To Peter's eyes they look positively lethal. Gingerly he picks one up, holding it carefully between forefinger and thumb. It's surprisingly thick and heavy.

'What is this, then? A piece of bomb?'

'No, that's part of an ack-ack shell-casing,' Tom replies with enthusiasm. 'Most of the shrapnel is, you know. On this other one you can see part of the lettering.' He holds out another piece for Peter to peer at. 'Look, there on the rim. See, it's in English.' His voice is vibrant with interest.

'Where do you find all these, then?'

'Oh, lying around all over the place…well, not exactly all over, but here and there. And we do swaps, you know. Look – I got this the other day.' He holds out a piece of white silk cord. 'I swapped an intact fuse-cap for that.'

'It's a piece of parachute cord, isn't it?'

'Yeah. But from a parachute mine. That's special, that is!'

'So do all your pals have collections like this?'

'Yes. Of course. But they're not all as good as this…although one or two are better.'

He's lost all his reticence, and is now bubbling with animation. For the first time he looks squarely at Peter, studying his uniform.

'I can tell the sound of a *Dornier* from that of a *Heinkel*, you know,' he says, trying hard to keep his voice modest. 'And I can recognise a *Messerschmitt 110* by the sound of its engines.'

'Can you indeed!' Peter, in turn, has to strive to keep any semblance of doubt from his tone.

'You're not in aircrew, though, are you,' Tom continues authoritatively, studying the front of Peter's tunic. 'Yet you're a Flight Lieutenant. How is that?'

'Tom!' his father says sharply, 'that's rude.'

'No, you're right,' Peter intervenes hurriedly, 'I'm not aircrew – you see, I'm a doctor.'

'Oh, that's good. I think I'd quite like to do that. When I'm grown up, that is.'

CHAPTER TWENTY-THREE

As they come out into the foyer of the cinema, at just after eight, Peter feels curiously disorientated. The auditorium of the *Astoria* has had something to do with it. On both sides, leading up to the proscenium and reaching to the ceiling, the construction and effect was that of rambling, white-washed houses such as might be found at a hill-top village in, say, Andalucía or Tuscany. Balconies had bougainvillea and wisteria twining around them, and decorative rugs slung over their walls, while shutter-framed windows were, in some cases, dark with mystery, in others picked out by the orange glow of subdued lighting from within. He'd expected that at any minute some darkly handsome senorita with flowers in her hair would saunter out onto one of the balconies to gaze at the scene below. And as his eyes had drifted up towards the roof, the blackness there had been as it were that of the night-sky, contriving the appearance of twinkling stars obscured from time to time by drifting clouds. He's never before met anything like it. It has been distinctly surreal.

But the film, too, has got to him, not only through spectacle and colour, but because it has brought back so many memories. All members of The Famous Four had at one point read Fenimore Cooper's *North-west Passage*, passed from one to another (Jamie had been the instigator, he seems to remember) and had on many an occasion played out its scenes in woods and on the lake, had become the buckskin-clad rangers searching for the Passage, defying and defeating the Iroquois on the way. Seeing it brought so vividly to life on the screen has brought back those memories – never really forgotten, only mislaid. Has Jamie, also, he wonders, felt the same? Have those long-lost excitements returned too for her? And has it, too, swirled her back into childhood, to the triumphs and turmoils of those now-long-ago days?

And then, also, Jamie had held his hand throughout most of the film, reaching out for him soon after they'd settled in their seats as though it were the natural thing to do. He'd not expected that, but, after his initial surprise, it had seemed natural to him as well, a form a sharing, just as they'd done in the past. He'd felt a tightening of her hand during tenser moments of the film, but otherwise she'd let her hand simply rest there, her fingers linked with his. It had been comforting – and, yes, exciting. And he'd been taken aback by that reaction – for, after all, it was only Jamie.

Now, as they pass through the foyer – empty of people, the only sound that of the fountains splashing into their marble basins and the muted clink of coins as the girl behind the glass of the ticket office counts her takings – he feels an urge to say something about the way it has affected him. But something holds him back: a dimly perceived awareness that to do so might perhaps take them over a borderline across which there could be no return.

So, instead, glancing at his watch, he says, 'Have we time for a bite to eat somewhere, d'you think?'

Jamie nods, and suggests a small restaurant that she knows of in Soho. They have a couple of hours yet before Peter's train, still leaving time for Jamie to catch the last tube.

Outside, the now-darkened streets of Finsbury Park are strangely quiet. Only half an hour ago, during the film, the message *Air Raid in Progress* had flashed up on the screen (this had caused hardly a stir apart from a few whispers such as 'They're late tonight' – whereas, he's been led to understand, only a few weeks ago there would have been immediate alarm, even panic leading to a rush for the doors). But out here on the streets all is quiet, the few passers-by certainly not dawdling, but equally not in any undue hurry. From somewhere not far away there comes the clangour of a bell, an ambulance or fire-engine perhaps, but somehow it gives the impression of having nothing to do with the cacophony of war.

As they head for the tube, she turns to him and says, 'I haven't thanked you yet for what you did at Daphne's.'

'I'm not sure that it was very much, in the end.'

'Oh, but I think it was. It had the effect of clearing the air. And of getting them talking – and got them to include Tom in their discussions. That alone should help. It was clear that the poor lad was worried stiff about being sent away. After all, he must have seen pictures in the papers of all those poor little evacuees standing lost and forlorn on station platforms – and they were only going out into the countryside, not out of the country. I know Harry Barton seems a bit insensitive and a bit of a boor, but as you rightly and astutely pointed out, he's really only covering up for his own weaknesses.'

'I didn't say that!'

'No, not in as many words. But you did ask him whether it was possible that he was transplanting his own fears onto Tom. That was good, I thought. And I could see that it certainly gave him food for thought. And you did it all with such quiet authority. I was very proud of you. And grateful.'

He looks at her suspiciously, but there is no hint of patronisation. There again, he wouldn't have expected there to be, from Jamie.

'I'm sure you would have done just as well without me,' he says.

'I'm sure I wouldn't. And you really must stop selling yourself short!'

Although she says it lightly, she sounds cross. He looks at her curiously; but she is looking straight ahead, and doesn't say anything more.

He too remains silent, baffled by her mood.

After a few seconds, she says, 'Anyway, it's been nice doing something like this together, again. Hasn't it?'

It isn't quite a statement. It's as though she is seeking confirmation from him.

'It certainly has,' he says. The words aren't well-chosen. He suspects they might be seen to be conveying a certain insincerity. But to elaborate now might only make matters worse, might carry a message that isn't really intended. The last thing he would want to do to her.

Prevaricating, he changes tack.

'The picture was good, wasn't it.'

'Yes. Wonderful.' Her reply is flat, in spite of her use of the superlative.

'I can't imagine Spencer Tracy being your type, though,' he persists, trying to tease her.

'On the contrary, he's precisely my type. Quiet, calm, courageous and dependable. So, you see, you don't know me as well as you think!' Her tone, too, is bantering. But the look she gives him is a level one.

Having by this time reached the booking hall of the Underground, the distant rumble from below of an approaching train hurries them towards the escalator, preventing further discussion. And, once settled into their seats on the train, he doesn't know what else to say on the subject. However, she seems content with their silence; so he lets his mind go into neutral as he gazes at the undulations of the pipes and cables streaming by outside the carriage windows.

As they draw into the station at Russell Square, though, his attention is drawn to the presence of a considerable throng of people on the platform. At the next station, Holborn, there are even more: a solid mass of men, women and children sitting and lounging the full length of the rear of the platform.

'Good Lord! What's going on?' he exclaims, as the train draws to a halt.

Jamie looks at him in some surprise. 'It's just the shelterers, of course.' She makes it sound like something out of *The Time Machine*.

'The shelterers?'

'Yes. The people spending the night here,' she explains. There is a surprised patience in her tone, as though he's newly arrived from foreign parts.

'But I thought that wasn't allowed? That the Underground was being "kept clear for transport in emergencies".'

'So it was. But people decided for themselves, as they're wont to do, that you can't get much more of an 'emergency' than the present blitz. And the authorities have had to relent. It's all becoming quite organised now.'

The train is still standing, its motors ticking, its doors open, so that a wash of warmth spiced with the odour of humanity permeates the carriage. 'Shall we get out and have a look?' Jamie suggests.

'Yes. Let's,' he says, picking up on her sudden enthusiasm; and they make a dash for the doors as they begin to close.

Their abrupt spilling out of the train is met by some expressions of curiosity – and by patent hostility from not a few. Looking around he concludes there must be a couple of hundred people in all, littered along the length of the platform. Now that he is able to study them he sees that they tend to be clustered in groups of various sizes. There are solitary couples; a good many more family units of three, four or five; and any number of larger collections of folk who, judging by their animated conversations, are friends or neighbours already known to one another. Some sit on cushions, a few on stools, but many merely sprawl on coats, rugs or blankets, with sometimes a second garment to cover them. However, it certainly isn't cold: the place is so densely packed that the warmth is almost stifling, the atmosphere catching at the nose. Among those passing the time by chattering are a few sitting quietly reading, peering in the subdued lighting at book or newspaper. Others are playing cards or draughts. He even spots two men playing dominoes, making space for their pieces as best they can. The crowd is mostly shabbily dressed, but standing out are just a few who look as though they might have come straight from Knightsbridge or Park Lane. However, with the general chatter and hum, and the nature of the gathering – giving the impression of animals having fled to the safety of their burrows – they do rather remind him of *Morlocks*.

As Jamie and he stand for a few moments absorbing it all, he becomes aware of a growing hostility from some of those around them. Jamie too must have picked up on this, for she mutters to him, 'I think perhaps we'd better move. I don't think they're too keen on sightseers'.

Then, as people take in his R.A.F. uniform, that hostility seems to increase rather than diminish. In fact one old man calls out to him, ' 'Ere, why aren't you up there knockin' 'ell out of those bloody Hun?' It is said good-naturedly, but there is no denying the animosity in it, and a number of women are nodding their agreement.

'He's just popped down for a bite to eat,' Jamie calls back, to a greeting of general laughter. But nevertheless she takes Peter's arm to guide him towards one of the connecting passageways.

'You've seen all this before, then?' he asks her.

'Yes. Well, I've been out to see Daphne once or twice over the past weeks. So I've watched the whole thing grow. As I said, the authorities are actually getting quite organised now. Did you see those two white lines painted parallel to the edge of the platform?'

'Yes. I was wondering what the idea is.'

'It's intended to leave room for people actually travelling on the tubes. The idea is that the one painted furthest away from the edge – eight feet in fact – shouldn't be crossed, by those sheltering, until after 7.30 in the evening; and the second one, which is four feet from the edge, is only allowed to be crossed after 10.30 p.m. From what I've heard, people are usually pretty good at sticking to those rules, too. Apparently once they've switched the power off on the rails, when the trains have stopped for the night, people actually spill over onto the track and bed down there as well.'

'Presumably someone comes along in the morning to tell them when power's going to be switched back on?' Peter quips.

'Presumably!' Jamie agrees. 'In fact, someone told me the other day that they've actually started running a supply train with refreshments, as well, to some of the stations, at around 7.00 in the morning. And the normal trains start running again shortly after that. At that point, from what I gather, everyone disperses pretty rapidly. But then a few start queuing again in the afternoon, and they allow them in once more from 4.00 onwards. All very sensible and orderly in the end, you see!'

By now she's led him up steps to the exit passageway leading to the lifts, and he sees that people are already settling down against the walls here, as well.

'Where are we going?' he asks. 'Shouldn't we be heading back for the trains?'

'In a minute. But I believe there's a Medical Centre been set up here, as there has been in some of the other stations. I thought you might like to see it?'

'Right. Yes.'

And a few seconds later they do catch sight of a crudely painted sign saying *Nurse Station*. This turns out to be a small room with an arched entranceway – what has been an office previously perhaps. The door is standing open, and inside the room, which has white-washed walls, a young man in a white coat and a girl in light blue nurse's uniform stand chatting. The only furniture is a rickety table, two chairs, a battered-looking surgical couch, and a tattered screen together with a glass-fronted cabinet containing a few bottles, bandages and one or two instruments. A sphygmomanometer, an auriscope, and a stethoscope stand on the table along with a few papers; and the only other bit of furnishing is a telephone which looks as if it might have seen better days. The two people look up as Peter and Jamie approach, studying them with interest. Then the young man, noting the medical insignia on Peter's uniform, comes forward with outstretched hand and a slightly querulous expression on his face.

'Hello. What can we do for you?'

'Just curious,' Peter says. 'Jamie...Jane, here, had heard about you, and we thought we'd take a look, if that's alright?'

'Ah,' says the man, his face clearing as he looks Jamie up and down with interest, 'I thought for a moment that perhaps the military were taking over!'

'No such luck,' Peter laughs. 'Tell me, where are you from?'

'From Guy's. We're just doing a three-hour stint, and that's quite enough, I can tell you!'

'Do you get many problems, then?'

'No, minor ailments mainly – some of which have been stored up from during the day. A certain amount of dehydration towards the end of the night

– it gets so warm down here. Minor injuries from falls, sore throats, that sort of thing. And mosquito bites. We have a big bottle of Calamine to hand!'

'Mosquito bites?'

'Yes. The warmth and high humidity, with all these people, seems to have produced a perfect breeding ground for the blighters.'

'For the mosquitoes, that is,' the nurse puts in with mock innocence.

'No malaria, though?' Peter jokes.

'Not yet! Could be just a matter of time!'

'And head lice,' the nurse says bitterly. 'Don't forget those!'

'Ah, yes. The dreaded lice. That's purely a nursing problem of course…' (and here he received a playful punch on the arm from the nurse)… but they fairly put off the toffs, I can tell you!'

'I can imagine!' Jamie says. 'But I did notice a few people sitting down on the platform who seemed to be, shall we say, out of place.'

'Just one or two,' the doctor replies. 'Those of a more nervous disposition. But most of the folk down here are from the East End. They're the poor blighters who're getting the brunt of it. Such a lot of them have lost everything – including friends and relatives.'

'I suppose it's quieter here for people, though, and cleaner, than in the public shelters up above, in spite of the mosquitoes and head lice,' Jamie comments. 'And safer.'

'I don't know about quieter – it can get pretty rowdy down here during the earlier part of the evening. But yes, it's remote from the noise of the blitz. Although I notice there's been a directive going around recently advising people to sleep with their heads away from the walls – apparently that way you're less likely to pick up the vibrations from the guns! And definitely safer, yes.' He pulls a face. 'But did you hear there was a direct hit on the Trafalgar Square station earlier this evening?'

'No! Good God! A lot injured?'

'Must have been, I think. From what I hear it came through into the booking concourse. Rotten luck. But that news has made us all a bit more nervous here, I can tell you. Although we are of course a good deal deeper down here.'

Some ten minutes later, as Peter and Jamie head for the Shaftesbury Avenue exit at Piccadilly Circus, both of them are in thoughtful mood – Peter, certainly, because seeing at first hand the almost troglodytic existence being forced upon many has been a shock. A new awareness that even then there was no real safety for these people, has for the first time really brought home to him the widespread impact this war is having. For all, for servicemen and civilians alike, the easy camaraderie, the jokes and the apparent disdain for everything about the war – the dangers, the hardships, and the well-meant but clumsy efforts of Authority – are merely a cover-up for the deep-down fears which now permeate their lives: the fear of death or injury, the fear of subjugation under the Nazis, the fear of fear itself.

The words scrawled on a notice-board at the head of the escalators leading down to the Bakerloo line bring a grim smile to his lips. It is stark in its simplicity: *Temporary Disruption to Southbound Services at Trafalgar Square*. The most terrible events could these days be dismissed as *Disruption*; and everything now, life itself, is *Temporary*.

And as they near the top of the steps leading up to Shaftesbury Avenue, expecting to emerge into the now-familiar near-total blackness of London at night, it is no longer black. For fraudulently conjuring up peacetime memories of the night-glow of Piccadilly Circus there is now a baleful presence of dancing flame. Where once, in memory, there would have been the excited chatter of traffic and people out on the town there is now an uproar of hurrying figures, of raucous shouts, of screams, of the brittle clamour of emergency bells, the sharp crack of shattering glass, and the roar and rumble of fire. And, as they emerge into the street, where before the war there would have been a kaleidoscope of coloured lights and passing traffic, there is now a clutter of fire-engines and rescue trucks, and a confusion of fire-ladders and hosepipes from which writhe jets of water made red by the presence of flame. Acrid smoke stings their eyes and catches their throats; billowing overhead, blacker than the night itself, that smoke too in places has a sullen redness as though tinged with blood.

Hesitating at the top of the steps, stupefied by the scene before them, they are accosted by a black-uniformed, tin-hatted A.R.P. man hurrying down. Under his arm he has a red-and-white board saying *No Exit*, which, it seems, he is to place at the bottom of the steps.

'I would turn back if I was you,' he says, his voice hoarse. 'There's nothing out there for you at present. And there's a probable U.X.B. further up the street.'

Looking about him Peter takes in the presence, across the way, of a broken building, glimpsed intermittently through the drifting smoke. It has been reduced to a mere bone-yard of tumbled beams and girders on which hang, flesh-like, the tattered remains of walls, floors and ceilings; a corpse of a building around which flames lick hungrily as though eager to consume the lot. His instinct until now has been to push ahead, to see what help he can give. But at the man's words, and at the scenes before him, common sense prevails: he would only be in the way, better to leave it to those whose skills have already been honed by numerous events of this sort. And there is Jamie to think about, too. So, his arm protectively around her, they stumble back down the steps, feeling as they do so that they are becoming one with the 'shelterers', the refugees. And he can't shake off the feeling that in his own case he's merely dredged up justification for what in effect is cowardice. Those people up there, grimly going about their duties, are after all ordinary men and women risking their lives doing what they have to do. They may be wearing uniforms, but many are volunteers, civilians who have no need to do what they are doing. The terrors of bombing and strafing on airfields are bad enough, the horrors of the battered bodies and minds of those returning from Dunkirk may have been difficult to face, but somehow all this is more obscene. This is indiscriminate. Here, the individuals being killed and maimed are passive victims, they have no way of fighting back; the buildings being destroyed are not the temporary edifices put up to fight a war, but the products of decades or even centuries of urban civilisation.

Back among the ticket machines, smoke now drifting around them, among the mundane mechanics of everyday life, once more remote from the chaos above, he is left with this sense of loss. It's as though having for a short while this evening rediscovered some of the sensations of childhood, the warmth of early friendship, of innocent youth reawakened, now it has all been wrested away. It could be difficult to regain, perhaps be gone forever.

He thinks he can see some of that pain reflected in Jamie. There is now an awkwardness between them. Abruptly pushed into parting, they are floundering. It is as though, caught in flood-water, they are being torn from each other's grasp. He wants to say something to renew that bond, to strengthen it. But that seems too desperate. It will, will it not, seem that he still needs to draw from her the strength and direction she's provided him with in the past?

So, instead, he reaches for the obvious, the superficial.

'I do hope the Bartons come to a sensible decision,' he says.

She looks at him blankly for a moment, as though not understanding. Her eyebrows draw together as she appears to wrestle with what he's said.

Then, 'I hope so, too,' she says, a sudden weariness in her voice. 'I think that now they probably will.'

She attempts a smile. 'Anyway, I'll let you know.'

Then, after a moment's hesitation, she reaches up and kisses him on the cheek. 'Thanks again, for today,' she says, and turns on her heel and walks away.

He waits, expecting her to turn round and wave. But she doesn't.

It is after two in the morning by the time he arrives back at camp, cold, hungry and dejected by all that has taken place in the past few hours. His parting from Jamie has left him distinctly unsettled, as though somehow he is guilty of serious failure, but is unable to put his finger on it. His train, having left King's Cross half an hour late, had then been delayed for another two hours further up the line. He'd alighted onto a deserted platform at Marwell, found no taxis or other available transport outside, and had had to walk the mile and a half in drizzly rain. Thoroughly weary and bad-tempered, he heads straight for his room, but is pulled up short by a light in the Mess. Putting his head around the door, he finds Stanton sitting there on his own, looking equally dispirited. This isn't a night when the padre would have been expected to be here in camp at all. And there is something about the padre's posture that is distinctly alarming.

'Hullo, Arthur,' he says. 'You still here?' Then, not really wanting to put the question, 'Is something wrong?'

'Yes. I'm afraid so, Peter. I've been waiting here for you. You're late.'

'Yes…the trains…you know.' He takes a deep breath. 'What is it?'

'Come and sit down.' Then, when Peter remains standing, he hurries on: 'David's squadron was sent to *Bremen* this evening. Short notice. Should have been Blenheims from Watton, but they'd had some sort of mishap at Watton...' His voice trails off.

Peter sits down. 'Heavy losses?' The question comes out hoarsely.

'No. Quite light, actually. They're all back, half an hour ago. Bar two, that is. David's bus is one of those two.'

Peter, already cold, feels his spine turn to ice. 'Well, there's time yet. Isn't there?' His words hold no more conviction than his thoughts. 'I mean, he could be limping back on one engine. Or have baled out.' There is rising desperation in his voice. 'Did anyone see anything? Whose is the other aircraft missing?'

'Dixon's. No, no one saw anything. And, yes, there is time yet. They'll still have fuel for another fifteen minutes or so. Anyway, a lot of the boys are keeping watch, along with the C.O., over in the control tower. I came over to see if you were back. And to intercept you if you weren't here in the Mess. Maybe we'd better get over there?'

'Yes. But I must look in on the Sick Quarters on the way. Make sure they're organised. Just in case...'

'Of course. Actually, I did look in myself, a short while ago, to see if you were there...and anyway to make sure they were all right – having been put on standby at short notice, you understand. Not that I could be a judge of that, needless to say, but I thought someone should do so. I must say they seem a good team, though. All three of them have turned out.'

'Oh well, thanks for that, Arthur. Yes, they've melled very well. And Bart Browning is certainly a lot more relaxed with Sue Broadley than he was with O'Connor.'

'I bet he is!'

But there is a twist of sadness in Stanton's grin; and Peter himself has felt his guts convulse on mentioning O'Connor's name. It is strange how, even now, he still prefers the use of her surname to that of her given name, that to his ears it still retains a ring of endearment in a way that it never had when she was alive. Sister Broadley, her replacement, couldn't be more different. In her forties, plainly pleasant, with spectacles and prematurely greying hair, she is quietly efficient and self-effacing. Rarely does she argue, but gets on with the job – although, he suspects, usually ending up doing that job in her own professional way, whatever suggestions he might make. He admires her, but remains emotionally detached from her. Yet he always thinks of her as 'Sue' and not 'Broadley'. The same can be said of Eileen Page, the junior nurse who's been brought in as an additional pair of hands. Young and fluffily attractive, somewhat scatter-brained yet with a good rapport with Browning, he always thinks of her, too, by her given name 'Eileen'. But there is no closeness to his relationship with her, either: it stays at the superficial level of friendliness between colleagues. In fact he knows little about either of these women, choosing to stay uninvolved. Whether his remoteness is consciously cultivated he can't say, and doesn't care. He doesn't want to go through with either of them what he's had to do with O'Connor.

The control room, when they get there, is crowded but strangely silent. One or two, including Beal, glance their way and nod as they enter. But then they turn back to continue their vigil across the blackness of the field, as though staring on its own might will the missing aircraft to appear out of the night. From time to time the wan face of a waning moon appears from behind clouds, silvering their edges and briefly bathing the field in its pallid light. But for most of the time the darkness presses in on the windows of the tower, adding to the claustrophobic atmosphere within. On occasions, one youngster or another, forgetting himself and relieved only that on this occasion he isn't one of the 'missing', will quietly make some quip, only to be instantly crushed by quick glares from others. But otherwise the minutes drag by without comment, broken only by the voice of the radio operator at intervals calling, 'Come in, please, Alpha Charlie X-ray – Alpha Fox Oboe. Are you receiving? Over.' But his exhortations are met merely by the hiss and squeak of static.

Someone opens a window, persuading himself perhaps that he's heard something. But the only sounds are those of the sibilance of light rain, the riffle of wind across the grass, and briefly the lonely call of an owl. And the silence within the room is broken only by the shuffle of feet, by the rustle of clothing as one man or another raises his wrist to peer at his watch, or more frequently by impatient sighs.

'Must be just about out of fuel by now,' someone mutters, but receives no reply: no one wants, yet, to face that fact.

Outside, the moon once more shows its face, seeming on this occasion that bit more determined to chase the clouds, to clear the sky; and, as though this alone has played its part in setting a more hopeful scene, at the same time there comes the sound of a distant drone. There is a press of bodies to open more windows, a collective holding of breath; and as the sound becomes more definite, draws nearer, several say together, 'It is!'

But instantly excitement gives way to uncertainty, to apprehension. One of the flight engineers gives voice to their doubt. 'It's a single engine'.

A few more seconds of tension, of silent listening, then, from someone else: 'But definitely a Wimpey, I'll bloody swear it.'

All eyes strain to part the darkness, to give shape to the sound, which by now is clear and ever nearer; while in the background the radio operator, striving to keep his voice calm, keeps repeating his mantra, '...This is Marwell control, come in please. Over'.

Again doubt is raised. 'It couldn't be a lone jerry, could it?'

A pause to consider that thought is followed by derision. 'No, I tell you, that's a bloody Wimpey. But he's coming in on one engine.'

The decision made, the cold moonlight is abruptly warmed by the runway lamps coming on, and in the diffuse glow, beyond the perimeter of the field at a height of no more than a hundred feet, there appears the shape of the plane – instantly confirmed as a Wellington. Clearly its pilot is having difficulty in keeping it under control, for as they watch it losing height it rocks and yaws; and the prop on the starboard side spins idly so that it is like a bird with a broken wing. Someone produces binoculars, and others crowd round him, urging, 'Can you make out the markings?'

'No…not clear…He seems to have lost part of his tail-plane, too…Yes, now I can see…It's…it's Fox Oboe.' There is a collective sigh. It can't be said to be one of relief, nor of disappointment, only an expression of acceptance. In a carefully neutral tone someone articulates what they all already know. 'Marty Dixon's.'

Desperation propelling them, several others demand of the fellow with the binoculars, 'Can you see another kite behind him?'

And for the first time Beal speaks up, his voice tired but carrying its usual authority. 'All right chaps, that's enough. One crew back for the present. Let's see them down safely, first. Then we'll perhaps learn about the others.'

Already, from the tarmac below, the crash wagon, fire engines and ambulance are making their way onto the taxiways next to the runway. Silence settles once more onto the control room as all eyes fix upon the aircraft now on its final lumbering approach to the ground. Immobilised by tension, they follow its uncertain descent as it threatens at one moment to plummet prematurely, at the next to lift nose-up and flip over. Looking almost spectral, its upper fuselage pale and ill-defined in the moonlight yet its undercarriage reflecting orange from the lights below, it seems to float towards them. And from those watching there come muttered urgings, 'Go on!…You can make it!…Don't let that nose drop!…You're almost there!'

Finally, as it draws level with the control tower, it seems to pause for a moment – until with a puff of smoke one wheel touches the concrete, then the other. It bounces violently once, and a second time, threatening to overturn as its starboard undercarriage suddenly gives way, before slewing and pirouetting its way for another three hundred yards along the runway until it finally stops, facing the way it has come as though looking back in disbelief at what it has just managed to achieve.

A ragged cheer breaks out in the control room, and there is a concerted rush towards the door. But someone in authority barks out, 'Attention! C.O. present!' And, admonished, they sheepishly stand back to let Beal pass.

Once out on the tarmac, though, it seems it is every man for himself. Stanton and Peter make to join the throng executing a mad dash on foot across the grass toward the distant outline of the crippled aircraft, which is now again in darkness. But at this point Beal, who is in the process of making a U-turn in his open-top car, with the Adjutant already on board, spots them and gestures for them to jump in, and they both pile into the back. By this means they are the first to arrive, to join the crews of the emergency vehicles milling around, having found that thankfully there is in fact nothing for them to do. Indeed Dixon and his crew are already leaving the aircraft, looking sombre and weary but clearly relieved to be down in one piece, and apparently unharmed. Beal is quickly out of the car, Peter and the others following more slowly. Impatient as they are for any possible news, still they appreciate the need to respectfully stand back while the C.O. goes over to Dixon to clap him on the shoulder and shake hands with the rest of the crew. Not quite in earshot, therefore, try as he might Peter can make little of the murmured conversation. For what seems an age Beal questions Dixon in an increasingly terse manner, but then his whole body is seen to slump, he shakes his head slowly from side to side as if trying to reject what he's just been told, and turns back towards the car. He looks first at Peter and then at Stanton, the muscles in his jaw working convulsively. Then he visibly straightens his back, and his eyes take on a steely look.

'I'm sorry,' is all he says, and gets back into the car.

The Adjutant, the padre and Peter follow wordlessly. The message is clear, yet incomplete, although they all understand it means more than just 'no news'. Desperate as they are for clarity, nevertheless neither of them dares question Beal just yet. He too needs moments to adjust. He will talk to them when he is ready. Meantime they must absorb the reality of their worst fears, shut out hope, and prepare to invite in the beginnings of grief.

It isn't until they arrive back at the main buildings that Beal speaks, his voice carefully controlled but gruff.

'They went in for a second run,' he says, 'followed by Dixon. It seems they both got caught in the same flak. David's plane blew up. No possibility of survivors.'

And with that he turns on his heel and walks away.

The Adjutant pauses and looked sympathetically at Stanton and Peter. 'I'm sorry,' he says. 'I believe Munro was a special friend of yours. He was a fine chap, and will be sadly missed. Hard to replace.' Then he too walks away.

Peter finds himself suddenly invaded by a jumble of memories – snapshots from the shadows of the past, like newly re-discovered photographs: of David in his first two weeks at school, desperately homesick, looking wide-eyed and trusting, as Peter reassured him it would 'soon pass'; of him washing Peter's rugby kit, pressing his cadet uniform and buffing his boots, and doing all those hundred and one other little jobs that was the lot of the 'personal fag', doing it willingly with determination, to the best of his ability; and of his first flowering of talent on the rugby field, when everyone began to sit up and take notice of this newcomer. And he's overtaken once again by more recent memories: of his own first, disastrous meeting with Athena, and the ways in which, in spite of that, they had gradually become friends; and of his chat with David, as the result of which the two had gone off and got married.

And his recollections are brutally interrupted by Arthur's voice, gruff but cold and hard as steel. 'Come on,' he says. 'I'm afraid you and I have a visit to make.'

Peter turns to him, startled, uncomfortably aware of cowardice whispering in his ear.

'It's after three,' he says. 'Wouldn't it be better to leave it until the morning? Anyway, Beal may prefer to do this himself.'

The look that Stanton gives him holds only the barest hint of compassion.

'It has to be done, Peter. And who better to do it than you and I?'

'Yes, but to disturb Athena with news like this in the middle of the night seems a bit brutal, doesn't it?' says Peter. He feels his face flush as he hears the note of desperation in his own voice.

'Look, I understand this is particularly personal for you, but neither of us is a stranger to having to break this sort of news, are we? And, from what I can gather, it seems you aren't aware that David, since they were married, has always phoned Athena as soon as possible after landing, whatever the time of night. She'll be sitting up waiting for that call, and already beginning to fear the worst. As for Beal, he already has enough to do. If I know him, he'll be up the rest of the night composing letters. He'll only be too glad for us to carry out this particular task for him.'

Resigned, Peter nods, and follows his friend towards the car park, dread sitting like a stone in his stomach. For he knows what, so far, only Athena herself also knows: that she's probably carrying David's baby. And whether that knowledge will ease the pain of her loss, or make it worse, he's no idea.

CHAPTER TWENTY-FOUR

On the 14th February 1941 my mother died.

The fact was entered in his journal in that form, stark and singular. But pasted on the page, beneath that plain sentence, was the telegram which had brought the news:

WITH GREAT REGRET HAVE TO INFORM YOU YOUR MOTHER PASSED AWAY THIS MORNING STOP PLEASE CONTACT URGENTLY STOP LOVE JOHN

It was as though, for the ever after, the official form – with its buff-coloured stuck-on tape and uncertain print – was necessary for the information to remain believable, to become acceptable.

Fortunately he'd been alone in his room when Barnes brought him the yellow envelope, unopened. Telegrams usually meant only one thing these days. Bad news. Unable to think what it could possibly be, his heart had lurched as, with shaking hands, he'd torn the thing open, his batman hovering in the background.

'Any reply needed, sir?' the man had asked, anxiety evident in his own voice.

For Peter at that moment, the words on the docket still swimming formlessly in front of his eyes, the enquiry had come as from a distance, also without shape. But he'd managed to gather his wits, to keep his voice reasonably steady.

'No. Thank you, Barnes. No reply.' Reply? What reply was possible? Certainly not "Roger" – 'message received and understood'. It was beyond understanding. Mercifully left on his own, he'd sunk onto the bed, head in hands. Unable to think, the sentences still reverberating in his head, he'd sat like that for some time – minutes? Half an hour? Finally he'd pulled himself together and gone off to find a phone.

He'd got through to home on the fourth attempt. It had been Jessica who'd answered, her words cracked and broken not only by the bad line but by obvious emotion. Uncle John, when he'd come to the phone, had been no better, the sound of tears in his voice.

'Peter, my boy, I'm so very sorry. It must be a dreadful shock for you. It's impossible for us, too, to take in.'

He'd gone on to explain that he'd tried and tried to get through on the phone, without success. Only in desperation had he resorted to the telegram. The story gradually came out, interrupted by pauses for intake of breath, for clearing of throat. Marjorie had gone down with the flu only four days previously – there'd been quite a bit about. At first she hadn't seemed too bad. Then, on the afternoon of the third day, yesterday, she'd taken a turn for the worse. Influenzal pneumonia. It had taken hold at frightening speed. By the early hours of the morning she was dead.

'I did my best, son – we all did. But there was nothing I could do.'

'I'm sure of that, Uncle John.'

He'd meant it. But the words had seemed empty.

On the train, going north, he's still dazed. At times he's locked into a roller-coaster of emotion: one minute down in the depths, the next experiencing a sense almost of relief in the knowledge that, as he persuades himself, she is no longer having to live with her 'unhappiness' as he's always perceived it. At other times he's stuck with sudden spells of numbness wherein he can retrieve no feelings at all. He doesn't know which is worse. One replaces another with bewildering speed. And suffusing it all is guilt. He knows it's irrational. But he can't seem to shake it off. His promise to himself, all those years ago, that he would take care of his mother now that his father had gone, has come to nothing. It doesn't help that he knows, of course, that it had never been possible for him to do that. That indeed it was never needed. His mother had had to steer her own path through life – just as had he and everyone else – and she had done that, with dignity and determination. Even so, he still sees it as yet another failure on his part, his failure as a son.

Is that then the main reason for this sense of loss? For, what *has* he lost? What indeed has *she* lost? – any chance of real future happiness? He doubts that. Indeed, can he know that she had been unhappy in the circumstances in which she'd found herself? When it comes to it he knows very little about her, about her thoughts, about her past. They'd never confided in one another. What little he does know of her, of her previous life, of her formative years, her life before he became conscious of her as a separate individual, he's gleaned from others, not by asking but in a purely passive way, absorbing a bit here and a bit there. Perhaps he should have asked more.

And what knowledge of him, her only child, has she taken with her to the grave? Probably very little, if the truth be known. All right, she brought him into the world, nurtured and protected him, watched him develop from infant to child, from child to man. She had knowledge of him that he doesn't have of himself other than through the artificiality of the odd few photographs

– meaningless as they are, like looking at a stranger, mere shadows of the real self. She had known his ways, his mannerisms, his character – but almost nothing of his thoughts, desires and fears. They had remained secret, just as hers had for him. Two people who, one might imagine, should have been the closest in the world to one another had remained worlds apart. At times indifferent, even antagonistic. There had been mutual affection, to be sure, love if you like; but little actual expression of that. Sympathy and concern, but no empathy. No real connection. And if that was the case, what hope is there for him in any future relationships? Perhaps though that is the way it is ordained? Apron strings designed to be fragile at best; the survival of the species overriding all else – future relationships the important ones, rather than those from the past? But in his case what of future relationships? He doesn't seem to be having much success in that department. He sees himself as isolated, surrounded by space. He remembers, from childhood, seeing luggage on a station platform somewhere, and a trunk labelled *Hold – not wanted on voyage*. He recollects being perplexed by it at the time. But he understands it now: that's exactly how he felt at the time, and still feels.

And now he's weary of these machinations. They serve no purpose; and anyway it's all well-trodden ground. He understands that to find himself now unexpectedly, prematurely parentless must inevitably increase his sense of isolation. It's how he's felt all his life; and all his life, he supposes, he's blamed his parents for that. But to thus accuse his parents serves no purpose. For they too could blame their parents for their own failures in that respect. And he has almost no information in that direction, is in no position to pass judgement.

But arising from these thoughts he begins to understand that some of these twinges of guilt arise from his feeling angry – hardly an appropriate emotion, surely, when one has just lost someone so close, the major part of one's life for so many years? – angry that his mother should be so inconsiderate as to die before he has had time to redress some of this ignorance, to make connections, to feel part of a continuum, to belong. (Was it Bart Browning – surely it must have been – who'd quoted, 'Without knowing the past we cannot understand the present.'?) But how can he blame her for that? It had been as much his fault. Perhaps he'd always thought there would be time, sometime, for all that. Well, now it's too late.

His acknowledgement of his anger allows him to identify some of the other causes for it, too. He's irritated by the presence of the 72-hour pass in his pocket – that the closure of a major chapter in his life has had to be officially countenanced in the form of a meagre three days 'compassionate leave'. It has had the effect of seeming to trivialise the whole experience. Yet he's immediately overcome by shame at his own self-pity: for loss is an all-too-common factor of life now; he's far from alone in this.

No, it's Jordan who is the main cause of his anger. And there's nothing new in that, either. But when she'd phoned him yesterday evening to express her sympathy, his heart had leapt. Now, at last, there was an opportunity for her to reveal at least her affection for him – feelings he's latterly suspected had always been there, though carefully hidden. His bereavement, their loss in common, would bring them closer. He'd anticipated they would travel home together, would have the opportunity, with all usual barriers down, to get to know each other better, to really recognise each other's worth. He'd been absolutely devastated, therefore, when, having made the usual sympathetic noises, she'd said, 'I'm sorry I'm not going to be able to get up for the funeral, but with my big rôle in this new show, which is at a critical stage of rehearsal, I simply cannot get away. I'm sure you'll understand?' At the time he'd stammered something more or less polite; but after he'd put the phone down his fury had erupted. Well, he thought savagely, at last the stage-like character of her name has come into its own – Jordan Webster, up in lights! And he remembers her first rebuff of him, when he'd queried the unusualness of her name.

Now, however, he *can* begin to see it all from a different perspective. He's been obsessed by Jordan for far too long. Woven a fabric of dreams around her, romanticising their relationship, making her into something she most certainly isn't. So to hell with her! That's all finished. But it increases his sense of remoteness.

He's been staring out of the window, not really seeing anything. Now he begins to take notice. It's cold in the carriage, packed though it is, but the air outside is much colder and the window has begun to steam up. He rubs at it with the sleeve of his greatcoat, feeling uncomfortably like a small boy rubbing the snot from his nose. At first he sees only a clearer reflection of the other people in the compartment, for although only 2.30 it is murky and dusk-like outside. The train is beginning to climb again, labouring on this trans-Pennine route, black smoke billowing past the window. He's aware now that the countryside over the past hour has taken on a harder aspect. Stone walls, hardly recognisable as such, made white and woolly by their thick covering of snow with bare patches of grey showing only here and there, snake untidily across fields which are mean and rarely level, sheep their only occupants. The snow lies deeply everywhere, in places piled high in drifts against the walls, forming a visual causeway from one field to the next, and only from the contours of the snow can one guess at the contours of the countryside. For the most part it remains undisturbed, a virgin land: only where the sheep have ploughed a path, creating a ragged furrow in the whiteness, or where the farmer has entered through a gate to deposit bales of hay, only then is there evidence of intrusion into this silent world. The sheep themselves, languid and resigned, might pass for grey boulders in this world of white. He dwells for a moment on the irony of the war having been accompanied so far by two exceptionally fine summers and, now, by a second exceptionally harsh winter: no opportunity to enjoy the one, and a diminished ability to cope with the other. But it dawns that in spite of the gloom of the scene outside and the glumness of his thoughts he's beginning to feel more alive again: that there's something about the loftiness of the hills and the robustness of the land, in contrast to the unrelentingly benign flatness of Suffolk, which has awakened something within him. It's as he used to feel when, at the end of each school term, the train was taking him home. Just as it is now.

But this time his mother won't be there; nor ever again.

As his spirits dip, he's drawn back into thinking about the war. It's difficult not to think about it. It occupies most of people's thoughts – the pages of newspapers full of nothing else, all else of little consequence. The ups and downs of it. Not that there have been many ups. They are at last going to be getting those fifty old navy destroyers from the States, which Winnie has been on about for long enough. That might help to stem the welter of disasters in the Atlantic. And other armaments have been promised. But hopes that Roosevelt's re-election as President would bring America into the war have been dashed (just as Bart Browning had predicted – 'no chance' was the expression he'd used). Thank God, anyway, that Joseph Kennedy had been replaced ('fled', some people said) as U.S. ambassador in London: he'd been a real thorn in the flesh, dismissive of British efforts, and defeatist through and through. Meanwhile, Bomber Command had 'upped the ante' in the bombing war by greatly increasing raids on Germany; but equally there had been unrelentingly devastating raids on London and, in recent weeks, also on Coventry, Birmingham, Liverpool, Manchester and Southampton, as well as attacks on other provincial towns. Browning (again) had argued that these raids couldn't be said to be a 'result' of our bombing policy, as some, accusingly, had claimed: that Germany, having failed so far to invade us, would have no option but to try to bomb us into submission. And with that incendiary raid on the City, at the end of December, they'd near as dammit succeeded – it had been a close-run thing, and no one could quite understand why they hadn't persisted. Mind you, the view was that the invasion would finally come ('try to...' was the stout phrase generally used) in the spring – a daunting thought. Once more, Browning was the dissenter, airing the opinion that Hitler need be in no hurry, now that it was clear that America (in spite of all Churchill's entreaties in that direction) was not going to come in. Browning's view was that Hitler would have to secure his Eastern boundaries with Russia before turning his attentions to Britain – and would have to do so 'by invasion, if necessary'. This had evoked some derision in the Mess, when Peter had conveyed those ideas there. 'Doesn't he know that Germany and Russia have a non-aggression pact, that they're hand in glove?', had been the comments of many; and some had scoffed, 'Who does this jumped-up corporal of yours think he is, anyway?' It was Arthur who'd quietly reminded them that it was another 'jumped-up corporal' who was responsible for the current goings-on, and the same who'd made a similar pact with Chamberlain – that maybe they'd become too hung-up on the idea of rank, or lack of it. This somewhat seditious judgement had stunned them into silence. But later, when Peter, with some amusement, had taken all this back to Browning, he'd added, 'I seem to remember that it was you, anyway, who said some time ago that Hitler would be an idiot to even think of invading Russia'. To which Bartholomew, as always blinking anxiously behind his spectacles, had replied, 'Yes. Well we can always hope…that is, that he *will* be such an idiot.'

Now made thoroughly morose again by the direction of his thoughts and by the sight of further flurries of snow sweeping past the window, he turns his head to see whether any of the other occupants might be persuaded into conversation. They're a mixed lot, all crammed close together along the plush-covered bench seat each side of the compartment, and all seemingly sunk into a condition of boredom and gloom similar to his own. On his immediate right is a large, comfortably overweight, middle-aged woman, made even bulkier by the thick overcoat she's wearing, so that every time the carriage sways he's in danger of having the breath crushed out of him (and he uncharitably wonders how she's managed to retain so much adiposity after eighteen months of rationing). She appears to have a cold, sniffling and supressing sneezes at intervals, so he's not keen to strike up a conversation with her. Without too-obviously craning his head out beyond her bulk he can't see who're sitting beyond her; but the six people on the opposite side, from left to right, consist of two army privates with R.A.S.C. flashes on their shoulders, a soberly-dressed elderly man who looks as if he might be a solicitor or a banker, a young couple with a small girl sprawled asleep across their laps, and, in the far corner, a Wren officer. All of them are either asleep or have their heads stuck into newspapers or periodicals. The Wren at present is one of those in the latter category, but he'd noticed her earlier and thought her attractive – and she certainly has pretty knees. He muses on the thought that if things had been as they should have been, both of them travelling First Class as befitted Officers of the King, they might possibly have been alone – and then, goodness knows what opportunities might have arisen? As it is, there wasn't a First Class coach on the train, so Third Class it had to be, and his First Class travel warrant is lying uselessly in his pocket – at which thought he allows himself a wry smile that he's become so accustomed to this exalted status that he's actually miffed at having to travel among the *hoi polloi*.

He wonders if he should get up and go out into the corridor to smoke his pipe. He daren't light up in here: apart from the offence it might cause anyway, there are stickers on the windows which clearly say No Smoking – which is ironic, as the compartment is already redolent with the stale smell of cigarettes as well as, inevitably, with that of grime and soot. But when he looks at the corridor it's still crammed with those not lucky enough to have found a seat: better to stay where he is, fortunate at least that he's not in that situation.

As his head turns back he allows his eyes to dwell for a moment on the pert knees of the Wren, made all the more seductive by the semi-sheer fabric of her black stockings – not an effect intended by whoever had designed the uniform, he suspects. At the same moment she lowers her paper to turn the page, and he glances up to see her giving him a contemplative look. It's a look that's more knowing than hostile, but nevertheless (or because of that) he hastily turns away, feeling like a foolish adolescent. He's too readily reminded, yet again, of Jordan at the top of the stairs.

But he's determined not to think about Jordan. Instead his thoughts turn to Athena Munro – and to David. He'd been to see Athena a couple of times since that night when Arthur and he had gone along to break the news of David's death. To his astonishment she had taken the news, if not exactly calmly, at least with dignity, not quite able to hold back the tears (they would have come in profusion later, he was certain of that) but with a quiet courage that had impressed them both. As a result, full of admiration and sympathy for her, he'd begun to entertain ideas of coming to her rescue. Foolish, romantic ideas that he could somehow step in and take David's place: ideas that make him now squirm with embarrassment when he thinks about it. On the second occasion, stumblingly he'd actually started to formulate those ideas to her, not in so many words, but by hints and gestures that she'd immediately understood. She'd instantly recoiled – then recovered sufficiently politely but coldly to indicate to him that, while she was grateful for his concern and indeed his friendship, his attentions in other respects weren't welcome, either now or at any time in the future. He can see now that, apart from any other considerations, his timing had been dreadfully wrong, that what he'd done had been insulting to her as well as to David's memory. He knows he's been an idiot, and wonders, not for the first time, why it is he's so fanciful, capricious almost, when it comes to women. He can't seem to prevent himself acting the fool whenever he comes up against an attractive female, as though, for that moment, she's the only one in the world.

It had happened with Anna Beal.

At first he'd been merely intrigued when, three or four weeks ago, he'd been called to the phone to speak to 'a lady who wouldn't reveal her name', as Barnes had delicately put it, indicating he had asked. His curiosity had turned to bewilderment therefore when, on reaching the phone, he'd discovered it was Anna. After all, there were a number of valid reasons why she might want to speak to him, so why create an air of mystery? – particularly since she must have had to use her acting skills to disguise her voice when speaking to Barnes.

Then, when she'd asked if they could meet sometime – somewhere discrete, not in London, and certainly not anywhere near Marwell, and please would he not say anything to anyone about it? – it was then, he now remembers that, unlikely as it seemed, he'd concluded this was to be some sort of romantic tryst. But why with him of all people? She'd been friendly enough in the past, but he'd always seen her mild flirtation as no more than that, purely for her own amusement and that of others. Mild panic had begun to fight with his excitement.

On that Sunday afternoon some ten days after her phone call, as he gets off the train at the village where they'd arranged to meet and finds his way to the one and only inn, his excitement is greater than ever (he's thought of little else since her call), but has by now also become overshadowed by feelings of both disloyalty (to Beal) and apprehension (as to whether he's making a dreadful mistake). Numerous other doubts, too, whirl in his brain. Will she have arranged a room, or will that be up to him? How does he approach it, and what name should they use? Will she expect lunch first, or will it be straight up to the room? Indeed, will he be up to it? Will she take the lead, or will she expect him to do so? He knows he's out of his depth – just as he had been with O'Connor that time. Clearly Anna, too, is much more sophisticated in these matters than he. This conclusion has not exactly come as a revelation. He's always seen her in that light; has always been somewhat overawed by her in fact. But he is surprised – and, it has to be admitted, more than a little disappointed – that she's so readily prepared to deceive her husband in this way. But, that being so, what does that make *him*?

On walking into the almost deserted lounge bar of the pub and finding her already there, he's decidedly deflated therefore when she greets him warmly enough but with only a handshake and a polite 'Thank you for coming'. Her attitude is no more than courteous – distant even. But she does seem a little anxious. A bit like many a patient in the consulting room, in fact. Perhaps that's all it is, then? A consultation of a sort? But in that case why this extraordinary secrecy? Why go to these lengths? Could it be, though, that it is only a front, in case anyone should be observing them? Maybe her true feelings will become evident later.

He doesn't know which way to view it, and can't dredge up the courage to come to a decision.

His mind in a whirl, he automatically offers her a drink, and whilst waiting at the bar surreptitiously studies her. As always he's bowled over by her – and, as ever, more than a little intimidated by her exotic beauty and her near-bohemian air of worldliness. She's wearing a green woollen sweater and darker tweed skirt, the clothes embracing her figure. A large oval pendant, amber he thinks, on a silver chain, hangs between the swell of her breasts, accentuating their heaviness beneath the sweater. He thinks she may have lost weight, however; even so, it hasn't taken away any of her voluptuousness.

And it's then, as he ponders these things, that a whisper of sanity suggests to him that it's not possible she's interested in having any sort of affair with him.

At her suggestion they go straight into lunch, taking their drinks with them. This serves to calm him a little: doing an ordinary thing in an ordinary way. But he still doesn't know why he's here. Over the meal – neither of them eating much – they talk in desultory manner about this and that. He learns that Jordan has been given minor star status at the *Windmill* (doing a solitary song-and-dance act, as opposed to being just a member of the chorus). What's more important, as Anna puts it, in spite of the blitz Jordan is still in work. Anna's play has closed, it turns out, along with many other West End theatres. He learns, too, that Jordan is still seeing Bill on a regular basis; not that that is any surprise. But Anna seems to put special meaning into that piece of information, as if to discover whether this has special significance for him. But why would she want to know that? Anyway, he does his best to remain expressionless: he doesn't want to reveal that particular weakness to Anna.

They chat on, and it is only at the end of the meal, when they are sitting on their own in a small coffee lounge, that, more out of desperation than boldness, he eventually puts the question.

'Anna, why have you asked me to meet you like this?'

For a second or two she looks defensive, frightened even, as though about to deny her reason. Then she composes herself, meets his gaze, her dark eyes seeming to draw him in.

'I am sorry to involve you like this, Peter. But I badly need to talk to someone, and I couldn't think of anyone else who might be relied upon not to blab about it to others.'

He doesn't know whether to feel disappointment or relief, that this is all she has in mind.

'But why here, like this?' he blurts out. Then hurriedly tries to recover. 'I mean, it's not that I mind meeting you this way…that is, it's very pleasant…but it seems…well…'

'It seems a bit like an…assignation, is that how you say?' She smiles, surprise and delight crossing her face. 'I hadn't thought of it like that.' Then her eyes are bright with mischief. 'But why not?'

Sudden consternation (or was it last-minute hope?) must have appeared in his own expression, for all at once she becomes solemn.

'I'm sorry. I joke. Of course. You wonder why I could not have made an appointment to see you at the base, in the ordinary way? Well, because I couldn't be sure that word would not get back to Jim, and he would have wanted to know why I had been to see you. And I wouldn't have been able to tell him that. And for that same reason I couldn't risk being seen with you outside of the base – after all, it might have been thought we were indeed having an affair.'

The archness is back, making it appear as though it could have been, could still be, a real possibility. She changes position, sitting back in her chair and crossing her legs, the movements suggestive without meaning to be, but enough to once more fill him with confusion.

She notices this, studies him curiously, a small smile still playing on her lips, then suddenly she's serious again.

'You mustn't mind me, Peter. We actresses and actors are all the same. Always wanting to have an effect on people, and always needing to know what that effect is. But then perhaps other people are the same? It's just that we make a profession of it. Anyway, as I say, I had to have someone to talk to, and who better than you.'

She stops, studying him again as though trying to decide how to continue. He wonders if she's been making a deliberate attempt to flatter him (in which case she's succeeded) and decides that, no, she's too honest for that. So he waits patiently.

Finally, hesitantly, she says, 'How well do you know Jim?'

The question stumps him. How well does he know Beal? When put to the test.

'Well…' he stumbles, 'I was at school with him, of course, and fagged for him – for two terms, that is, and he was much more senior needless to say. And I've seen him at work here, at Marwell – but also only from a distance, as it were. But…fairly well, I suppose.'

'So you would say that he's talented, capable, honest? Brave? Generous? Fair-minded?'

'Yes, certainly. All of those things.' By now he's thoroughly alarmed, once more, wonders where this is leading.

'Yes. That's what I thought you'd say. It's what I expected. And needless to say, you are absolutely right. That's what everyone would say, isn't it.'

'Definitely. He's an exceptional man.'

'Yes he is.' She gives a little laugh. 'I wouldn't have married him otherwise.' She makes a small self-deprecatory gesture. 'That sounds awful. But I hope you know what I mean.'

Again she pauses. Suddenly looks forlorn. Takes out a handkerchief, looks as if she's about to dab her eyes with it, thinks better of it, looks up and squares her shoulders.

'You see, that's the problem. That's what makes me question whether it is I who am in the wrong.'

'I don't understand.'

'No. How could you. How could anyone. But I will explain. You know of course I am Jewish. We have talked about this before. And that Jim's father – who has great influence on him – is not exactly pleased that this is the case. That there have been objections to my spending time promoting the cause of Jewish refugees in this country, for example. That they see it as the wrong sort of publicity, whatever they mean by that. You remember?'

He nods. He remembers it well.

'And now, you see, we have reached a point where Jim – and no doubt his father – would like us to have children.'

So that's it, he thinks with some relief, it is a medical problem of sorts, after all. He entertains a fleeting wayward thought that perhaps Beal has some difficulty or other in consummating the marriage. Hence the secrecy.

'And there is some…medical difficulty?' he asks cautiously.

'With the having of children? Oh no, at least not so far as we are aware. Although it hasn't been fully tested yet. No, the difficulty is in an entirely different direction. You see, before that could happen Jim – or more particularly his father, I suspect – would like me to change my religion, to become Christian.'

He's out of his depth again, can't see the connection, or the relevance of her coming to see him.

'Is that not possible?' he says, unsure of his ground.

Her eyes widen in surprise, whether at the nature of the question or that he should have asked it at all, he's not sure. But he's left in no doubt as her eyes then flash in anger.

'Possible? Of course it's *possible*. But, for me, impossible. I just cannot do it.'

'I don't understand.'

'Don't you? I'd hoped you, at least, might.' Her anger has grown, and with it has come a frown of disappointment. 'But perhaps you too, after all, are like the others.'

She makes it a disparagement, and he shows his consternation.

Immediately she's contrite. Puts a hand on his arm.

'I'm sorry. That's unfair. How could you understand. Let me explain. I have never believed that Christians are less favoured by God than Jews. If it were only that, I would have no hesitation in changing. But my being Jewish is more than a pact with God. It is more than being German or becoming British. It is a matter of being a member of a persecuted race. Persecuted not just now, and not just by the Nazis, but persecuted all over the world for many hundreds of years. At this moment in history I am in this country because of that persecution, which the Nazis have taken to new, unimaginable depths. Once again we have become the scapegoats for everything that is rotten in the world. We suffer for it. And how we suffer. All over Europe, men, women and children are paying a terrible price for what is for them a mere accident of birth, albeit something they are proud of – and quite rightly so, for we have nothing of which we need be ashamed, any more than other peoples. My parents, brothers and sisters even now are paying that price – may well have already paid the ultimate price. And I have deserted them.'

Here the tears begin to flow, unchecked, and through them she pleads, 'Do you think therefore that I could now finally abandon them, and all my race?'

He gazes into her tear-streaked face, at the appeal written over it, and is stricken by it, with a mix of compassion and desire. Across the coffee table he takes both her hands in his, clears his throat and says, 'No, Anna, I know you wouldn't – cannot.'

'Then what am I to do?'

To Peter the answer seems obvious. 'Have you explained all this to Beal...to Jim? He would understand, I'm sure.'

She shakes her head vehemently. 'No, he would not. And if you think that, you do not know him as well as you think.'

'But surely... It can't be of such importance to them...to him?'

Again she shakes her head, this time impatiently. 'You think they don't have their own principles, as I have mine? That theirs are less important to them?'

'But theirs are based on prejudice and nothing more.'

'And mine are not?'

He pauses, ponders on it. 'No. It's not the same. After all, you're not asking Jim to become Jewish. And presumably your children would not be Jewish.'

She stares at him for a moment, anger flaring once more. Just as quickly, it dies. She shrugs, says quietly, 'They would be half-Jew – of course; that cannot be altered. But, no, they would certainly have to be brought up as Christian. As I said, I have no great objection to that. But that isn't the issue. The issue is that their mother would be a Jewess, and marked as such. Believe me, for Jim's family there can be no question of children while that is the case.'

It is his turn to stare, he who is now at a loss.

She speaks his thoughts for him. 'So what am I to do?'

What indeed? Desperately he searches for ideas. 'Give it time?' he suggests.

'Time? What time? Who now has time? Jim wants a child. I want a child. Who knows what time is left to us. Already there has come a gulf between Jim and me. We no longer make love. I dare not. I suspect he thinks I no longer love him; that perhaps there is someone else.' She gives a hollow laugh. 'You see why it is so important for you and me not to be seen together like this!'

She is quiet for a moment, then says in a low voice, 'I am afraid that he might be beginning to think of having the marriage annulled.'

'Could he do that?' he asks doubtfully. 'Would he?'

Again comes that shrug, a gesture of helplessness – or resignation. 'With influence, anything is possible.'

'And would that be so terrible – under the circumstances?'

Already Peter is entertaining wild possibilities, carried away on a tide of emotion, of sympathy verging on devotion. Fantasy is again taking over; and he tells himself to grow up, to return to reality, not to be such a damn fool.

She looks at him sorrowfully – perhaps, by his manner, to an extent divining the direction of his thoughts.

'Yes, it would. For one thing, I still love him – and admire him – in spite of all this. For another, where would that leave me? Remember I am a German, here less than three years, and also a Jew. As a single woman – one seen to be somehow disgraced – that last fact would not evoke sympathy here, in spite of our treatment under the Nazis. Rather the opposite I suspect.' Here she raises a hand as he begins a protest. 'You may think otherwise, but believe me, I know! I experience it daily in spite of my...position. I would become an outcast, become interned perhaps. The social support I enjoy from being married to Jim would disappear. And if – God forbid – the Nazis should successfully mount their invasion of Britain in the next few months, what little protection I might have had would have evaporated. Jim knows that, of course. And frets about it, I know. But somehow, for reasons I still do not fully understand, it is still not sufficient to resolve the other problem. And it is making us both deeply unhappy.'

369

'Would you like me to try to speak to Jim about it?' he asks. He can hear the reluctance in his own voice.

She throws up her hands, a theatrical gesture of horror. 'God forbid! He would never forgive me for having told you any of this. No, I wasn't really expecting that you would have any answers. It is sufficient that I have been able to…unburden myself a little. It is a dreadful thing to feel alone, to have no family or friends to be able to talk to in such a way, you know? And, I suppose, I half thought that Jim might just possibly bring himself to talk to you about it at some point, you being, in a way, his doctor so to speak. In which case I should prepare you for that, put my situation to you? Anyway, thank you for being such a friend.'

If I *can* help…in any way…in the future…?' His voice is gruff with suppressed emotion, with annoyance at his own feelings of inadequacy: he wishes he could sound more assured, more decisive.

She puts an affectionate hand on his arm. She is the one who is now more self-possessed. 'I know that, Peter. You are a very nice man. An attractive man. Some girl one day is going to be very lucky.' She hesitates. 'Someone like that nice friend of yours, Jamie, perhaps?' She raises an eyebrow in mock archness.

He gives a surprised guffaw, genuinely taken a back. And is further discomfited because he realises that sounded unkind, unfair to Jamie, and reflected badly on himself: more evidence of a tendency to disloyalty. He tries to cover up as best he can. 'Jamie? Good heavens no. That thought would have her rolling in the aisles! No. We're close friends, that's all. I've known her since childhood, you know – well, since we were in our early teens, anyway.'

'And that makes some kind of difference?'

'Well, yes, of course. It's not the same, is it.'

She raises a questioning eyebrow again, but this time without mockery. 'You have known Jordan, too, for the same length of time. Is that, also, 'not the same'?'

He feels himself flush. 'What do you mean?'

'I think you know what I mean. I see I embarrass you. But Jordan does talk about you, you know? Oh, nothing derogatory, don't look so upset.'

She pauses, as if contemplating whether she should say more. Then, with a slight shake of her head, a gesture of denial, she looks at her watch and rises from the table. 'I must go. I have to meet Jim later. Thank you for lunch, and thank you again so much for taking the time to meet me, and for listening to me as you have. I appreciate it more than I can say.'

'I don't know that I've been any help.'

'Oh, but you have. More than you realise.'

'Well, just give it time,' he repeats, for want of anything better to say, knowing how inane it sounds. 'Things may change.'

She laughs, sounding more relaxed. 'That's certainly true!'

She sticks out her hand, immediately laughs again, lets it fall and instead leans forward to kiss him on the cheek. 'That's the least I can do,' she murmurs, the words, for him, as provocative as the fragrance she's wearing.

They head for the door, but before going through she turns. 'Jordan has been a very good friend to me, yet I know she can be silly and vain at times. But there are reasons for the way she is, and reasons for her behaviour towards you…' She puts a restraining hand on him as he starts to protest. 'No, it's alright. I have seen what I have seen, and have heard things from Jordan. But it's not all as it might seem. That's something, though, that you will have to learn from her, sometime, perhaps…And I don't think you know your Jamie as well as you think, either.'

And with wave of her hand she moves away.

Well, so much for Jordan, and Anna's soothing words about her, he thinks savagely. It's now quite dark outside the window, a darkness out of which formless shapes, made white and ghostly by the snow, come streaming past, identifiable only at intervals whenever illumination from the carriage windows lights up those closer to the line. The loss of perspective and the blackness reflect his thoughts. He wonders whether he should pull down the blind, but no one else seems concerned. Perhaps the blackout is seen to be less important up here; for by now they must be nearing Penrith, close to home. And the idea of coming 'home' does nothing to reduce the blackness of his thoughts.

Numb with desolation, he casts the first trowelful of soil into the ice-encrusted grave. The sharp sound of it striking the coffin gives rise to the sensation of it having struck him also. It's as though he himself is lying there, a weight of earth already pressing upon him, blotting out sky and excluding air, so that he can neither see nor breathe. Momentarily overcome by this sense of suffocation, he lifts his head with a gasp, takes a deep breath, steadies himself, and having regained his composure looks around him. Uncle John, head bowed, in the process of casting his own trowelful of earth, appears to be as much affected as Peter. More than that, in the morning light he seems to have aged overnight. Next to John, Aunt Mabel stands, rigid and aloof, her features largely obscured beneath a black hat and veil. Having initially expressed her sympathy on his arrival the previous evening, as only to be expected, this is how her manner has been ever since. Whether from grief or lack of it, he cannot tell; whether her affectation of the old-fashioned veil is to hide her grief or to cover the guilt she may feel from lack of it, he doesn't know. Of course he shouldn't be altogether surprised if she isn't altogether overcome by sorrow at the loss of her sister. He's always been aware of there being no real bond between them, just as, equally, there had never been any love lost between either of them and their younger sister Anne. Perhaps that is often the way among siblings? Certainly, in the course of his work, he has come across a number of examples of families constantly quarrelling among themselves. Yet he's always felt that in this instance there was more to it than that, no doubt the result of the thing between his mother and Mabel and Uncle John when they were young. The two sisters could hardly have been expected to be firm friends after that, and it was probably why there had so often seemed to be a certain wariness between the two older sisters, as though there existed, somehow, a lack of trust. At times, certainly, it would fade, both of them jolly together, affectionate even, as if some recollection had transported them back to a time when it had been different. But these brighter moods between them never lasted. Without Uncle John's moderating presence, he thinks, it would have become open warfare – and it must have been very difficult for him too. It was something that, on every occasion coming home from school, he'd dreaded: that he would find a situation in which the tension between them was so palpable that he might wish the holiday over before it had properly begun. Well all that's over now.

He lifts his eyes to the hills. A startling white, sparkling in the weak sunshine, clean-cut against the azure sky, their shadows are delicate shades of mauves and deeper blues. And for a moment his spirits rise. What is it, he wonders, that he finds so reassuring about these mountains? Their height perhaps? Their massive presence? Their permanence: looking down on this place for hundreds of millions of years before the existence of mankind, and likely to be still doing so for many millions of years after man has gone? Is it that they remind him of the sheer wonder of it, of Earth lost in Space, drawing him back to a consideration of what, he supposes, men call God, the creative energy behind it all? Or do the mountains merely remind him of the happier times in his childhood? Certainly, so serene and placid is it, this place could be on a different planet to that supporting the frightfulness of war. A place of peace on a tranquil day. A fitting time and place to be saying goodbye to his mother. A form of heaven on earth, in a way.

And that is a thought that brings in yet again perhaps his greatest regret: that he hadn't been able to be with his mother at the point of her death. And he wonders what her dying thoughts might have been; for, surely she must at some point have been aware she was dying – in his, admittedly limited, experience the majority of people are aware when the time comes. Might it have been that she felt cheated, as though having an interesting book abruptly snatched away, not knowing what the final chapters would reveal, whether for good or bad? Or, more likely, would the blanket of profound malaise have folded around her, bringing with it the desperate need to retreat into sleep, to accept release, to seek an end to things? And if he *had* been there, could anything meaningful have been said, anything that would have eased her passing?

He recalls how, in his early teens, he'd conceived the idea that the word Heaven might be a derivation of the word Haven, a place of safety. From this he'd evolved the idea of it denoting a place away from the crimes and calamities of man; not so much a refuge for Man away from the world as a refuge for the world away from Man. A tranquil and beautiful place, therefore, but a remote one – not embracing the human race but excluding it. Then he'd begun to worry (a little) that this was to be seen as heresy:

therefore, because of these ideas it might, paradoxically, be he, and he alone, who would be kept out of heaven. In fright he'd abandoned such ideas.

He has to admit, though, that his original childish concept of heaven still has a clinging appeal. Does he believe in Heaven now, though, as taught, any more than he did then? Does he believe that one day he and his mother will meet again, be able to redress all those omissions they had carelessly allowed to occur the first time around? That his father will be there to enfold him, apologising for his fatherly faults, and explain what those experiences had been that had conspired to make him the way he was? He would like to think so; but cannot persuade himself that it is likely, or even possible.

Wearily he mentally shrugs his shoulders, returns to the here and now – and catches sight of Cook looking at him across the open grave. Suitably solemn on this occasion, stolid and unperturbed as always, she's eyeing him speculatively as if she might have some inkling of his thoughts. He receives from her a compassionate smile, not merely expressed, but as one with him, sharing their grief with a single look – and, instead of being merely the recipient of her sympathy, his heart goes out to her, grateful for all her concern and commonsense advice over the years. In her simple no-nonsense way she has been his rock, a person to turn to not because she ever became involved but because she remained un-involved, down-to-earth, caring but dispassionate. More than any other person, even more than the relatively remote figure of Uncle John, she has been his mainstay, the person he would first turn to in times of trouble. It wasn't that Uncle John didn't care, he knows that. It was just that he was always so busy, not often there. It had been the problems of others, his patients, which had made the first demands on his time. Now he's busier than ever: the other GP in town having been called up into the army, John is having to run both practices, with only a little part-time help from an elderly formerly-retired doctor living in the area. In addition, in recent weeks there has been an increase of the town's population by an influx of refugee children from mainly Manchester, Liverpool and the North East; and they have brought with them their own unique emotional and physical problems.

To cap it all, John has been telling him, locally there have been one or two cases of poliomyelitis, with the result that worried parents have been calling him in as soon as their children have shown the slightest snuffle. However, in spite of this workload, with its accompanying preoccupation and weariness, and in spite of his undoubted grief (and sense of failure) at Marjory's death, he'd made sure of being with Peter the previous evening, not just physically, but emotionally, sharing sorrow, reminiscing, telling him something of his mother's younger days, allowing him to rediscover some joy at her life to balance the grief at her passing. More than that, on a number of occasions he'd addressed Peter as 'son', something he'd never much done previously, a gesture that had affected Peter deeply.

But now, he's drawn away from these thoughts by an awareness of Cook still repeatedly staring across at him. She seems to be trying to communicate something to him. Mystified, he watches as she turns her head, deliberately it seems, to peer to her right across the assembled throng (many of whom, he suspects, are there more out of respect to 'the Doctor' than for any other reason) as though intent on drawing his attention to something or someone. Curious, he follows the line of her gaze. At first all he can see is a blur of strangers. Then, all at once, a familiar face jumps out. For a moment he finds it difficult to believe. Then his spirits rise. For there in the crowd he recognises the familiar figure of Jamie.

Looking down on the lake, memories of that first time up here come swirling back. Unlike that first time, though, today the lake is frozen to an inky black, and on it the reflections of mountains and wooded shores, instead of being painted in the fresh colours of spring, are a monochrome white as though etched into its surface. This time, too, instead of the warm summery breeze of that day, an icy wind from the north shrivels their skin and tugs at their clothing, so that in spite of the sunshine and the hard going on the way up he's glad of the windproof jacket and the thick woollen pullover beneath.

Although the snow generally is lying to a depth of eighteen inches or more, with drifts much deeper than that, Jamie and he are not the first to have made their way up here: the path has been compacted and made slippery by the passage of other feet, so that progress has been difficult and he's been made aware of how relatively unfit he's become.

When she'd suggested yesterday, back at *The Beeches* after nearly everyone else had left, that if the weather held out they might this morning go for a walk together in the snow, he'd been delighted; her train back to London (she had only a 48-hour pass) wasn't due to leave until teatime, leaving them time enough. 'I'm afraid I had to resort to telling them a small lie at Uxbridge,' she'd told him. 'I said an aunt of mine, to whom I'd been very close, had died. Mind you, it wasn't altogether a lie, was it. After all, I'd always called your Aunt Mabel 'aunt', even though she wasn't a proper one, and your Mum was her sister, so it made her a sort of aunt, too, didn't it?' It was said in the amused manner familiar to him from their childhood; clear to both of them that she wasn't entirely concerned about whether it had been a lie or not. It left him with the impression that she'd been determined to be present at the funeral, come what may – which was a comforting thought. Nevertheless he'd felt compelled to test that out.

'It was good of you to come,' he'd said.

'Did you ever imagine I wouldn't have?' she'd replied – reprovingly, with an edge of irritation, as if his doubt disappointed her.

'Jordan didn't,' he'd pointed out, for no good reason.

'Yes. Well I'm not Jordan, am I,' she'd said flatly, and had turned away to speak to Uncle John who was standing silently gazing out of the bay window. Shortly after that, she'd left – 'I must spend some time with my Mum' – leaving him with the feeling, once again, that he'd said something to upset her.

However, this morning, which had dawned bright and clear with the promise of a fine day, she'd turned up as arranged, just as he'd expected. And when she'd suggested they go up onto "The Ramparts", the name they'd given to this spot in their Famous Four days, he'd more than readily agreed: it was years since he'd been up there, and it would be pleasant to revisit old haunts.

The route, as always, took them past Tyson's farm: had she been thinking about that when she'd suggested this particular walk? As they'd approached the gates of the farm, he'd recollected his first time there, and the hastily cut-short visit they'd had to the bull.

'Should we call in on George, d'you think?' he'd then said on this occasion today.

She'd made a show of glancing at her watch. 'We haven't really time, have we.'

'It would only take a few minutes,' he'd persisted.

She'd stopped and turned to face him, her eyes carrying that usual friendly sparkle, her expression open, patient; but signalling in that familiar way that her mind was already made up.

'How long is it, Pete, since you've seen George?' she'd asked.

'Oh, I don't know. Several years, I suppose.'

' "Several years" as in when you went off to University?'

'I suppose so, yes.'

'So, are you imagining him to be the same old George as when you last saw him?'

It had been said kindly, but he'd been able to see what she was getting at.

Flustered, he'd replied, 'No, of course not, not really. But...' His words had trailed off.

'But it would be nice to see how much he's changed?' she'd said gently. 'Well, I can tell you that. The last time I saw him, about twelve months ago, he was the same old George – matured of course, like the rest of us – but his outlook had changed. When the rest of us had gone away, to London and elsewhere, to college and seemingly to lead adventurous lives, George remained stuck here, working for his father. When the war started, he tried to join up – no doubt, knowing George, because he wanted to do his bit like the next man – but probably also to get away, to be his own man. As you already know, they wouldn't take him – for a number of reasons.'

This had evoked in Peter a vision of George with his permanent limp, and he'd stirred uncomfortably. Jamie, noticing his discomfort, had placed a reassuring hand on his arm. 'You really should let that go, Peter. That wasn't your fault, as I've told you. You can't go on blaming yourself for it for the rest of your life.'

Chastened, a little resentful, and still guilt-ridden, he hadn't said anything.

'Anyway,' she'd gone on, 'you can imagine how George then felt when he heard that the rest of us, you, Bill and I, were all in the RAF, presumably doing interesting and exciting things and our bit for the war, as it were. He felt left out.' She'd given a rueful laugh. 'No longer one of the Famous Four.

Mind you, it's not that he resents it. George doesn't have a resentful bone in his body. It's just that he feels…lessened. Out of our class, perhaps, it has to be said. Not that he needs to feel that, of course. In many ways George is the best of us – with all due respects!'

He hadn't entirely agreed there; but he'd been thinking of Jamie in that context.

'So, are you saying that he might not…welcome us, calling on him?'

'I don't know, to be honest. Perhaps if we hadn't allowed this long gap to develop, it would have been different. But to call now, after such a long time, might only reinforce his loss of self-esteem.' She'd given an awkward laugh. 'It might just be that he would see it as us merely 'slumming.' '

He'd been able to see the point. And they hadn't called. But once again he is left with this uneasy feeling of disloyalty to a good friend from the past.

Now, as they stand in the icy wind to admire the view and regain their breath, on impulse, feeling sudden affection for her, he moves behind her and enfolds her in his arms. She gives an elaborate shiver, says, 'Mmm, that's better.' She briefly turns her head to look up at him. 'Do you miss it?'

'The place?'

'Yes, the place – and other…things…' Her voice trails off.

'Yes, I do. Very much.' His words, tumbling out, have led his thoughts, crystallised his emotions. 'Do you?'

'Oh, certainly!'

'How is your mother?' His enquiry, jumping out, brings a pang; the realisation too that he hasn't given any thought at all to his own mother for the past hour.

She tenses a little, sensing, it seems, the regret implicit in the question. 'She's very well, thanks. Asked me to pass on her condolences.' She laughs, an apologetic note enclosed. 'I'm afraid she wasn't altogether upset about your Mum's funeral, though – after all, it had the effect of bringing me up here for a brief visit!'

He adopts the same tone. 'Ah, well, silver linings and all that.' Then changes tack.

'Does she mind living alone again?'

She knows what he's asking. 'You mean, does she miss my stepfather? I suppose she does. It's difficult to say. She was so much aware of the strain between him and me. It meant she was always on edge whenever I was around. Now she's more relaxed on the few occasions when I'm home. I do try to get up whenever I can. But, as you know, it's very difficult.'

'We always wondered, the three of us, what was going through your mind at the time. We could see how upset you were, wanted to help. But we didn't dare say anything, didn't know how to set about it.'

She turns her head briefly and smiles up at him, gratitude in her eyes. 'Yes, I realised that. And it did help, a little. But I couldn't bring myself to talk about it. Not even to you. Anyway, looking back on it, it was all foolishness on my part. But he seemed like an intruder at the time, you know, with no right to be there? I've given it quite a lot of thought over the years, and I've come to understand, too, that he was simply in the firing line of the anger I felt that Daddy had been taken away from us.' She laughs again, this time apologetically. 'I'm afraid God came in for some stick there, as well!'

He's not sure whether she's being merely flippant, or whether God is real to her, religion important. It's an aspect of her he hasn't considered before. Religion was not a topic they ever touched on as children. It would have been surprising if it had been. He wants to ask her about it now, but doesn't know why. He can't see why it should be of any importance to him what she believes. So he remains silent.

She's still standing encased in his arms, leaning back against him, quite relaxed. But the position has meant that their conversation has taken place with neither easily able to look at the other, leaving the impression that the physical communication and the personal communication have been on two different planes, one having nothing to do with the other. Now, as the silence that follows becomes drawn out, he becomes conscious of the intimacy of their posture, which suddenly seems awkward. She must have realised this as well because, taking care to appear casual, she releases herself from his arms, moves away a little, and turns to face him. He notices that in spite of the protection he's been affording her from the wind her cheeks appear flushed. So he suggests they move on.

As they struggle on through the snow, though, he's aware that the old easy atmosphere between them appears to have disappeared for the moment, and searches for something to say to break the silence. But it is Jamie, first, who does so, taking them back onto neutral ground.

'How're your uncle and aunt managing with their two refugees?'

He grins, not unsympathetically. 'I'm not sure that *manage* is quite the right word. Cook is the one who manages, even though she's no longer living in. Aunt Mabel supervises, with an air that suggests she's just passing through, not really meant to be there – just as she does with the problems of rationing: leaves it all to Jessica. What she's signalling about these children of course is that *they* shouldn't really be there. Don't get me wrong. She's kind enough to them. But it's all done at arm's length, as it were. Luckily they can fend for themselves in many ways. The girl's ten after all, and her brother's eight. Luckily. But they'd never seen a bathroom before, or an inside lavatory, so from what I gather it's taken them some time to adjust.'

'They're from...?'

'Liverpool. Poor little mites. Transported into a whole different world, away from their family, it must be very difficult for them. Uncle John does his best with them, needless to say. But he's not often there. And I think they're still rather in awe of him. The trouble is, when it becomes time for them to go home again – if they go home again – it'll probably be just as difficult for them to adjust all over again.'

A frown crosses Jamie's face. 'What d'you think the likelihood again is of invasion in two or three months' time?'

'God knows. There seem to be two schools of thought, don't there. Either that it's got to happen, sooner or later. Or, that having failed to gain dominance in the air in September, they are not any more likely to do so now, and are not therefore likely to try to mount an invasion in the foreseeable future. But, being at the centre of things at Uxbridge, you must hear more about it than we do at Marwell?'

She laughs. 'Not much of it reaches *my* ears, I'm afraid! But what people there can't understand is why jerry doesn't concentrate on the airfields again.'

'I suppose they think they can bomb us into some kind of submission by what they're doing now? And they could just be right. Plus the stranglehold they're getting on the Atlantic convoys, from all accounts. They could just manage to starve us into submission, instead. I must say, it must be a bit grim being in the Navy on those Atlantic routes. Bad enough in this weather anyway, without being torpedoed! Bart Browning, needless to say, has views on the invasion question, though… I've told you about him?'

'He's your Sick Quarters corporal, the one who was a History professor at Oxford?'

'That's right. A tutor in modern history, to be precise. Well, Bartholomew thinks that Herr Hitler will have to deal with Russia next, before he attempts to finish us off. To cover his back, and all that.'

'But he and the Soviets are supposed to be allies of a sort, are they not?'

'Browning thinks it's not worth the paper it's written on. Any more than Chamberlain's bit of paper was in Thirty-eight. He reckons that because Adolph is himself devious and conniving, he will expect Stalin to be the same – and Browning agrees with Adolph on that! Hitler's argument will be that if he ignores the Soviets, while dealing with us, Stalin will seize the opportunity to strike at his back.'

'But why would Stalin want to do that? What would it gain him? Anyway, the Russians surely aren't a match for the Germans.'

'Not in terms of military expertise and equipment, no. But they have enormous resources of manpower. Besides which, Browning argues, Stalin knows that Hitler has always had designs on the East, that he regards the Soviet races as being inferior, and that, having found how easy it is to subjugate Europe he'd expect Russia to be a pushover, thereby providing Germany with living space, mineral resources, and, in effect, slave labour. According to Bartholomew, Stalin will understand the inevitability of that, once Hitler's defeated us. So, if an opportunity arises to strike first Hitler will feel obliged to take it.'

'In other words the Russians will attack the Germans because they expect the Germans to attack them? And Hitler will attack Russia because he realises that otherwise Stalin will have an advantage!'

Peter grins. 'Something like that. According to Bartholomew Browning, corporal in the R.A.F., but also Oxford don whose expertise is History! Which, he assures me, provides lessons for the present – or, as he prefers to phrase it, 'It's the shadows of the past that reveal the light in the present'.'

'But surely Hitler's not such a fool as to walk into a war on two fronts? Even I know that isn't good military strategy.'

'No. You're right. And these are only Browning's views. It all seems pretty unlikely. But Bart argues that, probably, Hitler never expected to have to go on fighting us. That he would have thought we would either come to an accommodation with him early on, or else he would quickly defeat us. And if the likes of Chamberlain and Halifax had been in power, the former outcome would have been more than likely. The Browning version is that Hitler has simply miscalculated. He hadn't reckoned on events throwing someone like Churchill to the fore! Anyway, that's all as may be; I haven't found many who will side with Browning and his version of things.'

Jamie shivers, whether from cold or apprehension he can't be sure.

'Come on,' she says briskly, 'let's walk on,' – and seizes his hand, perhaps seeking solace. For a fleeting moment he's reminded of O'Connor – the same combination of boldness and a need for consolation.

Hand in hand they trudge on, slipping and sliding, the snow up to their knees, giggling like a couple of kids. The snow, though, as they go higher, is all the time becoming deeper, making progress ever more difficult. It's becoming clear to both of them that they aren't going to be able to go much further, although neither is willing to give in. Once again they stop, ostensibly to admire the view across the lake. Across on the far shore *Fairview*, 'Hammy' Hamilton's house, looks exactly as it did all those years ago, although today standing out more starkly than it did when nestling in new green foliage, that time in the Spring. For Peter, though, the sight of the house causes old doubts and jealousies to come washing back, carried on a tide of memories, and for a moment he's become a child again – skin prickling at the thought that on that day, still shy and uncertain, he'd continued to believe that Jamie was a boy.

He glances sideways at her now, wondering if the same memories are flooding through her as well, or whether she's truly left it all behind, has matured in a way that he's seemed, so far, unable to do.

Still pondering these things he's not aware of continuing to study her profile, until, becoming conscious of his gaze she turns her head, flushes a little, and says, 'What?'

His embarrassment grows. 'Sorry. I was just thinking about things.'

'About George?'

The question throws him. Why George? Does she think he's still dwelling on that? But he answers diplomatically.

'Yes, amongst other things.'

'Oh, don't worry about George. He comes from good old country stock. They're accustomed to just getting on with life. And he's not short of enterprise, as you know. Before long he'll probably've persuaded his dad to take on one of these Land Army girls they're talking about, and next thing you know he'll have upped and married her!... So? – what of the "other things"?'

He laughs, trying to sound casual, but not entirely succeeding. 'Oh, Roger Hamilton, for one... I wonder what happened to him?'

'Hamilton? I've no idea. Probably running the local Home Guard, I shouldn't wonder. Even more full of his own importance than ever, no doubt. Whatever made you think about him?'

'Oh, seeing the house, you know, and all that.'

She's silent for a moment, then says quietly, ' "All that" being the thing with Jordan, I suppose?'

Now he's thoroughly embarrassed. None of them – not even the three boys among themselves – had ever referred to that particular episode again afterwards.

'No. Well, yes …that is…'

Jamie laughs. 'I remember your faces that day when we caught them together, at his house, supposedly playing tennis! I think George was the only one of you who fully understood what might have been going on – although I don't think it was very much, actually. Bill, I remember, was absolutely furious, thinking that Hamilton was taking advantage of her. Although, in fact, it was Jordan who was leading him on, I'm quite sure: she's always known exactly what she's doing when it comes to men, what power she has over them. Even in those days. She was always fully in control. Although I think she might have met her match now, with Bill.'

'Bill? But he's always carried a torch for her. Besotted, I would have said. That's why he was so angry that day.' He can't quite keep the grumpiness out of his voice.

She looks at him curiously. I don't think Bill has ever been besotted, as you put it, about anything or anyone. Very much his own man, is Bill.'

It's her turn to sound irritable. And his turn to look at her curiously. Surely she hasn't got a thing about Bill, after all? He finds the thought strangely disturbing. Perhaps because he's always regarded their friendship, his and hers, as special: special perhaps because of their common circumstances, both having lost their father, but also because they seemed always to have a particular affinity which went beyond their friendship with the others. Although – he has now to admit to himself reproachfully – he hadn't given much weight to that in recent years.

'As for you, though,' she continues, 'I remember you looked thoroughly crestfallen and bewildered at that particular episode!'

'I did not!' he replies, stung.

'No need to be so indignant! We tended to forget, always, the three of us, that you were that bit younger than the rest of us. You always fitted in so well.' She looks at him mischievously. 'Even so, I bet it was because she was weaving the same spell over you, as well, all the time pretending to have no time for you? Some of that came out that week we all spent together at your Grandad's at Silloth. If you remember. In fact, come to think of it, she was all over you that time when the three of us met up in London, a few years ago, wasn't she.'

When, jolted by what she's just said and by the now uncomfortable memories of that day, he doesn't reply, she looks at him more seriously.

'She hasn't still got you caught up in her sticky little web, has she?'

He tries to utter a denial, but the words won't come. Unable to look at her, he can feel his cheeks burning. For some reason he's painfully reminded yet again of the day that Jamie and he first met, when he'd thought she was a boy, and he'd refused to climb the tree with her.

Abruptly she turns on her heel. 'Come on,' she says crossly. 'We'll have to be getting back.' And she stomps away through the snow, muttering something to herself as she goes.

Feeling every bit as foolish as he had that first day, he hurries after her. 'What was that?' he calls anxiously.

She swings round to face him, eyes blazing.

'I said, Men are such fools!'

CHAPTER TWENTY-FIVE

Arriving back at the door of his room, after breakfast, he met Arthur Stanton just coming out, towel and shaving kit in hand.

'Hello, Peter. Good to see you back...' The words, expressed in his normal hearty manner, faltered, then cranked down to a more suitably subdued tone. 'Things go alright?'

Clearly, for a split second there Arthur had forgotten the reason for Peter's three-day absence. Well, it was entirely understandable. These days the padre was beset by death and bereavement on all sides. In the dining room this morning Peter, having been away for only that short time, had seen at the breakfast tables several new faces he didn't recognise: the latest replacements – already, these days, to Peter's eyes looking raw and scarcely out of school (which, in fact, was probably the case). And at the next table to his, where normally sat one of the crews he'd got to know well, the table settings had lain forlorn and undisturbed, as though these inanimate objects could be aware that not again would they be witness to the boisterousness of those particular men. It was evidence of how regular this scenario had become that, after a momentary pang of sadness, he'd mentally shrugged his shoulders and grimly got on with his breakfast. But, as always, his self-consciousness with regard to his own relatively secure status had sat heavily on his shoulders.

'How are you?' Stanton was saying, the concern eloquent in his eyes.

'Yes, alright, Arthur, thanks.' He made a gesture of helplessness. 'Everything went much as expected.'

'Particularly difficult, always, losing one's final parent,' his friend said gruffly. 'A whole book closes at that point.'

The comment wrenched at Peter. Obvious as it was, it coincided so closely with those preoccupations of his own that had seemed to be walling him in, isolating him, that he felt a great sense of relief that someone else could see it the same way.

'Yes.' His voice caught, in spite of his determination not to let it happen.

Stanton moved in to fill the hiatus. 'Much snow up there?'

'I'll say! Several feet deep in places. And the lakes frozen over. Jamie – Jane Evans, that is – turned up. So we managed a walk together. Great fun.'

His thoughts returned to that. Her explosion of anger, something he'd not seen in her before: the fury with which she'd said the thing about men being such fools. For reasons that he'd been unable to fathom, his response to it had been to blurt out, '*My father shot himself, you know.*' He'd felt an idiot as he said it. He couldn't imagine what had prompted him to say such a thing. As a *non sequitur* it couldn't be excelled.

Her response, though, had floored him just as much.

'*I know that,*' she'd said quietly, her anger just as abruptly extinguished. '*I've always known it. And that wasn't your fault either.*'

'And cousin Jordan, too, no doubt?' The mock-malicious challenge in Arthur's voice, drawing him out of his retrospection, also threw him off-balance.

'Jordan? What?'

'On the walk with you.'

'Jordan? No, she wasn't there.'

'You mean you didn't invite her? Or was it that she had her Fighter type, Bill, in tow?' Again this teasing innuendo in Arthur's tone, this friendly challenge in his gaze. But it was as if he was seeing right into Peter, probing his innermost thoughts. It irritated him. To hell with it, he thought.

'No, I mean she didn't come up for the funeral.'

This time Stanton's eyebrows shot up, his expression amounting to one of disbelief. 'What, not at all?'

Peter didn't try to keep the sarcasm out of his voice. 'No, *not at all.*'

'I find that hard to believe.'

He had to grin. 'Yes, I can see you do.'

'What were her reasons? I mean…had you fallen out, or something?'

'No. The truth is, we were never really "in".' He suddenly felt – and sounded – tired. As though bandages had suddenly been lifted from his eyes. As if he was seeing clearly for the first time. And didn't like what he saw. 'It seems she didn't regard it as important enough,' he said. 'Not enough to jeopardise her newly-acquired leading role in the new show, anyway.'

'And yet your friend Jane – Jamie, as you call her – contrived to get away.'

'Quite.' He wondered about Jamie. If she was all right. She would have arrived back in London as the evening raids had got underway. He should phone to make sure she'd got back safely; although it was often so difficult to reach her by phone. Anyway, once she'd got to Euston, it was straight underground for the tube to Uxbridge. It was unlikely there'd been any problems; just the train itself would have been vulnerable on the approach into Euston. It was strange, now he thought about it, that he was worrying about her, unnecessarily, and yet never gave any thought to Jordan, who was in central London all the time. At risk from the bombing. Strange too how Jordan seemed to have come to terms with the raids. She'd been so anxious about it at first. Uncle John and Aunt Mabel worried, he knew. Had enquired several times if he saw much of her, and how was she coping? Evidently she'd been home only once in the past six months, and didn't communicate with them much. Uncle John had appeared just as concerned about him, though. Had said on two occasions prior to his departure, 'Take care of yourself, now, won't you, Peter.'

'Also preoccupied by her relationship with Bill Jackson, I suppose,' Stanton was saying.

'Jamie? Oh, I don't think so. Nothing like that. Not for one minute.' The suggestion surprised him. But it did again set him wondering.

'Jamie?' said Stanton, registering his own surprise. 'No, I meant Jordan.' He studied Peter for a moment. Then said carefully, 'I don't suppose you've ever regarded either of them as actual girlfriends, have you? Just…close friends.'

'Jamie and Jordan? Good Lord, no! They'd both fall about at the idea.' There was a trace of bitterness in his voice, thinking of Jordan. 'Anyway, Jordan's my cousin,' he added.

'That's somewhat immaterial, isn't it?'

'Yes, I suppose it is.'

'And there isn't anyone else?'

Peter began to bridle; then let it pass. He was only too well aware that Arthur had become a good friend and was merely concerned about his welfare.

'Now then,' he grinned. 'You're beginning to sound a bit like an old woman! I promise you'll be the first to know when the time comes.'

Stanton grinned back. 'Just checking, laddie. Sylvia gets very cross if I don't keep her posted about your comings and goings! Anyway, I must get off for my ablutions before the other buggers bag all the hot water. I didn't have time this morning before I left home. "t-t-f-n".'

'You've been listening to "ITMA" again,' he called after him accusingly.

'Doesn't everyone?' came floating back.

Fifteen minutes later, across at the Medical Rooms, while he was in the middle of his ward round with the Sister, they were interrupted by Browning hurrying in. 'Excuse me, sir. Telephone call for you.'

'Can't it wait?' he said with mild irritation.

'The caller says it's urgent, sir.'

'Oh, alright. Who is it?'

'A corporal Evans, from Uxbridge, sir. She wouldn't say what it was about. But, being from Uxbridge, I thought it was likely to be important.'

Peter didn't make the connection for a moment. When he did, he was filled with alarm. "Urgent", she'd said. Something about Jordan? (But why via Jamie?).

His fears grew.

Jamie's voice, close to tears, magnified them further. 'Peter? Thank God. It's dreadful news. Bill was shot down yesterday evening. I've only just heard. A friend of his from Church Wealdon phoned me.'

Why was it that, shamefully, a wave of relief ran through him before being immediately followed by a weight of regret?

'Is he...?'

'No, he's alive. But dreadfully burned, I believe. He's been admitted to St George's.'

Another thought struck him, one which, again, carried with it a certain ambivalence. 'Does Jordan know?'

'No, I gather not. That's part of the problem. Someone's got to tell her.'

The silence in the side ward is oppressive after the bustle of the main ward from which it is an annexe. In the second of the two beds is another pilot with serious burns. In both beds the occupants are made anonymous by the head-to-toe bandages in which they are swathed. Only by the labels affixed to the foot of their beds can one identify who they are. Both men are deeply unconscious – or, more correctly, are rendered deeply unconscious by the morphine they're having. Only the presence of the I.V. drips – their rubber tubes disappearing snake-like into the layers of bandages, the straw-coloured drops of serum falling second by second into the drip chambers from the glass bottles above them – only these otherwise-inanimate devices reveal that anything active is going on. Without them one might be forgiven for thinking that this is a room in the Egyptian section of the British Museum.

Nothing can be seen of Bill apart from two small apertures (from each of which protrudes a short tube) in the centre of the wrapped white ball which represents his head. Without these, indeed, there is nothing to indicate that Bill any longer exists.

Peter looks at Jamie, sitting on the other side of the bed, and knows that there is no way that either of them will be able to sit here in silence for more than a few minutes more. They don't speak, because there is nothing to say. It has all been said. And because it seems almost irreverent to break the silence. It's like standing watch at a vigil.

Given another day or two, the ward doctor had said, when their condition has stabilised, both men should be able to be transferred to a specialised burns unit. Possibly to East Grinstead, to McIndoe's unit. If they have any beds. (What was left unsaid, though tacitly understood, was that as well as providing expertise, being out in the country it would also remove the men from risk of death or further injury as a result of the ever-present dangers, here in London, of the blitz.) Since neither Peter nor Jamie are relatives of Bill's, the doctor had been reluctant at first to give them details of his injuries. It was only Peter's presence, in uniform, and his medical status (as well as the implication, without it actually being stated as such, that he was an M.O. in charge of Bill's case) that persuaded him to answer Peter's questions.

He's suffered 40% burns, they've been told, mainly to head and limbs – the typical pattern in such cases. Some of the burns are third degree, particularly on the hands, and will later require grafting. Assuming he survives. But the even more serious problems are the terrible injuries to the face, and particularly to the eyes. It will be some time yet before they can know whether he will ever see again.

Peter has visions of Bill, debonair, handsome and cocksure, a wow always with the girls. And he has a vision of Sinclair, that time at Church Wealdon, a human torch enclosing a scream – an agony not so much of the body, insufferable as that was, but of the mind; and then, the flames snuffed out, the wounds revealed, the features gone, the skull stripped bare. And he remembers Bill's reaction to that, his projected bitterness at Sinclair's survival: better to be dead than to have to live with that, he'd said. And Peter now cannot hold back a groan.

Jamie quickly looks up, sees the expression on his face, and quickly looks away. She has known Bill much longer than has Peter. Since very early childhood: they had played together, gone to school together, been together week in and week out when Peter was no longer there but away at school. Perversely he experiences a jab of jealousy. Immediately he upbraids himself. What is there to be jealous of now! All the parameters have changed. In one stroke relationships have been altered. Not just immediate ones, he realises, but secondary also. He looks at Jamie's face, at the distress and compassion there. No longer in minor key for himself, but in major key for Bill; it is no longer he, Peter, whom Jamie sees as the vulnerable one, requiring protection and support, but Bill. And he thinks about Jordan. About her refusal to come to visit Bill; about the way she had, apparently, received the news.

Neither he nor Jamie had been in a position to get away immediately, to break it to her, which had concerned them. The sooner she knew, the better, before she heard about it casually, unprepared, on the grapevine. (And, it had to be said, the sooner they could get it over with, the better.) How to get around it? Then he'd thought of Anna, wondered why he hadn't thought of her before. The perfect person: sympathetic, sensible, one of Jordan's closest friends, and – although they came and went, passing each other like ships in the night – seeing her anyway on a regular basis. When he'd spoken to Anna on the phone, once she'd got over her own upset at hearing about it she readily agreed; she would be able to see Jordan that afternoon, giving Jordan time to let the theatre know she wouldn't be coming in that evening. And she would be able to stay with her, go to the hospital with her, spend the night with her if that was what was wanted.

Anna had reported back, by phone, the following morning.

She had been mystified, and not a little taken aback (and still sounded it) by the whole thing. She had, she said, approached the matter carefully, trying to lead Jordan gently into the import of what she had to tell her. At first Jordan hadn't seemed to be taking it in, kept shaking her head as though trying to shake off a troublesome fly, repeating over and over, 'He's dead, isn't he.' Apparently, Anna had had the dickens of a job to persuade her otherwise, so much so that, once she had convinced her, then she had to do a bit of hard back-peddling to warn her that he was however still seriously ill. 'Ill? How?' Jordan had demanded. Anna, knowing what was necessary, however painful it might be, had gradually introduced the facts, as she understood them, about his having been 'badly burned'. Jordan, she said, had just looked at her uncomprehendingly, finally saying, 'His face too?' Anna had said, Yes, unfortunately, she'd heard that was the case. Jordan had then lost all colour, had shuddered and said, 'How horrible. I can't bear that,' and then, and only then, had started weeping. After a while, when she'd recomposed herself sufficiently for Anna to offer to go to the hospital with her, though, she'd started crying again, saying, 'No, I can't, I just can't.'

'That's alright,' Anna had said, 'I understand. We can leave it until tomorrow.'

It was at this point that Jordan had become angry, saying fiercely, 'You don't understand! I just can't face anything like that. I just can't!'

Poor Anna, totally perplexed and more than a little angry herself, had had to leave it like that. She'd offered to stay the night, however, and this had been refused. By this stage, she said, Jordan had become completely in control of herself again. Her features set, Anna said, it was as though she'd just been told that she was being replaced in her leading role, and had come to terms with it. After an hour or so of talking about anything other than Bill, silly inconsequential things, Jordan had looked at her watch, said, 'Well, I must be getting ready to go off to the theatre,' – and Anna, astounded, and even more angry and upset, against her better judgement had left.

Anna had then phoned Jordan the next morning, before phoning Peter, and had found her to be her normal self, but remote, with no mention whatsoever of Bill.

And Peter, phoning Jordan himself, later, had found the same. It was beyond him. He'd ended up, at that particular moment, feeling more sorry for Anna than he had for Jordan, had felt it necessary to again contact Anna to reassure her that she mustn't worry, it wasn't her fault – which had been tactless on his part, for Anna, a little cross, had replied that no, she was certain it wasn't.

When he'd passed all this on to Jamie, when they'd met up to come to the hospital, she'd merely shrugged and said in a resigned manner, 'That sounds like Jordan.'

He looks at Jamie again, now; catches her eye, says, 'Peculiar, Jordan's reaction, isn't it. Do you think she'll gradually come round, come to terms with it, in a day or two?'

She looks at him silently for a moment, pityingly it seems. Then, 'I doubt it,' she says drily.

'But…it beggars all belief.'

'Not when you know Jordan. Which, clearly, you don't.'

'What do you mean?'

'I mean that in Jordan's world everything centres on Jordan. She's been so indulged all her life that she lives in a make-believe world, in which nothing nasty must happen. No wonder she ended up going on the stage. It's just a pity she hasn't more talent for it.'

He looks at her in astonishment. She sounds quite waspish. He'd never have suspected she could be like that.

'But, let's be fair,' he says. 'It must have come as an awful shock for her. She probably just needs time.' It all tumbles out in rather a stammer. 'And…and meanwhile a bit of attention and affection.'

That sounds like Jordan,' Jamie says again, her voice this time expressionless.

A sense of triumph connives with recklessness, and vies with conscience. But to the extent that he is aware of these sentiments, it is only distantly. He has contrived, for this evening, to thrust aside any thoughts of it now being three weeks since Bill had been shot down; three weeks during which Bill had rallied, been transferred to Cambridge and then, two days ago, to East Grinstead; three weeks in which it has become clear that he will survive, but with terrible disfigurement and, probably, total blindness. Three weeks in which not only has Jordan never visited Bill but, to Peter's knowledge, has never even enquired about him. He's convinced himself that her behaviour is so extraordinary that there must be some deep-seated psychological reason why she is unable to face up to it: that her horror at what has happened to Bill is such that she's buried the fact, persuaded herself that it hasn't happened – even, that she's never known Bill. That she is in absolute denial. Without that conviction he couldn't have been here tonight.

Jamie of course doesn't buy it. Since their first visit to Bill, at St George's, they haven't managed to go along together again, but have gone separately – Peter once only, Jamie a number of times, whenever she's had time off. But they have spoken with each other on the phone on three occasions, and it is Jamie who has kept him informed about Bill's 'progress'; and about Jordan's intransigence. The contempt in her voice whenever she refers to Jordan has been all too obvious; and some of it, he suspects, is beginning to be directed at him by association. That upsets him.

But none of this can be allowed to intrude on this evening. For, tonight, they are celebrating Jordan's birthday. He looks across the table at her now, bright-eyed and as bubbly as the champagne in the glass in front of her. Wearing a clinging, low-cut, silvery evening dress held up, precariously it seems, by only two slim straps which show off her neck and shoulders to perfection, she is the epitome of loveliness. Is it his imagination, or are several men's eyes being turned towards him with envy, and not a few women looking at her both with interest and resentment? Catching his glance, now, she turns to smile impishly at him with a slight lift of her shoulders, a gesture that, to his enlivened mind seems to hold a wealth of promise. Then she resumes her activity of letting her eyes dart around the room, now and again lifting a hand in a wave to someone else she's spotted whom she knows. She seems to know an awful lot of people. This thought for a moment has the effect of somehow dampening his ardour. Grow up! he admonishes himself. Of course she'll know a lot of people. She moves in that sort of set. But it is him she's selected to come and help her celebrate her birthday.

When she'd phoned him a week ago, to invite him, his reaction had been firstly one of suspicion, followed by caution, then by delight, and finally alarm. He wondered: why him, after all this time? Then: was he to join a large party of her theatrical friends, only to become overlooked and forgotten in the melee? On learning that, no, there would just be her and him ('just an intimate little *tête-à-tête*' was how she'd put it) disbelief had fought with delight and lost. Then the panic had set in. What to get her as a present? Something to set the occasion. Having managed, with some difficulty, to ensure that he could have this particular night off, he had then had to butter up the Adjutant again to be allowed another half day to go up to London to find something suitable. In the end he'd come up with a silver chain with a simple drop pearl pendant – 'a little something' which he'd presented to her earlier in the evening, and which she'd accepted graciously but, it had to be admitted, with more amusement than excitement.

However, the evening has gone well enough so far. The *Cafe de Paris* had been Jordan's choice. 'It's a lovely place,' she'd said. 'Anyone who's anyone goes there. I go there all the time. You'll love it! And Snake-Hips Johnson and his Band are playing.'

He'd never heard of 'Snake-Hips Johnson', but he had heard of the *Cafe de Paris* nightclub, and, right enough, 'everyone' seems to be here. He looks around the room again now, something he's seemed to be doing for much of the evening. No one he recognises, but the place crowded, a high proportion of uniformed officers from all three services, a few of them French and Dutch, and a veritable cornucopia of attractive, elegantly-dressed women. Being situated beneath the Rialto Cinema, it does have the reputation of being the safest nightspot in London, and he supposes that this is at least part of the attraction. He looks up at the balcony: people are still pouring in, although it is well after midnight. On occasions like this it is indeed difficult to remember there is a war on.

The band strikes up again, and hurriedly he asks her to dance: he's learned by this stage that if he isn't quick enough some other man is likely to get in first – and it has done nothing for his emotional equilibrium to realise that in all cases she's appeared to know the man in question more than passingly well. He can't help but wonder whether Bill had been exposed to the same 'treatment' – although, knowing Bill, he would have been much more self-confident and relaxed about the whole thing. But, again, he doesn't want to think about Bill. Not tonight.

Unsurprisingly, she dances well, moving easily against him, applying her body (invitingly, it seems) against his – and, in all fairness (and no little surprise on his part) not complaining at his own clumsy attempts to move smoothly around the floor. He's taken back to that Christmas dance at the *Royal George*, and her belittling of him in those days: and she must have felt him tense, for she leans her head back to look into his eyes. 'What?'

'Oh…I was just thinking of the old days.'

She holds his gaze for a few seconds, a questioning in her own, then says lightly, 'We mustn't dwell in the past, though, must we. We must live for the present,' – and she glues her body to him once more, her face up against his, her breath warm against his neck, her perfume assailing his breath and his senses.

'The past is past, Peter,' she murmurs into his ear. 'We must let it go. Pretend it never happened. Life's too precious now.'

He wonders idly whether she thinks that life was less precious in the past, although he knows what she means: she means life is too *precarious* now. But it raises the possibility that this might be the clue to her otherwise inexcusable neglect of Bill. He asks himself whether this is the time to broach the subject. But he doesn't make any real effort to come up with an answer. It is enough for the moment that to all intents and purposes he appears to have benefited from Bill's loss. And to his own inner ear that sounds horribly callous, and he very quickly changes the way he puts it to himself – if 'Life's too precious now' is a good enough excuse for the goings-on of so many these days, then it is good enough for him. Anyway, the band has stopped. Not the time, after all, to introduce any form of sobriety into the proceedings. He shepherds her off the dance floor. The moment, thankfully, has passed.

Back at the table, as he settles her into her chair, she looks up at him and smiles, a slow, dreamy smile, contented, like a cat. 'Mm, that was nice. We should have done this more often.'

Floating with success, before resuming his own seat he reaches across the table and pours more champagne into her glass. 'We must get some more of this too,' he says, grabbing at the arm of a passing waiter.

It was then that everything went black. He was unable to breathe, his lungs and his head were about to burst. He was engulfed by sound: a sound so immense and so abrupt it was felt as pain, a roar which just as quickly was joined by an equally deafening high-pitched whistle erupting, it seemed, both from within and from without. He was aware of this and then he wasn't, for pain surged, pain everywhere, intolerable pain compressing his bones and boiling his blood, an agony so great that it excluded everything else, a gross entity that became the whole of him. Whether it lasted for seconds or minutes he couldn't have said. But gradually, timelessly it seemed, it receded, allowing awareness of other things. He had the impression of lying on his back, a great weight forcing him down, a particularly agonising ache in the middle of his spine. With supreme effort he managed to draw breath; suddenly the pressure was eased, and he was assailed by a smell so foul and foreign that he immediately retched. He wasn't aware of the passage of time, could comprehend nothing. Gradually, though, in darkness and isolation, as in a dream, he felt his limbs begin to move. Of their own volition it seemed. He tried, from a distance, to control those movements, to bend them to his will, but there was nothing to suggest connection between limbs and brain. The roaring in his ears subsided a little, and the whistling lessened, allowing other sounds to percolate, muffled, as through water: the clattering of falling objects, remote cries and groans, the creaking of timbers as in a ship at sea.

And light began to impinge, grey at first, like the light of early dawn through curtains, becoming that bit brighter and blood red as with the rising sun. Shapes came into focus, bit by bit, although at first he had difficulty making sense of what he saw. A woman's hand, it seemed, lay close to his face, nail polish bright red against the flesh, the glitter of diamond and gleam of gold startling against the grey; and as he peered, trying to understand, there appeared to be another hand that tugged and stripped the rings away. As he struggled with these images, he realised that he could feel, now, a weight across his legs. With difficulty he turned his head, saw what appeared to be a man, a man with khaki top and tartan skirt, his face leering, but nothing where the top of his head should be. And he thought, this can't be right. Then memory returned, and with it consciousness. The nightclub! Standing by the table. Jordan...Jordan! All at once he knew. Something terrible had happened.

With a groan he struggles to get to his feet (surprised he is able to do so, surprised too that the corpse lying across him is real) and wildly looks around him. Dim light suffuses the room from somewhere above, working its way through a pall of dust and wisps of smoke, so that it is like seeing the scene through mist by moonlight. It is a scene of total confusion. He can see that part of the ceiling has come down, beams lying split and twisted, jumbled across the room. Tables and chairs lie scattered, picked up and dropped, some broken, some surprisingly still intact; yet other tables still stand untouched, plates and glasses on their surfaces, as though just set, but now covered in a layer of that same grey dust. And, everywhere, people in every attitude – or the bodies that are no longer people. Of those still conscious some move, drawing upright as he watches, like figures climbing from the grave; others stir briefly, then flop, once more inert. And others just lie, bent and broken, draped and strewn across furniture, or part-buried beneath a rubble of beams, plaster and bricks; which of these are still alive and which are not, it is impossible to tell.

From somewhere beyond what had been the ceiling, he now sees a few thin shafts of light slanting down, only slightly less grey than the fog they penetrate. His eyes automatically following them down, his panning gaze is abruptly halted. For dimly picked out in the centre of the room is a large alien object. Rotund, with a threatening aspect, protruding at an angle half-in and half-out of the distended floor, metallic fins thrust into the air, it is immediately identifiable. The brown casing gleams defiantly, and from a jagged split along its side spews out a viscous yellow substance with that same rank smell that he is finding so repugnant. The cause of this chaos is now clear.

All this he takes in without seeming to. He isn't conscious of deciding that the bomb, being split, must now be harmless. He hasn't knowingly concluded from the scenes of havoc around him that there must have been, in addition, an explosion, another bomb. He hasn't stopped to analyse whether he himself is injured. His one thought, now, out of the fog of his mind, is Jordan.

391

He finds her lying on the floor, beneath an upturned chair at the far side of their table, which has stayed upright. Moving in a daze, he notes, as though in a still picture from a film, that her evening purse lies undisturbed on the table and that champagne still waits in a glass, bubbles forcing their way up through the grime which covers its surface. He notices, abstractly, the body of the waiter, sprawled to one side, mouth gaping, neck twisted, eyes open and glazed. But none of this distracts him.

Her head is turned away from him, the right side of her face nearest to him a mass of blood. Even as he moves towards her with single purpose, wanting to know, yet not wanting to, his mind automatically registers other facts. An arm lies near her head, its hand still clutching a broken glass, but attached to nothing at the other end. The corpse of a young woman sits nearby, upright in a chair wedged against a pillar, mere shreds of clothing clinging to her denuded frame, her open sightless eyes still registering surprise. And now comes, rapidly, a loss of quietness: shouts and screams beginning to rive the air, rising above the subdued sounds hitherto, announcing an awakening from the dream of night to the nightmare of the day. But this is background only. In a moment he is at Jordan's side – yet, it seems to him, standing back, detached, watching as the professional in him shoulders aside the panic and checks for signs. He sees fingers – his own, it seems – probing at the neck for the carotid pulse – and finding it, strong and sure. And yes, she breathes! Then stirs, her eyelids flickering. Careful not to move her; he calls her name. No response. He calls again, gently nipped the lobe of her ear; she winces, and moves. He tries again, harder now. Her head jerks irritably, her eyes fly open, staring. He speaks again, 'Jordan, are you alright?' – a silly phrase. Slowly she turns her head, looks up at him, uncomprehending. Then, 'Peter?'

'Yes. Don't try to move. Have you any pain?'

Still dazed, she appears to think about it. 'No. Yes. My head a little. And my face.'

She moves her right hand up towards her face, towards the blood which covers her cheek, and quickly he waylays it.

'It's alright. Can you feel all your arms and legs?'

She looks at him in surprise; then giggles. 'I've only two of each!'

Still anxious, he says tersely, 'Alright, so see if you can move them will you?' Then laughs at the absurdity. Her response has told him she is fairly *compos mentis*.

As though humouring a child, she smiles, a slow smile, one by one waggling her feet and hands at him. 'See?'

Then the teasing vanishes, her expression clouds, doubt crossing her face. 'What happened?'

'It's alright. We're alright. It was a bomb. Came through the roof. Luckily didn't explode.' He doesn't mention the probability of one that has, nor the casualties, which clearly are many. Nor the fact that it is miraculous that both of them seem to have escaped relatively unscathed. But there is still her face to be looked at. He thinks it advisable not to mention that yet.

'Do you think you can stand?'

She nods, groggily makes attempts to rise. With a hand under one elbow he helps her to her feet, where she stands for a moment, swaying. She's clearly still dazed, not really comprehending what has happened.

'Are you sure you're all right?'

Again she nods, then pauses. 'There's something funny with my face.'

Once more he hurriedly intercepts her hand before she can touch her cheek.

'I don't think it's much. We've been lucky. But you've got blood on your face. We'll see if we can get it cleaned up, then I'll take a good look at it.'

Her expression changes, horror quickly followed by fear. Her voice rises to a squeak. 'Oh my God!' She tears her hand from his grasp, and it flies to her face, coming away sticky with blood. She takes one look at it and screams, her hands pumping up and down in agitation.

He is appalled. She is like a child with a tantrum. 'For God's sake, Jordan! It's probably nothing. No more than a scratch.'

'Nothing?' she screams at him. 'It's not your face though, is it!'

'Don't be so bloody pathetic!' he snarls at her, now thoroughly angry, conscious of the dead and the seriously wounded all around them, which she hasn't yet seemed to have noticed. 'Come on!'

Grabbing her by the wrist, he yanks her in the direction of the Ladies' Powder Room, even though he has no idea whether it will still be there. After one startled look at him she becomes quiet, and starts to follow meekly. It is then that for the first time she becomes aware of the carnage all around them. She freezes, shrinking back on herself, expressions of disbelief then horror crossing her face. He thinks for a moment that she is about to start screaming again, but then it's as if she shut herself off from it all, and allows him to lead her forwards. Progress isn't easy, however. In the weak light filtering down from above (presumably from some lights still working in the cinema upstairs) they have to pick their way carefully, negotiating rubble, glass and broken furniture. Every few steps they have to walk around or step over pools and rivulets of blood, which she does fastidiously, on her toes like a nervous fawn, and this angers him even more. For on all sides are casualties, some alive, skin and clothes tattered, blackened and scorched; others clearly no longer living, and these she is avoiding looking at, as though they don't exist. And Peter, looking with a professional eye at all these people, finds himself wondering why the devil he is letting himself be so solicitous toward Jordan when he should be doing what he can to help those seriously injured. Then he reminds himself that a number of the corpses do have quite horrific injuries, and he can't blame her for not wanting to look at those: in more than one, torso has been separated from head or limbs; others are simply no longer recognisable as having been human. But, for every one of those are three or four who desperately need help, and these she is also ignoring. As is he, more or less – although automatically taking note of the kinds of things that will have to be dealt with. Some have obvious fractures or crush injuries; others

393

blood-soaked clothing, or clearly-evident bleeding wounds; while others have, in addition, nasty burns. These are the people for whom he should be doing something. With every step, therefore, his sense of guilt grows, feeding his anger. Yet still he feels he mustn't leave her.

However, he consoles himself, more and more people around them – those not injured, and those whose injuries are less severe – are starting to sort themselves out in dazed fashion, as though waking from sleep, and are beginning to go to the aid of those less fortunate than themselves. He will take a quick look at Jordan's face, hopefully be able to reassure her, and then return to do what he can. Anyway, he decides, although it can't have been more than a few minutes since the bombs struck, additional help from outside should be arriving soon.

Even as the thought enters his mind he hears shouts from above. Looking up through the gaping hole in the ceiling he sees torch beams playing on sagging plaster-work, beams and girders; then incongruously picking out a row of cinema seats hanging precariously into the void like some strange giant caterpillar. Only then does it strike him how vulnerable they still are, down here, from all the damage above. The sooner they all get out, the better. This clearly is the conclusion of the rescue teams, for there appears to be a particular urgency to their movements: figures carrying stretchers and other equipment can be seen scurrying down the stairway, which fortunately seems to be more or less intact. He realises, too, that thankfully the cinema would have closed an hour or two ago, otherwise there would have been a very considerable number of casualties there as well. As it is, the rescue services must have a major disaster on their hands. At least there doesn't appear to be any significant fire. One of the rescuers, in dark blue fatigues, has now reached the damaged balcony and is staring down into the dance floor. 'Bloody hell! – what state is that bloody great bomb in, down there?' he calls out anxiously to no one in particular.

'It looks all right,' Peter shouts back. 'The casing's split.'

The man peers around trying to identify the speaker, spots Peter in his RAF uniform, and is reassured. 'Right. Anyway, we'll have you all out of there in a jiffy.'

Peter isn't as confident about that as the man sounds, but confines himself to calling, 'There are a lot of serious casualties. And quite a number of dead.'

The man, who by now has been joined by several others, all now starting down the stairs, replies, grim of voice, 'Yep, we thought as much. Had to be. Don't worry, there are other crews on the way. Thank God there's no fire as yet, and the building doesn't seem to be too unstable.'

Peter doesn't bother to reply, realising that at this stage the chap is just thinking aloud, as much as anything to reassure himself and his mates. It isn't the time for casual conversation.

By this time, anyway, Jordan and he have reached the washrooms, which look reasonably intact. Jordan by now is strangely quiet, moving along in a fog of her own. He is thankful at least that her initial hysterics have subsided; whether that will hold true once he's revealed the wound to her face, remains to be seen. In the past weeks he's been shown a side of her he hadn't previously suspected.

He leads her, uncomplaining, into the Ladies. Not that it matters which they go into: men and women in various degrees of distress from shock and injury are milling around in the entrances to both places. Towing her behind him, he works his way toward the wash basins, where people are doing their best to clean themselves up and deal with their wounds; luckily, for the present there is still a water supply, but he can imagine it being cut off at any moment. Progress is frustratingly slow: it is like being carried along in a log jam, those reaching the front gradually rolling aside, allowing those behind to move that little bit nearer. And all the time every creak and groan in the fabric of the building makes him wonder whether the whole structure is about to collapse on top of them; makes him question what on earth he and all the others are doing here, licking their wounds; why the hell they don't just get out of it. Once they reach the line of basins, however, he becomes chastened: for most are in much worse state than is Jordan. One in particular catches his eye: a young Flying Officer, wings affixed to his tunic, who has lost three fingers from his right hand. He is being attended to by a middle-aged lady, evidently a stranger to him, who is busy fastening toilet paper to the bleeding stumps, using a strip of fabric – possibly torn from her petticoat. She is working efficiently and calmly, but tears are streaming down her cheeks; and the chap is saying to her, kindly: 'Please don't be so upset, my dear. After all, they're my fingers, not yours.'

The thought in Peter's mind is that the fellow is lucky to at least have retained his thumb and index finger for the future; but what an irony that, presumably, he has survived a significant number of hours of air combat only to be to be clobbered whilst relaxing off duty. It seems unlikely that he will be flying operationally again for quite some time, if at all – but, there again, look at that chap Bader, flying Spits with a couple of tin legs. He wonders whether he should offer to help with the dressing, but she is doing so well he leaves them to it. Witnessing this particular cameo, though, has once again made him feel a sham in this uniform: he is forever watching events from the sidelines, not properly taking part in this war.

Beside him, Jordan moans and sags against him. He hurriedly turns his attention to her. She looks pale, as though about to faint. Whether this is from seeing the man's fingers, or from taking note of the other casualties, or whether she is still concerned only with herself, doesn't matter. The sooner he sorts her out, the quicker he can get on and do something properly useful. He looks around for something with which to clean the blood off her face. The only thing available are toilet rolls, which people have brought from the cubicles. Wetted, they will do. He muses, sardonically, that it is fortunate the *Cafe de Paris*, like the armed services, is still being supplied with the real stuff, and not having to make do with torn-up newspaper much of the time, as are people at home. Taking a handful of the paper and soaking it under the tap, gently he begins to sponge away the congealed blood from her face. She winces as he touches it, but otherwise says nothing; and he suspects that her reaction is one of fear rather than discomfort. To his relief, as the wound cleans up it becomes apparent that although she has a superficial laceration running from the outer corner of her eye down to the angle of her jaw, it isn't deep, merely through the epidermis, and certainly won't require stitching. No doubt she'll be left with a scar of sorts, but probably not really noticeable – easy to cover up. His ministrations have started the thing oozing a little again, and he takes out his handkerchief and presses it to the wound for a minute or two before allowing her to turn and look at herself in the mirror.

She takes one look, closes her eyes, looks again, her mouth opens wide, and she begins to wail, jumping up and down. 'Oh my God! That's horrible! I'll be scarred!'

He explodes in anger. 'For God's sake, Jordan, you're alive and in one piece! What does that scar matter? It's minor.' He knows immediately he's chosen the wrong word.

She flies at him in a frenzy, hands up, nails out, like a cat, oblivious to those around her. 'That's what you'd want, isn't it, then you'd think I might bother to become interested in you!'

Infuriated, without stopping to think he slaps her hard across the left side of her face. Appalled, he steps back. There is a sudden quietness around them, an edging away, a momentary cessation of people's personal concerns as they take in the small drama in their midst. Only for a moment. Then they lose interest, and turn back to their own difficulties.

Jordan too has stepped back, eyes wide with shock, silenced. Grabbing her wrist, he yanks her non-too-gently out into the shambles of the main room. Spying a chair up against an intact wall he flings her down into it. 'Stay there!' he commands, while I go and see what I can do to help those who really need it.'

Without further glance he marches away, not knowing and not caring whether she'll be there when he comes back. Seeking out one of the tin-hatted figures among the score or so of rescue workers now toiling in the dim light, among the debris, he calls out, 'I'm a doctor. Can you do with some help?'

The man looks up in disinterested fashion. 'Have you got any equipment with you?'

'Well, no.'

'Nah. Not much you can do, then. We're well used to this. Put those alive but unconscious into a position so they don't choke, put a tight bandage or a tourniquet on those haemorrhaging, and start digging out those who need digging out. That's all there is to it – or as much as we're able to do.' His voice holds grim resignation, a deep-down weariness from hours and weeks of having to deal with the same sort of thing. 'Ambulance teams and hospital teams'll be here soon, likely. Best you get out of it, where you can do more good. You never know with these buggers. A place can seem safe, then the whole bloody lot comes crashing down. Best be out of it.' And he jerks his head in the direction of the stairs.

Fighting an ever more profound sense of uselessness, Peter hesitates, before resignedly turning away.

To his great surprise Jordan is still sitting where he's left her. She is holding his handkerchief up against the side of her face, taking no interest in the activities around her, the once-elegant silver dress, stained and torn, clinging to her and looking as forlorn and forgotten as does she. As he joins her, she looks up listlessly, almost fearfully, like a little girl lost, and at once he is overcome with compassion. Although he's always known there isn't much substance to her, he's never before been able to admit it. Now he sees. Take away her strikingly good looks and there isn't much left. That is the essence of her. Her beauty, and the vivacity and allure that comes with her knowledge of that beauty, is everything. Her apparent strength, her arrogance, is all pretence, play-acting. He feels at this moment that he's suddenly done a whole lot of growing up, that for the first time in his life he can look at her dispassionately and see her for what she really is. Yet he still likes what he sees. Now he can freely admit it. Over the years she's got under his skin to such an extent that, he now knows, he will never entirely rid himself of her. And having admitted that, he realises that he is ready, at last, to enter into a relationship with her, to pursue her, as an adult, on equal terms.

Taking her hand he says, gently, 'Come on, let's get out of here, and sort ourselves out.'

She look at him suspiciously; but he fancies that she understands exactly what he means by that. As they cross to the staircase he remembers that she'd been wearing a white mink stole when they arrived and had left it in the cloakroom, which they are just passing; like the rest of the place, everything in it is covered in a layer of grey dust, but they find what looks like it hanging at the back of the room.

'This yours?' he asks.

She nods listlessly, watches as he shakes out some of the dust, and allows him to put it around her shoulders. Then, still without saying anything she quietly lets him lead her up the damaged staircase, through the wrecked remains of the foyer of the cinema, out into the street.

CHAPTER TWENTY-SIX

Outside in the darkness of Coventry Street it was strangely quiet. That was not to say empty. At first just a few figures were seen, appearing like wraiths from the underworld and passing through areas of half light before disappearing again into the blackness; only as the eyes adapted to the night could one begin to see that many more people were bustling around in the darker periphery. And each person moved with purpose, each it seemed with an allotted task of which they had full knowledge. There were members of rescue teams, some in khaki fatigues, some in navy blue; there were firemen, many with the letters AFS stamped on their uniforms, proclaiming their voluntary role; there were soldiers, ambulance people, A.R.P. people, and several policemen. All of them working more or less silently, confining speech to occasional comments: orders, exhortations, oaths, words of advice, or simply suggestions, often pithy, of how to proceed. But there wasn't the hullabaloo Peter had been expecting. Nor were there even any idle passers-by: those few who might otherwise have been travelling from nightclub or bar at this time of night, or from work, to other duties or wherever their needs would normally have been taking them. Every one of the people here, without exception, had a part to play. There were no curious onlookers; if they had arrived as such, they hadn't stayed as such, but had got stuck in. Neither was there the expected crash and bang of an air-raid. Of course Peter, along with all those down in the depths and noise of the nightclub, hadn't been aware of the raid, anyway. The first they'd known of it had been when they'd found themselves on the receiving end. But, presumably, the raid must have passed overhead and the All Clear sounded some time ago.

He hesitated on seeing all this desperate activity, wondering if he should get involved. But the words of the rescue worker down below, his phlegmatic advice, still rang in his ears, still crushing in their dismissal of his ability to play any significant role. He looked around him. He could see in the gloom the outlines of a couple of ambulances drawn up in the middle of the road, and as he continued to peer into the darkness a third ambulance, *Charing Cross Hospital* emblazoned on its side, came up behind; and the clanging bell of yet another could be heard approaching. From out of the dark there appeared a blur of white, transforming itself into the figures of four nurses in a group, carrying satchels, picking their way across the rubble – they in turn being followed by a couple of doctors in white coats, also carrying cases. He turned to look at Jordan leaning heavily on his arm, the wound standing out darkly on the side of her face, which in the gloom was as white as the uniforms of the hospital teams. And he decided. There was no place for him here. And certainly not for her. His responsibility was to get her home.

He said as much. She nodded mutely. For the first time this evening he looked at his watch. Ten past one. The buses and tubes would have finished some time ago. Jordan clinging to his arm, they left the commotion behind and began to make their way, unsteadily, towards Leicester Square. Apart from emergency vehicles, he had seen no other traffic in past minutes but he thought there was a chance they might pick up a cab there. If not, perhaps they should turn back to Piccadilly Circus; they'd probably be able to get the night porter at the Regent Palace to order a cab for them. Otherwise they would have a longish walk in their present state, and Jordan in her spiky high heels, to reach her flat.

In spite of their unsteady progress, however, they covered the short distance to Leicester Square without too much difficulty. On the way, passing the Coventry Street Corner House he found himself strangely dismayed to find that its plate glass windows at ground level had been blown out, their erstwhile protective outer shutters lying splintered and broken on the pavement. Why this discovery should affect him, he couldn't say – until he remembered that time he'd first returned to London, newly qualified, the time he'd met Jamie and Jordan there. A whole heap of memories crowded in, but predominant was that of his delight in re-acquainting himself with London on that occasion, and particularly with the Coventry Street Corner House. He could recall the sights and smells of that ground-floor delicatessen as clearly as if he were still there. To see it destroyed in this way, and to be aware of the destruction being visited on the city in general, shattered also his carefully guarded selective memories of the past, together with what little remained of his faith in the future. It seemed, at that moment, as though the past itself had been destroyed, vanishing into the density of night. But then other memories of that particular occasion came sliding out of the shadows: the shameful way he'd behaved towards Jamie on the cusp of his infatuation with Jordan; and the way in which Jordan had manipulated the situation for her own ends. He glanced at her now. How things, indeed, had suddenly changed. His life might be said to have come full circle, yet arrived at a different place.

Having now reached Leicester Square, it was apparent that there had been a considerable amount of damage there as well. A partly wrecked taxi cab lay on its side at the edge of a crater in the middle of the road; and the windows of a number of nearby buildings had been blown out, shards of glass in some instances still hanging there grotesquely, suspended by the strips of sticky paper which had originally been fixed across the panes. The facade of the Odeon Cinema across the square looked distinctly pockmarked, as well – whether from this particular raid or a previous one, there was no way of knowing.

Apart from the two of them the Square was deserted – unsurprisingly, given the time of night and the recent raid. Besides which, everyone's attention would be on Coventry Street and in particular the results of the two direct hits on the *Café de Paris*. And there must have been considerable damage to other areas of the West End as well. However, the absence of people here meant they weren't likely to find any taxis either. At that point, he noticed the red glow of a cigarette-end in the deeper shadows at the entrance to the Odeon; and as he watched, a figure in khaki battledress stepped forward, followed by two more, all looking in this direction. He debated whether to go across and ask them whether they'd seen any cabs around since the All Clear. But he was all at once conscious of the picture he and Jordan must present: 'toffs', he on his own, Jordan vulnerable and most definitely provocative in her scant dress, with the added temptation of a valuable mink stole around her otherwise bare shoulders. At the same time it brought to mind that incident in the Club, when he was beginning recover his senses: the rings being stolen from a dead woman's finger. It was something he had thought he'd imagined. But, he now realised with revulsion, that it had actually happened. And, ashamed though he was to admit it, he now suddenly felt afraid. The fact that they were at war may have lessened the incidence of street crime in London, but it hadn't removed it; indeed there were reports that the presence of the blackout had actually increased the risk in relative terms. And the donning of a uniform didn't make an honest man of a potential criminal, rather did the trappings of war often have a brutalizing effect.

He glanced at Jordan. She was standing there not taking much interest in anything, but shivering slightly – whether from anxiety similar to his own, or from cold, he didn't know. For early March it was reasonably mild, there having been a sudden thaw in the past week, but in spite of her stole she'd little enough on, and he mentally kicked himself for not having thought about that before. He took off his tunic jacket and put it around her shoulders.

'Come on,' he muttered. 'We're not likely to find a cab here. We'd better get back to where there's more activity.'

She hugged the jacket around her, a gesture perhaps of gratitude, but didn't say anything. She still seemed to be in a daze, allowing him to make all the decisions. He wondered belatedly whether she might be suffering from a degree of concussion. But, he reassured himself, she seemed alert enough in all other respects – just uncharacteristically pliant, following him without protest.

As they moved back into Coventry Street, heading for Piccadilly Circus, he was becoming aware too that his present sense of vulnerability stemmed from another source also. For he was on the verge, for the first time, of committing himself to Jordan. Of that he was suddenly certain. His desire for her over the years had become stronger than ever (even though, he recognised, it amounted to obsession), and it was perhaps now no longer to remain fantasy. The conflicting sentiments that had at times made his life a misery were being swept aside. He could no longer find it in him to hate her, or even dislike her. He wanted her, that's all he knew. And might well be able to have her. But with that conclusion came new uncertainty. He was no longer sure about what else he did want; nor what the nature of that commitment might be. And, to be honest, he wasn't sure anyway that he wasn't on the brink of making a fool of himself yet again, misreading the signals she appeared to be giving him.

As they once again approached to within two hundred yards of the *Rialto* (now with rather more light surrounding it than before) out of the darkness, silhouetted against the glow, came a figure on a bike: an A.R.P. man sporting a white tin helmet, the shapes of gas mask case and rattle dimly visible slung over his shoulder. As he came up to them he drew to a halt, straddling the bike, and peered suspiciously at them in the gloom.

'Now then,' he greeted them without ceremony, 'where are you two heading, then?'

There was a certain belligerence in his tone, to Peter's ears all-too-characteristic of minor officialdom.

'We're looking for a cab,' he said stiffly. 'Any likelihood of one up there?' He tipped his head in the direction of the Circus.

'Shouldn't think so,' the man replied cheerfully (gratuitously so in Peter's view). 'Not if they've any sense. I should seek shelter, if I was you. There's likely to be another wave of those jerry buggers any time about now. Beggin' your pardon for the language, Miss, but it's the only word for them. Where d'you want to get to?'

'Oxford Street. That's to say, Harley Street.'

'Well I wouldn't go this way, if I was you. There's a U.X.B. at the bottom of Shaftesbury Avenue, so that's closed off. Regent Street's blocked – a whole stick of bombs dropped there in the raid a while back, just by *Liberty's*. And I've no idea what the side streets are like. As you can probably see, there's a real mess further along 'ere, too – the Rialto and the Caff di Paris 'ave caught a packet. I should cut through to Charing Cross Road if I was you – there 'as been the odd cab up at Cambridge Circus over the past few nights. Then if you need to find shelter on the way you can always duck into Leicester Square tube, which is open. Failing that, you might find a cab at St Giles' Circus – I think the Tottenham Court Road tube station's open as well, for shelter. And while we're on abart things like that, why 'aven't you got yer gas masks with you?'

The belligerence had returned, and Peter was about to give him a mouthful, when he thought better of it. The fellow was only doing his job as he saw it, as well as regularly risking his life in the process. It would be uncharitable to criticise him for it.

'We seem to have recently mislaid them,' he replied drily.

'Orlright, orlright, there's no need for sarcasm.' He fished out a flashlight and played it on them, peering at them more closely. 'Cor stone the crows! You do look a mess! What 'appened to you?'

Peter fancied that his tone had become more respectful on seeing the RAF uniform draped around Jordan's shoulders – although no doubt most of his interest was in the present occupant of it. But he realised also they must indeed look a mess, and did a quick check on Jordan and himself in the light of the man's torch. They were both covered in grey dust, with darker streaks of dirt here and there; Jordan's dress and his jacket on her shoulders were crumpled and stained, as well as torn in several places; and, apart from the laceration, now black in appearance, on Jordan's face, both he and she were covered in numerous other scratches and blobs of dried blood. The man was right.

'We got caught up in that lot along there,' he said, pointing in the direction of the Rialto.

'Bloody 'ell! – excuse the language, Miss – you've been lucky, no two ways abart it! Well, take care. Don't chance yer luck again. And I must be on me way – the bloody sirens'll be going again any time now.'

He seemed for a moment to be about to apologise to Jordan once more, but thought better of it, touched his helmet, and went on his way.

A minute or two later, passing through Leicester Square again, to his relief they found it empty, with no sign of the soldiery this time. As they turned into Charing Cross Road and headed north, passing the tube station as they did so, he wondered briefly whether it would be sensible to heed the man's advice and take shelter there. But all was quiet at the moment, and if they were to have any chance of finding a taxi it would have to be fairly soon. He elected to press on. There had been a subdued light deep inside the entrance to the station, but otherwise everywhere remained pitch black, and they had to make their way carefully, wary of the possibility of debris lying in the street. It reminded him again of the night-time pea-souper fogs of bygone days, having to grope one's way along. As then, it was difficult at times to know even where the kerb was, and given the absence of traffic he decided they should walk in the middle of the road: if any vehicles did come along, they would be heard before they were seen, and there would be time enough to get out of their way. He cursed himself for not having the foresight this evening to bring along a flashlight. He pondered again on the whole business of the complete blackout. Surely it would have been better to have put at least a few guiding lights at street corners, so that one could know where one was – after all, they had deemed it safe enough to leave the traffic lights working, albeit hooded and masked. In any case, from what the boys at Marwell said, on nine nights out of ten, even with an overcast sky, the Thames stood out like a silver ribbon below them – making it all too easy for jerry, also, to know exactly whereabouts over London they were.

Jordan had hardly said a word since they'd left the nightclub, which was most unlike her. And she was stumbling a bit, still a weight on his arm.

'Are you alright?' he asked.

Yes...Alright...Tired. And a bit head-achy. That's all. And my feet hurt. It'd be nice to be home.'

He smiled in the darkness. She sounded just like many a patient from the past, having just been spared death or serious injury she was still only too eager to trot out every remaining minor symptom. But, give her her due, she hadn't sounded altogether sullen about it – there had at least been a trace of her usual vivacity.

'Well, hopefully we'll be able to find a cab soon. Then...'

Further words were stifled as the air was all at once riven by the sound of the sirens, first one and then another, rising to their shrill crescendo before beginning to die away, only to lift again into a renewal of that lonely wail. The person who had chosen the patterns for the Warning and the All Clear respectively had chosen well, he decided. The undulations of the Warning were enough in themselves to strike dread, without the implications they carried. There was something primitive in the sound, taunting in the way in which at frequent short intervals it seemed about to go away, only to renew its cry, its warning of impending danger. The All Clear whenever it came, in contrast, removed the taunt, its high note reassuringly constant, triumphant it seemed in its proclamation.

His acknowledgement of all this was innate. There was no space for thought – only for the gut-wrenching rush of adrenaline brought about by the sound, and the desperate need for action. He tried to marshal his thoughts as he felt Jordan flinch at his side. He'd no idea how far they'd come, how close they might be to Cambridge Circus, couldn't remember how far it was from there to Tottenham Court Road and the tube, didn't know whether the tube station there would even be open, couldn't decide if they would be better to turn around and go back to the Leicester Square tube. There wasn't even any certainty that the *Luftwaffe* would come this way: it was just as likely, probably more so, that this time they would confine their attentions to the City, to dockland and the associated East End, as they most often did. In any case, it was senseless to have to retrace their steps, to head away from their goal.

'How do you feel about pressing on, regardless?' he asked Jordan.

Her reply was surprisingly decisive. 'Yes, let's. I just want to get home. If we're going to find a cab, it'll have to be soon. Any that have been around will be buggering off any time now.'

He was taken aback, even a little shocked, by her choice of language. Then he thought, How prim of me! He reminded himself that she was leading a far from sheltered life these days, that she must hear such expressions all the time – as likely as not from the showgirls she mixed with as well as from the men. Also that she must by now have become very used to the raids, whereas he'd had practically no experience of them: somehow he felt more trapped, here in the darkness of the city streets, than he had when he'd been at the receiving end on the airfields.

They increased their pace, Jordan clinging to his arm as she teetered along on her high heels. He thought of suggesting she take off her shoes in order to make better progress and to make it easier for her – but there was the probability of scattered glass or other debris on the streets.

As they hurried along his ears strained for the first sounds of planes. Already, high to the south-east, the probing beams of searchlights could be seen criss-crossing the blackness. And shortly after that his ears began to pick up, from a distance, the staccato thud of the ack-ack batteries as they opened up on the southern perimeter.

They increased their pace even more, and a minute or two later he became conscious of the dim shapes of the buildings on either side of them receding as the street opened out into what could only be Cambridge Circus. Here, there were a few people at least, hurrying this way and that – until then he'd begun to get the irrational feeling that Jordan and he were the only two not to have fled the town. But no sign of any cabs. From what he could remember it was about the same distance again up to St Giles' Circus. He checked this with Jordan, who muttered her agreement.

'Game to push on?' he asked her.

'Yes, let's.' Her voice reflected the impatience he himself felt.

They hurried on, the street again becoming deserted so far as he could tell. He once more cursed silently that he hadn't a torch.

A minute later he thought he was beginning to pick up the drone of the bombers. Another minute, and he was certain. The dysrhythmic throbbing of their engines was unmistakable: a contradictory combination of the monotonous and the menacing – *Dorniers* and, probably, *Heinkels*. Coming this way. Scarcely had he reached that conclusion than the first faint whistle of bombs reached his ears, followed by a series of muffled *crumps*, the ground shivering beneath their feet.

'Christ!' he said, 'That's not far away.'

Hardly had he spoken than a barrage of noise rolled over them, for a few seconds obliterating all other sound as well as thought. On regaining his wits, he realised this must be due to the opening up of the A.A. batteries in St James' Park and along the Embankment or elsewhere – and immediately it dawned on him that a succession of metallic thuds starting to hit the road surface around them must be due to falling fragments from the shells bursting high above.

'Bloody hell!' he exclaimed, 'That's shrapnel!' and grabbing Jordan by the arm he hauled her, caring not that he was dragging her off her feet, in the direction of the buildings nearest to them. To his relief, as they approached, the outline of a doorway appeared in front of them: furthermore, the door itself was recessed, with broad stone pillars on either side and a solid-looking stone canopy jutting out over steps. The entrance to an office block, it seemed; Victorian and sturdily built it would afford them as much protection as could be, here on the street. As they huddled into its recess, Peter enveloping Jordan in his arms hard up against the doorway, the din reached a deafening crescendo made up of aircraft noise now directly overhead, the barrage, and increasingly and ever more loudly the whistle and explosion of bombs. In the midst of this bedlam he caught himself muttering into her ear, repeatedly, 'We'll be alright, we'll be alright!' Whether she could hear him in this cacophony, and whether he himself believed the mantra, was irrelevant: for it was not of his own volition. Jordan, wrapped in his arms, was shuddering – as was the fabric of the building around them and the stone beneath their feet – and he could hear she was making small whimpering sounds, like a wounded animal. For all he knew he may have been doing the same. For long seconds that seemed like minutes they clung together, thoughts banished: life itself distilled into a microcosm of noise and fear, draining all will except that to survive – until even that had been taken away from them. At that point, emerging distinctly out of the clamour there appeared a sound that seemed to pierce its way into his skull, set his teeth on edge and to shred his skin. Lasting several seconds, it was like the tearing of fabric: as if silk were being ripped with increasing ferocity on a gigantic scale. Accompanied by a blast of hot air that threatened to tear them bodily from their refuge, it convinced him that the end had come. For simultaneously came a flash of light bright enough to blind him, a roar which deafened, a searing heat, and total pain as Jordan and he were slammed hard against the doorway and down onto the step. Then instantly, as quickly as it came, it was gone. Initially he was uncertain he had survived. He could see nothing other than a blood-red curtain, hear nothing but a ringing as if all the bells in the world had been set in motion, and feel nothing but pain. Yet, once the red aura began to clear and he could see shapes again, he was able to gradually take stock of his own survival and then of the surroundings. And things had changed. Where before there had been darkness there was now brightness. The whole street was illuminated, the buildings across the way lit by orange and yellow and flashes of bright-white flickering on their facades – facades in which the empty spaces that moments ago had been windows now glinted red inside like the sockets of a creature whose eyes had been put out. In that wavering light the roadway and pavements, too, glittered menacingly in odd fashion – revealed to be from scattered glass and metal fragments.

Still unable to hear anything other than his own roaring tinnitus, he quickly turned his attention to Jordan. Without being aware of it he'd already got to his feet, but she remained sprawled against the door, an arm clinging to his legs. She looked every bit as shocked as he felt, but was conscious at least.

'Are you alright?' he asked – or rather, mouthed: for he couldn't hear his own voice, and doubted whether she could hear either. He was aware it was the umpteenth time this evening that he must have asked that fatuous question, but it carried the same import and had the same urgency as before.

She seemed to understand, for she nodded – a little doubtfully it had to be said.

Carefully he pulled her to her feet and held her at arm's length to look her over. Unable to see any sign of injury, he turned her half-round to make sure, then relaxed his hold, whereupon she moved in and clung to him once more, her face against his neck. He looked out into the street again, studying it in its apparent silence. The raid (or, at least, this wave of raiders) had evidently passed on. But several other buildings were belching plumes of black smoke from every possible aperture, and from some of them too came the first flutterings of flame. Beyond the broken face of one, revealed in a momentary flare of light, there was a glimpse of a dark confusion of tumbled beams, masonry and girders. Cautiously he poked his head out beyond the door pillar, looking firstly in the direction of St Giles' Circus, then back toward Cambridge Circus, both ways now visible by the light of more distant fires. The way ahead seemed relatively untouched; but no more than twenty or thirty yards back in the direction from which they'd come an enormous pile of rubble now obliterated most of the street. He stared in astonishment: one of the buildings on that side had lost the whole of its frontage. If Jordan and he had been only a minute or so later in their progress up the road they would have caught the full packet. The remaining shell of the building was an intriguing sight: its interior opened up as if it was a gigantic doll's-house, the contents of offices and upper-floor apartments and storerooms displayed for all to see. Although tongues of flame were already licking in several of the rooms, the furniture, furnishings and goods looked otherwise intact. He almost expected to see similarly doll-like figures sitting at desks, or lounging at ease. But there was no sign of life, no figures at all. At this time of night the offices of course would have been empty of people, but some of the upper rooms clearly were bedrooms and bathrooms – was it possible that the occupants of those rooms had been sucked out by the blast, whilst everything else had been left more or less untouched? It was a grim thought: and he found it necessary to reassure himself that it was more likely that they'd left the building during the raid earlier in the evening.

But then he decided he wasn't really concerned about any of that, anyway, because he was now instantly filled with elation. For the second time that night he and Jordan in a strange and miraculous manner had survived a situation in which logically they should have been maimed or killed. It surely must have been ordained. And it was now, too, that he recollected that on this occasion, during those last long and desperate moments, he had been silently praying – not consciously so, but instinctively – and his prayers had been answered. Now anything was possible. Now, too, he was suddenly very much aware of Jordan's body glued to his – not in a contrived manner, as during their dancing that evening – but in a primitive way, out of a lust for life. And then they were kissing, frantically, violently, almost brutally, open-mouthed, as if trying to devour one another. He had a sense of power such as he'd never known before. She wanted him as much as he wanted her. He was convinced of it, that it had always been so. His arousal was total, beyond any previous experience, his passion soaring as his new-found delight in her was borne on the back of all those years of frustration. His hands were everywhere, exploring every nuance of her through her dress, these new sensations mingling with the fantasies of the past. And she continued to squirm and shiver against him. After long breathless minutes of this she abruptly drew back and said something to him. The ringing in his ears had diminished, but there remained a loud whistle which prevented him from hearing what she'd said. It didn't matter. The desire in her eyes, seen darkly, was as obvious as his. His urge was to haul up her dress and to take her there and then. But that would be shabby, would mar the essence of the moment. The time would come. Soon.

They stumbled out into the street, still clinging to each other, supporting each other, laughing from both joy and relief. Unable to hear properly, he didn't know whether the All Clear had sounded or not. It didn't matter. They had been tested and had won. They were immortal. Life lay before them. The world lay before them.

As they turned towards St Giles' Circus other figures started appearing in penny numbers; from where, he couldn't tell. Most were dressed in overalls of one sort or another, so he assumed them to be fire-watchers, A.R.P., that sort of thing. Then, from behind them, in the direction of Cambridge Circus, there came a rumble and a roar, startling in its suddenness, and the men in the road began running past them, heading that way. Presumably another building, or part of one, collapsing. He hesitated, Jordan tugging him in one direction, his professional instinct in another. The latter won and, dragging her with him, he too turned back. Their way was soon blocked. One small mountain of rubble piled onto another, men already clambering over the lower reaches, torches flashing. In the passing light an object caught his eye, and then another: the head and arms of a teddy-bear sticking out from the bricks, and a slipper. Then the beam of a torch picked out something else: a pale arm protruding, reaching skywards, a thin arm, a child's arm, hand flopping at the wrist as though beckoning for help – or waving farewell. In an instant men were around, throwing off stone and brick; then they stopped, peered – and turned away.

And he too turned away, obeying Jordan's insistent hands. There was nothing for him here, other than as another pair of unpractised hands; at present no call for medical skills – not his, anyway. And at that moment this too didn't seem to matter. This was part of another world, no longer the same as theirs, his and Jordan's. A protective arm encircling her, they continued their journey northwards, this journey which, for them, now had new meaning.

A hundred yards further on there were other damaged buildings, and another pile of smoking rubble partially blocking the street, all now bathed in a wan light. Peter, looking up, saw that the sky overhead had opened up to reveal a bright moon, almost full. And turning his head he saw – in tune with the secluded miraculous world he now inhabited, and therefore not in any way unexpected in its materialisation – a taxi cab in the process of doing a U-turn on the far side of the tumbled stone and brick. He waved frantically, at the same time letting out a mighty bellow – the sound reverberating in his skull. With his newly-found super-confidence he was convinced the cab would stop; and it did. Half a minute later, having picked their way over the debris, they'd reached the nearside of the vehicle, and were peering in at the driver.

'Where d'you want to go to, Guv?' the man said, peering back at them, his voice casual as though it were the most natural thing in the world to be touting for trade so soon after a raid. Peter noticed that he even had his FOR HIRE flag up on his meter. And although the man's voice had sounded muffled, he had been able to hear what he'd said.

'Harley Street, please. Is that possible?'

The driver looked at him in surprise. He was a man in his mid-fifties, Peter judged, thick-set, with short, wiry, silvered hair and a grizzled but amiable face. ' 'Course, why not?' he replied scornfully. 'Provided you've got the fare,' he added with a straight face.

'It's just that with all the damage around, streets blocked and so on, I thought it might prove difficult,' Peter said, feeling the necessity to explain. The all-conquering mood which had overtaken him during the past few minutes was rapidly evaporating, and his astonishment was growing that this man was so calmly driving his taxi around town with all that had been going on. 'When did the All Clear go?' he asked, for no particular reason.

The driver looked at him as though he might have come from a different planet, and for the first time seemed to be appraising the state of both of them.

'Blimey,' he said, 'where've you two bin? There ain't bin no All Clear yet wiv this particular packet, so far's I know. If there 'as, they 'aven't told me.'

'You mean the raid isn't yet over?' Peter asked, trying to keep calm (and aware how ridiculous the question must sound). He was beginning to get the feeling that a third time might not be so lucky; and now that his hearing was to some extent returning it came to him that he could hear guns, still, and the sound of planes in the distance.

'Let's just say that if it is, no one's told jerry, either', the driver said in kindly fashion, as though humouring a child. He peered at them again. 'Wot 'appened to you two, anyway? You look as though you've both bin run over by a train.'

Peter and Jordan looked at each other and giggled. 'Something like that,' Peter said. Then looked up as the sound of planes grew louder high overhead; and at once twisted around as from somewhere behind came a series of plopping noises immediately followed by a succession of sounds reminiscent of the shorting of electric cables. His eyes were met by the sight of a large number of incandescent objects lying scattered around the street and tumbling off buildings: fizzing and spluttering. The light they emitted was so bright that it hurt the eyes to look at them. He'd not seen such things before, but instantly knew what they were.

The cab driver put his thoughts into words. 'Bloody 'ell!' he said, 'Incend'ries. 'Op in quick! We'd better get out've 'ere.'

Peter and Jordan, needing no further prompting, hurriedly scrambled in as, with a lurch and a squeal of tyres, the driver set off. A hundred yards up the street he slowed to a crawl and, turning around and sliding back the glass partition between him and them, asked, 'Wot number?'

They looked at him blankly.

'Arley Street,' he said patiently. 'Wot number?'

They burst out laughing. 'Forty six,' Jordan said.

'I don't think you'll get much medical 'elp there at this time of night,' he said. But they could see him grinning in the mirror.

'Do you normally go on working during the raids?' Peter asked, curious.

The grin was replaced by a much grimmer expression, a turning down of the man's mouth.

'Yeah, well, I might as well, mightn't I?' he said flatly, in rhetorical fashion.

They waited for him to elaborate, but after a few seconds, when he hadn't done so, Peter ventured, 'Why is that?'

There was a considerable pause. Then, 'The missus caught it, you see, when Camberwell was 'it at Christmas. In one of them public shelters. Fat lot of use they are! I wus out at the pub. Anyway, I reckon, now, I might as well be out doin' somefing useful as sitting at 'ome waiting for the buggers to come again.'

To break the silence that followed, Peter asked, 'Do you have any family?' It was a 'doctor' sort of a question, almost out of habit, the kind of thing one asked the bereaved if you didn't know them well; but he wondered if this cockney stranger might see it as prying.

Indeed, he saw the man give him a keen look in his mirror, but he then shrugged his shoulders, and said, 'Yeah, a son. Nineteen. An''e's in the merchant navy. Atlantic convoys.'

There was tiredness and resignation in his voice. Peter knew his meaning. The U-boats were taking a heavy toll, and the chances of surviving more than a few convoys without being torpedoed were pretty slim. Not dissimilar to the bomber crews: and it was a toss up as to which would be the worse fate – being shot down in flames, or being pitched into the ice-cold sea where, as likely as not, there would be burning oil to contend with also. They were all heroes, these young men, doing their job with stoicism, knowing that their lives were probably destined to be cut very short. And more than ever it made his elation at surviving the last two raids seem petty; and revived his wretchedness at the relatively protected role he had in this war, observing it only, not really knowing how it was for these men. His father, Uncle John, Arthur Stanton, all had had to go through it in the last war, had had to cope with the fear, had had to discover just what they were made of, were capable of in the face of that fear. It didn't seem right that, from mere chance, he was able to avoid it – or be denied it. He would never know. Would never be put to the test. And in his eyes that made him less of a man.

Probably this driver, as well, had been in the last war. That was what had given him this toughness, the ability to accept whatever life threw at him, to go on in spite of it.

Strangely, it was Jordan who put the question to the man, in an oblique way.

'Aren't you afraid, driving around like this during a raid?'

'Nah. It's no different to all the other blokes – firefighters, A.R.P., fire watchers an' such like. At least I'm on the move, not having to 'ang around an' take it. Anyway, I 'ad three years on the Western Front in the last lot. The blitz is peanuts compared to that! And I'm dry! We never seemed to be dry in the trenches.'

They lapsed into silence after that. There didn't seem to be any more to say. Anyway, Jordan, who'd been lolling against Peter, his arm around her, ever since they'd got into the back of the cab, now impetuously turned her attention to him once more. Twisting around so that she was half-way across him, drawing one leg up across his lap, the hem of her dress high, she began to lavish kisses on his face and neck, apparently oblivious to whether the driver could see. Peter certainly wasn't objecting to this unexpected turn of events – indeed was relieved that, now things had returned to something like normality, she hadn't cooled off – but he did find it extraordinary. Besides which, he still harboured a wariness of her from the past. He couldn't help but wonder what devious motive she might have. Then, unable to stop himself making sure that the driver wasn't watching, and that the glass partition had been closed, he chided himself for being so pathetic. Why couldn't he simply let himself go, accept that for her, as with him, desire was still rampant? – resulting perhaps from their exposure to danger and survival of it. But even as he enthusiastically returned her kisses, his hands roving over her, he still had to torture himself with the thought that she'd no doubt done this sort of thing many a time with Bill, and as likely as not with Beal before that – and quite possibly with many others. Even now, the wretched jealousy of old refused to go away. And he was hard put to thrust away the image of Bill as he'd last seen him.

How far things would have gone there and then (Jordan quickly, gloriously, crawling all over him) he was never to learn, for the cab drew to a halt and the driver, without looking round, slid back the partition and said, 'Ere we are, then, forty-six, safe 'n sound.'

Peter must have paid him and thanked him, but didn't remember doing so. He was aware only of Jordan pulling him towards a front door, and fumbling with her key in the latch. He was vaguely aware too of the All Clear sounding somewhere in the background, and remembered thinking that the timing of it and its inherent note of triumph were particularly appropriate. Then he was willingly being tugged up a dark, narrow staircase, both of them stumbling as they went, Jordan's tipsy-sounding giggling music to his ears. Somehow reaching the top, clinging together they burst through another doorway and into a living room in which furnishings and furniture – a table, easy chairs and a settee – were identified in washed-out hues of mist-blue and grey from the moonlight coming through the uncovered window. He made as if to go across and draw the blackout curtains, but Jordan, still clinging to him, and reaching again for his mouth, urged him, 'No. Leave it,' her breath hot against his lips. The next thing her tongue was a wild thing inside his mouth, her lips clamped to his, and she was propelling him backwards toward the settee. The feverishness of her assault took him by surprise, but he was

410

instantly, fully, aroused. For a few seconds it was as if they were locked in combat, each fighting for supremacy, sprawling struggling half onto the couch and half onto the floor. She was making moaning sounds, almost as she had when they'd been cowering in the doorway during the raid; and he could feel her fumbling at the buttons of his trousers. Visions of the past came rushing in, crystal clear, visions of golden glow from skin and silk, of light and shadow on thighs and lingerie, on stockings and suspenders – the images which had haunted him over the years – and right away his hands were there, beneath her dress, and the sensations, the smoothness and the sensual textures, were as he'd always imagined. But there was lubricity too. The moisture over which his fingers slid beneath her pants was not unexpected to him now, but could never have been part of the dreams of callow youth; O'Connor had been his mentor there. And the lessons O'Connor had so briefly taught him he now applied, until, beneath his hands Jordan writhed and gasped. Her hands too had found their way in, grasping him and gripping him until he too winced and groaned, and became ever more desperate in his quest. For the cravings of his adolescence had become embellished by time and imagination: and now his face moved down to join his hands, to nuzzle and burrow beneath the upturned dress. His hands drew down the silk so that his lips and tongue could caress and probe, drinking in the scents of perfume and passion, finally fulfilling his wildest dreams. And he felt her fingers spread wide behind his head, controlling, guiding, one moment restraining, the next coaxing, as though pleasuring herself through him. Soon, beneath him, she became frantic, crying out as though in anguish, bucking as if at one moment trying to escape, the next thrusting as though trying to draw him in. Words came, released more than uttered, broken words, hard-to-hear words which seemed to come from her very depths, words of which she was probably unaware: 'I've always wanted this…go on…go on.'

And he could hold back no longer. This was to be the fruition of years of longing. Silk parted beneath his hands, he rose and stooped to briefly pass his tongue across her breasts, somehow, at some time, exposed, then moved on to kiss her mouth, odours mingling; and he was up inside her, sliding easily, engulfed, attained, transported, complete.

From somewhere came the incantation of an alien voice, 'I love you…I love you…' And, recognising the voice as his own, immediately came doubt. At the same time, too, Jordan went rigid, her legs kicked beneath his own, and her arms came against his chest, forcing him away. 'No!' she cried, 'No, we can't! We mustn't!'

Aghast, he drew back. 'It's all right,' he pleaded.

'No! It isn't! We can't! We can't!'

'Why not!' he objected, resentful, his voice as distraught as hers.

'Because I could be your sister!' she cried.

411

CHAPTER TWENTY-SEVEN

As the coast of England disappears behind them three hundred feet below, and they swing out over the dark waters of the Channel, he experiences, unexpectedly, a feeling of loss. Until now all he's felt has been excitement tinged with apprehension. And a sense of achievement. But now has come, suddenly, the realisation that he's well and truly committed. Through no one's doing other than his own. And the angry, devil-may-care attitude with which he's been imbued all week has evaporated. The bitter gall of fear that he's all day been expecting but which amazingly hadn't arrived until now, is there sitting deep in his stomach. What has he let himself in for? In the ten days since twice escaping with his life in such unlikely manner, only to then have Jordan drop that unimaginable bombshell, he's thought that nothing could affect him any more. But now, as the glinting white of cresting waves below reminds him that they are heading out into the unknown, he's starting to have doubts. There are still things that matter; and it may be that he's on course to now lose them.

He glances across at Beal sitting calmly at the controls; looking bored, even. What's going through *his* mind? Of course, he's done this many times before – though not for quite a while. Does he still feel fear? Does he, for example, wonder whether, this time, he'll be returning to Anna? Or has it become just another tedious chore to be got out of the way? And why has he volunteered at all to take this crate up on this occasion? Could it be that he also, like Peter, feels that these days he's a bit 'out of it', not doing his bit, sitting behind a desk, watching other go out to take all the risks? And does Beal, also, after his months of being 'grounded', feel vaguely disturbed by the constant shake and vibration of this Wellington, never mind the noise, or by the cold which is already beginning to make itself felt? Or does he simply rise above it all, as he seems to do with so many things?

At this point Beal's voice comes through on the intercom, hollow and foreign-sounding on the earphones that are integral with the helmet. 'Will shortly be crossing the Dutch coast. Starting to climb now, to twelve thousand. Time to get out the oxygen and the hot water bottles, gentlemen. Hang on to your pencils, Johnson.'

'Righto, Skip.' The chorus of acknowledgement coming back from the crew carries an assortment of inflections and intonations. Hard on the heels of that comes the unmistakable voice of Johnson, the Navigator, his Aussie accent identifiable even through the distortions of the intercom.

'Right on, Skipper. In approximately three minutes you should be able to identify the outlines of *Walcheren* and the *Westerschelde*. From there your heading is one-two-zero. Repeat, one-two-zero. Over.'

'Wilco, Johnno. One-two-zero.'

Peter, in spite of being prepared for it, can't help but be impressed by the laconic casualness of this scratch crew, and by the way they have all (including Beal himself) accepted that although it's the C.O. at the controls it's still all right to treat him in the familiar way that they would any other pilot regardless of rank. Although he knows a certain amount about all four of them, having seen them around on the station over several weeks, he's aware that only two of them have ever flown together before. 'Boomer' Johnson, a Flying Officer, is the most experienced of them, barring Beal himself. And it's Johnson he knows most about, being a fellow officer. He's been in since the beginning; indeed he's now well into his second tour. Although more usually addressed as 'Johnno', his second nickname perfectly suits his typically loud Aussie voice. Actually, though, it is short for 'Boomerang', an obvious choice perhaps, in view of his nationality – but attached to him, it is said, because 'he just keeps coming back'. That reputation has made him a welcome addition to any crew, given the level of superstition which pervades nearly all of them. Not only that, however, he's much sought after for his exceptional navigational skills. He's a particularly popular member of the Officers' Mess, as well, largely because of his lively personality but also because he's a talented pianist, able to switch from Classical, to Swing, to Ragtime, to Jazz with the greatest of ease. As a result he's been at the centre of many of the more lively shindigs down at *The Swan*. Those who know him well say that when he came over to join the RAF at the outset of war, he left behind 'a real peach' of a fiancée in order to do so; which has made many a man wonder why he's here at all. In keeping with his 'lucky' reputation he'd been away on a three-day furlough when his aircraft, B for Baker, had crashed on landing, four days ago, with the loss of all of the crew.

The other three members of crew are all Flight Sergeants, and therefore less familiar to Peter, although he's gleaned a certain amount of information about them whilst they've been at Marwell.

'Brummie' Baldwin, the mid-section gunner-cum-wireless-operator, has, as his nickname implies, a rich Midlands accent which makes him the good-natured butt of many of his colleagues, most of whom have just-as-recognisable accents of their own. He's a small, easily excitable man who nevertheless seems to possess an unflinching ability to phlegmatically take whatever life throws at him.

413

'Jock' Donaldson, a Glaswegian with a similar build to Baldwin (which makes him particularly suitable for his somewhat cramped role of front-gunner-cum-bomb-aimer) is in some respects the opposite of his Birmingham counterpart, being quietly spoken, slow and methodical, and a studied pessimist. He reminds Peter of Mrs Mop, the constantly miserable character in *Itma* on the wireless, whose catch-phrase is 'It's being so cheerful what keeps me going' – and, in fact, although he always seems to have a gloomy view of everything, he does also usually contrive a fairly cheerful countenance. He and Baldwin have done some twenty trips together as members of a crew that were badly shot up ten days ago, the pilot and navigator both dying from their wounds having first of all managed to bring the stricken aircraft safely home (for which Beal has recommended them for posthumous DFCs). How Baldwin and Donaldson can have so readily volunteered for this operation after what they've just been through, Peter can't begin to imagine.

The final member of crew, Patrick Mahon – a Liverpudlian with a taciturn demeanour amounting almost to sourness – of all of them is the least likely candidate for his role. He's the rear gunner. Being not much short of six foot in height, with legs to match, it appears improbable that he can ever fit himself into that cramped rear turret; but he seems able to fold himself up in a way that suggests he's made of India rubber, and then, according to reputation, relax into that position, uncomplaining, for hours on end. Indeed, he gives the impression that he actually relishes the job. And the reasons for his enthusiasm for his chosen task are not hard to find: his entire family had been wiped out during one of the heavy raids on Liverpool at the end of November, and he carries with him a seething hatred of all things German. He's just completed his first tour of thirty ops, and should have gone on leave, but it's in keeping with his attitude that he's refused his leave and has asked to immediately begin his second tour.

And as he feels himself being thrust back into his seat as the aircraft assumes an angle of forty degrees and, with an even greater roar from its engines, begins its climb, Peter continues to cogitate on the circumstances which have brought this experienced, yet patchwork, aircrew together and have resulted in his being here as well. Watching Beal, whose right hand is holding the throttle levers forward whilst his other hauls back on the joystick, he finds it difficult to accept that the conversation with Beal only this morning had actually taken place. If it weren't for the fact that it all now feels only too real, he would still be convinced that he'd dreamt it.

As it was, the call to Beal's office that early in the morning was so unusual that it had had an unreal aura to it from the start. He hadn't been able to imagine what it could be about. And when Beal had immediately launched into his narrative without any explanatory preamble, for a while he'd been even more perplexed.

'There's a big push on from Ops, tonight, Peter,' Beal had said, tersely, clearly not wanting to waste time. 'Maximum effort called for. One-two-eight squadron is more than a bit depleted in personnel, and we have a spare serviceable kite, K-for-King, without a crew. However, I've managed to scrape together a scratch crew with more than enough experience for the job, but we haven't any spare pilots, so I'm taking her up myself, with an empty seat. What do you think?'

Peter must have looked as blank as he felt (was Beal asking his advice, for heaven's sake?), for impatience had then injected anger into Beal's voice.

'I'm asking if you want to come along, for God's sake! Bloody hell, you've pestered me often enough for the opportunity. Well, now's your chance. It's not likely to come again!'

Peter had felt as if he'd been kicked in the guts. It was like being asked, out of the blue, for the first time ever, if you wanted to play in the 1st XV for the toughest match of the season (and he'd recollected what Bill had said about that sort of thing). Excitement had been followed by dismay. But, without thinking, he'd said the only thing possible, stammering the words out. 'Yes, of course. You bet!'

'Right, that's settled, then. I'll have to square it with the crew, of course. And warn them to keep mum. And not a word to anyone, mark you. We're both likely to be up before a Court Martial if this ever leaked out. As it is, the brass wouldn't look kindly on me going up, either, without permission – which I'm not intending to seek. Briefing is at sixteen hundred hours: you'd better sit in on that. You can sneak in at the back – which is something you sometimes do anyway, so no one'll take any notice. Then you'll know what's going on – and really get the feel of the whole thing. After all, that's what you're after, isn't it.'

Peter had half suspected that there was a hint of sarcasm in Beal's voice at that point, but the C.O.'s face had expressed nothing but professionalism and a desire to press on to deal with the no-doubt-hundreds of things demanding his attention before having to face the preparations that lay ahead. It had made Peter feel very small.

'As far as the Sick Quarters are concerned,' Beal had gone on to say, 'just say you'll be away overnight; cover will be arranged in the usual way. And I'll get Flight Lieutenant Johnson – who's going to be our navigator – to look out a flying-suit for you, and all the accoutrements. You'll just have to don those as best you can once on board the aircraft, and then no one's the wiser. You can come out in the car with me, and we'll sneak you on board from there.

Peter, understanding that Beal was sticking his neck out in providing him with this opportunity, had by then begun to be filled with gratitude – and a certain pride in the knowledge that it was all part of the 'old school tie' thing.

Now, he wasn't so sure that gratitude was quite the right word.

Indeed, as he was leaving Beal's office, he hadn't been able to resist voicing some hesitation, in the form of a query, saying, 'Does that mean you'll be without a second pilot?'

'Haven't I already said that we can't find any pilots for this aircraft?' Beal had replied testily. 'That's why I'm going – and why you're able to go. If you want to change your mind, let me know.'

The slight sneer in his voice had been unmistakable, and Peter, hot under the collar, had hastened with his reply, 'No, certainly not …I just wondered…'

Beal had relented then by saying, 'I've thought for a long time that a co-pilot is really unnecessary anyway, you know, and have said so. And I think that the powers-that-be are gradually, at last, coming round to that view. Better to take the time to train one chap really well than try to train twice as many indifferently in half the time. That's partly why we're losing so many crews – the damned drivers just haven't had enough flying time! And you can always give another member of crew minimal training in the basics of flying the aircraft: enough maybe, or maybe not, to get by in an emergency. All the pilot needs, really, is a spare pair of hands for the controls at times, and someone to keep an eye on the dials when the going gets tough.' Then, bending further, he'd made an attempt at a joke: 'But I don't think there's time to give you that training before this evening! Anyway, I mustn't let you get me onto one of my hobby horses. We must press on. Dismissed – and see you this evening. Take-off is 2200 hours, boarding at 2145.'

Well, all that's water under the bridge, now. He's got what he thought he wanted, and he's got to bloody well make the best of it. And when he stops to think about it, excitement is now overtaking nervousness. He peers out through the cockpit window, using his gloved hand to wipe away the condensation already forming on the inside of the scratched and bleary Perspex. They're passing through patchy cloud, the grey tendrils rushing in as if to smother the aircraft, before wetly streaming away down the side of the canopy. Above, there are brief glimpses of a half moon, a 'bombers' moon', its cold light throwing patches of white onto the clouds above and below and onto the starboard engine cowling. Now and again, through the cloud beneath, he fancies he can see the dark outlines of land, or the gleam of moonlight on water. Otherwise they could be alone up here, in a world of their own, droning on aimlessly with nowhere to go.

Except that they have somewhere to go: Stuttgart, still some six hundred miles distant – three hours or so there, and the same back. There'd been a concerted murmur, at the briefing, when this had been revealed as the target. The prime objective, the Intelligence Officer had declared dispassionately, was to be the Bosch works, a main supplier of magnetos and dynamos for the German war effort. A well-defended target, therefore, not only because of the presence of that factory, but because of other industries there as well. An important target, to be sure, but small in size. Every man in the room had known they'd be doing well if, with their present skills and bombsights, coming in at altitude, they managed to get just a few hits onto their target. Hence the 'maximum effort' that had been called for on this occasion: the more bombs that were dropped, the reasoning went, the more that some were likely to hit what they were intended to hit.

He looks at his watch. 2230 hours. Half an hour into the flight. A sixth or seventh of the way there. In spite of the anticipation, the adrenaline flowing, this bit is almost becoming tedious (there's little or no talking, for Beal had, from the start, cautioned them he didn't want any unnecessary chat over the intercom). Part of him is still surprised that they haven't already met with any flak. But the C.O. had previously informed them that he was going to pick his own route to the target – having cleared it with S/L Robinson, the 128 Squadron leader (in fact Jack Robinson was probably only too relieved that he wasn't going to have his C.O. breathing down his neck all night!). Crews choosing their own individual routes had been more or less the norm during the first year or so of the war, Peter knew, but increasingly now it was being frowned upon. He could see its merits, though. Goodness knows where the other kites of 128 were, never mind the rest of the bomber force; presumably on some parallel course somewhere. But they were probably drawing all of jerry's attention, poor sods – would be much more visible on the screens of the German equivalent of RDF (a piece of technology which, it was now clear, jerry certainly had) than would a single aircraft.

Mahon's voice over the intercom, from the tail, breaks into his thoughts.

'Could be a one-one-oh behind, above and to our port at seven o'clock from you, Skip.' His voice, although calm, has an edge to it. To Peter's ears it's as though the man is actually fearful that it isn't the case, that he's not going to be able to have a crack at a *Messerschmitt*.

'Righto, Pat.' Beal's voice is also matter-of-fact. Peter wonders whether these men really are as relaxed as they sound, or whether it's all studied, a learned reaction with the purpose of reassuring one and all that every man is up to the job. He suspects that it's the latter. Or a part of him wants to believe that.

The Wellington is banking hard to the right and climbing again, the throttle levers once more pushed forward to their maximum. Up ahead Peter can see a mass of cumulus, pale against the dark night sky: it is towards this that Beal is heading – whereas many a pilot might have been panicked into going into a dive. His voice now pays out facts in a monotone: 'New heading one three four, speed two-ten, climbing to fifteen thousand. Recheck your oxygen.'

'Gotcha, Skipper.' Johnson also sounds cheerful. The information is of course for him: he will have to re-plot, and be able to give Beal a new heading once (or if) they've shaken off the (supposed) *Messerschmitt*. It all sounds like a game. Which in a sense it is. But no consolation for the loser.

The next moment, as Peter releases his mask to check the oxygen flow as he's been shown, they are in cloud: thick adherent stuff, enveloping the aircraft like a great moist lump of cotton-wool. The effect is totally claustrophobic. Rather than being protective, Peter thinks, it makes one feel defenceless: all one's senses shut off, unaware of what's lurking in there, the predator able to pounce at any moment from anywhere, without one knowing it's about to happen. Except of course that he won't know where they are either. In the darkness, the only light, now that they're in cloud, a faint glow from the instrument panels, he peers around at the interior of the fuselage, unable to see much, but his mind's eye reminding him of just how cramped it all is. And so utterly fragile: a simple metal latticework with a covering of treated fabric, the beams and struts holding the whole thing together apparently so flimsy as to be incapable of doing their job. Further back the darkness is just as near-total, with only a faint orange glow emanating from the navigator's light behind the half partition. He pictures cannon-shell and machine-gun rounds blasting into the interior of this confined space, which even in daytime is dark, restrictive and full of obstructions, awkward corners and sharp edges, so that one can only pass along it with difficulty and in a half crouch; and he can picture the pandemonium that would surely result. Particularly if there's fire. But he doesn't want to think about that. Most of all not that.

His guts are tied in a knot. The oxygen is having a drying effect on his throat, the regular sibilance and click as he breathes through the mask sounding like a metronome counting down the seconds to oblivion. He shivers and is aware his teeth are beginning to chatter. He tries hard to suppress it: he wouldn't be able to live with the knowledge that he'd shown fear in front of Beal and the others. But when he thinks about it he realises that he's no longer actually feeling afraid. Indifferent, rather. Or even angry. But so cold: it's the cold that is producing somatic reactions that could be mistaken for fear. The intense cold is something that Peter has been prepared for: he's seen the effects of it on so many occasions. But actually experiencing it is a totally different matter. It's beginning to eat into his bones – in spite of the layers of clothing he's wearing, as they all are: the bulky, woolly-lined Sidcot Suit on top of their normal uniform and thick jumper, sheepskin flying-boots, thick leather gauntlets with silk linings, and leather flying helmet.

For the first time he's tempted to envy the cramped lot of the nose- and tail-gunners: they at least, these days, have electrically-heated suits. Mind you, they most certainly need them in those exposed turrets; on a number of occasions in the past he's had to treat the frostbite of rear-gunners.

He's mildly elated to conclude that he isn't, after all (so far) afraid. But bemused at identifying the anger; anger that's been seething within for the past week. He should by now have put it behind him, he decides, particularly now that his own life has more than ever been placed on the line. Of course, his anger at Jordan that evening had been justified at the time. Yet, seen in the cold light of day, what had she done, other than tell him what he should have been told a long time ago? She'd exaggerated and over-dramatised, of course. But that's Jordan. Something she's always done. He'd recoiled at her words, shock and disbelief further fuelling his fury at the time; and he'd stared down at her, struggling to decipher what she'd said, aghast at the enormity of it, and the implications, even whilst knowing that what she had asserted was clearly impossible.

Indeed it was. Yet not entirely. What she might have said – what she *should* have said – was, '*It's just possible that I might be your* half-*sister*.'

But that turned out to be even worse, because once she'd explained – once he'd eventually given her the opportunity to explain – it had dawned on him that her claim was just tenable. And the implications of that were so convoluted that he hadn't any longer been able to think straight. And hadn't wanted to believe it, for all sorts of reasons.

It had been their aunt Anne (of course) who, years back, had fed Jordan the information. Some of it Jordan had known from other sources, from hints and clues and guesswork. But, until that occasion when Anne (the worse for wear from drink, as usual) had chosen to spill the beans, even Jordan hadn't guessed the half of it.

The claim was that Anne had had an affair with Peter's father (or, as it now appeared, his assumed father). This had been in 1912, when Anne was only sixteen and still at school. Jordan had no idea who had started the affair, and hadn't asked; but Anne at the time had been pretty, flirtatious and impressionable; Gerald Waring had been handsome, already a Captain in the army, but also impressionable. Yet at the time he and Peter's mother, Marjory, had been married for not much longer than a year. The affair had, however, soon come to light – Anne again? – and (as Jordan put it) all hell had broken loose – which could be imagined.

Peter's mother had left her husband and fled home to stay with her father, and needless to say had been totally distressed and depressed. Anne and Gerald Waring had of course become pariahs to all who knew them. And the whole disaster had threatened to utterly destroy the family. They had however managed (more or less) to hush it up, although there had been any amount of public rumour.

And John Webster, Jordan's father, the caring doctor and an old flame of Marjory's, had been frequently on hand to offer Marjory comfort and counsel.

All that had been certain. What also was certain was that Marjory and Gerald Waring had eventually made their peace, it being the most pragmatic thing to do, and had got together again. But not, according to Jordan according to Anne (who, her tongue loosened by alcohol, had somewhat gleefully passed this on to Jordan) until the spring of 1913. And Peter had been born, full term it was thought, in November of that year. It seemed that speculation at the time, and since, as to who might be his true father, had not only been Anne's.

And it is this, all too obviously, which is the cause of his continued turmoil. His anger all week has been directed at all those concerned, a seething bitterness at the knowledge, out of the blue, that he is the subject of deceit and 'betrayal' not only by both his parents but by 'Uncle' John also. However, side-by-side with his anger there has also developed an inner conflict. For what is his anger about? About his mother? – or on her behalf – for having been subjected, by those closest to her, to such betrayal and unhappiness? Or about what was done to him? – that (albeit presumably with the intention of trying to protect him from similar distress) he'd been kept in the dark about it all; that he'd been allowed to grow up cocooned in ignorance, his life a sham, a family-outcast as it were, distanced from the truth of his origins, everything mere pretence. Or, there again, is his anger on a much more mundane level, in that all this has resulted in the shattering of his life-long dreams with regard to Jordan? He feels cheated. And sad. Sad that his mother should have gone to her death carrying that sort of secret with her, that she hadn't had the instinct (or courage) to understand that in order to truly make her son (whom she had created and borne and nurtured) a part of her for ever, it was essential he be a party to his own origins. To the truth, whatever that may be. He feels that if it were possible to go back, to do the whole thing again, he would want it to be done differently: not so much with regard to the facts of those human errors and weaknesses, but in the redressing of the effects of those errors.

Of course, it may all be a mistake. Or downright lies, given the source (neither Anne nor Jordan can be seen as being altogether reliable in what they say). Yet, if true, it would explain much. The stormy relationship between his parents; and the awkwardness, the lack of warmth, between him and his 'father'. The difficulties – guilt on the one part and antagonism on the other? – that existed between his mother and her sister Mabel, and their joint hostility to their sister Anne. And not least of all 'Uncle' John's warmth and solicitude towards his mother and to him: it being more than just for the 'son' he'd always wanted, perhaps, but for his actual son? It might also explain Jordan's attitude, her constant antagonism over the years – instinctive perhaps at first, but, later, more than just objection to this 'intruder' into her family life: suspicion leading to jealousy perhaps, that this 'son' that her father had maybe always wanted had legitimately usurped her position.

In the end, or course, his uncle will be the only person able to say whether it is likely that any of this is true. And Peter doubts he'll ever have the courage to broach the matter to Uncle John. Or even whether he would want to. For their relationship is as good and close as it could be: John has *de facto* been a father to Peter in every possible way.

And now, hot on the heels of this anger comes guilt. For he's been concentrating on the effect that all this has had on himself, without any thought for the way in which it must have affected the lives and wellbeing of those closest and dearest to him – just as, all his life, he's never previously given any thought to their past at all. So, they floundered their way through life, made mistakes, did things wrongly – as he himself has done. He's blamed them for his misfortunes, particularly blamed his father. But who could know what influences in their own backgrounds had given rise to the mistakes they'd made. As Sylvia Stanton had once said, if one wholly blames one's parents for one's own inadequacies and misfortunes where does the parcel stop? – it could go back endlessly over previous generations. And would he, in their place, have avoided those selfsame stumbles and wrong turns along the way? Alternatively, if he'd known any of this could he then have achieved glory at school, as opposed to his relative failures; if he'd learned what had made his father what he was, been able to understand why his father had done the things he'd done, been no longer under the shadow of his 'desertion', would it have made any difference? Somehow he doubts it. When it comes to it, he thinks, each has to be responsible for his own progress and his own destiny; one cannot go on blaming others, not even one's parents, for one's own disappointments and weaknesses.

Nevertheless, he yearns now to be able to go back, to have had the opportunity, insight and courage to talk over with them their failings and uncertainties, the influences in their lives which had forged them and deformed them. Too late now; and probably always a pipe dream. Is this the stumbling-block in the affairs of folk in general, he wonders, that they are too immersed, cannot look down objectively on what they do and why they do it? – the *Munich Agreements* of life, wherein personal needs and pretences get in the way of what is necessary, so that it is only later, when the vagaries of the photographic negative have been turned into the clarity of the print, that the true picture becomes clear? So that at Munich, for instance, Chamberlain had seen in Hitler only what he'd wanted to see, what his people had wanted him to see, resulting in their chasing shadows when they should have been staring into the fierce light of day?

Anyway, just where this leaves him so far as his relationship with Jordan is concerned, he doesn't know. Whatever the truth, she believes what she has told him, and there may be no altering that. Only time will tell. And he's not sure that he cares any longer. He's beginning to see her ever more clearly, in the 'fierce light of day'.

The intercom clicks and rustles into life, Beal's voice competing against the background hiss of oxygen intruding on his microphone. 'Out in the clear now: eyes peeled everyone.'

Peter peers out of the cockpit window and, as he mentally shakes himself out of his morbid preoccupations as a dog shakes itself free of mud and water, is vaguely startled to find himself here in the present. Yet his ponderings surely cannot have lasted long – as in a dream, thoughts seemingly protracted, but in reality perhaps lasting only a minute or two. Outside, the sky is now clear, moonlight pale on the propellers and engine cowlings; and small, broken clouds scud below like a shoal of silvery fish.

A tense silence is followed by the voices of the three gunners in turn. 'No sign of intruders, skipper.' In Mahon's case his voice on this occasion carries a distinct note of disappointment.

'Righto,' Beal replies, 'but stay alert. We'll descend to eight thousand. Will maintain this vector for another five minutes, Johnno, in case jerry is following our original course. Be ready to give me a new bearing, then, will you.'

'Right on, Skip.'

'Doc, put a hand on these two throttle levers, will you.'

Peter, taken unawares at being addressed in this formal manner with an unexpected demand by Beal, looks up in alarm, and sees Beal looking at him with that amused, slightly bemused, fashion so familiar from days of old. In an instant he's back at school. Clearly, Beal has the same thought. With a grin he points to the two levers in question, as though explaining something syllable by syllable, and explains, 'I need to balance the port engine, and need an additional hand. Don't look so worried, they won't bite. Just don't move them, that's all.'

'Good on yer, doc,' Johnson calls cheerfully. 'But watch out, he'll have you flying the bugger next... Mind you,' he mutters in mock *sotto voce*, 'that might be an improvement.'

'If you're going to slander your highly respected C.O., Johnson,' Beal says equally cheerfully, 'then you shouldn't do it over the airways. Consider yourself on a court martial when we get back.'

'You mean, *if* we get back, don't you, Skipper?' comes the lugubrious voice of Donaldson from the nose turret.

'And the same goes for you, Jock,' Beal says blithely. 'Anyway, enough of this chit-chat. Let's concentrate on the job in hand. We're now at angels eight. Come off oxygen.'

Peter, switching off his own and unfastening the mask, glad to be rid of the coldness wafting into his face and irritating his nose, is nevertheless interested to find that at first he begins to feel slightly breathless without it, even though he's sitting doing nothing. Only too well aware of the euphoria that can ensue as the result of even slight anoxia, he wonders whether it is entirely wise to be without it at this altitude; but he knows that the supplies have to be carefully husbanded. Anyway, he doubts whether anyone could become euphoric in this damned cold. For the first time he really begins to understand what these bomber crews have to put up with in sheer bloody discomfort, never mind the constant apprehension. He brings to mind what one of the blokes had said to him some time ago: 'Exciting? – no, Doc, it's ninety per cent utter boredom and ten per cent sheer terror!' Then he has the thought that it could all become a lethal cocktail: cold, boredom and relative lack of oxygen leading to dangerous inattention – particularly among the less experienced crews. Could that be part of the reason why crews on their first half dozen trips had four or five times the average risk of not coming back? Were they taught about any of these things during training? He doesn't know.

The Wellington drones noisily on, seeming at times to be in danger of shaking itself to bits. Outside, beyond the plane, with nothing to reflect the moonlight – at present not even any cloud – all is blackness, stars clear-cut, like diamonds. They could be alone in the world. Perhaps there is something to be said for flying in formation, after all? At least there's something else to see. But also something to bump into – he knows that collisions in mid-air do occur from time to time; it's just that no one wants to talk about those. He peers down toward the ground – or what he imagines to be the ground: a darkness seemingly deeper than that all around them. Then, as he looks, he imagines he sees pinpoints of light coming and going, wonders whether it's a trick of the eyes, or perhaps some carelessness in shielding lights on some road or other. The next moment the aircraft rocks violently, there's an almighty bang, heard clearly in spite of the background noise and the insulation of his helmet, and out of the window he sees a puff of black smoke, and then another. For a second he can't think what's going on. Something gone wrong in one of the engines? He looks across at Beal, who's looking in his direction, grinning. Beal holds his mask up to his face and clicks on the microphone. 'No need for alarm, Doc,' he says. 'Just a little bit of heavy flak. They got lucky with that one, though not nearly close enough; and they're not likely to trouble us much. There's never been a great deal around here. Don't worry, you'll see the proper stuff before long.'

Peter can imagine the grins on the faces of the other members of the crew, and braces himself for some verbal flak over the intercom. But Johnson inadvertently comes to his rescue.

'New heading, Skipper. One three zero. Repeat, one three zero.'

'One three zero it is, Johnno. Speed one-eighty – one eight zero.'

'That'll take us some ten miles south of *Koblenz* in about thirty minutes' time, Skip. You should be able to see the Rhine at that point, dead ahead. I'll give you our new heading after that, which will probably be one seven zero. That should take us to the assembly south west of *Karlsruhe*. ETA 0115.'

'Roger, Johnno.'

Peter is startled to learn that they are now actually over Germany – although why this should surprise him he can't think: Holland and Belgium are every bit a part of enemy territory as is Germany itself, so in effect they've been flying over 'Germany' ever since they left the Channel. But a part of him thinks that somehow the *Fatherland* will be more assiduously defended than will the occupied territories. He knows, though, that this info from Johnson is more for the benefit of the crew – and possibly for him – than for Beal. The navigator and the skipper would have discussed and agreed the plan of their route prior to take off. He's pleased to find they do take the trouble to keep the rest of the crew fully informed; shut off in their own private zones of responsibility it would be all-too-easy for the rest of the crew to feel isolated and therefore more vulnerable. He looks again at his watch. Twelve thirty. The time has indeed passed more quickly than he'd realised.

He allows his mind to drift once more into random thoughts: Beal at school, his resolute toughness, always a hard taskmaster yet never unfair. Then he remembers what Anna Beal had said about him, and wonders. Always difficult to truly assess people, particularly if the information comes through the eyes of others. A picture of David Munro floats before him, David in his first year at Bards, fresh, eager, and uncertain; finding Peter 'helpful' – although Peter has no memory, or awareness, of this. A pang of regret runs through him, of wasted lives, wasted opportunities, a cavalcade of imperfect relationships – and he flushes in the darkness as he remembers that evening with Athena Munro, following David's death. And his fantasies about Anna Beal, imaginings of what it must be like to make love to her, so that he was sucked into misconstruing her motives when she asked him to meet her that time.

He comes to with a start, comprehends that he must have dozed off, hopes Beal hadn't noticed. Bewilderingly, the cockpit is flooded with a dazzling light, the intercom a cacophony of curses. 'Shut it! All of you!' Beal's voice slams them into silence. 'Waring, grab those levers, will you!

Eyes peeled for bandits, everyone.' He feels the plane sliding sideways, turning, going down steeply, engines screaming, revolving on itself, so that he's flung sideways in his seat, straps biting painfully into his shoulder and chest, the plane turning more and more tightly, yawing as it does so, seeming to be about to go into a spin, and he knows it's out of control. He tries to look at Beal, but cannot turn his head, finds he's looking out of the side of the canopy down towards the dark mass of the ground, except that there's no longer entirely darkness but long beams of searchlights sweeping to and fro, bright banners of white and yellow splitting the blackness into segments through which strings of fairy lights in white, green and red are rising lazily to meet him in almost friendly fashion, seeming to whirl around the rotating plane, seeking him out, only to suddenly whip up speed as they draw near and then whizz past in venomous silence, dawning on him that this is tracer, already celebrating, he knows, his certain death.

'Keep those bloody levers steady!' Beal's voice is unrecognisable, a strangled snarl – and Peter is startled to find that he does indeed have his hand on the throttle levers, unaware of how it had got there – and he wonders What is the point? But they are now back into darkness, the light flak vanished, the instrument panels once more a reassuring glow; and with a final, wrenching, body-straining series of vibrations, as though the wings are about to come off, the Wellington levels out, its engines screeching their protest.

Peter's hand is unceremoniously knocked from the levers by Beal as he takes over; and someone says, 'Christ, that was like coming down a fucking helter-skelter!'

'More like a bloody corkscrew going into a cork,' Johnson growls. 'For crying out loud, Skipper, where did you learn to do something like that?'

'Jesus, where did that flak come from, anyway?' Baldwin exclaims. 'How the hell did that light fix on us so suddenly?'

'Aye, it came frae nowhere right into my fucking face!' This is Donaldson from the nose turret. 'Ah'm still blind frae it.'

'Well let's hope you stay that way, Jock,' calls Baldwin. 'You might actually manage to hit the bloody target then, when it comes to it.'

Shaky laughter follows, through which Beal's voice cuts sharply. 'All right, boys, settle down. Let's concentrate. We're not out of it yet. There could be night fighters around as well. I think they just got lucky there, but obviously they know we're here.'

Long seconds of tense silence follow, as the Wellington starts to regain height. Then Johnson's voice comes on the intercom. 'Your heading should be one-seventy, Skipper, one seven zero. Can you still see the Rhine? It should be on your port beam.'

'Confirmed. Tell me Johnno, what was all that light flak doing there? I thought you'd said we'd be well clear of *Karlsruhe*?'

And so we were, Skipper, by my reckoning. I can't understand it. You didn't see anything looking like invasion barges going down the Rhine, I suppose? They'd be pretty keen to protect those this time round.'

'Can't say I did. They'd be hard to spot by moonlight, anyway, I imagine. How about anyone else? You, Jock, for instance?'

'No, sir. Nae a thing.'

Beal glances in Peter's direction, but doesn't say anything. Had Beal noticed he'd been asleep beforehand? He goes hot and cold at the thought.

'Can you confirm present speed and height, Skip, please?' Johnson continues.

'Speed one-eighty, one eight zero; altitude just coming to niner thousand. Rendezvous height is twelve, correct?'

'Correct. At present speed and course we should meet up with the main stream in twelve minutes. Then five minutes to target.'

'Right we are, chaps, everyone on their toes. Eyes peeled for our own squadrons. And jerry will be well aware by now of where we're likely to be heading. Could be bandits from above or below before we hit the flak. Assuming we manage to join up with the squadron, we go in with the second wave, scheduled for 0120 hours, at eleven thousand. We'll go in then, whatever. We go for the red markers, which should be immediately behind the yellow. If they're any further back, we'll overshoot them by ten seconds, Jock – there's been far too much creep-back recently.'

'Wilco, Skipper.' Donaldson's voice carries all the enthusiasm of a man going to his execution; but Peter knows this is normal for him, that he has the reputation of being absolutely stalwart when it comes to doing his job.

He shivers, but knows it is from excitement rather than fear. He's pleased about that; but knows that fear is likely to follow. He can sense the rising tension among the crew: it's almost palpable. But again it's not from fear, he thinks, more from the adrenaline that will be surging through them, everyone keyed up in the hope of finding the courage to perform well, to 'not let the side down', to avoid being seen as the weak link. For each there will be no immediate thought of injury or death: at a young age those things happen only to someone else. And the thrill of the moment blocks out the intellect; if it were not so, all of them, at least the more sensible ones, would end up being branded as 'Lacking Moral Fibre'. The numbers of such would soar, the system would collapse. Only when the intellect kicks in, in those quieter moments, will the fear once more start to eat into them. For all of them know the statistics, even though they're played down. It's simple arithmetic. For each and every member of aircrew in Bomber Command at the present time the chances of surviving their first tour of thirty ops is not much more than one in two; for those who do survive and go on to do their obligatory second tour, it seems the odds against surviving become even shorter. Every man knows that the more time goes on the more likely he is to die or be mutilated. It does no good to point out to them that strictly speaking, statistically, it's simply not true – that, like tossing a coin, it doesn't matter how often you do it, the odds of it coming down heads or tails are the same on every occasion. Their perception of the contrary is unshakable. And that is the mark of their immense courage. For men like Johnson, Baldwin, Donaldson, Mahon and Beal (particularly Beal, who's had more exposure than any of them, and has no real need to be here) who've done this so many times before and yet continue to do it week after week, sometimes several times a week, it is bravery of the highest order, for it consists of a dogged determination to go on, in spite of knowing that one's life, precious though it is, is likely to be cut short. And Peter is swamped by an even greater clear-eyed admiration for them. All right, so there's nothing really new in that. He's always been full of admiration for them, envious almost. But it's different now that he's actually experiencing what they have to go through. Then, almost immediately, his paltry pride at being with them is cut short and he writhes in self-contempt which must mirror, surely, the contempt they feel for him. For suddenly it strikes him that he is being indulged, that he is having the best of both worlds: he is up here on a single op, his first and last whatever happens, yet has the advantage of being with a seasoned crew. Unlike them, the odds of anything happening to him are long indeed. Or are they? Reason reminds him that the odds are the same for each and every trip – but influenced by the nature of the target. And this one is known to be 'sticky'. His heart takes a lurch.

He looks yet again at his watch – surreptitiously, for fear that Beal might notice and recognise it as anxiety. Five past one. He is aware his hand is shaking. This is what it must have been like in the last lot, for his father and all the others in the trenches, waiting for the sound of the whistle which would demand that they leave relative safety and go over the top, knowing that shells, machine guns, grenades and, finally, if they make it, the bayonets, are waiting.

Now, all at once, he doesn't know which is the worst. The cold. Or the noise. Or the thunder of fear suddenly there in his chest, and the ice in the pit of his stomach. Beside him, Beal, hands quite still on the control column, peering to left and right through the Perspex windows, might well be out on a relaxed Sunday afternoon drive. It reminds him of Beal on the rugby field at school, going about his tasks in a calm business-like manner. Actually enjoying what he's doing. Of course he'd never been there to witness Beal in those pulsating minutes before the game, the team together waiting to come out, legs and arms jittery, adrenaline coursing through their bodies.

Silence ensues. For each man, time for thought? More likely the blanking out of thought; time spent in the struggle to deny emotion.

'Should be seeing the mainstream any time now.' Johnson's voice crackles like a gunshot.

'Blenheims below, one to two thousand feet, to port and to starboard.' Donaldson, from the nose turret, confirms almost simultaneously, for once sharp and positive.

'New heading ninety, skipper, niner zero.'

'Roger, Johnno, niner zero. Climbing to twelve thousand. Watch out for our chaps, everybody. We don't want to be mistaken for the sodding enemy – or to be colliding with them. Might make us a bit unpopular.'

'Target illumination at eleven o'clock, skipper, about ten miles away.' Donaldson says. In spite of a certain excitement in his tone, he still manages to sound morose about it.

Peter looks hurriedly in the direction indicated, the nose of the Wellington gently turning to follow his line of gaze as Beal makes the small correction. Trying to look in several different directions at once, Peter feels as though his eyes are coming out of his head. He understands that the risks of collision with other Wellingtons coming in at the same altitude must be very high indeed at this moment. But for the moment he can't tear his gaze away from the scene now straight ahead and below them. Coming from the ground, and reflected back by clouds, can be seen a great pulsating glow in ever changing colours of red, white and orange, just like the dying embers of a gigantic fire. Why he should be surprised to immediately understand that that is exactly what it is, he doesn't know – except of course that these are no embers but the advanced stages of conflagration. Another thought strikes him as he tears his eyes away to nervously look again for other aircraft: Beal just a minute or so ago had said 'climbing to twelve thousand', when earlier he had confirmed the attack altitude to be 'eleven thousand'. He ponders this for a few seconds, and it comes to him that the skipper must be anxious to get above any other Wellingtons that might be around, that coming up to join them at an angle from below would increase the risk of collision: far better to briefly pass through them until it is known exactly where they are. At least, this is what he assumes to be Beal's intention. Peter has heard, often enough, crews saying that glimpses of other aircraft on a raid are few and far between in the darkness, silhouettes seen only occasionally against the backlight of fires or searchlights. Indeed no one really knows how often bombers are brought down by 'friendly' bombs falling from those above them: it only needs a minor error in the timing of different squadrons and disparate aircraft going in at various altitudes for such mistakes to occur. And the same factors applied with regard to collisions. For, to all intents and purposes from a purely visual point of view they might as well be up here alone in the blackness.

'Confirm time.' (Beal's voice makes him jump, so immersed is he in these nervous thoughts.) '0113, agreed?'

'Agreed, Skipper,' Johnson replies.

'Righto, boys, then we'll begin our run, at eleven thousand. Donaldson, Mahon: any sign of aircraft below us?'

'No, none, Skipper,' they reply in unison.

'All right, here we go, then. Flak ahead.'

CHAPTER TWENTY-EIGHT

Peter closes his eyes and opens them again. Does he think that by doing this the scene would somehow have disappeared? For in front, rapidly approaching, is a widely spread curtain of light: a network of roving searchlight beams overlaid by a trelliswork of moving glittering tracer. On this are suspended, randomly, the yellow and orange blooms of shell-bursts, each of which hangs there for a moment before dispersing to a dysmorphic drifting black cloud silhouetted against the light. It would have a kind of beauty if it weren't for the knowledge of what it signifies. It seems impossible that anything can pass through this and remain intact. Also, oddly, it achieves the feat of making the night sky blacker whilst at the same time illuminating the scene around so that, silhouetted from time to time, ahead and below, briefly glimpsed, are the shapes of other aircraft, visually there one second, gone the next. And, even as he stares, now mesmerised, some distance below them and to their right comes a violent flash then a ball of flame which, slowly at first then gathering pace, falls away, like a meteor falling to earth. Yet there is no sound, only the background noise of their own engines. It's like watching a silent film. Over the intercom, voice thickened by repressed emotion, someone states the obvious: 'Some crew've bought it, poor buggers.' Left unsaid are the thoughts, Were they friends of ours? Is it to be us next?

And now, as they draw closer to this incredible scene, the sound begins to filter in, a muffled din growing in intensity, a series of bangs and reverberations, felt as much as heard, which seem at times to be coming from within their own craft, until they are surrounded by it, immersed in it, in total uproar; and the Wellington bucks and rocks as though possessed. Not far head of them another plane, now easily identified as a Wellington, becomes caught in a cone of three or four searchlights. As it manoeuvres desperately to break free, a second later an even brighter trace of cannon shell wafts across it, raking it from nose to stern. For long moments the aircraft seems to stand still. A couple of parachutes appear, canopies open, beginning their slow descent towards the hell below. Then the plane simply disappears, spiralling into the blackness. It seems to him at this moment that nothing, absolutely nothing, will be able to escape this conflagration.

'Right, Bomb Aimer, you now have command.' Beal's voice, calm and matter-of-fact as ever, jolts Peter out of his trance. Peering out of the side window down toward the ground a short distance ahead of them, he is somewhat surprised to find that what, a few minutes ago, had been an almost friendly glow in the distance has now become an inferno of brightness and colour, in places obscured by what can only be smoke, but stretching almost as far as the eye can see. The fires down there in one or two areas must surely be billowing to a considerable height. Yet from this altitude that isn't evident: the pattern is one of areas of red, white and orange coming and going, pulsating, becoming bright one moment, darkening the next. It's like looking down on a cosy fire in a domestic hearth. The reality is not imaginable. It is too remote.

'Roger, skipper.' Jock Donaldson's reply over the intercom is also amazingly calm. 'Port a bit. Bit more. Steady.'

'Speed one twenty-five – one two fifer – height eleven thousand, angels eleven.' Beal's voice in return is staccato, unemotional. 'Estimated wind-speed fifteen knots, one-fifer, from starboard.'

'Roger, skipper.'

Peter visualises Donaldson – flat on his stomach, peering down through his Perspex dome, making the last-minute adjustments to his bombsight, lining up the crosswires on his target – and wonders how he can make any sense whatsoever of the apparent chaos down there, or indeed fix on anything through the frequent pitch and yaw of the aircraft. He wonders also how the man can remain so calm when he must surely feel particularly vulnerable to all the flak that is being flung up at them, his belly bared to all as it were.

Then Donaldson's voice comes again, more urgent. 'I think the markers are all short, skipper. I can see the river, the *Neckar*. Target should be northeast of that, where it bends. Mostly everything has fallen south of that.'

'Can you attain?' Beal's voice is crisp, decisive.

'Negative. Too far right, and overshooting.'

'Abort. I say again, abort.'

Peter is flooded with relief. Good, let's get out of here as fast as we can! He's convinced that any moment they're about to be hit, some of the shell-bursts coming perilously close, the beams of searchlights momentarily touching them then moving on, tracer arcing up towards them missing them it seems by a hairsbreadth.

Then Beal speaks again; and Peter's blood turns to ice, he can't believe what he's hearing.

'Right, chaps, we'll go round again. That all right with you?' Beal's voice is light with irony, but determined.

Whether Peter groans out loud he doesn't know. Fear, a cold fist gripping him in a way he's never known before, and could never have imagined, brings with it the sudden certainty of his own death. And all at once he's no longer here, ridiculously suspended in an uncaring sky, but crouched in the mud of the trenches waiting for the whistles to blow. Beside him, his father, too, crouches, along with all the others, bayonets fixed, each man staring, features frozen, avoiding the eyes of others, seemingly gazing out but in reality looking inward, each man isolated, alone although sharing the moment with thousands. His father's face has that gaunt look, one of helplessness laced with anger, a look that reveals the certain knowledge that life has now been reduced to this: an ignominious farce in which all volition has been taken away, the individual reduced to the status of puppet, a puppet about to be tossed carelessly and uselessly, without purpose, into the flames. It's a look, he knows at this moment, that is surely reflected in his own features. It's a look remembered so well from childhood. And now, finally, he understands. It's a look that never goes away. The product of anxiously and repeatedly staring at the imminent likelihood of one's own death or dismemberment without it ever becoming a certainty, it becomes etched indelibly. It's a look that eats into the soul. Only when time itself has created some sort of hiatus between the events and the present can the memory become relegated to the past, and even then not truly so, for in the stuff of nightmares it returns to become once more the present. He knows now that this was the spectre – one of the spectres – that had haunted his father throughout Peter's childhood. He had always thought that it was because of his childhood presence that his father had been as he'd been; he knows now that it was in spite of his presence, his child's innocence. It had had nothing to do with him – other than that, in his innocence, he'd been incapable by his presence of banishing the past. For he understands now that a gulf exists between those who have been through the experience and those who have merely heard about it – a gulf that cannot be crossed, a wall that cannot be climbed; the means do not exist for it to happen. For, even those who have shared the experience usually cannot share the memory: to give it voice would be to re-establish its reality. His father's anger had in fact been projected far beyond his son: Peter had simply happened to be in the way.

The brief and sudden silence within the plane, created by Beal's words and occupied by Peter's thoughts, is broken when Johnson says, 'Oh, yes; bloody marvellous!' But there is humour there also, beneath the sarcasm. No one else says anything.

Already the aircraft is banking sharply to port and climbing. Momentarily it is caught in a beam of light, and then passes through it. Peter is aghast. It seems senseless. Why not just drop the bloody bombs, like everyone else, and get the hell out of it! And now, mercifully, they're in total darkness again: as the plane continues to bank he's looking down past Beal and there's nothing, only the peace of a void, no conflict, no inferno, no death, and he finds himself silently praying, Dear God, let it all stay away! And he sees again an arm protruding from a broken building, a child's arm, a life snuffed out before its time, and it strikes him, amazingly for the first time, what has been happening below. Those are not just buildings being obliterated down there, but whole families, consumed by fire and suffering, and by the fear of agony and death. And in that same instant he finds he cannot care. For, as the plane continues to turn, their own personal inferno swings once more into view, now distant but drawing closer, the tail-enders of the bomber force, dark shadows briefly glimpsed against the flare of destruction, undergoing their own purgatory; and even as he watches one more explodes in a ball of fire, and another declaims its end as it spirals downwards trailing smoke and flames; and Peter, too, now strangely all-too-briefly calm, is instead once more consumed by anger and hate for the enemy, for those below.

The Wellington has levelled out, has throttled back, and is dropping as though of its own volition. But Beal reveals his involvement as he speaks, a note almost of exultation in his voice. 'Right, boys, here we go again. We'll go in at six thousand this time, now that we're a tail-ender – no one above us and all that.'

It's Donaldson who breaks the silence which greets this statement, broadening his accent in comic style. 'Ye'll let us have a wee look at yon bar ye'll get to your DFC, will ye, skipper?'

Although said lightly it's spiced with resentment, clearly insulting and even more clearly grossly insubordinate. Peter imagines he can hear a sharp intake of breath from the rest of the crew – or perhaps it's his own. Any tension as a result of this is quickly broken, though, by Johnson.

'It's you who's to blame, you dumb Scot: it's you who just had to blab about us all being off target. Anyway, it'll give you at least a sporting chance to hit something worthwhile this time! In any case, you know what they say: the lower you are the safer it is.'

There's a concerted groan from the others. Peter knows what they're referring to. He's heard this debate on a number of occasions in the Mess and in the pub, usually after several beers. The theory promoted from time to time is that, because an anti-aircraft gun has a presumed vertical 'acquisition arc' of about 140 degrees, making it's 'killing zone' an inverted-cone shape, the closer one flies to the bottom 'point' of the 'inverted cone' the shorter the distance through it and the less time there is in which to be hit. It's full of fallacies, of course, and everyone knows it: not the least of these being that the lower you are the less time it takes for the shells to reach you – one cancels out the other. In any case, if it could be applied at all it could only be applied to a single gun and not to batteries of a dozen or more. That the argument cropped up at all was simply a reflection of the need they had to bolster their morale in the face of increasing pressure from above to make the bombing more accurate – which meant going in lower.

As it is, Beal sounds merely amused when he says, 'All right, Jock, let's see what you can do. The quicker we get this properly done the quicker we can all go home. Now at six thousand feet, speed one two five, wind speed and direction as before, fifteen knots from starboard. You have command.'

'Roger, skipper. Steady as you go.'

Peter suddenly feels as though they're now very much alone up here in an empty sky, the sole object of the enemy's spleen. He wonders if the others feel the same. Searchlight beams play briefly on them before losing them again. All around them are the flashes of shell-bursts and the deadly lines of tracer floating up towards them with spurious grace. Once more the plane bucks and heaves like a wild thing, the pitch of the engines fluctuating with the attempts by Beal to maintain as steady a course and attitude as possible. The overall noise is unbelievable, the din from outside now drowning the sound of the engines. Yet through it, on the intercom, Donaldson's voice maintains a steady stream of instruction: 'Steady. Steady. Port a little. Too much. Steady. Steady.'

A sudden bang is very much louder than the rest, and is accompanied by a symphony of whistling sounds clearly heard within the aircraft. Someone groans, a note of pain it seems – Peter thinks fearfully it might be Beal – and someone swears. The Wellington shudders, hesitates as though wondering whether it's able to go on, then resumes its previous rhythm. Above and behind Peter's head he's aware that there are a number of rents in the skin of the plane – he can feel cold air from outside blowing down on him. He realises, sickeningly, that they've been hit. He looks hastily in the direction of Beal, but is unable to make out any detail. He wonders whether to ask; senses that this is hardly the time.

Donaldson's voice at the same time is urgent. 'Veer right, Skipper! Right! More! Steady! Steady. I have the target.'

And reassuringly the plane responds.

Peter looks down towards the ground. The fires are so much more obvious from this height, one running into another. He wonders again how on earth Donaldson and Beal can make out any sort of useful detail in the tumult below. Or how anyone can manage to survive it.

There comes another enormous bang, and once again the plane staggers before continuing. Peter wonders if the others are praying as he is. Not consciously so – his thoughts are too preoccupied for that – but he is aware that in the deeper reaches of his mind there is a constant litany of primal pleas to God.

'Steady. Steady.' Donaldson is droning on, apparently oblivious to anything else, fully focussed on the job in hand. As, obviously, is Beal. Dear Christ, Peter thinks, let it be soon!

No sooner has he had the thought that as a prayer it was hardly appropriate, given what he was asking to happen to those below, than his plea is answered. The plane, suddenly relieved of its 4000lb burden, leaps upwards, accompanied by Donaldson's triumphant shout, 'Bombs away!'

'Well done, Jock,' calls Beal, as the throttles thrust fully open and the Wellington labours into a climb, at the same time banking to starboard. 'I should think that was bang on target.' Then, 'Perhaps we should go round once more to take photographs, d'you think?'

If it was meant seriously, which was doubtful, the chorus of protest is answer enough. And, as quickly as anything that has happened this night, they're away from all the sound and fury, alone in the darkness, the engines once more a steady drone, heading for home. Peter glances at the glow of the clock on the facia in front of him, then at the luminous dial of his watch. One confirms the other. 0129 hours. They've been over the target area – not once, but twice – a mere sixteen minutes. It's seemed like a lifetime. Yet now, with the coming of relief, it might never have happened.

Beal's voice all at once sounds weary, coming out of the darkness. 'Have you managed to set a course for us, Johnno?'

'Right on, Skip. Maintain two-six-niner until we've re-crossed the Rhine north-east of Strasbourg. That should be in about thirty minutes. And that'll then take us north of Nancy and south of Chalons, as agreed. Shortly after that, southwest of Epernay, we'll turn onto two-nine-zero to take us midway between Paris and Reims. I make it a tail wind now, of ten knots; d'you copy?'

'Affirmative.' There's an additional element now to the tiredness in Beal's voice, a something that Peter can't quite interpret. But the tone is still positive, tinged with irony. 'We've taken a few hits, as I'm sure you're all aware. Any damage reports forthcoming? Or injuries? Each in turn, please, according to drill.'

One by one, each crew member gives his report, lacing it with a humorous quip. This is followed by silence, until Beal says drily, 'Peter? – you're still with us, I take it?'

Peter, registering with a start that he still isn't thinking of himself as a member of the crew, hurriedly says, 'Yes. All right...Thank you.' He's aware that, given the context, his final expression, slipped in instinctively, sounds incongruous.

'Right, chaps,' Beal says. 'Switching to *George* for the moment. Peter, would you come and look at this for me, please. And bring the First Aid kit, and the torch – they're both in the cubbyhole on your right.'

Now he's able to identify that extra note in Beal's voice. It's one of pain.

Johnson also is quickly onto it. 'You been hit, Skip?' There's anxiety in the question.

'Only a scratch. Nothing to worry about.'

'Mm. Something to be said for bringing along your own personal physician, then, after all.'

There was no unkindness intended in the Australian's attempt at humour, Peter knows, born as it is out of nervousness at the thought of the potential loss of their pilot – but it is a reminder of just how superfluous he's seen to be by the others. And as he struggles out of his harness, finds the torch, and stumbles towards Beal, who is already making an attempt to shrug his way out of his flying jacket, he too is anxious about what he's going to find.

It quickly becomes obvious. Caught in the beam of the flashlight the already-congealing blood on the skipper's left hand and on the rim of the control column gleams in ominous fashion. Gently he helps Beal ease out of the bulky sleeve of his jacket. The sleeve of his uniform tunic also is sodden, and a jagged rent can be seen in the upper part.

'Shrapnel?' he asks. 'Or a bullet?'

'Must have been shrapnel. The only tracers anywhere near us were cannon. Would have taken my arm with it, together with the cockpit.' It is said without drama.

'Have we any scissors?'

'In with the kit.'

Of course.

'Need a hand, Doc?' This is Donaldson from somewhere below them, now back in his gun turret.

It's Beal who answers. 'No, stay put, Jock. And keep your eyes peeled, everyone. As you know, there've been increasing reports of night-fighters over France in recent weeks, probably using some form of RDF. We don't want to run into one of those at the last push; we need to see him before he finally pinpoints us. Remember, momentary exhaust flare is all you'll see of him, so keep alert.'

Having obtained the scissors, by the light of the torch which he parks on a convenient bulkhead Peter cuts away the sleeve of Beal's tunic and then that of his shirt and examines the wound on Beal's upper arm as best he can, swabbing gently with a gauze square. At least there doesn't seem to be any arterial bleeding, but the laceration looks horribly deep and it is evident that the lateral head of the triceps has been partly severed. Beal must be in considerable pain. Could the offending shrapnel still be in there, he thinks, and probes a little deeper, evoking a muffled curse and yelp of anguish from Beal.

'Sorry. Just wondering if there could still be anything in there.'

'Doubt it. There doesn't seem to be. These things come at tremendous speed. Probably would have broken the bone if it had lodged, and that seems to be alright.'

Peter puts a hand on Beal's shoulder and the other under his elbow, and applies cautious longitudinal pressure.

'Any pain when I do that?'

'No more than before, no.' (It's said with dry humour, but from force of habit Peter perceives a mild admonition at the imprecise form of his query.)

'No, well, as you say, the bone seems to be alright.'

He decides then that the injury is very close to the course of the radial nerve, as well. 'Any loss of sensation or of movement in your thumb and index finger?'

'No. I wish there were! It's bloody painful – seems to be going right down to that part of my hand.'

'That's alright, then.'

'It may be alright for you, but it bloody well isn't for me!'

At that moment to Peter it seems immaterial to explain. Instead, he says, 'It needs stitching and x-raying, but that'll obviously have to wait until we're back. I'll put a bandage on it, and that should stop the bleeding. Do you think you're going to manage?'

'You mean I've got a choice?' This time the impatience in Beal's voice is obvious. It had been a flabby sort of question.

Then Beal relents a little. 'I may need help with the control column from time to time, particularly when it comes to landing. But I'll let you know when and what when the time comes.'

'Would you like something for the pain?'

'A couple of pints of Burton's wouldn't come amiss! – but I don't suppose you've got anything that isn't going to make me drowsy?'

Peter considers. There's some morphine in the cupboard, but that clearly won't do. And aspirin wouldn't be much use for something like this. Feeling as impotent as ever, he replies, 'No, afraid not.'

'That's what I thought.'

At this point Mahon's voice comes over the intercom, from the rear of the aircraft. 'There's a persistent slick of oil on the port side of my turret, skipper. It must be coming from the port engine, I think?' It's said calmly, but there's a certain venom in his tone – yet another thing to hate the Germans for.

'Much, Pat?'

'A fair bit, Skip. It's running off in dribbles.'

Beal grunts both his acknowledgement and at the same time his irritation, and can be seen to be peering at the dials in front of him.

'Temperature and pressure seem alright at the moment. What distance and time have we got left, Johnno?'

'About four-forty miles, Skip. What are we doing? – two hundred knots, with still a light tail wind? So, two hours twenty or thereabouts.'

'Plus an hour if I feather it.' Beal's more or less talking to himself, thinking aloud for the benefit of the others. 'Cutting it a bit fine. It'll be pre-dawn before we're over the Channel. We'd be a sitting duck in half light. We'll just keep going for the time being. Peter, keep an eye on these two dials, here, will you – port-side oil pressure and engine temperature. If either starts to change, sing out.'

Peter, completing the bandaging, murmurs his acknowledgement and returns to his seat, re-fastening his harness. For a while he can't seem to tear his gaze away from the two dials in question; but after some minutes when the flickering needles have barely changed their position, he begins to relax. Perhaps things are going to be all right after all. With a little bit of luck they'll be safely back at base within two and a half hours. He experiences once again that end-of-term, returning-home feeling, a mixture of relief and elation (although experience in the past had taught him the effect was entirely ephemeral, soon overtaken by a sense of disenchantment with the routines of everyday life). And immediately once more comes the guilt, knowing that for the others, with the possible exception of Beal, it'll be 'back to school' again if not the next night then the night after or the night after that. And, anyway, making a comparison between that and going back to school is effete in the

435

extreme; there can be no comparison, and that the idea had entered his head at all simply emphasises how pathetic is his own view of himself. Nevertheless, he allows himself to bathe in those comforting memories of the past: the summer smell of bracken, gorse and pinewood, converting the skin-warmth of the sun into an olfactory experience as well; the contrasting coolness of water, the burbling of a mountain stream and the slap-slap of waves against the hull of a boat. And in turn he's gripped by the sweet pain of nostalgia. Angrily he tears himself away from his thoughts, and stares out of the cockpit window, past the outline of Beal's head to the blackness beyond. Something pale gleams out there, and it takes him a few seconds to recognise that it's the light of the moon, now low on the horizon, reflected off the engine cowling. It takes him a few more seconds to understand therefore that the cloud must have now considerably broken up; and that if he can see moonlight glinting on the skin of the Wellington, then so will the crew of any jerry night-fighter in the area. And there's something else out there, something which for seconds at a time obscures the reflected glimmer of moonlight. With horror he recognizes it as smoke. Hurriedly, fearfully, he looks at the instrument panel: the needle of the temperature gauge is up, not a lot, but definitely up; whilst the needle of the oil-pressure gauge is almost at zero. With a panic that is engendered not only by the present but also by recollections of the past, he turns to look at Beal: the pilot's head is slumped forward, his chin resting upon his chest, asleep – or unconscious.

'Skipper,' he says urgently, the term of address unfamiliar upon his lips. 'Skipper!' Then remembers he hasn't turned on his intercom. 'Skipper!' he repeats.

Beal's head jerks up.

'Skipper, oil pressure is down, temperature rising. And I think there may be smoke from the port engine.'

Beal visibly shakes himself, his head swivelling from instrument panel to port engine. 'Oh, fuck!' he says. It's more an expression of irritation than of alarm.

Peter braces himself for the follow-up question: How long has it been like that? But Beal merely busies himself with taking over from auto-pilot and flicking various switches.

'Johnno,' Beal says. 'You got that? I've feathered the port engine.'

'Yeah, Skip. Got it. Speed down to one-twenty? Confirm?'

'Confirm.'

A few seconds silence, then, from Johnson, 'I make E.T.A. around 0450, provided there's no change in wind direction – and provided this old crate doesn't tear herself to bits before then. There's a howling gale through a ruddy great hole back here. Bloody cold it is, too! Anyway, that timing should leave us more than enough cover of darkness. And the moon's about to set.' Then, with the first intimation of anxiety, 'You okay to manage the controls on one engine, Skipper?'

Beal grunts his reply. 'So far, at least. If it gets too difficult I can get doc, here, to give me a hand. Baldwin, you still with us? You've been amazingly quiet.'

'Yes, Skipper. Still here. Just thinking.' In spite of the apparent calmness of the words, the nervousness in the mid-gunner's voice is all too evident.

'Yes, well be careful, all that thinking can be bad for you. Keep a weather eye open on that port engine, will you. There's no sign of fire at the moment, but you never know.'

'Righto, Skipper. Will do. I'll let you know as soon as I see anything.'

'That's the ticket. But keep an eye open for jerry, as well – on both sides.'

'I know what you're thinking, Brummie,' Mahon, from the tail, cuts in. 'You're thinking about the bacon and egg when we get in.' It's said with good humour, but he still manages to make it sound like an accusation – as if to say, This particular op isn't over yet, we still might have the chance to get another crack at jerry. Nevertheless, for Peter it carries a welcome ring of optimism, a conviction that they're going to make it. More than that: the reference to bacon and egg for breakfast is a reminder that crews coming back from an op are treated to that perk in recognition that for the moment they stand apart from other men, having come through the ordeal of battle. And for that one moment he, Peter, will be one of them.

His elation, though, is short-lived. There's still a long way to go. It brings home to him the differing experience of bomber crews and fighter boys in the R.A.F. The fighter pilot is on his own in the heat of battle, almost entirely dependent upon himself and himself alone. But his spell of exposure, although at times frantic and terrifying, is relatively brief; and if he is shot down and lives to tell the tale he is more often than not over his own home ground. The bomber crews, on the other hand, not only are exposed to many hours of risk, albeit at a lower intensity most of the time, but if they are shot down (which, after all, happens with as much frequency as it does for the fighter pilots, and with several men involved) then the likelihood is that it will be into enemy territory; no bacon and egg for them, when it happens. Yet it's the fighter boys who have been accorded all the glamour and acclaim. That can't be right, he thinks, and wonders why it is the case. Is it because the fighter pilots are seen as purely protective, defending hearth and home against the bringers of death and destruction? – each heroic, a St George riding out alone against the dragon? But what of the bomber crews? What of their role? They are the carriers of death and destruction to civilians, men, women and children, in the enemy camp. A less honourable pursuit, perhaps? And to what purpose? Yet Churchill and others have spelled it out clearly enough: stuck here in our island, on our own in the world and expecting invasion at any time, our only way of taking the war to the enemy, of hitting back, is by means of the bomber. And these men are risking life and limb, day in and day out, in order to do just that. Not only that, their courage in attacking the ports, the enemy shipping and the invasion barges, against considerable odds, back

437

in August and September, surely played as much a part in preventing the invasion then as did those weeks of the more grandly titled *Battle of Britain*. And no doubt would do so again in the weeks ahead. God willing. Yes, to be sure, Fighter Command had to continue to keep control of the skies over Britain if Hitler were again to be thwarted in the days to come; but his means of invasion had also to be destroyed. And only Bomber Command could do that.

With these thoughts he's now convinced that he did the right thing in coming on this trip: it's given him a whole lot of new insights. More than that, he's actually glad he came: it will enable him, in his own view, to hold his head just that little bit higher in the Mess. When they talk about these things in the future he will more properly know what it is they mean. And he's grateful to Beal for having made it possible.

Suddenly anxious, he glances across at Beal. Is the man holding up?

As though conscious of being looked at, Beal turns his head in Peter's direction and grins, his teeth gleaming in the semi-darkness; with some difficulty, using his left hand, he puts his mask up to his face and speaks into it.

'Wondering if I'm going to conk out, doc?'

'No…that is…how are you?'

'A bit rough – but alright. I tell you what, though, all this beats an average game of rugby any day, doesn't it?'

'It certainly does.' He makes the correct response, but has difficulty in putting any conviction into his voice. However, gratitude for Beal having given him this opportunity comes to the rescue – although, he's about to say 'I wouldn't have missed it for the world,' when he thinks just how smug this would sound, and says instead, 'It's certainly made me fully understand just what you chaps have to go through time after time.'

Beal grunts a non-committal reply, before grinning again and saying, 'Who would have thought all those years ago at Bard's that we'd one day find ourselves together in this sort of situation.'

His comment imparts a warm feeling of inclusion for Peter, and brings home to him the ever-changing complexity of relationships over time. He mumbles some sort of response; but somehow is instead thinking about 'Boomer' Johnson, so far from his homeland and having had to forge new relationships with erstwhile strangers. But then, as well as being extremely gregarious he's the sort of bloke who thrives on excitement – why else would he be here? It strikes him he doesn't even know Johnson's proper first name; and finds himself wondering about the family and fiancée he's left behind and what they think of his being over here and into his second tour.

After this, silence descends upon the crew, the only sounds being the relatively subdued drone of the single engine, the rattle and creak of the fuselage, and the high-pitched whistle of wind through the rents in the fabric. Perhaps weariness and a sense of anti-climax (in spite of Beal's warning to remain vigilant) has taken over; and, anyway, idle conversation is always

438

somewhat hampered by the need for the process of switching on and off the intercom.

He's not sure how much time has passed, whether his thoughts had drifted, or even whether he'd once again nodded off. All he knows is that he's suddenly back to that morning when he was first arriving at Marwell: there's a similar hammering noise, though less metallic, within the aircraft, and at the same time the aircraft makes a sudden swerve, as did the car, and goes into a steep dive. He can hear Beal cursing, even over the general hullabaloo, which has now been added to by the rasp of their own guns. Fighting the centrifugal force thrusting him back into his seat, he turns towards Beal and sees, as expected, that his face is contorted by pain and effort as he strives to control the heavy stick. Mustering all his strength Peter releases his harness and heaves himself in Beal's direction. 'What can I do?' he yells in the pilot's ear.

'Haul back and help me keep the wheel to the right, but carefully!' Beal replies, his voice as hoarse and staccato as the guns which are still intermittently continuing their clatter.

At first it seems as if the plane is not going to respond. But, with the two of them pulling on the column and Beal controlling the wheel and the rudders, the starboard engine screaming its protest, the wings vibrating and the fuselage bucking as though the whole thing is about to fall apart, gradually the nose begins to come up. Then, just as they finally, slowly, come back to level flight, Beal bellows, 'Now, gently, haul right back!' – and they go instead into a lumbering climb.

That too seems as if it will never end. Their own guns are now silent, the only sounds being those of the struggling plane; and at last Beal indicates that they should level off.

There follows the intimate quietness of suspense, all noise seemingly excluded. After what seems a very long time, Beal speaks.

'Any sign?'

One by one the replies come from Mahon, Baldwin and Donaldson. 'No, skipper. He seems to have gone.'

'I don't know where the bugger came from,' says Mahon, his voice carrying a mixture of anger and apology. 'But I got a quick squirt at him.'

'Me too,' says Baldwin excitedly. 'I'm pretty sure I got in a few hits.'

'He looked all right when he passed in front of me, below.' This, sourly, from Donaldson in the nose turret. 'But I let him have it up the arse. Got a good look at him, too. It was a one-one-oh. Somehow, I don't think he'll be back.'

'Well, if *you* are actually optimistic about it, Jock, I think we can be pretty certain,' Beal says drily. 'Sorry if that's disappointing for you, Pat,' he adds, 'I know you're itching to have another crack at him. But keep on the alert, everyone. Now, damage reports, please. Mahon?'

'A few more holes in my turret. It's bloody draughty, I can tell you! But otherwise all right.'

'Baldwin?'

'A couple of spars fractured, Skipper, and a ruddy great tear in the skin – if Patrick thinks he's cold, he should bloody well try sitting here! Oh, and I think the starboard-gun mounting is buggered; it won't budge. And I think I can smell fuel.'

'Can you tell where?'

'Not really, no.'

'Well, see if you can find out, will you – and for God's sake look out for flame.'

'Will do, Skipper.'

'Johnno?...'

'Johnno?...' Beal repeats, when there's no reply. 'Johnno, are you receiving?...'

Still silence.

'Baldwin, check out Mr Johnson, will you, maybe his intercom's out...' But by now there is growing alarm in Beal's voice.

'I'm already there, Skipper...Oh, God, Skipper!...I think...I think...perhaps the Doc should come back here and take a look?'

Beal, grim-faced, urgently gives Peter the nod. But, still out of his seat, Peter's already hurriedly turning to do just that. Moments later he's crouching beside the navigator, who's slumped across his map table. Eerily bathed in the orange glow from the table lamp there's a large hole in his flying jacket, centred on the middle of his back, and a large stain, brown in the light of the lamp, can be seen spreading downwards. Around the hole the material of the jacket is shredded and blackened: clearly an exit wound; and from the appearance and position of that and the attitude of the body Peter hardly needs to feel for the carotid pulse to know that he's not going to find it. With a sick feeling he gently pulls Johnno back, so that he can see his face and chest. His fears are confirmed. The entry wound at the centre of his chest is not a lot smaller than the wound at the back. He turns to Baldwin, pulls a face, shakes his head in sadness, and gives a thumbs down.

Baldwin, dismay written all over his face, speaks into his intercom. 'Skipper, it appears that Mr Johnson's a goner. Nothing the doc can do.'

'Bugger,' says Beal, his voice coming tinnily out of Baldwin's flying helmet. Then, 'Can you make out where our last position was on his plot-map?'

Peter, experienced as he is, can still only wonder at the philosophical way in which these men have learned to accept the death of a comrade. But Beal is speaking again, and Peter hurriedly unplugs Johnson's intercom and plugs his own into the socket, in time to hear Beal say, '...should be a time and a heading on the plot line.'

Baldwin and he peer intently at the map spread out on the table: there is blood all over it, but the map having a gloss cover they're able to wipe away most of it. Sure enough, they can see the ruled pencil line running horizontally across the sheet, ending south-east of Chalons, and the figures 0315 and 270 pencilled underneath it.

Baldwin deferring to him, it's Peter who passes on the information to Beal.

'Right, Peter, can you take the ruler and measure the distance from the end of the line to a point mid-way between Paris and Reims, and also estimate the compass bearing to there?'

Peter thinks about it for a moment, then takes the measurement. 'Four point two inches, and I reckon the bearing to be about two-eight-zero.'

Silence follows, so that he wonders whether Beal has heard, or whether indeed he's still alert enough to be able to hear.

Then Beal says, in reality musing aloud, 'Right, so that was ten minutes ago, say twenty miles, so if we continue on this bearing for another twenty five minutes and then turn onto two-nine-five, that should be about right.' Then, decisively, 'Right, Peter, come back here and bring the maps and ruler with you, will you. Baldwin, you get back to your guns, just in case.'

'Right, Skipper. What about Mr Johnson, though?'

'Mister Johnson's not going to be going anywhere, Brummie.' It was said gently.

'No, sir. Of course.'

'Have you got any ammo left?'

'Probably half a belt on the gun on the port side, Skipper. More on the starboard side – but that's the one that's buggered.'

'Fair enough. Let's hope we're not going to need it.'

Back in the cockpit, Peter peers searchingly at Beal. 'How're you feeling, Jim?'

The use of the forename just slips out, without him thinking – it seems somehow more appropriate under the circumstances – and Beal gives him a quick look without making comment. 'Bloody awful, to be honest, Peter. But I'll manage. It's a bugger about Johnno, though.'

'Will we manage without him?' He winces as soon as he's said it – it sounds callous and self-centred.

It's a few moments before Beal replies, and when he does his voice indeed carries a sharp edge to it. 'D'you mean with the navigation? I assure you I'm quite able to deal with that.'

Peter, flustered, says, 'No, I meant with your arm and…and all that.'

'Well, I am going to need your help. So you see you have turned out to be useful, in more ways than one. For a start, you see that switch over there? – can you flick it across to the right. It's to transfer fuel from the port tanks to the starboard; we're getting a bit short on the starboard side, with that engine carrying all the load. Also, it'll help the balance of the aircraft.'

Peter does so, and for a good minute Beal peers repeatedly at the dials in front of them. Then, tersely, 'Right, Peter, do it again, will you.'

Peter complies. Again Beal stares at the dials; and after a long silence in which the growing tension in him is apparent, he says, 'And that's all we bloody well need!'

'What is it?'

'It's not working. Must be the pump. Probably hit when we were strafed.'

'What does that mean?'

'Unless we can do something about it, it means we won't have enough fuel to get us home.' It's said flatly, but with rising impatience. Then, 'Try it once more.'

'When it's apparent that nothing is happening, Beal says over the intercom, 'Baldwin, have you used the manual fuel-transfer pump in the past?'

'Yes, Skipper.'

'Well have a go at this one, will you. We need fuel for the starboard tanks, and the pump's gone for a burton. But it might only be the electrics.'

'Will that work?' Peter asks. His mouth has gone so dry that he has difficulty separating his tongue from the roof of his mouth.

'How do I bloody well know!' Then, relenting, 'It should do. The trouble is it's so bloody slow. And damned hard work, doing it fast enough. You and he and probably Donaldson will have to take it in turns, with each of you in turn continuing to help me here. It'll mean we'll only have Mahon at the back to watch out for bandits.'

Peter resumes his seat – no point in fastening his harness – and listens tensely to Baldwin labouring away somewhere behind him. His inclination is to join the man to see if he can help at this stage, but Beal may want him here; and anyway, knowing Baldwin's excitability, it may be more tactful to leave him to it for the moment.

As it turns out, it's not long before they hear Baldwin cursing roundly. 'The fucking thing won't budge! – 'scuse the language, Skipper. It seems to be completely jammed.'

'Try hitting it with the back of the axe; that should be stowed somewhere back there.'

There soon follows a series of bangs punctuated by Baldwin's curses. Then, 'It's no good, the bloody thing just won't move.'

'Peter, go back and see if you can give him a hand.'

He does so, as before using the torch to find his way. He finds Baldwin, illuminated by an emergency lamp, straining away at a two-foot metal lever sticking up from a compartment in the floor. He places his hands next to Baldwin's, and the two of them once more heave one way and then the other. It's as solid as a rock.

He speaks into the intercom. 'He's right, Skipper, it's absolutely jammed. Must have been damaged, I think.' He makes his way back to the cockpit, his heart hammering in his chest.

Silence follows.

Finally, Beal wearily says, 'Right, everybody, we'll get as far as we can – probably no more than half an hour – then, I'm afraid, it's everyone for the Caterpillar Club. I think I'm right in saying it's the first time for all of us?' He turns to Peter with a wry grin. 'So you won't be the only novice, Peter. And, don't worry, I'll tell you what to do when the time comes. Meanwhile,

Baldwin, just show the Doc how to get into his parachute harness, will you, then at least he knows that much!'

An odd noise comes over the intercom. It turns out to be Mahon clearing his throat. He says, 'There's just one problem, Skip. My chute's had it. Got shot up when we were strafed. Missed me by a hairsbreadth, he did.'

'So, that's alright, you can use Mr Johnson's.'

'No, Skipper,' Baldwin says, 'that's damaged too.'

A pause follows before Beal says, 'Alright, that's enough argument. Baldwin, take my chute back to Mahon. You'll all bail out when I tell you to. That's an order.'

It takes no more than a few seconds for the implications of that to sink in, and a chorus of protest follows. 'No way!'…'I'm not going to do that!'…'With respect, you can stuff that, Skip!'

Peter thinks quickly. He's the one superfluous member aboard. Should he volunteer to stay aboard? But the others, when they've bailed out, are likely to be captured anyway, aren't they, no more use to the war effort? He can imagine, too, what Beal would think of that sort of suggestion, can visualise the anger that would follow. He hesitates, torn all ways.

Beal sighs, a tired sound, one of resignation.

'All right, that leaves us with only one alternative. A crash landing. In the dark. Is that what you want?'

'It's the best offer we've had so far, Skip,' Donaldson says. 'Just give me sufficient time to get out of the nose!'

The others also murmur their assent.

'It is a possibility,' Beal says. 'During the daylight raids prior to Dunkirk I remember an area of flattish scrubland – what the French call *maquis* – on high ground just north of the River Marne, nor-nor-west of Epernay. It's not ideal, rather closer than one would wish to both Paris and Reims; but having said that, it did seem to be a fairly remote area. I remember bearing it in mind at the time! Anyway, we'll simply have to take our chance – at least we might get down in one piece. All agreed?'

Again they all murmur their acquiescence.

'Right, that's settled. It'll be about half an hour from now. I'm going to start gradually losing height, and will start dumping fuel from the port tanks; the less we have on board and the less weight we're carrying, the better.'

An uneasy silence descends. Time seems to tick by interminably. Peter finds that, amazingly, he no longer feels any fear: rather is he imbued with a sense of fatalism. What will be, will be. There is merely a lingering regret that there are things he would have liked to have done, people he would have liked to speak to, issues that he would have liked to address. They must have felt like that all the time, in the trenches. Or perhaps, like now, they simply wanted to get it over and done with.

Beal's words, when they finally come, do however cause a wrenching of the guts.

'Right, you lot, we should be approaching the river Marne any time around now. Sing out as soon as you see it; it's pretty big, you won't miss it, even in the dark. We're at four thousand feet and dropping. I reckon landing altitude will be at around fifteen hundred, so I'll have to put her down smartish once we see the ground. Peter, I'll need you to operate that throttle lever when the time comes: I'll say either 'half back', 'three quarters back', or 'right back', or a variation of that. Understood?'

'Understood'. It hits him just how difficult it's going to be for Beal to keep control of the plane with just one engine, never mind the problems he's got with his arm.

'There's the river, Skip!' Donaldson sings out a minute or two later.

'Right, Jock, got it. You get up here now, and strap yourself into Mr Johnson's seat. I'm beginning final descent. Brace yourselves, everybody! We don't know exactly when we'll hit, there might be practically no warning. Peter, look out ahead, will you. I need to keep an eye on these instruments. There should be enough light to see the ground, but it'll appear only as a darker area, like a shadow. Yell out as soon as you see it, even if you're not sure.'

Peter, peering out through the windows, starts to panic, thinking he can't see anything. But gradually things start to take shape, he can make out the lesser darkness of the sky and an horizon ahead; and suddenly there's an even darker shape in front of them, stretching away from them and not far below. 'Ground beneath!' he shouts, wondering at the same time if he's making a fool of himself.

Beal looks up sharply and peers out. 'Right, men this is it! Throttle right back!'

Peter yanks on the lever, hears the engine falter and slow, feels the aircraft lurch and drop, has an impression of dark shapes racing past below, and then, very shortly, coming towards them. The next thing there's an almighty bang and the plane leaps jarringly upwards. For a moment any view of the ground is lost; the nose dips sharply again, there's a cry of agony from Beal, the plane shudders and checks, lurches on, turning as it does so, to the accompaniment of horrendous screeches and bangs, suffering an agony of its own, tips sharply to one side, continues to slide, fast, bumping and shaking as though on the point of falling apart, and then comes abruptly, sickeningly, to a halt. He's aware of being flung violently forward, the seat harness wrenching painfully at his shoulders and midriff, of his head striking the top of the instrument panel, of hearing a further cry of agony from Beal, and then he sinks into unconsciousness. The last thing he's aware of is a smell of fuel.

CHAPTER TWENTY-NINE

The smell of fuel persisted. Coming, it seemed, from the oval shape looming over him. A head?...A person?...A person whose features, eerily lit by the glow of a torch, he couldn't quite make out. Then a voice, full of anxiety, a voice a bit like that of Brummie Baldwin. The words were hard to identify – distant and garbled.

It sounded like, 'Are you all right, sir?'

He took a few moments to digest what he'd heard. His head was thumping painfully and he was having difficulty keeping awake. It was as though he were struggling through glue. He made a supreme effort to grasp at something firm and solid, focussing hard on the features floating in front of him.

'Baldwin?'

Yes, that's right, Mr Waring. Are you all right, sir? We thought you was a goner.'

'All right? Yes, I think so.' Things were coming back to him now. With difficulty, he made to turn his head; and was mildly surprised when it actually obeyed him. His surroundings, by the light of the torch, were equally confusing. There was no identifiable form, just a jumble of broken struts, wires and bits of metal, interwoven with ripped canvas and shattered Perspex. He could feel cold air on his cheek, and concluded that somehow or other he must be out in the open. He tried to move, but couldn't.

'Just a minute, sir. We'll undo your harness.' This was a different voice.

'Jock?'

'Yes, sir.' Followed by, '...Donaldson, sir,' as though it were necessary to clarify.

He felt hands fumble at the release mechanism of his harness, and then he was free to experimentally move his limbs; this time it was with considerable relief that he found he was able to do so with only a minimum of protest from muscles. As his eyes became accustomed to the relative darkness beyond the sphere of torchlight he realised he was actually looking through the detritus of the cockpit, to the outside: he could make out the dark shapes of small trees and shrubs like an army marching through the landscape. Then he recollected. *Maquis*, Beal had called it. They were in Occupied France. And now he remembered the sounds of agony from Beal as they'd hit.

'How is Wing Commander Beal?' he asked urgently, thinking at the same time how odd it was that they should all have chosen to revert to formality now that the flight was, indeed, over.

'He's not good, sir. Unconscious, and his leg looks very odd. But we haven't dared move him. We were hoping…that is, waiting until you came round and could look at him.'

He struggled to rise, found that he could only achieve a half-crouch in the confinement of the wreckage; and at the same time there came another powerful whiff of aviation fuel.

Trying to remain calm, he said, 'There's an awful lot of petrol around, by the smell of things. We'd better think about getting out sharpish, hadn't we?'

'I don't think we'd be able to move the C.O. in a hurry, sir. His leg looks a right mess.'

This was Donaldson – was there a note of contempt in his voice?

'No, of course. I was just thinking about the risk of fire.'

'I understand, sir. But it appears that the skipper had managed to switch off the engines and fuel supply before we actually hit the deck. So I think the risk of fire, now, is small.'

Another thought came to him, also belatedly. 'What about Sergeant Mahon? Do we know how he is?'

'I'm here, sir. Alive and well – bloody jerry'll have to try harder than that to bloody well get rid of me!'

Oddly, Mahon's voice was coming from somewhere outside.

Donaldson, evidently anticipating the surprise this would induce, explained. 'Pat's turret came away with the tail unit on our first bounce, Doc. He landed separately from the rest of us. Trust a scouser to be stand-offish!'

'Well, shift over, then,' said Mahon, 'and let me get in. It's bloody cold out here.'

'The Skipper, sir?' said Baldwin impatiently.

With a nod Peter moved forward, his head glancing painfully off a spar as he did so, and leant over the crumpled figure of Beal. He felt for the pulse at the neck, and that was reasonably strong and regular; got Baldwin to shine the torch into Beal's eyes and satisfied himself that the pupils were equal and reacting; then turned his attention to Beal's legs, dreading what he was going to find. His worst fears were confirmed. The right leg, partially trapped beneath a beam, was strangely twisted and bent; above the knee there was a long rent in the leather of his flying-suit and also in the material of the trousers beneath, and through this could be seen an open wound with dark bubbles of blood and what looked suspiciously like the jagged end of bone.

'Christ Almighty!'

'What is it, Doc?' Baldwin's voice rose in alarm.

'There's a bloody awful compound fracture of his lower femur, that's what. And that's just what I can see. God knows what else there might be. I don't see how we're going to be able to move him. We'll just have to wait until jerry gets here, which presumably won't be long. Meanwhile I'd better try and get a tourniquet on it: it could be bleeding pretty badly, but there's no way of getting in to have a proper look.'

There was silence and a strange stillness from the rest of the crew, who had clustered in behind him. He looked around, but couldn't really see their faces in the dark. Something was wrong, though: it wasn't just concern about Beal.

Donaldson gave him the clue. 'Do what you can, Doc. I'll stay with him after that. The rest of you can scarper.'

He understood then. Whilst he'd been meekly accepting the fact that they would all now become prisoners of war, the others had had no such thoughts.

'No,' he said. 'There's nothing the rest of you can do here. I'm the one to stay with him. Just give me a hand to get this tourniquet on, and then you can all go. And that's an order.' He surprised himself with how imperative he'd made that sound; and certainly none of the others produced any argument.

But at that point another voice came from outside, a voice that was heavily accented, low and urgent.

'Allo, English! 'Ow injured are you?'

'By God!' said Mahon, 'that sounds like a Froggie!'

'*Oui*,' came the reply, in amusement, 'it is a Froggie! Several Froggies in fact! All 'opping along to get you out of 'ere! But there is little time. We must be quick. 'Ow well can you move?'

Peter took the torch from Baldwin and shone it through the gap in the fuselage. '*S'il vous plait!*' came the sharp command, 'put out the light! We do not wish the *Boches* to see us!'

Peter hurriedly did as he was told, but not before managing to get a glimpse of several figures crowded outside the wrecked fuselage.

'There are four of us that are all all right,' he said. 'But our skipper – pilot – is badly injured. Unconscious, and a badly fractured leg. And we have one man dead…before the crash, that is…' His voice tailed off. Then, even more inconsequentially he found himself adding, 'I'm a doctor.'

'*Un médecin? C'est vrai?*'

He could understand the incredulity in the man's voice. More and more he was feeling the same way himself.

'We'll need to put on a tourniquet; and something with which to splint his leg – 'splint', *comprenez-vous*?'

'Yes, I understand – pieces of wood. Better you speak English, eh?'

'Righto.'

'Righto! Then, let us 'urry, or the *Boches* will be 'ere to do the job for us.'

447

In no time at all, it seemed, the beam trapping Beal's leg had been removed, the tourniquet applied, and some lengths of spars produced. Under Peter's supervision, these were fastened to the injured leg. This done, they carefully and with some difficulty ferried him outside and laid him on the ground. With someone holding a jacket around him to shield the light of the torch, Peter briefly checked him over for signs of further injury. Finding none, other than a livid bruise on his forehead, and satisfied that there wasn't in fact a great deal of bleeding, he cautiously removed the tourniquet, took a few more seconds to ensure that all was still well, and, conscious of the growing impatience of all those around him, pronounced him fit to be moved.

'What transport do you have?'

'We 'ave a truck. A farm truck. With straw. That will do nicely, eh?'

'Very nicely. How far is it to the hospital?'

''Ospital? We cannot go to any 'ospital.'

Peter stared at him in the semi-darkness. For the first time since their arrival some ten minutes ago he took more notice of these people who had arrived, miraculously it seemed, out of nowhere, just at the right time. There were six of them: the man who had been doing all the talking, who also appeared to be their leader; four other men; and, to Peter's surprise, a woman. He turned his attention to the leader.

'But we have to get him to a hospital. It is essential.'

'It may be 'essential' for you, and for 'im, *mon ami*, but not for us!'

There was a new hardness in the man's voice, and an intransigence in the set of his head and shoulders. Peter stared at him. In his forties, swarthy, of medium height but thickset, he wasn't a man whom Peter would want to argue with. Come to that, as he peered again at the others and noted their watchful stillness, he decided he wouldn't want to argue with any of them, including the woman.

'Already we risk our lives, and our...work...to 'elp you,' the man went on. 'For that you are very welcome. Also we can continue to 'elp you, but on our terms. Otherwise you must take your chances with the *Boches*. But, I must warn you, whilst you may be reasonably all right if it is the *Wehrmacht* or the *Luftwaffe* who take you, I 'ave to tell you that there are units of the S.S. in the area, and from them it is likely to be a very different story. Now, you must decide. For we go.'

'Where would you take us otherwise?' Peter said.

'Somewhere reasonably safe. There, perhaps you can help your friend? You are a doctor, *n'est ce pas*?' There was still doubt in the man's voice.

'All right. We're in your hands. And, *merci*.' He glanced at the three crew. There was no disagreement. They had little choice.

'Good. Now we go. *Vite!*' He turned to his group, and three of the men carefully picked up Beal, two at his shoulders and one at his legs, and began to move away with him. Fortunately perhaps, he was still unconscious, although he did groan a little as they picked him up.

Peter remembered the injured arm.

'He has a wound, a serious flesh wound, of his left upper arm, as well.'

'*Très bien,*' the leader said. 'We will be careful. But we must get away now as quickly as possible.' He hesitated. 'There is one other matter. We 'ave to set fire to your plane.' He looked hard at Peter.

'But…'

'I know. You 'ave one comrade in there who is dead. But he must remain. We 'ave no time to bury him. It will be an honourable cremation. And later we can say words for him. But if the plane 'as been burned it will delay the *Boches* finding out that some of you 'ave survived, you understand? Jules here…' – he indicated the fourth man – 'will stay behind and do that once we 'ave got away.'

Peter nodded. He could see the logic of it. 'There are identification tags,' he said. Perhaps they at least would be some sort of memento for Johnno's family in Australia.

'*Oui.* We understand. Jules will remove anything personal from the body and let you 'ave it later.' He said something rapidly to the other man, then turned back to Peter and the crew. '*Alors*, come! It will soon be light.'

They hurried after the others, already some distance away and approaching a couple of vehicles – a small open truck and a car – parked behind thickets.

Once Beal had been placed in the back of the truck – the woman and two of the men getting in with him and almost completely covering him with piles of loose straw – the leader gestured for Peter to join him in the cab. Peter began to protest, thinking that he ought to be in the back with Beal, but one look from the man silenced him, and he did as he was told.

'Your comrades will go with the others in the car, and you will meet up with them whenever it can be arranged,' the man said. 'We go in different directions.' And with that they were off.

Later, he could recall surprisingly little of the journey. The man drove carefully but, in spite of not having any lights, at considerable speed. Peter could only wonder how he could possibly see where he was going in the darkness, following narrow muddy tracks over moorland and through woods, only occasionally making use of minor, metalled roads. Mostly they drove in silence, the only noise being the bumps, creaks and rattles of the ancient truck and the sound of the engine (deliberately kept low by dint of staying in as high a gear as possible without actually stalling). As they bumped bounced and slid their way along, Peter constantly worried about how Beal might be faring in the back. At one point, without apparent reason, the man abruptly drew to a halt and switched off the engine, holding up his hand for silence; and sure enough half a minute or so later, some distance away through the trees, could be seen the wavering headlights of some other vehicle, presumably on a nearby road. After it had passed they waited in silence for a full two minutes before continuing on their way.

In spite of the dearth of conversation, however, Peter managed to discover a certain amount about the man, whose name, he said, was Jacques – it was evident that this was a pseudonym: in this business, he seemed to be saying, we trust no one. Whether they were members of the Resistance, or merely racketeers of some sort, Peter hadn't yet decided – although it seemed to him that if it had been the latter they would hardly have interrupted their activities for the sake of a few British flyers. He learned (on asking) that they had just happened to be in the area when the Wellington had crashed – indeed it could hardly have been otherwise unless they had been blessed with a remarkable prescience; and, in complimenting the man on his English, he learned that in the mid-Thirties he had for a couple of years worked in Covent Garden Market in London. But that was all that was forthcoming; and he had more sense than to pry further.

After about an hour they crept out onto a main road, and shortly after that drew stealthily into what seemed to be a farmyard and then straight into the black recesses of an open barn. Without a word Jacques got out, gestured with the flat of his hand for Peter to stay where he was, and disappeared. When he returned a few minutes later he was accompanied by the shadowy figure of a woman.

'This is Marie-Louise,' he said in a low voice. 'She owns this 'ouse and farm. She speaks good English – even better than me – and she is a trained nurse. Your friend will be carried into the 'ouse, and will stay 'ere for as long as is safe. You also. I will return as soon as I can, perhaps later in the day. *C'est bien?*'

'*Très bon. Merci.*'

In spite of this attempt at a jaunty reply, Peter was full of anxiety as Jacques and his two male compatriots carried Beal into the house. Not only was he worried what further damage might be being done to the fractured leg, he was also still inclined to think that, whatever the consequences, it might be better if he were taken to a hospital. He could only be grateful at least that Beal was still unconscious and not suffering: although the fact that he still hadn't come round was in itself a further worry. Following them into the house and up two narrow flights of stairs, he had to stop himself from fussing around like a mother hen. Gently depositing their patient on one of two beds in the room, without more ado Jacques and the two men turned and left, and Peter found himself alone with the woman.

For the first time he was able to take note of her. Her features were softened and blurred in the subdued light of a nearby table lamp, but to his surprise she seemed quite young. Why he should find this unexpected he didn't know – until he took in the fact that she was also heavily pregnant, and realised that this must have been why she had seemed so clumsy in her movements across the yard and up the stairs, making her seem to be much older than she actually was. He also registered that she was decidedly attractive in a way that reminded him, with a jolt, of Anna Beal: not as strikingly so as Anna, but with the same dark hair and eyes and high cheek bones.

'Now, *Monsieur*,' she said, 'we must get your friend undressed and into bed, and see to his injuries as best we can. You are a doctor, I believe?'

He nodded, and was about to launch into another plea about getting Beal to a hospital, when, speaking rapidly, she interrupted him.

'We must see first to your friend, and then before long get you also undressed and into something less distinctive. Both sets of uniforms and clothes will be stored safely, hidden away from the house, in case you may need them later.' Seeing him stare at her blankly, she explained, somewhat impatiently, 'We cannot allow you to be arrested here, for then we will all suffer the consequences; but if you were arrested later, and not in uniform, they would have every excuse for executing you as supposed spies. *Parlez-vous Française?*'

'*Oui, Madame. Un peut. De l'école seulement.*'

She smiled briefly. 'Yes, I see what you mean. Nevertheless, your accent is not too bad – enough to fool most Germans. But you would perhaps have to confine yourself to one or two words only – enough to get by, if challenged. Anyway, first things first. Let us deal with your friend. What is his name?'

'Jim…'

'*Jim,*' she interrupted, using the French pronunciation. 'That will do. And your name?'

'Peter.'

'*Pierre*. Right, Pierre, would you perhaps again examine your friend, now that you have him in better circumstances, and then we can assess what are his needs.'

Already reeling under the brisk efficiency with which she had so promptly taken charge of things, he was even more surprised when she went over to a drawer and came back with a stethoscope, a sphygmomanometer, a tendon hammer and an ophthalmoscope – all the basic essentials for his needs. She watched intently as he went to work. There was an almighty bruise now apparent, in the better light, on Beal's forehead, which explained the severity of his concussion, but the neurological findings were all normal, and he was reasonably satisfied that his skull was not likely to be fractured. He didn't dare think about Beal's neck, with all that it had been subjected to. As for the fracture of his femur, although compound it seemed to be a simple fracture a short distance above the knee but clear of the joint, without any evidence of comminution, for which he was grateful.

The woman gave an audible sigh of relief when, a few minutes later, he gave his verdict that he could find no problems other than the obvious ones.

'*Très bien*. I can find for you suture materials here, for the gash in his arm. But we will need a Thomas splint, will we not, before we can attempt to reduce the fracture of his leg? That I can get, in an hour or two's time, from our clinic in town. Also some ether, which we will need if he regains consciousness before then – for it is possible he might do so, is it not?'

'Yes, it is, *Madame*. Indeed, I hope that will be the case, for I think he is suffering only from simple concussion. Yet it would be easier all round if he were to delay his recovery until we've got him fixed up.'

He was pleased to see that his gentle attempt at ironic humour was appreciated by her; although his own secret smile was at the way in which, under the influence of her somewhat precise speech, he too had slipped into a formal way of speaking. But all she said laughingly, was, 'Oh, please! Do not keep addressing me as 'Madame'. In English it makes me sound like a middle-aged frump. Or the manager of a brothel. Which you can clearly see I am not! My name is Marie-Louise.'

'Yes, Marie-Louise, I can clearly see that you are not either of those things! When is the baby due, by the way?'

'In about four weeks – just to complicate matters.'

It was said lightly, but a frown had crossed her face – indeed not so much a frown as an expression of pain.

'Perhaps we shouldn't have been brought here, under the circumstances,' he said.

'Under the circumstances, with your friend Jim as he is, Jacques had no reasonable alternative.'

'Would it not have been better if he had been taken to a hospital, anyway? Would it not still be better?'

She looked at him long and hard, anger in her eyes. Then they softened. 'You cannot be expected to understand. But let me explain. If your friend had been taken to hospital, once he had regained consciousness and his wounds treated, he would then have been interrogated by the Intelligence people from either the *Luftwaffe* or the *Wehrmacht*, or both. Interrogated harshly, but not brutally. No doubt he would have given them only his name, rank and service number, as is proper under the terms of the Geneva Convention, and that possibly would have been the end of it. He would have been taken off to some prisoner-of-war camp. But, here, we are not far from Paris, and there are units of both the S.S. and the *Gestapo* themselves operating in this area. Their methods are, shall we say, distinctly less civilised than the rest of the German military. I remind you also that Jacques and his people had already, very properly, become involved in his rescue. They would have found it almost impossible to have taken him to hospital without being discovered. And then all hell would have broken out…is that the expression? And what about the rest of you? Our friends in the *Gestapo* (here she imbued the term with such contempt that he thought for a moment she was actually going to spit onto the floor) would have wanted to know about you and your rescuers. And they would have had no hesitation in doing whatever was necessary to get that information from your friend. Do you understand what I am saying?'

'Do you mean they would have roughed him up to get the information? But he wouldn't have been able to tell them anything.'

'No he would not. But they could not be sure of that. No, they would not have roughed him up, as you put it. Not just roughed him up. They would have tortured him, and gone on torturing him until they were certain he had nothing to reveal. Would you have wanted that?'

He stared at her, aghast, unable to accept what he was hearing. 'Surely not! An R.A.F. officer? A senior officer, at that. It's unheard of. Surely. They must just be local…scare stories…propaganda?'

This time her anger was truly frightening. He thought she was going to strike him. Then she laughed, a bitter mirthless sound. 'You English, you know nothing! Nothing of how we are living here, under Occupation, of what we have to contend with – not just from the Germans, but sometimes from our own authorities as well. Do you know what will happen if they find you both here, now, under this roof? You, your precious senior officer and you, may well be all right – prisoners of war – but I, and my family, and eventually those who brought you here, will definitely all be tortured to find out more, much more, and then finally hanged or shot. I tell you, you know nothing!' And abruptly she collapsed into a chair staring into space as though a spectre had materialised in front of her.

Appalled by this sudden alteration in her demeanour, he went over and placed a hand on her shoulder, uncertain how to respond. Irritably she shrugged him off; and for long seconds he stood there, helpless and frightened. Finally he said, 'Well, I assure you we are most grateful for all you're are doing for us. I hate to think what would have happened to us otherwise. It is very kind of you to go to this trouble on our behalf.'

She stood up then and turned to face him, smouldering, the light hazel of her eyes hardening to dark flint, her voice filled in equal parts with anger and contempt.

'Do you imagine you are the only ones to know fear and tragedy? We, too, are exposed to such things. Kindness doesn't come into what we do. It is quite simple really. We have a common enemy, you and we, a brutal one who knows no pity. You, still, are in a position to carry the war to that enemy in a way we are not. It is to that end that we do these things.'

Then she straightened her back, brushing angrily at a suspicion of tears. 'I am sorry,' she said. 'That was not fair, taking out my anger on you. You cannot be expected to know about these things. It is when I think of Raoul, which I try to avoid doing, but without success, that is when my courage goes.'

'*Raoul*?'

'My husband.'

'I'm sorry, I didn't know. He's…dead?'

She swayed. For a moment he thought she was going to faint, and placed a steadying hand on her elbow. This time she didn't resist.

'I wish he were,' she said. Her voice had been so low he wasn't sure he'd heard her properly.

'What do you mean?' he said, hesitant.

She looked up, faced him squarely, sudden fierceness shining through the moisture in her eyes. 'You think that sounds awful? Well, it is awful. But, you see, the *Gestapo* have him. In the Rue Madeleine, where they have their headquarters. In Paris. *Doctor Raoul Pontet* – who only ever wanted to help his fellow man – in the hands of the *Gestapo*.' Tears forced their way through now, spilling down her cheeks, but the fierceness was still there.

'Your husband's a doctor?' It was a trite thing to say in this context, ridiculous, and he bit his lip.

'That surprises you?' She seemed to be pitying him.

453

'Well, no. Of course not. But, I mean…what has he ever done to be in the hands of the Gestapo!'

'He…he is accused of being involved with the *Resistance*. And that…is all I can say.' Her fierceness burgeoned. 'But we waste time! Come! The Germans will come here as a matter of course. It may be – probably will be – later in the day. But it could be sooner. Let me show you something.' She went over to a large old-fashioned wooden wardrobe standing against one wall, and opened it. A few clothes – shabby, men's work clothes – hung inside. 'This wardrobe is fixed to the wall,' she said. 'But let me show you…' She reached up inside, to one corner. Here is a hook. If you pull it outwards, see what happens…' She did so, and he heard a click. Then she pushed at part of the wooden back of the wardrobe, and the whole section swung away from her revealing a dark cavern beyond.

'This leads into the upper part of the barn next door,' she said, 'an upper gallery in which there are bales of straw. Once it's pushed to again, and with a few bales piled near to it, from that side it looks just like the planking in the wall of the barn. If you do hear a commotion downstairs – the Germans are always noisy about it! – then you would have to get Jim through here. You will have time, hopefully, to also tidy the bed once you've done that. The secret is in the timing. Usually they search the barn and then the house, or the other way round. But never the two at the same time – at least not so far! – and we have been searched three times.' She shrugged her shoulders – a Gallic gesture. 'It's not perfect, but the best we can do. Now, let us hurry and deal with Jim.'

There followed some small, reassuring successes. Armed with the catgut and needle provided by Marie-Louise, he was able to suture the wound in Beal's arm; and shortly after daylight Marie-Louise returned with the Thomas splint, and the two of them (with Beal mercifully still unconscious) managed to reduce the fracture of his femur into a reasonably satisfactory position and tidy up and bandage the associated flesh wound. That done, Marie-Louise disappeared again for a short time before coming back with clothes which, once he'd changed into them, she pronounced made him look tolerably like a French farm labourer.

'Soon,' she had added, 'we will provide you as well with a proper identity document.' Then, with another small smile, 'Also, I shall have to examine your underclothes at some stage.'

He looked at her blankly.

'To remove any labels which would give you away – and indeed to make sure they do not look too English,' she explained.

After that, they breakfasted together in that small attic room – coffee and croissants (only later would he discover that the coffee had been a special concession, taken from a dwindling supply). Both of them were on edge listening for any unexpected sounds from outside; and Peter, in addition, constantly wanting to check on Beal's condition, fretting about his continuing unconsciousness. Meanwhile he did manage to glean some more information from her.

The farm lay about four kilometres outside of town – a small, market town, it seemed, called *Sablemont-sur-Aisne*. The farm had been inherited from her husband's parents, and although still worked (by Marie-Louise and an elderly employee she referred to as *Hercule*) it was now not much more than a smallholding – producing enough for their own needs and for a small surplus to be sold in town. She had also, throughout their marriage, assisted her husband in his medical practice in the town; but now, since his arrest six weeks ago, and because of her advanced pregnancy, their clinic had been able to open only two half-days a week, and then most of the time for minor complaints only. There was no other doctor in town – another reason why Raoul was being so sorely missed by all and sundry (here she had to struggle once again to maintain a semblance of composure). However, she explained, a medical officer from the *Wehrmacht* garrison at *Soisson*, not far away, had kindly offered his services for a couple of hours once every two weeks, and that was some help – but she used the word 'kindly' sarcastically, and he noted that her facial expression and tone conveyed a confusion of doubt, gratitude and distaste. Then she revealed that since her husband's arrest along with a number of other men from town she had had no news of him, didn't even know whether he was alive or dead. This, in spite of many attempts to find out – including two trips to the Gestapo headquarters itself, in Paris. He realised that going to those lengths must nevertheless have taken considerable courage, as she herself had initially been under investigation as well. Indeed, at that stage she perhaps would actually have been arrested if it had not been for the intervention of this same *Wehrmacht* doctor who, as it happened, had been visiting the clinic at the time ('in order to inspect it; typical German thoroughness', as she witheringly put it). It seemed that he had been given the task by his superiors, anyway, of supervising the clinic and authorising the issue of certain controlled drugs by signing the registers.

After their discussion she excused herself – 'there is much I have to do' – but reassured him that she wouldn't be far from the house.

For Peter, the hours that followed were filled with anxieties. Every small sound, outside or in, made him think the S.S. were about to pounce. At intervals, in his imagination he heard the sound of jackboots on the stairs (even though Marie-Louise had told him that the S.S. favoured the middle of the night to make their arrests – no doubt surmising that this was the time when people would most probably be taken by surprise). Again and again he would fret about how he was supposed to be able to lug the still-unconscious Beal through the wardrobe and then cover his tracks before the troops burst into the room.

But nothing happened. As each hour ticked by it became ever more likely that at any minute the Germans would swoop on the farmstead. Yet still nothing happened. And that only increased his anxiety. From time to time he would pace the room in his agitation; only to become conscious after a minute or two of the fact that this might be heard from below. Then he would cross to the window and stand, staring out. At first this was done absent-mindedly, all his thoughts turned inward; but after a while he began to appreciate the charm of the surrounding countryside, in these more southern latitudes already adorned with advanced signs of spring. Below, the farmyard was bounded on its far side by low buildings, presumably byres. Beyond them, and past the gateway, ran the road, which then turned in a right angle to run away into the distance between an avenue of tall poplars. On either side were fields with thick hedges. Already the sun was well up, remnants of mist still clinging low down, the whole scene bathed in a golden glow. Cattle in the fields basked in the early warmth; a soft breeze gently ruffled grass and foliage. It all seemed a far cry from a theatre of war.

From behind him came a stutter of mumbles and moans. Turning, he saw with relief that Beal was beginning to stir, his right hand coming up to brush at some perceived irritation at the side of his face. He hurried over to the bed. 'Jim?'

Beal's eyelids fluttered. Then he sank back into sleep. It was encouraging, though. And, sure enough, ten minutes later he began to move again, and his eyelids to flicker open.

'Jim?' He not-too-gently squeezed the lobe of Beal's ear.

'Wharrisit?' His speech, though slurred, clearly denoted irritation, and he made an ineffectual swipe at the thing tormenting him, before firmly closing his eyes again, clearly determined not to be disturbed.

'Come on, man, wake up.' Peter this time gave him a series of tentative slaps across his face.

Beal's eyes flew open, comically attempting to focus on the figure leaning over him, as if he were drunk. For a time he stared in incomprehension, then awareness gradually dawned.

'Waring?...Peter?...is that you? What are you doing here?'

'I'll explain in a while, once you're more yourself. But we crash-landed, d'you remember? It was very well done, by the way. We all survived...apart from Johnno, of course...and that's thanks to you. But I'm afraid you've injured your leg. And you were knocked unconscious when we hit. You've been out about eight hours.'

Beal looked blank, not understanding, tried to move. 'God, my leg feels as though it's got a five-hundred-pounder lying across it; and it hurts like buggery.'

'Yes, well don't try to move it. It's broken, I'm afraid. And it's suspended in a rigid splint, with traction, which is what's making it feel so heavy.'

'Well, take the bloody traction off, can't you!' Clearly he was making a rapid return to normal.

'Not possible. Sorry. Your leg won't mend without it. We have to keep the thigh muscles a little bit stretched, otherwise the fractured ends would be pulled past one another. It'll have to stay on for a few weeks.'

'A few weeks? I can't stay like this for a few weeks. There are things to do. Is Anna here? She'll tell you.' He turned his head, wincing as he did so, and tried to focus on the room. 'Where the hell are we, anyway?'

Over the next half hour Peter patiently described the chain of events leading up to and following the crash-landing, repeating it, or bits of it, several times, until Beal gradually began to take it in. But when it came to telling him yet again about the rest of the crew, that they were all safe, 'apart from Johnno, of course.' Beal looked puzzled.

'Why isn't Johnno safe?' he asked.

'You don't remember about Johnno?'

'No. I don't. Are you going to bloody well tell me?'

'He's dead, I'm afraid. Got shot by that Messerschmitt.'

A look of pain crossed Beal's face; to be followed by one of concern. 'I don't remember any of that,' he said.

'What's the last thing you do remember?' Peter asked, curious.

The other man's brow furrowed in concentration. Finally he said, 'I remember starting the second run at the target... And that's all.' He looked at Peter enquiringly. 'That's bloody odd, isn't it?'

Not really. It's called retrograde amnesia: it's not uncommon following severe concussion. There's memory loss for events over a variable length of time prior to being knocked out. In your case it seems only for the previous hour or so, which is mild. In some cases it can be for days beforehand, or even weeks. In due course the memory often returns; for you it's almost certain that it will.'

'Bloody bad show about Johnson, though. Anyway, did we hit the target? I seem to remember we'd overshot the first time round.'

'According to Jock Donaldson we hit it fair and square.'

'Good show. And you say the others are all right? – but not here?'

'As far as I know they're all right. In a safe house somewhere else.'

At that point he was about to go into the dangers they all still faced however, and to explain the business of the wardrobe and the barn next door. But it was as though the gods were waiting for that moment: the words were frozen on his lips by the sound of a number of vehicles pulling up outside. Curbing an impulse to rush straight over to the window, instead he hurriedly sidled up to one side of it and cautiously peered out.

Immediately panic threatened to overtake him. Lined up in the road outside the gateway were three trucks, military insignia painted on their cabs. In the back of each truck, in two lines, one along each side, were a dozen or so soldiers in grey field uniforms, coal-scuttle helmets on their heads; they sat impassively, staring straight ahead, as though placed there and instructed not to move, rifles held in the 'order' position at their sides. Even as his mind raced, calculating how to respond, the thought struck him that this was the first time in eighteen months of war that he'd actually seen the enemy 'in the flesh'; it was like coming across, in the street, some famous person previously familiar only on film – it was hard to believe they were real. But real they were: and, as he watched, the cab door of the leading truck opened and an officer in grey uniform, peaked cap and jackboots, jumped out and strode into the yard.

'What is it?' Beal's voice hissed across at him.

'Jerry troops. But *Wehrmacht*, I think, not S.S.' Whether the significance of this was lost on Beal, he didn't know. Already he was feeling calmer, deciding that he could deal with the business of getting Beal through to the barn once it became clear which way the thing was developing.

The officer meantime had disappeared from view, probably having crossed over to the front door, which Peter couldn't see without revealing himself at the window. At that point, though, the figure of Marie-Louise appeared from around the corner of the building, and the figure of the officer came back into view. For a minute or so they stood in animated conversation – Peter bracing himself for the order that at any moment would come for the troops to spill out of the trucks. But, to his amazement, instead the officer clicked his heels, courteously saluted Marie-Louise, strode back to his truck, and a few seconds later the convoy was driving off, to disappear into the distance down the road.

A very short time after that, whilst the two men were still congratulating themselves on the unexpected turn of events, Marie-Louise burst breathlessly in through the door and flung herself at Peter to wrap him in an exuberant embrace.

'I thought we were for it, there!' she exclaimed shakily, her face against Peter's chest. 'All they wanted was directions! They're a new unit to the region. Had got themselves lost. Even the Germans can do that, it seems!'

'Do I get one of those hugs, as well?' Beal said.

She looked across at him in surprise, at the same time thrusting herself away from Peter, seemingly now impatient with herself. '*Ah, bienvenu, Monsieur Jim!*' she said, '*Comment allez vous?*'

'*Bien, merci, Mademoiselle.*'

She broke into a peal of laughter; the first time Peter had seen her actually laugh. It transformed her. From having merely attractive features, her face shone with beauty.

She looked up at Peter, still laughing. Either your friend Jim is a great flatterer, or else you have already impressed upon him that I do not like to be addressed as *Madame*!'

CHAPTER THIRTY

The days slid by, carrying March into April, the weather staying balmy, colours golden and light green. Throughout those first days Peter stayed in their attic room, deeming it safer to do so. He spent long periods sitting near the window, caught midway between apprehension at the prospect of troops coming to arrest them and boredom at this forced restriction: he longed to be outside absorbing the spring air. Day by day his frustration grew. Yet on each of the few occasions that a cloud of dust appeared in the distance on the road coming towards the farm, fear would take over, the taste of it remaining even after the inevitably innocent vehicle had passed by; and for a while, then, he would be content with the status quo.

Sporadically he would chat to Beal, none of the talk meaningful: Beal remained drowsy much of the time, anyway, or disinclined to talk. His leg seemed to be mending satisfactorily according to Marie-Louise, whose information on that was more up-to-date than Peter's: for, after watching his clumsy attempt at re-dressing the wound on the first occasion, she'd impatiently insisted on doing it herself thereafter – and, it had to be admitted, had made a more professional job of it. From time to time, on these occasions, she would stay and talk a little; but she clearly had much to do, and although he found himself more and more looking forward to her appearances, whenever she was there he felt increasingly guilty at wanting to delay her departure. Over those days he came to admire, more and more, her courage, her spirit, and the way in which she remained bright and purposeful in spite of the anguish she must be suffering at her husband's plight, imagining what might be happening to him at the hands of the Gestapo, knowing that he may not survive, that he may never get to know their as-yet-unborn child. And he remained a little bit afraid of her.

He took pleasure, though, in studying her appearance whenever he thought she wasn't aware of his doing so: he was enthralled by her vivacity, by the way in which her features were constantly changing, her emotions clearly displayed in them, so that she could be seen to move from enthusiasm to uncertainty, from excitement to stillness, from quiet prettiness to radiant beauty. Not only that, and contrary to the impression he'd at first gained the night they'd arrived, in spite of her pregnancy she was never without poise and grace: he delighted in watching her every movement. But the knowledge that every hour Beal and he were there was putting her life and that of her unborn child at risk, began to weigh heavily upon him. It was clear, from the arrangements that had been put in place in this room, that she (and her husband Raoul) had sheltered people in this way before, yet although he'd made a number of attempts to get her to talk about it, she wouldn't do so. Mistrust, or at least caution, ran deep. Clearly the tenet, What people didn't know, they couldn't divulge, had become their first commandment. He, and those at home in Britain, had over the past eighteen months become used to war with all its terrors and privations; but here in occupied France was a different kind of war, a war in which secrecy was everything, one in which the terrors were of a different dimension, not out in the open but lurking, evil and not fully imaginable, in dark places.

Usually, in their conversations with her, by and large they all by tacit agreement steered clear of talking about the war: it already impinged enough on them in their thoughts, waking and sleeping, without bringing it out into the open. But on one occasion, when she stayed to talk to them a little longer than usual, the discussion had, inevitably, drifted that way. And it soon became apparent that, contrary to his assumptions (and, it turned out later, those of Beal also) in general the French attitude towards Britain was not as benign as they'd fondly imagined. It seemed that, given the present situation in France, many people were contemptuous of Britain. Anger arose firstly from the fact that the British Expeditionary Force had not, in the final phases of the battle in France, hastened north to the side of hard-pressed French forces standing in defence of Paris, but had instead in 'cowardly' fashion retreated to the coast and the chance of salvation. Secondly, that at the Dunkirk withdrawal, the majority of those saved had been British troops at the expense of French, who had 'bravely stood back to cover the British retreat'. And, thirdly, that in any case Britain had 'dragged France into the war in the first place', by recklessly and unnecessarily invoking the treaty with Poland after the Germans had invaded that country. Finally, there was great bitterness at the way in which Churchill in July had ordered the destruction of the French fleet in harbour at *Oran*, resulting in the deaths of over a thousand French sailors. In actual fact, from what Peter knew of it, there could have been no question of allowing those ships to fall into German hands, and the French had been well aware of that and had been given every opportunity to either bring the ships to a British or American port, or to scuttle them – but he kept those views to himself.

In any case, Marie-Louise made it clear that she didn't hold these opinions with regard to Britain, that indeed in her view the majority of French people didn't hold these opinions; although it was a significant minority who did. She also was quick to acknowledge that much of this stemmed from despair; and, it had to be said, from guilt – guilt that with an army big enough, on paper, to match that of Germany, France had failed to stem the onslaught and, in the end, had covered herself in ignominy by capitulation.

'Also, you see,' she said, 'we are jealous. Jealous that Britain has, yet again, escaped enemy occupation, as she has done so many times in the past; whereas France has, over the centuries, been occupied again and again – this time being probably the worst. We look across the Channel and see Britain safe and sound. All right, I know, there are hardships there – shortage of food, all the terrible bombing – and sacrifices, but nothing in comparison to what we here are having to suffer.'

'Britain may not be safe and sound for much longer,' Peter said, somewhat angrily.

'You mean invasion?' Marie-Louise said, making a little moue.

'Yes. Hitler can't afford to leave it any longer than the early summer.'

'Oh, I do not think Monsieur Hitler will try to invade England again. We see no evidence of preparation for that, here in France. He's made a half-hearted attempt once to do so, and failed. Anyway, why should he bother? England can be no real threat to him, in spite of all your bombing – with due respect. He only has to wait, and Britain will have to come to some sort of accommodation with him, or be starved into submission. And on his Eastern borders, Russia is no threat to him: for they have their non-aggression pact, do they not? You see, that also is part of our disenchantment with things, here in France. Beneath our bravado lies despair. We try to actively resist, but these Nazis are so...so crafty. We kill one of them, and at random they take ten, sometimes fifty, of our men, some mere youths, and shoot them out of hand. They understand only too well how to undermine the will to resist – one merely has to be ruthless in retaliation. And that's just the *Wehrmacht*. The *Gestapo* and the S.S. are the real thugs. They have taken us back to the middle ages with their cruelty and their tortures...'

Here she broke off and turned away for a few seconds. Then he saw her shoulders straighten, and she turned back, brushing angrily at her eyes. Peter was disconcerted. This was a side of her he hadn't detected before. She'd seemed to be totally resolute – hard, even.

'And in the end,' she went on, 'in spite of all the brave words by your Winston Churchill and by de Gaulle, what possibility is there of France ever becoming free again, this time? If Hitler cannot manage to invade Britain, then presumably the same applies the other way round: Britain cannot manage to invade mainland Europe. Not without America, anyway. And this time the Americans do not seem to want to be embroiled again in the quarrels of Europe. All this is, after all, our own affair.'

'I agree with Marie-Louise.'

Beal spoke for the first time on this particular occasion; until now he'd more often than not seemed content to merely listen to their conversations whilst displaying a combination of condescension and amusement. But now there was a note of resignation in his voice, indifference even. It was most unlike Beal, as well. Peter, looking at him curiously, thought he looked

461

unnaturally flushed. But he seemed well enough otherwise; and returned Peter's gaze in a neutral enough manner, as it were with a metaphorical shrug of the shoulders.

Whatever the case, Peter now felt himself being overcome again by despair. If these two, with all their grit and determination, felt that way, what hope was there? Yet, somehow, he couldn't quite accept it. What was it Bartholomew Browning was prone to quote? *History is not only about the past. It's also about the present and the future. For peoples, over generations and centuries, have gone on repeating the same patterns. Driven by the three universal forces of greed, fear and the lust for power, they have followed the same paths, and made the same mistakes, over and over again. There may be variations in the patterns, but in general terms what has gone before will come again. For we never seem to learn, never change. Only by studying the lessons of history can we learn how to change the future.'*

So, if Bart was right in what he said, could it be that history had a more encouraging view to offer? After all, the Americans had been (understandably) very reluctant to become involved in the last war; but in the end events had conspired to make them do so. Perhaps the same sort of thing might happen again this time? But when he really thought about it, remembering just how isolationist the Yanks had become, he couldn't convince himself.

A couple of days after this particular conversation Jacques appeared, bringing forged identity papers for them. He also brought news of Baldwin, Mahon and Donaldson: they remained safe and well, and were soon to be 'moved', the implication being that this was a first step towards attempts to repatriate them. It was proposed, therefore, that Peter should go at the same time – so that they could travel from location to location in pairs, this being deemed to be the most practical and inconspicuous combination for travelling in such circumstances. The only person apart from Jacques himself to show no consternation at this suggestion, was Beal. Peter, after initial excitement at the thought, began to feel more and more alarmed; and Marie-Louise, he suspected, was also perturbed, though she tried not to show it. And the more Peter thought about it, the more impossible it seemed. Yes, Beal seemed to be on the mend, but there was something about him that was bothering Peter – and should complications occur what would become of him then? For the moment, therefore, no decision was made and Jacques went off, muttering to himself, thoroughly disgruntled at this hiccup in his plans.

The following evening Peter's diffidence became vindicated in a most disturbing way. When Marie-Louise had taken down the dressings on Beal's leg she came over to Peter and quietly asked him to have a look at the wound before she put on fresh dressings. Sure enough, the edges of the wound, always a little inflamed, were now angrily red and beginning to blacken in places; and when he gently pressed on the sides globules of green pus oozed into view. Quietly he turned his attention to the foot. As he feared, a number of the toes looked decidedly dusky, and when he felt for pulses on the dorsum of the foot and at the ankle none could be found.

Neither he nor Marie-Louise made comment, but when he caught her eye she made an almost imperceptible movement of her head before saying, perhaps a little too loudly, 'I'll have to cut up another sheet for some fresh bandages, Pierre. Perhaps you would come and give me a hand?'

As they went out of the door, Beal, who all this time had been chatting away perfectly cheerfully, said, 'I hope you two aren't sneaking off for a quiet tipple without me?'

Marie-Louise, archly raising an eyebrow and managing to produce a grin, said in mock indignation, ' "Tipple"? *Qu'est-ce que c'est que ça*? I hope it doesn't mean what I suspect it might!'

'It means a drink,' Peter said hastily – and then felt rather foolish.

'That's *tant mieux* – even better, do you say? That's a good idea, Jim. We'll bring you one, as well.'

But outside the door they looked at each other sombrely. And Peter suspected that Beal, too, was well aware of what this was all about.

As he followed Marie-Louse down the stairs, it was with some surprise that he recollected that this was the first time he'd been out their attic rooms since their arrival ten days ago. The two flights of stairs led straight down into a spacious kitchen. A blackened cast-iron range ran along one wall, plain wooden racks and cupboards occupied another, and in the centre of the room stood a large scrubbed table. At the table sat a fair-haired girl in her late teens, her head close to a big old-fashioned wireless set, from which he could just hear a voice droning on in French.

He rocked back on his heels. He hadn't for one moment expected anyone else to be there.

Marie-Louise, noting his consternation, said, '*C'est très bien*. This is Jeanette. She's my niece, and helps me with the house. She knows all about you, and it's quite safe – but we thought it wiser for her not to make your acquaintance unless it became necessary. And, anyway, she speaks no English.' She said something rapidly to the girl, who turned off the wireless, before turning to look at Peter.

'That's London she's listening to,' said Marie-Louise slightly apologetically. 'They broadcast at this time every evening – news, and messages of various kinds. Strictly illegal for us to be listening to it, of course, but everyone does it, and the Germans must know that. They try to jam it, but with varying success.'

He inclined his head at the girl, who smiled back pleasantly while studying him with open curiosity. He then turned again to Marie-Louise.

'There's infection, isn't there,' she said.

He nodded. 'It's more than that,' he replied grimly. 'There's early gangrene as well.'

She turned away in distress. 'Am I responsible for this?' she said, her voice muffled.

'Good heavens, no! It's nothing to do with you. You mustn't for one minute think that. Your handling of the dressings has been very professional. No, it's the nature of the wound, and the manner in which it was caused. Purely that. As I'm sure you know, it's always a risk in a compound fracture, anyway, open as it is to the outside. And so often the blood supply becomes impaired in a fracture of this sort.'

'Can it reverse?'

He was silent for some seconds. 'Possibly.'

'But not likely?'

'No.' The word was dragged out of him. 'Not here, anyway.'

'You mean…it might be possible in hospital.'

'I think you know that. Surgically there are things they could do that we can't do here.'

'You mean amputation?'

'Well, before that. But, yes, in the end, amputation, if it became necessary.'

'Otherwise…septicaemia?'

'That's right.'

'And that would be the end.' It was a flat statement.

They stared at each other in silence. Then the girl, who had been listening intently to all this presumably without understanding anything of what they'd been saying, but who must have picked up on the growing tension, said something angrily to Marie-Louise. There followed a fiery exchange between them, too rapid for him to know what was being said, and then the girl got up and rushed out of the room.

Marie-Louise, looking pale, clutched at the table and then sat down. 'I'm sorry,' she said. 'Don't worry, she'll soon calm down. But she had to know what the situation is. You see, it affects her as well.'

He was riven in two. If he didn't get Beal into a hospital, then the man would die, he was sure of that; once infection set in to a fracture of this kind, particularly where the blood supply was precarious, then the only possible course of action was surgical. If he followed his instincts and did push for him to go into hospital, he suspected that Marie-Louise herself might not refuse – but Jacques and his crew most likely would, in no uncertain terms. Of course, it might be possible to get her to arrange something without the others being told. But that wasn't the point: the point was that if he was able to do that the possible repercussions for her and for those around her didn't bear thinking about.

He looked at her sitting there, white as a sheet, hands covering her mouth as if trying to prevent herself from saying what was in her mind; and he thought about the risks she'd already taken for them, thought about her husband's situation, and about her unborn child. And he knew he couldn't do it.

She looked up and met his gaze. It was obvious the same sorts of thoughts were in her mind.

'We'll have to talk to Jim,' she said.

'To Jim?'

'Of course. This is all about him, isn't it. He has to decide.'

He looked at her in astonishment. With all the problems she already had, and with the enormity of the threats now hanging over her, she was still capable of saying that it was Beal whose life was first and foremost at stake – that was the immediate problem – and that he had the right to be involved in the decision. Her generosity of spirit astounded him. What's more, it was something that hadn't crossed his mind: all his training had brought him to the belief that it was his job as a doctor to make such decisions for other people, to take everything into consideration, to advise them accordingly, and to metaphorically walk away with a shrug of the shoulders if they chose not to take that advice. Yet she – who, if they went ahead, would risk an outcome far more horrible than Jim's would be if they did nothing – still was willing to take that risk. Her moral strength astounded him.

On the other hand, though, was it fair to put Beal in the position of having to make the decision himself? Wasn't it, in reality, simply asking him to sacrifice himself, in effect to commit suicide?

But he looked at Marie-Louise again, and he knew she was right. For she was prepared, it seemed, to risk far greater sacrifice. He had no right to argue against that.

And as soon as they re-entered the room, it became clear that it was the correct decision. Beal looked at them steadily, and said, 'It's infected, isn't it.'

'Yes,' Peter replied. What more was there to say.

'Am I going to lose it?'

This time there was no ready answer. '...It's probably going to have to come off, yes.'

'...But?...' It was Beal who broke the further silence.

'But...there are problems.'

Beal could be seen thinking about it, without fuss, his gaze fixed firmly on Peter, then switching to Marie-Louise, who was quietly gnawing on her bottom lip.

'Yes, I understand. Of course. There can be no question, at this stage, of my going into a hospital.'

'Well...' Marie-Louise began.

'No,' Beal cut in, 'it would risk giving away the whole game here, I can see that.'

'More than that, Jim,' Peter said tetchily; did Beal really think it was so simple? 'It's not just a question of spoiling escape-line operations here. Apparently it's the Gestapo who are likely to question you. Then, it seems it's not just a matter of name, rank and number, but a great deal more than that. Evidently they'll go to any lengths to find out what they want to know.'

'You don't mean torture?' Beal said in mock horror.

'That's exactly what he means,' said Marie-Louise, an angry note in her voice.

Beal immediately sobered, looked at her carefully, said slowly, 'You're serious, aren't you.'

'Yes, I'm afraid I am.'

'And that wouldn't end with me?'

'No. You'd be just a means to an end. It would be the *Résistance* they would be interested in. They would realise that you must have had help over the past days since the crash, that you would be the link to us – to me, and then, eventually, to the others. Once they'd been led to us, then each of us would be subjected to the same sort of interrogation.'

Peter looked at her with renewed admiration. Well aware of what the Gestapo would have been meting out to her husband, she was still able to talk about it with apparent dispassion. But he knew how much she must be suffering beneath that calm exterior.

'I see…Well that's it, then.' Beal turned to Peter. 'For if the leg doesn't come off?…'

'The infection will almost certainly spread, in spite of what we can do to try to prevent that. There's already some early gangrene, and I'm afraid it's more than probable that you're going to lose the leg in any case. But before that happens…'

'…before that happens the infection will finish me off, anyway,' Beal completed for him.

'Yes.' The word was dragged out of him. He was back at Bard's, Beal dispensing a heady mixture of firmness, fairness and kindness, inspiring them all to greater things, hero-worshipped for his sporting prowess, god-like; and he saw Beal at the controls of K-for-King, steady as a rock in spite of everything being chucked at them, in spite of his wounds; and he thought of Anna, waiting for her husband back at home. Who would have thought it could ever come to this.

Beal had said something else, something he hadn't taken in. He had to ask him to repeat it.

'I said, amputation is the answer, then. Would solve the problem?'

Peter looked at him uncomprehendingly, wondering if perhaps the man was becoming confused, hadn't he really understood what they'd been saying?

'Yes, but…'

'…and it would be mid-thigh, fairly straightforward?' Beal interrupted him, his voice suddenly decisive and full of expectation.

'Yes, but I don't see…'

'Then why can't you do it?'

Fright gripped him. Was the man mad? He took a deep breath, spoke as though explaining something to a difficult child.

'It has to be done in hospital, where they have the equipment, can provide the anaesthetic, have surgeons who are sufficiently experienced in doing these things.'

'But you're a surgeon, M.B., Ch.B. are the qualifications, are they not? Unless I'm mistaken, that stands for Baccalaureate in Medicine,

Baccalaureate in Surgery, does it not? And you know how to do it, have assisted at such operations, or at least seen it done?' There was now that familiar toughness in his voice, that 'I'll brook no argument' ring.

Peter was suddenly aware of the pressure of responsibility bearing down upon him, of reverberations from the past, of being asked to 'stand up and be counted'; felt he needed somewhere to hide.

'It's not the same, though,' he said with growing desperation, 'it requires a specialist surgeon to do an operation of this kind. And, anyway, it's out of the question to do it outside of a hospital.'

'Why is it?' Beal persisted. 'Go back to the Crimea, the Boer War, even the last war, and it was being done all the time outside of hospital.'

'But they had the proper equipment, and the skills.'

'I'm not convinced their skills were anything to write home about; but I see what you mean about equipment. Nevertheless...'

'There's no problem about the equipment,' Marie-Louise interjected suddenly, her voice rising with growing interest. 'At the clinic we have a full set of surgical instruments. It's many years since they've been used – the doctor before us had been Surgeon to the Mines – but I know they're in good condition. And we have a portable surgical lamp.'

'And the anaesthetic?' Peter said, trying to prevent his own voice from rising in pitch, but making no attempt to avoid a touch of sarcasm. 'What do you propose to do about that?'

'We have ether at the clinic,' Marie-Louise said quietly. 'And I've had some experience in giving it as an anaesthetic – for tonsillectomies, circumcisions, that sort of thing.'

'But those are relatively minor operations,' he countered, 'taking only a few minutes. There's far greater risk during an operation of this magnitude.' He felt as though waters were closing over him.

'Oh, for God's sake, man! What are you afraid of?' Beal's voice was loud with anger and contempt. 'That you'll botch it? That I'll sue you! That I'll die? What choice is there? Either we put me first, take me to a hospital – which probably wouldn't be possible anyway – and throw these kind people to the wolves. Or else I'm going to die anyway! It's I who have to decide about this particular risk – which in any case seems to be Hobson's Choice. All you've got to lose is your precious self-esteem. And that's not worth a damn!'

Peter shrivelled, forced himself to meet Beal's angry stare. Marie-Louise turned away in embarrassment.

'All right,' he said, grasping at the last shreds of dignity. 'Let's do it, if that's your decision.' He turned to Marie-Louise. 'From what you've said, it is possible?'

She hesitated only a moment. 'Yes. Yes, it is.' The light of determination was there again in her eyes, adding to his sense of shame.

'It'll have to be fairly soon,' he said. He looked at Beal and then at Marie-Louise. Not only was he thinking that Beal could deteriorate quite

467

rapidly, but also that she could go into labour at any time. And in a sense the whole thing depended as much upon her as it did on him.

She hesitated. 'You'll have to come to the clinic to show me exactly what you'll need,' she said thoughtfully. 'My next normal clinic day is in two days – Wednesday afternoon. It would look too suspicious if I went any other time, particularly if I've got you with me. It would draw too much attention to us. If I go at my usual time I can simply explain that you have recently come to work at the farm, and that I've brought you along to help carry supplies. We can take some boxes along with us, to make it look more realistic. But that would mean we wouldn't be able to do the operation until Thursday. We'd need daylight for it, I think. Would that be too long to wait?' She glanced apologetically at Beal as well as at Peter.

It was Beal who answered before Peter was able to. 'The greater risks are to you and your people. I think we should take all the precautions we can, in that respect. Thursday will be fine, regardless.' He looked challengingly at Peter – who paused only briefly before going along with it.

Marie-Louise left them shortly after that – although she briefly reappeared soon afterwards to leave them a bottle of wine. All three of them it seemed needed to be alone for a while with their thoughts. Stuck as they were in the one room, for some time Peter and Beal sat in silence, quietly enjoying the wine. Then Beal self-consciously cleared his throat and said, 'Peter, I'm sorry for what I said to you before. You didn't deserve that. You'll understand, though, that it was said in the heat of the moment, and wasn't entirely meant.'

Peter, while noting the use of the word 'entirely' as a qualification, accepted this to be true. He could only imagine what must be going through Beal's mind, knowing what he had to face in three days' time: for, in spite of his show of confidence, he must share Peter's doubts about how competently the operation would be carried out, and must be equally nervous about the anaesthetic. No doubt the same kind of thoughts would be pre-occupying Marie-Louise.

As if reading his thoughts, Beal went on, 'I have to admit that I am more than a bit afraid of Thursday, and I can see why you might be nervous about it too: it is, after all, a big responsibility to land you with…' He grinned. '…And that makes me sound like a self-important arsehole! Anyway, I think it was fear making me speak as I did. I suppose I was just anxious to get the decision over and done with.'

He paused, then continued thoughtfully, 'You know, I've sometimes thought that fear and courage are strange bedfellows. In one sense they are antagonists, but at the same time the second is dependent on the first, can't be said to exist without it. In the time I've been in the RAF – and indeed before that, at school, on the rugby pitch for example, or the cricket field – I've seen many forms of heroism, and various degrees of cowardice. Now and again – rarely, actually – I've seen chaps who didn't seem to know the meaning of fear: whether they just had no imagination, or were carried along by their thirst for excitement, the rush of adrenaline, I've no idea. Some of them were awarded medals or other such honours – man-of-the-match, that sort of thing. But are we right to refer to them as 'heroes', I wonder?

'That as may be, the fact remains that for the vast majority of us fear is an all-too-familiar companion. Granted, it's an emotion that more often than not is in minor key, easy to overcome, hardly requiring what we call courage, but merely a bit more determination. But what about real fear, the fear of death, of pain, of mutilation, of ignominy, even? The fear of losing those whom we love, whether by their death or by their rejection of us? Those sorts of experiences can sorely test our courage, and then all of us may to some degree be found wanting. So, then, who's to say who is a coward and who isn't? How can we know what is in another's mind, what torments they suffer? How can we define 'cowardice'? – and that being so, how do we define 'courage'? It's a question I've had to ask myself on many occasions as commanding officer – for example when it comes to making decisions about whether a particular bod should be withdrawn from active duty, as likely as not to be stuck with that awful epithet 'lacking moral fibre'; or alternatively whether another chap be recommended for a medal.

'Of course we can all recognise a 'coward' or a true 'hero' when we see one. Or, at least, we think we can. It's easy enough at the extremes. For example, when a fellow deserts his mates in order to save his own skin, abandoning them to their fate when by staying he perhaps could have helped them all to survive, then that is cowardice by anyone's book. At the other end of the scale, when someone knowingly risks his own life to save the life of another, that must be recognised as heroic. But what about the sort of situation we had over Stuttgart, when I made the decision to go around for a second run, as indeed skippers of aircraft quite often have to do? Who's being the more courageous there? The skipper? Or the crew, who have no choice in the matter? Chew on that one if you will. I seem to remember Donaldson making some sort of pertinent remark along those lines, at the time!

'And, while we're on the subject, I think what did take courage was when you set out to try to save Flight Officer O'Connor that time we were under attack at Marwell.'

Now Peter started to protest. For the last two or three minutes he'd been listening restlessly to this homily. It was most unlike Beal, who was as a rule a man of relatively few words, preferring action instead. As a result, his suspicions had been aroused, wondering where this was leading, wondering in characteristic fashion whether it was going to come back to some adverse observation about him. So it was with surprise that he heard it suggested that what he'd tried (and failed) to do that day had been in any way heroic: for at the time he had in fact acted purely instinctively. Indeed, he couldn't have done any other once he'd seen who it was and the danger she was in – and, truth be known, he hadn't fully realised at the time that he himself had been in any particular danger – until, that is, Mitchell had scrambled out after him. If anything it had been Mitchell who'd been the hero; or, more specifically, O'Connor. And, as he remembered that day, the pain returned.

469

Beal meanwhile had held up a hand to stem the beginnings of his protest. 'I know what you're going to say. That it was all done on impulse. And I think – thought at the time – that that was probably the case. And that's why, when Warrant Officer Mitchell recommended you for a medal, I decided against it. It was, though, a brave thing to have done. But it's an illustration of the sort of things I've just been saying.'

So that was how Beal knew about it. Mitchell had reported it. And his distress deepened, to think that an episode in which he'd been so impotent should ever have been considered to be anything other than tragic; and that O'Connor's greater courage at the time had been entirely overlooked.

But, coming back to the present, intuition told him that this, still, was leading to something else, and he continued to look at Beal with suspicion.

Beal must have sensed this, because he gave a knowingly-wicked grin, then immediately sobered and said, 'I know you must be wondering where I'm going with all this. To tell you the truth, I've debated whether to bring it up at all. But it's something that's been on my mind for a long time; and, speaking of fear, as I've said, I am anxious about the outcome of Thursday – not that I don't have absolute faith in you, of course! – so I feel I must get it off my chest.

'It's to do with your time at Bard's.'

Peter inwardly cringed. He could sense what was coming.

'You mustn't take this amiss, Peter,' Beal went on. 'But I know you had a difficult time at school. When you were fagging for me, I was aware that you had acquired the nickname, 'Wary', which was obvious enough, I suppose, given your surname…'

(*Oh, that's not fair,*' Jamie had said. '*Wary' means sort of 'fearful', doesn't it? I don't think you're that, at all. Cautious, perhaps. I shall call you 'Cautious'. Just between you and me. No one else to know.*)

'…but I learned later, after I'd left, that you had indeed developed the reputation of being a bit of quitter.'

He didn't know where to look, wished the ground would open up and swallow him. Could one never shake off the past?

'I'm sure you yourself must have been conscious of that at the time, without understanding the whys and the wherefores,' Beal continued, 'but I think you should now know that there were one or two other people who did sort of understand. One of them was Richard Wilson. And once I'd chatted to him, when I returned to an Old Boys' Day a couple of years after I'd left, I became another who began to understand – whereas I hadn't done before. Of course, we knew about the death of your father, that he'd committed suicide …don't look so devastated – it's something we had to have been told about. When I say 'we', I mean Jack Roberts, of course, as your Housemaster – although I don't think he had enough sensitivity in him to be able to interpret any of your hang-ups on the basis of that information; and Wilson, as Assistant Housemaster, as I've already said. And then me. You may wonder why me, as opposed to Jenkins, who was Head of House. Well, Richard Wilson took upon himself to tell me, in the strictest confidence, because he thought someone among the House Prefects should know, and he wasn't willing for it to be that chap Jenkins. But we were the only ones: it was never passed to anyone else, and I for one regarded it as such a privilege to have been told that I certainly wasn't going to blab about it. That's largely why I picked you to be my fag: I felt sorry for you – and I apologise if that now sounds more than a little patronising!

'Wilson, as he told me later, could see you were fighting your own private battles, but thought also that you were in denial. I knew, whilst I was still at school, that there were these stories circulating – presumably from you – that your father was not only still alive, but operating as some sort of spy: 'a secret agent' was the term used, I seem to recollect. And Wilson afterwards, at that Old Boys' Day, told me that he thought that, in the years that followed, you had to some extent retreated into your own private world in a number of other ways. He was concerned that this was to some extent impeding your progress through school in many respects, and he simply wanted, I think, to share these concerns with someone who might understand – which I think I did; although neither of us could come up with any answer to the problem.

'I can see how mortified you are by these revelations, Peter – this unholy delving into your personal affairs – and in a sense I'm sorry to have ever brought it up. But you see, you and I share a bond in all this – because it was under the influence of my father that I was similarly driven. Not the same, of course, but similar because it has been his presence in the background – very much alive, in my case – and the complexity of that relationship, which has driven me to being the kind of man I am, and made me behave at times in ways of which I am ashamed.'

Here, he stopped, and looked at Peter carefully. 'You look surprised. Is it such a surprise?'

No, not a surprise, Peter was thinking – remembering the occasion on which Anna had asked to meet him in order to unburden herself – more the light of revelation, of pieces falling into place; of relief that another, even someone like Beal, had an aspect of himself of which he could feel ashamed. But Beal's conclusions, he was sure, were still to come.

'No, not entirely,' he replied, adding, as a kind of sop, 'I've learned never to be surprised at what people reveal about themselves.' The temptation was there to reveal what he already knew from Anna's lips; but he knew that couldn't be. Instead he let his own unspoken question hang in the air.

Beal must have picked up on it, for he said, 'You're still wondering, though, why I'm telling you all this now? Well because…suddenly I could be running out of time…' His hand came up again to quell Peter's objection. '…It's all right, I'm not over-concerned about that, just being pragmatic…And I want to set the record straight while I still can. Just as, I suspect, you've carried your burden of shame and regret over the years, I'm now carrying mine. And, in our different ways, I think we should now do our best to expurgate it. For your part, I hope it will be sufficient to have the knowledge that others have seen and understood your difficulties, and have not thought any the less of you for it, rather indeed have admired the way in which you've managed to recover. That too has taken guts and determination.

'For my part, I'm not going to bore you with details: that isn't my objective. What I do need you to know, though, is that more than anyone it is Anna who has suffered from my behaviour. And she hasn't deserved that. If for any reason I don't make it home – and, God willing, *you* do – I want to ask a favour of you. Anna will very possibly be left in a highly vulnerable position – that will be so, whether the invasion comes about and succeeds or not. What *is* certain is that she won't get any support whatsoever from my dear family – again, I won't go into details. If you, therefore, could be there for her as much as you can I'd be eternally grateful.

'And now let's put all that aside and just get on with this bloody good wine, shall we?'

CHAPTER THIRTY-ONE

Sunlight, slanting through lazily-waving poplars, cast dancing images on the dusty road stretching ahead of them. On each side, glimpsed between the trees, fields were dazzling in their brightness, cattle and the green of corn appearing insubstantial as though seen through chiffon. It was hard to remember it was still only April: at home this could only have been the appearance of early summer.

So far, apart from a single cyclist who had dipped his head to avoid their dust, they had seen no traffic. For Peter, this was a boon. At first, as they'd started off, he'd felt an immediate sense of freedom. It had reminded him of the occasion during his first House Job in hospital, when for the first time in four weeks he'd had time off and gone out into the outside world: everything had seemed novel. Today, on stepping into the fresh air he'd experienced the same rush of exuberance. It hadn't lasted. When, after only five minutes, they'd met the cyclist – a harmless local who had ignored their passing – he'd suddenly felt conspicuous, naked. He was sure the eyes of the whole world must be upon him. This had prompted a belated thought which, alarmed, he'd put to Marie-Louise.

'What about your tame German officer, the doctor, won't he be at the clinic?'

She'd answered tersely, some of his nervousness having transmitted itself to her: '*Mais non*. It is not his week. He comes only once every two weeks.'

After that they'd continued in silence, each of them pensive. There was much to occupy their thoughts.

They came, now, to a fork in the road. A signpost indicated, to the right, *Soisson*; and straight ahead, *Sablement*. It seemed strange to see the sign there, the suggestion being that things here were more settled than at home, where all the signposts had been uprooted long ago. Here, it seemed to imply, the invasion has come and gone, but yours is yet to come: we at least know our lot, you still live with uncertainty.

This aura of being resigned to fate was repeated a few minutes later on their approach into the town, for at the side of the road the name of the town was calmly stated, set in stone for all to see: *Sablement-sur-Aisne*. And now that they were here his nervousness increased.

As they covered the short distance through narrow streets into the centre of town, the atmosphere here too appeared anything but relaxed. Few people were out in the streets, and those who were moved around it seemed in a nervous way, hardly ever stopping, and then only briefly to converse with one another, moving hurriedly in and out of houses and shops, rarely pausing to peer into shop windows. The town centre itself consisted of a vast cobbled square, on all four sides of which were shops and other buildings. In the middle stood an ancient market hall of modest size, the side facing them open to the street. Standing prominently beyond that, on the far side of the Square, was a building of much grander proportions, occupying most of that side. Carved into the stone lintel above its imposing portico, lest there be any doubt, could be seen its statement of purpose: *Hôtel de Ville*. Peter took all this in, reminding himself that this would be the town hall and not an hotel in the English sense; but his gaze was held by the red, white and black of a Nazi flag. Some six feet by eight feet, flying lazily above the entrance, it totally dominated everything around; and it struck him that nowhere was to be seen any semblance of a French *Tricoleur*. A lesser building next door had a more modest sign: *Gendarmerie-Sablement* – and the Swastika above its door, whilst only in the form of a large disc fixed to the wall, still managed to convey the same presentiment of evil. On each side of the steps leading up to the town hall stood a German sentry, rigidly to attention, rifle grounded; and at several street corners were other armed sentries, these standing at ease but watchful. For a moment Peter was back in Berlin five years ago. And the same chill crept into his bones.

Marie-Louise, who meanwhile had drawn up on the near side of the square, next to a haberdashery, said, '*Merde*, the bloody *Boches* are everywhere! There must be something going on.'

'It's not usual to find them here?'

'Outside the Town Hall, yes. The Germans have taken that over as their local headquarters, needless to say. But they're not usually all over the place, like this. That happens only when they are doing a trawl.'

'A trawl?'

'Yes – that is the right word, is it not? – fishing. Looking for something – or, rather, looking for certain people. Anyway, we are here at the clinic, now. Try to act normally. And stare briefly at the nearest sentries – it seems to arouse their suspicions less than if you avoid looking at them. Thank God, at least there doesn't seem to be any sign of the S.S. at the moment. They're absolute shits.'

As she carefully manoeuvred her pregnant bulk past the steering wheel and clambered awkwardly out of the driving seat, he made haste to follow her, staying close at her heels as she unlocked a door at the side of the haberdashery and clambered up a flight of stairs. Halfway up he remembered the cardboard boxes left in the back of the van, and reminded her.

'Oh, yes. Could you get them, please? It will look more purposeful if anyone has been watching us – and, anyway, we may need them. And leave the street door open when you come back, would you – that way, again, it will look less as if we've got something to hide. The clinic will be due to start in about forty minutes, in any case.

Arriving back at the top of the stairs with the boxes, he found himself on a wide landing, against one wall of which was a short row of chairs. Off this a doorway led into a large room with a window overlooking the square. The window was covered by a net curtain, and through it the sun streamed brightly to light up the room.

Like any doctor's surgery, this was furnished sparsely with a desk, a few chairs, a screened-off surgical couch, and a number of tables, cupboards and cabinets. At the back of the room, on the opposite side to the window, a door, which was ajar, led into another room. Marie-Louise was crouching in front of an open cupboard, tugging at a heavy-looking wooden box. He hurried forward to help her, stopping himself from using the phrase, 'You shouldn't be doing that', and saying instead, 'Here, let me.'

Giving him a brief appreciative smile she moved aside to allow him to carry it over to the desk, then followed behind to move in and lift the lid. Inside, as he had surmised, was an assortment of surgical instruments.

'There should be another box at the back of the cupboard, on the bottom shelf,' she prompted.

It too was significantly heavy, but as the desk was cluttered with the bits and pieces she was already sorting out he placed this second box, for the moment, on the floor. Straightening, and about to join her, he paused for a few seconds to study her as she worked, stopped in his tracks by the way the sunlight was catching her face, highlights and shadows constantly changing her features like a work of sculpture in progress, strength and beauty in every nuance. All her attention was on what she was doing, but conscious perhaps of his gaze, she turned her head suddenly in his direction. He felt like a little boy caught with his hand in the biscuit jar, for her eyes narrowed, momentarily taking on a look of surprise and then immediately becoming guarded as if his interest was somehow distasteful to her.

'What?' The sense of irritation was in her voice also.

'No. Nothing.' Perceiving that wasn't enough, and increasingly flustered, he added, 'Just admiring the proficiency with which you're sorting those out.'

That sounded even more lame; and she gave him a thoughtful look before saying, 'Come on then, you'll have to tell me what you need, and whether any of these will do. There'll be people turning up for the clinic before long. And the less time we spend here, the better.'

Chastened, he turned his attention to the instruments. Many were of an obsolete design, but they were for the most part in good condition. Somewhat unenthusiastically he picked up a large, curved, amputation knife, cautiously testing its edge with his thumb.

'I don't think I've seen one of these outside a museum, until now.' He had a mental picture of one of these sweeping through skin and muscle, down in the gloom of a mine, the only light most likely that of a lantern held aloft, the knife wielded perhaps by a man who'd never done an amputation before; and as he pondered on the raw courage of surgeon and victim alike, his own muscles tensed at the thought of the task he had to perform tomorrow.

'Don't worry, we do have some more modern scalpels,' Marie-Louise said drily. 'They'll need sharpening, but Hercule will soon see to that, he's a marvel with a whetstone.'

'How are we going to sterilise them?'

'Carbolic acid? We have some of that. Then, in the kitchen oven?'

'Yes, that should do.'

He sounded nervous, he knew that. She glanced at him, spoke with some impatience. 'You'll be all right, don't worry. Once you get going it'll be second nature. And, when I did my training I assisted at one or two mid-thigh amputations; so we'll cope between us.'

He did his best to smile at her. Whilst he couldn't help but admire her grit and determination – 'spunk' was a more fitting word, he decided – he was finding himself more than a bit in awe of her. At times she could be utterly, beguilingly, feminine; at others she demonstrated a not-inconsiderable streak of ruthlessness. Not for the first time he wondered about her excellent English, and where she'd learnt it; he still hadn't got around to asking, and now wasn't the right time. He was as much concerned about the anaesthetic as he was about the surgery, and deliberated whether to mention it. As a student he'd had a little instruction on the use of ether, but it had all been theoretical, and he'd never seen it actually used. Was she going to be sufficiently capable for him to be able to concentrate on what he was doing, without having to check all the time on Beal's condition? But she might easily take offence, and then refuse to do it. He decided to approach it in a roundabout way.

'Do we have a proper pad and mask for the ether?'

She gave him a look of deliberation, then nodded. 'I know you're anxious about that side of things, too, but I assure you I am quite good at assessing the depth of anaesthesia; and if I've any doubts, when it comes to it, then I'll sing out. We can both only do the best we can.'

After that they concentrated on agreeing what would be needed and finding instruments in sufficiently good condition to meet those needs. Gradually, as they identified each type, counting aloud as they did so, the little heap grew: 'Four pairs artery forceps...four pairs skin forceps...needle holder...two large scalpels...one smaller scalpel...two retractors...' He had a sudden thought, and spoke with some alarm: 'Bone saw? We haven't got a bone saw.'

'I think you'll find one in the other box,' she replied calmly. 'It's probably of the same era as the amputation knife, but a saw's a saw, and I think it'll be in reasonable condition. Also in that box you should find some curved needles of various sizes – they might need sharpening, but again Hercule will see to that. In there as well there should be some reels of catgut of various strengths, and some suture silk. And we've plenty of gauze swabs here in the clinic.'

Another thought struck him. 'What about morphine? We're going to need that.'

There's a certain amount in stock here. Half-grain and quarter-grain ampoules. And I can spare a 2 millilitre syringe and a couple of needles.'

'Won't that be eating into your supplies of morphine, though? I imagine that it must be difficult to get replacements, these days.'

'Yes, it can be. The Germans have taken control of virtually all medical supplies in France; and, needless to say, they consider their own needs before distributing the rest. But I haven't done too badly here, so far. Particularly since I've been on my own.'

She'd given a certain inflexion to the last statement, which he picked up on. 'Is this due to your tame army medical officer? Perhaps he fancies you?'

He'd meant it as a joke; but the look she gave him was bitter and angry. Then, as so often seemed to be the case with her, she softened: it was as though her hardness was of an assumed nature, difficult to maintain.

She pulled a face. 'I don't know about "tame". And as for the other, he's cold and efficient like so many of the *Boches*, but never anything other than absolutely correct. However, yes, he has been fairly helpful – for a German. Particularly since he suspects, I think, that I'm part Jewish.'

He looked at her with new interest. 'And are you?'

'You sound surprised. Can you not see it in me? I had a Jewish grandmother, on my mother's side.'

A certain defensiveness had accompanied her words, her expression resentful. He realised, too, that in telling him this she was putting a certain amount of trust in him. He hastened to placate her. 'No, not surprised.' He thought of Anna Beal, how like her she was. 'It's simply that it had never crossed my mind, one way or the other. Anyway, what does it matter?'

Anger flared again, and disbelief. 'You're not trying to tell me you don't know what they are doing to the Jews?'

'Well, in Germany, and in Poland from what we hear, yes. But not here in France, surely? I thought that France had been given a certain amount of autonomy, under the terms of the armistice, at least with regard to domestic government – not as much as in Vichy France, admittedly, but nevertheless…'

'Huhh!' she interrupted him in disgust. 'In certain respects the Government here are every bit as complicit as Petain's government is. They are arresting Jews – goodness knows what happens to them, you never seem to hear anything of them after that – and it is the *gendarmerie* in many cases who are doing the arresting. As often as not they take their orders directly from the Gestapo. And, in any case, they seem to have been given broad instructions to seek out Jews. Admittedly an awful lot of the *gendarmes* – the majority probably – turn a blind eye on that, whenever they can.'

'But they wouldn't be interested in you, anyway, surely?'

'No. Probably not. It's two generations back, and the Jewish surname hasn't come down, seeing that it was on the maternal side. But if they care to look back into Registration records, they'll find the connection. In fact they may already have done so.'

'But why would they bother to do that?'

'Because when Raoul was arrested they tried to implicate me also. They couldn't find any evidence to do so. But they would be able to use my Jewishness, however remote, as a pretext to take me into custody. After that, no doubt it would just be a matter of time until they managed to make me confess to almost anything.'

A distinct shiver ran through him. More and more he was grasping just how much raw courage it was taking for her to do the work she was doing.

'Anyway,' she went on, beginning to pack instruments into one of the boxes they'd brought, 'enough of that. We must get on. You've still to find the things in that other box – and if they're not there it might take us quite some time to find them elsewhere.'

As he rummaged in the second box, he had another thought, and paused to ask her. 'What about the drug register, with regard to taking out the morphine? Doesn't this German bloke check that, each time he comes?'

'Yes, he does. But there's a certain amount of…shall we say …leniency there, too. I can usually fiddle it.'

Satisfied, he continued his search, and to his relief soon came across the things he was looking for. He peered dubiously at the bone-saw; but, as she'd said, a saw was a saw, and it seemed to have retained most of its sharpness. Although he still had considerable misgivings about his task the next day, his confidence was now beginning to grow.

He was about to say so, hoping to mollify her somewhat, when from out in the street there came a sound that stifled the words in his mouth: the roar of trucks entering the square, rumbling and rattling over the cobbles and then skidding to a halt. Marie-Louise rushed over to the window and cautiously looked out, keeping well back from the net curtain. 'Mother of God!' she said. 'It's the S.S.!'

He hurried over to join her, his heart hammering to the extent that he thought it must be heard outside. How on earth could the S.S. have got onto them so quickly? – unless someone had seen them coming in and reported it. As he reached the window Marie-Louise put out a restraining arm, pulling him back to the side. 'Careful! I don't think they'll be able to see us through the curtain – but the sun is shining into the room, and you never know. We don't want to draw attention to ourselves.'

Cautiously peering out, he saw there were two army trucks pulled up along the side of the market hall, black-uniformed troops, rifles in hand, already tumbling out and racing across the cobbles.

But in a direction away from the clinic.

Marie-Louise had backed up against him as they huddled into the corner, her hair brushing against his chin. There was a hint of some discrete perfume. Instinctively he'd placed his hands on her arms, and could feel her shivering. Here he was, still in a blue funk even though there seemed now to be less cause for alarm. But what must it be like for her? Had there been a similar scene when Raoul had been arrested? That memory must be with her for all time.

Now, as they continued to watch, their breathing coming raggedly, they saw people – two men and a woman – being dragged and driven out from one of the houses, violently pushed by both hand and rifle butt so that they staggered and stumbled, hardly able to keep their feet. Marie-Louise, with an animal moan, started to turn away, then froze again as one of the SS troops, clearly an officer judging by his high-peaked cap, broke away and strode purposefully in the direction of the clinic. But at the same time another figure, this time in the grey uniform of an officer of the *Wehrmacht*, came into view from beneath the window and took a couple of steps to meet him, saluting as he did so.

'*Mon Dieu*!' exclaimed Marie-Louise.

Peter's heart gave a leap. 'What is it?'

'*C'èst le médecin*! The doctor! But he's not due this week! Quickly, into the back room! And take those boxes. I'll try to stall him down at the door. But he knows there's a clinic this afternoon, so he'll probably come up. Just push the door to, without fully closing it, and try to look busy, but quietly! He probably won't have reason to come in there, but if he does then I'll have to come in with him and introduce you. His French is very poor – we converse in English – so if he says something to you try to pretend you can't understand. Just keep saying *Excusez moi?* And for God's sake don't give any indication that you understand English!'

With that, she made for the stairs; and Peter scooped up the various boxes, putting the original ones back into the cupboard and taking those they needed into the back room. This, about half the size of the main room, had a small window with grimy, frosted glass through which grey light filtered uncertainly. Once he'd pushed the door to, it was distinctly gloomy therefore, but when his eyes had adjusted he could see that there was a clutter of bits and pieces of equipment and furniture, and a number of stacks of other boxes. They at least might provide him with something with which to look busy.

Hardly had he got started on this than he heard muffled footsteps and the murmur of voices in the main room. Curious, he tried to make out what was being said, but it was all too indistinct, and he didn't dare get too close to the door for fear of being discovered. This went on for a few minutes, voices rising and falling but still unintelligible. Then, suddenly, he heard Marie-Louise cry out as though she'd been struck, and this was followed by silence. Heart in mouth, he expected that at any moment the jerry officer would burst in through the door, revolver in hand (did medical officers in the German army carry revolvers?). For a few seconds he dithered. Was Marie-Louise being physically hurt, and if so to what extent? Should he rush out there and try to protect her, or would this only turn what was in fact a minor problem into a disaster? He prevaricated, creeping nearer to the crack in the door to try to discover more. At this point he could hear the man's voice again, and the sound of Marie-Louise weeping, something he would never have expected of her. Anger rose within him, weakening his self-restraint. Agitated, he shifted position, trying to make a decision – and as he did so, his foot struck something metal on the floor, which rolled away with a sepulchral ring.

As he backed away, holding his breath, there was sudden silence in the room outside. This was followed by the man's voice, and then that of Marie-Louise. And the next moment he heard her call out, '*Pierre, entrez ici, s'il vous plaît.*'

It took a few seconds for him to understand what was expected of him; but her voice, although shaky, had been calm and clear, and the instruction definite.

Cautiously he opened the door and moved into the room. Marie-Louise was sitting by the desk, her face pale, her eyes red, and tears still glistening on her cheeks. The German officer, silhouetted against the sun-washed window, stood looking down at her, his right hand resting on one of hers. He looked up as Peter entered the room, stared for a moment, and then took a step back, his eyes widening in horror and disbelief.

For a second, against the light of the window Peter didn't recognise him. Then it sank in. He was staring into the face of Hans Kolber. It was his turn to be rent by horror.

Marie-Louise meanwhile, who had briefly lifted her chin towards Peter as he came in, as if to indicate that he should remain calm and follow the plan, now began to look from one to the other with growing concern, clearly baffled as to what was taking place.

'This is Pierre Lebrun,' she said to Hans, uncertainty evident in her voice in spite of an obvious effort to keep it firm. 'He's recently come to work for me at the farm.'

Hans meantime had turned his back on Peter, and was staring out of the window, his body rigid. This gave Marie-Louise the opportunity to mouth a silent question at Peter, her bewilderment all too obvious. Her face was so stricken, his heart went out to her: gone was all the toughness he'd become accustomed to over the days. But he in turn was paralysed by doubt. Fate had turned up the unlikeliest hand possible. What the implications were – all the permutations racing through his mind as to which way it might go – who could tell?

However, Hans then fed him a clue, abruptly swinging around on his heel and saying, with feigned disinterest, '*Bonjour, Pierre, comment allez-vous?*'

His accent was awful, even to Peter's ears, and his expression one of indifference; but those remembered brown eyes carried amusement as well as a lingering astonishment.

'*Très bien, monsieur,*' Peter stammered. '*Merci.*'

480

He wasn't sure where Hans was taking this, knew only that he'd better go along with it. It was Hans who held all the cards. Covertly he studied him for a moment. In spite of the severe military uniform, which made him look slimmer, he'd changed very little in the five years.

'*Eh, bon. Dîte moi, parlez-vous l'allemande?*' The amused expression had changed to one of mischief.

'*Je regret, non, monsieur.*'

'*Je regret aussi, Pierre. Mais, parlez-vous anglais peut-être?*' His eyes now fairly twinkled; and Peter began to think perhaps this was going to be all right. But then he remembered what had happened to Hans's mother, and the apparent lack of compassion on that occasion. And caution returned. But, whatever Hans's game, he had to go along with it.

'*Non, monsieur. C'est-à-dire, un peut seulement.*'

'*Un peut?* A little? Well, that will perhaps suffice.' He turned to look at Marie-Louise, who was still sitting there looking confused and distraught, and his expression changed to one of concern, tenderness almost. 'I'm afraid I've had to bring bad news to Madame Pontet. I'm sure she would like some minutes to herself, so we will leave her and go into that other room. There are some things I would like to ask you.'

Marie-Louise began to rise, desperation in every line; and Hans put a reassuring hand on her shoulder.

'It's all right, my dear. Do not distress yourself. Nothing terrible is going to happen, to you or to Pierre. You have suffered enough already.'

Peter could see that Hans's attempts at reassurance were having little effect. She still looked frantic, and clearly mystified, her eyes beseeching Peter to do something, or at least to provide some explanation. Still unsure of the outcome himself, he could only hold up his hands in a small placatory gesture and give her a smile, hoping that she would take comfort from that. And, needing some explanations himself, he allowed himself to be propelled away by Hans, who, apparently wanting to maintain some sort of subterfuge, uttered the one word, '*Venez!*'

Once inside the back room, Hans closed the door and turned on the light. Gripping Peter by both arms, he fiercely hissed, 'What the devil are you doing here?'

'I was shot down,' Peter said, following Hans' lead and keeping his voice low. Whatever Hans's intentions, he had to go along with it. But how else was he to answer except with the truth?

'You're in the R.A.F.?'

'Yes. Obviously.'

Hans ignored the mild sarcasm. 'As a pilot?'

'No. Like you, as a medical officer.'

'Then how the devil did you get yourself shot down over France?' There was disbelief there.

'That's a good question. I've asked myself the same thing many times over the past days.'

Hans allowed himself the semblance of a smile, but there was still suspicion. 'Go on.'

'I thought I should experience what the aircrews were experiencing.'

Hans stared at him for a moment, then broke into a grin. 'Trust you to get it wrong!'

But Peter had something else on his mind. 'What's this bad news you've brought Marie-Louise, then?' he demanded.

Hans immediately sobered. 'Her husband, who is also a doctor, was arrested by the Gestapo, accused of working for the Resistance.'

'Yes, I know about that.'

'You do? I hope that is all you know. Anyway, I learned this morning that he…died in custody, shall we say. It is very sad for her.'

Peter stared at him. 'Is that all you can say? "Very sad"!'

Hans stared back. 'Peter, you do not know this Doctor Pontet. I do not know him. We both know Marie-Louise Pontet, who is a good and courageous woman. As, no doubt, was her husband. And she is now a widow, expecting his baby. As I say, it is very sad. But these things happen all the time, in the present circumstances. What happens when you drop your bombs, huh? Yes – I know – or when we drop our bombs? People die, people become bereaved, people suffer. We have tumbled into a mad world. And we find ourselves on the opposite sides of a wall from one other. We who are friends, who are doctors, who are here to help people, to save them, who inhabit the same world, the same ethics, the identical profession of which we are both so proud. And we look on helplessly. But what are we to do? There are many bad things going on, but you or I cannot stop them. We are swept along with everyone else. We can only do our little bits here and there to try to correct things. In the face of this tempest we have to hang onto the things which truly matter: only by doing that can we mitigate the terrible effects of the storm. Which is why we are having this conversation now, like this. Do you understand?'

He was beginning to. If he was hearing Hans correctly, Hans was going to go along with the pretence put forward by Marie-Louise and him. As a friend he was not about to throw Peter and Marie-Louise to the wolves. And in taking this stance, he was doing so at some risk to himself, believing that was the right thing to do.

'Yes, Hans, I think I do. What I think you're saying is that there are things which ride above the awful things of the present time; a spirit which flies above the baser aspects of mankind, and which must be made to survive?'

'Yes!' said Hans with fervour. 'Exactly that. I knew you would understand. Do you remember those lines from those verses about Kate Kennedy, at St. Andrews, which you quoted to me at the time?'

He didn't; but clearly Hans did. 'Go on.'

'If I remember correctly, they go, …*I shall not perish – nay, I shall enjoy while years exist*…And then, …*I am your past delight, your beauty lost; all that you saw and all you failed to see; plaything and price, the purchase and the cost – I am them all...I am Kate Kennedy.* I've thought about that often, found it poetic, but not really understood it – until recently. I think – now – this Kate Kennedy represents the spirit of mankind – flawed as it is: the high aspirations, and the lost opportunities; the beautiful and the ugly; the successes and the mistakes; the good things and the bad. An understanding of that is probably more relevant now than it's ever been. There is much evil around; but there is much good. I think, probably, Marie-Louise and her husband – her late husband – represent much of the good. Who knows who will win this terrible war. But whoever it is, that spirit, that better aspect of mankind, must be made to survive; there must continue to be people who will search it out and carry it forward.'

He stared at Hans with new respect – and not a little astonishment. He remembered the conversation about Hitler that he and the others had had with him, that evening in 'Sallies', and the naivety with which Hans had approached the subject, not willing to believe anything bad about Hitler. And he recollected again the dispassion with which Hans had related, on Peter's visit to Berlin, the facts about the loss, through divorce, of his mother. Dare he now ask about her? Would Hans now see it in a different light?

'Do you hear anything of your mother, these days?' he blurted out.

A look of pain crossed Hans's face, and for a moment also one of displeasure. Then his face softened. 'Yes. I have regular letters from her. She has settled well in the United States. In New York. She is quite happy, I think.'

And your grandmother was going with her, I seem to remember?'

The look of pain returned. 'I regret to say my grandmother... died. In Germany – before she was able to go.' He grimaced, a private gesture; then with forced lightness, said, 'That was a good week, was it not, that week in Berlin, during the Olympics? Do you remember all those pretty girls in the Tiergarten? How they smiled at us? We missed our chance there, I think, did we not!'

'Yes,' he replied, with equally forced enthusiasm.

'You are married? Or have a girl?'

'No. And you?'

Hans shook his head. 'No. Me neither.' He laughed, an attempt at gaiety, but instead managing to sound only sad. 'Perhaps they weren't smiling at us, after all, those girls, do you think! Not handsome enough for them!'

Peter laughed back, politely; but the nostalgia was all too plain. And the conversation was becoming sticky again, uncertainty building up tension. Hans too was aware of it, for now he retreated into the persona of *Wehrmacht* officer, stiff and upright.

'But we must leave all this until another time. Those *verdamt* S.S. are crawling all over the town, and if I stay longer it will put us all in danger. Also, it would be wiser not to reveal to Madame Pontet that we already knew each other – just in case, you understand? You will perhaps be able to make up some story about our topics of conversation in here?'

'Yes. I understand.' (Only too well, he thought bitterly. Hans was worried that if Marie-Louise were to be arrested, then as a result of what was forced out of her he, Hans, too might well become implicated.)

'Well, old friend, I wish I could say it's been good to see you again – astonishing as it has been! Perhaps the next time will be in more pleasant circumstances? You notice I do not ask what plans you have – but I wish you luck. And, whatever the result of this war, God willing we will meet again.'

'Yes, Hans, I hope so. And thank you. You are indeed a good friend.'

Hans started to salute, then changed his mind and shook Peter's hand. '*Auf Wiedersehen*, Peter.'

CHAPTER THIRTY-TWO

He came to with a start, almost falling off the stool; understood to his horror that he must have nodded off. How long had he been out for the count? Not for more than a few seconds, surely? Guiltily he looked across at Marie-Louise, partly hidden by Beal stretched out on the kitchen table between them, the blood-soaked sheet covering him like a shroud. Wearily he got to his feet so that he could see her properly. She at least was still awake, sitting listlessly the other side of the table, staring into space, her hands cradling her belly as though wanting, if nothing else, to protect that life within. Both of them were totally exhausted by their efforts and by the nightmare of the past thirty-six hours; yet, although her ordeal had been infinitely greater than his, robbing her of sleep during the night even more than it had him, it had been she who had driven them on, resolutely repelling despair. Only when all was over had she allowed her own sorrow to enter in. Now, he let his gaze dwell on her face. Even though she was, at the moment, dejected, he thought how lovely were her features in repose, shed of all that energy and anger.

His admiration of her had now become immense. After Hans had gone, the previous afternoon, other than a few hasty words of what he'd hoped would be reassurance he'd had no time to explain anything to her before the first patients for the clinic had arrived – a clinic she had been determined to continue in spite of all that had happened. How she'd got through the following half hour, devastated by grief at the news of Raoul's death and in addition fearful of what might be about to happen to her, he couldn't imagine. But get through she did. She must constantly have been expecting that at any minute there would be the rush of jack-booted feet up the stairs. Fortunately however, as a result of the activities of those same S.S. outside, patients had been few in number; and as soon as the last had gone she'd wasted no time before bursting into the back room to discover from Peter just how bad his grilling by Hans had been.

At that point, even although Hans had impressed upon him the need to keep her in ignorance of his and Peter's prior friendship, he'd felt there was no alternative but to breach that unspoken promise of complete confidentiality. For how else was she to believe that this Major Kolber's perplexing approach to Peter had not only *not* had sinister implications, but on the contrary had been for the protection of all three of them (for Peter was in no doubt that, whatever the sincerity of Hans's actions, his decision had been as much in his own interests as in theirs). Equally, once she'd heard the facts Marie-Louise had needed no prompting for her to realise she must never reveal to Hans that she knew anything of this. There was no telling then what even he might do about her if he thought he was being put in jeopardy.

Even so, she'd taken some persuading that this most unlikely turn of events was anything more than a figment of Peter's suddenly deranged imagination. And only after she'd got over her astonishment and her face had momentarily flooded with relief, only then had she allowed her personal grief to fully take hold. At first he'd watched, ineptly immobile, as she'd slumped, face in hands, and sobbed uncontrollably. He'd quickly understood, though, that there was more to it than pure grief: mingling with sorrow were undoubted signs of relief. For some seconds he'd found this difficult to believe. Then the penny had dropped. For one thing, Raoul's undoubted suffering had ended. But more than that, Raoul's life may have been snatched away, but the life of his unborn child, for a while seemingly threatened, had been given an unexpected reprieve. And, at that point, more than ever he'd appreciated just how much courage it was taking for her to do what she thought was right. In helping to conceal R.A.F. personnel she was willing to risk not only her own life, but, far more importantly, the life of her child.

Only then had his feeling of impotence vanished, so that he'd been able to go to her, gently lift her to her feet and enfold her in his arms for her to weep against his shoulder, her tears of both sadness and transient relief mingling with his own.

After that, the journey back to the farm had been comparatively sombre. Marie-Louise's need to come to terms with the loss of her husband, as well as the contemplation by both of them of the dangers and difficulties that lay ahead, had driven them into silence. Theoretical planning, thought-provoking as it had been, had been completed: a far more frightening challenge still faced them. For not only would there be the uncertainties of the surgery itself, but there was a growing awareness of just how vulnerable they were going to be over the coming days should the S.S. come sniffing around: whether it was by being caught *in flagrante* during the course of the operation itself, or during the days afterwards when it would be virtually impossible to get Beal into hiding at short notice.

Then, too, he hadn't yet been able to come to terms with what was about to happen to Beal, and his own central role in that. Having a limb chopped off resulted in a kind of bereavement in itself, didn't it? But it also had more practical implications for Beal. It was going to clobber Beal's chances of getting back to Blighty in the foreseeable future. And what about his own

486

chances, come to that? – for he couldn't very well go off and leave Beal in this predicament, nor for that matter leave Marie-Louise to cope with him.

All these thoughts had gone through his mind. And he'd decided the whole thing was a mess, good and proper – so that by the evening he hadn't been able to shake off his moroseness. It must have been all too obvious, for it was then that Marie-Louise and Beal had both lost patience with him. Marie-Louise had simply walked out of the room. Beal had exploded.

'For God's sake, Waring!' he'd burst out. 'You'd think it was your bloody leg that's about to come off; or, your loved one who's just been murdered by the fucking Gestapo! Give some thought for the rest of us, will you!'

It had brought him to his senses. Full of contrition, he'd apologised.

After a few minutes Beal had simmered down sufficiently to say, 'Look here, Peter, I do understand how difficult it is for you as well. But you're allowing yourself to fall back into the pattern of your youth. It's the same old problem, isn't it? Too much introspection, too much self-criticism leading to loss of self-confidence? As I must have said to you in the past, if there's a job that has to be done, however difficult, there's a lot to be said for just bloody well getting on and doing it, and to hell with the consequences! You're far too self-deprecating for your own good, you know. For a change, why don't you try believing what's all-too-obvious: that in your own personal way you're every bit as capable as the rest of us. Each of us has his own strengths and talents, as well as his weaknesses; the differences between us don't necessarily make one better than another. Good God, man, you couldn't have succeeded as a doctor if that weren't so! All you need to do is take that final step out of childhood.'

He'd thought about that during the sleepless hours of the night. (Too much thinking again! – but at least he'd come to some sorts of conclusions.) Inevitably it had taken him back to his parents once more. Throughout his life, the only person he'd ever remembered giving him any sort of encouragement had been Uncle John. However, that very thought had pulled him up short. For there he was again, putting the blame on others for his own mistakes and inadequacies, without giving any consideration to the flaws and failures that they themselves had had to contend with in their lives. Furthermore, as he'd listened to himself silently voicing these ideas, it had struck him just how self-pitying and pathetic it all sounded – and after that he'd drifted into a kind of restless sleep.

Now, as he stared at Beal's amputated leg lying in ghoulish isolation by the sink (waiting for Hercule to come and take it away), he thought it might serve as some sort of a metaphor for his own life. For he knew, inside, that he'd tended always to see himself as cut off, unwanted and unloved.

And his thoughts inevitably turned once again to his father (his supposed father, Gerald, that is), whom he'd come to regard, early in childhood, as being an uncaring and arrogant bully. Gradually, though, he was beginning to understand that perhaps the man himself had suffered from all-too-familiar shortcomings: lack of self-esteem and all the rest of it – no doubt compounded by his experiences during the war. Was it this that had partly led him into having that disastrous affair with Anne – a liaison which had verged on the incestuous – and to all that had followed, so that finally he'd hated himself to such an extent that he'd had to end it all?

He remembered only too well that final act (since that evening with Arthur, when he'd excavated the memory from his subconsciousness, it wouldn't leave him alone). Deep down he'd always blamed himself for it. But now at last he'd come to the conclusion that at the most he'd merely been a catalyst; if what happened hadn't done so at that particular crisis, it would have done so at another. His father simply hadn't been able to learn to 'just bloody well get on with it'.

Anyway, he wondered, how many of his father's defects were to some extent the responsibility of *his* own parents? Was there no limit to that endless cycle? Perhaps not, in one sense. But, when all was said and done, every individual had to walk the earth alone, did they not? Was it not up to each to find their own way?

So. It was time for an amputation of his own. Time to cut out all these thoughts. Time to finally grow up. Time to get on with it and to hell with the consequences. And that was what he'd just done.

Now that it was all over it was with curious detachment that he stared at Beal, lying there inert on the table. He would be hard put to clearly recall the sequence of events during that three quarters of an hour of surgery.

It had begun well enough, once Marie-Louise and he, after a little bit of trial and error, had been content with the level of anaesthesia; and once he'd plucked up courage to take scalpel in hand and make the first incision. The cuts had been clean and well-shaped, though, to form the future skin flaps for covering the eventual stump. He'd been pleased with that. And, having already applied a tourniquet, there had been little bleeding at this stage, just a gentle, capillary ooze. But he remembered thinking he would have to work fairly fast: the tourniquet would have to be released before long if damage to surviving tissue was to be avoided.

Cutting through muscle, though, had required more courage, for it was then that important structures had had to be identified. And it was at this point that memory now became confused. He remembered finding and tying off the femoral artery and vein at the appropriate level: that had been relatively straightforward. The tricky bit had been identifying the main branches that came off the proximal, upper, part of the femoral vessels, all of which had to be tied off and severed at just the right level for an adequate blood supply to be preserved to the stump. He'd searched back in his memory to anatomy classes of ten years ago, and thought that he'd brought to mind two of the branch arteries – the profunda femoris and the descending geniculate. Had he adequately traced those and ligatured them? When he thought about it now, it wasn't clear in his mind. But he must not have done, or else had missed one he'd forgotten about, for when he'd got Marie-Louise to cautiously loosen the tourniquet there had been an immediate gush of blood filling the whole area so that he'd no longer been able to see what he was doing. That was when he'd been on the verge of panic. Without Marie-Louise's presence of mind all might have been lost right then. Fortunately she hadn't let go of the strap and had been able to fairly quickly reapply it. Then, eventually, he'd regained his senses, found the offending vessel and dealt with it. But the damage had been done. In those few seconds Beal had lost a lot blood.

He must have completed the operation in a daze. He did remember sawing through the bone. That had been every bit as gruesome as he'd imagined, the now-severed limb coming away in his hand. But he had no recollection of sewing up muscle and skin. All he could remember was that by then it had all seemed rather pointless.

Yet, against all the odds, Beal had survived. His blood pressure was frighteningly low, to be sure. However, his pulse, though fast and weak, was regular. And his breathing was even. But the operation had been finished fifteen minutes ago and, as yet, Beal had shown no sign of coming round from the anaesthetic. Marie-Louise was blaming herself for that. She'd said as much; that she must have given him too much. But he knew that without the haemorrhage Beal would probably have been all right, and had emphatically said so.

He was about to say so again when the outside door flew open and Hercule's stocky figure burst in, Jeanette close on his heels, both of them gabbling something at Marie-Louise.

She sprang to her feet. 'He says there are German patrols in the area. Quickly! We must at least get Jim out of here, preferably up to your room. That at least will give us a chance.'

He hesitated. Moving Beal now might jeopardise any chance there might be for his recovery.

'*Dépêchez-vous!*' she spat at him. 'Do you think we have any choice! If they find us here, we will all die! You and Hercule take him upstairs. You can carry him on the sheets: the groundsheet underneath will be strong enough. Jeanette and I will clear up here as best we can.'

She said something rapidly to Hercule; then to Peter: 'Hercule will stay up there with you and help to move Jim through to the barn if it becomes necessary. *Alors, allez! Au plus vite!*'

How they managed to get Beal up the two flights of stairs without finishing him off there and then, he'd never know. Even more astonishingly, he seemed none the worse for it. Although still deeply unconscious, his pulse continued to be regular and if anything felt a little stronger. But the next few hours – if indeed they were to be allowed them – would be critical. If only there was some way of giving him a transfusion. But there wasn't. They had, the previous afternoon, discussed at some length the advisability of being prepared for that necessity; but it had turned out there was neither equipment nor suitable intravenous fluid at the clinic, and no possibility of getting it from anywhere else without raising considerable suspicion.

Over the next few hours he hovered between concern for Beal and that of the vision of grey-uniformed troops at any minute storming through the yard and into the house. He patrolled constantly from Beal's bed to the window and back again, finding solace from neither. He was uncomfortable too with the presence of Hercule, who remained at all times skulking by the window, as though daring the Germans to come anywhere near the place. He'd had little to do with the man, before this, but had found him to be a forbidding figure at the best of times. In his late fifties or early sixties, thickset and swarthy, with beetling brows and what appeared to be a permanent scowl, Hercule gave the impression of being monosyllabic even in his own language; and he affected not to understand a word of Peter's stumbling French, never mind his English. So the time was spent in silence, the minutes ticking by fraught with tension. Gradually the daylight dwindled, adding further gloom to the room: they felt unable to draw the curtains, which would have meant losing that sixty seconds of advanced warning of any threat; and therefore they were unable to put on the light, sensing that to do so would draw unwanted attention to an upstairs room. And all this time Beal's condition remained obstinately unchanged, Peter fretting about his pulse, blood pressure and respiration, and not daring to venture downstairs to see how Marie-Louise was faring.

It was virtually dark by the time they heard footsteps outside the door. But to his surprise it was Jeanette who entered, switching on the light and going over to close the curtains. She was clearly agitated, and spoke rapidly to Hercule, who then grunted, got up, and left the room. Jeanette turned to Peter, and he saw that she had a piece of paper in her hand, from which she began to laboriously read in fractured English. 'No German now. All gone. Madame baby coming. Hercule gone for midwife.' Then she did a curious little bob and fled the room.

He swore beneath his breath, thought: This is all we need! – did a quick check on Beal, and hurried after Jeanette.

He found Marie-Louise in the kitchen, sitting crouched over on a chair. She gave him a wan smile. 'Sorry about this. How is Jim?'

'About the same. No worse, but still out for the count.' He glanced around the kitchen – they'd done a remarkable job of clearing up. 'How are you?'

'All right. My waters broke – is that how you say it? – about an hour ago. And I've had the pains since. Quite strong and frequent.' She gave a rueful laugh. 'I thought with a first baby it was more gradual than that.'

'How often are the pains?'

'About every three or four minutes. I haven't counted.'

It surprised him that they were already as frequent as that, but he made light of it. 'Well, you're certainly not wasting time! You've sent for the midwife?'

'Yes. Jeanette delivered the message all right? I didn't quite feel up to coming upstairs at that moment. But the word had just come down the line, as it were, to say the patrols had gone away – we have a sort of network which keeps track of what the Germans are doing all the time – and I needed Hercule to go for Madame Jouet.'

490

'Madame Jouet is the midwife? Is she all right?' He wondered whether to offer to examine her at this point, but felt a bit reticent about that.

'You mean, is she any good? Yes, I think very good. She has no formal qualifications, but is in her fifties by now and must have delivered hundreds of babies around Sablemont over the years, so she has much experience. She lives not far from here, so should be here soon. And also absolutely "safe" from the point of view our security.' She grimaced, and bent over again, staying in that position for a good minute before straightening and giving him a weak smile. 'Sorry.'

'Where are you feeling the contractions?' he asked.

She pondered his question for a moment, an amused expression on her face as if to say, You men, you know nothing about it! Then she became serious as she understood his concern. 'Mostly in front, low down. But also quite a lot in my back.'

He had the thought again that he should offer to examine her. But as he was about to say something, she continued more briskly, 'I'm all right. Jeanette will be back in a minute, and then I think I'll get up to my room and rest for a while. You get back to your patient. And let me know as soon as there's any improvement, won't you.'

'Of course. And you'll let me know if I can be of any help?'

'I will be good, don't worry.' She sounded almost embarrassed.

Back in the room, for something to do he checked Beal's blood pressure again. To his surprise and delight the systolic had come up a little, to 80. But he still couldn't find a definite diastolic. And couldn't get any response from him. Despondent, he lay down on his bed.

Over the next few hours his mind wandered over this and that. Memories of schooldays kept coming to the fore, in spite of his attempts to shut them out. Drowsy, he drifted in and out of half- sleep, so that images passed in an erratic manner, not clearly recollections and not clearly dreams. Unsurprisingly, much of it included Beal; but at times Beal's presence became confused with that of Peter's father, and with that of Uncle John. He heard sounds which must have been those of the midwife arriving; and at intervals muffled voices filtered up from the floor below. At one of his more lucid moments he came awake wondering about Donaldson, Baldwin and Mahon. Since word had arrived here that they were 'on the move', they'd heard nothing more of course. Were they still free and on their way home? Or would they be holed up somewhere else, with no prospect of getting any further?

Then, all at once he finds himself looking down on Beal. Beal at the controls of a plane – not clearly the Wellington – Beal doing a sort of jive as bombs are spewed out of the plane's belly and fall to the echo of his glee. He, Peter, is somewhere above it, outside, looking down. The next thing, he too is down there in city streets, falling with the bombs, the bombs floating down in a black cloud, like rooks; flames and rubble are everywhere, people screaming and running, horror in every line. Stunned and helpless, he stands and looks; and as he does so a hand and arm, somehow familiar, a child's arm, thrust out of some fallen brickwork to mutely hold something aloft. At first he can't make out what it is. Then he sees. It is Beal's leg. The screaming all around rises to a crescendo.

And he came awake, thrashing and sweating.

But the sound continued. Not the same, but a distant shriek subsiding into silence. The sound of Marie-Louise, it dawned on him, coming from the floor below. Guiltily he looked at his watch. Three a.m. Groggily he got to his feet and hurried over to Beal. Surely he would have regained consciousness by now? He only had to do that, Peter knew, and his fighting spirit would see him through. But there was no change.

Then the noises from Marie-Louise's room again, a combination of agony and fear. There must be something wrong. She was too much of a stoic for that to be the sound of normal labour.

He headed for the door; and barged into the girl, Jeanette, who was on her way in. '*Monsieur, venez vite, s'il vous plaît!*'

Without waiting for response she turned and raced back down the stairs. He hurried after her, agitating as to what might be going wrong.

Marie-Louise lay on her back on a large double bed, a cotton nightgown up around her waist, her breasts tumbling carelessly from its open neck. Her face, which was turned his way, was as bleached as the pillow against which it lay, and taut with fatigue. A stout grey-haired woman wearing a stained white pinafore over a black dress, stood near the foot of the bed, leaning over Marie-Louise, whose knees were up and apart in the classical delivery position. The woman, Madame Jouet presumably, turned a flushed face in his direction as he entered. Her expression, initially registering some surprise, however remained calm and determined as she gave him a curt nod. But there was something else there as well, something also reflected in the face of Marie-Louise, and in that of Jeanette who was hovering uncertainly between bed and door. It took him a moment to realise what it was. Fear bordering on terror.

Even as he took all this in, Marie-Louise's mouth started to contort, her thighs, supported by her hands, drew up against her belly, her head and shoulders came up off the bed, and she began to moan – low, animal noises, a primitive sound with a life of its own. Madame Jouet said something to her, fierce and urgent; and it was then she began to scream. It seemed to go on and on, a sound surpassing that of pain; a heartfelt cry for help. A sound that in his experience he'd heard only once before. And he knew there was something terribly wrong.

Hurrying over to the bed, and almost brushing aside the midwife in his haste, he felt for Marie-Louise's pulse. So rapid and thready was it, it took him a few moments to find it. By now the screams had subsided, and she had fallen back, exhausted – so drained that at first she was unable to speak. But her eyes spoke for her. Startling against the pallor of her face, the pupils dilated, they were eloquent in their terror. More than that, they held a desperate plea. And he thought he understood then. Her fear was not for herself, but for her unborn child.

The midwife was still gabbling away, directing the words at him; whether to inform him, or whether to get him out of the way, he didn't know. He leant over Marie-Louise.

'Marie-Louise, you have to help me here. What is she saying?'

Silent, in the coils of her fear seemingly withdrawn into herself, she looked up at him beseechingly.

He shook her gently. He had to know, before the next violent contraction took her even further away.

'Marie-Louise. I can help you. Just tell me what I need to know.'

It was then that he saw that familiar light of determination re-ignite in her eyes; although her voice, when she spoke, was so weak he had to lean down to hear what she was saying.

'Lucille – Madame Jouet – tells me the head is well down, and the cervix fully dilated. ...She says that I'm just not pushing effectively enough. But I can't do any more. It just seems to be stuck. ...It feels as though I'm killing the baby.'

He straightened and looked around. The trumpet shape of a foetal stethoscope stood on a nearby table. Grabbing it, he placed it on the bed and hurriedly began to feel her tummy. And as he did so, the midwife seized his shoulder, her fingers like iron, and tried to pull him away.

Marie-Louise weakly held up a hand to try to stop her. He turned to the woman with what he hoped was a reassuring smile. '*C'est bien, Madame. Je suis médicin.*'

She looked at him in astonishment. '*C'est vrai?*'

'*C'est vrai,*' said Marie-Louise with effort.

One of Madame Jouet's eyebrows lifted in uncertain disbelief, but she stood back and allowed him to continue his examination. Right enough, he couldn't feel the baby's head, which must indeed be well down into the pelvis, but he could feel its feet up near the fundus of the uterus, so at least it confirmed it was a normal cephalic presentation. It took him a while to find the foetal heart, with the stethoscope; and when he did so, it was disconcertingly higher up towards the fundus than he would have expected. More worryingly it was very rapid – difficult to count, in fact, but he made it to be 170 or 180 per minute. A distressed baby, at some considerable risk.

'Marie-Louise, I'm going to have to examine you internally – do you understand?'

She gave a small nod, her eyes fixed on his; and she made an equally small dismissive gesture. I don't care what you do, she seemed to be saying, as long as you save this baby.

He quickly found some carbolic soap together with a nail-brush by a bowl of water on the side table, and scrubbed up. While he was doing this there were the alarmingly upsetting sounds of her having another contraction, and he knew he must get her examined before the next one could arrive. A quick look around confirmed what he expected: that there were no surgical gloves available. Without more ado, therefore, his hands still wet, he went over, waited a few more seconds for the spasm to subside, and then slipped his hand inside.

Sure enough, what the midwife had said, was so: the cervix was fully dilated, a thin rim applied to the presenting head, which was well within the pelvis. But he couldn't find on the surface of the skull the telltale softness of either of the fontanelles, which would tell him whether the position was the normal one of occipito-anterior, or the more awkward occipito-posterior – for the baby face-to-front always made delivery that bit more difficult. If this was the case, it might explain why there'd been so much hold-up. He pushed in a little further, which made Marie-Louise cry out. He apologised to her, explaining that he was trying to establish the position of the baby's head. Then, as he slid his hand up the posterior curve of the pelvic wall, he felt a soft indentation appear beneath his fingers. Was this one of the fontanelles? And if so, which? But something wasn't right. It was too small and too soft for it to be either of them. Straining a little more, he come up against something even softer, and flabby. Then it came to him what he was feeling! – an anus and a scrotum! It was a breech presentation – what he and the midwife had thought was the baby's head was in fact one of its buttocks. At the same time he registered that this was a boy, the significance of which for Marie-Louise was all too obvious. For a moment he was tempted to tell her. But then the full implication of the situation hit him: for he'd thought he'd felt feet up near the fundus of the uterus; and he couldn't feel feet here in the pelvis. The baby must be lying with legs extended up the length of the womb. And with its legs lying straight like that, acting as a rigid splint, that was what was preventing delivery. He groaned inwardly. A breech-with-extended-legs was notoriously difficult to deliver. One leg had to be manipulated so that it bent sufficiently at the knee to be able to perhaps grasp the foot and draw it down into the pelvis; then it had to be followed by the other. This was demanding at the best of times. He remembered that the problem always was dealing with the first leg, for the second one, lying alongside, interfered with the procedure. In fact, not infrequently it proved impossible without an anaesthetic which would relax the mother's musculature sufficiently for all this to be done.

And even when that had been achieved, there was still the difficulty, with any breech, of delivering the after-coming head: the head, coming first, as in a normal vertex delivery, being the broadest part and round and smooth, was what stretched the passage for the baby's body to follow. In a breech delivery that wasn't the case. Sometimes forceps had to be used to deliver the after-coming head. He looked around and couldn't see any obstetric forceps. Of course it wasn't likely that there would be.

But they did have some ether.

Marie-Louise meantime was being tortured by another contraction, her shrieks piercing him through. Not only was the baby in jeopardy, she was becoming dangerously exhausted. Furthermore, there was the risk that her uterus might rupture.

He had to get on and do this.

When the contraction had subsided sufficiently, therefore, he gently explained what he was going to have to do. 'Also, I'll have to do an episiotomy – to cut you – do you understand?'

For a moment she stared at him uncomprehendingly. Then with an enormous effort she seemed to rally. 'Just do it,' she said. 'I don't care about myself. But our baby must live.'

He swallowed hard. The chances of that seemed to be getting slimmer. But he couldn't say that to her.

'I'm going to give you a whiff of ether,' he told her.

'*Non!*' She spat the word out. 'No. It might finish the baby.'

'But it will relax your pelvic muscles, make it easier.'

'No!' she repeated, fury in her eyes. 'You are wasting time! Just get my baby for me!'

He quailed before her anger, for a moment angry himself: she was expecting too much of him, was being idiotically unrealistic.

Then Beal's words hammered at him again: Just get on and do it.

She was retreating now into the agony of another contraction. This was the time to act, while she was in the throes of her pain. He'd already spotted a pair of large episiotomy scissors among the other instruments on the table, had been intending to find out whether they'd been sterilised. Now he cast caution aside, grabbed them, placed the fingers of his other hand into her vagina to protect and support, and made the cut at the base of her vulva, through skin, muscle and vaginal wall in a backward direction at an angle of forty-five degrees – the words of Hamish MacGregor, Prof of Obstetrics, resounding in his ears: *The worst kind of episiotomy is the one that's too cautious.*

Her shrieks split the air; but it was probable she hadn't felt it: her pain had already reached its acme.

The ten minutes which followed would remain the longest ten minutes of his life. Her contractions, lasting almost two minutes each time, were now coming no more than a minute apart. In each of those brief intervals, while the uterus was relatively relaxed, he fought to bend the knee of the nearest of the baby's legs in order that he might reach its foot. And as he did so each time Marie-Louise frantically tried to get away from him, retreating up the bed, her screams revealing the inevitable torment he was subjecting her to; and now she had no respite from pain. It was torture for him also. He was tempted to give up; but didn't dare. And suddenly, unexpectedly, the knee gave. Straining upwards, following Marie-Louise as she involuntarily retreated from him, he was able to nudge it a bit more, to grasp the lower leg just beyond the knee and draw it down until he could seize the heel and bring it all the way. The second leg followed more easily, and with the gentlest of traction and a rush of fluid the rest of the body slid into view.

Without forceps, the head was more difficult. Fortunately the nape of its neck was facing him, so that with a bit of manoeuvring with one hand on the back of the head and the fingers of the other hand in its mouth, he was able to flex the head downwards and manipulate it through the vulval opening.

And the baby was grey and floppy, not moving. The umbilical cord was however pulsating. No time to waste. Quickly he clamped the cord and cut it. Hardly had he done so than from over his shoulder the baby was roughly seized by Madame Jouet and taken from him. However, he had no time to concern himself with that, for already there was bleeding, a swift trickle coming down the posterior vaginal wall and dripping down onto the bed. He peered past Marie-Louise's legs, up the length of her body to her face. And was shocked by what he saw. She appeared to be unconscious, in such a state of exhaustion that she might be on death's door. But for the moment no time for that either, for the trickle was becoming a gush. One hand back into the vagina, the other on her abdomen, on the fundus of the womb, compressing and massaging (wishing that he had some ergotamine available). And then the bleeding slowed. And stopped. He paused, waited, took a breath. Still all right. Hands bloody, not caring, he rose and rushed to her head, could hardly feel a pulse, couldn't tell if she was breathing. From across the room came a squawk, then a brief querulous cry. His eyes followed the sound, saw to his immense joy that the baby held unceremoniously in Madame Jouet's arms, was already beginning to kick and squirm. The next moment the room was rent by a series of angry wails.

But his joy could only be brief; reality struck back. His spirits plunged again, relinquishing hope. He grasped at what little of it he could. If only Marie-Louise could survive to at least see this.

And as he looked down on her once more her eyelids flickered and opened. Unfocussed at first, staring out at the unknown, listening, it seemed, to the unfamiliar sounds, her eyes gradually formed a question, one of bafflement and then of hope. Quickly and quietly he moved in to fill her silence.

'You have a boy, Marie-Louise.'

At first he didn't know whether she'd understood. Then tears appeared and spilled over. '*Merci, Pierre.*' The whisper was so weak he had to strain to hear it. Then, 'Thank you... Thank you.'

No time to do anything but give a brief squeeze of her hand, before returning to check what was happening below. And all was well. No further loss. He tried a gentle pull on the cut end of the cord. No movement yet. *The most important skill in the third stage of delivery is that of patience*, Prof MacGregor used to say. *The afterbirth will come when it's ready. Simply wait for a slight lengthening of the cord, then the only help it needs is a gentle pull, the other hand steadying the fundus of the womb.*' It wasn't always the case, of course. And there were some who advocated a more active approach. But on this occasion he thought he would take the Prof's advice.

He looked up as Madame Jouet abruptly appeared on the other side of the bed with the baby wrapped in a towel, and proceeded to place him, ever so gently, in the crook of Marie-Louise's arm. Then she stood and watched mother and baby with more tenderness in her face than he could ever have imagined. What the woman had done to resuscitate the baby in the way that she had, he didn't know; but it had been truly astounding. He got up from the foot of the bed, and stood also, watching Marie-Louise with her son. And as he watched he saw something remarkable happen. Her features took on a renewed strength, and the light of determination re-appeared in her eyes. The thought came to him then that if only Beal could regain his awareness, he too, in the same way, would be certain take up his own fight for recovery.

He must return though to the job in hand. The placenta had yet to be safely recovered; and Marie-Louise would need to be stitched before her traumatised perineum regained its full sensation. In fact, to his great relief, the afterbirth came away quite readily at the first attempt.

Over the next twenty minutes, as he sat at the foot of the bed working between her legs which were splayed and drawn up, methodically suturing the three layers – first the perineal muscles, then the vaginal wall, and finally the skin – he pondered once again the mystery that was childbirth. There was Marie-Louise, having gone through hours of torture – insupportable pain and the fear of what was to happen – and having been subjected to so much trauma that she had given indications of being unable to survive; yet instantly, once her child had been born, she had been transported to a state of ecstasy, all her torment forgotten. Even the suturing, a painful, undignified experience in itself, had elicited no more than an occasional grunt.

When he'd finished, and cleaned up, he went over to examine the baby, then, that done, he went up to her and briefly took hold of her hand. 'Well done, Marie-Louise,' he said. 'You have a fine boy.'

She looked up at him, and at Madame Jouet, her eyes brimming again. 'Thank you both, so much. *Merci beaucoup.* You have brought me new life.'

'What will you call him?' he asked. He thought he knew the answer to that. But still she surprised him.

'Raoul,' she said. Then, after a pause, 'Raoul Pierre.'

Later that morning, Beal died.

CHAPTER THIRTY-THREE

The hot June sunshine beating down on him did nothing to disperse the chill within, produced he knew by a sense of anti-climax. Arriving back at Marwell had turned out to be like arriving back at school as an Old Boy after several years' absence. The environment was the same, but the populace had changed. He'd fondly expected the place to be full of familiar faces all eager to greet his arrival, 'back from the dead' as it were; to be greeted as a kind of returning hero. Instead, there was hardly anyone he knew; no one to hang on to his every word, to hear about his experiences. He'd been away less than twelve weeks, yet there seemed to have been a wholesale change of personnel. The Stantons had gone: Arthur posted to Scampton, in 5 Group; and Sylvia – well, no one seemed to quite know about her, whether she'd gone with him or whether she'd gone back to Edinburgh as Arthur had for some time wanted her to do. The new C.O. was someone he'd never heard of, and who wouldn't, he was assured, be in any way interested in learning about Peter's exploits. (This information, such as it was, had been relayed to him by Matthews – he, at least, was still the Adjutant; and he'd given the impression of being even more harassed than before, thereby not inclined to spend much time chatting.) At the Sick Quarters a new M.O. had of course been appointed (but hadn't been there when Peter had dropped in); the Sister-in-charge had been replaced by someone he didn't know (and who was only vaguely interested in his pedigree); and Bart Browning, whilst still in post, was on leave. And when he'd popped into the Officers' Mess, the few faces in there were those of strangers. He'd trotted out a few names to them, in the hope of at least learning something of the old crowd, but all he'd been met with had been blank expressions. That, too, had been a chilling experience. Presumably those he'd known before were either posted elsewhere, dead or hospitalised. And with that depressing thought he'd come back into the sunshine to wander aimlessly around the station like a sheep separated from its flock.

What would he have had to tell them anyway? That his life had been saved by the skill and courage of their erstwhile C.O. – whom he'd repaid by allowing him to bleed to death? That over the past three weeks he'd been transported (somewhat unwillingly) across France, passed in succession from one person or group to another like a parcel? That, sometimes in the dark recesses of the night and sometimes in the bright exposure of day, he'd been taken on trains and buses, on bike or on foot, by strangers who, in most cases, spoke little or no English, and who'd seemed efficient but indifferent – and now and again scared out of their wits? That most of the time he hadn't known where he was or in which direction he was heading, and had half-expected that at any moment he might be abandoned into the arms of the Gestapo? That when, after eventually arriving at some fishing village on the Channel coast, and after sitting shivering for several hours in a damp hold smelling of fish and diesel oil, and then bounced around for a considerable time on a choppy sea, the sound of marine engines coming alongside had persuaded him that this, at the last gasp, had to be a German E-boat (whereas in fact it had turned out to be an R.A.F. rescue launch)? That when, exhausted and disorientated, he'd arrived at Portsmouth, instead of cheering crowds, banners and a band, he'd been met by the police, held in a cell overnight, and the following morning been interviewed at some length by Special Branch officers before being released and given a railway voucher to take him to London?

Hardly the stuff of heroism. Already, in his mind's eye he could see eyes starting to glaze over. 'Hair-raising exploits' of this sort were common currency, these days – not enough even to raise a solitary eyebrow.

What he wouldn't have told them was that he'd been reluctant to leave *Sablemont* in the first place. Now, when he looked back on his attitude then, he was mortified. That he could ever have entertained such an idiotically romantic notion beggared belief. But he recognized now that it was familiar ground, he'd been that way before, all too often. On this last occasion he'd cultivated this fond idea that he had become indispensible to Marie-Louise, that she'd developed a misty attachment to him, which would soon develop into love, enabling him to take on the role of replacement husband, father and local doctor. What had possessed him to think like that, he couldn't now imagine. To say it had been unrealistic was a gross understatement, particularly as it had totally ignored the inconvenient fact that this was Nazi-occupied France, and could very well permanently remain so. His only excuse, repeated to himself over and over, was that they had all just passed through a very emotional time, a psychologically unhinging experience. It could hardly have been a greater shock, though, when she, quickly picking up on his thoughts, led him to understand in no uncertain terms that not only were these ideas abhorrent to her but that she now regarded his continued presence a threat not only to her but also to her newborn son, and that the sooner he was out of there the better.

He could hardly blame her. She was right of course; and the restitution of her inherent toughness, now additionally bolstered by maternal instinct, had rapidly shouldered aside any erstwhile feelings of gratitude she might have had. He had discovered, however, that it was largely down to her influence (as well as the fact that he was being taken on his own) that he'd been taken to the Channel coast rather than via the much longer and more uncertain route over the Pyrenees, which was the usual method. He comforted himself also with the thought that she had at least named her son Pierre (at the time leaving no doubt in his mind that it had been a gesture of gratitude) and therefore would be permanently reminded of him. And why was that important to him? Out of nothing more than pure romanticism? What on earth was wrong with him? (Nevertheless, he promised himself, if, God willing, this damned war should one day be over, he would look her up again. And Hans, too – and what was that if it wasn't also pure romanticism?)

In foul and desolate mood, he looked around the airfield, at the bombers drawn up on the tarmac, and thought: it's just about as likely that those bloody planes will one day drop their bombs on the Pontet household, and that'll be the end of it. There was no order or reason to anything any more.

But when he stopped to take a hold on himself, he knew why he was in such a black mood. Nothing was going right for him. He'd hoped to quickly link up with the past, to re-connect. And it hadn't happened. None of his friends were here. He'd tried to phone Uncle John and Aunt Mabel, but in spite of several attempts hadn't so far been able to get through, the Long Distance Operator telling him again and again, 'All lines are busy'. Screwing up his courage to face Anna Beal, he'd tried to call her, to no avail. He didn't even know whether she was still at the same address. Then her name had stared out at him from a newspaper: she was starring in a new play at the Adelphi Theatre. But several attempts to get hold of her there had also come to nothing. So this evening he would have to go and try to see her at the theatre.

Unannounced. If his courage held.

He'd thought also of trying to get in touch with Jordan – but something in him had made him put that off. And he'd tried to get hold of Jamie at Church Wealdon, finally to be told by some officious-sounding WAAF officer that 'Corporal Evans was granted an honourable discharge from the service, on compassionate grounds, in the middle of May.' That had floored him – had she been wounded, was she ill, or was it something to do with her mother perhaps? Once more he'd tried to phone home, again without success. He felt as though he was having to drift, rudderless, without sense of direction or purpose, and without the necessary information to enable him to make decisions.

When he'd been at the Air Ministry yesterday, he'd tried to discover what people would have been told about his and Beal's disappearance back in March. First, though, he'd been immured all morning with the Intelligence bods, who'd been interested only in what he could tell them, rather than the other way round. They'd kept on and on trying to pump him on what he'd learned about the bits of Occupied France where he'd first of all stayed and then those he'd passed through en route back to Britain. And because he'd been unable to tell them anything of much interest they then seemed to regard him as somehow incompetent, even negligent – the fact that he'd survived (and Wing Commander Beal hadn't) had appeared to be of no concern to them whatsoever. All they'd been able (or willing) to tell him in answer to his own questions was that 'by the end of April, with no news coming via the International Red Cross, nearest relatives would have been informed of their being still missing, believed killed'. His exasperation, when they'd then been unable to say whether relatives would have now been informed of 'new developments', had seemed to mystify them. (He would have liked to have known, in particular, whether Uncle John and Aunt Mabel would already have been notified of his reappearance; and similarly whether Anna Beal would have had confirmation of Jim's death). He had, though, gleaned from them that only the previous week there had been notification via the Red Cross that the other crew members, Baldwin, Donaldson and Mahon, were prisoners-of-war in *Stalaglufte 2* ('...presumably, therefore fortunate enough to have been picked up by a unit of the *Wehrmacht* or the *Luftwaffe* and not by the S.S.').

With that, he'd been dismissed, but further floored then by being told that he was to face a 'Disciplinary Tribunal' in the afternoon, and therefore must not under any circumstances leave the building. It being by then lunchtime, and there being no evidence of anywhere to snatch a bite to eat, he'd had to spend the next two hours loafing in a corridor, brooding on what might be in store for him next. He had however had the comfort of his pipe. Whilst in France, he had managed to scrounge the odd pipeful of tobacco. He'd been most grateful for this, even though it had proved to be decidedly pungent. Then he'd come to understand the extent to which it was in short supply there, and thereafter had felt obliged to tactfully decline any further supplies. So, having been deprived of it for all those weeks, he was now thoroughly enjoying having it again.

What's more, during those two hours of waiting at the Air Ministry he had been entertained by a Fighter type killing time in the same fashion whilst waiting to go into an '...Intelligence debriefing, isn't it, boyo.' This was a red haired Welshman sporting a handlebar moustache, who turned out to be in Reconnaissance, flying Spitfires. Curious to know why the fellow had had to come all the way to the Air Ministry in London for that, he'd asked the question.

'They don't believe what it is I've had to say in my reports, isn't it?' the man had replied cheerfully, evidently not at all put out by his integrity being put into question. 'But I know what I saw – and I have the photographs to prove it!'

'Which is what?'

The chap had hesitated, then replied (without much conviction, it had to be said), 'I don't think I'm supposed to tell you that.'

It had been obvious he was dying to do so, however, so Peter had bided his time by taking the conversation in a different direction.

'That must be a risky business, flying reconnaissance?' he'd suggested.

'Not really. It tends mostly to be early morning or late evening: the angle of the light is better then, for the pictures, look you. So jerry isn't ready at those times for a lone aircraft coming over; and a single Spit must be pretty difficult to pick up on their R.D.F. or whatever it is they have. If they do spot me, by the time they've scrambled I'm in and out. And I always take a different route home. Also I'm going flat out, mind you; that is, as flat out as one can, carrying auxiliary tanks under the wings. And by the time I'm coming home I've ditched those, anyway.'

'How far can you get, then?' he'd asked, intrigued by the idea of a Spitfire doing long-range stuff, albeit with extra fuel on board.

'Depends on weather and winds and whatnot, look you, but a fair way into Germany. I fly in at what is reckoned to be the optimum height for economy, come down to take the pictures, and then get out again as fast as possible!'

By this time he'd peered with some interest at Peter's medical insignia. 'You're a medic, then? With our lot, or with Bomber Command?'

'Bomber. With Three Group.'

'Ah. Well, of course it's mainly the work of your boys that I'm doing the checking on. To see in daylight what effect they've had from some of their sorties. Not so much, in many cases, I'm afraid!'

'Must be difficult flying for you, though, on your own, having to navigate, take the pictures, and watch out for bandits, all at the same time?'

The man had dismissed that idea in a nonchalant manner – but nevertheless shown signs of being flattered before going on to change the subject. 'What have Intelligence wanted from a medic, then?'

Peter had told him.

It had been the Welshman's turn to look impressed. And it had broken through his professional caution.

'Look you, what I'm going to tell you is strictly on the Q.T., boyo. But being a doctor you'll know how to keep confidences?'

Here Peter, thoroughly intrigued, had given what he hoped was a reassuring nod – which must have worked, for after the briefest of hesitations the man had continued, 'Well, on three occasions over the past ten days I've come across large-scale enemy troop movements, in France, Belgium and Germany. Twice, big military convoys; and once, a whole Panzer division on the move.'

Peter hadn't been slow to take in the implications of this.

'Preparations for invasion?' he'd said in considerable alarm.

'Well, yes, you would think so, wouldn't you. After all, it's no more than we've been expecting. But there's the rum thing! In every case they were moving in an *easterly* direction, *away* from the Channel coast. As if they were *withdrawing*. And, as I say, I have the pictures to prove it.' Here he hesitated, then with an expletive he picked up his briefcase and without more ado spread a whole sheaf of photographs out on the table in front of them.

'See you. There in black and white! But the brass hats won't believe it. They're saying I must have got my orientation wrong. I ask you! If I was capable of doing that I'd have been a goner months ago!'

'I can see why they're thinking it doesn't make sense, though,' Peter had said. 'After all, why would jerry want to move so many troops back into Germany at this stage?'

'I don't know. Maybe it's a deliberate feint, to try to put us off? – maybe we were *meant* to see it? Maybe they're going back to refit and retrain? – after all, they've got the best part of three months of good weather yet, before they need to invade. If they're going to. But I know one thing. Something's afoot!'

'Why wouldn't they invade, anyway?' Peter had said, by now thoroughly alarmed but still grasping at slivers of hope. 'After all, they've got to do so sometime!'

'Exactly. But another weird thing is that as far as I can see – and I've talked to my chums in Reconnaissance, and they agree – there're no signs of movement of invasion barges like there were last autumn.'

'Perhaps they're better camouflaged? Perhaps they learned a hard lesson last time? – after all, we fairly blitzed them!'

'Could be. Anyway, it's not for the likes of us to decide about it. It'll all become clear in the end.'

Shortly after that Peter had been called in to his disciplinary tribunal, when his thoughts had perforce taken a different direction. However, the 'Tribunal' turned out to be two senior officers only – a Group Captain and a Wing Commander – both of whom he judged to be in their mid- to late-forties. Stern of face and correct in manner, they'd started off waspishly, asking him what on earth he'd been doing, 'a non-combatant going off on a bombing raid,' and hadn't he understood that it was contrary to the terms of the Geneva Convention for him to have been 'bearing arms', which in effect was what he'd been doing? He'd replied by saying that from what he'd been told the S.S. were sometimes torturing and executing British air crews, which also, presumably, was against the terms of the Convention; that he'd gone along to gain experience of what aircrews were having to go through during their sorties. The more senior of the two had responded to that by saying, 'I assume that, as a doctor, you don't have to have had pneumonia to know what the symptoms are?' To which he'd replied, 'No, sir. But I do know that, having now experienced what they go through, I will in future regard so-called 'Lack of Moral Fibre' in an altogether different light.'

After a hard look from the Group Captain he'd received merely a '*Huruumph!*' and they'd quickly passed on to ask was it Wing Commander Beal who'd 'knowingly' arranged for him to go along as a 'passenger'? To which he'd answered that he'd 'constantly pestered' the C.O. to allow him to have that experience, and he'd then gone on to detail the circumstances in which it had occurred. 'It wasn't as if I'd taken the place of the second pilot,' he'd added, 'because there wasn't one available. And W/C Beal took the view that having a second pilot on board was unnecessary, anyway.'

To which the Group Captain had replied, slightly sourly, that Wing Commander Beal had made those views known only too clearly in recent months – adding, more graciously, '...and I think many of us are now persuaded of that.'

After that, they'd become surprisingly avuncular, almost kindly, and had put him at his ease by congratulating him on his safe return, as well commiserating on the loss of Beal and Flying Officer Johnson.

Finally, before being dismissed with a 'token Official Reprimand' (as they had put it), they'd listened as he'd put in a plea for a posthumous 'gong' for Beal, in acknowledgement of what he'd achieved, even though seriously wounded, both during the raid and afterwards. To his astonishment, the 'Groupie' had then asked him, somewhat drily, what he had in mind? When he'd said, tentatively, that he'd thought perhaps a bar to his D.F.C.? The officer had merely nodded sagely, and let him go. Whether anything would come of it, and whether, in the face of Beal's death, anyone would really care, least of all Anna, he didn't know. However, it was the least that Beal deserved. (Yet he couldn't quite shake off the suspicion that he'd made the request partly to assuage his own sense of guilt.)

It had been well after 5.0 pm by the time he'd finally got away from the Air Ministry (having been granted two weeks' leave and told that he would be informed of his new posting in due course), and he'd been so weary by this time that once he'd eventually found a suitable hotel, he'd been only too glad to simply crash into bed. So he hadn't 'been able' to do anything about Anna (and deep down he knew he'd been relieved about having that short reprieve).

But it couldn't be put off any longer. This evening he'd have to try to do something about it. The longer he delayed, the more cowardly it would seem (and the more contemptuous Anna would be).

In an attempt to rid himself of this feeling of chill he turned his face once more to the sun. Heat was shimmering off the tarmac, and already the field was looking parched. It seemed as though it was set to be yet another long hot summer. In more ways than one. He thought of what the Welshman had said, of those signs which might well be heralding a coming invasion, however odd that might seem. How would Anna fare then? With her smoulderingly dark beauty, no Nazi would fail to regard her as anything but 'Non-Aryan', and would soon discover the truth of her Jewish background. Indeed, no doubt many of them would remember her and her film-star status in the pre-war years. Without Beal to protect her, what chance would she have on her own? And remembering what Beal had got him to promise about Anna, over that last bottle of wine, already the germ of an idea was growing inside him. Impatiently he brushed it aside as yet another example of his misplaced romanticism. Anyway, once she'd heard the truth about her husband's death, she would want nothing more to do with him. If, that is, he told her the truth. And how pathetic a thought was that?

He looked at his watch. Lunchtime already. Should he get something in the Mess? No, he didn't think so. His eyes travelled again around the empty expanse of field, at the grey ribbon of runway stretching into the distance, at the Wellingtons (along with six of the new, four-engined Stirlings) lined up, seemingly abandoned, on the tarmac. As he stared at them he found that misgivings about some aspects of Bomber Command's role in this war were once more edging in. He recalled the reconnaissance photographs that Taffy at the Air Ministry yesterday had been prevailed upon to bring out of his briefcase. Among those pertinent to his 'case', those that the Welshman had specifically wanted him to see, had been others – 'before' and 'after' shots of various targets in Germany. Truth to tell, Peter had been unable to make much of them. To him they'd seemed to be simply splodges of black and white, light and shade; no connection with anything actually on the ground. Were those dark areas the shadows of buildings still standing, or were they the outlines of where they'd once been? He hadn't wanted to ask. Those photographs were too remote to be associated with the reality of what must have happened in each of those places down there. Not for a moment could they begin to represent the agony and the actuality, the burned bodies and the flayed limbs of women and children, the careless extermination of men merely going about their lives. He understood, though, that it was the only way to fight this kind of war: to have symbols and icons representing 'the enemy', to have the enemy faceless, to imbue him with all the evils of the world so that he became a 'thing' to be stamped out.

He'd come to see, too, that if were theoretically possible for bomber crews to go over in absolute safety they wouldn't be able to carry out their mission: it would be seen as being too cold-blooded, too ruthless. They had to be driven by fear – fear so intense that it led to hate and anger; they had to be persuaded of the notion that it was 'kill or be killed'.

What, though, would future generations make of all this? What view would they take of this mutual wholesale destruction and slaughter from a distance? That would of course depend to some extent on the outcome of the war. But Bart Browning had always taken the view that what future generations think is not what's important. That the task of historians is to sift out, analyse, and learn – not to pass judgement. That one cannot moralise out of one's own place and time; that one cannot step into the shoes of the past.

Again, as he turned to look at the station buildings behind him, no one around, apparently deserted, he was overcome by desolation. It was only 'yesterday' (wasn't it?) that he'd originally arrived at Marwell, full of apprehension at the prospect of his new role, among people he didn't know. And now here he was again, with that very same feeling of isolation. It was like being in one of those dreams in which one is precipitated alone into an empty space that is all-too-familiar yet where one knows full well that the people who will soon appear out of nowhere will be total strangers. His first coming here, the 'Yesterday', had been an entry into the future; his leaving, now, was immediately relegating it to the past. It was as if present, future and past had been instantly compressed into one.

However, it was the present that had to be dealt with. This evening he would have to seek out, and face, Anna Beal: a prospect attended by both excitement and misgivings. Straightening his back, he headed for the gate; he would pause only to pick up his belongings from the Adjutant's office.

He arrives at the Adelphi in something of a lather: unable to find a taxi, he's had to jog some of the way, fearful of missing her. Standing in the foyer, regaining his breath whilst listening to prolonged applause from inside the auditorium, he's reassured that his timing is in fact about right. Around at the Stage Door, however, things seem less certain. The door-keeper, when he finally responds to Peter's knocking, is adamant. 'Sorry, guv, Miss Newman isn't seeing any visitors this evening.'

'Just give her my name, will you? See what she says?' The desperation in his voice must sound pretty pathetic. Of course, he can just hang around the Stage Door until she comes out, but there's no certainty she'll leave by this route; and anyway there are likely to be a whole lot of other Johnnies standing around by then.

The man hesitates, studies Peter's uniform dubiously, then makes up his mind. 'Alright, guv, but I know what she'll say.'

It's a few minutes before he returns, looking disturbed. 'What was that name again?'

'Peter Waring.'

'That's what I thought you said. Follow me.'

The door has her name painted on it, befitting the star of the play; but when the man knocks cautiously on it there follow several seconds of silence. When, at last, she answers, the thrill of hearing that familiar voice, with its husky tones, is almost too much for him.

The porter opens the door and ushers him in.

Anna is standing, wide-eyed, in the middle of the room. Wearing a silken robe, evidently she has just removed her stage costume and her make-up. Her face is unusually pale, and drawn; and there are lines of suspicion, and a lurking anger.

For a moment she stares at him in disbelief. Then she is in his arms, embracing him, her tears wet against his cheek.

'Oh, Peter! I couldn't believe it. I thought you were dead! I was certain this must be some dreadful hoax.'

He wasn't expecting this. Hadn't even known whether she would want to see him. Then he remembers. She doesn't know the circumstances of Jim's death. No one else knows. Only Marie-Louise.

She steps back to study him. He looks at her uncertainly. Has she even yet had final confirmation of her husband's death? But yes. Her expressed joy is fighting through a mask of sadness.

'You've heard?'

She crumples. 'Yes. This morning. One of those dreadful telegrams again. Of course, it was only what they'd led me to believe some weeks ago. But I hadn't entirely given up hope. One doesn't, does one? Now…well, it's better at least to finally know.'

She begins to weep again, this time giving way to her grief. He marvels that she can have gone on stage this evening, having been given the news only hours before. Courage, he thinks, can take many forms. And he thinks once more of Marie-Louise.

Anna turns away, brushing angrily at her tears. 'Look at me!' she exclaims shakily. 'A fine way to greet you, when I'm so very delighted that you're here! Forgive me. There is so much to talk about! So much for you to tell me.' She looks at him doubtfully. 'You can stay? You don't have to rush away?'

'No, of course not. I've come to see you.'

'Well, let me get dressed, and then you'll come back to the flat with me? Have you eaten? No. Well I have supper prepared at home – just something simple, cold. We have so much to say, for you to explain. You must tell me everything. But later, when I'm more able to take it in.'

The words are tumbling over each other now; she's becoming excitable. Not like her at all. But it's entirely understandable. She must have been on an emotional see-saw in recent weeks, particularly today.

He turns and makes to go out of the room while she dresses; but she puts a restraining hand on his arm, makes a little moue. 'Don't be silly. We're old friends! – and you are a doctor, after all. Just try not to stare.' It's all said teasingly, but there's nothing coquettish about it. Merely warm, friendly, feminine. He experiences a rush of tenderness towards her, thrusting aside any apprehensions he still has. All that can come later.

She continues to chatter whilst she slips off her robe and reaches for her clothes. He discretely turns to one side as she does so, but not before he has had a glimpse of what's on show; and as she dresses he cannot prevent himself from taking quick glances.

If she notices, she gives no sign – or doesn't mind.

Afterwards, when they leave the theatre, as they look for a cab, and during the journey across town to her apartment in Harley Street, she keeps up this banter in a nervous sort of way. It's almost as if she senses he has something important to tell her, and she wants to shut that out. He lets her talk, relieved too that she's keen to turn away from more important matters. He's happy anyway to just listen to her voice.

He learns that Jordan has gone home, and that it is uncertain when, or if, she will return to London. This in spite of the fact she had acquired star status at the Windmill, and is now the toast of many of the beaux in town. Evidently there had been a most dreadful raid on the city in the middle of May, going on all night, with hundreds of fires reaching into the West End. It had finally all been too much for Jordan, and she'd fled. Ironically, things in the city had been very much quieter since, 'as though jerry had lost heart', as Anna puts it, '…or, more likely, is gathering strength for another onslaught.'

He receives the news about Jordan being at home in a strangely disinterested away. Earlier in the evening he had finally managed to get through to Uncle John, but by the time the whoops of amazement at the other end had subsided, followed by expressions of delight that he would also be coming home for a few days, the rest of the conversation had been necessarily brief. There had been no mention of Jordan, therefore. But for him the events of the past three months seem to have relegated her from the forefront of his mind (where, he now perceives, she had been for most of his life) to somewhere much further back. He's not sure how he views her. Hardly as a sister. Certainly not as a friend. But it no longer matters. He will find a proper place for her in due course.

By the time they settle to the cold repast at Anna's, she has quietened down, appears more contemplative. This in turn makes him more nervous. But she is waiting, he realises, for him to begin to give her the detail of the past three months; it's simply that she cannot quite bring herself to ask about it, about Jim's last days. Slowly, therefore, he begins to tell her, starting at the beginning, relating the story of those events in the order in which they unwound. Occasionally she interrupts with questions, but otherwise she listens in silence. He tells her about the sortie, about all that happened there, about their rescue, and about Jim's wounds. He tells her about Marie-Louise, gives her chapter and verse of her situation. He even tells her about the extraordinary meeting with Hans. Haltingly, he tells her about Jim's operation, explains the whys and wherefores of his not being able to go to a proper hospital. He tells her everything. Everything, that is, apart from the one thing he knows he's going to have to tell her at some point.

He finds it difficult to meet her gaze, the forlorn expression she wears as if now, and only now, can her grief really take shape. The subjects he really needs to discuss with her are struggling to be heard. But this is not the time. He can see that. This, at any rate, is his excuse. He looks at his watch, is astonished, pleased perhaps, to find it is almost midnight. He will be glad to have reason to get away. To run away.

'Anna, it's late. I really must go. Perhaps I can see you again soon?'

'Where are you staying?'

'At the Regent Palace. I was lucky to land a room there. Town is packed out.'

'You can't walk all that way at this time of night.'

'It's not far. And I need the exercise.'

She looks at him long and hard. He can't quite read her expression. Pleading?

She speaks with hesitation, reluctantly. 'Peter, I don't want to be on my own tonight. Please stay.'

He expects her to show him to the spare room. Jordan's room. But instead she leads him, wordless, to her own. To her bed. Hers and Jim's.

They make love with quiet passion, their hunger not so much carnal as rather a mutual desire for reassurance in the face of an increasingly hostile world. Throughout, before and after, there appears to be a tacit understanding that this is not in any way to denigrate the memory of Jim, but instead is to be interpreted as a kind of celebration of how much he has meant to both of them through important periods of their lives. It's as if (he persuades himself) they appear to be telling each other he bestows his blessing on them.

Afterwards, nothing is said. They sleep, wrapped in each other's arms.

It is some time later that he comes to, perhaps driven awake by the heavy weight of conscience that seems to be sitting in his chest and throat. Also, as if he's been expecting something that's failed to appear. This he quickly identifies. For the best part of a year whenever he's been in London there has previously come, sooner or later, the sound of the sirens – and this night there has been none. As for the feeling of guilt, that needs no identification. As he lies there, thinking, in the darkness he can sense her near him. Now she stirs, murmuring.

'Anna?'

For a moment she is silent, then rolls against him, her breasts pliant against his chest.

'Are you awake?' he says.

'I am now.' He can hear in her voice the semblance of a smile breaking through her waking sadness; can detect the rising of her nipples against his skin.

'I have something to tell you.'

'Mmmm. Go on.'

'I was responsible for Jim's death.'

'What do you mean?'

'I killed him.'

She stiffens in his arms. Then, without a word she moves away and with one fluid movement gets out of bed. He hears her don her robe and, still without saying a thing, she walks out of the room.

For a short time he lies there, abject. Then he too gets up, slips on his shorts, and pads after her. She is sitting silently in a chair near the window. She has opened the curtains and through the window, from a clear sky, the delicate light of early dawn casts thin shadows into the room, high-lighting the generous curves of her figure under the silk robe. She has lit a cigarette, and in the dimness the tip glows brightly each time she draws upon it.

'Go on,' she says, her voice flat with weariness, or disbelief. Half of her face is in shadow, the other half blurred, as pale as the light. She is looking up at him, but in the half-light he is unable to discern her expression.

He sits down opposite her, and tells her again about the surgery on Jim. This time he explains about the overlooked blood vessel.

When he's finished, for long seconds she says nothing. Then, 'Is that all?'

'Isn't it enough!' He doesn't try to keep the anger out of his voice.

'Oh, Peter!' is her exasperated cry. 'You can be such a fool! You had me wondering all sorts of things.'

He doesn't know how to take this. He's been expecting anger, even hatred and rejection. Instead she sounds relieved, almost amused.

'If it wasn't for me he would still be alive.' He knows he sounds defensive and petulant. Which he is.

Now she's cross. 'Would he? It all depended on you, did it? You know, that sounds pretty egotistical to me! Tell me, what would have happened if you hadn't operated? He would have died, wouldn't he. And what would have happened if you'd taken him to a hospital? But then you've already told me about that! He failed to come round from the anaesthetic, didn't he? Why don't we blame this Marie-Louise, then, and not you?'

He remains silent, sullenly mulling this over.

'You did your best, Peter. Both of you did. Maybe there were mistakes. Maybe there weren't. Perhaps it was just inevitable, what happened. So, tell me, are you going to carry around this petty and gratuitous burden of guilt for the rest of your life? Does everything have to revolve around you?'

Suddenly, in spite of still feeling defensive, he knows she's right. A great burden lifts from him, not just with regard to all this, but in a much broader sense. He can begin to see himself in a different light. A flood of relief and gratitude sweeps over him, carrying with it his desire for her. She's a truly remarkable woman.

He hesitates, then brings to mind once again Beal's last few words to him about 'looking after Anna', and he plunges. 'There's something else I want to ask you, Anna. What will you do now?'

'What will I do? I'll carry on. What else?'

'Will you get support from Jim's family?' He already knows the answer to that, remembering what Beal had confided in him.

She gives a tired smile. 'Very little, I imagine.'

He teeters again, uncertain about the moment. But this thing that's been building inside him for long enough is now determined to break free. And Beal would have said, 'Go for it'.

Stumbling, he rushes in. 'I was wondering, would you marry me?'

For long seconds she stares at him, astonishment bordering on dismay, perhaps unable to take it in. When she finally answers her voice is hard with anger.

'You think I can't look after myself? After everything I've survived already? – things you've absolutely no idea about! I don't need your charity, Peter. Especially so soon after my finally knowing about Jim.'

Embarrassment is countered by desperation. 'I didn't for one minute mean it that way, Anna. And I didn't mean immediately! – I understand it's far too soon. But I'm in love with you. I would be the happiest man if you would consent, in due course, to be my wife. And I do know that under the circumstances Jim would have wanted it.'

She looks at him long and hard, searching for something. Then her features gradually soften. 'Forgive me for talking like this, Peter, but it has to be said. And from the experience I've gained from literature and drama, on the stage, as well as from real life, perhaps I have learned things about relationships that you haven't? I think you haven't yet learned the difference between infatuation and love. And there is a world of difference. It seems to me as if you think that every woman who attracts your attention – whom you fancy – has to fancy you back. It's as if you need that for your self-esteem. It makes you very vulnerable, you know; and must unnecessarily complicate relationships. It makes you read into people – into women – things that aren't there.'

Irritated, he says, 'I don't know what you mean.'

'Don't you? What about Jordan, for a start? And Shevaun O'Connor – yes, I know about her, Sylvia Stanton told me. And this Marie-Louise, in France – it's clear you're very emotional about her. And perhaps others. You know, there are some people who go through life content with a series of encounters, and the variety and excitement that goes with that. Others of course do seek relationships that they hope will be deep and permanent. It seems to me, though, that you have become confused, found yourself hovering between the two?'

He thinks about that for a minute. Decides. 'You may be right in general, Anna, about the difficulties of separating love and infatuation. But I know that as far as my feelings for you are concerned it's a lot more than just infatuation. I think you're wonderful in every way. I know I would be delighted to be able to spend the rest of my life with you.'

The early morning sun is beginning to cast its rays into the room, dusting contents with rose gold. In its light he can see that she's now smiling, that a similar warmth is reflected in her eyes – and in her voice when she eventually replies.

'My dear, I do find that very reassuring – and flattering. I do like you, very much, and admire you. It's true that I'm fond of you, even. But I'm not in love with you. Would you want marriage under those terms?'

She holds up her hand as he begins to speak. 'No. Hear me out first. If I were to agree to marry you, it would be as a marriage of convenience – like an old-fashioned arranged marriage, I suppose. In a sense, that's what I had with Jim. There's no need to look so shocked! I loved him in as far as I'm capable of loving anyone in the romantic sense that you mean. But I've never experienced that form of love with anyone – that is to say, 'swept away' by them. However, when I met Jim, remember, I was in a very distressed and lonely state, carrying a whole heap of guilt at having abandoned my parents, and everywhere meeting suspicion and hostility because of my being German – and Jewish! Jim became my saviour. He was attractive and exciting, and gave me respectability – opened doors for me, both socially and professionally. For that – and his love – I will always be grateful. And I miss him dreadfully. As far as you and I are concerned, I think it could work. As I've said, I like and respect you enormously. You're attractive, kind and considerate, and – to be thoroughly materialistic for a moment – as a doctor you would have money and standing in society. Many a woman would give her eye-teeth to have all that. And, given time, I'm sure that love could grow. But there's one – major – obstacle. And that's Jane.'

Jane? He thinks, What on earth is she on about?

His expression must reveal that, for she goes on, ' "Jamie" then, as you call her.'

'What about her?'

'You love her. And she's in love with you.'

511

He stares at her as if she's taken leave of her senses. Then laughs.

'What on earth gives you that idea?'

'I've watched you whenever you've been together. Seen the way she looks at you. I can assure you, a woman knows about these things. She's in love with you. Probably always has been?'

'But she's just a good friend.'

'Just a good friend? Or your best friend? Since you were children?'

'Well, yes…'

'You like her, then? Are fond of her?'

'Of course. Very much so. But…'

'And you think her attractive, as a woman? She has a good figure, an exciting one, does she not?'

He doesn't need to think about that, has always admired that in her. 'Certainly…'

'And a nice, pleasant face? You wouldn't say that she was unattractive in that sense?'

'No, of course not…'

'But not perhaps exceptionally pretty like, say, Jordan? Not altogether a beauty?'

She doesn't say, '…like me?' But that thought springs to mind. He feels himself going onto the defensive, on Jamie's behalf.

'No, I suppose not…' He hesitates. He's having difficulty in bringing details of Jamie's face into focus. He knows it so well, that he's never really thought about it. Has sort of always taken it for granted. Perhaps Anna believes he's thinking in the negative, because before he can continue, she says, 'You know, some are *given* a kind of beauty, and some contrive it. But some have beauty, true beauty, that shines from within. I see your Jamie as being in that last category. Would you agree?'

He dwells on that for a few seconds, knows she's right – it sits easily with him, strikes a chord.

'Yes, that's true.'

'So you agree with all that? All that I've said? That's what *you* think about her, also?'

'Yes. I've said so.'

'And what's that if it isn't love?' She sounds almost triumphant. As though she's given him something important.

He stares at her. The sun has by now risen high enough to fully illuminate her face, and he thinks again how strikingly beautiful she is. But he's thrown into confusion, dreadfully disturbed by what she's just said. Looking at Anna, a part of him doesn't want it to be true. But increasingly, overwhelmingly, he knows suddenly that it is. And that fills him there and then with a profound knowledge, and satisfaction, and excitement such as he's never known before.

All this must be showing in his face, because Anna now says, in fond fashion, 'You men can be so obtuse! It's true, isn't it?'

Unable to speak, he nods.

'Well, as soon as you can, tomorrow, go off and find your Jamie, and tell her what you've just learned.' She smiles, a broad delighted grin. 'And if, for some obscure reason, I'm wrong about her, and she doesn't want you, come back and see me, and I'll reconsider your proposition!'

She gets up, holds out her hand. 'And now, come back to bed.'

CHAPTER THIRTY-FOUR

Never before has the rhythmic clatter of the train been so musical. Never before has the cadence of the wheels beneath his feet filled him with such joy. The tune of *A Song In My Heart* keeps looping through his brain. This time, he's truly and finally Coming Home. They are close enough now for him to be able to recognise landmarks; he can count the miles and the minutes to his destination. And his destiny. For that is how he now sees it. This conclusion, to which he's been led so adroitly and so selflessly by Anna, no longer amazes him. It's as if, having had it pointed out to him, he's always been aware of it. So, how could he previously have been so dim? He consoles himself that so often one fails to see the thing right under one's nose; familiarity breeds not so much contempt as an inability to stand back and take a broader view. And of course there had been distractions – or, more particularly, one distraction – along the way. But that's no excuse. And he's lucky that he hasn't left it too late.

For if it hadn't been for Anna, he might never have seen what is now so blatantly obvious. And his thoughts turn yet again to Anna, on her immense generosity of spirit to have pointed all this out to him, regardless of her own possible interests. But then, was this in fact pure pragmatism on her part? Her outlook on life must surely have been forged by the hard road she had been forced to take, on the harsh experiences along the way. Not for her the impetuosity of others, but everything thought through, to arrive at the most sensible solutions to the difficulties ahead. He had seen evidence of this on many occasions.

But – and only for a brief moment – he can't help but think somewhat wistfully how exciting might have been a life spent with Anna.

He muses for a moment on the multitudinous pathways in life, the many crossroads that crop up on the way, and the factors that dictate whether one goes along one path or another. At each junction, the route chosen will lead to a completely different set of crossroads, to a whole new set of possible destinations. And what would be the likelihood of sooner or later ending up at a single specific place, regardless of the route taken? – very little, he imagines. How much of a role does Chance play, in this cross-country hunt through life, he wonders; and what proportion of it is the result of conscious decision? Moreover, how many decisions are 'conscious', and how many are actually subconsciously taken because of experiences from the past?

But enough of this rumination. He isn't in the mood for it, does far too much of it anyway. He is certain of his destination. Home. It has taken him a long time to accept what is 'Home'. It was Uncle John who'd started it, paved the way. But he now knows that, although he was unaware of it at the time, all along it has been the presence of Jamie who has gradually drawn him into thinking of the place as Home.

He wonders, now, who will be at the station to meet him. Wonders if he will be able to contain himself if Jamie is there but accompanied by others. For when he'd got through to home yesterday morning, to say that he was catching the midday train, it had been Jessica who'd answered the phone, everyone else being out. Once she'd composed herself sufficiently to be able to answer his questions, he'd learned that Yes, 'Miss Jane' was home, had been for a month – to which she'd added, with something that sounded suspiciously like a sniff, that Jordan ('full of London airs and graces') had also come home, for how long no one was sure. On being further pressed, she'd said that Yes, Miss Jane had been informed about his having turned up alive and well, and that Doctor John (who, almost as soon as he knew, had called in to give her the news) had reported that on hearing this she'd burst into tears – and that, every day since, she'd been round to find out when he might be coming home.

His sense of excitement therefore is hard to keep in check. Pictures jostle for a place in his mind's eye. Yet again he returns to those images that have accompanied him for as long as he can remember: Jamie, grubby and bedraggled like any 'boy', up a tree on the morning they'd first met; Jamie, arms and legs swinging gracefully as she climbed with ease up a fellside; Jamie lying with him in the shade of a tree on that hot summer's day when they'd gone haymaking for George's dad. In his imagination he can again see sunlight glinting on the surface of a lake, feel the breeze brushing his cheeks and see it ruffling Jamie's hair, and can again physically experience the various scents of spring and high summer – and the scent of Jamie.

Then, too, there are other, less distinct memories – memories of times when she had seemed angry with him for seemingly no good reason, small incidents when she had seemed to be implying that he was irritatingly living up to the 'Cautious' nickname she'd bestowed upon him, and occasions (particularly whenever Jordan had been present, or if there had been reference to her) when she'd teased him, even goaded him about little things. At the time, although baffled by it, he'd not attached any great significance to this behaviour. It had been one of those 'girl' things that clearly were impossible to understand. But now the pieces begin to fall into place. Had it all, in fact, been due to a tinge of jealousy? Jealousy that he'd paid Jordan more attention than he had her, that he'd placed Jordan on a pedestal whilst taking Jamie for granted? Had her irritation with him arisen from the fact that he'd seemed incapable (or careless) of interpreting the signals she was giving him?

And why was it that he'd not been able to see that for himself? (*Obtuse* was the word Anna had used – tactfully as a generality, but tangentially directed specifically at him.) Has he all these years confused himself by continuing to see her as 'a boy up a tree', as just one of the gang? It is difficult to understand now, from his present vantage point. Borne on a wave of elation, his vision is now clear. She is such a wonderful person. Revelling in the process, he mentally ticks off just a few of her qualities: bright, kind, considerate, adventurous and exciting; full of good humour; and loyal to her friends to the last breath.

And yet…and yet, from one minute to the next old doubts *will* sneak in. Suppose Anna is wrong? Suppose that, just as he was accused of seeing in women what he wanted to see, he is now being persuaded to see in Jamie what he, suddenly, more than anything desires? Suppose that Jamie's being in love with him is all a figment of Anna's, and his, imagination? How embarrassing will that be for Jamie. To what extent then will their old relationship disintegrate, their close and easy friendship, that sense of companionship, vanish into thin air? But there's nothing to be gained by dwelling on that possibility. One has to grow from the past, not stagnate in it so that the future becomes stillborn. Anything else would be to deny Jamie the chance of her preordained future, as well as his own. One had to find out. Anything else would be rank cowardice.

And all at once they are there, the train drawing into the station. Among the few figures waiting on the platform only one standing out. Jamie. He looks at her with new eyes. How very attractive she is. How could he have not seen that before. Grabbing his holdall, he heads for the door.

Looking in the wrong direction, she doesn't see him at first. When she does, for a second she stands stock-still as though making sure that he's real, that it is all true. Then she is in his arms, her lips against his, kissing him as she's never kissed him before, hugging him as if she never wants to let him go. Finally, laughing, they break apart, stand back to drink each other in. Those wonderful eyes of hers, he's almost forgotten about them, full of sunshine and colour, full of life.

She's the first to speak, her voice shaky. 'I never quite gave up hope, Peter. Yet I feared the worst. I had to try to cling to hope, though – I couldn't have coped otherwise, to lose you after what happened to Bill.'

He hadn't given a thought to Bill; but he, too, had been a close part of her life, for the whole of her life. 'How is Bill?'

'Oh, all right. Doing the best he can. He's lucky, I suppose, although it's been difficult to persuade him of that. But he's more or less completely blind. And has very little use in his hands. However, he can walk now, albeit with difficulty. He's changed, you know? He's not the old Bill, ebullient and self-centred. He's much more thoughtful, more caring I suppose. But immense courage, still. Rarely lets any of it get him down. He'll have to go back for a whole series of operations, yet – to his face and his hands.'

'He's out of hospital, then?'

'Oh yes, for the past six weeks.'

But he doesn't want to talk about Bill, doesn't want to hear the pride and enthusiasm in her voice when she speaks of him.

'Uncle John and Aunt Mabel send their love, couldn't come but can't wait to see you back at home...' she starts to say.

But for the moment he can't even pay attention to that.

'Jamie, there's something important I want to say to you.'

'Come on, then. We can talk on the way.' She links her arm into his, and they begin to move off down the platform, which by now is practically deserted. 'I haven't got the car – I thought we might walk. We'll talk on the way.'

But this won't do. It can't wait. He stops her and turns her towards him.

'Jamie, I love you.'

'She laughs in delight, leans up to kiss him again, briefly, on the lips. 'I love you too.' She laughs again. But does he detect an edge of uneasiness in that laugh?

'No – more than that. I mean I'm in love with you. Always have been. Will you marry me?' He has to blurt it out.

He might as well as have struck her. She goes ashen, and visibly staggers, so that he thinks she is going to faint and hastens to place a supporting hand at her elbow.

'You haven't heard,' she says dully, in what is little more than a whisper.

He's overwhelmed by fear. Something is terribly wrong.

'Jamie, what is it?'

She doesn't answer. Instead, she continues in that same dead voice, devoid of emotion, 'I didn't know...I couldn't even be sure of ever seeing you again.' Then, angry, 'If only you'd given me some indication over the years! Some reason to hope. I would have waited until the end of time!' It was a cry of anguish.

'Jamie, I don't understand! Tell me! What's wrong?' He's desperate now.

Throughout this exchange, she's avoided meeting his gaze. Now she looks at him, chin up, and her face displays a confusion of sadness, anger and defiance.

'Peter, I've married Bill. Three weeks ago.'

POSTSCRIPT

With a conscious sigh I'd put aside the last of Peter's diaries – or 'Journals', as he'd preferred to call them.

Over the three weeks following his funeral, I had turned to them whenever I could. At first I'd dipped and delved, but after a while I'd gone back to the beginning and read through them chronologically. Only then had I perceived that his recorded memories also bobbed up at random, understood that time has no relevance when it comes to recollection.

And my preoccupation with them had verged on becoming an obsession – perhaps fuelled by guilt: for I'd become very aware that most of what I was learning about him I hadn't known before, and more importantly hadn't sought to know.

However, although always engrossing, reading through the journals had been time-consuming. Altogether there were sixteen of them, one a year from 1926 through to 1941. The first two consisted merely of school exercise books, rather tatty and dog-eared. Although expressed immaturely and written in a childish hand, still they were not only amazingly thoughtful but also, unexpectedly for a boy of not yet fifteen, remarkably frank with regard to his emotions. Of course, at the time he'd written them he wouldn't have envisaged anyone else ever reading them. By 1928, however, he'd already progressed to proper, hardbacked, foolscap-sized, page-a-day diaries.

A lot of what he'd written was very detailed (although some of it, surely, could only have been written later, from memory). Considering the circumstances during most of those years, this revealed how astonishingly dedicated to this pastime he must have been. Much of it however contained only the bare bones of events and relationships, so that as time went on during my reading, and as I'd gradually become immersed in the situations and in the personalities of those involved, I'd found myself more and more using my imagination to 'flesh out' what he'd written, to imagine how people might have looked and what might have been said.

At first, my growing obsession with the diaries had started to irritate Sue; but then she too had begun to look into them, and soon had become as enthralled as I had, with the result that increasingly we had long discussions about the content. Now that I'd finished them, she'd had some catching up to do.

And my thoughts had gone back yet again to that morning after the day he and I had gone up to the funeral in Cumbria: a Saturday when I wasn't on duty but had stirred with the thought that I must call in on him before the day was much older, having left him alone with his thoughts the previous evening. His housekeeper Martha, though, had beaten me to it, and it had been her frantic phone call that had roused me from my lethargy and abruptly uncovered the true nature of the vague misgivings I'd had ever since the previous evening.

Arriving at his house, to be met with a still distraught Martha, I'd found him sitting in the chair where I'd left him, at first glance still asleep. Except that there was about him that special stillness which is unique to the dead. The whisky bottle was there on the table beside him, but was now empty. Scattered about him on the floor were his journals; and on the table with the bottle and a glass was a letter addressed to me, and a framed photograph.

And, prompted by those recollections, I'd then, for the umpteenth time, re-read that letter.

My dear Peter,

My apologies for leaving you with this burden. I know that you will handle it with your usual honesty and tact. I hope, too, that you will not think too badly of me. But, as you will gather, yesterday was the final straw. For when the past has become so remote that it no longer seems like one's own but that of someone else, when it has no more relevance for its own generation than it does for the present one, then it is time to say Adieu. I do so with as good a heart as one can muster on coming to the end of what one, for much of the time, thinks of as permanent. In my mind there is an uncertainty of what might follow. It may well be, I suspect, that it is entirely a matter of coming to the end of a long road (with hindsight, over too quickly!), weary in mind and body so that one is only too thankful to lie down and sleep. However, if Providence does have other plans, then that too should prove to be a fascinating journey; one for which I shall doubtless find, from somewhere, the courage again to follow.

My life, the one that is now ending, has I suppose been an eventful one. I have made many mistakes, and have had not a few disappointments – not least the gift, then loss, of love, and the lack of children and grandchildren whose progress I could interest myself in. But, it has, I have to admit, been an interesting one. Above all, I can still vividly recall, from time to time, the excitement that I and my fellow students felt at being privileged to study Medicine: we felt as though we were learning the secrets of the universe.

I leave you my Journals, to do with as you wish. They started as a childhood fancy, and for some reason continued, until finally ending abruptly (for reasons that will become apparent if you can be bothered to delve into them). Perhaps they will explain much to you – but not everything. I don't really know why I went on writing them for as long as I did. It was a kind of conceit, I suppose. I rarely re-read them afterwards – too much indulgence in nostalgia is not a good thing, for therein lies the path to melancholy and madness. However, I hadn't the heart to destroy them.

Thank you for all you have done. You have been a fine colleague and a good friend...

Well, had I? There were so many issues left unresolved, so many questions left unanswered, particularly now that I'd read his journals. Had he returned to Anna? Had she then agreed to marry him? Anna, the wife who'd 'died young', as rumour had it? It would be a simple matter to find out. Perhaps, one day, curiosity will take me there. But I wasn't sure then, and am still not sure, that I want to know, one way or the other. I'd wondered, too – and still wonder from time to time – if for a while at least, he'd kept contact with Jamie and Bill. I'd never heard him refer to them. Had he therefore cut himself off from them, finding the associations too painful – selfish though that might have been?

There had been so many neglected opportunities when I could have chatted to him as a true friend, could have allowed him the means to share with a person close to him some of those 'mistakes and disappointments', if that was what he would have wanted. For to have to confine such things – those issues which are the true milestones of life – to have no one to whom one can perhaps confide and relate, to be required to keep them imprisoned within, must surely emphasise one's own sense of isolation. My friendship in the end had been revealed to be all too shallow.

Plagued by guilt at my poor support of him, over the years, I had therefore struggled only briefly with my conscience about what to do on that Saturday. The Saturday of his death. I had, after all, treated him for some years for cardiac dysrhythmias associated with mild ischaemic heart disease, which might at any time have resulted in his death. The empty bottles might merely imply that he'd run out of his pills. He had died without dependants, had no life assurance, and I knew, as his sole executor, that he had bequeathed the whole of his estate to various charities. There was no one, therefore, who had any genuine interest in the cause of his death; nothing there of concern to a coroner. I signed the death certificate with a quiet heart. It was the least I could do for him at the end.

I'd paused then to dwell again on all that I'd read in his journals. I'd perceived, running through them, a kind of disenchantment with his life and with himself at that time. But he had lived through particularly interesting times; something I'd found myself envying. The War, for example, had been fraught with uncertainty, privation and fear – but, for those whom good fortune carried through, it had also been filled with excitement and adventure. It is intriguing, too, that his diary had ended on a note of uncertainty - not only to do with his personal affairs: for, at that point in June 1941 when he'd stopped writing about it he couldn't have known that within a week Hitler, against all likelihood, would invade Russia; nor that by the end of the year, following Pearl Harbour, America (again against all odds) would be dragged into the war, hammering the final nail into the coffin of Nazism and that of Japanese tyranny across the Far East. The hindsight that is 'history' is a cosy affair: the outcome of events is already known.

I'd been curious, too, at the thread of low self-esteem to be found in his writings – a view of himself of which, in all the years I'd known him, there had been no indication. At his funeral the church had been packed to overflowing. On the way out I'd been approached by one of his patients, a woman, who'd said, 'You know, for many of us the sun shone out of Dr Waring' – adding hastily, 'Not that you're not all right, Dr McMichael.' That was how I'd always seen him to be perceived by others. And that was how I'd perceived him: as a reliable, self-contained, contented bachelor-type, comfortable with himself and with the world he lived in. How little one can know someone unless one takes the trouble to delve beneath the surface.

Once more I'd picked up the photograph, which I'd earlier taken out of its frame in order to be able to look at it more closely, the photograph that had so fascinated me earlier on, on the evening prior to his death. I hadn't needed to refer to his letter again to know what he'd said about it.

'...I leave you, too, the photograph, the one you showed more than a passing interest in, yesterday evening. Again, if you care to read my journals, you will understand its significance for me, and to the funeral that you so kindly took me to yesterday, in Cumbria. Perhaps you will then care to keep it? – in memory of me, and to preserve, as it were, in some small way, my own memories?...'

Well, Sue and I had already agreed that we would find a place for it on one of our walls, next to the picture of the young Peter in his R.A.F. uniform. And there they hang still, side by side.

Even then it had been too faded to be able to clearly see her features, which are glazed over by a slanting sun. One couldn't say whether she could be called pretty or not, therefore; but her overall attractiveness, her vivacity and her obvious love of life had seemed again, and still seem, to leap from the flat surface. Then, too, as I'd studied it I'd noticed for the first time the shadow running diagonally from left to right across the foreground. It appears to be that of the person taking the photograph: which couldn't at that time have been Peter, I'd decided – she would hardly have given him a picture he'd taken himself. For I'd already discovered what is written on the back of the photograph:

To 'Cautious',
Happy 16th Birthday!
With all my love, always,
Jamie. x x x